CUCK

Kiran Nagarkar was born in Mumbai. He wrote his first book in a language in which he had never written before — Marathi. The book was called *Saat Sakkam Trechalis*, recently translated as *Seven Sixes are Forty-Three*, and is considered a landmark in post-independent Indian literature. His novel in English, *Ravan and Eddie*, acclaimed as a literary bestseller, has been translated into Marathi.

Nagarkar's writing has a lightness of pace coupled with a clarity which enables him to illuminate the most subtle and complex philosophical concepts with a directness and intimacy which linger in the mind long after you've finished *Cuckold*.

PRAISE FOR *CUCKOLD*

(*Cuckold* is) a fascinating book, a sort of fantastic marriage between the Thomas Mann of Royal Highness and the Lady Murasaki.

Gore Vidal

Here is writing so immediate and sensuous it leaves the reader with almost physical memories... This is a very important book, one which is deeply relevant to the contemporary world and yet will undoubtedly stand the test of time.

Dr. Susan Daruvala, *University of Cambridge*

Cuckold is so totally different from anything I have read in Indian English fiction that it deserves special notice and praise.

If bringing the past alive in such a persuasive manner was its only achievement, this would still be a great book. I know of no other Indian English author, Khushwant Singh included, who can write about another epoch in so confident or convincing a manner... Nagarkar not only has all the talents of a novelist, but also a philosophy of history.

Makarand Paranjape, *The Pioneer*

A tale of astounding power, grace and wit. Nagarkar takes us on a dazzling literary adventure, in language that is hypnotic, sensuous, irresistible...

Manjula Padmanabhan, *Outlook*

Miraculously liberated of all linguistic obstacles, unfettered by inhibitions of sacrosanctity, *Cuckold* is controlled by a truly renaissance imagination.

Subhash K. Jha, *The Hindustan Times*

Cuckold is a historical fiction at its best.

Khushwant Singh, *Sunday Despatch*

CUCKOLD

KIRAN NAGARKAR

HarperCollins *Publishers* **India**
a joint venture with

New Delhi

Published by
HarperCollins *Publishers* India
a joint venture with
The India Today Group

First published in Hardcover 1997
First published in Paperback 1999
Third impression 2003

HarperCollins *Publishers*
1A Hamilton House, New Delhi 110 001, India
77-85 Fulham Palace Road, London W6 8JB, United Kingdom
Hazelton Lanes, 55 Avenue Road, Suite 2900, Toronto, Ontario M5R 3L2
and 1995 Markham Road, Scarborough, Ontario M1B 5M8, Canada
25 Ryde Road, Pymble, Sydney, NSW 2073, Australia
31 View Road, Glenfield, Auckland 10, New Zealand
10 East 53rd Street, New York NY 10022, USA

Printed and bound at
Thomson Press (India) Ltd.

One of the premises underlying this novel is that an easy colloquial currency of language will make the concerns, dilemmas and predicaments of the Maharaj Kumar, Rana Sanga, and the others as real as anything we ourselves are caught in: a birth, divorce, death in our families; political intrigue, a national crisis, or a military confrontation in the life of our nation. The idea was to use contemporary idiom so long as the concepts we use today were available in the sixteenth century. For example, the measurement of time, theories of education, war strategies, music, the functioning of bureaucracy, etc. I was striving for immediacy, rather than some academic notion of fidelity, at best simulated.

Acknowledgements

'There's no way we'll publish an acknowledgement as long as your book,' my publishers told me. This was a gross misrepresentation of the facts. First of all, Cuckold is not a long book, just a bare 600 pages when the norm today in turn-of-the-century fiction is 670 to 1437 pages. Secondly, my original acknowledgements were not even a round five hundred pages. Since publishers have the last word in all matters, I'm constrained to do an abridged and utterly inadequate page and a half of thank you's. My apologies to all those good people who the publishers will not allow me to name and thank.

Ramchandra Rao had no idea of what I had in mind (nor did I) but he was instrumental in organizing my visit to Udaipur and Chittor and placed me in the hands of Nitin Tirpude and Rajiv Sharma. Why Nitin and Rajiv should have put themselves out to such an extraordinary degree will always remain a mystery to me. I wouldn't have had the help of these gentlemen, and all the other kinds of help without the silent support of my old friend, Daljit Mirchandani.

Sunanda Herzberger got loads of reference books from the library. Out of the blue, Tulsi Vatsal — I'll come back to her again — bought me a copy of Baburnama. Fate, serendipity, the grand design, whatever you choose to call it, the book was coming together.

If Babur plays a crucial role in my novel, it is due, to a great extent, to Annette Susannah Beveridge's translation of the Baburnama. How does one doff one's cap to a dead author except to recommend her to all those who are interested in exceptional literature?

Nancy Fernandes got acidity, lost her 20:20 eyesight but typed and retyped the manuscript without complaint. Rekha Sabins, the translator of my novel *Ravan and Eddie*, was the willing(?) victim of my first, and largely incomprehensible readings from *Cuckold* as it was being written. Tulsi Vatsal played Mahmud of Ghazni, Timur and Jenghiz Khan rolled into one and lopped off close to a hundred pages. Her sharp critical insights and cuts made *Cuckold* a tighter and far better book.

I'm grateful to my friend Pervin Mahoney for her comments, initial editing and encouragement. And to Nita Pillai for further vetting the book. How shall I thank my friends Hira and Adrian Steven? Their patience was close to infinite. Every word, line, paragraph and chapter was scrutinized, every suggestion annotated and discussed. Never mind the inadequacy of the words, thank you both, again. Meena and Vijay Kirloskar have stood by me, and when the going's been tough, given me a sense of perspective with wry humour and encouragement.

Whatever the shape of my gratitude, most of it is related to the fact that these people believed in the venture. Among the believers, I must especially mention my friend, Octavia Wiseman. She has stood by *Cuckold* through some difficult times. I'm grateful that she never gives up. That leaves my editor at HarperCollins, Priyakshi Rajguru. Like most soft-spoken people, she knows her mind. I'm glad that her mind was set upon *Cuckold*.

Major Characters

RAJPUT KINGDOM OF MEWAR · CAPITAL: CHITTOR

Maharana or Rana Sanga	—	King of Mewar
Maharaj Kumar	—	The Rana's eldest son and heir apparent
Vikramaditya	—	The Rana's third son
Rani Karmavati	—	The Rana's favourite queen and Vikramaditya's mother
Kausalya	—	The Maharaj Kumar's 'dai' or the woman who breast-fed him
The Princess	—	The Maharaj Kumar's wife
Kumkum Kanwar	—	The Princess' maid
Adinathji	—	Finance Minister
Leelawati	—	His granddaughter
Lakshman Simha	—	Home Minister
Rajendra	—	His eldest son
Tej	—	His younger son
Pooranmalji	—	Prime Minister
Mangal Simha	—	Head of Intelligence; Kausalya's son
Sunheria	—	A washerwoman
Bruhannada	—	Rani Karmavati's chief eunuch
Rao Viramdev	—	Ruler of Merta and uncle of the Princess
Puraji Kika	—	A Bhil chieftain

MUSLIM KINGDOM OF GUJARAT · CAPITAL: AHMEDABAD

Muzaffar Shah II   — Sultan of Gujarat
Bahadur Shah (Shehzada) — His second son

MUSLIM KINGDOM OF MALWA · CAPITAL: MANDU

Mahmud Khalji II — Sultan of Malwa
Medini Rai   — His Rajput prime minister and later, his enemy
Hem Karan   — Medini Rai's son
Sugandha   — Medini Rai's daughter

MUSLIM KINGDOM OF DELHI · CAPITAL: DELHI

Ibrahim Lodi — Sultan of Delhi

Babur   — Invader from Central Asia and founder of the Moghul dynasty
Humayun   — Babur's eldest son

Chapter 1

*T*he small causes court sits on Thursdays. When Father's away I preside. There were fourteen plaints to be heard. I dealt with them all, albeit as the sun rose to the meridian and then crossed it, I became impatient. The seventh was the most interesting, perhaps because it was not about being done out of money or land but afforded a change of pace and a bit of humour.

An old, bent dhobi, I would have sworn it was the same washerman who besmirched Sita's name and obliged Lord Rama to banish her into the wilderness some two thousand years ago, was now casting aspersions on his wife's virtue.

'She has a lover, maybe several,' his voice was thick with chronic bronchitis and he had to clear his throat many times before he could speak.

'Do you?' I asked his wife. She couldn't have been more than sixteen or seventeen. How naive, or hypocritical, can one get in court? Did I really expect her to smile demurely and tell the court who she was sleeping with?

I was sitting in a small semi-hexagonal balcony which jutted out from the sheer rear wall of the palace my great grandfather Maharana Kumbha had built. She and the other litigants stood fifteen feet below. Her head was covered with a green and yellow bandhani chunni which was tucked into the cleavage of her blouse. I was sure I had seen that chunni before. The sun got into her eyes when she raised her head to answer me. She bent forward and drew the silk covering her head down, to shield her eyes. Her ivory bangles, each bigger than the previous one, clattered down into the angle at her elbow. Her breasts, the colour of fine sand at Pushkar, were exposed for a brief second. I could feel Mangal's eyes at the back of my neck.

I still couldn't figure out why that chunni was so familiar.

'Ask him,' she ignored my question, 'if he has performed his husbandly duty by me even once after my father got me married to him two years ago.' Her forthrightness was as unsettling as it was unexpected. Her eyes held mine. There was no bitterness in her voice; a matter-of-factness, that's all.

'Is this true?' I asked her husband.

'What do you think? Would any man, least of all her lawful husband, be able to keep his hands off such succulent fruit?'

'What is your age, old man?'

'What's that got to do with her infidelity?'

'Don't be impertinent or I'll have you thrashed.'

'I was washing clothes before His Majesty, your father, was born but I'm still able. I was the Hatyara's dhobi. Never was a king so obsessed with cleanliness. But he could never wash the blood off his hands. He was always on the run. Where he went, I went.'

'You have a loose tongue, old man. It'll tie a noose around your neck one of these days.'

'I know the Hatyara's name is taboo, but his father had no intention of dying or relinquishing his throne. Thirty-five years is a long time to wait. Do you blame him if he lost his patience and got rid of Rana Kumbha? Would you do any the less if Rana Sanga, your father, may he live forever, hangs on to his crown thirty, forty or fifty years from now?'

'Were it not for your age, old man, you would die for treason. Even so, you'll receive ten lashes after the court rises.'

'That will not dampen my virility, Your Highness.'

I was beginning to tire of his garrulousness.

'That remains to be seen. Go to the brothel at the end of Tamarind Lane on Monday night and prove your prowess in Rasikabai's bed. I'll defer my judgement till she gives me her report.'

'And were I to fail, and I say this merely as a point in rhetoric, does that justify my wife's infidelity?'

'Even if you prove your virility with Rasikabai, you'll still need to produce proof of your wife's unfaithfulness.'

*　　*　　*

I like to be at work by six thirty in the morning. That gives me an hour and a half to scrutinize the papers, appraise individual issues, take decisions, jot down my remarks in the margins and move on to more pressing matters. Around nine, while I was conferring with Sahasmal from the Department of City Planning about digging a couple of wells, since the population of the town had risen by over a thousand in the last year, a courier from Father arrived. The confrontation with the Sultan of Gujarat was proving to be more difficult than Father had anticipated and he now needed money to pay the troops, buy victuals and enlist the support of two score and ten rawals and rawats and their garrisons.

There was of course no money in the exchequer. We fought endless wars so that our enemies would sue for peace and fill our coffers, and immediately emptied them to pay back the interest — settling the original sum was out of the question — to our gracious financiers, the Mehtas. And borrowed from them on the instant to finance further wars which, in turn, would fill our treasuries to bursting and ease the pressure of interest payments, and so on and so forth, till the vicious circle had become the web at the centre of which we were stuck like flies being slowly sucked of all juice.

I sent a message to the treasury, Kuber Bhavan, asking the grand old man, Adinath Mehta, to do me the favour of conferring with me in my private chambers. Adinathji had refined the game of protocol, wherein he had the upper hand but placed himself in the position of a supplicant, to a minor art form. Would I do him the honour of going over in the evening for a game of chess followed by dinner? His wife, happy coincidence, had prepared my favourite sweet, rabadi. It would be a change of atmosphere from the affairs of state and his great-granddaughter, Leelawati, would be delighted to show me how much progress she had made in embroidering the royal insignia for the flag which would accompany me when I led our troops in battle.

The rabadi was a nice touch since Adinathji was only too aware that I had taken a dislike to all sweets made from milk in recent years. But who was I to refuse an invitation from the great Adinathji? Besides, the nine-year-old Leelawati, if she was allowed to be around by the patriarch, would more than compensate for any discomfort

3

suffered in the financier's company. She was a superb mimic, quick-witted, precocious in the extreme, obstinate and a surprisingly shrewd judge of character.

'You don't have to dine early, Your Highness. There's some dispute about whether Mahavirji really enjoined us Jains to eat before sundown but as you know, I like to play it safe. I try to rationalize and tell myself it's good for the digestion, especially at my age. You, of course, have no such problems.'

What would happen if I said, 'Yes indeed, I will eat later' and added as an afterthought, 'After I've had a few drinks'?

Needless to say, nothing would happen. The absolutely unlined face of Adinathji would not furrow or show the slightest sign of discomfiture. Were I to ask for a woman from the sweet and sour Tamarind Lane, he would respond with a 'How thoughtless of me not to have made arrangements,' and proceed to instruct one of the security personnel to send for Kajribai or someone as expensive. After a decent interval of say, forty-five minutes, he would let me know that he was extremely sorry but the carriage had met with an accident and the poor lady had broken her seventh vertebra or cracked open her skull or lost all her teeth.

The food, as usual, was good without being fussy. I marvel at a cuisine which is so circumscribed; no garlic, no onion, no root-vegetables and of course, no game or mutton, fish or fowl, and yet seems to suggest that what it lacks is but superfluous. Daal bati, rotis of cornflour, khatti daal chawal, gatte ki sabji, kanji wadas, and maal pohe. I knew that the meal was not complete and did a good imitation of surprise and delight when Adinathji's wife brought out my favourite sangri beans boiled and then fried in oil and spices. Ghee, I'm aware, is the mark of hospitality but I wish Shrimati Mehta was a little less prodigal with it. I felt bloated as a dead ox which has been water-logged for a week or two but there was no gainsaying the lady of the house when she sent for the dessert, bundi sheera.

We moved to the drawing room and sat down to play. I had the curious feeling that life itself was a game of chess for Adinathji. Every move was planned in advance: the invitation, the bait of Leelawati (I had asked for her twice and was told she was coming

4

but there was no sign of her), the food, the chess. If the whole ritual was familiar, it was because I had played the game often in the past. Skip a step and the game would never end. Adinathji, more than most people, knew that ends are what games are played for.

This was good training for me. When in a hurry, take it easy, breathe deeply, go slow. I knew I was playing well but I also knew that he was playing with me. Perhaps it had something to do with the non-violent creed of his religion. The only battles that he and his kin fought, the only blood they spilt was on the chessboard. Massacres and carnage were not to his taste. He preferred the long, slow, tortuous death. I knew that he had designs on my vazir, which is why he left him alone.

It was ironic how all the kings in India, at least all those I knew, were financed by Adinathji's kinsmen, the Jains. His son-in-law, Sahadevnath, stood surety for the Sultan of Gujarat whom my father was fighting. Ibrahim Lodi in Delhi leaned on Shrimati Adinath Mehta's brother. Adinathji's youngest son had relocated in Malwa and was lending money to the chief money-lender to the throne there. The ironies resonated a little more deviously than that. The Jain mind is an abacus. It sees everything in terms of numbers. Like interest, you earn merit.

You give alms, you earn merit. You feed the poor or the Digambaras, you collect some more merit. Pacifism is a capital investment of the highest order. It's a kind of super-compound interest scheme with an eye on both heaven and earth. Extend the metaphor and it has a foot in the here and now, and the ever-after. Let's look at the latter first. The more merit you earn, the more you are likely to abridge the number of reincarnations you have to go through to reach the kind of enlightened state which gets you to moksha. In the meanwhile, just see how profitable the fruits of non-violence are in this life. You stay pure while someone else, someone like me and my Rajput clan, does the sinning and the killing. While you religiously refrain from bloodying your hands, you lend vast sums of money to finance the mightiest armies at minuscule decimal point percentages which add up to monstrous sums as interest. Whatever the outcome in the killing fields, we warriors protect you. We often die; you live unscathed to finance another war. And here's the best part: thanks to in-laws, nephews, cousins and the whole unbelievable complex of the extended family, your interests are safeguarded in every way, and you emerge substantially richer whoever wins, be it friend or foe.

I seem to have got my knife into Adinathji and his tribe today. Why do I become so unreasonable in his presence? He's never self-righteous and he would just as willingly — perhaps far more happily and with a clearer conscience — put his money into building forts or dams or business ventures as he would into bank-rolling wars. Perhaps it's because I see myself crawling or maybe it's the fact that we need him more than he needs us.

There, he has made his penultimate move. By various feints and manoeuvres and the sacrifice of pawns and horses, he has got my vazir to expose the king. Now for the swift kill. But, of course, the elegant fell stroke is never administered. Having established his Grand Master status once again, he'll now let me win through a transparently bogus mistake. But Leelawati has rushed in, scattered my embattled and besieged king and Adinathji's hordes and jumped straight into my lap. Her knee squashes my left testicle while she beats a tattoo on my chest.

'You didn't even tell me you were coming.' I try to breathe. The universe is out of focus. I cannot tell whether it is my groin that hurts or my chest or throat. 'You must have come to borrow money from great-grandfather. That's why you came furtively and will leave shame-faced.'

Adinathji's waxen face with its butter-soft complexion colours slightly. I am pleased to find traces of blood and humanity there. His great-granddaughter has truly embarrassed him.

'Leave us, you hussy. I never thought I would live to see the day when my own blood would insult the heir-apparent. I will never be able to raise my head in front of you, Your Highness.' Adinathji was not feigning chagrin. He may reserve his opinion of me but his loyalty to the House of Mewar was unqualified.

'Let her be.' I had finally found my voice. 'I asked for you. Twice. They said you were coming but you were playing hard to get like the Id ka chand.'

'Nobody told me. I bet Dada wanted to talk business with you, tell you how short money is these days and raise the interest one seventh of one percent and that's why I was kept in the dark.'

Was it possible for the great Adinathji, the financier of last resort to the prime financiers of this country and others, to squirm after he had already been subjected to the indignity of blushing? Leelawati, you may pound the other testicle to a nice round coin and I'll still owe you one.

'What have you got for me?' Her arms were around my neck.

'What have you got for me?' I was fully recovered.

'Ha, I have something for you even though I didn't know you were coming.' She was up and away and back in a trice with a piece of cloth. It was a red pennant with my ancestor, the Sun-god, embroidered in gold brocade. The eyes, the moustache, the haughty lips, the thirty-six rays, she had got them all to perfection. 'Damn,' she snatched the flag from my hands. 'I wanted to first see what you'd got for me.'

'Whatever it is, it couldn't possibly compare with your gift.'

'Let me be the judge,' Leelawati cut me short. 'Show me.'

I gave her the present I had brought. She undid the silk scarf wrapping and stared in disbelief. 'It's a sundial. Did you make it with your own hands?'

'I wrapped it with my own hands.' I tried to make a joke of it but was conscious of how cold and dull my present was, compared to the effort and affection she had expended on hers.

'Great minds think alike. See, both of us had the same motif in mind. Are those real rubies that mark the hours?'

'You've got to be joking. Just ordinary pieces of broken glass I picked up in the garden.'

That disconcerted her till I smiled.

'They are, they are, you liar.' She hugged me tightly.

Adinathji and I settled the business of the loan quickly. One eighth of one percent less interest than the last time.

*   *   *

It was late when I returned home. I let Mangal stable the horses and slowly climbed up the stairs. Queen Karmavati was waiting for me. A little unusual to see her at this hour and that, too, in my chambers. Normally she would have summoned me to her wing. Was Father all right? I saw the vermillion sindoor on her forehead and the bangles on her hand and relaxed.

'Why are you limping?'

I wasn't. More like shuffling, trying not to agitate the soft swollen rocks at my crotch. 'A little weary, I guess. Could do with some rest.' I thought that was neatly done. A subtle hint to postpone the interview to a more sanguine hour. She was not about to fall for this pathetic ploy.

'How did the meeting with Mehtaji go? And what rate did the two of you decide upon? I bet he took you for a ride and we are all going to have to pay for it.'

No point asking my second mother how she knew that I had gone to Adinathji's and what I had discussed with him. Mother made it a point to know anything and everything that happened in Chittor or outside, if she felt that there was an ultra-remote chance that it might affect her future. Information, she believed, was not everything; it was the only thing. The sad part was that she often lost sight of the fact that it was a means and not an end in itself. If she had it, even if it was useless, she felt in control. There was no point getting mad with her. I have, to this day, not understood why Father didn't appoint his favourite queen head of intelligence.

Queen Karmavati had a complicated network of spies and the most tortuous but fail-safe way of checking whether the information she received was a hundred percent reliable. Add to that, her astounding arsenal of grilling techniques. She was single-minded, uncouth and effective. She would stoop or rise to any means; tease, coax, cajole, threaten, blackmail, broker, barter, whatever it took to elicit some inane, nasty or critical tidbit.

She wasn't likely to leave until she had stripped me of the entire day's details. I was too tired to be perverse and parry her queries. I made a clean breast of everything. There was nothing I could do to assuage her voracious appetite for gossip, hearsay, rumours, omens, insinuations, arcane references and obtuse offences.

'Surely you didn't come at this time of the night for this inconsequential tittle-tattle.'

'Let me be the judge of that. You may be heir apparent but, let me hasten to add, more apparent than heir, at least so far.'

The rivers of maternal affection were in spate tonight. I was the first-born and Queen Karmavati was not about to forgive me that. It is her son Vikramaditya she favours for the crown.

'I came about the nautch girl in your harem. Are you man enough to keep her under control? Or do you want me to do it for you?'

The nautch girl she was referring to had just drawn in a soft sibilant breath of pain and hurt. After years of abuse, my wife had still not got used to the Queen's endearing references to her. She had been standing behind the curtain of coloured glass beads for at least half an hour now, waiting patiently with a silver lota of water. She had spent over a month threading the musical beads. If you stood at a little distance from the curtain, you could see a peacock with a telescoped neck and a very long feathery tail. There was something queer about its left eye. She had inserted the wrong shade of bead there; it looked as if it was walleyed.

I have told her not to wait up for me. Today, yesterday or ever. But she does as she pleases. My wife has a mind of her own. When Mother Karmavati leaves, she'll come out, pour the water into the intricately carved gold tumbler which also serves as the lid of the silver lota, hand it to me, and then remove my shoes.

I can do no wrong in her eyes. That is not quite true. She has a highly-developed ethical sense but I am permitted anything, well, almost. I am certainly forgiven everything. Tantrums, ill humour, physical violence, the crassest of behaviour, politeness, bewilderment, despair, wild and vile swings in moods. What I bid her, she'll do uncomplainingly, except for one thing. I am treated as a child. What I do, say, or think, does not affect her.

'In the last six months alone, I have brought you no less than seventeen proposals.' It is my second mother who cuts my pointless meandering short. 'Even the most conjugally happy princes marry several wives. Look at your father. He loves me dearly but he knows his duty. Marriages are political alliances. They are also a safeguard. They ensure a long line of succession and they prevent any queen from getting too big for her shoes.'

Mother should talk. She's got feet bigger than Chittor, bigger

9

than Rajasthan, bigger than the throne of Delhi, and she's constantly putting them in her mouth. Where was this homily on marriages leading to? I have been married once and I'm sick of it to the pit of my stomach. Does the queen really love my father? I respect him as I respect no other man but then I don't have to sleep with him. How can any woman bear to look at him, let alone make love to him? My wife fainted the first time she saw him. Father pretended that it was the heat or maybe the effect of one of those long and dire fasts young women undertake before marriage. But he is too shrewd not to know that nightmares and the villains in Pataldesh look less terrifying than him. One eye he lost to his brother, an arm to the Lodi of Delhi, the drag in his right foot he owes to Muzaffar of Gujarat, and as to the cuts and nicks and wounds and slashes on his torso, the dummies we use for target practice are more whole than him. There are few men braver or more driven than Father. Perhaps bravery is the ultimate addiction.

'Are you listening, you fool? I can see your eyes floating in sleep but there are matters here that need urgent attention. The nautch girl.'

I was wondering when you were going to come back to my wife, for this nocturnal visit could only be inspired by your daughter-in-law. 'She has cut off our noses. And our izzat. Our illustrious family name is mud. While Chittor burns, your nautch girl continues to dance.'

Anything for a vivid phrase, Mother. No flames here, though; the last ones were quenched over two hundred years ago when Rani Padmini and her women jumped into the johar fires the day Alauddin Khilji captured Chittor. But the phrase which the visitor from across the seas used, I believe, was Emperor Nero sang and fiddled while Rome burnt.

The eunuch, Bruhannada who was a silent party to our conversation had a slight, supercilious smirk on his lips. I would have preferred it if Queen Karmavati had not spoken about these things in front of him; or the eunuch had had the decency to excuse himself while matters of state or the business about my wife was discussed. But that would only amount to deluding myself. There's hardly anything that transpires in the palace and at Chittor that the Queen's eunuch is not privy to. He is clever, devious and I sometimes suspect, he is the Queen's evil genius. His etiquette is impeccable and he is always careful to do the bare minimum of bowing and scraping that protocol says is the Maharaj Kumar's due. I am never less than civil to Bruhannada but there is a coldness in my heart that would rather not utter his name or deal with him.

'Dance? You mean bathroom singing?' I had vowed not to utter a word but the queen always succeeds in subverting my silent resolves.

'The tawaif has graduated from mere singing to dancing. She was swirling on the first floor of the Tridev Mandir while the crowds, eunuches, princes, servants, maids, princesses and queens watched from below. A fine view from under the latticed balustrade as her skirts rose and billowed. A riveting sight even for weary eyes like mine.'

The Tridev Mandir. My grandfather Raimul built it for the family when he beat the forces of the Hatyara Uda and was crowned. One of my favourite temples. Nothing elaborate. Delicately but not excessively carved. Serene. Private. It has a terraced structure. Eklingji Shiva on the ground floor, the Flautist on the first and the Sun-god on the second.

'I'll wager my brother Vikramaditya had ring-side seats.'

'Leave him out of this. He is not the issue. The tawaif is. Besides, if his wife was dancing, you too would have been there gaping.'

'She's not even fourteen yet.'

'What difference does her age make? The older you men get, the younger you want your pleasures. Look at your uncles. They want girls before they reach puberty.'

Was this true? Would I too end up like them?

'Get rid of her before she makes our family the laughing stock of Rajasthan.'

        ✳   ✳   ✳

She placed my foot on her knee to remove my mojari. I raised it and lifted her face up. She did not withdraw her eyes.

'Did you? Did you actually dance?'

'I don't remember.'

11

My foot slammed into her face. It was not the hardest of blows but it knocked her down. The lota rolled over several times before it clattered to a halt. Her lower lip was cut open, the blood had stained her blouse, the water from the lota had wet the back of her petticoat. She took my foot in her hands again, disengaged the shoe and brought my toe to her left eye first and then let it touch her right eye. I was her lord and master and she would not do me out of acts of obeisance. She did not ask why or wherefore, nor look aggrieved or wipe the blood from her lip. She was unconcerned whether I kicked her again or not.

I must have groaned.

'Are you hurt?' she asked me and wiped my brow. I winced at the touch of her hand. Was ever a human hand so soothing? I could have wrenched her arm from her shoulder and flung it out of the fort. She picked up the lota, went out, filled it up and came back. She began to unbutton my duglo. I strode out in a dudgeon but was sure that she hadn't noticed my theatrical exit.

I went to the stables and got the syce who was asleep to saddle Befikir. Mangal hurried after me. He looked puzzled and unsure of himself. Perhaps my sudden departures and swings of mood were taking their toll of him too. But his anxieties lay in another direction.

'What should I do with her?' he asked softly.

I gaped at his presumption. I may be livid with her but she was my wife. How dare he concern himself with her. 'Who are you talking about?' I asked brusquely.

'The woman whom you saw in court the other day.'

'Which woman? Can't she wait till Thursday for me to look into her case?'

'It's the woman whose husband was complaining that she had been faithless.' He was still talking in conspiratorial tones.

'I didn't ask for her.'

'I know but I thought Your Highness might perhaps enjoy a new face.'

'Did she want to come?' That was the trouble with trusted old retainers. They think they know your mind better than you.

'Gladly.'

'And what about her husband? What if he cites me as the

co-respondent in the case?'

'He'll be away all night. He's being tested at Rasikabai's.'

'You are a clever fox, Mangal, but I hope not too clever by half. What if she's promiscuous and has some disease?'

'Trust me, Highness.'

'What does that mean? Like Shabari, have you tasted the fruit before your master?'

'The Lord be praised. I thought you had given up wit and smiling altogether.'

'You haven't answered my question.'

'She's a virgin.'

'Oh no, not a virgin please.' He caught the dismay in my face and interpreted it as a moral scruple.

'And in a hurry to lose her innocence. I have left her in the Chandra Mahal.'

'Have her sent to the palace.' Mangal looked as if I had singed him with a hot iron rod.

'My prince, ghanikhama, but isn't that going too far?'

'You heard me.' At least this one wasn't a dancing girl like the one at home. 'What's her name?'

'Sunheria.'

The syce had gone back to sleep. I kicked him, not too hard. He woke up and looked bewildered. The timekeeper's bell tolled for midnight. The sentry called out darkly, 'Jagte raho.'

'Have you saddled her yet or not?'

'I have, my Lord.'

'Then what are you waiting for? Hold her steady.'

Mangal caught up with me in a minute; and the two of us rode out of the fort. The sentry at the Suraj Pol would not allow us to pass until I gave him the password. Since last year, we've initiated the system of leaving a different password for every gate to tighten security. Too many mercenaries and spies doing the rounds these days. Must pull up the sentries at the other three pols we passed. Should have seen the smirks on their faces. I'm sure they think we are going to ride to the next town for a night of debauchery.

The Ganga may be a holier river, it certainly is mightier but it is not my river. The Gambhiree is my mother and my memory.

13

As she is Chittor's mother and memory. They bathed me with her waters when I was born and, God willing, they will wash me with her before placing me on the pyre. She is privy to all my doings, my innermost thoughts and the dilemma that wracks my soul. She is not judgmental and she has no answers. Her role is to witness all but she may not interfere. Perhaps she has opinions, even strong views, but she holds her tongue forever. Where do songs go when you cease to hear them? Where does the turbulence of the air disappear after thousands of birds flap their wings homeward at eventide? Where are the cries of the Rajput women who spatter their red palm prints on the wall and leap into the flames of johar? Where is my childhood, my catapult, my broken slate, my first parrot, my youth and first sin and all those that followed, where is my old age and the first time I saw the woman from Merta? Ask Gambhiree. She knows it all. We are all safe because Gambhiree will keep her secrets. She is, as her name suggests, deep and sombre and meditative.

There is a mist on the river. The air is stifling, the moon is marooned in dark, sinister clouds. I take off my clothes, say my prayer and slip into Gambhiree. The water is black and cold. I sink in it like a stone. I let go. I float up. The waters swish around me. The strands of my muscles uncoil and my thoughts unravel. Black oblivion runs through my veins. Beware the river tonight. The tall ebony grasses sway sinuously and ensnare my feet. They call to me to come and forget the world above. Yama is abroad on his buffalo tonight. The river is his sister Yami. She is the temptress Death. Who can say no to Yami? Even her brother lies with her.

Flimsy phantoms rise to meet me. The watery faces of my ancestors scream soundlessly, their fluid octopus hands stretch and coil around me. Bappa Rawal, Rana Hameer, Rani Padmini, Hatyara, they all have urgent business with me but I can no longer lip-read their cacophony of demands. Perhaps if I sink deeper into the underworld, I'll be able to help them.

Somebody's pulling me up against my wishes. The gentleness of the undertow of the currents is deceptive. It's going to kill me softly, sucking me down a spiral vortex. I can hear Mangal calling my name now. I do not respond. The river is my quietus and I have no intention of surfacing again. Mangal's cries become more urgent and desperate. I wish he would leave me alone. He has spotted me and is forcing me up. It's raining heavily. The raindrops pinch the skin of the river in a million places. My skin smarts as they pierce it and go right through. I am awake. Mangal calls out my name as if I had died. The water laps gently over me. I am exorcised of my demons. The moon is out and Gambhiree is a slow silver enchantress.

As Mangal and I ride back, I have no memory of swimming in the river. My body is the ebb and rise of black water.

The lights are on in my palace when I return. It's like Diwali. She is awake. She's wearing a screeching yellow silk ghagra with a pink chunni. Her blouse is the green of first grass. She has dressed Sunheria, the ancient dhobi's wife, in new red brocade clothes and made her up to look like a bride.

Chapter 2

$\mathcal{I}$t's such an elementary rule, I wonder why almost nobody follows it. If you want to find out how a department's functioning or how the work's progressing on a project, go unannounced. It has nothing to do with catching people with their pants down or with their hands in the till. It's simply that that's the only way you can see them as they are, normal people. Normally efficient or normally sloppy. Give them notice and they'll get out the red carpet and put on a big show. But if all you want is to feel important, call them over. It is less trouble; your managers or ministers will be only too happy to take the day off and doctor the facts efficiently and you'll never have to deal with unpleasant or intractable problems ever again. Sycophants are a king's first line of defence. They protect him from the truth and build a fine mesh around him which filters all information. It's not just that bad news stays out. Often good news and good people too are disallowed entry. Because what you hear and see is what they want you to hear and see. When the end comes and the chair is pulled from under you, take heart, your free fall will be swift and irreversible.

The problem, of course, is how to keep all your channels of information open without being overwhelmed by them. Is there any way to institutionalize sources of criticism? But even if there was, it wouldn't help much because human beings are so adept at ignoring any point of view or opinion we don't care for. Do I have any other ideas on the subject? None whatsoever, except one small, unhelpful hint. Nobody can help you keep your communication systems open. You've got to work at them yourself, reach out and most of all, listen.

I was at the Institute of Advanced Military Tactics and Strategy before the sun was up. One of Father's oldest and most loyal followers is in charge of the place. Jai Simha Balech had known my father when he was in hiding and incognito, a long time before he became king. After ascending the throne, Father bestowed twenty villages on Jai Simha and gave him the title of Rawat.

'Your Highness, what a surprise.' The Rawat looked ill at ease. I had no reason to doubt Jai Simha's integrity or loyalty. I was paying a routine visit and he had no cause for alarm or discomfiture.

'I thought I would come and see how our future commanders and strategists are doing.' I was not being entirely truthful. The Rawat's approach to military tactics was far too conservative for my liking. Besides, I was keen to enlarge the scope of the Institute to encompass the latest technologies. I had heard vague rumours of advances made by the Arabs, Turks and Portuguese in war materials and I wished to enlist the Rawat's support in the matter before broaching the subject with Father.

We watched the field exercises first and then sat in on a class by Shafi Khan on classic attack formations. It was a lucid talk with ample diagrams and case-studies. When we were about to leave, I asked Shafi Khan if he conducted any courses on the techniques and mechanics of retreat. The class thought my query uproariously funny and guffawed while the teacher, I could see, had taken umbrage, thinking that my remark was a reflection on his teaching.

'I did not pose that question as comic relief. In the business of war, you may be surprised to learn, one party wins and the other loses. If the art of retreat is studied scientifically, you'll not only reduce loss of life dramatically, you may also live to fight another war.'

The teacher was mollified and the students were subdued. They may not have been enamoured by the prospect but a discussion on orderly and tactical retreat was a new idea as much to the instructor as to his pupils.

I could not fathom the cause of Jai Simha's stubborn uncommunicativeness. Everything in the Institute was in order. I thought it wise to ignore his taciturnity and broach the issues which were on my mind as we went back to his office. But the dam cracked before that. It was a trickle, the man's voice a mere whisper, but

I knew that something was terribly wrong.

'Your Highness, I was coming to see you later this morning.'

'I trust you haven't changed your mind and will allow me to reciprocate your hospitality. Will you join me for lunch?'

'That is kind, very kind of you, but I cannot.'

His body trembled and when I put my hand on his back, he shook his head from side to side. I could feel the intensity of his distress but in Father's absence, I am the court of final appeal. And I will not make a move, lend a solicitous ear or give a helping hand till the aggrieved party sees fit to ask me to intercede.

'I will leave instructions in my office to let you in even if I am busy.'

*   *   *

It was Thursday again. Pyarelal, the dhobi, was first in line today. There were bags under his eyes but there was also triumph in them. His wife, Sunheria, was standing a little behind him. She would not look at me. Did she hate me? Would she find it in her heart to forgive me? And yet it was to this white-haired, toothless and turbaned ruin of a husband that my heart responded. He had had six wives and five had borne him sons and daughters who had innumerable grandchildren. Some of the wives had died, others had left him. He had taken on a seventh and was now eaten through with suspicion and the fear of defeat. Who should know a faithless wife better than I?

'Master, Your Highness, I am a man.' His voice was high-pitched and accompanied by a thin wheeze. It was obvious his bronchitis was never going to leave him. 'I have done as you had bidden me and proved my manhood.'

'Yes, it is true that you are a man, Pyarelal. Rasikabai vouches for that. What do you wish to do now?'

'That proves beyond the shadow of a doubt that my wife is guilty, doesn't it?'

'Guilty of what?'

'Of cheating on me, what else?'

'Who is the co-respondent?'

'How would I know? Ask her.'

'Is it possible that she has a lover and is yet a virgin?'

'What do you take me for, a fool? She is no virgin, that's for sure.'

'How do you know?'

'Don't make me laugh. I am her husband, aren't I?'

'Why don't you drop the case, Pyarelal? Your wife's faithful to you, which is why she's a virgin.'

'What are you trying to suggest, Highness? That I'm impotent? Did I not prove my manhood with Rasikabai?'

'You did. You most certainly did. But it took a while, the whole night as a matter of fact and much coaxing, I believe. Rasikabai tried every trick in her book and you know she wrote the book, if all the reports are to be believed. I grant you there's a flame, however feeble, burning in you but your wife's too inexperienced to stoke it.'

Pyarelal was crestfallen but he was not about to give up.

'I'm telling you she has a lover. The night I was with Rasikabai, she was gone the whole night.'

'Wherever she was last Monday, Rasikabai examined her yesterday and declared her a virgin.'

'She has a lover. I know it in my bones.'

'Find him,' I told him, 'and we'll prescribe the harshest punishment under the law for him.'

Pyarelal finally went home. Virgin or no virgin, he knew his wife was cheating on him.

* * *

I had kept the afternoon free for Sahasmal, the head of city-planning. I had heard they were using ceramic channels for aqueducts in the kingdom of Vijayanagar and wanted to ask him why we couldn't adopt the same system. The second problem was the drains. The roads in Chittor were fine in summer and winter but come the monsoons, the only way to be happy was to become a buffalo. The place was full of puddles and ditches. Swarms of mosquitoes hung above one's head like a sizzling black muslin turban. The roads, at least, were a seasonal problem. The drains, unfortunately, were a nuisance round the year. Nuisance is a particularly inadequate and

19

imprecise word in this context. They were a disaster.

For some bizarre reason, all my ancestors, great and small, could not see or think straight when they discussed the population problem in our kingdom. They always ascribed it to the wars that we were forever fighting. War certainly decimates us (the dead are nothing compared to the maimed, crippled and disfigured in every warrior family, not to mention the hundreds begging for alms on every street, lane and by-lane), but it is endemic and epidemic disease which wipes out a quarter or half of our population every few years.

Maybe nobody dwells upon the subject of sewers because it is an untouchable matter. But if we don't pay heed today and bring the weight of both technology and the royal imprimatur to bear upon the problem, we are all going to be awash in our excrement and sewage.

The town-planner, Sahasmal himself looked a little abashed and was making genteel squeamish noises and wondering why we didn't discuss architectural plans for a new complex of marble temples of the order found in Ranakpur or a new Victory Tower that would be twice as tall as the one that the great Rana Kumbha had built. After all, Father's victories are no less than my great grandfather's. I told him that they were excellent ideas and I was sure that he could find the finances for these projects from the generous denizens of our city as well as from the wealthy and far-flung citizens of Mewar, but that as far as the exchequer was concerned, it would stick to more mundane matters like discharge and outlet systems.

I think he got the drift and said he would look for the maps of the city's drainage network, when Jai Simha Balech was announced. I excused the town-planner and asked him if he would find six that evening convenient to examine the maps. His jaw dropped in dismay and he started mumbling about the problem of locating such old documents. Besides, he wasn't even sure if any such maps existed.

'Good, that's settled then. Six o'clock sharp.' I wished him good day.

*   *   *

Jai Simha Balech was in better control of his emotions. I had a little difficulty keeping an opaque face. While I paid close attention to what he had to impart — how would I not, I could hear the rumblings of a crisis brewing — I resolved to sit in front of the mirror every day and practise the composure of the dead while I went through a litany of the most vicious scandals, disasters, setbacks and humiliations I could invent or perhaps merely recount from my own rich and variegated experience in these matters.

'Your Highness will recall that Prince Vikramaditya visited my family five weeks ago. We were greatly honoured and though I was unable to look after him personally because of my commitments at the Institute, my family felt privileged and went out of the way to make him feel welcome. He returned to Chittor about a week ago.'

Yes, I was aware of that. Since then he had not only had the pleasure of peering under my wife's delirious petticoat, he had composed doggerel of such scatalogical merriment that the whole town was gyrating to it.

'He came over personally to the school and thanked me in the warmest terms. He felt invigorated by the country air and by all the hunting and riding that he had done with my four sons. "You must come again. Soon," I told him. "I intend to, Uncle, I intend to," he said and left. Almost on his heels, I am sure they crossed each other, my two eldest sons rode over to Chittor.'

Balech stopped. I closed my eyes for the punch line. It did not come.

'Highness, I do not know how to proceed.'

I kept my eyes closed. This is good training for a future king. I willed myself not to conjecture. Flow with the tide, hold your tongue, relax every muscle in every part of your body. Go dead, go dead. Never show surprise or any other emotion.

'I beg your forgiveness if what I tell you now gives offence to your ears. But tell it I must. You are aware that we run a stud farm in our estates which the Rana, your father, bequeathed to me for my loyalty many years ago. By the grace of Shri Eklingji, the stud farm has done well. We supply horses to the army and to the gentry. Your own Befikir is from one of our most prized lines.

'A year and a half ago, the Solankis of Godwar reserved a filly called Kali Bijlee. She had come of age and we were about to dispatch her to the Solankis when Prince Vikramaditya espied her. She's a fine mare, one of the finest we've bred. The Prince wanted her. My sons offered him any horse on the farm but this one, since it had already been sold to someone else. The Prince graciously declined the offer.

'After he left, my sons discovered that Kali Bijlee was missing and so were nine other horses.'

I had seen my brother with the new horse. A bit too flashy and high-strung for my liking but a beauty if I have ever seen one.

He was playing some game he had learnt recently, where you hit a puck with a wooden stick while riding horseback, when I first saw her.

'Where did you get her?'

'Picked her up at a horse fair in Ajmer from a Pathan. Like her?'

'Must have cost you an arm and a leg. Make it two arms and two legs.'

'It's not the money which matters, it's the pleasure of riding such a fine, highly pedigreed creature, brother. But what would you know of pleasure?'

He had a point there but I was not sure how he had raised the monies to buy her. He was overextended as it was and in debt to almost everybody in the family, including, believe it or not, to me. Well, there was always his mother, Queen Karmavati. She had her sources, not to mention her own private cache, hidden, god knows where.

'That is not all. The night before he left, he bribed my horse-breaker who's reputed to be the finest in the country; even better than the one in the service of the Emperor in Delhi. I cannot trace him but suspect that he and his family are under the Prince's protection.'

I didn't have to will myself to be dead. I was numb and cold. Father, and I, and I think almost anybody who's had anything to do with Vikramaditya know that he is not a man who's waiting for trouble to happen. He makes it happen. We all know what to expect and yet none of us can keep pace with my brother's inventive ways.

'I want the mare back. As to the horse-breaker and his wife, I'm sure you'll do the just thing.'

Just thing, just thing. Just the thing I need. Do I know what is the just thing? Leave alone for anybody else, for myself? And even if I did, how do I go about getting the just thing done?

'Jai Simhaji, why did it take you close to a week to report the matter to me?'

He hesitated. 'If I had had my way I wouldn't be here today either. I went to Adinathji, then took the matter to the Pradhan Mantri. They commiserated with me but hinted that I would be better off if I forgot the whole business.'

I wondered if Jai Simha Balech would have taken up the matter with Father if he had been around instead of me.

*   *   *

I went to see Vikramaditya. There was no point summoning him. He might refuse to come. I could at least spare myself that humiliation.

'I urge you to return Kali Bijlee to Jai Simha Balech immediately,' I saw no reason to beat about the bush, 'and he'll not file criminal charges against you for theft.'

'Who's Kali Bijlee?'

'The horse that you stole from Jai Simha Balech's stud farm.'

'My horse is called Kajal and I bought it from a Pathan near Ajmer.'

'You have papers to prove the purchase of the animal?'

'Sure. But I threw them away.'

'Any witnesses?'

'It's not a wife I bought, just a horse.'

'Will you give the mare back to Rawat Balech?'

'No, I will not.'

'Do you realize the consequences of this? The Rawat is a friend of Father's and one of his trusted lieutenants. Do you want to alienate him and his clan for a mere horse? The mare was sold to Godwar's Solanki who's fighting on our side against the Sultan of Gujarat. Do you have the faintest inkling of the political

23

repercussions of your actions?'

My tongue tasted like dry ash. What an ass I was to try to reason with my brother.

'The horse is mine. And even if it wasn't, no Rao, Rawat or Raja for that matter could take it from me. Pusillanimity is your second name, brother, but I am the King's son. I will take what I want.' He smiled. No, he's incapable of that; he leered. 'Including the throne.'

*   *   *

I went back to my office and got hold of Mangal.

'Can you find out where Prince Vikramaditya's new mare is? If you can locate her, tell me how many men are guarding her. I know you don't have to be told this but can you do it without raising suspicion?'

I knew it was pointless but I recalled that ancient master states-man, Kautilya's advice. 'Never dismiss the obvious because it is obvious. Make a checklist and go over it point by point meticu-lously.'

I sat down quietly and wrote down three alternate scenarios: 1. We do not find Kali Bijlee. 2. We find her and confiscate her. And 3. We find her but cannot take possession of her. Under each of the three alternatives, I made a list of possible actions to be undertaken. It took me the best part of an hour to make corrections and additions and shuffle some of the points around. At the end of the list, I wrote in a bold hand: Time is of the essence. I will think things through. Act swiftly. But within the framework of the law.

Writing something down doesn't make it happen, but at least you know what you expect of yourself.

'She's not there and the syce, stable-keeper and anybody con-nected with the mare won't talk.'

'Post two of your people to watch Prince Vikramaditya's move-ments. I want to know who visits him and for how long. If he goes out of the house I want to be told on the instant. Inform the Prime Minister, the Chancellor and the Home Minister that there will be a Security Council meeting at nine tonight at my office. Ask the

24

captain of the guard to report here at the same time and await my instructions. Tell Rawat Jai Simha Balech that we will require his presence at ten past nine. Go. A crisis is not the time to feel self-important. You'll only end up giving the game away.'

I pored over the drainage network with the town planner. My interest in sewage must have been contagious. Instead of plumbing and excrement and dirty water, he began to see it as a problem. He was going to be all right now. He was already looking for the other part of the problem: the solution.

I was interrupted twice, both times by Mangal who took me aside into the antechamber. My brother Vikramaditya was conferring with his three closest cronies, Fateh Simha, Sajjad Hussein and Mahesh Gaur. The second message was that Sajjad Hussein had left Vikramaditya's residence in a hurry.

'If Sajjad Hussein leaves the fort, he is to be intercepted after he has crossed the Gambhiree, not before. I repeat, not before. Let your men make sure that this is done when no marriage party or nautanki troupe is in the vicinity. Sajjad may have an escort. Ensure that our men are not outnumbered. Strip Sajjad and dispossess him of all missives and monies. Incarcerate him and his men in Kumbhalgarh fort. You are not to leave Chittor, Mangal, or lead your men on any forays. You'll only co-ordinate my instructions, and see that they are carried out to the letter.'

The town planner was in a state of elation. I asked him to submit his plans for rehauling, extending or totally replacing the old sewage system in a phased manner and to write a report on costs and raising funds for the project either in terms of a new water tax or whatever optimal scheme he could devise. I had a quick bath, changed and composed my mind.

Adinathji was the first to arrive. If he had an inkling of what the emergency session was for, he had no intention of sharing it with me or probing me. All in good time. It was odd how much I learnt from this man whom I had no reason to dislike and yet wasn't overly fond of. His virtue was not that he held his tongue but that he listened. It was not a passive listening. I suspected that

25

our Prime Minister Pooranmalji did that. He too heard people out, but with a closed mind. Adinathji, on the other hand, notwithstanding his cold fish expression, would take his time weighing the pros and cons, but if he found reason in what he heard, would not think it a matter of honour to stick to his opinion merely because it happened to be his or because it was the received wisdom on a subject.

'What, what is all this ado about? Whatever it is, couldn't it be put off till the morning?' My uncle Lakshman Simhaji couldn't wait for the door to close before putting me on the mat. As an afterthought, Lakshman Simhaji added, 'Your Highness.'

The Home Minister was a large man gone to fat. I remember him from the days when I was a child. He was trim and tall and in a perpetual rush. He was one of our best commanders and had been deeply offended when Father placed him in charge of the Home portfolio.

'Shall I ask our womenfolk to lead the troops if, God forbid, Chittor is besieged when we are out fighting elsewhere?' Father had asked him. 'Besides, even when I'm at home, I still need someone I trust to take care of internal security.'

Lakshman Simhaji had grunted and his nostrils had flared. He had huffed and puffed as he was doing now but for very different reasons. He had become so bulky after he was forced to abandon the rigours of a soldier's life that he needed someone to ease him down on a seat and to lift him up. He spoke fast and that, combined with his breathlessness, made it difficult to follow him.

'Do you expect me to rest my butt on a seat higher than yours?' I had got Mangal to pile four mattresses on top of each other to make things easy for him. 'I may be old and fat and fart ceaselessly but my brains have not been addled to the point where I'll insult the Maharaj Kumar.'

I was being merely selfish, nothing more. The last time Mangal and I had to raise him, the two of us had almost keeled over.

'You are like my father, Uncle. It makes no difference if I sit at your feet.'

'Like, yes. But not an iota beyond that. Hold on to your seat and your dignity, Maharaj Kumar. Only then can the stars and the sun keep their places in the heavens.'

'I see that the Home Minister is already waxing eloquent,' Prime Minister Pooranmalji had slipped in without any one of us realizing it. Now here was an enigma. Not sinister but stealthy. Urbane, suave and utterly bereft of emotion. A very advanced instinct for survival. Not just for himself but for Mewar. I think he deliberately promotes the impression that he cannot be trusted. That way he is able to keep his distance and his options open.

'May you live long, Your Highness and may my life be added to yours.' I bent my head slightly to accept the Pradhan Mantri's benediction. We have two prime ministers among us Suryavanshis, the descendants of the Sun-god. Father is a Diwan or prime minister to Eklingji, the five-headed Shiva who is our family-deity and whose kin and representative he is on earth. Pooranmalji who had just entered is PM to the Rana, my father.

'I will dispense with small talk and come straight to the point. I may have acted in haste in calling this meeting of the Security Council. If it proves to be so, I apologise to you in advance. But I wanted time and secrecy on our side. In the first part of our session, we sit as the court of final resort in Mewar. I myself will take minutes of the proceedings.'

'Who, who is the plaintiff?' Lakshman Simhaji interjected. 'And what, what is the offence?'

'Call Jai Simha Balech.'

Neither Adinathji nor the Prime Minister betrayed the slightest trace of foreknowledge of the Balech affair. How would they react now that matters were about to come into the open, I wondered. Mangal showed Jai Simha Balech in. The Rawat looked cowed down. He had obviously not expected such a high-powered reception.

'Rawat Jai Simha Balech,' for once Uncle Lakshman Simha spoke without stumbling, 'you stand before the highest court of the land. Speak now or hold your tongue for evermore. If you decide to speak, then speak the truth. For if you fail to do so, you could not only lose your life but the state will also dispossess both you and your children of all estates, land, property and titles.'

The Rawat had the look of a trapped animal. He had not courted

27

trouble. Trouble had been visited upon him. Whatever the outcome, he knew he would be the loser. If he spoke up now, we would resent him for forcing our hand. The Rana who had once been his companion would grow distant. If he held his tongue, he would earn the enmity of the Solanki of Godwar. Worse, he would dishonour his clan and never be able to face his children. When you deal with naked power from an inferior position, perspectives get distorted. He was the aggrieved party and yet he felt guilty and would continue to do so all his life.

He spoke quietly. He did not leave anything out. When he had finished, he looked at no one in particular and said, 'I want justice done regardless of the rank and position of the accused.'

I knew we had arrived at the trickiest part of the session. I had been waiting for this moment. If I did not wrest the initiative now, Adinathji and Pradhan Pooranmal would leave me holding the bag. Lakshman Simhaji was a decent man but naive in matters of intangible nuances and subtle statecraft and he would, willy-nilly, follow their lead.

'Thank you, Jai Simhaji. Will you wait in the antechamber while we confer?' When he left, I briefed the court about my conversation with Vikramaditya.

'Are you sure that the mare you saw was Kali Bijlee?' The Pradhan Mantri's strategy, as I had expected, was to pick holes in the evidence till it became too shaky to prosecute the prince.

'No, I am not. At the same time he admitted that he had not bought the horse he called Kajal at Chittor. Besides, the horse he claimed to have bought would have cost a king's ransom.'

'I'm sure the Rana's son can afford that, wouldn't you say so?' Pooranmalji turned towards the Finance Minister. Adinathji smiled faintly but declined to comment on that rhetorical remark.

'Adinathji, is it true that my brother has been heavily in debt to your house for some months now?' It was my turn to pin him down to some concrete information.

'I wouldn't say heavily. A little, yes.'

'Has he applied to you for a loan recently?'

'No.'

'Had he done so, would you have lent him the money?'

28

'I cannot give an opinion on a conjecture.'

'Is it not true that when his IOUs came due, you not only refused to extend them but also told him that you would not give him any leeway in the matter of interest payments?'

Adinathji shifted just a little and considered his answer for almost a minute. 'Yes, that is true.'

'What, what has all this got to do with the case in hand?' Lakshman Simha asked impatiently.

'Almost nothing. I'm just trying to plug all the alleys and byways down which we can spend the rest of the night giving ourselves a way out of not confronting the issue at hand.' I was treading dangerous ground. Both the Pradhan Mantri and Adinathji were watching me carefully to see when I would overstep myself and move beyond the vigorous prosecution of the case into personal hostilities. 'And is it true that Prince Vikramaditya has not been able to raise the funds to pay even your interest?'

'He has not paid it yet. Whether he was unable to find the money, I do not know.'

'I do not know whether His Majesty, Rana Sanga, will take another month, two months or a year to return. You, as well as I, have been put in charge in his absence with the express purpose of not allowing affairs of the state to come to a standstill. I do not need to stress the seriousness of the charges the Rawat has brought. I would, however, like to point out that if there are other ramifications to this case beyond that of a simple but egregious theft, then the gravity of the offence as well as the responsibility placed upon us may be more substantial than we are, at first glance, willing to grant.'

I had gone to orotund lengths to avoid being precise while hinting at complexities about which I was, like them, clueless. But even if the arrow had been shot at nowhere in particular, it had certainly found its mark.

'Pooranmalji, what course of action do you and the other elders suggest?' Lakshman Simhaji burst in where the two foremost advocates of caution in Chittor feared to venture. 'Is there any option apart from summoning Prince Vikramaditya?'

There was a pause before Pooranmalji spoke. 'I was thinking more along the lines of sleeping over the problem tonight and then

29

meeting again tomorrow.'

'That would successfully subvert the purpose of holding this court at night so that we avoid undue publicity. And thereby also lose the great advantage of having time on our side.' I was putting up a good fight but I knew I was no match for Pooranmalji.

'And what if,' Pooranmalji smiled urbanely, 'what if there is a simple explanation to everything that sounds so full of sinister portent?'

The Home Minister rose to the bait but his hard commonsense did not get caught in the hook. 'Why sir, that is an outcome and a mercy that all of us are even now praying for.'

'I think we are all agreed then that the Captain of the Imperial Guard along with a select band of lieutenants should fetch Prince Vikramaditya,' that was the redoubtable Adinathji at his best. Think. And then think again. If you decide to act, no halfway measures. Act with the full force at your command.

I had hoped that Mangal would interrupt us with some news of Sajjad Hussein. I looked at his face when he entered now and realized that I had either gone on a wild goose chase or Vikramaditya was playing a more devious game than I imagined.

'Show the Captain of the Guard in.'

'Doesn't he have to be sent for?' Lakshman Simhaji asked a little puzzled.

'His Highness, the Maharaj Kumar took the precaution of having him on hand in case of just such an exigency.' Pooranmalji was loath to let me go that easily.

'Go silently and inconspicuously. Take enough guards to overcome resistance, if any, from His Highness, Prince Vikramaditya or his personal guard. You are to produce him before us. Do not use force unless necessary. Give him this warrant and bring him back.' The Captain of the Guard didn't bat an eyelid when I mentioned Vikramaditya. I wondered what kind of a moral dilemma he was trying to resolve in his own mind while keeping a straight, expressionless face. He was the head of the elite guard trained for one purpose and one purpose alone: to safeguard His Majesty and his family. What if Queen Karmavati told him that he would be court-martialled for endangering, instead of protecting, His Majesty's son who may very likely be the next Rana?' 'Take the Prince,' I could hear her saying with formidable imperiousness, 'yes, take him. But be warned, only on pain of death.'

The old men were yawning away by now. Had to keep them going till they got their second wind. Mangal had arranged for refreshments and light drinks. The operative word was light. I didn't want the food to sit like dead weight in their bellies and put them to sleep. I had not realized how tense I was until the food arrived. I couldn't bear to look at it. 'The mind must have the final say and sway over the body and not the other way round,' I could hear my yoga teacher telling me softly. 'Let there be no doubt in anyone's mind about who's the master and who the servant.' I forced myself to eat. I envied my uncle, Lakshman Simhaji, not because he ate heartily and picked up either his left or right buttock to allow for a smooth passage when he broke wind, but because he alone out of the four of us, was not exercised by the implications of what we were doing. Of course there would be consequences, maybe there would be hell to pay but that is the nature of action and authority and responsibility, and nothing more. Cast a stone in the pond, there were bound to be ripples.

*   *   *

Vikramaditya strode in. My heart missed a beat when I saw the manacles around his wrists.

'We had no alternative, Your Highness. His Highness Prince Vikramaditya resisted all our pleas to bring him here.'

Before the captain had finished Vikramaditya had come to the point.

'You old flatulent dogs, how dare you bring me here under duress? I promise you, you'll pay, each one of you will pay a price so heavy you'll rue the day you were born. And as for you, Prince aspiring, with your obsession for the letter of the law, for spirit you have none, I will reserve a special place in my heart for you. Every minute of my waking hours, I will invent a new and more deadly torture for you. Consider your life and career over. The rack will be sheer pleasure compared to what I'll concoct for you.'

'If you assure us that you will conduct yourself with decorum and uphold the dignity of this court, I'll ask the Captain to remove your handcuffs.' I had no intention of responding to his elaborate threat. 'If you so much as swear once more or misbehave in any other fashion, we'll be forced to chain and handcuff you again. What will it be?'

'What court are you talking about? This sad circus with three superannuated clowns and a spineless prince whose wife is a common nautanki girl? Look after your own affairs, heir-aspirant, instead of pretending to look after the business of the state. I have a suggestion for you. That wife of yours, the whole city knows, dances for free. Why not become her pimp? That way you'll have something more worthwhile to do with your time and you'll even earn some money.'

I thought I had scraped the bottom of the barrel when I was in the bath trying to figure out the full spectrum of my brother's repertory of insults, taunts and jibes. I had, of course, missed the obvious. He could twist an innocent remark, an awkward or embarrassing moment in childhood into a lifelong source of scorn and jeer. He was a master of puns, innuendoes and double meaning and would zero in on friend or foe alike when his guard was down and he least expected it. It didn't matter that his humour was always of the lowest order or that it mimicked and satirized physical tics, frailties and handicaps. If you were his victim, he drew blood and had you in tears and rubbed salt and chillies into your wounds by pointing out that you had no sense of humour and fun.

I looked at him. What a handsome head my brother had. He had piercing eyes and straight hair that sat in place until he was mad at something or laughing and threw his head back. Then it rose like a fisherman's black net and fell all over his face till he ran his hand over it and put it back in place. He is tall, a good two inches taller than I am — and I'm not exactly short at six feet and one inch — and even the most dishevelled and disreputable clothes only enhance his casual and offhand charm. When we were children, he was my favourite brother and even today I feel the loss of our friendship.

He had fixed his eyes on Pooranmalji and paused for effect. I'm familiar with my brother's mannerisms and bag of tricks. He was about to sow consternation and doubt in the mind of the court.

'Take heed all ye who sit in judgement here,' he had selected a low, velvet smooth and dark timbre from his wide range of voices, 'take heed that I do not recognize this court for there is no court in this kingdom nor anywhere upon earth which is fit to try me. I am a Prince, the Rana's son. Remove my handcuffs and let me go in peace. Because if you do not, you'll be responsible for the chaos and anarchy that will visit our land.'

There was an unholy silence for a minute and more. Then the Pradhan spoke. 'Remove his handcuffs.' Vikramaditya looked triumphant and made ready to go as Mangal unlocked the cuffs. 'Sit down, Prince. Not a word from you now till you are spoken to. Fetch Rawat Jai Simha Balech.'

Laxman Simhaji read out the charges.

'How plead you, Prince Vikramaditya?'

'I refuse to answer that question except to say that one cannot steal from one's own house. All the Raos and Rawats and Rajas in our kingdom are so by our decree and our pleasure. There is only one authority above us. That is Shri Eklingji whose vice-regents we are on earth. To him alone are we accountable.'

I was in the direct line of descent and would one day, God willing, be absolute monarch because my father was the Diwan of the god Eklingji. But this is the crux and paradox of Eklingji's legacy. We are his representatives on earth. Were he to appear in person tomorrow and demand the kingdom, we would have to hand it to him because we hold it in trust for him. Whereas the lands that we give to the nobles and loyal citizens are gifts. The only way we can take them back is if they misbehave or are disloyal or rebel against Mewar. Then alone does the law allow us to annex their lands by force. At least that is my reading of the law.

'Did you steal the horses, Your Highness?' Pooranmalji asked.

'I have committed no theft.'

'Are the ten horses which are missing from Jai Simha Balech's studfarm in your safekeeping?'

How subtly and beautifully the Prime Minister had phrased that question. If I was ever in trouble, I would want Pooranmalji as my defence lawyer. You could see Vikram squirming in the narrow confines of his mind, for it is a very limited mind that can accommodate at best three or four ideas in a lifetime and those, too, not simultaneously. It seemed like such a friendly, well-meaning, innocuous question. Should he answer, should he not? Was there a catch? There must be if it came from Pooranmalji, where the waters ran deep and the undercurrents were always invisible.

'I will refrain from answering that question.'

'Could you, through your good offices, arrange to return them either to this court or directly to the Rawat?'

'It's too late for that.' Vikramaditya had slipped up but I knew that nothing would come of it. It was uncanny, how without any prior understanding, we had let the ablest and most experienced lawyer among us take charge of the proceedings.

'Would you have been able to do it if the court had sat yesterday instead of today?'

'I don't know what you are talking about.'

'The horses, Your Highness, about whom it would appear, it is too late to do anything now. Have you lost them? Sold them? Or gifted them to anybody?'

'Don't try your tricks with me, Pradhanji, I am not about to fall for them. How can I lose, sell or gift what I never had?'

'How about the horse-breaker, Pathak? Can he be returned to his lawful employer?'

'No, he may not.'

'Where is he?'

'I am not at liberty to say.'

'Is he in your employ?'

'He is not.'

'Have you given him to somebody else?'

'He is a free man. He can take up a job where he wants.'

There was a soft knock on the door. It was Mangal.

'Maharaj Kumar,' Pooranmalji turned to me 'this investigation is not getting anywhere. Shall we recess and decide on our next step?'

'That seems like a good idea.'

'Take the accused to the antechamber. If he gets boisterous, handcuff him. Guard, make the Rawat comfortable in one of the adjoining offices.'

I went out and joined Mangal. He handed me a letter with Vikramaditya's seal on it.

'Sajjad Hussein and seven of his men are in custody in the imperial guard rooms.'

'What took you so long? If he left the fort, and he must have for you to have intercepted him, it must have been at least four hours ago.'

'My instructions to my men were to apprehend him only after he had left Bagoli.'

'Why is that?' I was willing to strangle Mangal for having countermanded my orders. Getting too big for his boots, he was. I must cut him down to size, the bloody ass, keeping me on tenterhooks while Vikramaditya played cat and mouse with us. 'I could have you in lock-up too for insubordination.'

'Sajjad Hussein has a farm at Bagoli.'

'So what's it to me? Do you want me to go and sow maize ... oh my God, how blind, how unforgivably stupid of me. Did you find Kali Bijlee?'

'And the other nine horses and the horse-breaker.'

'You should be in the crime branch, Mangal. You have an instinctive feel for how criminals think and work. I am going to recommend you to the Rana for this year's honours list.'

Mangal was not listening. If he was, he was not elated. His mind was somewhere else. 'Don't you want to find out what's in the letter?'

I took the royal letter back to the courtroom.

'How do you suggest we deal with Prince Vikramaditya now? All the circumstantial evidence points to his masterminding the theft but we have no proof.'

I interrupted the Pradhan. 'We have, Pooranmalji. We have recovered the horses, all ten of them, the horse-breaker and a letter from the Prince to Prince Bahadur Khan of Gujarat. With your permission, I am going to open it.' I thought the better of it and passed the letter around so they could all see the seal.

' "To His Highness, Prince Bahadur Khan," ' I read from the letter, ' "I trust this missive finds you in good health and in fighting spirits. You are right, we are not first-born and so will have to seize the initiative and then the throne. I think this is the opportune moment for it. Both our fathers are busy fighting each other over Idar. My brother, the putative Maharaj Kumar, is in charge at Chittor. He is weak and unassertive; his wife is a national scandal and while she leads him a song and dance, he broods and vacillates and is, even after so many years of marriage, without issue. That is neither here nor there. I believe that if you ride posthaste to Chittor with a force of two thousand men, my men will throw the gates open to you and I think we can restrict casualties to double figures and no more. The populace of Chittor is solidly behind me. They are tired of the one-eyed, one-armed and one-legged King and will any day opt for a dashing, debonair and daring prince who can laugh heartily and has a hearty appetite for fun, games and pleasure.

' "When I am consecrated upon the throne, we'll proceed forthwith to Idar. Your father's holed up in Champaner while mine's fighting against your father's general Malik Ayaz. Can you imagine the surprise and confusion in both armies when they see us together? We'll speedily rout them and take my father prisoner. Thence we'll force-march to Champaner, imprison your father and crown you King of Gujarat.

' "I have already set the wheels of disaffection and rebellion in motion here. I urge you to leave as soon as you receive this communication. My trusted lieutenant, Sajjad Hussein, will guide you here safely. As an earnest of our eternal friendship, I am sending you ten of the finest horses of Mewar, the crown and glory of the lot being a mare called Kali Bijlee. She is, I assure you, the finest horse bred in the land. I would not part with her for the world. It is indeed a measure of my regard and affection for you that I gift this black lightning to you.

' "The horses are accompanied by the man who bred and broke them. He is by far the finest horse-breaker in the country. He too is yours.

' "God speed. I look forward to greeting the King of Gujarat in the coming weeks.

' "I am, as always, your true friend,

' "Vikramaditya Sisodia." '

The court returned the horses and the horse-breaker to Rawat Jai Simha and then confronted Prince Vikramaditya with the evidence of his treason. By rights he should have been put to death. But he was a prince and my brother and while Father lived and was sovereign, it was only right that we should leave it to him to do what he would with his son. Perhaps it was a grievous error not to have made an example of him. Perhaps we should have treated him exactly like other commoners and noblemen who had committed treason and paid for it with their lives. Perhaps the course of history would have been different if the court had acted in concert and forcefully. Perhaps. Instead, all four of us signed the order for his internment and sent him under heavy escort to Kumbhalgarh fort where he was to be imprisoned till Father's return.

When anybody asked where Vikramaditya was, we told them the truth. Half the truth. He was at Kumbhalgarh. Recovering from a nasty wound inflicted upon him in the course of his favourite sport: hunting.

*   *   *

I had no wish to go back home. I was exhausted. I tried to count up to ten but couldn't remember the number that followed three. I did not want to see her face or be subjected to her solicitous care. I didn't need her to take my shoes off and then my turban and the angarkha. There were servants to help me disrobe. And who wanted to disrobe anyway? All I wanted to do was to get into bed and stay there for the next two hundred years.

I went to Chandra Mahal. My head must truly be badly damaged. I was hallucinating. That dhobi's wife, I can't recall her name, was standing by the bed in my room. I ignored her.

Mangal spoke to her. 'Not today. Some other time. He's exhausted.'

'Who are you talking to?' I asked Mangal irritably.

'I'll look after him,' she said.

'I asked you who you are talking to? Can't you answer?'

'Sunheria, Maharaj Kumar.'

'What the —,' I swallowed the obscenity, 'what is she doing here?'

'She comes here every night.'

I was half-awake now. 'What for?'

'She said you asked her to.'

I couldn't handle this. The phantoms in the Gambhiree were beckoning me. 'Go away. Both of you.' I dropped on the mattress and passed out.

I woke up at five. The Gurukul and its military training had ruined my sleep forever. Whatever time I went to bed, I was up at five. Sunheria was sitting in the corner.

'Do you always fold dirty clothes too?'

'Did I make a mistake?'

'What do you do with your dirty clothes?'

'I have just two pairs of clothes. I wear one and wash the other.'

'So whose chunni were you wearing that first day in court?'

She blushed. 'Her Highness, your wife's.'

'You must have more clothes than any other woman in the fort, more than even Queen Karmavati since the entire household seems to send its clothes to you.'

'I thought I was going to court, so I should dress well. That's the only time I have borrowed anyone's clothes.'

'A likely story.'

She smiled. 'Well, sometimes I borrow clothes for a while. But I always return them.'

The curtain moved almost imperceptibly. I put a finger on my lips and looked at Sunheria. I got up softly and in three strides was in the next room.

I barely got a glimpse of her back. She was running fast and her long thick plait slapped hard against her bare back. Kausalya.

I came back.

'Do you realize that you are putting me at grave risk?'

She looked puzzled. 'How?'

'If your husband were to name me as co-respondent?'

'Oh, those are the laws for common people like him and me. You are above all that.'

Vikramaditya would certainly have agreed with her.

'Weren't you angry with me the other night? At the palace?'

'Why would I be upset?'

'Because Mangal forced you to come.'

'Nobody forced me. I came because I wanted to.'

'Then you must have been all the more angry when I turned my back on you.'

'How could I be when your wife was so kind to me?'

'Are you going to stay in that corner all night long?'

She got up shyly and came forward. I untied the strings of her blouse at the back and tried to pull it off but the nine or ten bangles stopped me dead.

'Are you trying to tell me that every time you take your blouse off, you have to first remove all these ivory bangles?'

She laughed. I got hold of the bangle closest to her wrist and tugged at it. It was the narrowest and effectively held up the others which grew progressively larger. It was no use, I would just end up breaking her wrist and a couple of her fingers. She pressed the index finger and thumb of her left hand around the knuckles of her right and slipped the first ivory band out. The second one took the same kind of coaxing. The rest fell out rapidly, all she had to do was hold the forearm and hand down. When she had repeated the process on her left arm, I gently pulled the choli off. I thought of Pushkar again and the hills of sand that the previous night's winds leave behind. I passed my hand lightly over them, almost as if I was afraid to change the contours of the dunes. But that slight breeze generated by the lambent hand was enough. The sands shifted, ripples ran through them and the purple pinks which had lain slack and slumbering rose slowly till they came to fine tremulous heads.

I undid the knot of the ghagra and let it fall to her feet. I picked her up in my arms and laid her on the mattress. Her eyes were wide open. There was no trepidation in them. They were watchful, they wanted to know what my next move was going to be. I flicked my tongue between her breasts. She shivered. I took off my clothes and lowered myself down on her, the weight of my body on my elbows. Her body smelled of freshly pressed clothes. My head dipped and the tongue slipped over her right nipple. Another tremor.

I raised my body up all the way to the ankles before plummeting down. And froze.

'Are you a virgin?'

39

Chapter 3

 Let nobody fool you, most couples are conjoined on earth.
The mismatches, now they are a different story. They are
made in heaven.

$\mathcal{H}$e had been the most eligible bachelor in this part of the world.
It took them a long time to find a bride for him. Two or three
proposals along with horoscopes arrived every day. They had to
appoint a full-time priest to go through the horoscopes and decide
which matched his. There was no point in looking at the proposals
first and getting excited about a few of them only to discover that
Saturn was in the wrong house in one princess's case and another
princess had a malevolent Mars dogging her.

Marriage is a two-way street. The girl's people make overtures.
But the boy's relatives don't sit on their behinds and wait for a pari
or an apsara to drop out of the heavens. You make your moves
too, prepare a list of the houses you would like to be allied with,
then find out if there's a suitable unmarried girl there without a
limp or a cleft palate or polio legs. Do you remember the time the
Maharaj Kumar's father, the Rana, got married? The king of
Mandasaur had a fine, vivacious daughter with a complexion that
would put morning dew to shame. She was there right under
everybody's nose and nobody noticed her. No malice aforethought
or any question of 'let's teach Mandasaur a lesson, we too can get
even with them' or 'let's reserve her for the second son'. Nothing
of the sort. They just forgot all about her. When the Rana didn't
marry her, the others drew their own conclusions. They surmised

40

that appearances were deceptive, that there was something fatally wrong with her, why else would such a fine match be passed over. Soon everybody was staying clear of her. She was never rejected because she was never considered. The girl was not bothered the first four or five years. Then she realized that nobody was ever going to ask for her or even look at her. She took it ill. She knew something was terribly wrong with her even though she couldn't tell what it was. In time something did go wrong with her, something terrible happened to her, in fact. She got a tic in her face, it spread to her hand and then to the knee. She couldn't sit still, her elbow pulled in one direction and her leg in another and without realizing it she was making faces all the time. She stopped going out. After a while she didn't come out of her room. Then she tied a rope to a beam and kicked the stool from under her.

It was his grandmother, the Queen Mother herself, who found the girl for the Maharaj Kumar. She was from Merta, a principality under Rao Ganga of Jodhpur. She was born in a village called Kurki and was the only daughter of Rattan Simha, the second son of Rao Duda of Merta. Since she had lost her mother as a child, she grew up at her grandfather Duda's house. She had skin the colour of light golden honey. Her eyes were green and her manner was quiet. Her father was always away, travelling, fighting wars.

When she was no longer a girl but could yet hardly be called a woman, her grandfather, whose pet she was, looked for a suitable boy for her. Her grandfather, her uncles and aunts, even her father Rattan Simha made enquiries, short-listed four princes and then because their horoscopes were matched in heaven and because he was the heir apparent of the most famous Rajput kingdom of the day, they approached his grandmother. Maharana Sangram Simha or Sanga as he was known to his people, thought it was a worthy match for his eldest son. Even the most impartial and critical observers had only the most glowing things to say about the girl. She was beautiful, devout and obedient. She would make a fine wife and God willing, a fine queen for Chittor, in the fullness of time.

As a token of confirmation of the betrothal, the girl's uncle, Rao Viramdev was deputed to go to Chittor with the tika presents. A retinue of noblemen and servants on horseback and camels carried

41

three coconuts and eleven betelnuts covered in thick gold leaf; two hundred coconuts, ten pounds of jaggery, ten pounds of betelnuts, ten pounds of dates, ten pounds of sugar, ten pounds of pistachios, fifteen pounds of almonds, seven pounds of lac and seven pounds of betel leaves. There were twenty-one seed pearls to be stuck on the boy's forehead over the vermillion tilak. For the bridegroom and his relations, there were a hundred and one suits of gold thread, turbans, dhotis, balabandis, goshpechs, and cloths of various designs, with precious stones embedded in them. The last of the gifts was fifteen horses with velvet and jewelled trappings and one hundred thousand tankas in cash.

The Maharaj Kumar sat on a pedestal. He was fidgety, a strand of brocade from his duglo kept chafing the nape of his neck. At the end of a long drawn-out ceremony, the purohit put a tilak on his forehead. The gold coconuts and betelnuts were offered to him and the other presents displayed for everybody to admire. Finally the Rana saw the gifts. The marriage date was fixed and Rao Viramdev returned home with a hundred tankas in cash and several baskets of sweets. ·

* * *

It seemed as if the whole of Chittor was going to Merta for the wedding. Other people's marriages, your brother's, sister's or friend's marriages are fun. Not your own. Prior to the marriage, Ganapati, the Auspicious One, sat in the palace for seven days. Each day, they fed the groom such rich food, he would soon sport an enormous paunch and become the twin brother of the elephant-headed god himself. The women in the family danced and sang every night, their men watched from the terrace and when a singer, instrumentalist or drummer had outdone herself or himself, they went down and gave a tanka coin to the artist.

There was much drinking, merry-making and badinage. The butt of all the humour was the bridegroom. He smiled, he laughed, he bore it all philosophically.

It took weeks to reach Merta. Rao Dudajee, Rattan Simha, Viramdev, everybody came to receive the Maharaj Kumar and his wedding party at the border of Merta. The baraat went round the village with great fanfare and came to a halt at the Arjun Simha Palace. There was talk of whether everybody would find a bed, forget a room, in the Palace. But they needn't have worried. Merta was not about to be awed and patronized by Chittor or known as the poor relative who had married rich. The Palace which looked unimpressive from the outside, went on forever once you entered it. New wings had been added and the rooms well-appointed. They relaxed till sunset.

Why can't they have marriages at a decent hour in this part of the country? The reason is they just don't. Full stop. End of matter. Huge trunks were opened and everybody wore brand new clothes. Two darzees attended upon the Maharaj Kumar to make last minute adjustments and fittings. A dhoti which came down to the knees and a fine and intricately brocaded emerald green duglo on top. The most ornate and flashy piece of clothing was the turban. It was red in colour with a mighty turra of gold thread. Seven strings of pink pearls, the smallest at the top and the largest ones the size of marbles at the bottom, hung from the Prince's neck.

It was time to go to the bride's house and get married.

He was suddenly at the threshold. He had alighted from the elephant. The priest had performed the puja and tied a string around his father's silk purse to make sure that the Rana didn't spend even a copper coin while he was a guest of Merta. The drums and the trumpets were still blaring. If he turned round he would see his father, close family and half the clan behind him. But he felt cut off from them. He would have to make it on his own from now. There was no returning to his youth. His carefree days, the occasional wild parties, the absence of responsibilities, he had left them behind. Walk under the lintel and he would step into full-grown manhood. He felt abandoned and alone. Surely two steps in either direction couldn't make such an irreversible difference. It was absurd but true nevertheless. He thought of his bride whom he had never seen. When she took those two steps out of the house, she would exile herself almost permanently from the people and the house and the trees and the birds and the temples and the town where she had grown up. In one stroke her past would be severed from her and turned to the ashes of memory.

He would stand by her, put his arms around her and protect her. They would make a life of their own. He touched the toran on the lintel of the gate with his sword seven times — why do symbols like the threshold or the toran carry such a burden of meanings — to signify that he had fought and won his bride in battle. He crossed over.

His aunt, his father's sister who was married to the bride's uncle Rao Viramdev and had brought her up, made him sit on a low wooden bajot, and put a tilak on his forehead. 'Open your mouth,' she said and fed him curds and sweets. Then she took out a gold tanka from the purse at her waist and stuck it over the tilak.

She led the way inside the house to the mandap. He sat down on a carpet. His bride walked in. The chunni which covered her head fell over her face. The marriage ceremony took forever. First his left leg and then the right thigh went to sleep. He had to be helped up and steadied for the saat phere. The girl's odhani was tied to the siropa cloth in his hand. They walked seven times around the fire. He was in front of her on four of the circumlocutions and she thrice. At the end of five hours they were man and wife.

It must have been two, maybe two thirty when they were locked into their bedroom. He held her hand. She withdrew it. He held it again. 'Sit,' he said and gestured towards the bed. There were strings of mogra and marigolds hanging from the frame of the bed. She shook her head. He thought he saw a passing smile on her face. Was she laughing at him? She pointed under the bed. A toe was sticking out. It was one of her cousins lying in wait to surprise them as they became intimate. The cousin laughed and cursed himself for being spotted before the time was right. The crowd outside the door was just as disappointed that they hadn't got the laughs they had anticipated. They took their own time to open the door and let the intruder out.

She sat on the bed. When he approached her, she shrank within herself. He was surprised to find that she was terrified of him. She

was trembling and her teeth had set up a low percussive rhythm.
'I will not hurt you,' he said, 'ever'.

She looked at him gratefully but the fear was still there. He pulled
the chunni back from her head. Her hair was parted in the middle.
It was tied in a plait that reached below her waist. There was a big
red tikka on her forehead. Her nose was long. She had a wide
mouth. The lower lip was large but delicate. It was her green eyes
which held him. They shone with fear. They had the look of a
hunted animal who's waiting for the final blow and the agony to
end. He realized that her fear made him clinical. He saw the pale,
exposed flesh of her midriff. He wanted to bend down and kiss it
till he had gentled her and her breathing became easy. He put his
hand on her back. She shuddered and moved away.

He wanted to take her in his arms as he had promised himself
when he was at the threshold. How could he convince her that he
would protect her from all harm? He wished there was a lion or
a tiger in the room. It wouldn't matter to him if he was mauled,
lost an eye or an arm, so long as he could kill it with his sword
and make her understand that he was her shield.

The bell in the palace compound struck five. Most of the strings
of flowers had come undone and been crushed on the bed. They
were still playing hide-and-seek.

'Please don't run away. I am very tired as I am sure you are too.'

She had pulled the pallu back over her head and her face.
Nobody had told him this is what husbands and wives do, at least
newly-weds. Kausalya, the only one with whom he could talk freely
about these matters hadn't said a word. He felt empty and lost. He
sat in the middle of the bed sunk in despair. Another minute and
he was going to pass out. He lunged at her. She almost escaped
but her plait flew into his hand. He pulled her back. She resisted
but he jerked her sharply by her hair. Whimpering in pain, she
walked backward till the bed stopped her. She fell on her back, her
legs hanging outside the bed.

'Please,' she whispered, 'I'm spoken for.'

What did she mean? Hadn't they got married today? Wasn't she
his bride and virgin? He pinned her hands back, scooped her legs
up from the ground, snapped the string of the ghagra open and

45

half tore it pulling it down. 'We are man and wife, man and wife,' he was trying to persuade her as much as himself of the fact of their marriage. She said it again. 'I'm betrothed to someone else.'

He crashed into her. She was tight and unyielding. He guided his member with his hand and slammed into her. Again and again. And again. She was crying. He had broken the barrier and gone through clean. He drew back and lunged all the way in. He had found his rhythm. Plunge, retract, out. Plunge, retract, out. She was limp, he went on maniacally. He missed the downward stroke by a fraction and hit the flat of her thigh. He withdrew and lunged again.

He was aghast when he saw his penis. It was broken. There was a jet of blood flowing out of it. It burst forth in spurts. Her choli, sari, ghagra, bed, everything was wet and red. She couldn't take her eyes off his member. He looked at her in terror. He didn't know how to stanch the flow of blood. There was sweat on his brows, he felt weak and yet the blood kept welling up. He knew he was going to die. He held his member down with his hands but they were so wet, it kept slipping. She pulled her chunni from under her head and wrapped it rapidly around his penis and held it up so that its mouth was pointing towards the ceiling of the room. After a couple of minutes, the spasms of blood subsided but she continued to hold it gently till he fell asleep.

Chapter 4

Who makes up or invents proverbs? They are so often a crockful of never-mind-what. They pile up platitude upon platitude which the officious and unctuous mouth in and out of season and are taken to be the distillates of wisdom. But proverbs are sagacity after the event. Homilies, truisms, adages, maxims are the work of the glib, the undecided, the ambivalent and of those who would have it both ways. Show me a proverb and I'll show you its antidote. When I was in the second grade we had two stories cheek by jowl. The title of one said 'If enough people say it, there must be truth in it.' The next one immediately proceeded to contradict it. 'Listen to everybody but do what you think is right.' When I pointed out to my teacher — may he rot in hell and prosper in heaven — that one negated the other, he took me on his knees, my head and feet dangling, and caned me till he had completely cross-hatched my buttocks. 'You buffoon,' he told me, 'they complement each other.' Do you wonder that our people have the intelligence, analytical ability and the steadfastness of the weather-vane? They endorse and propagate the views of the last man they've seen. 'Unity in diversity. Diversity in unity.' We don't see any contradictions because we love to believe that antitheses, polarities and the one and the many are the same.

What does it matter one way or the other? In the long run we are all going to end up dead.

What was this long tirade in aid of? I am about to mouth a proverb.

Life is stranger than fiction.

I was feeling good. I felt like seeing our kingdom. (I was about to say my kingdom. Is that a sign of love, power, possessiveness or just being wishful?) I ran up the Victory Tower. That's not quite

47

true; the stairs are too narrow and dark. I took the steps at a brisk pace and did the forty vertical yards in four minutes flat. How can you not love Mewar from here? The view is breathtaking. Sometimes you can see all the way to Kumbhalgarh. It must have rained all night long and then stopped in the early hours. The sky is transparent. You can see the gods behind the clouds. I bow my head and ask my ancestor, the Sun-god to bless me. I thank him for his munificence. The land of the fort is verdant. The birds are out making a racket. Seventy parrots wheel in the sky and come straight for me. At the very last minute, they turn an invisible corner and alight on the parapet of Rani Padmini's palace.

The pujari at the Kalika Mata temple lightly tolls the bell and then in a voice that is as clear and crystalline as the sky this morning sings the Surya Stotra. (Did you know that the Kalika Mata temple was originally dedicated to the Sun-god?) He sings of the brilliance of Surya Deva. He tells of the god's chariot, its seven horses and his charioteer, Arun, whose torso ends at his waist. He marvels at the journey the god makes every day across the dome of the sky. His speed is light and his medium is light and his message is light. I stretch my hands out and gather an armful of the sun's rays.

In the thick forests on the slopes of the hill on which Chittor stands, the lions and the tigers, the deer and the boar are calling it a day. I can see one of their watering holes from here. A male antelope with magnificent antlers drinks unhurriedly and then looks up. Was that a footfall or just a dry branch falling down? The muscles in his neck are taut. He looks around carefully just in case there is an unwelcome visitor. Everything seems to be all right. He calls his mate. She comes out shyly, rubs her flanks against his and drinks from the pool. A tribe of monkeys swings off the branches and lands at the opposite end. They are a noisy, cantankerous lot. Soon they settle down to remove lice from each other's hair.

I'm doing a three hundred and sixty degree swivel. The township within the fortress walls is slowly coming to life. It's always the women who wake up first and come out to fill water. If someone were to ask me what is Mewar, my first answer will be Mewar is colour. There will be other answers, some of them more important, like our blind and indiscriminate bravery or valour. But that's not a spontaneous, instant reaction. When I close my eyes I see colours leaping at me. They skid and lurch and shove and push everything else out. Have you seen the reds and yellows and blues and greens in Mewar? There's the sun in them and a rawness that's like an open wound. I know that muted colours are a sign of sophistication. They are pleasing and beautiful, I won't deny that. But the daring and sheer nerve of the hues and colour combinations of Mewar is like a punch in the solar plexus. In the most ordinary and quotidian moments of life, my people rewrite the dynamics of colour every day. They are profligate and prodigal and yet so controlled, they re-invent colour every time they use it.

Look at that woman rubbing charcoal powder mixed with a bit of opium into her gums. I can't see her features but that kind of slow, suffused pleasure in your waking moments can only come from a border-line addiction that's been inherited over generations. Her red and black ghagra is topped by a banana skin yellow blouse and the phosphorescent green of a new mango leaf in spring. Her two companions at the well are lightning blue, pomegranate seed pink and eggplant purple. Who needs lassi when these colours can slap you awake first thing in the morning? The lord and master of the hut on the left is up and Mrs. Eggplant Purple is pouring water out for his bath.

Something moves at the corner of my left eye. Far in the distance I see a group of men riding hard from the southwest. They are blots and blurs just now but I suspect that they are outsiders. It's odd that they are without a flag.

I came down and told the sentry to notify the guards at the check-point to look out for about thirty foreigners and send a message to me at the office as soon as they learnt the visitors' identity and mission. But something about that flagless group kept gnawing at me. I rode down to the check-point to find out who the visitors were. One of the guards on duty was asleep. I woke him up and told him he no longer had a job. He begged me to pardon him. I turned away. The riders were crossing the bridge over the Gambhiree with a white flag.

It couldn't be, could it? It was. Prince Bahadur Khan of Gujarat in person. Had Vikramaditya sent two messengers to him anticipating that one of them may be caught? How could the Prince have travelled from Ahmedabad in a matter of eight or nine hours? Was his army in hiding somewhere close by? I hid my surprise. He was little short of alarmed.

'How did you know I was coming?'

'I have my sources.'

He racked his brains. 'We didn't tell anyone.' He looked suspiciously at his companions. 'And for the last couple of weeks we rode nonstop except for resting at night.'

I didn't respond.

'Your Highness Maharaj Kumar, in the absence of your father, His Majesty Rana Sanga, I wish to apply to you for asylum and protection at Chittor. I hereby formally surrender my sword, my shield and my person to your care. And so do my companions.'

'Why don't you ride in with me to the Atithi Palace, take a bath, change, have breakfast? We'll have all the time in the world to talk then.'

Even if his army was in hiding, once we had him, they would think twice before attacking. As it turned out, it was nothing but a banal coincidence that Vikramaditya had written to Bahadur Khan to bring his army to usurp the throne and that Bahadur Khan had turned up seeking asylum the very next day.

I installed Bahadur Khan in the Prince's suite of rooms in the Atithi Palace and replaced the servants with intelligence men who were also trained to be excellent cooks and personal valets. I shut myself up in my office. What was going on? This is daylight, nine seventeen in the morning. I can't be dreaming this up. What was Prince Bahadur doing at Chittor as a supplicant? He had sworn to raze Chittor and subjugate the whole of Mewar in revenge for our sacking of Ahmednagar.

Obviously he had had to defer his resolve. Later on I would be criticized by a group of nobles, Rani Karmavati and Prince Vikramaditya himself, for being weak-willed and for nursing a snake in our bosom. Did we really have a choice in the matter? Oh yes, we could have shut the gates in his face or better still, bumped him off, with his companions. The former course would have further alienated the Prince and the second would have pushed his father, Muzaffar Shah, over the edge and enraged him to the point where it would have made a material difference to the outcome of the war Father was waging against him. This way he was our guest and hostage. It would humiliate Muzaffar Shah and in case things went badly for us, we would have an ace up our sleeve. Besides, if ever in the future, Bahadur became king of Gujarat and conquered Chittor as he had sworn, he might perhaps think kindly of its people and spare them.

He slept through that day and night and the next day. I got Mangal to wake him up in the evening and asked him to join me for dinner. At seven o'clock Bahadur presented himself at my palace. He had brought a few gifts with him: a set of six gold goblets from Istanbul for me and, for my wife, a wonderfully carved statuette of the Flautist in green jade from Gujarat.

Can we read the character of a person from his face? Perhaps there's a science to it and the thickness of the eyebrows, their angle, the width of the forehead, the curve of the nose and the contours of the lips, the colour of the teeth, the placement of the ears and their size are all precise signifiers of the man or woman within. It's not as far-fetched as it sounds. At Chittor itself, Makhanlalji can tell a person's future merely by looking at his face. And there's a Chhayashastri at Merta who measures your shadow and looks up an old treatise and traces your vocation and your past. I have no such hidden talent or prowess. All I can do is conjecture which is at best a highly unreliable business. And yet from the moment one sees a face, one is almost involuntarily drawing up a profile of the person and locating him on multiple polarized axes: like-dislike; trust-distrust; dull-bright; open-devious. If I am often a good judge of people it is because I go by my instincts while simultaneously distrusting them.

I like Bahadur Khan but I don't trust him. It's not so much that he is unreliable as that he is impulsive and impetuous and won't give himself time for second and third thoughts. And yet I suspect that he is capable of maturing. Which is why, I think, he is going to be dangerous in the long run. He is spoilt and his ambition is the work of an idle and over-reaching mother. He is impatient and like most would-be usurpers has no sense of the quiddity of life: that sons become fathers and must face the same dilemmas that they had visited on their parents.

We sit opposite each other on the thick Persian carpet which is a gift to Father from our common enemy, the Sultan of Malwa. The Shehzada is enjoying the meal. Our intelligence in such matters is fairly good and I have got the cooks to prepare some of his favourite dishes, Afghani tangdi kebabs and ghazab gosht along with a Gujarati sweet dish called shrikhand made from yoghurt that's been strained in muslin to rid it of water and then slowly stroked with sugar and saffron till they disappear. We make small talk. I know there's something on his mind that he wants to spill out but his good breeding prevents him from doing so till we are through with the meal.

'You must be wondering what brings me here on a sudden visit.' We were having paan when he broached the subject.

'It's a rare pleasure to have someone as distinguished as you amongst us.'

'You are very kind and I hope I can repay your hospitality one of these days. Very soon, as a matter of fact, if I have my way.'

'Rest, relax, we would like you to stay as long as you want. Consider Chittor your second home.'

'Maharaj Kumar,' he'd had enough of this polite sparring, 'forgive me for dispensing with niceties and coming straight to the point.'

'Please. There is no formality between friends.'

'My father's armies are engaged in battle with Mewar's near the kingdom of Idar. If you'll lend me just twenty thousand cavalry, I will seize our capital of Ahmedabad with the support of my sympathizers and followers there and unseat my father, Sultan Muzaffar Shah. I will relinquish Idar. In one swift move, Idar will become part of your father's domain. Gujarat and Mewar will sign a peace treaty and your country will gain a lifelong friend in me. Needless to say, I will also compensate you for your forces at the rate of fifty thousand tankas for each day of service.'

Great to get Idar on a platter. The fight for Idar goes as far back

52

as my very first memories. Bahadur has set up a nice series of 'ifs' but it does not suit his purpose to dwell on the imponderables. Can I raise twenty thousand cavalry? Will that number be enough? Does he have a substantial following in Ahmedabad? Will Ahmedabad fall like a ripe and rotten custard apple into his hands? And what if our forces are vanquished? What did I know of Bahadur as a military strategist? It's heartening to learn that he's going to finance the expedition but where was he planning to get that kind of money from and against what collateral? My own dealings with Adinathji have taught me that he needs castles and lands and forts, not in the air, but on solid ground to lend a ear to any proposal for a loan. Whatever monies he had lent to Vikramaditya was on the sound reasoning that at a pinch, the Prince's mother would come through with the original sum and some highly compounded interest. As to a lifelong peace treaty and friendship, it was a happy thought but for the moment a rather far-fetched one.

Every single one of the objections I raised in my mind was good enough to cool my ardour, if any, to help the Prince. But all those fine points of rational analyses and logic were merely skirting the issue. Even if there was a hundred percent guarantee of Prince Bahadur winning the throne of Gujarat, it would not alter two facts: one, his father, the legitimate king is alive and two, he is number two in the line of succession.

Not a line moved in my impassive face but I could barely restrain myself from picking him by the scruff of his neck and giving him a couple of hard slaps followed by a memorable whipping and then throwing him in the dungeons and letting him rot there till he had lost his teeth and his vision and begged on his knees to see the sunlight and breathe fresh air and swore to follow the laws of primogeniture.

Chapter 5

$\mathcal{I}$ have avoided speaking about the rights of succession as much as the other forbidden subject which tears my guts and paralyses my mind. But Prince Bahadur has touched a particularly raw spot and the least I can do is to gain a degree of relief by talking about it.

I am a self-conscious person. Loners usually are. Often, though not always, I know how my mind works and I have a fairly good idea of the kind of person I am. I am ambitious. Ambitious enough to want to be king today. In matters of policy and state, I have few scruples. If there was gain, solid gain in backing the sons of one of our archrivals, Prince Bahadur Khan for instance, I would gladly do it, however much it hurt me to go against the few principles I have.

But I am the son of Mewar and a Guhilot Sisodia to boot. It's the only family tree in Rajasthan that can be traced all the way back to the seventh or eighth century and through an unbroken chain of thirty or forty kings. We are a country of bards and minstrels and story-tellers and troubadours. They never tire of telling stories of the heroic exploits of my ancestors. Of Bappa Rawal, Rana Hameer, Choonda and Rana Kumbha. I think we breathe in less air than we inhale these stories. Our anecdotes are all history. The bed-time stories of our children are about these larger-than-life monarchs and warriors from the past. Our arteries and veins are clogged with them. Sometimes I think we have no present, only the past.

They paint a rosy picture, these tellers of tales and very sensibly, don't dwell too long or too often on the bad guys. That's not quite true. What they do is far more dangerous. They turn the fratricidal and bloody struggles that always preface the assumption of the throne after a king dies, into a hundred or thousand pretty couplets about heroism and valour. They cannot see death's head above the crown of each king. And nobody calculates the cost of all this insane and internecine bloodshed to Mewar. We are our enemies' best friends. For what better chaos and anarchy can they wish upon Mewar than that which we wreak upon ourselves? Only a short-sighted fool will take solace from the fact that the same deadly struggles take place in the kingdoms of our neighbours.

I am the first-born and heir apparent and Maharaj Kumar. It can be said that the reason I'm so interested in primogeniture is because I stand to gain nothing less than the crown, the throne and the kingdom of Mewar. But it's a little more than that. I am constantly aware of how fraught with uncertainty the future is for Father, me and my siblings. Because I cannot forget how red and sticky our hands are with the blood of our fathers and brothers. We don't have to go too far back into the past. Take my great-grandfather Maharana Kumbha. Some say he is the greatest king Mewar has seen, greater than even Bappa Rawal and Hameer. This is fruitless speculation. What is of moment is that when Kumbha came to the throne, there was not a single axis from which he did not perceive either present or imminent danger. Our current foes, Delhi, Gujarat and Malwa were forever snapping at the flanks of Mewar, seizing huge chunks of its flesh or going for its throat. But as always amongst us Rajputs, it is not the outsider who is to be feared, it is our own blood and kith and kin who'll undermine our power far more effectively than any foreign enemy could. The Rajput ruler of Sirohi, the Hadas of Bundi and Jodha of Marwar, not to mention the Rana's brother, Khem Karan, often joined forces with our enemies and kept Kumbha on a short leash.

Be that as it may, Kumbha was the only Rana in living memory who waged a simultaneous battle with Gujarat and Malwa on two different fronts. It is true that he did not annihilate either of them, but he managed to keep each of his predators at bay, and enlarged the boundaries of Mewar as no other previous king had. He annexed Sarangpur, Gagrone, Narana, Ajmer, Mandaur, Mandalgarh, Khatu, Chatsu, Abu, Ranthambhor and other forts and towns, many of which have, since his death, changed ownership several times. He was forever on the move. And he seems to have had his hands more than full. So it's difficult to imagine how he found the time to build thirty-two fortresses which are, to this day, bulwarks against the foreign invader. Building must have been his passion. He built temples, palaces and the Tower of Victory. He thought of geography as the timeless architecture of the cosmos. The only way a man could defy time was to leave behind buildings that would not die. He spent a great deal of time with his favourite architects, Jaita and Mandan. He suspected that some enemy would cut his life short but hoped that the work of his town planners would ensure him a place in Chittor's posterity. His architects did not fail him. When you walk through Chittor today, you are stepping into Rana Kumbha's vision of it.

He was shrewd, sensible and knew when to leave well enough alone. Forget all his achievements and successes, just the fact that he was around gave the country stability and continuity. They say he was built like Chittor, wide and tall and almost impregnable. He had not been ill since the day he was born. He had been on the throne for thirty-five years and looked good for another thirty or thirty-five. That's when his son Prince Uda, whose ambition and impatience got out of hand, murdered his own father.

It was a shaky throne the Hatyara acquired and an uneasy crown he wore. Criminal careers prior to royal investiture were not unknown in Rajasthan and yet there was such a wave of revulsion against Uda, he felt threatened by his own people and feudal lords. To curry favour with princes and maharaos and rawals, he began to disband Kumbha's acquisitions with such celerity and abandon that Mewar soon shrank to the size of a third-rate principality. He gave Abu back to the Deora prince, and bestowed Sambhur, Ajmer and the adjoining districts to the fledgling king of Jodhpur as the price of friendship. They accepted the bribes of entire provinces gladly but didn't extend either loyalty or support to the self-orphaned king.

You cannot be unnaturally ambitious and soft-hearted at the same time. Uda should have scotched dissent with an iron hand. He had taken a drastic and dastardly step but he didn't have the gumption to follow it through ruthlessly. Remorse is a powerful hallucinogen. He saw dangers and revolts brewing across his kingdom and was insecure to the extent that he went and prostrated himself before the Emperor of Delhi and even offered him a daughter to obtain the Sultan's sanction for his acts and authority. It took barely five years of running from pillar to post to prince for Uda's life to give out.

Which brings me to a brief digression. Being in the right has got nothing to do with courage or exceptional bravery. The forces of evil will fight just as enthusiastically or fiercely as the armies of righteousness. Again, people talk with a sense of wonderment about the incredible bravery of us Rajputs. This is missing the obvious. Whether it's Father, my brothers, my ancestors, I or my countrymen, we are, it goes without saying, unsurpassedly fearless and valiant. There may be merit in this but little room for wonderment. From childhood, personal courage is taken for granted amongst us. I use the words taken for granted advisedly. No one in Mewar brainwashes children or stresses the importance of courage. It is all in a day's work. I remember standing at one end of a large circular wooden enclosure when I was fourteen. The gate at the other end was opened and a tiger who had been starved for a week was let in. No, I was not expected to fight him with my bare hands. I was wearing steel armour, my arms were heavily cushioned, and I had a bow and arrow, a sword and shield.

Have you seen a hungry tiger? He is hyperactive, ferocious but unfocussed. I was a week's lunch, dinner or whatever tigers have and he made straight for me. I aimed, not too carefully, I'm afraid, and shot an arrow. It should have pierced his heart or brains but it lodged in his rump. He turned round to check what had hit him and see if it could be got rid of. My tutor Rawat Jai Simha Balech was about to throw his javelin when Father stopped him with a wave of his hand. I was relieved. I took a second arrow from my quiver; the tiger was incensed with pain, rage and hunger and racing towards me. I rested my weight on one knee and let go of the arrow at an angle of thirty degrees. It went through his right eye and into his brain. He had an epileptic fit, he thrashed his limbs and rose. But the fire had died down and his vision badly impaired. I took the sword and brought it down on his neck. Father jumped over and helped me sever his head.

'There, you are a real lion now, just like your name says.'

It had not occurred to me till then that the Simha in my name, as well as that in all Rajput names, signified that my people and I were lions.

The options of doubt and fear and retreat are unthinkable because these areas in our minds have been sealed off. In truth, they are no options at all. There is no discrimination or willingness in our valour. It is blind, headlong and unflinching because we don't know any other way of reacting in a confrontation.

If the story of Uda is a grim comment on unchecked ambition, his brother and successor, Rana Raimul's three eldest sons did not seem to have learnt any lesson from it. Their abominable impatience to discover who would inherit the throne even while their father was young and in complete control of his senses, is a curse that will blight all future generations of the House of Mewar.

My grandfather Rana Raimul had fourteen sons and two daughters from eleven queens. The eldest, Prithviraj and the third, Sangram Simha or Sanga as he came to be known later on, were the children of the Jhali princess, Ratan Kanwar. The second son by another queen was called Jaimal. To this murky cast of characters, add the young princes' uncle Surajmal, a man of devious gifts and a talent for inflaming passions and one whose aspirations did not preclude the throne of Mewar. Who would be king was a subject that took precedence over all else and preoccupied the minds of the princes, yet none of them had ever dared to voice their innermost thoughts until one day Surajmal said: 'Who will win the prize for archery, who will grab the tits of the luscious maid-in-waiting, Satya Kanwar and bed her, whose elephant will dash the hopes of the others in tomorrow's elephant fights, who in God's name gives a damn about the outcome of any of these? Don't look so shocked Sangram, there's only one question and one question alone that is the companion of your waking and dreaming hours.'

The princes looked away till Prithviraj, the impulsive one who could hold neither his tongue on a leash nor his sword in its scabbard, looked defiantly at his uncle and asked, 'And what question is that?'

'A simple question, who will be king when your father is no more?'

There, the sacrilegious, forbidden words had been spoken and the earth hadn't cracked open, their uncle had not been smitten by lightning and the heads of the three princes were still on their shoulders.

'You have any answers?' it was still Prithviraj talking, 'Because by right it's mine and nobody else's.'

'By law, yes. After all, you are the first-born male in the family. But who knows, the plague could kill you, your father may banish you, or you may meet with a fatal accident. Or there's always the possibility that one of your dear brothers who loves you so inordinately and indiscriminately could arrange to have you murdered.'

'I asked you if you had any answers, not this prattle about accidents and disease.'

'It's a damned shame, isn't it? Time alone knows and he will not reveal his secret till he thinks the moment is ripe.'

The young princes looked at their uncle in disgust. He was a Naradmuni and nothing more. He named the unnamable, mentioned the unmentionable, and after he had roused your curiosity, left you on tenterhooks.

'What precious words, the very essence of sagacity. Uncle, spare us your philosophical homilies,' Jaimal spoke witheringly.

All three of them turned away and were about to leave.

'There is,' their uncle's voice was soft and laggardly, 'there is one other way.'

'Good for you. Keep it to yourself.' Prithviraj said. 'I'm not interested in your childish games.'

'Very well then. I'll go to the priestess of Charani Devi at Nahar Magra with Jaimal and Sangram.'

The audacity of the thought was breathtaking. No, it was a little more than that. It was an awesome idea, one that froze the blood in your veins, gave you cramps in the pit of your stomach and made your tongue so heavy, it was impossible to utter a word. There was terror in the hearts of the princes for you did not take Charani Devi's name lightly and you did not take it in vain. They were off to Nahar Magra, the tiger's mount but even the bold Prithviraj would rather be riding back home. What kept them going was the fear that the others would penetrate, at whatever risk to their persons, the mystery at the heart of the future.

There were many legends about the Devi. One of them Kausalya told me when I was a child. Time was suffering from advanced symptoms of megalomania. He was the framework or the boundaries within which everything that happened, happened. The demons, the gods, space and the cosmos were time-bound. Nothing – not even nothingness – existed beyond the limits of time. Little wonder then that Time began to perceive himself as cause and consequence, the begetter and begotten, as the beginning and the end. It was not just that he had delusions of grandeur, it appeared that he was what he claimed to be: omnipotent, omniscient and omnipresent.

The gods including Brahma, Vishnu and Shiva had seen many crises, they had often been on the verge of defeat or extinction and yet always at the last minute, through imagination, guile, trickery, or the clever use of power, they had pulled back from the edge of chaos and won the day. But Time had been on their side then. Things were a little different now. They sent embassies of goodwill and reconciliation to Time, they held war-councils, they intrigued and thought of double, triple and even quadruple crosses. They had a vast repertory of feints and sleights-of-hand, bribes, betrayals and treachery. Time might take the bait but he could also outlive it. They had to seduce him. They rendered his dreams pornographic and when his passion was aroused, they sent him apsaras and Vishnu in the form of Mohini.

To no avail. The moment of truth for the gods who had survived all manner of travails and calamities, was at hand. Time was about to ingest the three worlds when Charani Devi hurried past. She was gathering together the million and one strands of Time, here, there, up, below, before, yonder, next; she didn't look to the left or the right, her hands stretched, foreshortened, her fingers picked up the loose ends and the unbroken threads, endless stretches of prehistory, history-to-be and the simultaneous present that is the same

60

second multiplied by all the points in space, she must have put glue on the tips of her fingers for not a straggly piece of raveled warp or woof escaped her, she bundled it up helter skelter, no beginning, no middle, no end, no order, just one monstrously big ball the size of the cosmos. Then the Devi opened her mouth and swallowed all of it in one gulp.

But just as the gods were about to rejoice and celebrate this greatest of victories, they realized that they had circumvented one calamity to fall prey to another that was even more devastating. Time had stopped dead. And so had everything else. Because life, as we all know, can only occur on the axis of time with its three sharp and fluid divisions: the past, the present and the future. With Time sitting confused and muddle-headed in the belly of Charani Devi, life would cease to be.

So the gods went into a huddle once again. They could tear open Charani Devi's stomach — with her consent of course — and let Time out. But that would get them back to square one. Or worse, since Time would know that the gods couldn't do without him. There was one other solution, an unthinkable one since nobody, not even Brahma had the courage to approach Charani Devi. She had just done the impossible, performed a service that had saved the universe. And now they wanted her to do something even more impossible, something that would deprive her of sleep forever; something that would never, never end; something that would be the loneliest job in the world. When no one else comes forward, Shiva takes up the challenge. He went over to the Devi's mansion in the heavens. She was larger than any pregnant woman ever would be for she had Time in her belly.

'You know what I've come for, don't you?' Shiva asked her.

She looked at him with her large, limpid eyes. She had always been one of the liveliest and most restless goddesses in the heavens. But the knowledge of her fate did something strange to her face. It gave her a composure and stillness that wrenched at Shiva's heart. Shiva gently took her hand in his. She held it tightly as if she would never let go of it.

'You want me to unravel the tapeworm of Time. You want the present back.' She spoke after a long time.

'Will you do it?' he asked her. It seemed as if she would never answer.

'It is going to be a long, lonely and loveless vigil,' she said.

'Long and lonely, yes.' Shiva told her, 'but not loveless. No one will ever part us. You have but to think of me and wherever I am, I shall return to you.'

And he embraced her forever. For that is what the conjoining of the ling and the yoni is, a timeless union. And so Charani Devi sits in the temple and delicately, oh so delicately, coaxes a fraction of a millimetre of the worm from her mouth. She can never close her mouth for if she does, all mankind and devilkind and all godkind would be forever frozen in suspended animation.

*   *   *

No, it certainly wouldn't do to earn the Devi's displeasure.

The Devi has an assistant, a priestess who keeps a watch over her. She helps her when the Devi wants to take a bath, change her clothes or put some soothing unguent in her eyes. And because she is so close, because of her sheer physical proximity, she can look into the Devi's open mouth, all the way back to where her tonsils are and as far into the future where her mouth turns into her gullet. And that is how the priestess has the powers of an oracle and a seer.

Prithviraj and Jaimal entered the dark, cold and underground temple of the Devi first. When they could see a little clearly, they seated themselves on a pallet. Sanga, who followed them, stumbled in the darkness. He didn't wish to give offence to the Devi and sat down where he was. Surajmal came after him but he waited till he could see better and then surveyed his surroundings. Prithviraj spotted the priestess behind a curtain. She was standing still as a tree and her eyes were closed but he knew that she was watching them. It's now or never, he told himself. Surajmal chose a spot next to Sangram. He had barely put his knee down when Prithviraj spoke.

'Priestess, we've come to find out who amongst us will be the next king of Mewar.'

Prithviraj had sprung the question, as was his wont, impulsively and without waiting to do obeisance to the Devi and without greeting the prophetess or paying his respects. The dread query had been shot like an arrow from a bow. There was no going back now.

Surajmal, with one knee set down and the rest of him in mid-air waited for the sibyl's response. How could he have missed the Priestess, he asked himself, despite careful scouting? Was she amused, was there a sardonic line of irony between her lips? Her eyes passed over each of them and then came back to Sangram Simha.

'Sangram could not see and sat down where he could. He is not even aware that he is sitting on the Devi's panther hide,' the Priestess spoke almost inaudibly.

Sangram looked down. He really was sitting on the panther hide. Had he insulted the Devi by presuming to occupy her seat? Was she angry with him? And what form of punishment would she prescribe? Everyone knew that since the day she had saved the cosmos, she had developed a terrible temper and could consign the object of her wrath to a fate worse than death. He hurriedly raised himself, then realized it was too late and sat down again.

'Strange are the ways of Fate,' the priestess' eyes were still closed, 'it has chosen him to be the next king.'

Who was she talking about? Obviously she was doing things blindly, talking of the strange ways of Fate when it was she, the soothsayer, who was muddling things up. Prithviraj was sure she was making a mistake. He wasn't going to permit that. He would open her eyes and make her look at all three of them and then foretell the future. Surajmal was, anyway, not in the line of succession and was merely accompanying the young princes.

'As to the uncle,' she interrupted Prithviraj's train of thought, 'he didn't lurch around and fall, he waited like a wise man to look before he leapt and then deliberately chose the spot next to Sangram. But all Sangram had left him of the striped skin was room enough for a limb. The throne will be within your reach, Surajmal, you may even graze against it but your hold on it will always be precarious. Ah Surajmal, if only your destiny had been as bountiful as your aspirations.'

'What about me?' Prithviraj had got his sword out of its scabbard. 'What about me, old woman?' There was so much rage and disappointment in his eyes, he must have been as blind as she was. 'I'll make you change your accursed prophecy even now,' he was half-crazed as he brandished his sword. But the oracle was no longer there. The curtain fluttered and try as he might, Prithviraj could not part it. 'I'll prove you wrong. I was born to be king. No one else will take my throne, least of all this little runt of a brother of mine.' The sword came down hard. Sangram drew his head away sharply. His left eyeball sat dead on its blade. Dislodged and set free from its mooring in Sangram's eye socket, the soft egg-white with its black yolk surveyed the scene disinterestedly. Prithviraj brought the blade down again but Surajmal's sword halted its progress. Blood poured from the hole in Sangram's head. Prithviraj's sword caught him above the right shoulder and below his ribs as he ran blindly out of the door of the cave.

Surajmal and Prithviraj fought without let. It was evident that they would not stop till one of them was dead. Was there any reason why they were fighting now? This, as time was to prove, was but the first of their confrontations. It became an addiction and an obsession. At least later on there were pretexts — land, kingdoms small and big, territorial imperatives. But the unmentionable truth was simple. They enjoyed it. Mauling each other had become an end in itself; it gave purpose to their lives. It's curious that they never did manage to kill each other. Or perhaps, not so odd after all. For what would one have done if the other had fallen?

'While you fight our uncle,' Jaimal spoke to Prithviraj, 'the usurper has flown.'

Prithviraj came to his senses. The wounded Surajmal was happy to get a respite. Jaimal asked the villagers the direction in which their brother had fled. They pointed towards Chaturbhuja. Prithviraj and Jaimal mounted their horses and the chase was on.

* * *

Rathor Bida Jaitmalot and his two sons had come to the village of Sevantri to visit the shrine of Rup Narain. They had prayed there, made their offerings and were about to return home when Sangram rode into the compound of the temple, his clothes bathed in blood.

'Rathor Bidaji, I, Sangram Simha, son of Rana Raimul, beg you for asylum and protection from my brothers Prithviraj and Jaimal who are in hot pursuit of me and wish to kill me.'

Sangram had lost a lot of blood. He fainted. The Rathor and his sons took him inside the temple, washed his wounds and bandaged them. They revived him with water and strong medicinal herbs. They were about to ask him the why and the wherefore of his feud with his brothers when they heard the sound of galloping horses.

'Have you seen our brother?' Prithviraj asked Bida who was saddling his horse. 'He rode in five minutes ahead of us.'

'No,' replied the Rathor, 'no one's been here. My sons and I are on our way home after visiting Rup Narainji.'

'And whose horse may that be, Bidajee? An extra steed you brought along for the journey, just in case one of your other horses tired or had an accident?'

'Yes, just as a safeguard.'

'Then why is he foaming at the mouth and sweating so copiously? And why do I keep getting the feeling I have seen him before? Not once but very often?' Jaimal's sword was out. 'Hand over my brother, Sangram Simha. Whatever the cause, the fight is between him and us. It has nothing to do with you. All I ask of you is to give Sangram to us. After that take your sons and go in peace.'

'I am a Rajput like you, Prince Jaimal. I gave my word to Prince Sangram Simha to give him shelter and protect him. The only way you can take him is by killing me and my sons.'

What was a Rajput's word worth? Not much. It cost Rathor Jaitmalot and his sons their lives. They did brave battle. They stood their ground while Prithviraj and Jaimal slashed and struck them from their horses and Sangram Simha made his escape.

Should Rathor Bida not have given his word? Should he have broken it? Where does one draw the line? When my own mother, the Maharani and at least nominally, the first among queens, told me this story and she told it often and when she forgot to, I forced her as a child to tell it again till I had fallen asleep, there were no villains, only heroes. Prithviraj, Jaimal, Surajmul, Bida and his sons, Sangram Simha, all of them. Would it have made a difference if Father had died at the hands of his brothers? Would they have been any the less heroic? It would have been all the same to her and to all the other Rajputs who live to tell the tale. Perhaps it makes no difference to Father either. At least he never shows it. He certainly never mentions the subject. Perhaps I am the only one who gets all hot and bothered with the thought of such wanton blood-letting.

Father waited till the wounds in his eye and the rest of his body had healed. He changed his attire and lived as a cowherd in Marwar. They say he was dismissed from his job because he was thought to be stupid and was pulled up for eating flour cakes when he was supposed to have guarded the animals. He left Marwar and travelled incognito towards Ajmer. On the way, he enrolled in the army of Rao Karam Chand, the Parmar chief of Srinagar, the ancient capital of the Parmars about ten miles from Ajmer. The Parmars were now a spent force, but Rao Karam Chand had still an army of about three thousand Rajputs and Father was just another soldier among them.

Years went by. Rana Raimul banished Prince Prithviraj from Chittor when he heard of the quarrel between the brothers. Prithviraj took off in a dudgeon but in no time at all made a name for himself. Strife was his element. In a race of braves, he outshone everyone with his courageous deeds and spectacular exploits. It appeared that Prince Jaimal, the silent spectator at Charani Devi's temple would inherit the Rana's throne. He was circumspect and he bided his time. But he ran out of luck when he affronted the princess he loved, and her father killed him on the spot. Prithviraj was back in favour and recalled. The throne and the crown would now surely be his. He married the woman that Jaimal had desired. The two of them, Prithviraj and Tara, continued their dare-devil exploits, repossessed kingdoms, drove their enemies to despair and built up an entire mythos around their careers, becoming the darlings of mass imagination.

My father remained faceless until one day — take the story anyway you want, with a pinch or a fistful of salt since it's been told about many a prince in hiding — until one day Jai Simha Balech (yes, the very same one whose hospitality my brother Vikramaditya had so abused) and Janna Sindhal discovered him sleeping in the fields while a snake reared its head over the exile. As if this was not symbolic enough, a bird of omen alighted on the snake's crested head and chattered away. The omens were duly deciphered and Karam Chand learnt that no less than a prince of the house of Mewar was serving him. Father must have regretted the loss of his anonymity deeply for soon the news had spread and Prithviraj was on his way to settle old scores and wrongs that none other than he himself had initiated.

What would have transpired if the two brothers had confronted each other after so many years must remain a matter of conjecture since Prithviraj's progress was halted by a letter from his sister, Anandabai. She recounted how badly her husband, Rao Jugmal of Sirohi was treating her. She begged her brother to free her and take her back to the paternal roof. Uncle Prithviraj, who I never did meet, was in a rage and swore vengeance on the Rao of Sirohi. A slight change in plans and routing and the Prince was at Sirohi by midnight. He did not knock. He scaled the palace walls and Jugmal woke up with a start to find a dagger at his throat.

My uncle would have slit the offending throat without compunction but his sister, responding to her husband's appeals for mercy, beseeched him to spare Jugmal's life. Uncle agreed on condition that Jugmal hold his wife's shoes over his head, touch her feet and beg her forgiveness. Jugmal complied immediately. All was forgiven and forgotten. The next day Jugmal feted his royal guest at a great party. All the noblemen of Sirohi were present on this occasion of reconciliation. Soon it was time to bid Prince Prithviraj goodbye. Jugmal presented the Prince with three of the confections for which he was so renowned.

Uncle reached the shrine of Mamadevi and was in sight of his beloved Kumbhalgarh, but realized that he would never make it. He sent for his wife who was at the fort but Jugmal's poison had worked its way to his heart and brain before Tara Bai could bid him farewell. She had no wish to live on without the husband who had been her companion in the great adventure of life. Prince Prithviraj's pyre was lit. As the flames shot up, Tara Bai embraced him and ascended to the regions of the sun.

The road was clear now. Rana Raimul was ill and it was time to call Prince Sangram Simha from Rao Karam Chand's estates in

Srinagar.

Blood. Will we ever be able to stanch the rivers of blood? How often have I pleaded with Father to issue a royal proclamation, once and for all, that anybody but the heir apparent, who has designs upon the crown will be put instantaneously to death?

Father listens and nods his head in assent. He understands how many lives this will save, how many misfortunes it will avert, and how much our sovereign kingdom will stand to gain. Who can appreciate the implications of my proposal better than he who had suffered so many indignities for so long? And yet he will not put his seal to such a decree because Rani Karmavati stands over his shoulder.

*　*　*

'You do us a signal honour, Prince, by offering us the hand of friendship. There is nothing more valuable that either His Majesty, the Rana or I would want in our relationship with the kingdom of Gujarat. I think all of us have, in the process of being constantly at war, lost sight of an extraordinary simple truth. That the dividends of peace are greater than all the plunder of victories. But I must beg your indulgence in two matters.'

Did the Shehzada Bahadur know what was coming? He hadn't once mentioned or asked for Vikramaditya. Butter, as they say, wouldn't melt in his mouth. His sources, I was sure, had already informed him of Vikramaditya's imprisonment. He knew that we could not but be aware of the dialogue that my brother and he had started about carving up Mewar and Gujarat among themselves. Something had obviously gone wrong at his end that had made him bring forward his departure, without prior notice to his co-conspirator in Chittor and without the forces which were supposed to owe allegiance to him.

Young though he was, certainly younger than I, he was too steeped in the arts of diplomacy to let on that he had suffered setbacks at home as well as after his arrival in Chittor.

'It is I who am the suppliant and must beg your indulgence. Pray, what are the two matters?'

'I need to inform His Majesty, the Rana, of your arrival and of your proposals. He is, as you are aware, the final arbiter of all matters in Mewar.'

'Yes, of course, that goes without saying. Please tell His Majesty that I send him my greetings and wish him success.'

'I am certain of his warm reception to both, your presence here and to your very interesting proposition,' I continued as if he had not interrupted me. I was not about to tell him that I had already dispatched a letter to his father, the Sultan of Gujarat. I too sent him greetings but desisted from wishing him success in his war with Mewar. I said that he must have been not a little anxious about the disappearance of his second son, Prince Bahadur and that I was happy to rid him of this source of worry. Prince Bahadur was with us, he was well and would continue to be our guest for as long as he wished. Yours sincerely, etcetera.

He was bound to hear of his son's presence in Chittor. Might as well get some benefit from it.

'The business of the troops that you require may pose a slight problem. Your intelligence is precise. We do have about twenty thousand troops in Mewar. But you'll be the first to agree that it would be unwise to enlist them all in the expedition to Ahmedabad and leave Mewar exposed.

'But, and let me stress this, the last thing I have in mind is to throw a damper on your scheme. What I suggest is this: as an earnest of our intentions and commitment, I will write to the Rana asking him to spare ten thousand troops from our forces here. While we await his reply, you could spend that time raising another ten thousand troops from your friends among the nobles and vassals of Gujarat and, needless to say, from your loyal forces in Ahmedabad and in the rest of the kingdom. Our combined armies then would make short work of capturing Ahmedabad.'

Was I lying? No, I wasn't and he knew that. At least I hoped he did. What I was doing was hedging Mewar's bets. Of course, we could raise more than twenty thousand troops in our kingdom and from our dependencies but that was neither here nor there. It was crucial that if the attack on Ahmedabad took place, it should look like a spontaneous revolt or uprising from within Gujarat itself and not from an established and old foe like Chittor.

He knew that I had him in a bind but as his reply showed, he was also astute enough to realize that I was talking sense. 'I think you've got a point there. Without my own troops and the backing of a section of the nobles, I might just end up alienating the people of Ahmedabad.'

I hoped that I had bought time and had come across as supportive but not over-eager or impulsive.

'Now that we are through with business, perhaps we can turn our attention to some pressing matters like pleasures. We have had a drought here since His Majesty, the Rana left. You are just the excuse I needed. How would you like to go hunting one of these days? I know that you are an ardent patron of wrestling. I am afraid our wrestlers won't be able to match the skill and speed of your stalwarts but you could assess our teams and advise us on how to improve them.'

I rose to leave soon after and then deliberately turned around at the door. 'Oh, I forgot a little something. Whenever you feel like company, just inform Mangal Simha here. He will see to your needs instantly. Perhaps if you are specific about your requirements, he might even guarantee satisfaction.'

Chapter 6

 *Ah yes, the truth. What a to-do we make of this word when
we all know we would be so much better off without it.*

The wedding party returned home. Her favourite uncle, Rao
Viramdev accompanied her to Chittor. She was allowed to bring
a friend or servant along with her who would stay with her all her
life. She brought her childhood friend and maid, Kumkum Kanwar.
They had never been outside Merta and Kumkum was full of wonder
and alarm at the sights, scenes and smells of Chittor. Merta was
a small town compared to Chittor. Chittor was wealthy and worldly.
It was filthy, spacious, corrupt, crowded and self-assured. Kumkum
Kanwar could not keep a lid on her excitement. She tugged at her
friend's sleeve, pointed breathlessly at the Victory Tower, she
screamed with delight at the size of the custard apples, she was
horrified at the boldness and number of the beggars, her eyes
enlarged in disbelief at the variety of precious stones, pearls and
jewellery exhibited so casually in the market-place. Her mouth
remained agape that whole day.

Her young mistress was quiet. But she was neither snobbish nor
supercilious from a sense of inferiority. She was as eager, impres-
sionable and excited as her maid. Since the time she reached her
teens, she had always been shy and quiet. Her new status as bride
to the Maharaj Kumar of Chittor had added an edge of reserve to
her temperament because she did not understand the implications
and nuances of entering such a large and alien household. She was
at the epicentre when she would rather not even have been on the

71

outermost periphery.

Her husband did not speak to her the first six days of her stay. He looked pale and anaemic and hurt beyond mortal help. She tried to do things for him, get his slippers, fetch his saafa, button his kurta, dry his wet hair after a bath. He turned away. If he needed something he asked Kausalya. Kausalya, she learnt, was his dai, the one who had breast-fed and looked after him. Kausalya was silent and aloof though never insolent or disrespectful to her.

On the seventh day she went back to Merta with her uncle. Her husband came to see her off. He did not speak to her nor did he wave goodbye. How lonely, how desolate he looked despite that deliberately impassive face. She felt his pain but did not know how to reach out to him. She was happy to be going back. She could stay two or three months with her family in Merta. If she set her mind to it, she could charm her uncle Viramdev, and extend her stay by another month. This was the last indulgence she would be permitted. It was meant to soften the severing of all connections with her maika. Whoever designed and wrought the fabric of tradition understood that you cannot be a girl one day and a wife the next; that the distance between your parents' home and that of your husband is farther than infinity; that if you try to bridge it overnight, the effects may be traumatic.

She knew what she had to do on this visit. She must brand in her memory the images of her village, of her house, of her horse, of her favourite people, of the well, of her father and grandfather and aunts, of the god in the temple, of the sands and the trees and the kumatiya, khajri and kair of the desert. And the sound of the school bell and the sound of a sandstorm and of rain hissing into the sand, her aunt beating the water out of her hair with a thin towel, the bucket at the well hitting the water some hundred feet below. And the smell of the sun burning the sand, of dry kachra frying in oil and spices, the powdery, bleached smell of her father's armpit when he came back from a long day of surveying their lands, the fierce smell of the kevda leaves in their garden. All these she must etch on her memory. They would have to last her a lifetime. Of course they would permit her to come back and visit. But this was definitely goodbye, her last long stay at the home of her grandfather and father.

She did not have to coax and cajole her uncle into allowing her to stay an extra month. He could not bear the thought of her leaving home. He had never prospect of her as his niece. She was his daughter, not her father's. Which is why her father and her uncle were at loggerheads when the subject was the daughter one had fathered and the other one was father to. But the month was soon over and neither father nor uncle had the heart to argue.

'Who is it?' his voice was low.

She did not answer. She had been back for seven weeks now. Every night he asked the same question. He looked more haunted than before she had left. There was a tightness to his mouth and his eyes were the water at the bottom of the hundred foot well in her home. He no longer tried to sleep at night. He held himself erect, it was something his body could not unlearn after so many years of military training. But it was an empty shell that managed to be at work at six; conducted the affairs of the ministries under him, talked business, assisted his father in formulating strategy, attended official functions, presided at the small causes court on Thursdays, played cards on new year's night. But there was no person there, only the pain of not knowing and the fear of discovering the truth.

'Who are you betrothed to? I have a right to know.'

He did, he did, he had every right to know. Would to God she could clutch him to her breast and cool his searing brow and soothe that racked body. But didn't he know that you cannot take the name of the beloved?

He came home late in the evenings. As soon as he got in, he told the maids and the eunuchs and even Kausalya to leave. They giggled and smirked. They thought the Prince was besotted with his wife. She brought his food in a silver thali. He kicked it away.

'Why did you get married? I didn't force you to.'

No, he hadn't. She had tried to tell her aunt but she had looked puzzled at first and then laughed it off. When she had broached the subject again, her aunt had lost patience. 'Enough of this childishness. He is a fine young man, a prince. Not just a prince, the Maharaj Kumar. Don't be an ingrate. It's not just you who's getting married. The betrothal will bond the two houses.'

Then he stopped kicking the plate. His body shook with rage. He turned away.

Kausalya came into her room one afternoon as she sat writing by the altar when everybody in the palace was asleep.

'What are you doing to the Maharaj Kumar, Princess? What wasting disease have you visited upon him? Speak woman.'

She put aside the quill and closed her papers.

'What spell have you cast upon him? You are going to kill him with love-making. I've watched you for weeks now. He comes home from work in the evening, throws everybody out, and locks the door. There's never any talk between the two of you, is there? What insatiable appetites you must have, woman, that you keep him up all night long, night after night? And what strange witchery do you practise upon him that he shuns all those who love him, even me, who would give my life for him?'

* * *

She was back a couple of months later.

'How is it that you are always writing when he is not' here?'

She raised her head slowly and put her writing materials away. Kausalya looked uneasy. She was silent for a long time. It was as if she had something on her mind but didn't know how to find the right words to unburden herself.

' 'Why do you deny him?' Kausalya couldn't hold it back any longer and didn't care how she phrased it.

The Princess didn't know how to react. This was a completely different tack from the one Kausalya had taken the previous time. She was thrown off her guard. How did she know? Was it a shot in the dark? Or had he spoken to her? He was so proud, that didn't seem likely. What was the point of answering her? No amount of explaining was going to make anyone understand.

'Are you frigid? Do you not like your body? Why do you make

him suffer so? What ails you, woman?'

Kausalya stretched out her hand and touched her cheek gently. 'Are you lonely, child? Do you miss home? Look at you. There's not a line or blemish on your face. I'll wager your life is as flawless and untouched as your complexion. You've led such a sheltered life, you don't know what cruelty or hatred is. There is no pride in you but innocence, which maybe is a pride of sorts, I do not know. Has anybody been mean or nasty to you? Have we said something to hurt you?'

She shook her head but did not speak.

'You are killing him, you realize that, don't you? Oh, I know he'll live but more dead than alive.' Kausalya held her by the shoulders and shook her hard. 'If something should happen to the Maharaj Kumar, I'll kill you.' Kausalya let go of her. There was no resistance in the Princess, just the despair of the cornered animal. 'Is it me? Do you loathe my presence? Would it help if I went away? Forever. For if it is so and however difficult it may be for me, I will leave. I will never again show my face to him or to you. Tell me, just tell me, woman, put an end to the Prince's agony.'

Kausalya gave up. She walked out. She was back the next minute.

'I won't leave. I don't know what black magic you have worked upon him. Beware Princess, I'll keep a watch on you. You are bound to slip up some time. Whatever your devious designs, and however subtle, I'll get you. Then God help you.'

Kausalya was as good as her word. She was not in the Princess' hair all the time nor did she watch her like a comic spy in a high drama of intrigue and discovery from a bhavai. She was around, if anything, even less than she was before.

Kausalya wasn't quite sure whether it was something about the Princess' writing or the way she put it away that struck her as odd. She knew that her mind was working overtime these days imagining clues and omens in everything and everywhere. But you had to admit that it was a little unusual for a Princess, even a literate one, to be always writing. The Maharani, for instance, or even the favourite, Queen Karmavati, never wrote, they got some scribe to do it.

It was a mystery where she hid all her writing material. Kausalya had gone through almost everything in her rooms. It had taken a long while. The only time you could search the place was when she was having a bath and when nobody was around. It was a little disconcerting to find that she did not keep anything under lock and key, not even her jewellery. She was a trusting fool, she was. But after you had said that, the question still remained: where had all those months of writing gone?

Kausalya made friends with Kumkum Kanwar. It was not difficult one day to casually broach the subject of her mistress's constant scribbling.

'Who knows? To her father perhaps. Or her uncle and aunt. But how would I know anyway? I can't write or read.' There was no prevarication or guile in Kumkum Kanwar's face.

Neither can I, thought Kausalya.

Kausalya found the material in the last place she would have imagined. In the Princess' prayer room. Her gods and goddesses sat on a yellow pitambar which covered a raised platform. There was a black stone Shivlinga, an exquisite Saraswati in bell metal, a foot high marble Shri Krishna, a copper Eklingji, the triumvirate of Ram, Laxman and Sita, a gold Surya and a jade Vishnu and a fierce Chamundi made from black marble. The pages were wrapped in muslin and, along with an ink-pot and quills, were stowed away in a drawer under the platform and the holy silk.

There must have been at least four or five hundred pages there of which more than a half were full of written matter. The individual letters were beautifully formed like black studs carved with infinite care and often an entire sentence stood out like a necklace of black pearls. But if you took in all the lines together, the total filigree work on the page looked a confused and convoluted mess. There were long stretches which seemed to have been written in a scrawl that was trying to catch up with her frenzied thoughts. Kausalya could not relate the writing to its mistress. She was so neat, tidy and unruffled. She had to have things just so and no other way. And to make sure that she got what she wanted, she almost always did everything herself. If you looked at the writing, what you saw was a person of extremes, of violent swings of mood, confused and chaotic.

Kausalya laughed. For someone who could not read, and the letters, for all she knew, may have been in some foreign tongue, she wasn't doing badly at all as a quack character-reader. She might as well set up shop interpreting the lines on the palm of a hand, or the signs of the zodiac in a horoscope. She didn't want the Princess to find out that some of the pages were missing. She chose a wad of fifty from somewhere in the middle and stuck them inside her choli which came down all the way below the navel. She put the pile of writing papers back in the drawer and covered the platform with the silk pitambar. Then she carefully placed the gods back in their original positions. As far as she knew, it was impossible to tell that someone had tampered either with the idols or what lay under.

Now that she had the papers, she was at a loss to understand why she had gone to such lengths to find and steal them. What was she going to do with them? She could show them to her son Mangal. He knew how to read. He had attended classes with the Maharaj Kumar. But there was a grey and grim distance that had come between the mother and son over the years. Nothing had been said, there was no single cause but Kausalya suspected that her son hated her. They had one thing and only one thing in common: the Maharaj Kumar. There was not much else they lived for. Kausalya didn't find it improbable that one of these days the two of them might kill each other because of him.

She kept the papers with her for a week. Then she stood outside the entrance to the Prince's palace. He was late. She had to wait over two and a half hours. He saw her and turned his head away as he had been doing since his marriage. He was about to disappear behind the doors when she called out to him softly, 'Maharaj Kumar, I have something to show you.'

'I'm not interested.'

'How would you know till you see what it is?'

'Leave me alone.'

She grabbed his hand. He tried to shake it off. She held on to it. 'Let me go Kausalya, for if you don't...' he had raised his hand.

'If I don't, you'll slap me, right?'

He took a deep breath. He would not look at her. 'No, I would not.'

She shook her head. 'I don't know whether I would mind it so much if you did. It would be some kind of conversation at least, something which you and I seem incapable of having nowadays.'

'May I go now?'

'You don't want to see what she writes?'

It was as if she had stuck a dagger in his heart. He stood motionless. His shoulders drooped. He closed his eyes.

'Who are you talking about?'

'You know who.'

'Is there something exceptional in that? People who know how to write, an illiterate like you might find that a little difficult to understand, may want to communicate with their relatives and friends at home.'

What had happened to him? Why this wanton and superfluous cruelty which was so alien to his nature?

'Write every afternoon and not send these communications to anybody but hide them from all eyes?' She took the papers out from under her choli and handed them over to him.

'I am not interested. I am not.' He clutched the papers in his hand and walked in.

*　　*　　*

He did not pretend to lie down that night. He told the eunuch on duty not to let anyone enter his room, not even the Princess, and sat down at his low desk. He went through the pages, ten, fifteen, a hundred times. There were places where he couldn't link the zig-zag of her writing. It rose from the middle of the page, went to the next one, came back to the margin of the previous page, gave up the sentence, started another, abandoned that, and tried to revive the earlier one. But disconnected and disjointed though the writing was, it was all addressed to one person. It was a delirious raving, a mad outpouring of passion and plaint, the most abject grovelling and fits of temper and tantrums. Haughty rejections, passages of fierce and naked eroticism, begging and pleading with him to come and visit her, take her away once and for all from the rest of mankind, hold her in his arms tightly, giddily, till every bone in her body was broken. Why did he not come, wherefore this arrogance, this playing hard to get, she could do without him, she had no need of him whatsoever, she was sufficient unto herself, she would commit suicide, plunge the Maharaj Kumar's sword into her heart, free the Maharaj Kumar once and for all, the poor dear man, how she had made him suffer. Enough is enough. She was going on a fast unto death, today was her fifth day, she was so thirsty, she had a little water to drink, then the maid brought some cold fresh lime juice with honey, it was like amrut, oh forget it, why should she starve herself for someone who didn't have the courtesy to reply to her letters, answer her urgent calls, admittedly there were at least a dozen of them every day but was this any way to treat your beloved? Sometimes she thought love was just a blind alley. She gave her all and he didn't say yes or no, he didn't accept it, neither did he reject it. What was she to make of him and of her unrequited love? What was the point of being betrothed if your beloved never thought of you, never called out your name, never remembered your birthday, didn't remember the first song she had sung to him? And then suddenly, out of the blue, the skies darkened, and the thunder was a python crushing and grinding mountains, and the lightning was a scorpion that flashed and flared and stung her and the rain pierced and raked her flesh and there he was, the love of her life, the undertow of the sea, the spirit of the drifting sands, the tongue of the wind in her ears, the caress of the peacock feather and the hardness of the flute was against her.

There were quatrains and broken verses and entire poems. There were padas that she had started and scratched out. The lyrics were the only text that he didn't read. Poetry left him cold. His curiosity was intense but try as he might, he couldn't overcome his resistance to verse. And anyway there was so much prose, he decided to look at the poems later. There were invocations and laments and requiems and hymns and soliloquies and excruciatingly detailed descriptions of her life at Chittor, her aloneness, her conversations with Kumkum, brilliant pen portraits of the Rana, an insightful assessment of Queen Karmavati, aching and unflinching introspections about the magnitude of the pain and suffering she was causing the Maharaj Kumar and her inability to reach out to him or bring him peace; sharp memories of her uncle, her grandfather and her father's guilt that her mother had died and the child deprived of her love and also his own guilt because he didn't know how to talk to her. She told her lover everything, about the tiny, almost invisible tentacle that a seed was tentatively sending out as a feeler into the universe and why did the woodpecker's beak not wear out or lose its sharpness although it had been boring a hole for its nest for the past seventeen days and did the phases of the moon have anything to do with the state of her moods and whether her love for him was flooding the plains and making the rivers change their courses. She couldn't stop talking about the greenery and woods and forests of Chittor. She wondered if there were two earths, one for Merta and one for Chittor. She had never seen so much green. She tried to take it all in with her five senses. Her greed was insatiable. She described trees and branches and leaves and flowers as if they were creatures with whom she could talk. Each branch was an arm and a tree was a thousand-armed goddess and the leaves were her brood of children. She could look at a leaf for hours, dilate upon its network of arteries and veins, draw it and distinguish hundreds of kinds of greens. The wind was a flute at times and a shameless intruder at others. Its lambent touch gave a tree goose pimples and it talked dirty and roused the tree and became frisky and felt it up and down till the tree told the wind to leave it alone, but that only made it bolder and it was all over the tree and then there was no stopping it and the tree didn't want it to stop either.

The eunuch was dozing. He woke him up and asked him to fetch Kausalya.

'Where's the rest?'

'I thought you weren't interested.'

'I asked you where's the rest. Please Kausalya.'

Oh God, what had she gone and done. What was this arrow stuck in his soul? Where was this wound that bled day and night and yet had no mouth? What had those scribbled pages told him that there was now a hot fever on his brow and his breathing was shallow and his eyes blind with hurt?

'My Prince, my precious one,' she touched his hand, 'is there anything I can do to relieve your agony?'

He did not push her away when he disengaged himself.

'Yes, you can. You can tell me where the rest of the papers are.' She showed him.

There was more of the same. It went on. Dogfights and torrid reconciliations.

At three o'clock he dismissed the eunuch and went into the Princess' bedroom. She lay on her side. You couldn't have known that she was alive unless you placed your ears against her breast. The faces of human beings are lies. She lay quiet and dreamless as a child. Who would have guessed what tumultuous upheavals took place beneath that calm? He shook her awake. She was awake instantly without the disorientation that gives you time to adjust from one consciousness to another.

'I am going to kill him,' he said. 'Whoever he is, I am going to kill him.'

She smiled.

Chapter 7

$\mathcal{T}$he news from the front hasn't been either very bad or very good. Sometimes I think that Sultan Muzaffar Shah has lost his nerve and that's why he has retired to Champaner instead of leading his armies against Father. But the Sultan of Gujarat is a wily man. It would suit his purpose to make us believe that the fight had gone out of him and that power was slipping from his hands. Perhaps he knew a thing or two that we Rajputs had not learnt and were unlikely to. He appreciated the fact that not every skirmish was a battle and not every battle was a war. Secondly, he understood the benefits of delegation. He figured why pay your generals hefty salaries and award them vast jagirs if you were going to end up doing all the work anyway? Thirdly, if the Gujarat troops lost, the shame and dishonour would accrue to the generals in charge and not to him. And lastly, the fortunes of the war Father and he were fighting had seesawed long enough, going his way for some time and ours at other times. It seemed unlikely then that it would have a definite and lasting outcome. So why get worked up and lay one's honour and life on the line?

Father has maintained a studied silence on the subject of Vikramaditya's treason and imprisonment. I know that Rani Karmavati has sent embassy after embassy to him accusing me of overarching ambition; of rigging up false charges against the naive and innocent Vikramaditya and pleading with him to free my brother. At times she threatens to go to Kumbhalgarh and personally unlock the triple latches and locks that imprison her beloved son. I wouldn't put the last beyond her. And I frankly wouldn't know how to respond. The soldiers in the Kumbhalgarh fort can't possibly deny her access to Vikram. She hasn't left me alone either. She has been coming over to my office and challenging me in a stage whisper that will carry a good mile or so to put her behind bars now or else ... I daren't put her behind bars for an offence she has not yet committed and I doubt if I would, even if she did set the Prince free. Sometimes she is all honey and charm and enquires after my welfare and brings over a savoury that she claims she has cooked herself. For a whole week she won't refer to Vikramaditya and then suddenly she pleads his age and lack of experience and won't I forgive him just this once? When I mention that the matter is out of my hands, she starts screaming and reminds me that I am a twit, an avaricious and ambitious twerp who's so afraid of his brother's outstanding leadership qualities and the love the whole populace bears him that I've thought it in my interest to keep him locked up.

Where does Father stand in all this? Does he see it as treason or merely, as the Queen says, as the impetuous behaviour of an energetic and impatient youngster who is but following in his father's footsteps? Does he appreciate that a legally constituted court of the highest personages in the kingdom voted to send the Prince to prison? Will he stand by our decision?

In the meantime our guest, Prince Bahadur, is a great success in Chittor. Even the Queen Mother has grown fond of him. His smile, his prodigious courteousness, and his generous nature, never mind who is financing it for the time being, have swept aside all earlier reservations in the minds of those who had objected to my proffering him protection and hospitality. Bahadur is well-read and well-informed. He is curious about almost everything which is new to him. He is intelligent and sharp, and under his own roof, I'm sure, will not suffer fools gladly. But he never talks down to anybody at Chittor and has the knack of adjusting his intellectual pitch to whoever's around.

He has a broad and bawdy sense of humour which, moreover, does not give offence. His repertoire of jokes is staggering and he never repeats himself. He tells Gujarati jokes, Malwa jokes, Delhi jokes and once he was sure of himself and of his reception here, he started telling Rajput jokes.

You have to see him do an evening with his five mothers. He

does them individually and with different voices and he does them bitching simultaneously. Out of the blue, the chief eunuch of the zenana appears. He rails at them lasciviously and tells libidinous stories. The Sultan is away at war or preoccupied with some odalisque and the starved queens suddenly fall upon the sexless intimate who must now perforce unmanfully appease their concupiscent frenzy. My cousins, colleagues and nobles laugh rowdily (so do I), little realizing what an accurate portrait he is painting of our zenanas and what wondrous tales he would have to tell back home of all our tics and idiosyncrasies, fragile egos and risible follies.

There's a rich timbre to his voice and his laugh is deep and infectious. For the moment he is the toast of the town and his engagement book is full for the next fortnight.

The women in the palace gossip endlessly about him and the company he keeps at night. They watch him from their jharokhas when he leaves the Atithi Palace in his smartly tailored white clothes, bottlegreen or pink sash around his waist and a fancy saafa on his head. He knows he's being watched and he deliberately overdoes the airs of a rake. When we go for dinners together, I notice the women of the house fighting to be closest to the curtains that sometimes perfunctorily separate them from us, as much to see him as hear him. Bahadur's opened my prudish eyes. Women enjoy the double-edged joke, bawdy and sexual humour far less self-consciously than men. You can hear them laugh their hearts out and stop all of a sudden because they realize the men are watching them.

He hasn't been idle, our friend Bahadur, but to be fair, Vikramaditya's mother was the first to make overtures to him. She has promised him twelve thousand horse and ten thousand infantry if he gets together a small group of his people and frees the Prince. Bahadur has shown interest in the scheme but he is no fool. He knows he can't afford to align himself with a down-and-out friend, at least not yet. Yesterday, Rani Karmavati raised the ante further and told him that she would provide the men if he provided the leadership to spring her son from jail. I like that. I am sure that he'll wriggle his way out of that one too but am keen to see how he's going to do it. That's being over-confident. I'm slipping up. He may just decide to take her up on her offer.

However dashing and popular, Bahadur's not without problems. He can't hold his drink well and sometimes his mouth runs away with him. Nowadays I make sure that when he begins to get out of hand, one of my people adds a little opium to his drink. That settles matters quickly for he is fast asleep in the middle of a sentence. But once in the early days when I too was feeling my way with him, we were invited to dinner at the house of the Minister for Home Affairs, Lakshman Simhaji. My uncle loves company and keeps open house. The trouble is he can drink anyone under the table. By the third drink, Lakshman Simhaji's son Rajendra and Bahadur who have become good friends, were slapping each other's backs. When they were on their fifth drink the Minister and Bahadur were exchanging anecdotes about the hilarious blunders committed by the Malwa and the Delhi armies. It was Bahadur's turn to one-up Lakshman Simhaji. He remembered a trick that his father had played about the time that Bahadur was eleven.

'On the eve of the battle, Father sent his emissary Shaist Khan with a white flag to the enemy camp. There was much speculation about the Khan's visit: What did he want? Was Gujarat suing for peace? Did the Sultan want to strike a deal with the enemy? Nothing of the kind. The Sultan had a small request to make, a mere trifle. "The next day is a feast of Islam. Would Mewar be so kind as to defer the fighting by a mere twenty-four hours?" (I should have realized instantly when he switched to tales from closer home that the Shehzada was about to enter dubious territory.) The commander of the Mewar armies was a pompous windbag, the kind who believes in large, magnanimous gestures. "Tell His Majesty," he said, "we are civilized and chivalrous people and would be happy to oblige. We'll treat tomorrow as a day of rest and join battle with you at 9 a.m. the day after." There was much drinking and merriment that night in the Mewar camp. The next morning, when the soldiers were suffering from a hangover and taking it easy, the Gujarat armies attacked. It was slaughter, unprecedented slaughter. Close to three thousand Mewar soldiers were massacred.'

Lakshman Simhaji fought hard to keep an impassive face.

'And do you know who we owed our triumph to?' The Shehzada was getting repetitive. 'To the Commander of the bravest army in the world. The fool believed there were rules and codes of conduct in the prosecution of a war. There's only one rule in war. It's called victory. Victory at any cost and to hell with the rest.'

Bahadur laughed his hearty laugh. My cousin Rajendra excused himself and went inside. I was too embarrassed and angry to look up. The massacre was one of the blackest days in the annals of Mewar. Later on, Lakshman Simhaji more than paid back the Sultan of Gujarat for the three thousand soldiers he had lost that day but the people of Mewar never forgave Gujarat for its dastardly act. Bahadur, however, was right. The Sultan understood the meaning of war as Rajputs even today cannot. One must conduct war as if the life of one's country depends on it. It often does. Conduct it then with every means, fair and foul. If you can, go for the kill. If you can't, bide your time.

The Minister for Home laughed too, a choking, mirthless kind of laugh. He poured a big drink for Bahadur and an even bigger one for himself. Bahadur asked him to top his story. Laxman Simhaji smiled a little ruefully. 'Prince, I've laughed so much today, I'm close to tears. Some time in the not too distant future, I hope I can tell you of a rout that will make you laugh till it hurts. Let's drink to that.'

*　*　*

I was with the town-planner, Sahasmal, that morning. He had been hard at work and had come up with two schemes, one for sewage and another for potable water. His plan comprehended two new networks of piping for the whole city but at significantly different levels. Since seepage is mostly downwards, the clean water pipes would be at least three feet higher than the ones that carried the dirty water. The new waterworks and drainage systems would be executed in phases and would be financed in two ways. The first was a scheme whereby whoever invested money got four percent interest and four percent tax benefits. The rest of the money would be raised by an annual water cess to be paid in advance every year.

'I like them, I like your plans for the water systems,' I said. 'Let's refine them a little more in the next couple of months and present them to His Majesty when he's back. Thanks.' He was at the door when I called out to him, 'Sahasmalji, I assure you your work will be far more beneficial and lasting than that of Rana Kumbha's architects, Jaita and Mandan. Come back next Tuesday. We'll spend some more time ...'

I did not complete that sentence. Mangal had walked in. What was he doing here? Shouldn't he be with Bahadur at the hunt? One look at his pale face and exhausted eyes begging me to forgive him and I knew that something terrible had happened. I motioned to him to wait outside and said goodbye to Sahasmal. I collected my wits and walked out quietly. Mangal had untethered Befikir and was waiting for me.

'Where to?'

'The Atithi Palace.'

'How badly is he hurt?'

'Very.'

'Did he have a fall?'

'No, my Prince.'

I should have gone. Too late to say that now. I had had the feeling I had been mothering Bahadur too much. He had asked for protection when he came over but I was being too literal and he was chafing under my vigilant eye. He was an avid hunter and since the jungles around Chittor have some of the best game in the country, I arranged for a royal hunt. I was sure that he would be happier on his own and have a good deal more fun if I was not around. Besides Mangal would keep an eye on him. It had not occurred to me that Prince Bahadur could get hurt in a hunt.

'Weren't Rao Bharat and Hada Komal with him?'

'They were, Your Highness. So was I. I have failed you.'

'We'll look into that afterwards. Have you called the Raj Vaidya?'

'Yes. And the hakim too. He has lost an enormous amount of blood.'

We were at the palace. Bahadur had been transferred from the make-shift stretcher to his bed. There was a strong smell of infected wounds and I was already beginning to feel nauseous.

'Clear the room,' I said hoarsely. 'All except the Raj Vaidya, Hakim Altaf Hussein and Mangal.' The members of the hunting party, the servants and the spectators disappeared. I felt Bahadur's

87

forehead. It was hot enough to boil water. 'What are you two planning to do?' I had woken the two medical men out of their reveries.

'Ghanikhama, Sarkar,' the hakim said hesitantly, 'but I have taken his pulse. It's too late to do anything.'

'And you, what conclusion have you reached?'

'I don't know, Your Highness, but it seems that the patient is past recovery.'

'Sit down,' I said softly to both of them. 'If he was not a Prince but a common man from one of our villages, what would you do? He may not have a strong pulse but you did find remnants of a feeble pulse in him, did you not, Hakim Altaf Hussein? That would mean he's alive, right? Would you permit a seriously ill villager who is not yet dead to lie in his own muck and not even change his clothes? My friends, you've been overawed into inaction by his royal pedigree. Consult with each other, treat him as any other human being in desperate straits and get to work. Do your best and let God do the rest.'

I got out of the room, walked through the endless corridors of the Atithi Palace into the garden and took several quick, long inhalations of the wonderfully pure, unfetid, fresh air of Chittor.

Chapter 8

 It was the stuff of bad nautanki plays. Man. Woman. And lover. Except that the last one was an almighty god.

'You think this is a laughing matter? You are going to tell me who it is. Now. I'm going to kill him and then I'm going to kill you.' His voice was a strange and violent inhuman screech. 'Have you no shame carrying on under your husband's roof? Speak bitch, speak. Who is it, who is it who ravishes you in this very palace while you deny your husband his conjugal rights?'

'Calm down, please calm down,' she pleaded with him. 'You are going to wake up the whole palace.'

'I don't give a horse's soft grassy green shit who wakes up. I don't mind waking up the good Lord of the universe Himself and telling Him what a great time my wife's been having right here under His very eyes.' He had, however, lowered his voice. Here's this slut carrying on merrily, he thought, a consummate dissembler, if ever he had seen one, never a hair on her head out of place or a line of anxiety on her forehead, leading a double life and she's worried someone might hear him. Well, she needn't worry, he had sent off all the servants. She was all his now until he had wrung the truth out of her.

'Is it my younger brother, Rattan? Or my debonair paternal cousin, Rajendra? Or is it Vikramaditya who's always hanging around in your vicinity salivating at the sight of your exposed feet with their gold anklets and when he thinks nobody's watching, peering into his bhabhi's blouse to see if he can delve a little deeper

89

into the cleavage?' He was suddenly silent, aghast at how low he could stoop. No one, but no one was beyond suspicion. Could anyone bring himself to believe that the Rajkumari pure-as-virgin-snow was such an uncontrollable whore? Anything was possible. 'Is it Father? Is that why you fainted when you first saw him?'

'Stop, please stop. You are going to regret your words and hate yourself.'

'Or is it that uncle of yours, the one you went back with to Merta, Rao Viramdev? Is it him you've been betrothed to while he's supposed to be married to my father's sister? Did he start you young, such a fine, handsome man, so much dignity and such a noble face. And that handle-bar moustache on which you used to swing as a child, did he tickle your ears with it and then tickle you all over? Did he say, this is our secret, only you and I will share it all our lives?'

She was crying now. Soundlessly. Her chest went through paroxysms, she was trying to speak but her tongue seemed to have retracted. Her breathing was erratic. Her eyes turned upwards and only the whites were visible. Her hands and feet tensed and twisted while her mouth started to lose its alignment.

'Ah, woman, this is one trick you are not going to pull on me. No hysterical or histrionic fits, if you please.' He slapped her hard. He slapped her again. Her breathing improved and her eyes focussed but she was still disoriented.

'No more, please,' she said suddenly. 'I will tell you who it is.'

It was his turn to lose his tongue. He looked as if someone was strangling him. For seven or eight months, or was it a year, the one thing he had wanted to know was the name of the man to whom she was betrothed. Now she was about to tell him and he had lost his nerve. He didn't want to know, shut up you harlot or I'll pull that tongue out, shut up, I don't give a damn who it is, just so long as I can carry on being ignorant.

'It's him,' she said and pointed to the small marble statue next to her bed.

'Who?' he asked her.

She pointed at the statue again.

'That's Shri-Krishna. What's he got to do with this?'

'It's him.'

'Is this your idea of a joke?'

She shook her head.

'You take me for some kind of fool? Are you going to confess or do I have to strangle you to get the truth out of you?'

'It is the truth.'

He struck her then. Her chin opened up. His next blow caught her on the left eye. 'Rajputs don't ever raise their hands on their women,' he didn't stop hitting her. 'But neither do their women make out with men from the very first year of marriage.'

'I thought you went through all my writing.'

'What?' he was not sure he understood what she was saying. Her words were as indistinct and swollen as her lips.

'Never mind.'

'Yes, I read everything barring the bloody verse. Can't bear the stuff.'

She smiled.

*   *   *

She was lying. Trust her to come up with someone as absurd and incredible as Shri Krishna for her paramour. A simple straight-forward man was not good enough for her. Only a god, one of the most powerful, important and beloved of gods would do. You couldn't fault her for under-reaching, lack of imagination, or low self-image. It was so far-fetched, so utterly beyond the probable and the possible, some credulous fool might just give it credence. Shri Krishna. Ha. Make it a ha, ha.

He took the sheets back to his rooms to start reading the poems but he dozed off. It was one in the afternoon when he awoke. He picked up the top fifty pages.

Get him on the double
Tell him it's an emergency
The doctors have given up.
I can't bear it
I think I'm going to die
It's a slipped disc

A shooting pain up the spine
A fire in the brain
A comet bursting in the kidneys.
Is he here?

Call him, tell him to rush
Tell him, it's the end
I've got galloping TB
The left lung's collapsed
The right one's dead
And the soul, it's fled
Has he come?

Sound the alarm
Knock on the door of heaven
Get him out of bed
It's terminal
Cancer of the upper intestines.
It's spread
Into the esophagus.
Spilt into the lower bowels,
The liver, the bones, the breast.
What? Hasn't he come yet?

Ask him to come fast
I'm about to breathe my last
Nothing serious really
Just a routine heart attack
Tell him I died
With one eye open.
Lying on the pyre
Just to check
If he came
With a smirk
On his face.
And a tart on his arm.

If he won't come soon,
Let him come late,
I'll wait.
If it makes him
Feel important
To be inconstant
Why, of course
I'll indulge him.

Because Giridhar
Lover
Move over
I've got another.

———————

Stop him, stop that arsonist
Pin him down, manacle him.
Put him in solitary. Give him the third degree.
He set fire to me, in broad daylight.
Made a raging torch of me.
People watched, he laughed.
'Try and put that one out, it's spontaneous
    combustion.
It's self-immolation but she'll never burn out.'

So, resident incendiary, Shyam, Philanderer,
What's the score? Seventeen thousand ladies incinerated
    to date.
Died of puppy love, infatuation, yearning,
Flaming dervishes of desire and illicit passion.
Calling and cursing you, your infidelity stoking the fires
    further
The simpering fools, I'll not say a requiem for them
Better dead than pining for a lecher
with a third-rate ditty on his lips
and the disrobing leer in the eye.

But there's news for you, my god,
I'm closing down spectator sports.
About time too.
I'm going to turn the heat on you, my friend.
A nice change of pace, don't you think,
Your turn to roil now.
Light the spit please,
Let's have a nice slow fire.
Turn and turn and turn
The Blue One a soft golden brown,
Nice and juicy like a sheish kabab.
This time around, I'm going to rip that heart of yours.
A little more than a heartburn, I would say.
A heart-attack really.
Fatal. Call it love.

Shyam, Giridhar, a likely story. Tomorrow she'll call him Rama, Partha, Sanjay, Kanhaiyya or by any name she can think of, he thought, just to throw me off the scent.

Chapter 9

$\mathcal{J}$t was physically impossible, at least so I thought, but the Shehzada's body was even hotter than before. They had changed his clothes and someone was applying cold compresses to his forehead. There was a strong smell of rose-water in the room but the sour odour of flesh rotting managed to leak through.

'Have his wounds been cleaned?' I asked the vaidya.

'Superficially. The cloth of his shirt, earth and sweat have formed a hard crust. If we tear if off, he'll start bleeding again.'

I had walked back into the Prince's room hoping for a miracle. What I beheld was the slow progress of infection and the deterioration of his physical condition.

I went back to my office, hurriedly wrote a note in my own hand, affixed the seal of the state and sent Mangal to Kathoda, the Bhil kingdom in the mountains to the north of Chittor. Mangal was demoralized and exhausted but this was a mission I could not entrust to anybody else. Mewar and the Bhils of Kathoda had been close for generations. It was an unlikely friendship, tribals and city dwellers, but enlightened and mutually beneficial self-interest prevailed over the omnipresent snobbery and superciliousness of the Rajputs, and the Bhils had got over their natural distrust of urban sophisticates. When war clouds gathered, they sat in on our War Councils and were our closest allies on the battlefield. Their weapons and war tactics are different from ours but they are every bit as brave as us Rajputs. Nobody knows the Aravali mountains better than them. When they fight on their own, their strategy is to draw the enemy into the jungles and hills. However powerful the foe, he doesn't stand much chance against the Bhils in their home-territory.

We trade in times of peace, attend coronations and send embassies to Kathoda and other Bhil kingdoms. They send their princes for studies at our Gurukuls — that's where I met my friend Prince Puraji Kika. Whatever I know of the jungle, its sounds, its smells, its silences, its worms and maggots, its weeds and grasses and trees, its birds of prey and birds of carrion and about animals, big and small, I owe to Puraji Kika. He taught me that herbs and seeds can anaesthetize, revive and kill. They can put you to sleep, cut off blood supply, reverse the course of scorpion and snakebites as well as make you delirious, attack your brain and turn you into a vegetable.

My note was to Puraji who was now King. Our relations were a little strained because some of our nobles in the vicinity of the Kathoda border had, according to Raja Puraji, appropriated Bhil lands and were killing game indiscriminately. Since game is what Bhils live on, the decimation of the deer, boar and neel gaya population was affecting their very survival. Raja Puraji Kika is not just a neighbour and a king and all other kinds of formal things, he is first and last, my friend. I had been a little too preoccupied with the Vikramaditya imbroglio and then with Bahadur's arrival and had not looked into and redressed the wrongs perpetrated by the local jagirdars.

There was no point mincing words. I told the Raja that I had no excuse for the delay in attending to his complaint. I would do so in the next few weeks. Right now I was in trouble, deep trouble, to put it mildly. A royal guest, a Prince of Gujarat, had been mauled by a lioness. The Chittor doctors did not seem too hopeful, read, had given up on him. Would he please send his personal physician, Eka by the fastest steed at the king's disposal? The Prince's life and my honour and reputation were at stake.

On the fourth day I knew the end was near. The odd thing was that in many ways the Vaidya's and Hakim's medicines had been remarkably effective. The fever had come down, Bahadur's pallor had improved, he was not as restless and he seemed to be in less pain. But even as I entered the compound walls of the Atithi Palace, the overpowering miasma of rotting flesh and putrefaction too far gone hit me. I knew that cloying, giddy smell which clung to your nostrils for days and weeks and infiltrated the lining of your brain and lingered in your memory forever, so well.

My little sister Sumitra, of whom the finance minister Adinathji's great-granddaughter Leelawati reminded me so much, fell off a swing when I was fourteen. I guess she was my favourite though I never admitted it. She drove me mad wanting to be with me everywhere I went, including the bathroom and the toilet. She wanted to do everything I did. She came to the Gurukul, she came to wrestling matches, crashed into stag parties, wanted to hang out with us boys when we went over to the whores' lane. She was a pest and I was the object of her hero-worship.

We were worried because she always swung too high and had fallen on her head. She was unconscious for close to forty-eight hours but she came to and was back to her old self. We had forgotten about her fall when I noticed that she had begun to walk on her toes. Another fad, I said to myself, it will pass. There was a time a few months ago when her only mode of locomotion was cart-wheels.

On the third day I realized how unobservant I was. Her right foot was swollen, she had been in pain for days and hadn't mentioned it because she didn't want to bother us. I looked at her heel and found a soft, squelchy swelling at the core of which was a sharp point. Even if you brushed against it with a finger, she would weep from the pain. We called the Raj Vaidya. He thought it was an abcess of some sort and applied poultices to the foot and gave her potions.

Her whole leg was swollen now and she would lapse into a semi-conscious stupor from time to time. She woke up one afternoon and said to me, 'I know why I fell down. There was a thorn in my heel and it hurt so much when I put pressure on my foot, I let go of the swing.'

'Why didn't you remember it all these days?'

She looked puzzled for a while and then she smiled. 'I didn't think about it till you asked me just now but when I woke up from the fall, I lost a couple of tables from my memory. I tried hard to figure what 3 times 7 was and I couldn't. I remembered my tables up to 5, and from 8 to 12, but 6 and 7 had just gone out of my mind. That's why I got such bad marks in my last test.'

'Do you remember them now?' I asked her just in case she was hallucinating. She was not. She reproduced them perfectly. 'You lie down quietly and I'll run and tell the vaidya that it's nothing but a thorn in your foot.'

'Will you hurry because otherwise I'll be asleep by the time you return?'

I had every intention of slouching through the whole of Chittor before getting back to her but for some reason I ran back all the way from the doctor's. She was already unconscious and the smell had begun to ooze. She was fighting armies of demons which swirled through her mind and there was no way I could cross over into her nightmares and fight alongside her and bring her back.

Her leg had become black and purple and shiny. The vaidya called the surgeon. He was ready with his instruments and about to make an incision when she tensed up and her limbs and her neck twisted at inconceivable angles and stayed that way for a long, long time. The poison had reached the brain, the Raj Vaidya told us. He tried to force her mouth open to pore a calmative down her throat, but it was no use.

The next day it was impossible to stand even a quarter of a mile away from Sumitra and not slump down to the ground with the heavy scent of her festering foot. The bloody girl was unconscious but if I was not holding her hand she didn't stop calling my name till I arrived and took her scrawny palm in mine. She opened her eyes as the falling sun flooded the room with light.

'They are going to cut off my leg, aren't they?'

'No way, child.' Father spoke to her though the question was addressed to me. 'Nobody's going to cut off your leg while I'm alive.'

Should Father have died and let the surgeon cut off her leg? How I hated Sumitra for forcing me to swim through the dead pools of her malevolently sweet and sickening odour. I cursed her and swore I would never return. I was under no compulsion, nobody else went, not her mother, none of my other brothers or sisters, not even the servants. The vaidya got bulletins of her health every four hours and he dished out the same medicine without venturing near her.

I never did ask him what he was giving her but I am almost positive it was some derivative of opium. I knew I ought to be grateful to him for keeping her unconscious of her agony but I hated him for not doing anything more. He was a doctor, wasn't he and aren't doctors gods who can save your loved and dear ones? I had not learnt then that even gods who pretend to be all-powerful cannot save anybody.

On the eighth day of the large, looming, imponderable millennium of the deadly scent, I swooned while going to see her. I had stayed away the previous night and the whole day while the little slut had relentlessly kept up the litany of my name. Oh sweet sweet forgetfulness, if this is death let me drown in it just as long as I don't have to go back to that little girl with the black edema that is a flower that keeps blooming and will one of these days drive out all the inhabitants of the earth and still keep growing till it has blotted out the sun.

For seven days and nights all those who loved her and did themselves the great and sensible favour of not visiting her, paid the brahmins to knock at the doors of the gods and wake them up and ask them to relieve the agony of my sister Sumitra who I was willing to kill with my bare hands but her throat was so tiny, her voice such a whisper and her body so dark and bursting with pus, I didn't dare touch her.

Was it because the priests in the temples smelled death that they had accelerated the tolling of the bells? They rang at the Kalika Mata temple, at the Eklingji temple, at the Jain temple and the Kumbha Shyam temple. Was it for her or for me? No, I was not going to die if she too was going to accompany me in death. It's either her or me, make up your mind. When I came to, I pretended for an eternity that I was either dead or still in a dead faint. They held onions and the soles of shoes and the essence of the most dark and priceless attars from Shyamaprasad Ramlal's collection of perfumes which he exported to the far corners of the earth, to my nose. And all the while I heard her calling my name.

What was the point, the bitch would never die and let go of me. They said you don't have to go. You are unwell. You haven't slept for days. Not go? You think that witch is going to let go of me that easily?

Inside Sumitra's room, there was just one person. Kausalya. She had been there all week long swabbing Sumitra's brow and applying cold compresses, covering her when she threw off the soft cotton coverlet, changing the bed linen into which the suppuration leaked continually. She fed her water with a spoon and occasionally tried to coax some suji or kanji into her mouth. She mixed the powders the doctor sent with milk and if she threw up, she cleaned up the mess. Nobody asked Kausalya to take on this job. She was far too well respected and important a person in the palace hierarchy to be doing such a thankless and repugnant task. But Kausalya did not seem to be aware that she was doing anything special. She loved Sumitra and was doing what she thought had to be done.

Did Kausalya expect me to come earlier? Or not leave at all? For it was she who had to keep answering Sumitra's calls and tell her that I was on my way and would soon be with her; she couldn't imagine what could keep me away from my beloved sister. But Kausalya never said a word to me about my comings and goings and my duties. She never put a name to any of her expectations of me.

I drew the curtains and let the light in. Then I came and sat by Sumitra. You could barely hear her now but I could see her lips moving with my name. Kausalya had done her hair the way Sumitra liked it, in one plait. She had sponged her and dressed her in the aquamarine chanderi choli and ghagra that was one of her favourites, though if she had had her way she would have worn my clothes. There was a tiny red tika on her forehead and Kausalya had matched it with delicate ruby earrings. She must have known I had come. She had stopped her dry whisper and her palm had opened. I placed the index finger of my right hand in it and she clenched her fist around it. Her breathing seemed to settle down into a more regular pattern. The most unlikely thought crossed my mind. There are some people you can afford to lose only by your own death. I let it pass.

Kausalya came over and changed the soiled cloth under Sumitra's leg. She groaned in pain. I soothed her with my free palm and kissed the red dot. She opened her eyes, took in the room and looked steadily into my eyes. I smiled slowly. Her face lit up and she smiled back, her left cheek dipping in the middle to form a dimple.

'I am going,' she said and was gone.

Chapter 10

 He was my best friend. My confidant and preceptor. This Blue God with the flute and the peacock feather stuck in the band around his head.

She was a deep one. He had to hand it to her, it was, frankly, close to a master-stroke in the escalating war of nerves between him and her. You want a name, say it again, you want a name, you really and truly want the name, how many months had he pursued her with that one single question, here it is, she had thrown a name at him casually, like a bone to a dog, go ahead, chew on it for the next seven hundred or a thousand years, for all I care.

What a name. She must have planned and chosen it carefully and with such cruel pleasure. It was one name and a hundred names. It could stand for the one and only one or for anyone. One poem had Giridhar, the other Shyam, the next Gopal and the one after that spoke to a nameless one. It could be a pseudonym, a pet name or a private code name for a beloved. It could be one or all the people she had referred to or none of them. She had kept her part of the deal, now he was left to stew in his own juice.

He threw his head back and laughed. A loud, unambiguous, unforced laugh. The bride of god, how's that for a conundrum? Try and figure that one out, my friend. You had to admit that she was a wizard at sowing confusion and slipping away. Put yourself in her shoes, you are having one hell of a roaring, ear-splitting, torrid affair, they get you married to some young bloke, the future king of the most prestigious kingdom in the community. Do you keep your secret to yourself, no sir, you are a plain-speaking, honest person. On the night of your wedding you tell your husband the truth, and nothing but. He wants to know who the other man is. He wants an answer to that question so badly, he is shrinking, literally dying from curiosity. You hold your silence till the man is about to go completely berserk. And then when you can't put him off any longer, what name do you tell him? Would any woman barring her have thought of telling him that she was in love with a god?

Why had she not chosen Shiva, Brahma, Indra, Agni, Varuna, Vishnu or any of the other gods? How did she pick the name of the *Gita*-god, Shri Krishna, Krishna, Bal Krishna, Flautist, Giridhar, Gopal, Govinda, Atmaram, Shyam, the Peacock-feathered One, Vasudev, Kanhaiyya, Kanha, Murlidhar, Kaliya Mardan, Nagar, Madhusudan and a thousand other names and aliases? Did she know what the Blue God meant to him? He had never told her; what conversations had they ever had that he could have revealed the special corner Krishna had in his heart? Besides he was not demonstrative and never singled Krishna out for any special form of public worship. He did his sandhya in the mornings after he had his bath, put the red tilak on the foreheads of the gods and goddesses, said his prayers, prostrated before them and went off to work. He doubted, no, he was absolutely sure, that neither his mother nor Kausalya was aware of the closeness between him and Krishna. How had she found out? Was she a clairvoyant, could she peer into a man's mind and see its innermost secrets? Had she chosen Krishna deliberately knowing how vulnerable her husband was and how confused and hurt he would be? He felt exposed. His wife was an unknown and uncharted territory. What little he had seen of her told him that she was devious beyond anyone he had known. She was full of surprises, each greater than the previous one and they were all unpleasant and disturbing. He felt a shimmer of fear under his skin. Who was she? What was she up to? What other fearsome wonders and shocks were in store for him?

Whoever had heard of falling in love with a god, for God's sake? Gods were for worshipping, praying, interceding, invoking in times of distress and calamity, begging favours. Sure, Krishna was the most loveable of gods and if one were to believe the stories about him,

103

he was more than a little soft on women. The endemic promiscuity of Krishna was one aspect that he did not quite understand and, truth to tell, he wasn't terribly interested in it either. The Blue God had, quite apart from his wives, a seraglio bigger than those of all the other gods and every shepherdess in Brindaban was infatuated with him.

One of them, Radha, was closer to him than any of his wives, which is why Krishna is worshipped often as Radheshyam. But the gopis and Radha and all of Krishna's wives spoke to him, heard his beautiful voice, played with him, danced with him, listened to him play his flute, saw his beautiful eyes and his glowing blue complexion, saw him pick up the Govardhan mountain on his little finger to save them from a deluge, witnessed him vanquishing the evil on this earth. To cut a long story short, they saw him in the flesh. That's the only way you can fall in love. Not by seeing a carving or a statue or a painting.

*　　*　　*

In love with Krishna, he laughed again, a likely story.

He was a lonely boy. His father was away at war most of the time. Even when he was at home he was taciturn. He was the king and always preoccupied with the affairs of state. The Prince was not sure whether he was a stern man or just looked forbidding. He came down to the Gurukul when there were competitions or sports, not really to watch his sons' progress but because he was the patron of the academy and that's what patrons were supposed to do. Sometimes his eldest son won a couple of medals; in one particular year, he walked away with the first prize for archery, military strategy, swimming and riding. If the Rana's breast swelled with pride, the only way he showed it was by being more awkward than he normally was with him. He should have felt alienated from his father, neglected and ignored. But he didn't. He knew his father kept an eye on him. Part of the problem, he grasped when he was fairly young, was that he and his father were not demonstrative because they were clumsy when it came to matters of emotion. Both by temperament and by their calling, they kept a close watch on themselves, and very rarely let themselves go. Often just looking at him, he got the drift of what was going on behind his father's quiet visage. He had the feeling that his father too read him with accuracy and insight. It wasn't that they were cold fish. Quite the contrary, they were men of intense feelings and sentiment. But they understood that if you were to be a good leader you did not allow your emotions to come to a boil, and even on the occasions when they did, you took care to separate the emotional from the rational and opted for the latter. He knew his father thought a lot about him and that was about as close to paternal love as he would get. Or perhaps thinking about someone was the same as loving.

His mother, the Maharani was certainly a loving person. He was her son, her first-born and he thought she loved him more than she loved his father. She asked him if he had had his milk and had he eaten his breakfast, eggs, cornflour chapatis dripping with ghee, almonds and sheera. Then she told him the menu for lunch. After lunch she enquired whether he had had enough dal, roti, cabbage, green peas and okra shakh and most important of all had he eaten the mutton masala, the chicken tikkas and the three varieties of fish.

'You must eat the greens but if you want to be king, you must eat mutton and cashew nuts and pistachios and almonds and fish and drink lots and lots of milk but never with fish, mind you.'

It was always at lunch-time that she took it upon herself to tell him what she was planning — perhaps it was conspiring since she spoke in hushed tones — to give him for dinner. Food, he grasped early on, was in his mother's eyes as perhaps in the eyes of many other mothers, the essence of love.

His mother had little else to do the whole day and that seemed to keep her busy. He was singularly lucky that she did not have the patience to sit in on his meals because as a child he was a finicky eater and whatever little he ate, it was because of his grandmother's and Kausalya's stories. They were stories from the *Ramayana* and the *Mahabharata*, from the *Puranas* and the *Panchatantra* and of course stories about his ancestors and their heroic deeds. They must have told him the same tales over and over again but it was also true that they both had an inexhaustible repertoire of stories. As he grew up, he often said, 'Oh, you've told me that one before.'

Without losing their temper or batting an eyelid they moved to another story. Often the Queen Mother and Kausalya told the same story, sometimes on the same day. What struck him was how differently they told it, not just their intonation, manner of telling, their pauses and the build-up towards climactic scenes, but the content itself varied. His grandmother, paradoxically, was the more matter-of-fact: who did what and how; who was right and who was wrong; she went straight for the jugular. Kausalya, on the other hand, told a story from different points of view. She always seemed to be asking the question, why. And when you asked why, it was not so easy to find one party right and the other wrong.

He had many heroes, some from his family tree and a great many from the *Ramayana* and the *Mahabharata*. Bhim, Rama, Shiva, Lakshman, Bhishma, Hanuman, he dreamt of them and their exploits during the day and at night. But when he grew up, he realized they were all static. They may have grown up physically and in years but they were the same at the end as when they began. What changed was the plot-line; the events and the circumstances altered, they remained steadfast. They went from extreme luxury to acute poverty, from war to peace to war, they renounced their kingdoms, or undertook the severest bachelorhood because of a promise their father had given, their foot touched a stone and brought a woman to life, they prayed to the gods and won so many boons that the gods themselves feared them. Their lives were turbulent but the quality of their experience rarely warped, bent or changed the way they looked at things. Their minds were impervious. Little, if anything, seeped in. They had experienced much but experience did not alter them or reshape their outlook radically.

The one exception was Shri Krishna. The god seemed to grow with him. There was not one Shri Krishna but at the very least, three or four. He was protean and he changed his role according to the circumstances in which he found himself. You could not put your finger on his character and say, yes this is him. He defied definition. You could never predict how he was going to act or react. Did he have principles? Yes, he did. And yet if the occasion called for it, he kept them in abeyance, changed them or forgot them. Was he ruthless and unscrupulously opportunistic? Sometimes. But the

Flautist wouldn't have framed the questions quite that way or would have subtly side-tracked them while answering them. Over-simplification was easier to handle but it was also dangerous. Nobody had a monopoly on truth. And your perception of the truth changed depending on your past experience, your family, clan or professional loyalties, your cultural background and what you wanted out of life. Was Shri Krishna dynamic because he saw the larger picture or did the canvas grow wider and far more complex because he responded differently to each set of circumstances and problems?

Bal Krishna was everything the Maharaj Kumar was not as a child. He was the ultimate brat. Mischievous, obstinate, disarming, cocky, exasperating, loveable and gregarious. The whole of the under-fifteen population of Gokul were his buddies. He was what most boys in villages were: a cowherd. He was their leader. He called to them on the flute and they followed him everywhere. Everything he did was an adventure. He was always in trouble and barely managed to squirm his way out. Because he was always stealing freshly churned butter from the kitchen, his mother hung the butterpot high up. He aimed a stone at the pot and stood under it with his mouth wide open. Or made a pyramid of his friends and climbed on it and stuck his fingers inside the pot and licked all the butter. When he was caught and he almost always was, he denied being anywhere near the kitchen. 'I? I was busy grazing the cattle.'

There were all the incredible feats that he performed as a child. He destroyed the demons Trinavartta, Aghasura and Dhenukasura when he was still lisping. By the age of seven, he had saved all the villagers of Vrindavan from the deluge that the god Indra had visited upon them to teach Bal Krishna a lesson. The boy-god's response was a little drastic. He lifted the entire Govardhan mountain on a finger and sheltered his people under it.

His foster-mother Yashoda caught him stealing laddus. As usual he looked innocent and aggrieved. She ordered him to open his mouth which he nonchalantly proceeded to do. What she saw inside was a vision that she was never to forget. The whole universe, the cosmos itself was enclosed in his mouth.

How do you do all the things you do and get away with them,

he often asked Krishna. When he was growing up and getting to be uncontrollably randy, he wanted to watch all the women in the palace bathe naked and then steal their clothes, just as Krishna had done sitting on the branch of a tree on the banks of the river Jamuna. He had actually gone down to the Gambhiree when the townswomen were bathing in it. They had their clothes on but you could see their breasts and nipples through the wet fabric. He was starting to get a painfully tight hard-on when he was spotted and got the thrashing of his life from Kausalya. He wanted to say to her, you yourself told me the story of Krishna and the maidens in the river, so what's wrong if I do the same. He didn't because she would look him in the eyes, grunt and slap him once more.

The Maharaj Kumar didn't forget Bal Krishna but he left him behind as the years passed. He read the *Mahabharata*, especially certain sections of it, again and again and was deeply puzzled and intrigued by the mature Krishna. He seemed to have severed almost all connections with his miracle-performing childhood. Unlike the Maharaj Kumar's ancestors and all the other Rajputs, Krishna was loathe to indulge in heroics. Most of the time he preferred to wait and watch, play the game of diplomacy, negotiate, avoid confrontations as far as possible, hold out for the longest time and give a long rope to people to hang themselves with. Time, he seemed to think, was not only a healer, it also had a way of resolving issues and problems of their own accord. It was curious, frankly it went against the Maharaj Kumar's grain and everything he was taught to hold sacrosanct, that Krishna did not very often pick up the gauntlet thrown at him. However provoked, he played for time. And here was the crux of it. Bravery and gallantry he seemed to eschew as far as possible. If his statesmanship did not work, he became wily and devious. War was never an alternative, it was always the extreme resort when every other means of persuasion had failed. He was, from one point of view, responsible for the greatest, longest and the most annihilating war ever fought — the Kurukshetra war — but he tried every trick in the book to negotiate peace before he finally gave up.

It took the Maharaj Kumar a long time, years and years, to understand that at the very core of his being, Krishna did not worry about what people thought of him. The god was sure of himself and knew what he wanted. He did not need to prove himself at any point in his life. Unlike Krishna, his own people, despite their great valour, needed to convince themselves almost on a daily basis that they had not lost their spirit. Whence this insecurity, he wasn't able to say. Why did the Rajput code of honour and chivalry always devolve upon the sacrifice of their own lives? Why were they always afraid of being seen as pusillanimous? It left no room for manoeuvring and for any other options including machinations, a concept which the world owed largely to Krishna.

Krishna had no problems putting his tail between his legs and retreating. One would have thought he would be in one hell of a rush to terminate his uncle, the tyrant Kansa who had killed every one of Krishna's seven siblings. Instead, Krishna stayed away from him as long as he could. When Jarasandha, perhaps the most fearsome of all despots, the one who aimed at becoming king of all kings, threatened to attack Krishna and his people at Mathura, Krishna didn't just back off, he packed his bags. He took all his subjects and fled to Dwarka. Finally when it was time to settle scores, he got the mighty warrior Bheem to fight Jarasandha. Jarasandha was very much on top of the situation when Krishna took the twig of a tree in his hand and clove it in two. Bheem understood the unspoken message. He got hold of Jarasandha's legs and tore him apart straight down the middle.

Perhaps what the Maharaj Kumar owed most to Krishna was a habit of mind: don't take anything on authority. Received wisdom is a very good thing, it is after all the distillate of centuries of experience. But because someone says so or it has been so since as far back as memory can stretch, that doesn't make it so. Re-examine. Question. Doubt. And if need be, but only if the advantages more than outweigh the ill-effects, don't hesitate to swim against the tide. He talked often to Krishna, discussed the pros and cons of a situation or a problem, and set forth his arguments. It was to Krishna's acts that he referred when planning strategy and in times of crises, drew out their meaning and their implications. That he had learnt his lesson well was evident from the fact that he was willing to question and modify the teachings of Lord Krishna himself.

And now out of the blue, this wife of his was claiming the Blue God for her own.

Chapter 11

His new-found friends, his well-wishers, even his old cronies had abandoned Bahadur Khan. That isn't quite true. It was the stench that had driven them away. He would surface out of his fever and the toxins that had laid siege to his brain from time to time. Sometimes he didn't know where he was and asked for his father. The only person around to take care of him in the past three days, apart from me, was Kausalya. He asked me several times if I had reached a secret agreement with his father and was keeping him imprisoned. He wasn't quite sure if Kausalya was his wife, mother, courtesan or spy. He looked at her pitifully and begged her to use her good offices with me to have him released. She nodded her head and told him that she would speak with me the moment I was alone.

'My father is no ordinary man,' he informed her, 'he is the Sultan of Gujarat. He'll pay whatever ransom the Prince wants. Jagirs, elephants, horses, you mention it, he'll give anything because, Sikander may be the eldest but I am his favourite.' He held Kausalya's hand and kissed it with his lips and his eyes. 'You will, won't you?' he started crying. 'I have nobody but you and if you let me down, the Maharaj Kumar will leave me to die. Have you seen what he has done to me? He tried to kill me.'

'How did he do it?' Kausalya asked him. He thought about it for a long time, then whispered to her, 'He knows the lions and lionesses of Chittor and its environs. He paid one to kill me but I fought with it with my bare hands.'

The rest of his semi-conscious time he howled. I wanted to cut his tongue off, ram a thick wooden ruler down his throat. Kausalya sat immobile making me feel like a spoilt child.

Bahadur is fast receding into the sleep of the immortals. He hasn't been conscious for at least thirty-six hours. The doctors came twice daily because they were afraid of my displeasure. They changed the medicines from time to time but that was more for my sake than the patient's. In my sister Sumitra's case, I was sure now that she would have survived if Father had let the surgeon amputate her leg. What was the surgeon going to amputate in Bahadur's case? His rotting guts or the chest cavity above his heart?

My thoughts went back to Sumitra. I knew what was in Father's mind when he told the surgeon to leave her be. She would hop and limp about when she recovered and some Rao or Rawal would force his son to marry her because an alliance with Chittor was desirable and her husband would treat her like a cripple, abuse her and humiliate her by mimicking her gait. Even now I catch myself telling Father in the privacy of my mind that I would have gone from any corner of our country and skinned her husband if he had so much as raised his voice at her. Why could she not have stayed with us? I would have looked after her.

I would have too, but that's nonsense because Sumitra is not here and I am using her constantly as a decoy not to look at what is staring me in the face. Where had that bloody Mangal gone? Was Puraji playing a game of tit for tat, teaching me a lesson in kind for not taking prompt action against the Rajput poachers? Had the tribal doctor Eka died a couple of years ago and I didn't know about it?

I'll do almost anything to get Bahadur to live and yet there are times when I imagine the great relief that would accrue from his death. I would be free, free, free from the gruesome rot.

We'll build a tall and wide pyre and I will go forth like a man to his appointed task, pour the ghee, say the prayers wishing his soul eternal peace and light the pyre at the head, at the feet and the sides till there's such a mighty conflagration that the very sky will go up in flames. I realize I'm not in my right mind. The Prince is a Mussalman and we'll have to bury him but no amount of earth can get rid of that bilious perfume. I ask the labourers to dig deeper. How deep, they ask. I think of the well with perennial waters my great-grandfather built at Kumbhalgarh. Two hundred and seventy feet. More but not less. They are making slow progress. The Prince's corpse has begun to go rancid in the sun under the white sheet that is wrapped tightly around him. I remove my duglo, hang on to the rope and descend. I dig like a mad man, shame the workers into digging and shovelling faster. It's night. We don't stop. Someone brings a tape measure. Two hundred and seventy feet. We stop and climb out. The body is lowered. I can hear it plunging, hitting the sides of the pit like a haphazard bucket in a well. There's a deep low thud. We throw the ropes in and start shovelling the earth into the hole. It takes us three days and three nights. I pat the earth hard and lie down on top of it exhausted. I am about to fall asleep. I sense something in the air. It's uncoiling like a snake from its subterranean nest. Bahadur's malodour, how eagerly, affectionately, it rises to embrace me. We start digging again.

Mangal. Followed by a man who I can only hope is none other than Eka. I am about to go off the deep end and ask 'Where the hell have you been?' Fortunately Eka ignores me altogether. Mangal draws me aside and tells me that Puraji's doctor took a full day looking for the shrubs and herbs for treatment. Wherefore the relief, I ask myself. Nothing has changed. If anything, the Prince is twenty-four hours closer to death. I am about to leave when the doctor calls out to me. 'You'll wait outside till I've finished my examination.' It's a long, long time since anyone has spoken to me without my honorific. I am upset at his lack of manners and grateful. If I am ordered around, someone else must be in charge.

Eka took his time, about thirty minutes. Off and on, Bahadur's shrieks damaged the fort walls. Eka was precise. 'He has multiple infections. The lioness' teeth, the dust and the dirt. His wounds should have been cleaned at any cost. But what is not done cannot be undone either. He's suffered a tremendous trauma and he's lost a lot of blood. Plus he has had fever for days. I am going to make him unconscious, otherwise he will not withstand the shock to his system. Then I am going to clean his wounds. If he survives and if the poison has not done irreparable harm, then I'll apply poultices and cover the wounds with bandages.

'What are his chances? I would rate them very low. Twenty to twenty-five percent on the outside. The only thing in his favour is his youth. Anybody who can bray like that after what he's been

113

through, must have the health of an ass.

'Should I proceed? Or would you rather that I concentrated on reducing the pain?'

He had thrown the question and the responsibility of taking a decision back at me. Is this what kingship meant? I guess it did. 'Will reducing the pain make him come through?'

'No. But as I have explained, the first option does not guarantee that either.'

'Whatever slim chance there is, does it lie in the first option?'

'I see that you are looking to me to make your decision...'

'I am not.' I put him down firmly. 'I need to have the facts before I decide either way.'

'There is a good chance that I may hasten his death by all my probing and cleaning but there's not much else going for him.'

'All right. We'll take our chances. Clean him up.'

*   *   *

'Are you saying prayers for the recovery of His Highness, Shehzada Bahadur?' I asked the mullah who was waiting for me about five hundred yards down the road from the palace.

'Yes, Your Highness, five times a day.'

'Not very effective, are they? Maybe you should say them oftener and a little more fervently.'

'They come straight from the heart, Master.'

'And do you ever pray for our health, mullah?'

'Everyday, Maharaj Kumar.'

Maybe he did. Unlike me who didn't pray for my soul's redemption or his.

'I came to ask a favour, Master.'

I should have known. You don't get a favour for free. What did he want? A job for his son in the army? Or out of the army into the civil services? I waited for him to speak.

'Our mosque, Sire, is in a state of disrepair. Would His Highness consider giving a donation for rebuilding it from the state treasury?'

'No.' I was sharper than I had meant to be.

'But just last year, His Majesty, the Rana gave a big sum for the construction of a Shiva temple and a Jain one.'

'Mullah, tell me something. Will a Muslim king consider giving a little donation towards the upkeep of a Hindu shrine?'

He looked crestfallen and turned to go. 'But let me give the matter some thought.' That seemed to touch him after my rebuff. 'May Allah look after you.'

I stared at his receding back and called him again. 'Mullah, it is not conditional but I would appreciate it if your prayers helped repair my friend, the Shehzada's health.'

It's the seventh time in seven days I have been to the Eklingji temple. The guards beat the crowds back as I entered. I paid the head priest for the abhishekh and asked him if I could have some privacy for a few moments. After he had left I prostrated myself. My mind was numb. Shiva is the Destroyer but they say he destroys to create anew. I find it impossible to barter with God, you give me this and I'll give you that and I hate to treat him as a petition box. I lay on my stomach and took his name seventeen times, then I said, 'I wish you well, O God. I hope you'll keep us well too. Bahadur is as much your guest as mine. We've always treated our guests with honour and generosity. I trust we won't fail them now either. May your blessed hand rest over my head and Bahadur's.'

I circumambulated ten times around Eklingji and went home.

Leelawati was sitting on a swing in the palace. Without meaning to, I ran towards her. She flung herself from the swing straight into my arms and hugged me. She wouldn't let go of me and I wasn't about to let go of her. To be trusted so, without any reservations, I too must have been up to some good in my past lives.

'Where have you been all these days?'

'You should ask. You never come home. Never send for me.'

'Look who's fishing for compliments?'

When in the wrong, take the offensive. 'You could have come over too.'

'I asked Father and Dadaji every day. They said you were busy and not to be disturbed.'

'If I am as busy as they say, how is it you are here today?'

'I was invited if you please.'

I caught a fleeting glimpse of her behind the curtain. What was she up to? She had already driven a wedge between the Flautist and me. Did she now plan to deprive me of this child too? Leelawati is my only living link to my sister Sumitra. I had no intention of losing her. I must have felt truly threatened. I was about to ask Leelawati the same asinine question that a child is asked at least once a day. Who do you love more, her or me? Fortunately Leelawati interrupted me.

'What have you got for me?'

I gave her the prasad from Eklingji to gain time to think. She hadn't come for so long I had stopped stocking up on chikki, halwa and other sweets.

'You wait here. Close your eyes. Don't move. Not an inch. Not a millimetre.'

'What if I do?'

'You'll turn to stone.'

She opened half an eye to check if I was watching her.

'No cheating, madam.'

She quickly closed her eyes. I ran out into the garden, picked a dozen roses, then doubled back, went to the attic where my toys were stored and got ten marbles from the bottle in which I had hoarded them many, many years ago. She was standing still with her eyes closed.

'May I open my eyes?'

I kissed her left eye and then her right. 'Now you may.' I gave her the bouquet. It was such an unexpected present, she stood there a little hesitant and thoughtful.

'Does this mean you love me?'

'But I always did and always will, stupid.'

'Forever?'

'Yes. Seven lives and more.'

'Now look who's silly. Not you, but it is I who must ask for you as my husband in my next seven lives when I tie the string around the banyan tree at the festival of Vat Savitri.'

The curtain moved almost imperceptibly. Greeneyes was

116

listening to Leelawati's and my conversation. Leelawati did not miss the tightening of the muscles in my face.

'These flowers are a token of our betrothal, aren't they?'

Is that what flowers are for? If I give some to my wife, will we be married too? Leelawati was distraught by my silence.

'Yes.'

She smiled and gave me back a flower. 'There, now the marriage is sealed.'

'Are you going to keep jabbering or do I get a chance to give you your second present?' I gave her the marbles. Her eyes lit up with incandescent pleasure.

'Veerdev, Raghudev, Ashok Simha, Pratap can all go to hell. I don't need their marbles any more and it's okay if they don't play with me. I can set up my own game now. You haven't asked what I have got for you.'

'I'm sure you'll part with the information, anyway.'

'That does it. I will not tell you what it is and I won't give it to someone as snooty as you.'

I apologized. I begged for mercy.

She was not about to forgive me. 'I made them with my own hands.' She added just in case I had lost interest.

'What?' I asked innocently.

'Hopscotch shells.'

'There, you told me.' That brought on a shower of blows.

'You made me. You tricked me.'

'More fool you.'

'I'll get you for this. I will too.'

'Are we going to play or just blabber?'

'Are you really going to play hopscotch with me?' She couldn't contain her delight. She brought out the shells. She had painted them with phosphorescent sindoor. 'See, you can play with them even at midnight and you'll see them.'

She watched us play through the evening from the window. Once when I stumbled and sprawled on the ground, I thought I heard her laugh.

It was the first night after the Prince's illness that I had slept. I was woken up around one thirty. There was a message from the tribal doctor. He couldn't get a reading of the Prince's pulse. If I wanted to say goodbye to him, now was the time.

'Is he awake?'

'No, Highness.' Was the honorific back as consolation for his inability to change my guest's fortunes? If he was not awake what was the point of calling me? Was I supposed to keep vigil? Say a prayer for his soul? He must have read my thoughts.

'Sometimes they wake up and are absolutely lucid before they venture to other worlds.'

Don't I know it? But once was enough. What shall I say to him? The Shehzada didn't wake up that night. Or the next.

I didn't see the point of going back to bed. A dip in the Gambhiree, phew, the water was cold or perhaps I'm not in such great shape, and I went over to Lakshman Simhaji's office.

I had discussed Raja Puraji Kika's complaint with him about a month ago but had not followed it up. He felt we should call our nobles from the border areas to Chittor and ask them to clarify what was going on.

'Are they likely to confess to poaching if, and I grant you that it's a big if, they really have been?'

'I would like to think they are honest men. And even if they are lying they are bound to slip up.'

'If they were honest men they would not be grabbing Bhil lands. Raja Puraji is not likely to have made this complaint without checking the facts first. But there's another matter of some urgency here. Apart from the fact that we have both been lax, I want to send a signal to all our neighbours that we value their friendship, if it is proffered, and will do everything in our power to cement it.'

'Fair enough, but why the urgency? Merely because the Bhil king is your Gurukul friend?'

'No. I listen to the heroic tales that the Charans and the other bards sing of and I am aghast. Do you know just how many of our wars in the last fifty years alone were due to some petty frontier dispute provoked by a small-time jagirdar whose greed got out of hand? Every friend that we make and keep is at least one war less.'

He was silent for a minute.

118

'I will send for Hada Parbat.'

'Won't that give the game away?'

'Give me some credit, Maharaj Kumar. He'll meet the erring landlords and be sympathetic to land-grabbing and poaching and worm out all the information we need. When instructed precisely, he's a capable man. He'll leave tomorrow.'

He was right. I sent a courier to Raja Puraji Kika telling him that I was instituting an enquiry as of immediate effect and would keep him posted of developments.

At ten o'clock I had a meeting with Rao Jai Simha Balech. He owed me one and I wanted to strike when the iron was hot. I enquired after his family, especially his sons and then moved straight on to business.

'I have been through your report. I agree with your analysis that given the state of technology in the weaponry and equipment in our neighbouring kingdoms, we are, at the very least, at par with them. In many instances, our elephants have proved to be a major factor in our favour. But do you remember what you taught us at the Academy? The difference between bronze and iron was a phenomenal leap in war technology, not a matter of degree but almost of a different species. Both the opponents fought with swords but against iron, the bronze swords were soft as clay. From the reports that have filtered down from the north-west, from Turkey and beyond, the technology of war materials seems to be undergoing revolutionary changes. I am not talking about matchlocks. I have heard that they now have some very, very big guns, I'm not sure what they are called but just ten or twelve of these massive guns can play a devastating role before two opposing armies can join hand-to-hand battle.

'Unless we are familiar with the new equipment we'll find ourselves in the position of the soldiers with bronze swords confronted by iron ones.'

He was respectfully attentive, I was after all the Maharaj Kumar, but I didn't want him to humour me.

'All this will take time. How soon do you think you can get all the information on the subject? Names, diagrams, effective range, the chemistry of the gun powder, and the metallurgy for the guns.

119

Who has the expertise and who is selling it? Let's have competitive figures and last but not the least, where can we hire experts and teachers to train our men?'

He looked dumbfounded. I had overdone it. Perhaps I should have gone about it in stages.

'Will your father approve of all this?'

'Whether Father approves or not, the new know-how will overtake us all. That is the nature of technology. The least we can do is to keep abreast of it. Otherwise someone else will and that will be the end of us.' I decided to deadline the project to conclude the discussion and underline its seriousness. 'I have set aside thirty thousand tankas from the defence budget for the project. I would like to have a preliminary report within two months and a detailed one in five months' time. I suggest you treat this as top priority.'

I opened the mail after he left. Two letters about tithe payments. One from Sirohi saying that they regretted the delay but the dues would be paid in the next fortnight. The other one was from Mandasaur, excessively courteous, so one knew that they were stalling. They said the usual thing, the monsoons had failed and there was no harvest plus recent wars had left the treasury empty. Would we please reschedule their debt and waive the interest? No way. I would write to them tomorrow. The monsoon had failed at the beginning but picked up very well later, so the rabi crop would be just fine and the wars they mentioned had taken place a year and a half ago. As a mark of the special regard in which we held them, we would give them a grace period of sixty days.

There was a letter from Father. He had heard that Mahmud Shah Khalji of Malwa was once again getting restless and wondered whether we could have some of his mail intercepted, read, re-sealed and sent to its proper destination. Could we also send along reports of the reconnoitring activity in the north-east? What was in his mind? Ibrahim Lodi, the Sultan of Delhi, was certainly losing his grip but was Father finally planning to move against him?

You had to hand it to Father. Unlike his predecessors, his relationship with the other Rajput principalities and kings was exemplary. However gravely provoked, he avoided military confrontation with them. Look at the records and correspondence of my grandfather Raimul, even of my uncle Prithviraj; they are constantly at war with their own kindred. If Father gets a chance to rule another forty years, he'll not only set a precedent for peace among Rajputs, he'll prove something far more fundamental, that given the will, we don't have to fight with each other to the death to confirm that we are alive and that the dividends of peace can be invested in the progress of the state. Isn't it ironic, I would never dare to voice these thoughts to anybody, least of all to Father? They would sound patently false. The greatest living apprehension of Father or any other ruler for that matter must surely be the eldest son.

I find it tragic that Father and I can never be close. He must suspect my every move. It must have taken unusual courage to appoint me acting Head of State in his absence. Does he worry every night that I will raise the flag of rebellion and usurp his throne? Or that my men are even now poisoning his cup of wine? Am I plotting the murder of my siblings? After all, the memory of the Hatyara Uda will be fresher in his mind than mine, and the race to the throne between him and his brothers Prithviraj and Jaimal must be a nightmare that he must live through every day. Besides, patricides and fratricides are not a Rajput monopoly. Look at our guest Bahadur and his ambitions to the crown though he is son number two.

If Father had several enemies abroad and seven at home, I was at risk from six of them: my brothers Rattan, Vikramaditya, Karan, Parvat, Krishnadas, and Uday. Vikramaditya had been caught in the act. The others were innocent only because they had the good sense and good fortune not to be caught, at least not yet. And what would happen when I had children? Nothing much. The risk factor would rise in proportion to the number of sons I fathered. The only remedy was to kill them all at birth or lock them up in some distant prison and throw away the key.

No, sincerely, how do I persuade Father to think sanely and sensibly about a subject that, I'm sure, he never ceases thinking about? How and when will this sword hanging over all our heads be removed?

*   *   *

I waited for Sunheria at the Chandra Mahal. Sometimes she came, sometimes she didn't. I was terrified when she did and distraught when she didn't. She did not expect anything, she did not wait for anybody, she was never disappointed. Is that what you call a strong woman? If her husband found out, if I slipped out of her hands tomorrow, if my wife laid claim to me, so be it, she would move on. Move on where, go in which direction, she did not know and did not care. Because knowing and caring didn't help much either. She wore all those expensive clothes in a casual careless fashion and that made her – without her realizing it – even more desirable and provocative. She loved eating pickles at the oddest hours. She dropped mango pickle on an expensive silk chunni the last time she was here. 'I'm going to be hauled over the coals anyway,' she said. 'Might as well wipe my hands with it.' She did. Was she doing it for effect? She looked at me and said, 'Don't worry. I'll wash the stains off. And I won't touch you with my sharp, pungent fingers.' That last bit relieved me. I can't stand the smell of food on my fingers or anybody else's.

When she came back, her hair was loose and dripping with water. She took off my clothes and eased me down on the bed. She closed my eyes and swept the hair softly over my legs, my stomach and my chest and then over my face. I was not aware of the healing powers of water and the gentle crawl of hair over the body till then. She let the hair drip for some time over my eyes. It seemed to suck the heat and the fatigue and the tension out of them. She went out again, wet her hair and came back. She turned me on my back. This time she started at my buttocks and let her hair take sharp drunken turns over my back. My body tensed up wondering whether she was going to turn a corner or just float on my skin. The water seeped in and the muscles relaxed. Slowly I went limp in every particle of my flesh and bones. 'Sleep,' she said, 'we'll make love when you wake up.' Because she did not think of the next minute and the next meal and the next day, there was never any rush.

Whatever she had to do, she could do today, tomorrow, maybe never.

Would she come today? What was the rationale behind her visits? Was it a whim, a sudden impulse or something as simple as her husband falling asleep early on a particular night?

'Never the last. That's putting too much pressure on chance. When I want him to sleep, I give him milk and sugar and mix a little something in it. He sleeps like a baby.'

'You should give it to me too.'

'There is no child in you. My husband is more fortunate than you. Even at his age, he can fall asleep and sleep for hours. You will wear sleep down. You care too much, Maharaj Kumar.' My head was in her lap and she was stroking my forehead.

'Is that good or bad?'

'To each his own. Let go Prince, let go of so much unhappiness.'

Her bangles were an object lesson in discipline. However impatient I was, they put the brakes on me. The more ragged and frazzled I got taking them off, the more intractable they became. There would be no one around, that's not true, there's always someone around in Chandra Mahal or any other palace, but I hated the clatter they made. It made me terribly self-conscious. The only way to do this, I would tell myself was to relax, calm my nerves. She would offer to remove them herself the way she had done it the first time. But I wouldn't let her. There was something mysteriously erotic about pressing her wrist ever so gently from side to side and when it had turned to putty and gone lax and limp, to let the bangle tinkle down to the tiled floor. And then gradually like the moon slipping out of a cloudbank, see her arm unveiled. Is the mystery of the body in the clothes? Is it in the knots that tie the strings that tie the clothes? Is it in watching your fingers slip the blouse off and drop the skirt and slip them on again? Is it in moulding your hands to the dips and swells and hollows as you pass over them on the other's body? Is sex watching Sunheria put on her anklets? Is it seeing her shake her hair loose, gather it together and twist it into a bun? Is it taking vermillion powder on her right index finger and zeroing in effortlessly to the dead centre of her forehead and spreading a perfect tika on it? Is it her hands cupping

123

together to hold water from the bucket, closing her eyes and splashing the water on her face? Is it these unconscious and almost involuntary gestures that she goes through every day?

Untense me, Sunheria. Press your hands upon the tight sinews in my back. Pull your thumbs down in deep furrows on the sides of my spinal chord. Rub your fingers into my temples till they spring a leak and the coils of my brain come out unsnarling from within. Dig into the depressions in the soles of my feet, uncork my pressure points and let me flow.

She did not come that night.

* * *

I knew it a good half mile before I reached the Atithi Palace. The smell had lifted. Khuda hafiz, Shehzada, I said and walked on briskly. I was suddenly bereft of fear and the cares of declaring Bahadur dead. It had happened and I knew exactly how to proceed. The letter to his father was ready in my mind. There would have to be a royal funeral. Perhaps this might stop the war between Sultan Muzaffar Shah and Father. Bahadur might have his uses after all.

Instead he was sitting up leaning feebly against a couple of pillows. There was a pre-morning light in his room. I took him in my arms, hugged him and kissed his forehead. 'Oh Bahadur, I thought we had lost you.'

'Forgive me, Maharaj Kumar for what I have put you through. No brother of mine would have done what you did for me. I owe you one, a very big one.' He passed out.

'Let him rest now and recover,' Eka told me quietly.

'The House of Mewar is beholden to you, Ekaji. You have saved our guest and our honour, I believe I've got my priorities right this time. You will be Honorary Royal Physician to Mewar from today. In appreciation of what you have done for us, the state bequeaths you Mujadi and ten other villages on the banks of the Gambhiree where it touches your Bhil territory.' I let go of his hands. 'Please don't go yet. Stay till he is completely out of danger.'

'I intend to, Maharaj Kumar.'

124

I went down to the Eklingji Temple and said my prayers and thanks. Shiva had nearly destroyed the Shehzada and now he had recreated him almost from his ashes. It is not pride, I told him, that prevents me from asking you for anything. It is the fact that you are all-knowing. Thank you again.

The next seven days the shehnais played in the Naupatkhana and every morning I offered my prayers to the founder of our dynasty, the Sun-god himself from the suraj gokhadas which projected like balconies from the palace walls and faced the rising sun. 'May your light be upon us always and may you always rescue Mewar from its darkest hours.'

Chapter 12

 It was an unequal fight. No Armageddon this, just the sport of a god.

He was returning from work when he first heard the singing. It was faint and very distant and he didn't know whether it was coming from the heart of the town or from one of the exclusive areas of the citadel a little beyond the Khetan Rani Palace. That was an odd coincidence. He had been thinking that now that the Shehzada was improving, he must arrange a jalsa to celebrate his recovery. He had not heard the voice before. There were just two people apart from his father who were crazy enough about music to import new talent from outside the kingdom: his uncle, Lakshman Simha, the Minister for Home Affairs and Narbad Simha, the commander of the infantry. Since the latter was away with his father, it had to be Lakshman Simha. Who could it be? It was unlike any of the voices of the great singers of Chittor.

He stood still and let the voice wash over him. For some reason that he could not explain, he always found both the sound and the raga itself far more moving if he heard them from outside someone's window or as he was going up the stairs or climbing the shoulder of a mountain. His great-grandfather had been a fine musician and musicologist. Great singers, even those under the patronage of other kings, thought it a rare privilege to be invited by Rana Kumbha. If one was down and out or there was a rift with one's patron, there was always room in Rana Kumbha's court.

Nobody had taught the Maharaj Kumar the intricacies or the

126

finer qualities of raagdari music. When he was a child of four, he sat in padmasan, his backbone a relaxed ninety degrees to the ground, for five or six hours while the singer or instrumentalist expounded a raga. God help him if he got restive or started to bawl, his father's head would turn slowly and the one good eye would come to rest upon him. It took a couple of seconds for him to turn to ash. All that was left of him was a pool of pee in his seat.

If a prince or princess' interest in music continued, then a teacher would come over at six in the evening twice a week for an hour. The Maharaj Kumar learnt the basics of classical music for barely three years. His voice, as the teacher politely told his mother, was passable but not special. And yet his grasp of the subject was remarkable. He had an unerring ear and could tell how and why a series of notes was to be sung just so.

If at a jalsa or mehfil, the audience was a little over-appreciative and kept the beat with their hands on their knees and nodded their heads and exchanged complacent glances of wonderment and plea-sure as the singer came full circle after a complex progression simultaneously with the pakhawaj player, the Maharaj Kumar left in disgust. Grammar, he felt, was a sign of competence, not of excellence. Do you congratulate your colleague, bob your head, pucker your mouth and smile approvingly when he constructs a sentence of seven or nine clauses without missing an article, mis-placing an adverb or bringing the whole superstructure down with a verb in the wrong tense? An audience which is easily pleased is congratulating itself on its own taste as much as the artist. It is a fool's game where the artist is a willing party to the audience's chicanery. It is not enough to love great art, the least you can do is to separate it from the mediocre and the competent; the virtuoso performance which is self-centred brilliance from an exposition that transports and transforms both the artist and the listener. He was not stinting of praise; it was merely that the praiseworthy was not a quotidian phenomenon.

Chittor had its crop of greats and even the occasional genius. It was not just a matter of equipment like the lungs, the diaphragm, the vocal chords and how much work and training had gone into it; it was also a question of what the mind, breadth of experience and the imagination of the artist could do with them. Shalivahan Samant, Rajab Ali and Rasoolan Bai had voices as deep and varied as the ocean and a range of emotion and meditation that was like a vision of life itself. He didn't know anything about the range of the voice he was hearing now. Besides, while first impressions were valuable and had their place in life, he was wary of them. It was only when you heard an artist over a period of time and in different contexts that you could tell whether he did the same thing over and over again or whether he was versatile and his range protean. He would withold judgement for the moment but he had to admit that the intensity of this new voice was unsettling. She flung it as if she would encompass earth and heaven. It was a javelin whose flight path was unaffected by storms and hurricanes because its own element was the flash and turbulence of lightning. It was difficult to imagine how anyone could sustain such raw power. What struck him suddenly was how easy it would be to mock that voice, and burlesque it from one's own sense of acute embarrassment because what it did was to expose the innermost being of the singer, no half measures, no private spaces, no room for equivocation. It bared all in public. It exposed itself without the common courtesies of concealment and dissembling that are essential for the smooth running of society. It was dangerous because it did not respect your mores and your hypocrisies and had no room for compromises.

Surely, a voice coming from nowhere and without a body or a face attached to it can't tell you so much, he said to himself. He smiled wryly, why does my imagination always run away with me? There was only one way to verify all the romantic nonsense he had been reading into that voice. Get to know its owner and after a period of a few months judge how far off the mark he had been. Whose voice was it anyway? He stopped every few yards. If there was one major shortcoming in his appreciation of classical music, it was that he rarely paid attention to the words. Maybe it had something to do with the fact that he couldn't bring himself to read poetry. If it was a folk song or a popular street melody, his ears pricked up and he wanted to know what it was all about. He was amazed at the bawdy vitality of some of the courting songs that the

Bhils sang and the pungency of the satirical verse that went the rounds of the city as a comment on the current political situation, the sexual peccadillos of some well-known person or on the volatile loyalties of some of the neighbouring kingdoms. In classical music, on the contrary, he tended to think of the words as a peg on which to hang the song. He realized that he was being unfair but in most cases where he had understood the words or had had them explained, he found them banal in the extreme.

It had begun to drizzle. He loved Chittor in the rains. Everything, even the stones, were just a little out of focus. The Tower of Fame and the Digambara temple were lost in low-flying clouds. He always thought of the grass in the monsoons as an actor waiting impatiently in the wings to make his appearance. A knock, a slight drizzle and entire armies of grass showed up overnight. Why does green mean so much and make such a difference to men and women? Why is it that no one sings of the dry brown of summer with the same joy and excitement? Is green the colour of life or is it the colour of madness? The green of grass is a possessive, greedy colour. It doesn't leave an inch of space for anything else. I want, I want, I want. It takes over and like the salesman at a cloth shop, unrolls yard after yard of grass till all the three square miles of Chittor are a waving field of green blades. Every now and then you come across a puddle of sky. Suddenly there's a chink in the heavens from which light tumbles out. Somewhere in the distance, I'm sure, there will be a rainbow.

The light and the rain affected the quality of the woman's voice. It became purer and there was a shard of sorrow in it. He was completely wet now. Lightning tore through the sky soundlessly. Later, much later, thunder grumbled irritably at the eastern corner of the fort. Twilight had a strange effect on him. His senses were sharpened and he felt distanced from everything around him. He could hear the words of the song now.

> The rocks have risen to the sky. Heaven has been
> relocated. It's gone under.
> The points on the compass have skidded and let go
> of their bearings.

The underworld has levitated and the demons are
    abroad.
Beware Blue God, someone may mistake you for them
    and slit your throat.

Stand on your head Flautist, it's a topsy-turvy night.
My arms are a black snake. Come, I'll wrap them
    around you.
I'll slither and slide inside and over you, twist and
    cling to your limbs.
I'll be your masseuse, the black rain my healing
    unguent.

Body on body, breast on breast, tongue coiled with
    tongue.
We'll tie a knot that can never be untied.
We'll intertwine into a double helix.
Weave vein, artery and capillary into an inseparable
    plait.

Everything has a place and purpose, you told us.
A viper must be true to his creed.
The fang needs sharpening, the lethal venom a victim,
Come my beloved, lie with me today and always,
No telling if poison and ambrosia are the same
Unless you savour them both.

It's a black snake, it is, this song of night and longing. When
someone departs, you are exiled. Would one be as alone but for
the people one loves? Oh God, I am not yet twenty-seven. How
did I make such a mess of my life? Does Sunheria think of her
life as lonely or a mess? Be my teacher Sunheria, teach me to, what
were your words, oh yes, let go. Come my friend, he said to himself,
self-pity is an indulgence you cannot afford. He started walking
towards the palace. It had begun to rain heavily and the skies had
darkened again. The voice became stronger and stronger. The
servants ran hither and thither, asking him why he had not ridden

home or sent for an umbrella. There were people standing all around and listening just as he had. He brushed them aside. He walked in a daze up the steps of the staircase. His wet feet slipped and he barely managed to keep his balance. He scraped his right knee but he kept walking. Who had had the temerity to hire a singing girl and bring her to his suite of rooms in the palace without his permission? Surely his house had not yet become a kothi.

His wife sat in the middle of her room in front of the marble Shri Krishna. The fingers of her right hand were strumming an ektara. Her eyes were closed. Her face glowed and she swayed just a little from side to side. He watched her as if she were an apparition. He waited for it to disappear, for disappear it would. It is fortunately the nature of hallucinations not to linger and turn into the substance of reality. He must be a sick, a very sick person to think that a Princess of the House of Mewar, the wife of the Maharaj Kumar, no less, would be singing like a tawaif in the palace itself with an audience of forty or fifty down below and a few just outside his private chambers.

'No telling if poison and ambrosia are the same
Unless you savour them both.'

She picked up the last line again and began to embroider on it. He kicked the ektara. It broke in two and slipped out of her grip. Her eyes opened slowly. He knew she wasn't seeing him.

Chapter 13

$\mathcal{I}$t took Adinathji close to a month to recover from a mild case of bronchitis. It must be different with younger people, especially active ones like Bahadur. He was walking around in ten days and playing chess with me late into the nights. He was a better player than I, except that he became impatient or lost his nerve at the last minute. My only strength, if you could call it that, is that I am a steady plodder.

'Have there been any letters for me?' he asked me in the midst of a game. He tried to make his voice sound casual but I could feel the tension in it.

'I don't know. I don't think so. At least not lately.'

'Not lately and not before that either. Was I putting too much faith in my friendships with the amirs and nobles of Gujarat or is the timing all wrong?'

I didn't know what reply to make. Sometime or the other, he was going to discover that a revolt is easier in theory than in real life.

'I wouldn't go that far. It takes a long time for mail to reach Chittor especially since the courier must make a long detour to avoid the battlefield. And then there is the matter, Prince, a thousand apologies for mentioning this, of your elder brother Sikander. However capable you are, do you think it might give the nobles pause?'

'No offence taken. I am no reader of the future but this I assure you, I will be King of Gujarat. When is merely a matter of time.'

I poured both of us drinks. 'Let's drink to that. Because quite apart from the fact that we have become close on a personal level, I believe that the peace treaty you mentioned between Gujarat and Mewar will prove a boon to both countries. May you indeed become the king when the time is right. I wish you every success, Shehzada.'

By the fifteenth day he was riding with me. 'Come I'll race you to Rani Padmini's palace,' he said. We were on the road near Bappa Ka Raj Tila, the platform where my ancestor Bappa and other earlier kings were crowned.

'Maybe you ought to wait another week or so, till you are completely recovered.'

'Nonsense. Don't make excuses.'

He took off like the wind. I tried to overtake him but didn't even manage to come abreast of him at any point. Winning put him in a good humour.

'A delicate matter, Maharaj Kumar,' he took my hand, 'and I don't quite know how to approach it.'

'In that case you would do well to say it as plainly as possible.'

That didn't seem to help him much. His eyes wandered all over the place. 'Can we go inside the Palace?'

'I suppose we could but some of the queens and their women may be bathing there.' Just as I said that, the Maharani's palanquin left the palace.

'Oh, I'm sorry. I hadn't realized that Rani Padmini's palace is still being used.'

'But that's not what you wanted to ask me, was it?'

'No, I didn't.' He hesitated for a moment, then spilled it out. 'That woman, the one who looked after me during my illness, I believe she was your dai.'

'Yes, she was.'

'She's stopped coming.'

'I suppose it must be because you are well and don't need her any more.'

'Yes, that must be the reason.' He was still having difficulty coming to the point. His eyes held mine. 'May I have her?'

And you think you've seen everything and what you haven't, you've had the sense to imagine: every possible scenario for anything and everything in the world. He caught the hesitation in my silence.

'Not for ever but while I'm here.'

'That's between you and her.'

✶   ✶   ✶

Kausalya breast-fed me. Later, when I was thirteen or fourteen, she introduced me to sex. Everybody learns about sex, one way or the other, early on or later. How you do it is a matter of detail.

I have no idea of Kausalya's antecedents. Rumour has it that a couple of years before he died, my grandfather Rana Raimul had a brief affair with a maid-in-waiting who caught his fancy. Brief may mean one night, a couple of nights or a few months on the outside. Well, maybe a year. The outcome of the fling was Kausalya. That's one story. There are five or six others. Perhaps Kausalya may be able to throw some light on the subject, but I am not exactly dying of curiosity. When she was twelve, she was married off to a courtier in the service of Father. Kausalya and the courtier had a son, Mangal, who was born ten days before I was. When I arrived on the scene, Kausalya was entrusted with the task of nursing the heir apparent and hopefully the future King of Mewar. I cannot very well recall whether she was partial to her son or to the Maharaj Kumar in the matter of breast-feeding. Perhaps I got preferential treatment; it was after all a major honour to be chosen as the dai of the King's first son. Perhaps she was impartial and whoever bawled louder got fed first. Or more likely, there was more than enough for both children and we suckled simultaneously at her abundant breasts.

Mangal and I must have been about a year old when Kausalya's husband accompanied Father to do battle with the Malwa forces and died with honourable mention. Kausalya could have left service then. She had over a dozen villages to her name which had belonged to her husband, plus some money of her own. But she preferred to stay. She had got used to city life and Mangal wouldn't get the kind of education he was getting at Chittor. She kept an eye on her property though, and started a poultry business there. Ever since I can remember she has been one of the major suppliers of poultry to the palace. She has diversified considerably since then. I'm sure at least five percent of the mutton and over ten percent of the vegetables we eat are from her farms. I think she must now be a woman of very substantial means, especially since she's branched out into money-lending to the queens and odalisques in the palace.

Even after she had withdrawn into the shadows, I have often thought of Kausalya. She was very likely born in the palace. She has certainly spent most of her life there in close contact with the queens and their servants and sahelis and all the important women at court, but she is unlike them. I think of the queens in the palace and my heart sinks in despair. Can you imagine the endless, the relentless, ever-stretching boredom of being a queen? After you've had a bath — how long, after all, can you prolong washing your hair — and dried yourself and eaten your breakfast and two meals and discount the eight hours of sleep, that still leaves twelve hours a day to do absolutely nothing. If you are in favour, in great favour, the king may turn up fifteen days in a month but he's out of town at least six months of the year. Father has twenty-seven wives, not to mention over a hundred concubines. What happens to the other twenty-six queens and to the odalisques? Doesn't the monotony of their vacant time drive them crazy? Sure, there are rumours now and again of a concubine or a queen having an affair. But a queen's worst enemies are all the other queens. Can you imagine how difficult that makes things? Because while a maid may find privacy for herself, the queens are always keeping a watch on each other. They don't want anybody falling out of line.

They can't spend time with the children because there are maids to do that. They can't even breast-feed their own babies because it's not done. I have seen queens howling in pain because nobody told them to squeeze the milk out of their breasts and they have become so distended and sensitive that the merest whiff of air is excruciating. Most of them don't read. They play hopscotch or some such children's game. Or they play cards and gamble and get into enormous debts with the wealthier queens or a branch of Adinathji's family. They talk, they gossip, and they intrigue. There are many camps in the seraglio but the most enduring one is the division between the favourite and the rest put together. The favourite changes, the one that has permanency is the opposition camp.

The big prize, obviously, is the throne. Any queen who's given birth to a son wants the crown to sit on her son's brow. But the crown is just the beginning of the deadly enmity among the queens. Allowances, the size of the wardrobe, who gets to sit where, whose child is doing better at studies, who has more eunuchs and maids-in-waiting, whose father or family is more powerful, whose hair is

135

longer, whose skin is flawless, any, but any pretext is good enough reason for feeling slighted, deprived and nursing grudges. Sexual allure certainly helps, but it's a long time since Rani Karmavati was the favourite with Father. And yet she has a strange power and hold over him which is difficult to explain or understand. Father is a cautious man, someone who weighs matters carefully and hardly ever acts on impulse. And yet if Rani Karmavati is around or has had a chance to work on him, this highly pragmatic and sensible man is capable of abandoning all sense. It is fortunate that so far, she has had her way in mostly trifling issues. But it's a bad precedent and one of these days she may force his hand in matters which affect the future of the state.

A long circuitous digression that nevertheless reflects on Kausalya. She has no time for gossip or politicking. I think when I was fairly young, she decided to make me her life's work. This is hindsight talking, of course, but Kausalya is clear-headed and she can take a long-term view of matters. It was, admittedly, a narrow canvas she was working on but it gave her a sharp focus and besides, if one day, I do become king, something of her slant and colouring and world-view would affect a whole people. Power, even if it's behind-the-scenes power, is its own reward and end and it certainly must have played a role in her choice of subject. She is also ambitious, more for me than for herself. I think it will take me a long time and a great degree of maturity to sort out what I inherited from her. Off the cuff, I think she gave me a sense of perspective. There is right and wrong in the world and there is always an ethical choice involved. The art of statesmanship is knowing how far you can side with the right and when to abandon it in the interest of the polity. For her, ruthlessness is a virtue. It has nothing to do with cruelty or torture. Ruthlessness was paring down issues to their essence, so that you did not get caught or influenced by the abracadabra and the side-shows of life. Woolliness was unforgivable.

But for her, I would have had the same contempt for literacy as the rest of the men in my family have. Intellectuals are never at a premium among my fellow Rajputs. They are not shunned, but they are objects of fun and a little despised. A life of action for them is the one and only goal of life.

Kausalya herself could neither read nor write. When she was a child she used to accompany princesses of her own age and shared their tutors. But she had some learning disability and was not able to master reading and writing. She was sensitive and proud and suffered because of the handicap. It was to compensate for this failure that, I suspect, she has almost total recall. She was not devout or overly religious but she went to temples and kirtans regularly. She said the brahmins and the charans liked to talk and show off their knowledge. Often they thought they could rule better than the king. And to support their arguments, they quoted from all kinds of sources, mythological, historical and secular. One of the persons they quoted most often was Kautilya from his *Arthashastra*. When I was fourteen, she made me borrow the *Arthashastra* from Father's library and read out a couple of pages to her every day. While its significance and meaning escaped me to a great degree at that time, it was one of the most fruitful experiences of her life. Since she always went to the heart of the matter with a parable or a paradigm, she demonstrated Kautilya's teachings to me with the real-life situations and crises from Mewar's own political events.

I remember those days clearly. I couldn't seem to attend to anything. Even when I read to her, my mind kept wandering. She pulled me up sharply because while I saw and reproduced the words, the sense escaped me and that affected my reading.

My friends including Mangal, were heavily into masturbating. They did it with such intensity and earnestness, it was almost like a religious ritual. But it was not a mass activity where everybody got together and thrummed their members. You could, but it was not mandatory. This was fortunate for me not for reasons of snobbishness or superiority, but because I couldn't work up any enthusiasm to play with myself. I can't say with any authority whether it was as a consequence of this or not, but I had wet dreams almost every night, sometimes twice in the night. I started wearing a loin cloth even when I went to sleep. It helped but not always and whatever the substance of the ejaculation, one thing was certain, it was not water. The damn thing invariably left a starchlike stiffness in the cloth.

I removed the sheet in a rush, took it to the bathroom and

washed it. When I got back I realized that it hadn't been a very smart move. The mattress was stained anyway and part of the sheet was wet enough to make Kausalya believe that I was peeing in the bed. That first day I pretended to be unwell and pulled up a thin coverlet all the way to my neck.

'Maharaj Kumar, don't you know what time it is? Get up and get dressed or you are going to be late for class.'

I opened my eyes and looked mournfully at her. 'I'm feeling feverish, Kausalya.' She came over and felt my forehead. 'Doesn't feel hot. Don't tell me you haven't done your homework or want to miss a test.'

I shook my head. 'Ask Mangal. No test today.'

'See how you feel by noon.'

I closed my eyes. She kept pottering around tidying up the place. I didn't realize when she left because I fell asleep. I woke up around ten thirty. The water had dried but there was an oasis in the sheet. I had had another wet dream. What was I going to do? Would Kausalya tell my mother, who in turn would inform Father?

There was no way Kausalya couldn't have noticed my hyperactive night life but she did not ever mention it.

Looking back I sometimes wonder whether, as the months passed, I didn't really want her to notice. This was about the time she caught me in the branches of the peepul tree a good mile and a quarter up river on the banks of the Gambhiree, spying on the women who went there to wash their clothes and themselves. This was my seventh time in the last fifteen days and I was absolutely sure that no one had spotted me. There was not much I could see. The tree was not exactly on the edge of the bank of the river and the women never really took off all their clothes. Even when they changed into dry saris, they did it discreetly and in one seamless action let the new clothes flow into the wet ones which dropped to the ground. I have no idea how Kausalya discovered my whereabouts. She waited till they had left and then got me down.

'If I catch you here again or anywhere else clandestinely watching women bathe or undress, I will thrash you till there's no skin on your body and then inform the Rana.'

Kausalya and Mangal had a room across the passage from mine.

138

It must have been a week or ten days after that incident that Kausalya told her son that he was a grown-up young man now and got him a room on the ground floor in an adjoining wing. A couple of nights later I woke up to find my fingers wet. They were deep in Kausalya's skirt.

I don't know to this day whether her son knows that his mother and I were lovers. His relationship with me certainly didn't change. If anything, he has become more devoted to me and more vigilant about my safety over the years. We have never discussed the latter but he keeps a hawk's eye on all my brothers and anyone who is their friend. He has his own intelligence network, one which is far more efficient and reliable than the state's, and has a good idea of my programme for at least the next seven days so that he can post his men at vantage points.

I am not thinking straight, am I? If he's half as good at spying as I am making him out to be, then it seems unlikely that he doesn't know about his mother and me. He has always had an uneasy relationship with his mother. Did he regard me as an intruder? But for me, he would have been the one and only one in her life. They are both naturally reticent but in the last few years, there's a coldness between them that's close to bitter hatred on his side. Kausalya does what duty demands of her as a mother. She got him married, but only after I was, to a girl from one of the prominent families of Sirohi. Kausalya bought him a fine house, a stone's throw away from the palace. The dowry that her daughter-in-law brought, she has invested for her son and bride in real estate in the town. She's not over-friendly with her son's wife but neither does she interfere in her affairs.

Thus far and no further. Kausalya has an acute sense of boundaries, not just physical and geographical, but interpersonal ones. More often than not, she is the one to draw them so that you might not always agree with their rationale, but once they are drawn, she sticks to them even if they end up inhibiting her own freedom or hurting her emotionally. When I grew up and my eyes started wandering, she sent me to Chandra Mahal. Sooner or later I would have gone to Chandra Mahal anyway. Many of my brothers and cousins, not to mention Father and my uncles, had suites with separate entrances there. You took a woman with you or asked one of the servants or security guards to get one for you. Kausalya made sure that the girls who visited me were clean and didn't have some infection. Was she jealous and resentful? Did she feel insecure and hurt? I'll never know. Perhaps she was sure that I would always go back to her.

I did. Until I got married. She decorated the bridal bed in Chittor and she took my wife under her wing. I had never needed her as much as I needed her then. I wanted to bury my head in the fork of her legs and squeeze, compress and force it all the way back into her womb. I wanted to cling to her and bash my head against her breasts till they burst and my head cracked open and I couldn't feel anything anymore. I wanted to tell her about the blood and my bride's earlier espousal; ask her about what I should do and where I should hide my face and why she didn't tell me beforehand and how I was to find my way out of this insupportable quandary not of my making. But I couldn't go to her and expose my shame. Was it pride, humiliation, a damaged and traumatized ego? Who knows? If anybody knew my secrets, Kausalya did. She knew my great and lasting anxieties about Father, the succession, the future of the country, my misgivings about the state of our armoury and my ideas about escape strategies during sieges. She alone knew my sexual pleasures and preferences, a great many of which I had no doubt learnt from her. It may not have resolved anything but talking about my bizarre relationship with the Princess to someone who had made my life her mission, would have taken a load off my mind. Perhaps she would have reasoned with the woman who everybody thought was my wife. Maybe she would have made her see the light. If not that, she would have dispelled the darkness of the woman's past and revealed who the secret and nameless stranger was.

Kausalya stayed in the wings not wanting to intrude upon me. The four months that my bride was away, she got the water for my bath ready and put out the clothes I was to wear to court or for an official function. She served me food and sat quietly while I ate. She slept in her old room and if I paced the room all night long, brought a glass of hot milk with turmeric powder in it. But we didn't exchange a word. She could have come at night and pressed her nipples into my mouth, pulled out my tongue and let it forage in her dark and mysterious ponds and rejuvenated me. But she kept back and I remained aloof till my need of her became a cold and hard rage that I could not understand nor overcome.

Mangal, doubtless, had sensed the abyss opening up between his mother and me a long time ago. Sometimes I thought that he rejoiced at her defeat and was happy to be even with her and to watch her suffer silently. For suffer she did. She did not know what had earned her my wrath. She did not know where she had gone wrong. Had I told the new woman about the wet fingers? Had I revealed the quasi-incestuous bond between the two of us to my wife on our first night? Had my wife forbidden me to have any truck whatsoever with her? Would she let it be known abroad that Kausalya had seduced me when I was fourteen when I should have been making out with girls of my own age who should have been abundantly available to the Maharaj Kumar? Would she be evicted out of the palace, dispossessed of her belongings and properties and exiled forever? But I am missing the point. For her greatest fear, and there was hooded terror in her eyes, was that she would be made to part company from the one most precious thing in her life: me. Never mind if I did not talk to her, see her even when she was in front of my eyes; it mattered little or not at all that the new woman had turned my head and there was nothing but cold hatred and a disowning of the past in my eyes, just so long as she could get to see me every once in a while.

She thought she knew me. She discovered that she didn't know the beginnings of me. Things at home went from bad to worse and I seemed to withdraw and curdle in her presence. There was high intrigue abroad in the kingdom. In the past, I would have bounced ideas off her or at least divided my cussed silence between us. Now I neither shared my bed nor my confidences with her. However much I tried to persuade myself that she nursed Bahadur through the worst days and sat through those dreadful nights at his bedside because she wanted to prove what a martyr she was, I knew in my heart that that was not how her mind worked. There were boundaries and there were duties. You did not cross the first and you performed the latter, regardless of the consequences and interpretations put upon them.

*   *   *

'The Shehzada Bahadur wants you,' I had summoned Kausalya to my room. It was an ambiguous statement and she could have played around with it to vex me and to cause me more embarrassment and discomfiture. She got the sense of the statement instantly. Quibbling and hair-splitting were not her way.

'Do you?'

'Do I what?'

'Do you want me to go?'

'I told him that was between him and you.'

We might as well have been enemies. My mask of cynical indifference didn't have much effect on her. She turned her face away to hide her contempt and disappointment and left the room. I went about my work; two meetings with the Prime Minister Pooranmalji about defence systems for Chittor and the other with Lakshman Simhaji about the action to be taken against the two nobles who, our investigations showed, had indeed encroached upon and annexed several villages from Raja Puraji Kika's territory. Another meeting with the minister of commerce about falling revenues and the short-term and long-term measures that needed to be taken. All these years I had been a proponent of octroi and sales taxes but I wondered if we had overdone it a bit and it was affecting our exports. I was attentive at all the meetings, interrupted proceedings when I thought we were not getting anywhere and tried to get the ministers and myself to look at old problems in a fresh and constructive fashion. We decided on the punishment and penalties for the two raos and constituted a committee to formulate a new taxation policy within thirty days. But something had happened. It took me over twenty-four hours to realize it.

How can another man's desire rekindle a passion that you thought was dead and even the memories of which had flown away? Something that I had killed deliberately and without any reason was rising phantom-like and haunting me. I gritted my teeth and pursed my lips and put Kausalya away. But Bahadur's interest in her was like a brushfire. The more I tried to put it out, the more it spread. Memories of Kausalya's body and our lovemaking seemed to interfere and impinge upon my conversations, the memos that I was writing, the preliminary budget for next year that Adinathji presented. Then the unexpected happened. My tortured and ravaged mind which had been run over, usurped and vandalized by that woman at home, the one they called my wife had now, however fleetingly, room for somebody else. Kausalya. Damn my pride. Why hadn't I said no to the Prince? He was aware of Kausalya's anomalous position, that she was my dai and had felt compelled to ask my permission. I had merely to mumble something about the mores and traditions of Mewar and its taboos. I could have embarrassed him and even elicited an apology from him for suggesting something so profane. Kausalya herself was waiting for me to say no. She would have thought of something, I don't know what, to put him off: she was infinitely resourceful. But I was so busy playing a role, 'I don't give a damn, do what you please, what's it to me,' that I had not bothered to ask myself what she meant to me and why I was so hell-bent on losing her.

There were at least a dozen or two girls available to the Shehzada at the Atithi Palace. Besides I was told he had also tapped other sources. Some of the families from his own community were keen on earning his favour and dreamt, I am sure, of tying up with the royal family of Gujarat.

Why did the Shehzada want Kausalya when he had all these girls at his disposal? What had he seen in her anyway? I was aware that it was a hypocritical question even as I asked it. She didn't just look young, she was young. If you saw her just once and that too fleetingly and didn't have time to notice her eyes, the facets of her face or her bearing, she would still make a lasting impression. Because above everything else, Kausalya had presence, a charisma that stayed in your mind. If the men in my own family had kept off her, it was not only because she was withdrawn and was the Maharaj Kumar's dai, it had something to do with fear. If you knew what was good for you, you did not cross Kausalya. She had the most direct eyes I had seen. They saw through you and your intentions and told you to stay off.

143

What was Kausalya going to say to Bahadur? How was he going to broach the subject? How does one break the barrier with a woman one does not know and has never spoken to? Sure, he had seen her but he was barely conscious then. Would he ask her pointblank? Take off her chunni and choli? Grab her breasts, stroke her nipples till there were shallow craters at their centres, suck them and suddenly bite into them, rip off her ghagra and while she was trying to get out of it throw her back on the bed, tie her hands to the bedpost, and ... and lunge into her? This was odd, very odd because I did not normally spend time thinking of the sexual proclivities of others. And then it hit me. I was not making any of it up. I was merely reproducing a secret report given by one of our people about the Prince's nightlife. In the middle of foreplay or sometimes at the very end, Bahadur would become violent and try out various experiments in a cruel kind of lovemaking. One of the cautionary suggestions made by the reporter was that the Prince seemed to want to test the limits of pain in human beings and sometimes ended up going beyond the limits of endurance. As such he needed to be watched. What the paid voyeur meant by 'he needed to be watched' is anybody's guess. Were we to wait outside Bahadur's door and when the lady in distress had abruptly stopped screaming and was losing consciousness, break it open, doff our caps to the Prince and say 'by your leave, your Highness' or 'excuse the interruption but we think the lady needs a bit of resuscitation?' His other recommendation was that we should select such partners for His Highness who were not only old masters, or rather mistresses of the art of receiving such treatment but were also adept at meting it out. A nice touch, that. I was sure that our internal intelligence service had a list of the twenty or thirty such experienced and desirable performers in Chittor.

The Shehzada had fallen ill soon after the report and in all the tension, it had gone out of my mind until now. Damn my asinine show of indifference. I told my amanuensis to cancel my appointments for the afternoon and rode home. That woman was singing. I closed the door of her room and locked it from outside. I searched high and low. No sign of Kausalya. I asked a maid to look for her in the queens' palaces and in the servants' quarters just in case she had gone to give some poor sick soul homemade medicines. Almost an hour passed but she didn't get back. I sent another maid after her and told her if she wasn't back within ten minutes, I would dispatch her to Kumbhalgarh jail. I went down with her and turned left before the zenana. I took off my shoes, and touched the feet of Annapurna Devi who rested in a niche outside the underground storehouses of grain. I made my way through the passages between the tall columns of gunny bags which contained enough lentils, dry beans and corn and jaggery to last the palace occupants for at least six months in case of a siege. I knew I was taking a chance just in case she was supervising some deliveries from the farms. She was not there and when the second maid returned with the first (she had got engrossed in a game of chowpat Rani Karmavati was playing with my mother, the Maharani, for some preposterously high stakes) she said that Kausalya was not on the premises.

I sent for Mangal. Was his mother visiting his family by any chance? No, she was not. I went past the Atithi Palace. I found it humiliating to ask the security guards which woman had visited the Shehzada last night. Was the Prince there? Yes, Your Highness but he has left strict instructions not to be disturbed.

Was she with him? Had she gone to him last night and not come out since then? Had they found so much in common? Had she discovered that she too had a taste for leather, whips, tongs, and cinders? Was she getting even with me for all the weeks and months of sullen silences and cold-shouldering? Was he pouring honey into her navel and licking it as I had done? Was he caressing her back with a peacock feather? Had she run her fingers slowly through his hair and massaged his scalp till he lay in a semi-comatose state only to be woken up suddenly by her tongue playing over his nipples?

There were other highly charged and utterly unmentionable things that Kausalya and I had invented and perfected between ourselves. Was she sharing all this with Bahadur, giving him a condensed course in what we had taken over ten years to explore and chart?

What was the matter with me? If I had missed Kausalya so much, why hadn't I known about it? And when I discovered the truth, why had my randiness gone completely berserk? It was as if I was trying to whip myself into some kind of sexual frenzy by deliberately regurgitating the intimacies I had shared with her. And what if she lay unconscious somewhere? What if he had hurt her beyond the point of no return, not just physically but far more importantly, in her soul?

Oh God, wherever you are, keep her well. And if it's possible, let her be mine and not the Shehzada's.

Where was she?

Chapter 14

We were that rarest of couples. Even after years of marriage we were madly in love. I with her and she with somebody else.

Should he pull her tongue out, he wondered, or stuff a large silk handkerchief into her mouth? Was she perverse? Was she doing it deliberately to annoy him? He had broken the ektara into two. That didn't seem to make much difference. She sang without it. Despite his resolve to make her stop singing at any cost, he listened intently. Would she go off-key without the ektara, sing a false note? If only he could catch her hesitating for the tiniest fraction of a second as she nose-dived into a glissando. She did not. Her voice was steady as a surgeon's hand. When it zigzagged, it was because she wanted to take a taan that slithered like a desert snake as it flashed past, progressing sideways across the sand. Where did she get that voice from? She was five feet two with a little bit of imagination. She was slim and slight. That range and fluidity of registers required a voice box made from tensile steel and it had to be attached to bellows the size of the palace.

He sat her down. He controlled the pitch and timbre of his voice. 'Do not sing. Is that understood? I will not have you sing under my roof.'

'Why?' she asked innocently or at least she did a fine imitation of innocence.

'Because princesses don't sing for the public, at least not in this house. Tawaifs do.'

'It was only a bhajan.'

'Rasikabai ends every mushaira of hers with a bhajan. Like you, she also gets an audience of a hundred or so to stand under the windows and balconies. Soon they'll be throwing coins at you too.' I had got carried away by my rhetoric. 'But they won't if I have anything to do with it. Today's was your last concert, is that clear?'

'If it upsets you so much, I won't sing.'

'It doesn't upset just me, it upsets the whole family. My mother, the other queens, the princes and their wives and it upsets Father.'

'Forgive me, I didn't, I didn't realize it would get to be such an issue that the whole family would be exercised by it.'

'Rani Karmavati called me over yesterday and told me with her usual straight face that the Rao of Chanderi had asked whether he could borrow the new singer we had acquired from Merta. He said he would pay well.'

'Do you want me to go and sing for him? I can't, I'm very shy.'

He was sure she was putting him on, no question about that. Was she crazy? Was she naive and stupid or did she take him for a fool? How was one supposed to talk to this woman? He could feel his temper rise and the blood throbbing in his head. Easy, easy does it, he told himself and found that despite the proffered advice, he was getting madder and madder.

'Just forget it. I don't want to talk about it, so long as you understand that from now on, you'll not, under any circumstances, sing for your pleasure or anybody else's.'

He should have known better. She sang every day. His wife was the talk of the town and there was nothing he could do about it. Not that he lacked the imagination or the initiative to think of extreme options. But there was a stray remark of hers which kept surfacing in his mind.

'I didn't know I was going to sing. I sit down to pray and I lose consciousness of my surroundings. When it's all over I discover that I have once again disobeyed your injunctions.'

He abhorred people who did not take the responsibility for their actions. He believed that all of us know what we are up to even when we tell ourselves that we drifted into something.

'I didn't know what I was doing, I swear I didn't. I found myself

148

in his bed and the next thing I know is I had slept with him.' Or, 'I didn't know what was happening but one thing led to another and before I knew what was what, I had stabbed him.' A likely story. And yet he wanted to believe her desperately.

After all, it was not so uncommon to be possessed. Everybody knew that smallpox was nothing but the visitation of a devi. She could kill you, blind you or being a goddess, she could leave you permanently marked with craters on your face and body. If someone else was perchance responsible for his wife's plight, this other one whom she called by various names, then maybe it was possible to be rid of him. And then maybe, just maybe, he and his wife could settle down to a normal, average married life.

In a cave some forty miles from Chittor, there lived a woman called Bhootani Mata. Nobody knew her antecedents. She lived alone and performed arcane sacrifices and ceremonies. Sometimes if the mood was upon her, she might decide to help a person. But there was no forcing her, nor was there any possibility of getting her over to the palace.

Bhootani Mata was not the kind of person he would have turned to, ever. But 'ever' is a flexible and finite word. Whether he knew it or not, he had crossed the shifting line that separates the sane from the unbalanced. Anything, he was willing to do anything, to retrieve his wife from the forces that had robbed her of her will and set her on a path of collision with the whole of Mewar. He set out to visit his Bhil friend, Raja Puraji Kika with Mangal and the usual retinue of ten or twelve others. On the way, they made a detour. Ordering Mangal and the men to wait, he climbed up the steep side of the mountain to Bhootani Mata's cave. He stood at its mouth and whispered: 'Mata, my wife will not cohabit with me. She says there is another in her life and she is his. I fear she is possessed for I have never seen her with another man. Please help me.' It must have been a long and twisting cave for her voice took a while to reach him. Her message was short. She used an obscenity and said that she had no time for him or his faithless wife. He started to plead with her. She threw a stone which hit him on the forehead, and told him to get out because if he didn't she would throw another one at that thing between his legs and then

149

it would make no difference whether his wife slept with the whole world because he would be of no use to her. He thought of retreating but then decided against it. What did he stand to lose any way?

'I'm coming in,' he told her and didn't wait for her answer. After ten or fifteen minutes he realized he was lost. At each turning there was a fork, sometimes three or four. The passages were black and mouldy, some of them had the overpowering smell of bat droppings. Sometimes he thought his hand brushed a lizard, at other times hairy tarantulas crawled over him. He wondered why his eyes hadn't become attuned to the darkness. He should have been able to see at least vaguely but the longer he stayed, the less he saw. He found it difficult to breathe. What time was it? How long had he been here? Was it just five or seven minutes or a couple of hours? He had given strict instructions to Mangal not to follow him. How long would it take Mangal to transgress his orders? Would he have the sense to bring a light? He himself certainly hadn't thought of it. And would a torch really help? Or would its flame also turn black? Was he going to be responsible for the deaths of Mangal and all the others? He felt a sense of panic at the thought. He had to find his way back.

He strove to calm his agitated mind and to think back carefully. He had entered from the west, the first two turnings were to the south, then to the north, he couldn't remember how he had navigated after that. He was getting disoriented. If you enter from the west and want to retrace your steps, do you go east or do you go west? It was a complex question and though he thought hard about it, he couldn't come up with a definite answer. Perhaps all directions vanish in the blackness of Bhootani Mata. He remembered something from his geometry lessons. If you went in a circle, you would get back to where you started. He would go left and at every crossroad he would take the extreme left turn. There was one more rule he would follow: he would count the number of steps he took.

He counted up to seventeen thousand and collapsed. Forget it. His fate was in Bhootani Mata's hands, if there was such a person as her, and he didn't care a damn what happened to him.

'Are my companions in danger? Did they enter the cave too?

Whatever you do with me is all right but you can't make them pay for my actions.'

A hand made of cast iron hit him in the face. 'Don't tell me what I can or can't do.'

'You've been following me throughout, haven't you?' he asked after he had caught his breath from the blow.

'You've been following me, or trying to.'

Eight hands picked him up. Four supported him, one touched his face as if to learn its features, one groped around his chest and shoulders, the seventh felt his member and the last one pulled his hair. He felt a tongue lick his face, the hands ripped off his clothes and the tongue touched his feet and his neck. How long was it? Was it one tongue or many? The hands sat him up.

'Scared shitless, are you? What happened to the cocky "I'm coming in"?'

He heard the sound of water falling off the edge of the earth and a distant screaming of voices in perpetual pain. He saw dismembered heads held up by the hair with the blood still dripping from them. He saw black feet stomping on the back of a demon lying on his stomach. He heard the sound of lips slurping blood, he saw the coitus of the earth and the sky, he heard the slow moaning of pleasure. There were severed limbs writhing on the floor, a hand came down, picked up a leg, shoved it into a mouth without a face which started crunching on it. He opened his eyes. In front of him was a hollow cavern with a platform in the middle. A toothless and blind old crone was sitting naked on it.

'There are others. Why don't you make it with them? You can marry again. Ignore her till she dies.' There was a pause. 'How about me?'

His body tensed with revulsion. 'Ghastly thought, isn't it?' As she spoke she turned into a young woman. She had a lush body, her breasts were full and firm, held tightly by a kanchuki that exposed her shoulders and arms. She wore a clinging sari. It had gold bands spiralling upwards, a gold waistband hung casually below her belly-button. She shook her hair loose. It cut the light. He heard the sound first. It pierced the eardrums with a sharp high-pitched note. She was whirling her head in circles, the hair swished through

151

the flesh of his face like a rake with a million thin needles. Her head rotated faster and faster. His body was being whipped and his skin shredded so fine, each strand by itself was invisible. He stood up in an attempt to run but the long hair kept whooshing past reaching deeper and deeper into his raw red flesh.

'Is she possessed or are you possessed by her? How many days, weeks, months is it since you had any thought barring hers in your mind? I would say that it's you who needs to be exorcised.' She paused in her gyrations and let the thought sink in. 'We are always trying to cure other people when we ourselves need the cure most. What do you say? You are here, it will take a minute and you will cease to think of her. You'll be a free man.' She paused again. 'Would you like to be a free man?'

He wanted to say yes, every bone and pore in his body said yes but he couldn't bring himself to utter the word.

'I thought as much. Who wants freedom when you can have perpetual bondage?' There was a weighty pause with some tortuous breathing. 'How far are you willing to go?'

He was intrigued by that last question. He wasn't sure he understood its thrust either.

'Money is no consideration,' he blurted out.

'You can shove your money you know where. What do you think I can do with it, make a chain of it? Eat it? Spin yarn from it and cover my knockers? There's only one question in life. Once you have the answer, you know everything that you'll ever need to know. It is this: Just how far are you willing to go to get what you want?'

'Pretty far, I would think.'

'Go home, you fool. When you know the answer, I'll be there. But by then you may not need me.'

'Who is it? What is the name of her lover?'

'What difference does it make?'

He had many more questions to ask. The light at the entrance of the cave blinded him.

Chapter 15

'Who was with the Shehzada on the night of the seventh?' I finally lost my patience and better sense and called the head of the security guard.

'I don't quite recall. That's a week ago, Sir. If you want to know I'll have to go and look up my records.'

'Yes,' I kept my voice under check.

'Right now?'

'Yes.'

He was back within twenty minutes.

'Yes?'

'It was a woman, your Highness.'

'What was her name?'

'We don't have it, Prince, because the Shehzada did not ask us to engage the services of a lady that night.'

'What did she look like?'

'There's just one sentence here under the column Description. "Woman with cowl covering her entire face." She was shown in at ten past nine.'

'What time did she leave?'

He fumbled for some time, making a show of going over the log. 'There's no entry here, Sir, for some reason.'

'For some reason, I don't exactly know why, sergeant major, I have a feeling you are about to be stripped of your rank and your job. It could be a man, woman or eunuch who may have wanted to give his regards to the Shehzada, steal a few art pieces from the palace or kill the Prince. Your log doesn't say and you don't care. He, she, it could have stayed the whole night, abducted the Prince but you and your subordinates don't know because they and you were playing cards, whoring or sleeping while on duty.'

He tried to protest. I'm sure he had a string of excuses but I was not interested. 'I'll review the matter with your superior officers within a fortnight. Till then you and the guard on duty are suspended.'

I cornered Mangal that evening. 'Aren't you worried where your mother is? She's been missing for seven days and nobody knows whether she's dead or alive.'

He shrugged his shoulders. 'She's an adult. She can take care of herself.'

I would have liked to have shaken Mangal's brains and his indifference. I didn't want to see the malicious look of satisfaction on his face. I turned around and left. Kausalya, I had to grant, was capable of looking after herself under normal circumstances. But an invitation to sexual congress was hardly normal and the Shehzada, I was beginning to appreciate, had a side to his nature that was on the far side of wild. That night at the wrestling matches had given me a new insight into the man.

He had mentioned more than a couple of times that he was missing wrestling. One of his companions who had accompanied him to Chittor was supposed to be one of the best wrestlers in Gujarat. A few days ago, I finally arranged a full evening's programme. Bahadur was in a great humour. Of the ten matches, the first nine were between Mewaris, the last between the Shehzada's man and one of our local stars. The Prince was in luck. Of the first nine matches, he had bet his money on seven participants who won.

'What are you going to bet, Your Highness? What are you going to bet against my man?' There was a mad gleam in his eyes. 'He's going to trounce your man.'

'How would you know?' I asked him.

'Because I saw him in action yesterday. My man will dismember him.'

'Have you fixed the fight, Shehzada?' I asked light-heartedly. He gave me a look of such contempt, I wished to God I had fixed it so that our man would lose early enough. It was too late to do anything about that now.

'Gujarat will cow down Mewar any time, Prince. On the battle-field or anywhere else. My man, rest assured, will annihilate your wrestler before the poor man makes his first move.'

There was a crowd of at least five thousand people. The noise was deafening and the excitement a little out of control. It was the rainy season and we had put up a big shamiana around the open-air pit to accommodate everyone. The sand-pit was the only part that was exposed. Everybody was sweating and eating massive quantities of cholle-bature, samosas, kaju chiwda, tawapudi, malpohe, bundi laddus. Bahadur had obviously had a few drinks plus I suspect some drug that was making him highly tense and restless. His pupils were dilated and his hands were shaky.

'What, what will you bet?'

'How about a hundred tankas on your man?' He was looking for a fight and I was not about to oblige him.

'On my man? Don't you have any pride and patriotism?'

'I like to be on the winning side.'

'Then you'll have to abandon your camp and country. Hundred tankas. Is that all Mewar can put up?'

'Your Highness, you seem to have forgotten that when it's our turn to be kings, we are going to sign a peace treaty.'

'Peace treaty be blowed. How much? And remember, you can only bet on Mewar.'

If only, I thought, wrestling could replace wars, I wouldn't mind if Bahadur and Gujarat won every fight for all time to come.

'Five hundred.' I gave the money to the bookie.

'No, no, no.' There was a thunderclap and it began to rain heavily. The two wrestlers were out. 'I have put ten thousand. You'll have to bet at least that much.'

Fortunately it was too late. The two men in the sand-pit had come to grips with each other. I understood why the Shehzada was betting so heavily on his man, Aslam Jaffer. He was tall and built like a mountain. His opponent, Bharat was half his size and more to the point, looked a little intimidated. They were both heavily oiled and the opening of the sluice gates in the sky didn't exactly help

155

matters. For the first minute and forty-five seconds, Bharat's only ploy and preoccupation was to slip out of Aslam's cavernous arms.

'Rat,' Bahadur said to me, 'the Chittor rat doesn't have the guts to give a fight. Look how he's avoiding Aslam. But Aslam is like fate. He cannot be postponed or put out. You watch, he's got a series of holds of such lightning speed, once he locks in, your man will beg to be let off. All he'll want to do is rest his back on the sand and give up.'

That's just what was happening, but not to Bharat. He was a wiry man who used his body rather than fought with it. The fighting he left to his mind. And his mind was an uncanny liar. It sent contradictory signals to the opponent. He came through on some and let his adversary down on others. He was compact rather than fast. The time to get him was when he was sizing up your game and frame of mind. After that things got a bit tough as they had for Aslam. Aslam had used a Bakasur hold and pinned Bharat so far back it would take just a couple of seconds for him to land on his back. Those few seconds were critical. Bharat's toe smashed into Aslam's kneecap. Aslam struggled for balance; Bharat was up, his foot jerked Aslam's leg forward, his head hit Aslam on the chest so that he was falling, falling, falling and was flat on his back.

Bahadur Khan was up and screaming dementedly. 'Foul. Cheating. This is no match. Disqualify Bharat. That referee is a partisan.' The mass of five thousand Chittorites watched him in surprise, dismay and with a rising sense of indignation. Bharat looked at me wondering whether he had done something unforgivable. I saw no point in eye contact. The crowd had begun to boo. The Shehzada noticed the turn in the tide and sat down. Time to diffuse the crisis, I thought and got up. 'Good night. Thank you everybody. It's late and we should all be going home. Tomorrow is a working day. Thank you Aslam, thank you Bharat for a wonderful evening.'

The crowd had already started to disperse when the Prince leapt out of the royal enclosure into the sand-pit. It was still raining and everything looked fuzzy and unfocussed. Aslam Jaffer was sitting up a trifle dazed. As Bharat gave him a hand to help him up, Bahadur

Khan's foot connected with Aslam's mouth. Seven broken teeth sprayed out and Aslam was once again flat on his back. The Shehzada's foot kept coming back at regular intervals. The cracking of the ribs was amplified by the sudden silence of the crowd. Five, six, seven times the foot slammed into Aslam's rib cage. Then it turned him over and hit him in the kidneys. Two firmly aimed kicks in the small of the back. The neck was next. 'You failed the Sultan, me and Gujarat. The izzat of our kingdom is mud in the infidel's eyes. The only honour left to you is to die.' I thought it time to intervene. He swung at me but I ducked and said, 'Time for the fifth namaaz of the day, Prince.' He stopped.

I changed horses twice and reached Rohala within five hours.

'You are not going alone, Your Highness.' Mangal ran after me as I mounted Befikir late at night.

'I see that you've made much progress since we last met. Do I now take orders from you?'

'Forgive me for presuming to advise you, Highness,' he knew perfectly well that I was deliberately distorting his statement of concern, 'but it is dangerous for the Maharaj Kumar to be abroad all alone at night.'

'Your solicitude for my safety is praiseworthy, but it may have been more apposite had it been exercised on your mother's behalf. If I need an escort, I will ask for one. For the moment, I would appreciate it if I could have some breathing room as well as a little freedom of movement.'

There was an unfocussed anger in me and even as I was regretting my petty sarcasms, it felt good to hit a man when he was down and could not retaliate. It was a long, long time since I had been to Rohala and while I recalled some of the rooms and the courtyard with the fountain and the tulsi plant, I had no memories of the exterior of the house I was looking for. It shouldn't be so difficult, I kept telling myself, to find the largest and most affluent house in a place like Rohala, but it was a moonless night and I was loath to run into the night watchman and have him find out that a prince of the realm was paying a secret visit to his village. I had

157

to get out of the maze of lanes and by-lanes and attain a vantage point from where I could get an overview of the topography of the place. The question was how? The land was as flat as my belly. The ever-present guardian Aravalli mountains undulated in the east but they were a good five or six miles away.

I tied my horse and did what any child of seven would have done right at the start. I spat on my palms and climbed up a peepul tree. When you grow up and return to them, you find that your school and classrooms, your home, the long and forbidding administrative block of buildings, your own father and mother, everybody and everything has shrunk. Unless my memory was playing tricks on me, Rohala had gone against the grain. It had prospered and grown into a town. The semicircular Mayura lake by which it was situated was a good mile and a half long. The slate-grey glass of the water looked solid enough to walk on. It was a mystery why the houses stopped exactly at the diameter of the lake but the effect was to turn Rohala into a toy town. Just in case the Mayura ever went dry, the town had its own river, a tributary of the Banas. There were at least forty two-storeyed buildings, a mosque with a minaret and on the left bank of the river, a temple.

Does a town, city or village have a heart and a soul and a mind? Who decided that the lake was for leisure and that the town should grow around the river? I felt I was caught unawares, as if Rohala had hoodwinked me and grown and spread behind my back. How was it I was so uninformed about our kingdom? How many other villages had burgeoned into towns? And how many had atrophied? I knew what I had to do. I must tour every part of Mewar. I wanted to see the faces of my people. I must talk to them, ask about their crops and industries. What were their problems? Were they good tax-payers? Were our revenue officers corrupt? That old fox Adinathji was right. Not war, but agriculture, manufacture and trade are the fuel of progress. What was the secret of Rohala's prosperity? Could it be replicated? Or was the trick to study the genius of each place and .... Chamundi. The temple on the river bank was a Chamundi temple and the house next to it was the one I was looking for.

I knocked for a long time. Was she there? I could feel the hostility of the house. With every tap of the knocker, it shrank back from me. The two-storeyed mansion was now a tight little ball of malevolent intent which swung back at me.

'Who is it?' the retainer asked. It didn't look as if he had been sleeping the sleep of the dead. He was alert, truculent and itching for a fight.

'Dai Kausalya. Is she here?'

'No, Your Highness, she is not.'

He was a professional bouncer, the kind that can deal with any manner of trouble and if need be, put an end to it. But I am a handful, and besides I never forget that I am the future king.

'Wrong answer. You should have said "Who the hell are you?"' I pushed him back and entered. The fountain was playing. The geography of the house came back to me. I turned right. Kausalya's room was on the first floor. I went up the stairs, turned left, ran along the balustraded passage that looked out on the courtyard and knocked on the fourth door. No response. I knocked again. Silence. I pushed the door hard. It didn't give. I was relieved. She must have locked it from inside.

'If you don't open the door, Kausalya, I'm going to break it open.' The retainer watched me from downstairs. Three other servants, two of them women, had joined him. I turned back to the door. It was latched from the outside. Neat trick, I said to myself, removed the latch and threw the door open. It was dark but I knew there was no one inside. I went in and slipped my hand under the bed. She was not there.

'Give me that lamp, you dolt,' I snapped at the watchman. He ran upstairs hurriedly and handed me the lamp. I went through every room. I scoured the bathrooms and the water-closets, I ransacked the servants' quarters. I took off my shoes and stepped into the prayer room with its stone icons of Shri Ganesh, Vishnu, Chamundi and the Flautist. I went back to the ground floor and combed the rooms once again. Oh God, oh my dearly beloved God, where was she, my one-time mother-sister-woman-lover-confidante and preceptor. The worst of my fears had come true and however violent I felt, I knew I could not touch the Shehzada.

I saw the household watching me as if I was an actor from a play. I asked for a drink of water both for myself and the horse.

We had a long journey back. They were closing the front door when I threw it open again. There was a room on the terrace.

She was lying naked on her back in a bed. The flimsiest of muslin cloths covered her. Her eyes were glazed with fever. There were welts and blisters and hives all over her body. I stood in the doorway. My arrival had generated a draft and the flame in the brass lamp trembled like a frightened bird and then died altogether.

I knew then what she had done. She had rubbed the poisonous weed called Maa ka Krodh or Mother's Wrath which grew in the marshes on the eastern slopes of the Ramkali hills and which all animals instinctively kept away from, on her body before going to see Prince Bahadur on the night of the seventh.

She was red and black like a bruised and broken tomato with fungus growing on it. Edema had disfigured the angles of her face and inflated it till her eyes, nose and lips were misaligned and yet level with each other. I took my clothes off slowly. Kausalya tried to sit up in bed but fell back exhausted. 'Don't Maharaj Kumar, I beg of you don't. You know how infectious the itching is.' I lifted the muslin sheet from her body lightly and then gently, very gently lay on her.

'I'll never leave you again, Kausalya.'

*　　*　　*

Jai Shri Eklingji

Our blessings be with you.

A worthy king must divide his time between his kingdom and the battlefield. It is time we came home and took the reins of state in our hands once again.

The conduct and direction of a war are good and essential training for a prince. It is our wish that you now take charge of our armies and do battle with the enemy, the forces of the Sultan of Gujarat.

Celebrate the festival of Janmashtami, pay
homage to the gods and proceed forthwith to Idar.
We await your arrival.

Shri Surya Namah
Your Father, His Majesty Rana Sanga

Ever since the day I could separate my childhood from my youth,
the one wish uppermost in my mind was to lead the Mewar armies.
I had accompanied Father on five major campaigns, participated in
strategy-planning and on the last two occasions led the main attack.
But that was all under Father's watchful eye and under his command. Now I was to be the sole commander of the Gujarat campaign
and yet I couldn't bring myself to rejoice without reservations.
Within a matter of hours, the news would spread and every minister,
secretary and under-secretary, anybody who was somebody in the
government and the civil services and the populace of Chittor would
arrive to congratulate me. But I know that it is not in Father's nature
to drop a job, especially such an important campaign, half-way. I
have often heard him say that change of leadership midway on any
project, particularly when you are fighting a war, confuses and
ultimately demoralizes not just the soldiery but the officers and
commanders too. There's a change of style and substance in the
thought processes and concepts, in the way a problem is identified
and a solution worked out, all of which affect the thrust and
cohesion of a team adversely. He has often given credit for our
victories against Malwa, Delhi and Gujarat to the sudden switches
in command effected by the sovereigns of these states, when the
war had not been going well for them.

Why was Father abandoning one of his basic tenets? Did I owe
the honour of becoming the commander-in-chief of the Mewar
forces to Mother Karmavati's good offices?

She had been sending an endless stream of missives to Father,
two a day in the past month and a half. I had thought about
intercepting and eliminating them but once you indulge in surveillance in personal dealings, you enter a bottomless pit of suspicion

161

and persecution. What is important is that I must not confuse Queen Karmavati with Father.

It's not the person who tells tales who is the culprit, it is the one who listens to them. What I must never lose sight of is that whatever the Queen, her chief eunuch Bruhannada, her long train of sycophants or any minister of state may whisper or insinuate in Father's ear, the responsibility for listening and acting upon it, instead of going by his past experience of me and assessing the evidence impartially is his, and his alone. For the moment it seemed as though the Queen's entreaties, warnings and counsel were fighting against Father's own conscience and sense of fair play. He did not wish to displease either of us. The middle path, the golden mean, is a fine principle but in the business of politics, you can't keep everybody happy.

But perhaps what he was doing was playing one against the other, making me commander-in-chief and getting me out of the way while he came back, regained his putatively threatened crown and set Vikram free.

There were, however, other reasons for my not wanting to leave immediately. I had initiated a project which I believed was of crucial importance to the future of Mewar.

The health of my people and consequently, the drainage system were top priority for me. But the water and sewage schemes were also a smokescreen. My primary concern was with the fort. For several years now I had been exercised by the one problem which even the strongest, soundest and most spacious fort poses. Chittor was just such a citadel. It was at a commanding height, the plateau on which the town sprawled was three miles long, it had its own perennial water-springs and it had large granaries. If there was a fort which was indomitable and unassailable, it was Chittor. And yet a long-drawn out siege like the one Alauddin Khilji of Delhi had laid, had brought Chittor to its knees and killed off almost the whole contingent of Rajput warriors in the fort.

For a while I was convinced that the problem was the institution of the fort itself. The safe haven, I was almost persuaded, was really nothing but a trap crying to be snapped shut. That's just what we did when hostile forces approached. We locked every gate and threw away the keys. Beleaguered, starved and exhausted after months, our only hope and way out of the predicament was the enemy. He alone could release us, either by raising the siege, or by storming the gates. I was, needless to say, throwing out the baby with the bath water.

I thought about it for months and re-invented the wheel. A fort was not the ideal solution but however inadequate, it was still the most viable. Was there no way out then? I realized there was, if I concentrated my energies and imagination on the phrase 'way out'. One of Chittor's greatest assets is that its slopes are covered with dense jungle. My plan was this: under the guise of digging sewer systems, engineer a secret but extensive network of broad tunnels with doors that would open out but not inwards, at seven or more deeply concealed and forested points along the base of the hill on which Chittor stood.

When a siege seemed imminent, the first thing to do was to evacuate all children and women. (The women may valiantly jump to their death in the fires of johar when all was lost, but in the meantime concern for their safety weakened the resolve of the men.) Stockpile as much food, wood and arms and ammunition as the fort could hold. But despite the fall in the population, the resources in a fort are finite. When the enemy was convinced that we were low on victuals, water and morale, move half the forces out at night, through the tunnels, if possible on a stormy and thunder-ridden night. In the absence of thunder, create a deliberate and effective diversion for the troops to escape. Once outside, regroup at night and take the enemy by surprise from the rear and cause havoc in his ranks. If the nocturnal assault fails, the remainder of the garrison too would vacate the fort the next night.

The enemy will discover a ghost town and fortress the next day. Sure, he'll loot whatever he can and set fire to everything in sight. That he would do even if you fought to the death. Now when his troops leave Chittor loaded with every kind of booty while a small contingent holds the fort, attack the over-burdened, lax and weary, home-bound divisions with everything you've got. You better make a rout of it because the day after, you besiege your own badly damaged fort which is almost bereft of supplies and take it back as quickly as you can.

163

I had barely forty-eight hours in which to settle my affairs, do my packing and say my farewells. But I had to find the time to meet my new proselyte, the town-planner Sahasmal, before I left Chittor. When I first outlined my ideas about the tunnel project to him, he sounded sceptical. He was worried about the time it would take to complete such an ambitious project.

'Rana Kumbha didn't build the Victory Tower overnight.'

'Your Highness, building in open space on firm rock is a far easier proposition than excavating rock for miles. In the former you just place stone upon stone. In the latter you chisel for days and make an inch-wide dent.'

I must confess that the elementary example he cited brought home the problem of the labour involved far more graphically than I had envisaged.

'So it will take longer to build than the Victory Tower, what of it? We hope the tunnels will prove useful to our children's children over the centuries. Besides if the scheme is going to really save us in times of a siege, then we can double or triple the work force we would employ for overground construction.'

'The second problem's more intractable. I'm worried about the air in the tunnels.'

'While digging or afterwards?'

'In both cases. But especially afterwards when it's been closed for years. It could become toxic and prove fatal.'

'Chittor is high but not so high that we'll have to dig a mile or two into the bowels of the earth. Perhaps we need to work out a system of vents and lower birds in cages to see if they can survive. I'm improvising, you understand? I'm not discounting or belittling your reservations. Perhaps there will be other more obdurate problems. But I would leave it to you to resolve them. Just think Sahasmal, if we can see this plan through, how many lives we can save. And if we survive, we may yet end up defeating the enemy. It's not exactly the Victory Tower you wanted to build when we first met. But we could call them Sahasmal's Victory Tunnels. Imagine how grateful future generations are going to be to you.'

'When do you want to see the first plans?'

'You tell me.'

'Four weeks from now. My son will personally bring them to you.'

'I don't want them to fall into anybody else's hands.'

'I'll do them in code. All the tunnels will be shown above ground so that the whole thing looks absurd and is completely indecipherable.'

'All right, let's see what you can do for us.'

'Godspeed, Your Highness.'

One last job remained. I sent for the mullah. 'Was it your prayers or the prayers of the priests in our temples which worked? Was it our gods or your One Single God who saved the Shehzada?'

The mullah looked perplexed. He didn't want to displease the Prince but he didn't want his Lord God to be angry with him either.

'Never mind, mullah. Here's the money for the repairs in your mosque.'

Since the Flautist was born at midnight, the official puja for the Janmashtami festival should have been at that auspicious hour. But as Shri Eklingji is our family deity, he is the first among equals and the honour of a night-long wake belonged to him alone. The family puja for the Flautist was a private affair at night and the public ceremony was held the next evening. I had almost entirely severed relations with the Flautist but this was official business. The kings of Mewar always visited the Brindabani Temple, did arati, touched the Blue One's feet, ate prasad, and distributed largesse amongst the subjects of Chittor on Janmashtami. Whatever my personal quarrel with him, I was not about to break with tradition. A kingship survives on institutions, and there's no greater institution than tradition.

It was a state occasion. Kausalya helped me put on the full royal regalia: yellow silk dhoti, a sandalwood-white duglo with some fine silver thread embroidery, nothing fussy, almost the subtleness of white on white which only a very few discerning courtiers would notice and appreciate and a green saafa topped with a flourish of white feathers. I bent my head for Kausalya to put on the fourteen-stringed meenakari gold necklace.

165

'Shall I fetch the mirror?' she asked.

I shook my head. I do not care to look at my own reflection. 'You tell me how I look.'

'Like a future king. And a king must always know what impression he's making on his subjects.'

'All right. Fetch it.' I saw a young man with an intense, thoughtful look. Deepset eyes, eyebrows that kept their distance from each other, an assertive nose and a wide mouth; the loose shock of hair was well-behaved since it was hidden under the turban. Why have I become such a painfully serious person in the last few years?

My brothers, Prime Minister Pooranmalji, Adinathji, the Minister for Home, my uncle Lakshman Simhaji and other cabinet ministers and dignitaries were waiting outside the palace. Each did obeisance to me, and I mounted the royal elephant, Toofan. I was relaxed, confident and as always, keeping an eye on myself. This was the first time I was standing in for His Majesty at a public function and I was conscious of the pomp and gravity of the occasion. The roads were thronging with townspeople. They were leaning over balconies, standing precariously on ledges and peering down from terraces. They wished Father and me long lives. I was moved by the warmth and openness of their affection and overwhelmed by their trust. If I were to ask them to go with me tomorrow and give battle to the Gujarat armies, they would come without question or hesitation. They threw flowers at me and the women pressed their knuckles against their temples to ward off the evil eye. I wanted to wave out to them and embrace them all. Instead I smiled slightly and raised my hand sedately every now and then as a future king should.

We had turned right into Maharana Kumbha Mahapath when I heard the voice, the same as on that rainy day when I had first heard it. I was daydreaming of course, no question about that. What would she be doing in this part of town? What in God's name was she up to? Since we led separate and independent lives, I had no idea of her whereabouts or how she occupied herself. That sounded lame. It would be a risible and inadmissible plea even in my own Small Causes Court. If the Maharaj Kumar of the realm was going to be in the dark about his wife's movements, he had better become a hermit and go into the mountains. Because if he couldn't take care of his wife, how was he going to look after his subjects and his kingdom? Did I not know it was Janmashtami, the Flautist's birthday? Did I expect her to have a change of heart, disown the Blue One and come and lie with me? I had no one to blame but myself. If Vikramaditya hadn't already helped me become a household name and the gossip of the town, I was about to make myself the cuckold, jester and fool in every bhavai, nautanki and farce in Mewar.

I knew what to expect. I kept a straight face and looked straight ahead. If you look haughty enough, I told myself, no one will dare make fun of you or crack a joke, at least not to your face. But the people of Mewar were in a good humour and willing to ignore the public humiliation of their Maharaj Kumar. We were now on the central avenue, Bappa Rawal Path, the one that divided Chittor into two almost equal halves. Every fifty yards, there was a pot tied at a height of some twenty-five or thirty feet with ropes that had a profusion of vines and flowers entwined around them. This was a piece of decoration I was unfamiliar with. Did the pots contain, I wondered, the Flautist's favourites, curds and butter-milk? I did not have to wait long for an answer. I heard the sound of a tugging at the neck of the pot above me. My first impulse was to duck my head. I was in no mood to be spattered with dairy products. Fortunately I kept my head and did not make an ass of myself. There was a shower of petals and by the time the seventh pot had emptied, not just Toofan and I but the entire road was a mosaic of pink, yellow, white and red.

Where were all the peacocks? Why weren't the parabolas of their lonely cries drowning out the song of my wife?

Seen the sun today?
It's gone peacock blue.
Looked at my tongue this morning.
Same thing. Stark blue.
Blue marigolds. Blue ravens. Blue grass.
Must be a blue cataract in my eye, I said.
Glanced, by chance at the calendar then.

167

Watch it impatiently for 364 days of the year.
Except today, of course.
Wish you a blue birthday, my love.
(Can gods have birthdays,
Thought they were without beginning or end.)
Blue is the colour of my beloved.
Blue is the colour of my universe.

They call me tart, harlot, whore
Slut, strumpet, fornicator.
Tell them, I beg you.
I beseech you, tell them.
Save my honour, beloved, save my honour.
Tell them who I am,
A god's wife, nothing less.
(Are you ashamed of me,
Why have you kept me your dark secret?)
Tell them, I'm yours.
Legally married to you before the gods.
As the sun, moon and stars are my witness
Tell them, to my last breath,
I'm a true blue.
Save my honour, beloved, save my honour.

Seen the sun today?

The song and the voice rose to a frantic chant of one of the Flautist's thousand names as we stopped at the portals of Brindabani Mandir. I alighted slowly from Toofan's back. 'Save my honour,' she cried again and again. 'Save my honour.' There is some misunderstanding here, my dear wife, I believe it is my honour and the honour of Mewar which need safeguarding. I took off my shoes. I could feel the Pradhanji and the Chancellor avoiding my eyes. Did they know? Did all the courtiers and the raos and rawats who were accompanying me know the identity of the singer? I was willing to delude myself even now. Of course they knew. An old man bent down and touched my feet. I took his hands and lifted him up.

He looked at me sadly, shook his head and said to no one in particular, 'Princess, part company with the saints. Your own Merta is ashamed of you. And so is Chittor.'

If his commiseration for my plight touched a chord within me, I was not about to show it. I climbed the hundred steps solemnly and walked across the mandapa and the kalyana-mandapa. The guards were having a difficult time keeping the thousands of towns-people in check. My wife had worn a nautch girl's bands of bells around her anklets and was dancing in full public view. Her skirts were a red blur, she was gyrating like a dervish in a trance. She was wet with sweat though her chunni and blouse had not yet turned translucent. How long had she been dancing? Only a woman possessed could have this order of preternatural energy. I have kept my peace all this while, Flautist, but I have a score to settle with you now.

How far was I willing to go to get what I wanted, Bhootani Mata had asked me. And my inane answer was 'pretty far'. No wonder she thought me a fool who spoke without due thought.

Now I couldn't go far enough. All the way Ma, all, all the way. As far as it takes. Whatever it takes to eliminate her but not without all the torture and suffering and pain that this world and every other is capable of. Do it Bhootani Mata, do it and give my soul peace. I have earned it.

I will make a covenant with the gods and the devils. Anyone you say. With Brahma, Vishnu, Mahesh, with Indra, Varuna, Agni, with the dread Yama himself. If need be, with the gods of a prior and primal time. I will not stop there. I will embrace evil and the black arts. I will blacken my heart and of a dark night open the gates and invite a black pestilence upon her and her kind. Open your treasure trove of death's heads and parasites, Bhootani Mata, of the numerous hordes of worms and weevils, maggots and termites and let them cover the earth and eat through the substance of the three worlds till there is neither stone nor clay, neither sky nor water, neither air nor fire, neither god nor rakshasa, merely a ceaseless tumult and simmering proliferation of the creatures of the under-world. Let them eat through flesh and bone and crawl out of eyesockets and other orifices of the mouth and ears and nostrils and

169

the anus till there's nothing left for them but to devour each other. Let there be nothing, nothing, nothing.

* * *

'Throw her at Toofan's feet. Let the elephant trample her to death. Tie her up in the public square and whip her till every drop of blood in her veins has dripped to the ground,' Queen Karmavati was screaming at me. The other queens and maids were in a state of shock. Even Kumkum Kanwar with her inordinate and blind love of her mistress looked distraught and on the verge of tears. 'Do you see to what depths your spinelessness has brought us? I warned you when she was dancing at home. I told you to get rid of her, banish her, lock her up forever, get rid of her once and for all but you didn't listen. How will we ever survive this shame? How will His Majesty, the Rana, your Father hold his head up again? I will tear her apart, limb from limb. Get up, you pansy and drag her home.'

'Not now, Mother,' my voice was low and dangerously calm. 'I will have silence. I have come to offer greetings and prayers to the Blue One. I will have peace. Each of us,' my voice was resonating and echoing now, 'must pray in his own fashion. This is her way. We'll all respect that.'

The Rani was speechless at the effrontery of my snub. It was as unexpected as it was unanswerable. She looked at me with ill-concealed hatred. She would get back at me yet for my insolence. But, for the time being, she was silenced.

Bhootani Mata was standing next to me. I felt the opaque white excrescence of the rock of the cave on my back and the wet slime of her palm as she took my hand in hers. 'Why not take your time before taking a decision, Prince? In life there is no going back. You cannot undo any act, however much you may want to later on.' I threw her hand off in disgust. Did the old crone really understand who I was up against? 'Think about it, Maharaj Kumar.' Her shrivelled flapping breasts slapped against my face. 'Act in haste and repent at leisure. What do you say, Prince?' I turned away and entered the Flautist's sanctum.

Is there anything more painful and lonesome than betrayal? Yes, there is. It is loss. And worse than loss are the tricks that memory plays. I looked at the Flautist. It was like meeting a dear friend after a period of years. My first impulse, it was hardly an impulse but the most natural thing in the world, was to touch him as I had done when I was four or five years old, but the priest came forward to greet me and the spell was broken. We were finally face to face. Two mortal enemies. Correction. One mortal and the other divine and immortal. I was overtaken by such a strong wave of loathing, I wanted to strangle him till the last breath had gone out of him and then snap his neck. What was I doing here? I didn't want to see his face again, not be anywhere in his vicinity for the rest of my life. It would be rhetorical and asinine to ask him 'Why?' Even on the rare occasion when someone proffers a reason, a sound reason, does it ever get to the heart of things or reveal the truth?

The Flautist's weakness for women was legendary. There were always women hanging around him. But what was astonishing, disconcerting and inexplicable was the curious nature of his attraction. The more women he had, the more women wanted him. When he discarded them, or rather, just plain forgot them, the more desirable and attractive he became. The truth is perhaps simpler than that: women love a philanderer.

But all that was a thousand or two thousand years ago. He had died a tragic earthly death and gone. Why after all these years ... forget it, there's no purchase in that line of thinking. I did what I had to do, the abhishek, the puja, the arati, the prostration and the circumambulation. I ate the prasad. When the senior ministers were done, we left.

*   *   *

The august gathering at my cousin Rajendra Simha's rose to its feet to greet the Maharaj Kumar and the Shehzada. The invitation was from Rajendra but as the patriarch of the family, his father Uncle Lakshman Simha came forward to welcome us. He embraced me and then turned to Prince Bahadur.

'Salaam alequm, Prince. Greetings to you on the mischievous Bal Krishna's birthday. Treat our house as your home. Make merry and may the child Kanhaiyya's blessings be upon you.'

My heart skipped a beat. Bahadur and I seemed to have put the

171

Kausalya incident behind us. He was no man's fool and was not deceived, I was certain, by Kausalya's ploy. I'm not sure whether she said anything to him on the night of the tryst, something about her gonorrhoea flaring up or just stood there mutely in the full and livid flush of her flesh's diatribe against her. He had been rejected and the Prince was not one who could conceive of anyone saying no to him. The offence had been noted and been kept like a scented flower from one's beloved in the pages of a much-thumbed book. He would take it out one day, look at the dry and desiccated petals aimlessly and strike. When I reached the Atithi Palace to pick him up, he was his normal affectionate and warm self. No point ruining the pleasure of the present for the distant future. When the latter came to pass, he would exact the price of vengeance.

Was the mention of a Hindu deity going to stick in his craw? Was he going to come up in a rash and make an issue of it? He smiled a disarming, winning smile. 'Wale-e-qum salaam,' he triple-embraced my uncle in the custom of his faith. Lakshman Simhaji wasn't doing too badly either. The funny anecdote Bahadur had narrated on his previous visit had been shelved and though the Shehzada couldn't quite encompass his girth, Uncle dutifully put forth his left cheek, then his right and left once again.

I am rather fond of my uncle as I suspect he is of me. Don't be put off by the enormity of his corpulence, his jiggling breasts, or the ripples of flesh that swim across to the distant shoreline of his body when he exposes himself to the masseur in the evenings. He is a man of great taste, puckish humour and a highly sensual softness that some women find irresistible. He is the only true hedonist in Chittor. He loves his food and wine and his bodily pleasures including farting in various keys. He is also a fine musician and has a deep, resonating timbre to his voice, which in the days when he was slim and active, made him one of the most sought-after amateur singers at parties. He didn't ever make a fuss about singing. He likes himself and he's sure that others like him too. He is Father's cousin and since Father was away often and his son Rajendra and I were the same age, he took it upon himself to be my guardian.

Rajendra is his father's son. He loves the good things of life.

When I was young, I would go to him when I needed cheering. When we grew up, we drifted apart. No fights or falling out, just the normal going our own ways which didn't seem to bring us together too often. We are going to be constantly in each other's company from tomorrow since Father has appointed him head of a division of cavalry. I'm looking forward to getting close to Rajendra again and not only because I need friends and allies. I like Rajendra. As with many gregarious and loquacious creatures, you never know what goes on in his mind or why he hurts. A good man and a loyal one. At first I was a little wary of his hot-house friendship with Bahadur but part of it, I suspect, was nothing more than possessiveness. I felt left out but was not willing to join them on their nights out on the town. We are always laying claim to those whom we have not bothered to stay close to and nurture. Bahadur and he are still close as you can see by the way they greet and hug each other. Bahadur's going to be a little lost from tomorrow.

The Pradhan Mantri Pooranmalji, Adinathji, the other cabinet ministers, my cousins, nephews and brothers came and greeted me. This is an informal function but I'll mingle with them later on. As my Father's representative in Chittor, etiquette demands I stand on my dignity till the performance starts. I know what they are thinking about but barring Vikramaditya, who, fortunately, is still in jail in Kumbhalgarh, no one, I'm certain, will refer to my wife's song and dance at the Brindabani Temple this afternoon. I chat with every-one, ask after their wives and children and pointedly talk of incon-sequential things.

The house is lit as if today is Diwali. My uncle is a collector of lamps and this is the ideal place to show them off. Sky-blue chanderi curtains are kept on a short leash in the huge windows but cross ventilation makes them strain and protest till they slip free and billow and reach for the ceiling. We may have more expensive carpets at home but the Persian and Afghan carpets at Lakshman Simha's always seem more springy and inviting. You can sit on them, loll on them or snore away and no one's going to come running and tell you to be careful because this one's a gift from the Raja of Kashmir and the other one on which you are resting your mud-caked shoe is a collector's item worth a king's ransom and is from the Sultan of Turkey. There are hundreds of cushions strewn across the carpets. Some are round, some square, some are fat cylinders. I would prefer a more inconspicuous place to sit so that I can slip out if I get bored. But you can't be cock-of-the-walk and expect to be ignored.

There is no formal dinner tonight. Whenever you feel hungry you go to the shamiana that has been set up in the courtyard. You may have a full meal, one of the best in this part of the country or make a meal of the endless varieties of snacks and savouries.

The pakhawaj player and the sarangiya enter and do namaskar to me and Bahadur Khan, to my uncle and Rajendra and to all the dignitaries, then settle down to tuning their instruments. Everybody has to wait on the Rana (or in his absence on the Maharaj Kumar) but there is one exception to the rule. An artist like a singer or dancer, or even the nautanki player, will not appear till the king is seated. This is the signal for the women to take their seats in the side wing. A red flash jumps over the extra sets of percussion and stringed instruments and is in my lap, its arms wound around my neck. Adinathji starts to protest but I raise my hand. Leelawati, as always, does wonders for my ego, spirits, heart, soul, and whatever bits and tatters of mind that are still around.

'You are going tomorrow without even saying goodbye.'

'That is not true. You are the guest of honour tomorrow at dawn. It is you who will present the pennant of Mewar to me.'

'You could have come home.'

A year or two and Leelawati will not fly into my arms. They'll marry her to some financier and we'll hardly ever run into each other.

'You haven't done adaab to His Highness, Prince Bahadur of Gujarat,' I changed the subject since I was not about to go into a long explanation about how little notice Father had given me to leave Chittor.

'You haven't introduced us.'

'Shehzada, this is Leelawati, Adinathji's great-granddaughter. Leelawati, His Highness Prince Bahadur.'

Leelawati got up and curtsied to the Prince.

'I was wondering whether the Maharaj Kumar would get around

174

to introducing me to the lovely young lady. Are you his favourite?'

'Yes. And he is mine.'

What a fine head Leelawati had. The Prince must have read my thoughts. 'She is going to be one of the most beautiful women in Mewar.'

'She is already one of the brightest.'

It was a tradition at Lakshman Simha's Janmashtami celebrations that the name of the artist was never revealed before the performance. Part of the fun of the evening lay in trying to guess whether it was a man or a woman, a singer, instrumentalist or dancer and his or her name. People laid bets, a cask of wine, a thousand tankas, a horse, a camel and sometimes a couple of villages. Almost everybody had his private grapevine and wanted to check out if his information was right. Rajendra nodded his head and went along with every speculation. Uncle declared solemnly that there was a major shift in the policy of the house and a half-man and a half-woman named after the bisexual deity, Ardhanareshwar, was going to recite hermaphroditic verse and sing simultaneously in male and female voices followed by a dance duet given by the same person.

'I'll bet you my diamond and emerald necklace,' the Shehzada told Leelawati, 'that it's going to be a dancer, obviously a female one.'

'Wrong. Partially wrong. It's going to be a woman singer.' Leelawati told him.

'Empty words won't do, Leelawati. You've got to put your money where your mouth is. What are you betting?'

'I have nothing to bet with.'

'How about that gold chain around your waist?'

Leelawati hesitated. 'Your anklet will do just as well. I'll wear it around my wrist.' Bahadur was tying Leelawati up in knots and for once she was not sure how to respond. 'What about weaving a pennant for me?' I hadn't realized how deftly the Shehzada had tied a noose around Leelawati.

'Yes, I would love to. Will you join the Maharaj Kumar or ride with Uncle Rajendra?'

175

The entire mehfil was babbling away but Bahadur's tense silence rang like an alarm in my head. I took off my belt and gave it to Leelawati.

'We'll bet His Highness, the Maharaj Kumar's ruby and pearl belt. Does that sound fair to you?" Leelawati did not wish to dwell on what a close call it was.

The Shehzada put the necklace around Leelawati's neck. 'You've won this round anyway, Leelawati.'

As luck would have it, I wouldn't have lost my belt.

'The name's Sajani Bai,' the woman said after she had made herself comfortable in front of the pakhawaj player and the sarangiya. 'Are names deceptive or do they reveal something vital about a person? Some people think I am every man's Sajani, and beloved. Others think I am theirs and theirs alone. You are welcome to your opinions, my lords. For as you know, a woman is like a throne. However large she may be,' she smiled and with a gesture of her hand pointed to her wide girth, 'she may enjoy one man and one man only at any one point in time. So while I enjoin each one of you to take his pleasure from me, my pleasure is for the one who gave me the gift of life. Adaab, Maharaj Kumar, adaab Prince Bahadur, adaab Lakshman Simhaji and adaab, all you lovers of the arts. Since you would not come to see me in Awadh, I have had to come to see you.'

She placed the string drone in her lap and closed her eyes. Her fat fingers strummed the strings softly. The moment of truth. The alaap is the part of our classical music that I like best. It is an inward voyage, an odyssey into the unknown. You are alone, truly alone, in the cosmos, no pakhawaj and no sarangi, just your voice feeling its way. It is a wordless meditation, a rumination on matters that human thought cannot encompass. Anchored in the schema enunciated at the very start, you are free to explore the full range of the human condition. It is the quality of the probing and the free-wheeling that exposes you and decides your worth as an artist.

It is men and women who consciously and fortuitously take an art-form in one direction or another. If I had been born in an earlier

176

age when our classical music was taking shape, or if I could devote myself to it even today, I would enlarge the scope and emphasis of the alaap, and make it mandatory as the true test of the artist. For like all meditation, an alaap has the solitude and form of a prayer. It is a cathartic and purifying act. You are blessed, touched by the divine and made to partake of the sacred.

There is good reason why the seminal artists of earlier times kept the alaap short and switched to the easier pacing of the vilambit where the beat of the pakhawaj is your guide. They knew the limitations and fears of the majority of singers and instrumentalists. To plumb the depths, you must leave the safety of the shallows, the easy sentiment and the company of others. One's own frailties, mediocrity, shortcomings and the fear of the abyss, one must dare them all.

There's only one test for Sajani Bai today. Not so much a test for her as the hope of a lifeline for me. Will she cast a spell on me and draw me down into the wells of oblivion? Will she release me from the torment of this afternoon? Will she heal me? Will I be made whole again? She struck a deep, low, majestic note and held it for a long endless moment till it seemed to slip out of time, then almost imperceptibly shaded into another. She states the scheme of the raga in crystalline phraseology. Then she sets out on her own.

To speak of music is to speak of intangibles. To attempt to catch its essence in words is foolhardy and doomed. The images music conjures in my mind and on the screen between my eyeballs and eyelids are not of a coherent extended metaphor. They are dissonant and diverse but coalesce with a natural dynamic that has its own internal logic.

She lays out her palette, the range of colours she'll be using. With measured strokes, both subtle and broad, she sketches in her themes and concerns though there is nothing sketchy about this. Her voice is still a rumble, brief glimpses of well-springs and fledgling currents that may or may not meet up. There's a sylvan stretch, broad beams of slanting sunlight broken by a million leaves and bushes, which turn into a moody, brooding bottle-green forest. Mythical beasts prowl sinisterly in the jungle. Deep down, the waters are linking up. There's a blinding vista of sky and V-formations of migratory birds in silent flight. A couple disengages and sinks down in a giddy glissando. Suddenly the voice is a full-fledged river, strong, wide but still unhurried. The water trips over dips and stones playfully, soon it's accelerating and the rapids froth like hot wild horses. I open my eyes. Sajani Bai's left hand is pressed against her left ear in search of an even purer note. The boneless fingers of her right hand undulate like fluid branches under water. Her eyes pass over my face unseeingly and withdraw into darkness. The piercing cry of a bird who's lost its mate scars the air. My eyes close. A red's on fire. I press my eyelids tight. The incandescent red trickles down my face. Her voice is leaping, speeding, rising high, ever so high, it arches upon itself like a curving wave and breaks in a trillion points. I release the pressure on my eyelids. Midnight blue is crisscrossed by jets of iridescent stardust. The lines sizzle and shift and race at breakneck velocities. They loop and link and skate and swing. Darting greens turn to raging sun flares to whistling purples to ruptured yellows. A white mist is coming in from the left corner of my eye. It rises swiftly. The underground river surfaces through it. It is in flood. I'm tossed and twisted, broken and bruised and reconfigured. My arms are as wide as the Gambhiree which I swallow entire.

Is it possible to make love to a disembodied voice?

I am washed ashore and am strangely at peace.

It is midnight when Sajani Bai winds up her concert. Leelawati is fast asleep with her head on my lap. I was not destined to keep the belt after all. Rajendra handed the purse of money to Sajani Bai. Adinathji picked up Leelawati and I walked over to Sajani Bai. I took off my belt and presented it to her. She touched my feet and said something. I had to bend to hear the words. 'I sang for you today, Prince, just for you. If it will help you to forget, perhaps even cure you, I will sing again for you some other time. Don't be alarmed, Maharaj Kumar, your face is not transparent, my mind is. You have the gift of genuine enjoyment. Don't lose it.'

'Two announcements. There are snacks and dinner downstairs in the shamiana, ladies and gentlemen. If you haven't already had them, please do not insult our house, especially my mother, and

178

refuse our hospitality. The other announcement will please you no end. There will be a surprise recital after an hour.'

I had not realized how hungry I was. Rajendra was right. The food was so good it fuelled my appetite further. Everybody was jovial and friendly and I was in great spirits. Rajendra had decided that Sajani Bai and I had a little delicate something going between us. Soon Bahadur had joined him and they did magnificent imitations of her voice, her ample bosom and at least fifty alternative versions of the indecent proposals Sajani Bai was supposed to have made to me. Each proposal was more outrageous and lewd than the previous one and almost everybody was doubled up. Without meaning to, we had formed a semicircle around the Shehzada and Rajendra. The only thing that worried me was that Bahadur was drinking steadily. He was looking for a refill when I tried to draw his attention to something else.

'Aren't you going to tell us what I said to Sajani Bai?'

Did I really believe they had been lubricious before? They were improvising wildly now but with such perfect timing, it was as if they had rehearsed their act for months. Where could the clandestine lovers meet? 'The Victory Tower. On the very top floor. There will be no one there. The whole of Chittor will be at our feet and if we raise our hands, they'll touch the sky. Well, mine will. Yours, I guess will come to my waist.' There's some problem about Sajani Bai squeezing into the entrance of the Tower. They resolve the quandary by making the lady edge in sideways. Not a very wise move. Madam is evenly distributed and is now lodged immovably at the entrance. A gang of prisoners is deployed to break down the wall to let the dear lady out. A child thinks that if the new central prop is removed the Tower will come down. His father smacks him. But the child is right. When Sajani Bai is finally able to make her exit, the great Tower begins to totter and wobble and comes crashing down. Fortunately the lovers escape unhurt.

'Why didn't I think of it?' the Prince asks himself and his inamorata. 'There is a solution to our problem. We'll send the Minister for Home Affairs, none other than the stupendously voluminous Lakshman Simhaji, to war against our Rajput cousins and appropriate his bed. It alone will hold us both.' 'But Sire,'

179

Sajani Bai protests, 'you and your cousins are the best of friends, you have recently even signed an eternal amity pact with them.' 'Little matter, I'm willing to sacrifice friend, foe and family for your sake, my Sajani.' And so Lakshman Simhaji is dispatched instantly and unceremoniously. Finally, the two are alone and in bed. They are locked in a long, torrid embrace. Then something terrible happens. The bed breaks? You've got to be joking. It's strong enough to hold two Sajanis. It's just that Sajani Bai can hear the Prince but cannot locate him. Oh God, where could he have disappeared? She picks up her right arm and checks under it, then the left one: is he, the poor little darling, lost in her armpit? No sign of him. She picks up her petticoat.

It was at that delicate moment that the Queen Mother, my grandmother herself walked into the magic circle. She had a frown on her forehead and her lips were clenched tight. 'Disgusting. Disgraceful. Is this how the younger generation entertains itself?' Everybody freezes. No one dares look up. 'Leaving the women out of the fun? What happens then, beta?' She asks the Shehzada. 'Does she find my Maharaj Kumar or not?'

It was time to go back to Deep Mahal.

We were all highly keyed up by now. There's usually just one performer at Lakshman Simha's Janmashtami party. What's up today? Who, what, when, why, how? As bookie for the latter half of the evening, Rajendra, the shrewd so-and-so was raking it in. Jugglers, acrobats, performing hijras, bards, dancers, lion-tamers, wrestlers, you name it, the more unlikely the suggestion, the more people were willing to bet on it. And lo and behold, guess who turned up? In the right-hand corner here, ladies and gentlemen, what we have is none other than the seven hundred and odd pounder, the one and only Sajani Bai. There's horror-stricken silence. Then everybody was crowding Rajendra Simha and yelling for his blood. I can't wipe the smile off my face. The swine, the shameless rogue, what a ride he's taken us all for. After all, he had merely said 'surprise'. That didn't rule out Sajani Bai.

But Sajani Bai had already begun her song. And suddenly there was absolute silence. It was about Dhola and Maru, our legendary star-crossed lovers. Maru has just seen Dhola for the first time and her friends are teasing her. We all know the folk song, we've heard it a million times but what Sajani Bai does with it is to give it her own twist, almost create it anew. We are just about to bask in her magnificent voice when there's the sound of anklets and seven apsaras make their way through the sprawled and stunned menfolk. They start dancing. Catcalls, whistles, clapping, applause. Most of the girls are barely seventeen or eighteen, some are exquisite, others are shy and self-conscious, but every one of them is an apparition. Those of us who leave tomorrow morning, hell no, this very morning know that they are the stuff of wet dreams. We will ache and pine for them, both in our waking and sleeping hours. Oh God, to be young and lovely. I feel old. When the song comes to the refrain, all of us, the women's section too, join in spontaneously and sing the chorus. It is impossible to sit still when a folk song from Rajasthan is being sung. We are all seasoned clappers and along with the pakhawaj, we give the beat. Song follows song and there's a masti and khumar in the air. We are drunk and high with the songs, the women and the sheer joy of being alive.

They are all wearing chanderi ghagras and cholis of deep earth colours. Sheer chunnis cover their hair and are tucked in at the necks of the blouses. All are wearing silver jhumroos around their ankles. There's one girl-woman here, the one in the dark snuff-coloured choli-ghagra who's perhaps the shyest of them all. Is she the youngest? There's no way of telling. What I or anybody else can tell for sure is that despite her bashfulness, she's smitten with the Shehzada. She keeps looking down into the middle distance while stealing as many furtive glances at him as she can. The snuff of her clothes clashes provocatively with the peach of her complexion. No ordinary nautch girl, this. None of the other girls either.

The Shehzada has been imbibing steadily and has a beatific look on his face. He has, needless to say, noticed the girl's inhibited – and hence all the more enticing – fascination with him. No explicit overture could be more persuasive or compelling.

'What's her name?' Bahadur lurched a little unsteadily even as he sat in the namaaz position.

'You are asking the wrong man, Prince. I'm just as ignorant as you are.'

181

'Isn't she something else?'

'Who?' I asked innocently.

'Is there anybody else here but her?'

'Seven of them, not to mention the love of my life, Sajani Bai.'

'Yes sir, Sajani Bai's the one for you,' he laughed unsteadily.
'That match, Your Highness, take my word for it, was made in
heaven. But I say, would you happen to know who the girl in that,
I don't quite know how to describe the colour, in that lustrous
brown, is?'

'You mean the third girl from the left?' I deliberately pointed
to the wrong girl.

'No, you fool, I said lustrous brown,' he half-rose, stumbled, then
stood up and directed his index finger waveringly. The girl was by
now blushing furiously and looking at her big toe as if she had just
discovered it. The blushing did her looks and face a world of good.

'That's not brown, lustrous or otherwise. It's snuff.'

'Do you think I give a damn whether it's brown or snuff or violet
for all I care. What is her name?'

'Shhhh, softly Shehzada,' I appealed to him, 'come and sit
down.'

'Only if you will tell me her name.'

'Please, Your Highness. Do come and sit with us.' Everybody
was enjoying his boisterousness. He had had that extra peg which
makes people happy and repetitive. I thought it wise to get the Prince
to bed now and signalled to Mangal to get a drink for him. He
knew what I meant, but adding the shot of opium was going to
be a little tricky with so many people wandering in and out. As
luck would have it, Rajendra got one of his servants to fill the
Prince's glass.

'Now you know who I'm talking about. What's her name?'

'I'm afraid I don't know, Shehzada.'

'Don't know the name of someone from your own house?' He
was not pleased with my answer.

'Not mine, Prince, this is Lakshman Simhaji and Rajendra's
place.'

'Oh, of course. Then I better ask Rajendra.' He turned to
Rajendra.

182

'Sorry to disturb you, when you are having such a good time friend, that too in your own home, but would you be so kind as to tell me the name of the girl in the snuff-coloured dress?'

'I don't quite remember, Highness. It's either Salma or Nikhat,' Rajendra smiled and went back to the business of watching the girls dance.

'Salma? Nikhat? Not a Hindu girl?' Bahadur looked puzzled. 'Why are you pursuing her so single-mindedly? Do you recognize her?'

'Should I? Have I had my pleasure with her?

'No, Sire, all the girls are virgins.'

'Then why would I recognize her?'

For some reason my cousin found the question hilarious. 'I don't know, I thought you might have played with her when you were a child.'

'Played with a Mewar girl, how's that possible?' The Shehzada was beginning to sound vexed. I was, I must confess, just as foxed as he was. 'I'm afraid you are speaking in riddles, Rajendra Simha.'

'She's the daughter of the qazi of Ahmednagar. I imagined that you must have met her when you visited Ahmednagar as a child with your Father.'

'Then what is she doing here?'

The singing had stopped. The girls were standing still, hugging each other. They looked frightened. There were drops of sweat on Salma or Nikhat's upper lip. Her armpits were sweating with the exertion of dancing so long but she was shivering. Her doe-eyes darted all over the place. Though her hands held her companion's arm tightly, she would have run all the way back to Ahmednagar if she could have got away from Deep Mahal. What was Rajendra up to? Did he know what he was saying? Why bring up Ahmednagar now? Then it dawned on me. I recalled his face when the Shehzada had told the story of the massacre of the Mewar forces and of Lakshman Simha's debacle. Rajendra had planned today's party with a single purpose in mind. He was going to have his vengeance by reminding Bahadur of the time we turned the tables on Gujarat, sacked Ahmednagar, destroyed their mosques, marauded their gold and silver and massacred thousands of their townspeople.

'Rajendra, I urge you to come to your senses and stop talking nonsense.'

He ignored me.

'Do you remember the time when the Mewar forces routed your Father's armies and sacked Ahmednagar, Prince? It was a slaughter and the qazi fell too. But we are a chivalrous people. We brought the ladies and their daughters back with us and are now training them in a new profession. We hope they'll give us pleasure, as they've done today and we'll give them hefty recompense. We...'

He did not get around to finishing the sentence. Would that I had pulled out his tongue or kicked him in his face. That way at least my dear cousin Rajendra who took his father's humiliation so much to heart would have fought by my side against Gujarat.

Bahadur leaned forward as if he was in pain. It was such a common old trick but I fell for it.

'Are you all right, Shehzada?' I asked him.

'Yes, I am. It's your cousin who is not.' Seven swift blows with his dagger and Rajendra was no more. There was the stillness of death amongst us. Salma or Nikhat, the poor girl crumpled to the ground. I picked up Rajendra. My clothes and hands were bloody. I wanted to bring down the gods in my impotent pain, I looked at the ceiling, at the lamps, at Sajani Bai whose voice had seen everything there was to see, feel and experience in this world and yet had missed out on Rajendra's death, I looked at my uncle, I looked at my dead cousin. My body shook and shivered but would not release the scream in me. Oh Rajendra, why did I not get closer to you earlier instead of waiting for our Gujarat campaign to start?

I heard the sound of metal leaving its scabbard once, twice, thrice. Rao Surajmal, Narbad Hada, Rawat Jodha Simha. They had encircled the Shehzada. The others were unsheathing their weapons. I eased Rajendra to the floor, got out my sword and stood in front of Bahadur.

'I don't need any protection, Maharaj Kumar. If they have the guts and the honour, I'll take them all on, one after another.'

'In my father, Rana Sanga's kingdom, you'll hold your tongue, Prince, and give me your weapons.'

'Do you expect me to die without defending myself, Prince?'

184

'There will be no more killing, Shehzada. Hand your weapons to Mangal.' I knew that if I looked at him, he would start a who-stares-whom-down contest. Instead I held the three potential leaders of retribution in our camp with my gaze. I could feel the heat of the Shehzada's internal conflict. Could he trust me? He himself had attacked an unwary man. Would turning defenceless be his best defence? Perhaps the enormity of what he had done was beginning to dawn on him. I doubted if he was given to introspection or regret. He would rather fight but he knew I was his only hope.

The Shehzada handed his dagger and sword to Mangal.

'He'll not leave Deep Mahal, alive, Your Highness,' Hada Narbad advanced on both me and the Shehzada.

'He is our guest. Anybody who dares so much as touch the Shehzada's hair, I will kill him first.' Was it tall talk? Was I going to take on the hundred-odd people in the hall. 'I am the Maharaj Kumar.' I spoke each word separately. 'Put your weapons down and go home.'

They stood undecided. Would they have listened? Or would they have revolted? Either way, I would never forget the look of loathing, contempt and animosity in the Hada's eyes. The Queen Mother walked towards us along with my aunt.

'Did you not hear the Maharaj Kumar? Sheathe your weapons and go now. Give us time and room to grieve for our grandchild.' Grandmother turned to Prince Bahadur. 'You have the Maharaj Kumar's and my word that no one will harm you. I loved you, beta, but you've dishonoured both Mewar's and my hospitality and affection. Go in peace.'

Perhaps Mewar and its people will never forgive me for not avenging Rajendra's death. Had I too just sealed my fate?

Chapter 16

 You can exorcise the devil. But how do you rid yourself of a god?

When the Maharaj Kumar reached the palace, the guards on duty saluted him. Should he dismount? Why had he come home anyway? Befikir stood patiently while he tried to figure out what he was doing at the gates of his own home at three in the morning. He was hopelessly confused. All he wanted was to go to the carpenter's workshop, pick up a long sharp saw, come back and lie in his bed. When he had settled down comfortably, he would take the saw and, starting from just above his eyebrows with steady, even strokes go all the way round his head. When the top one-third of his head along with his brains had fallen off, he would finally be able to sleep peacefully. No more thoughts, no more questions, never mind his wife and her tiresome romance and to hell with this terrible blight called life.

'Sire, Your Highness,' the sergeant major asked him, 'do you wish me to leave Befikir in the stables?' Why send Befikir to the stable, he wondered. The horse had more sense than he did. Befikir knows where his home is, who his master is, he understands technical terms like trot, canter, gallop and stop. He obviously knows his dharma. He was the Maharaj Kumar and he didn't know why he was at his doorstep. And having got there, what he was expected to do. Well, there was nothing to do but get down and climb the stairs to his wing and sit down on his bed and resolve what he was to do with his life next.

He was about to fall on his bed when he heard his wife's voice. Who could she be talking to? He had given strict orders the previous evening that the doors of her rooms were to be locked in perpetuity from the outside. Kumkum Kanwar could cook for her, bathe her and do whatever else her mistress wished but whatever happened, even if a fire broke out, she was not to be let out. The eunuch outside her door was fast asleep. He had a soft downy snore. When he exhaled, his mouth worked furiously to grab the air and eat it. Was he the one who was talking? No, he was far too busy eating some ambrosial stuff of which he could not have enough. The Prince could hear his wife's voice better now. It seemed unlikely that she was conversing with this corpulent dead weight through a locked door. Not bad looking though. Must have cut a fine figure when he was young and despite the absence of extended genitalia, was sure to have been popular with the queens. The Prince was not quite sure about the institution of eunuchs. Granted, they could not beget and procreate but barring that, no royalty had as much time and opportunity to make out with some of the most beautiful and aristocratic women in Mewar. That voracious mouth had kissed and known and slept with God knows how many of the Maharaj Kumar's mothers. Men are strange. They prefer to make believe that people make love only at night and that only the act of penetration is sex. The tongue, a truly penetrating instrument if ever there was one, and the rest of the human body, hands, lips, ears, the insides of thighs, toes, the belly button – was there any accounting for taste and erogenous sites – were discounted.

For some reason, the thought of touching that genderless flesh was repulsive. The Maharaj Kumar had to grit his teeth when he bent down and slipped his hand in the eunuch's pocket. It took some time and trying for the Prince to figure out which of the two dozen or so keys fitted the lock on his wife's door. He opened the latch softly. Her bed was made as his own had been on the night of the wedding. Flowers were strung from the four posters and lay crushed on the mattress. She was lying on her back, not a shred of cloth on her. Her clothes were thrown helter-skelter as if someone in a rush of indelicate impatience had disrobed her. He stepped over the eunuch and lightly closed the door behind him. When he turned round, he froze. She was staring at him. What was he going to say to her? Just dropped by to see if you were all right? No, honest-to-goodness, I had a terrible nightmare and was a little unnerved and was wondering if I could sleep in your bed, no hanky-panky, promise. He realized then that she was totally oblivious of him. When she slept, her eyelids came down only three-quarters of the way. That left her eyes slightly ajar with white crescents showing at the bottom, so that you had the uncanny feeling that she was watching you with hooded eyes.

Against the opposite wall was a low, red stool barely three inches from the ground. In front of it was a gold thali filled to overflowing with all manner of food, most of it sweets and pastries made from milk and curds. No, he said to himself, it didn't look as if the meal was laid out for him. In one corner of the room she had drawn an incredibly elaborate painting with rangoli powder of the Flautist and herself dancing the raas on the banks of the Jamuna.

He could not take his eyes off her. Her head stretched back pleasurably as if someone was running his fingers through her open tumbling hair. Suddenly she twisted and jerked away. 'No, no, no, no, no, you are tickling my ears. Please, stop it. Are you going to listen to me? Anytime I ask you to do something you do exactly the opposite. Stop being perverse. Let go of me. Or I'll pull your hair hard.' He knew she was all alone but he also knew exactly what her lover was up to. He was caressing the inside of her outstretched arm, the peacock feather in his hand was now in the dip of her armpit and flowing down her left breast and across her navel while he was nibbling at the nape of her neck. She was kissing him now. Her hands were wound tightly around air. She called out to him, two of the god's thousand names. 'Girdhar Lal. Ghanashyam.' There was such longing and love in her voice, it pierced the Prince's heart.

Get out, leave while you can and while you have an iota of dignity left in you. But he couldn't move and he didn't want to either. It

188

was torture and it tore him up and he didn't want it to stop. He had always thought that sensuousness was an over-inflated word, but she made him feel its force and flooding rapture and its place at the heart of the arcana of pleasure. He remembered the first time he had heard her sing. There was no withholding, nothing halfway, she gave it her all. She was doing the same now, staking everything she had.

The ecstasy her face and body radiated brought him up short. Even as a child he had not known anything so complete and profligate. She seemed to be the fountainhead of joyousness. Whence her abandonment and exuberance? How could a mere human being be capable of such consuming rapture that she was not even aware of the world around her? She was a closed and complete circle in which he had no place. She and the Flautist were sufficient unto themselves. It was impossible to break in. He was excluded. Out.

He was struck then by a terrible realization. So far, however much things had gone wrong, at least he was in control of himself. The Flautist was his enemy. He hated him with a passion that went well beyond an obsession. His hate was the only polestar and steadfast beacon in a world that had turned topsy-turvy on him. But the truth was, he didn't give a damn about the past, all the humiliation and pain he had suffered, not even the shameless exhibitionism of emotion he had witnessed today.

He wanted in.

He closed the door quietly and slipped the keys back into the eunuch's pockets.

189

Chapter 17

I felt exhausted and empty. How could a bare twenty-four hours pile up so many upheavals, calamities and tragedies? It didn't stand to reason. A curse upon you, Bahadur. We had lost you. Only God, Kausalya, and the Bhil shaman and I know how far gone you were. But we managed to bring you back from the clutches of Yama. If only fate or I had let you die. Damn you, Rajendra. You are no more but look at the havoc you've wrought. Mewar had spent months forging ties with the Shehzada Bahadur even as we were fighting his father and the Gujarat armies. Why? Because if there's no chance of a clean-cut victory, let alone the conquest and annexation of an entire kingdom, then it makes better economic, political and military sense to make peace with your neighbours and live amicably with them. And then you throw wisdom and caution to the wind, dump all that careful work and nurturing down the gutter and wipe the slate clean. Now you'll not be with me when I need you on my campaign. The honour of the venerable elders of our society is deeply wounded and if they could, they would be happy to have my head along with Bahadur's. What honour are we talking about? Surely Mewar is larger and more important than a personal slight delivered many moons ago by a Prince and guest who had imbibed too much.

You were going to avenge the death of three thousand Rajputs by telling the Prince that the dancing girls at the Deep Mahal were the Ahmednagar qazi's daughters. Bravo. Your thirst for vengeance must be shallower than the foreskin of your genitals. If you had had a little patience, not to mention an iota of brains, you would have stuck around with me and I would have made sure that you got your three thousand heads at least twice over. I loved you, cousin,

190

and I'll miss you but I don't need adolescent hotheads with me on my first campaign. One last thing. I was wrong, you didn't wipe the slate clean. It was clean when Bahadur rode in through the Suraj Pol that first morning. We didn't know each other. We were at best and at worst indifferent to each other. All his life now the Shehzada will recall his utterly disproportionate, hasty and immature final act in Mewar with loathing and disgust. He will never be able to forgive himself for paying back so much warmth, affection and kindness with blood and death. Infinitely worse, he'll never forgive me for saving his life twice. Mewar will stick in his side like a festering thorn and he'll bide his time to destroy a fond memory gone irretrievably sour.

'Stop thinking about Rajendra Simha and the Shehzada, my Prince. Rest awhile,' Kausalya patted my head.

I cannot leave the subject well enough alone and return to it as to a scab on a wound that must be teased and prized open. Why can't I be a good Rajput and see things simply, in black and white? There's no gainsaying that a swift and just trial will earn me a high profile and much popularity. But surely, statecraft is a little more complicated than that. Bahadur is not the Sultan, at least not yet. His father is. If Bahadur is put to death in Chittor, not only will the honour of his father, Sultan Muzaffar Shah be wounded, the people of Gujarat will be affronted. That may prove to be dangerous. The inexorable logic of retribution and national pride will demand satisfaction and roll its armies towards Mewar. But aren't we already at war? Yes. But the battle for Idar is a matter of territorial influence, that's all. Neither Gujarat nor Mewar are fighting for their life or land. We are backing different claimants to the throne of Idar and are skirmishing on foreign soil. A war on our home ground is a different matter altogether. We may perhaps even inflict a terrible defeat on Gujarat. But at what cost to Mewar? Villages, towns and cities will be razed, a year's crops burnt, the economy will be in shambles and tens of thousands of our people, farmers, artisans, traders, not to mention our soldiers, will lose their lives and be maimed. Spare the Shehzada and we'll at least have a grateful father who might just remember that he owes us a favour, a very big favour.

And yet, I ask myself, is it really reasons of state that demand

191

a more mature and wise response? Or am I just out of touch with reality and my people? In my preoccupation with larger issues, have I lost sight of a simple truth? No leader can afford to scoff at populist measures without forfeiting his constituency.

'Sunheria's waiting for you at the Chandra Mahal,' Kausalya told me as I changed into the white of mourning. 'She's been coming every day the past four days. See her today. At least talk to her or she'll think you didn't care to say goodbye to her before you left.'

I marvel at Kausalya. She's as possessive as they come but she never allows her biases to interfere with what she sees as her duty. I am the Maharaj Kumar. I need variety, change, a new face. She knows about Sunheria and over the past few months, has made it a point to be out of the way when the laundress has turned up. She wants my marriage to work. She's one of the least religious women I know but she has undertaken three sets of the most rigorous fasts without telling me. Even now she doesn't eat on Mondays and Thursdays. All this so that my wife will bear me a son and heir.

'Are you really going, Maharaj Kumar?' This was unlike Sunheria. She was not one to be easily depressed, certainly not by my departure. She had always, subtly but pointedly, asserted her independence with and from me.

'Yes. His Majesty is waiting for me to take over command. I thought I explained it to you the last time we were together.'

'May I come with you? You'll want company. I'll try and help you forget today's terrible tragedy.'

'That is thoughtful of you. But I'm going to war. What will you do there?'

'I'll wash your clothes. I'll do anything you ask of me.' She would not look up.

'What is it, Sunheria? There's something else on your mind.'

'How blind you are.' She had spoken simply, without any rancour. 'I love you, Prince.'

And I thought I could read people.

I thought both of us, but especially Sunheria, had made it a point to treat our affair casually and disclaim all emotional involvement.

'Don't be alarmed, Prince. I'm not about to cling to you. You were the first person who treated me as a human being and did it as if it was the natural thing to do. But it's not gratitude I'm talking about.'

'I am coming back, Sunheria.'

'I'll pray every day for your safe return. But I doubt it if you will return to me.' As always she hid her rough, working hands with her chunni.

I reached Lakshman Simhaji's house at five forty-five in the morning. I should have gauged the mood of the crowd on the lawns when it took its own time to part and let me in. Inside Rajendra had been placed on a raised bier. I waited for everybody to leave so that I could be alone with him. He was wearing the saffron robes that a Rajput warrior wears on his last battle and journey. He still had the look of fatal surprise he had on his face when the Shehzada drew his dagger and plunged it in. In a few moments he would be buried under five or six feet of flowers. I took his hand in mine. My eye fell upon the gold kada on his right wrist. I had completely forgotten about it. I had given it to him the year we completed our studies. I slid it off. There was a legend carved on its inner wall: "We'll grow battle-scarred and old together, my friend." And all these years I had believed that affectionate words cannot pierce and kill. I wanted to swing his arm to the ceiling and back and shake him awake. Get up, get up, get off your arse, you lazy wastrel, get dressed and let's make a move. There's a war waiting to be fought. It was not as civilized as that. It was a string of dirty words from our Gurukul days. I had certainly shaken him up. His left leg was bent at the knees and his torso was no longer aligned with his head. But it was no use. He was not about to budge. I let go of his hand. It flopped awkwardly outside the bier and rested on the floor. I put the kada back.

I came out and stood on the steps of the house. According to protocol it was the signal for the rest of the family and all the other mourners to say goodbye to him. Over a thousand people were

193

waiting outside. They pressed forward menacingly. Someone set up a chant. 'Blood for blood. Mewar's honour calls for Bahadur's blood.' Soon everybody had picked it up. It was obvious that if they didn't get what they wanted, they would be willing to settle scores with me. 'Free Prince Vikramaditya and lock up the traitor Maharaj Kumar.' It was not difficult to guess who had inspired this novel idea. The calls for my imprisonment rose by the moment. Good move, Mother Karmavati. Where the hell was that Mangal? Nowhere in sight. But I was in luck. If the situation seemed close to hopeless a second ago, it was now utterly beyond repair and redemption. Instead of Mangal Simha, God Almighty help me, the Shehzada was walking towards the mob. The bloody fool, as if he hadn't caused me enough trouble. Was it a case of belated conscience or, as I suspected, he couldn't forsake his theatrical bravado even now?

'Leave the Maharaj Kumar alone.' He had a resounding voice and he used it to magnificent effect. 'You want me, here I am. I am ready to sacrifice my life for the honour of Gujarat and Islam. Only cowards will attack a single man, ten to one, hundred to one or as you are now, a thousand to one. If you have the courage, come forward, one at a time and fight the fair fight. Let the righteous win.'

The crowd was now roaring alternately for my head and that of Bahadur's. The men had smelt blood, it didn't matter whether it was mine or the enemy's, they were not going to be deprived of it.

'Perhaps you are under the impression that you are at the amphitheatre watching competitions. And soon the wrestling matches will start.' It was such a low voice, it was a wonder anybody heard it but heads turned slowly and listened to Lakshman Simha. 'I would, however, like to remind you that my eldest son Rajendra is dead and but for your antics, we would be at the burning ghats by now.'

After the funeral I bathed in the Gambhiree and went to the Eklingji temple. I prayed hard. It was but recently that I had shifted my allegiance from the Flautist to our family deity. I begged him to

194

embrace the slain Rajendra and free him from the cycle of reincarnation. As for myself, I asked for light and wisdom and the greater glory of Mewar. The head priest suggested that Rajendra's death could be an ill-omen and it might be a good idea to leave a week later; ten days would be even better since that was an auspicious day. On some other occasion I may have been in two minds but fortunately I had no choice in the matter. You don't keep His Majesty waiting.

The sun was already halfway to the top of the dome. If things had not gone awry, we would have left by six thirty in the morning. I wanted to hurry but I was not leaving without going up to the Victory Tower. There's no need to be melodramatic about war. But it is reasonable to accept that a warrior cannot afford to put too much trust in return journeys. I make quick jottings. The Digambara temple which the Minister of the Exchequer, Adinathji, visits every morning was originally, they say, a Vishnu Temple. I have never understood how temples switch religions or worship one god for centuries and then overnight change to someone else. Next to it is the Tower of Fame, another Jain landmark. The merchant Jija Bagairwal Mahajan built it in the twelfth century to commemorate his visit to the shrines of the twenty-four tirthankars. It is about seventy feet high and has seven storeys. When my great grandfather Kumbha built the Tower of Victory, it was to upstage the Tower of Fame. The Jain tower is shorter and does not have any carvings inside.

I concentrate on the Chaturang Maurya Talab next. The Shiv Mandir at the centre of the lake has such strong Buddhist features, I suspect that here again there has been a change in divine tenants. Rao Ranmal's house. Badshah ki Baksi where, local lore holds, the Sultan of Gujarat was imprisoned in Rana Kumbha's time. Rampur Bhanpura's palace from around the same time. The Bhanpuras are today old nobility without old money. Rani Padmini's Palace with its Jal Mahal, the miniature jewel of a water palace that Queen Karmavati so often commandeers for her ladies' get-togethers. Kalika Temple. Haath Kund where our royal elephants are washed. Behind Rani Padmini's Palace is the Khatan Rani Palace. No queen this, but a lowly woman from the carpenter caste who caught Rana

195

Khshatra Simha's eye and became his favourite concubine. The Sas-Bahu Kund, the only place where mothers and daughters-in-law meet on an equal footing since both come to bathe here. Its springs are a mystery to this day since nobody knows their source nor the secret of their perpetual waters. Sattabees Devari or the twenty-seven tiny Jain temples built in the eleventh century. Last stop on my panoramic whirlwind tour of Chittor is the complex of the royal palaces where I have lived all my life.

I feel like a camel greedily stocking up at a water hole. Not very discriminating, I'm afraid. But I'm not looking for elegiac or epiphanic moments, just snatches and fragments of the life and rhythms of Chittor. Look at that group of women sitting in a circle with piles of cloth. They take little pinches of the cloth, tie knots around them with pieces of string and soak them in vats of dyes. Behind them extend row upon row of crossed bamboos with ropes stretched between. Any moment now bands of tight-rope walkers will climb the poles and walk nonchalantly on the taut ropes. Instead a woman hangs the 'tie and dye' cloths on them to dry. The wind fills the flamboyantly coloured sails and there's a full-scale regatta five hundred feet above sea-level. Down on the terraced slopes a pair of bullocks and a farmer walk backwards. I can hear the distant splash of the buckets hitting water in a well. Now they go forward and the water wheel empties the buckets into shallow channels. My eyes track the Gambhiree and come to a stop at the dhobi ghat. She is so far away but there's no mistaking her. That easy, unselfconscious grace of limb and movement could belong to no one but Sunheria. What did she mean by that cryptic remark early this morning? Is she a clairvoyant? Why won't I come back to her? Is this campaign which has begun so badly going to claim my life too? Her arms and hands swing up and the dhoti or sheet she's washing does a double loop and crashes on the wet black rock. Her arms don't look muscular but they must be made of corded steel to beat hundreds of clothes effortlessly hour after hour. Then it hits me, the black bruises on her back and her legs, the welt on her back, the missing bangle on her left arm and the swelling on the bridge of her nose which she said she got from a fall in her house seven days ago. She is right. I'm not just blind but dumb too. Her old man can't make it with her or anyone else for that matter, but that's all the more reason to beat her up with a stick. Why didn't she break his bones? She surely has the strength. Those hard adamantine palms of hers which she's so conscious of and is forever trying to hide, one whack from them and her husband won't be able to get up for a week or two. I'm talking rubbish. For all her independence and willfulness and although she does a man's work, Sunheria is tradition-bound and will not retaliate.

The custard apple trees are weighed down with fruit. Not yet ripe but I must take a few dozen along with me. Nowhere, at least nowhere I have been to, do you get custard apples like the ones from Chittor.

I called Mangal over when I got down from the Victory Tower. 'Put the fear of the devil in Sunheria's husband. If he touches his wife again we'll put him in solitary for assault and battery. I know you are discreet but let him not know the source of the threat.'

Leelawati, the royal household, the Queen Mother and all the other queens, Adinathji, the Pradhan and the gentry and denizens of Chittor were waiting at the parade grounds. I had asked my uncle Lakshman Simhaji to rest and not come to the ceremony for the presentation of the colours. Did I really expect him not to come? I had appointed his younger son, Tej, in Rajendra's place and he stood at the head of the contingent I was taking along with me.

Leelawati waited solemnly under the pavilion. No throwing herself at me or hugging me this time. She stood there like a little queen. She was wearing a bandhani ghagra-choli with a Dhaka chunni. My troops and I marched past the whole congregation and came to a halt in front of Leelawati. I executed a left turn and held out my spear. She unfurled the pennant she had embroidered for me and slipped it up the brass shaft. A maid passed her the gold thali with a lamp and kumkum and turmeric powder in it. Leelawati did the arati and put a thumbful of red and yellow powder on my lowered forehead. 'The honour of Mewar is in your hands, Maharaj Kumar, preserve it. Conquer the enemy and return unconquered. God speed. Jai Eklingji.' I stood up straight and saluted the pennant

197

with the Sun-god.

We were on our way. But not before I had performed one small errand. Something about Sunheria's strange words kept bothering me. I dropped in at the office and with Mangal and another clerk as witnesses, transferred two villages from my own property to Sunheria and sent the deed along with a note to Kausalya. The elite Guard brought the Shehzada and his companions to the main gate and handed them over to me. Neither Prince Bahadur nor I were unaware of the ironies of the occasion. Months ago, the Shehzada had ridden in, asking Mewar for asylum from his own father. He was leaving now under escort because his new friends did not care for his company any longer. He was as much an enemy of Mewar's as his father's now. We would part company at the border of our kingdom. What he did then was his business. It was possible that instead of going home to Ahmedabad or Champaner he would join the Gujarat forces and we would meet in hand-to-hand combat in the next few weeks.

Chapter 18

When I look at my peers, friends, colleagues, cousins and brothers, I realize what a dullard I am. They carouse together, they go out whoring, they are lively and full of fun and pranks. I would like to join them once in a while but am rarely invited since I am prematurely serious, and would very likely dampen their high spirits. But I am a plodder in other ways too. Even my elders find me a bore and a little too earnest. War is fun and games for them. They dress up, wax their moustaches, ride their steeds and charge blindly. They kill or get killed. Life is simple and far more exciting that way.

War is not my favourite pastime. I would resort to it only under exceptional provocation or if, after thorough planning, I was going for the big kill. The fact is, in the long run, most wars lead nowhere but back to where you started. If I am to fight, I want to make major and if possible, lasting changes in our political geography and fortunes. Otherwise I would rather sit at home and be at peace with my neighbours. I like to prepare myself before a confrontation. I need to do my homework. I want to know every single detail and fact I can lay my hands on about the enemy: the monarch, his generals and his army. I want to learn their likes and dislikes, peccadilloes and predilections; their mental make-up, their previous campaigns, what they eat, their notions of hardship, their sleeping habits and any other trivia you can think of. Most of all, I'm interested in finding out how they think. What about contenders and pretenders to the throne? Why fight if you can help along a civil war and get someone else to do all the fighting for you? If internal jealousies and power equations are germane to the final outcome of any war and need to be exploited, it is just as relevant to know the state of mind of the ordinary citizenry. Are the common people tired of conflict or supportive? What was the harvest like in the current year and in the previous three? Not just the state of the economy, trade, too, has an indirect but very substantial bearing on the enemy's — or for that matter, our own — capacity to fight a long war. None of these propositions are very original but I am perplexed by how reluctant most strategists and military commanders are to follow even the most basic principles of preparing for war. I'll grant you this, collecting information, more precisely reliable information, is laborious, time-consuming and a bore. Besides it's effective only if it's done in a sustained manner. Imagine studying the enemy's economic, political and military abilities for months, sometimes years when all that the decisive battle itself will take is three, five or seven hours at the most.

I have had such short notice this time, I feel particularly at a disadvantage. A fine way to assume the reins of command for my very first campaign. How am I going to lead my men if I don't know the lay of the land, let alone anything else? I'm not even too sure why we are fighting the war with Gujarat over Idar. I'm exaggerating of course. But the reasons are emotional and tenuous rather than political, economic or strategic. My sister's husband Raimul has a claim to the Idar throne but is rarely seated on it. Idar is a ball in perpetual motion between Gujarat and Mewar. Sometimes it is with us and sometimes, with Gujarat. How did Idar get to be so fickle and inconstant? You'll have to do a bit of back-tracking to the time when Prince Bahadur's great-great-grandfather, I am not too sure about the number of 'greats' there, Sultan Muhammad, was in power. Idar had for some time been a thorn in Gujarat's hilly western frontier and none too forthcoming with its stipulated tribute. Matters, however, became a little tricky when Har Rao, the chief of Idar realized that if he shilly-shallied any longer, Sultan Muhammad might just snap up Idar whole. He then did what was most uncharacteristic for a Rajput ruler. He bought his way out of the quandary by offering his daughter's hand in marriage to the Sultan.

The matrimonial alliance bought peace for Idar for a few generations until Raimul became Rao of Idar. But soon after he came to the throne, the young Rao was deposed by his uncle Bhim.

Raimul took refuge in Chittor and married my sister.

Meanwhile, Rao Bhim embarked on a policy of confrontation with Gujarat. He stopped paying tribute, raised the standard of rebellion and plundered Gujarat east of the river Sabarmati. Not a wise move that. Bahadur's father, Muzaffar II, was the Sultan now. The wrath of Muzaffar was the thin, long blade of a scythe that swept across Idar as if it were the tall, brittle yellow grass of autumn. The Gujarat armies sacked the capital of Idar, laid low temples and buildings and ravaged the country. Rao Bhim paid a heavy price for his little adventure. It took twenty lakh tankas, and one hundred elephants to appease Sultan Muzaffar.

Two years later, Rao Bhim was dead and his son Bharmal succeeded to the throne. Things had come full circle: Bharmal's accession was challenged by his cousin-in-exile, Raimul. When Father sent a strong force to support his son-in-law, Bharmal approached the man who had rubbed Idar's nose in the dust, the Sultan of Gujarat. That, in short, is how we got embroiled with Gujarat.

We had ridden hard for days and were finally at the border. I asked Mangal to see to Bahadur's needs including provisions, water or whatever else he required and to let him and his friends go. Mangal came back with a message: would the Maharaj Kumar be so kind as to give Prince Bahadur a brief audience?

'It does not behoove a prince of the royal blood to regret his actions. I do not. But I am sorry that I will no longer have you as a friend. You were a better host than I could ever have imagined. I owe you my life, not once but twice over. It is a debt that I'll never be able to repay. There's much that I or anybody else has to learn from you. I'm not blind, Your Highness. You are the loneliest man I know. No slander nor ridicule can touch you because you do not let the personal affect your professional life. It is in the latter sphere that I respect you most. I doubt if you'll ever be a popular king when it is time for you to ascend the throne, because you do not know how to make unpopular measures palatable.

'You've taught me that sewers are a subject worthy of a prince's attention. Shit, they say, is your element. If I gain the throne, some day in the distant future, I'll take it as a compliment if my subjects say the same about me. I'll not embarrass you further. All these years I had believed that money was a royal privilege and it was the duty of the king to spend it. I now know that to become king, one must master money. Economics and commerce, you've taught me, are more important than war and victory.

'I will not wish you well on this campaign but Godspeed and may God be with you. Khuda hafeez.'

'Where will you go Prince?'

'My brother Sikander seeks my head. I would rather keep it on my shoulders. I fly to Delhi, Your Highness.'

'Goodbye, Prince. I was serious about peace with Gujarat.'

'I know you still are. It took me a long time to realize it.'

*　*　*

Father. Why do I feel like a greenhorn at his first job interview? Perhaps it's because he's behaving like a king and employer and has kept me waiting in the antechamber of his sprawling tent for the last fifteen minutes. It's a good ploy. Makes the subordinate nervous as hell, his mind runs amok and his imagination works feverishly. Am I out of favour? Did I say anything to upset the great man? Have any of my actions in the last twenty-seven or thirty or hundred years given him offence? (Or perhaps I earned his enmity while I was still in Mother's womb.) Perhaps someone's been telling tales behind my back. I could see it in the sentry's eyes, I'm bad news and no one wants me.

Good tactic, that. Let the arrogant son-of-an-untimely screw stew in his own juice. These youngsters think they own the earth including their elders. Best to take them down a peg or two before they get completely out of hand. By now I'm really getting into stride, doing a piteous number that would make stones weep: you never loved me, Father. Where my soul was, there's a void and scar tissue.

But all my tomfoolery can't conceal my anxiety about this meeting. I have not exactly had a run of great good luck in my time as regent, have I? What with a prince of the royal family, Father's very own son Vikramaditya committing treason, and now Bahadur killing Lakshman Simhaji's son, Rajendra. Lakshman Simha is Father's closest ally and confidant and oldest friend. All this is bad enough but I can weather it. It's just so much inert fuel till you introduce the mother of all inflammatory substances into the scenario: Queen Karmavati. We've ridden almost non-stop. We've halted for barely a few hours at night and stopped to eat and let the horses graze. I have goaded everybody on in the hope that no one but I will break the news of Rajendra's murder. But I know it's a futile attempt. I'll bet Queen Karmavati's man's been here before me and Father's already heard.

I'm called in. I'm right about the Queen's man but wrong about Father deliberately keeping me waiting. The surgeon's been with him dressing his new crop of wounds. I wonder how he holds his water or blood or any other fluid. The man should be a veritable fountain with close to a hundred spouts all over his body. Why he has to be in every charge or fray is anybody's guess. Is it arrogance, megalomania or is it fear? Fear is a strange and, perhaps, the last word that would occur to anybody in speaking of Father. But Father is afraid as no other man in Mewar or anywhere else on earth is. He has been afraid from the day his brothers chased him from Charni Devi's temple. He's afraid someone will call him a coward because he didn't make a stand while his deracinated eye swung like the flesh and seed of a custard apple from his eye-socket, and fight his brothers. Somewhere deep in his heart Father subscribes blindly to the Rajput code of heroism and honour and is ashamed that he did not die an utterly pointless death.

We are face to face finally. He embraced me briefly and awkwardly; I was going to say reluctantly, but that would be incorrect. Awkwardness is what binds father and son together. For I am perhaps even more ill at ease with him than he is with me. I love him dearly and don't know how to express it and so make all kinds of wisecracks about him to myself. I give him a short, succinct account of the major actions I have taken and the events which have overtaken me since his absence. I do not stint on the unpleasant bits, neither do I wallow in them. He listens impassively, but not irritably or with hostility. At the end of it I am none the wiser. I hope he is. Does he approve, disapprove or is he indifferent? Did

I behave and act responsibly? How would he have responded had he been in my situation? What now? I need to have an answer to these and a few million other questions urgently, desperately. I know he'll not let on, now or ever. He doesn't disappoint me. What about Vikramaditya, what are his plans for him? Here, too, I can guess his game plan. He'll play his cards close to his chest and I'll know his mind and his moves only when the rest of Mewar discovers them.

'We have been away for months on this campaign. On a couple of occasions we've given the Gujarat forces a drubbing. To what effect? Muzaffar Shah has changed the command of his armies from one general to another and our son-in-law, Rao Raimul's morale has certainly taken a turn for the better. That's about it. We can't stay here forever. Neither can we post our armies here permanently. I want a decision. You are the one who has new ideas. Give us a decisive victory, son. Let Idar revert to its rightful owner and let us move on to other pressing matters.'

I did not speak. 'I like the work you have been doing on our water and sewer systems. I'll go back and study the plans and then together, you and I will take a decision. So you have reservations about a decisive victory?' I should have known better. He had diverted my attention only to get me into a corner. I had not uttered a word but he had interpreted my silence rightly. There was no point mincing matters now.

'May I speak frankly, Father?'

'Better be blunt now than when it's too late to retrieve the situation.'

'If you want to get a decision on Idar, you'll have to take Gujarat first, Father.'

'You mean take on Gujarat?'

'No, Father. I said what I meant. We have been taking on Gujarat for years. And where's it got us?'

'You are serious about this, aren't you?' He was not posing that as a question.

'I am not proposing that we attack Gujarat. I am merely clarifying the precondition for getting Idar for good.'

'Supposing I agree with you, what would you propose?'

'I would suggest we do our homework carefully. I'm taking it for granted for the time being that whatever the costs, we'll win against Gujarat. But is Gujarat worth the trouble, expense and the death-count? Or, all things considered would it be less expensive, less trouble and far more profitable to attack the Delhi Sultanate which is in an advanced state of decay and decadence? Or are we missing something south and south-west of us? I am, as you are aware, talking of our other neighbour in Malwa, Mahmud Khalji. Muzaffar Shah of Gujarat is a strong, active and dynamic ruler. Mahmud Khalji is weak and vacillating and possessed of little beyond personal bravery. Besides, we could exploit his troubles with his Prime Minister, Medini Rai.'

'And you think the time is ripe to strike?'

'No, Father. It's time to plan and form a strong and indivisible confederacy of Rajput and other like-minded interests under your leadership. The only reason the Sultan of Gujarat has not fought with and annexed Malwa is because it's a Muslim kingdom. If we attempt to take Malwa, we must move with care and yet suddenly. We don't want Gujarat joining hands with Malwa.'

'I had forgotten how deep still waters run, son. I had not realized that your ambition had taken the form of such clear long-term planning.'

'We are kings before we are warriors. Which is why it is our task to have a vision first. And then a policy to translate that vision into reality. Whatever ambitions I have, Your Majesty, are for Mewar.'

Did he believe me?

'Take back Idar. Talk to me when you return. You'll have plenty of time to consider the various options and make your recommendations then.' He rose and the brief meeting was at an end. I bent down and touched his feet. His hand brushed my head and in an uncharacteristic gesture, ruffled my hair. 'May the blessings of Lord Eklingji be upon you.'

'Is there anything special you wish me to bear in mind about the Gujarat army?'

'The key to it is their commander, Malik Ayaz. He's a Russian by birth and was taken into slavery by the Turks. Eventually he became the ward of a merchant who presented him to Muzaffar Shah's grandfather, I think. He's bright, ambitious and has a chip on his shoulder. He has had to work twice, if not thrice as hard to move up from being a slave to a free man and then to his current position as one of the most trusted generals of the Gujarat Sultan. He has more at stake than any other general in Gujarat, or Mewar for that matter. He needs to prove himself and the rightness of Sultan Muzaffar's choice of him. The other generals look down upon him and would be only too happy to see him fall and may even help to trip him. Somewhat overeager, he has the recent convert's excessive zealousness. A good commander.'

Father is laconic beyond words. He would literally eschew words if he could. He had said more to me today than he had spoken in all these years put together. He has a knack of zeroing in on the pivotal issue in any discussion. Having thrown a brief beam of light on a subject, it is his policy to withdraw.

There was one more occasion when we met. It was the march-past on the morning he left. He and I together took the salute and then he officially handed over charge of the command to me. The minor and major raos and rajas and rawals including my brother-in-law Raimul, the Rao of Idar, were all gathered at the farewell breakfast. Father was about to bite into a samosa when he lowered it. It was one of his quaint or deliberate quirks, no one knew which, that everybody was familiar with. It suggested in the most polite and indirect of ways that he had something on his mind and it might be well worth everybody's time and effort to listen carefully to him.

'Almost everybody here,' he said in his hoarse whisper, 'is older and wiser than my son. You have seen more monsoons and seasons, more wars and have far more experience than him. All this will be invaluable to him. I advise him to make use of these resources. I have one thought to share about him with you and then I'll leave. Don't go by his years. You are in good hands. Jai Eklingji.'

*　　*　　*

I spent the day conferring with the elders and the heads of state whose advice Father had asked me to take. Some I was meeting for the first time, others I knew well from childhood or had worked

206

under on other campaigns. But I was the commander-in-chief now and like the Gujarat commander, Malik Ayaz, I too had to prove myself twice over. I introduced them to my Bhil friend, King Puraji Kika and to my cousin, Tej. Bringing Tej along with me was a politic move. As Rajendra's brother, his presence did not fail to impress them. But both Puraji and I knew that he was my biggest gamble. It was not his loyalty to Mewar that was in doubt, his opinion of me was. He thought I was a coward and a blackguard. We had a little under fifty thousand cavalry and infantry with us. Rao Ganga of Jodhpur had brought a contingent of seven thousand and my wife's uncle, Rao Viramdev of Merta, one of Father's closest associates, had come at the head of five thousand. Rawal Udai Simha of the state of Dungarpur and Ashwin Simha, the ruler of Banswara were both fighting under Mewar's standard with small armies of their own. Even without the hundred-odd elephants, we were not an unimpressive force and were well matched with the Gujarat troops which according to Rao Viramdeo were in the region of sixty thousand.

Malik Ayaz had four deputies under him, all of them seasoned commanders who had fought our armies on several occasions. I asked Rao Ganga if he could compile detailed profiles of them, along with Malik Ayaz's, especially their previous battles and the strategies they had used. He was not sure what purpose they would serve but he was willing to oblige me.

'How many Mussalmans in our armies?'

'Under seven hundred, not counting the fifty you brought with you,' Rao Viramdev informed me. 'They are good fighters and loyal to us, I assure you.'

'That is not the reason for my question. Is it possible to augment their numbers without compromising our security and safety?'

'How many would you want?'

'Five thousand would be a good number. For the time being two thousand will do.'

'We are better off without them.' That was Tej's first remark of the session.

'If I could, I would get Adinathji's Jains to fight with us. Fortunately our Muslim citizens are not pacifists. They'll only be too happy to do their bit for their country.' Tej could barely conceal his contempt for me. 'But there is another reason. We would like to avoid, if possible, Malik Ayaz or his sovereign, Muzaffar Shah converting this war into a jehad against the infidels. They may do it regardless, but it will be difficult to sustain their case if we had a substantial number of Muslims fighting on our side.'

As a matter of fact, I, too, had my doubts. Was having more Muslims in our forces really going to scotch the fanatical and incredibly effective appeal of Muzaffar Shah or any Muslim potentate to go after the kafir? I had spent sleepless nights in the past wondering how to combat such a potent call to arms. The truth is, I know of nothing in our scriptures which could compare with the motivation and power of Islam. We, too, could and do fight holy wars but there's no mechanism for conversion in our religion. The urge to convert is, definitely, one of the driving forces of Islam.

Our greatest call to war is the *Bhagavad Gita*. And what does the *Gita* say? Fight the war or perform the duties of your vocation, whatever they may be, but without thinking of the fruits and consequences of your actions. Compare this with what Islam codifies and spells out in the most precise and factual manner. If you die fighting for your God, you go directly to heaven where houris and other vividly-described indescribable pleasures await you.

What is the afterlife the *Gita* offers? For the great mass of us unenlightened souls, there's nothing but an endless cycle of reincarnation. Unless we deliver certainties in the afterlife and be specific about the preternatural joys which await those who fulfil their duties, I doubt if we will be able to match a Muslim's zeal or commitment. It is a wonder then that Hindus win as many wars as they do.

I sent for Shafi Khan, our Muslim strategist from the military academy. He entered hesitantly. His first encounter with me had not gone well and it was obviously still on his mind. He did adaab to me, then to the rest of the Council and stood wondering how he had fallen foul of me now. I pulled out my sword suddenly. The sound of unsheathing would have jangled a dead man's nerves. I pointed the sword at Shafi Khan and switched it from hand to hand.

'We plan to kill you now, Shafi,' I said softly to him. 'How would you run?'

'For what offence, sire?' He was shaking.

'Because I don't like your face.' I raised the sword. 'Answer me.'

'You expect me to retreat and leave by the regular parting in the shamiana from where I came in,' he was on to the game I was playing. 'Instead I'll run to my right, kill Rawal Udai Simha and Tej Simha if they come in my way, but only if they force me to. I'll then tear open the side of the tent and flee.'

'Why not to your left?'

'It would be risky to take on Rao Viramdev and Rao Ganga.'

'And you think I'll be easy to get rid of?' Tej was incensed. 'Try me.'

'You have a bad temper. I'm counting on it to help you make mistakes. As to Rawal Udai Simha, I would never venture against him when he's on horseback. Standing, he has a wooden leg. It's a weakness I'll exploit to my advantage.'

'How far has your treatise on the science of retreat come, Shafi Khan?'

'Halfway, Maharaj Kumar.'

I needed to enlighten my companions about our private conversation.

'Shafi Khan has spent the last fifteen years studying and innovating war strategies. I believe Father used one of them in the last battle he fought here. I have set a different task for Shafi Khan. To work out strategies of retreat.'

Rao Viramdev was, as almost always, the first to get my drift. 'That makes a lot of sense. We lose more men while falling back than while fighting.'

'Extend your right thumb, Shafi Khan.' I passed the blade of my sword over it. I dipped my thumb in the large bead of blood that had welled up and put a red tilak on his forehead and then on mine. 'I hereby appoint you member of the War Council for this campaign. Do you, Shafi Khan, on pain of death, swear to total secrecy and allegiance to the kingdom of Mewar and none other?'

'I do, your Highness.'

After lunch Raja Puraji Kika, Tej, Shafi Khan and I went with Rao Raimul to get a feel of the lay of the land. We were about seventy miles north-west of Idar. While it was mostly hilly, some of it was densely wooded. The ground rose and fell steeply. One last treacherous dip in the land and we were on a plain that stretched for a couple of miles to the north.

'What's at the edge of the flatland?' I asked Rao Raimul.

'Valleys, hills and forests. To the west, the country is mostly deceptive quagmires and marshes. They are a legacy of the earthquake which churned up and displaced the inland seas three years ago.'

'Let's go west and then skirt around the sands.'

The Rao and I rode ahead. Puraji Kika and the other two followed.

'You don't think Idar is worth fighting for, I believe,' my brother-in-law, the displaced Rao of Idar said bitterly. 'When do you plan to abandon the pretense and give up on Idar?'

'The trouble with appointing stupid spies to do a job, Rao Raimul, is not that they misinform you but that you trust them.' I was curt and cutting with the Rao. 'So that's what made you sulky and silent this morning. If you were not married to my sister and if this war wasn't being fought on your behalf, I would have you suspended from the War Council for eavesdropping on His Majesty. What I said to the Rana is none of your concern but I will tell you what the Rana said to me in the hope that you may behave a little more responsibly. He said , "Win Idar and then come back".'

'I beg your pardon, Maharaj Kumar. I beg you not to hold it against me. You know how much I respect you. I would never do anything to upset you. I'll sack that spy as soon as I return. I'll have him whipped for slandering you.'

'Restrain yourself, Rao Raimul. Your apologies are worse than your accusations against me. And before you whip your eavesdropper, ask yourself who gave him the assignment.'

I slowed down and waited for the others to join us. I did not wish to hear any more of the Rao's talk. The hills and valleys proved to be almost a replica of the land we had traversed when we started out. We changed course quickly and rode towards the quagmires.

210

They stretched for at least a mile and a half and, but for the Rao's warnings, we would have blithely entered them. Raja Puraji Kika and I dragged a heavy branch weighing as much as a normal man and threw it as far in as we could. It fell about eight feet from us. In a few moments, it had been sucked out of sight.

The next morning, I rode before sunrise to the tallest hillock nearby to get a panoramic view of the bits and pieces we had seen yesterday. For ten minutes the sealed ball of the night would not let in the light except at the razor-thin line of the horizon. Then the sun broke through and flooded the undulating land. Violet and purple were the colours of the sun's waters and they rose in the sky in alternate bands. Soon the waters had commingled and deep red wine lapped at the edge of the earth. I looked to my right. Malik Ayaz's armies were falling into place on the plain. Oh, what a sight it is to see a disciplined army do its work with precision. Malik Ayaz, you didn't waste any time. The only way to greet the enemy is to catch him napping. I swept down into our camp and asked Mangal to have the leaders of the War Council in my tent in five minutes. What would have happened if I had not been atop that knoll this morning? I'm not talking about a stationary and unprepared army being an easy target for a massacre. Quite the contrary. My question is very different: what if we had not turned up to face the Gujarat armies? Would Malik Ayaz have waited four hours and then gone back in disgust? Would he have advanced? Would he have sent a message to us asking us whether we planned to join him in battle? Would he have assumed that Gujarat had won an unconditional victory? Would he have been confused and irritable and his armies bored and hungry and dispirited after a pointless wait? What is the secret and unspoken covenant between warring armies? It's not as if they have decided to meet at an appointed time like trysting lovers or duelists meeting to settle matters of personal honour. Who decides the time? Why do both armies range themselves against each other? What if one or both of them decided they don't want to fight that day because the general has got a cold or because the niece of one of the soldiers has eloped with a brigand and she needs to be brought back and brought to her senses? What if one of the parties does not care for the site or the angle of the sun in their eyes? Why do we feel honour-bound to fight that very day at that very time? What would have been the outcome of the great decisive wars if one of the armies had stayed put in its camp or chosen to wait at a different site of its own choosing?

Rao Viramdev, Rao Ganga, Rao Udai Simha, Raja Puraji Kika are old hands and so are their troops. They know the tricks of the trade and they don't get fazed easily. They have seen too many wars and there's not much that surprises them. Perhaps our Rajput ancestors knew a thing or two about fighting the Afghan hordes who came down the Hindukush mountain passes which other Hindu rajas didn't. Their antidote to the Muslim passion for jehad was to glorify death in war to the point where any other mode of dying was a lesser form of life and close to dishonourable.

We fought well, all fifty thousand of our warriors. But on the enemy's terms. By noon we had lost seven hundred and fifty men.

It was then that I took the fateful decision which has put all the raos and the elders in such a dudgeon with me and earned me the obloquy of all our armed forces. Rao Viramdev refuses to speak to me while Rao Udai Simha can scarce restrain his contumely. Raja Puraji Kika tells me that the budding poets in the army are busy composing limericks about the cuckold and coward.

I guess my first act and crime set the tone for what followed. I was not at the head of the troops at the outset and I did not lead the first charge. I wanted to but what I wanted more was to get a feel for how the different contingents from Mewar and its protectorates worked together and to observe Malik Ayaz's game plan from some elevated place. The right time to have done this was halfway through the battle but that, as any urchin in the streets of Chittor will tell you, is inconceivable. The troops think you are mortally wounded if you disappear and there's chaos and pandemonium leading, more often than not, to a rout. God knows I was unsure of myself but I decided to take my chances and I informed the War Council of my intentions. They were not pleased. They distrusted my new-fangled ideas. I was showing off, they didn't say that, but implied it. This one time, however, they were willing to indulge me. Except for Raja Puraji Kika. 'Don't do it, Highness,' he told me in front of the entire Council.

Malik Ayaz, I discovered from my position on the hill, had arranged his armies with precision following proven classical strategies. He had chosen his ground well, so that the sun was behind his troops and straight in the eyes of our army. He was a meticulous man, yet not conservative as he had shown by his wily move to engage us on the heels of Father's departure and while we were still getting our bearings. A man to respect and not take chances with. His elephant was tucked in an inconspicuous place and there was a clutch of twenty dispatch riders waiting at his side. They brought him news from the different divisions and he sent instructions to them as the battle progressed and the patterns of attack and defence changed.

We were at the height of the melee now, two battering rams trying to crack the other's defences. It looked like a deadlock, neither side willing to give an inch. If only we could continue to hold our ground, we could, in time, neutralize the Gujarat army's advantage. But I knew even then that I was fantasizing. Mewar, Merta, Jodhpur, Banswara, Dungarpur were all putting up a terrific front but they were pulling in different directions because we were not one army but many different units ranged on the same side. True, we were united by common sympathies and loyalties. But when did sympathy win a war? I knew what my first task was going to be when we were through with this engagement. It would take months, perhaps years, but we had to forge our various forces into one great fighting machine whose actions were as cohesive and single-minded as its intentions.

We were disintegrating imperceptibly like a sand wall. It was curious, now that the cracks were widening, the different divisions were no longer even pretending to be a single army. I raced downhill. The chances of my being able to stop the damage and reverse the tide were remote but I was going to give it a good try. I got hold of Raja Puraji Kika and told him to ask his forces to chant 'Jai Maharaj Kumar' vociferously so that our armies would know that I was in their midst. The cry was taken up none too enthusiastically and I could see in the distance soldiers standing in their stirrups to get a glimpse of their prince. I raised my sword and whirled it over my head and was about to yell 'Jai Mewar' when I realized that it was not just the Mewar armies which I was leading and changed my call to 'Jai Rana Sanga'. That got a good response. I repeated Father's name like a mantra. It seemed to revive everybody. The people around me were charged up now and we managed to break through the enemy's ranks. We kept up the pressure and penetrated deeper and deeper. But our progress, it turned out, was not echoed in other sections. What we had on our hands was a disaster: a comparatively small band of Rajputs forming an island in an ocean of the Gujarat army. We suffered heavy losses all round and I got a few nicks and slashes, one of them rather deep to prove that I was my father's son. I decided to call it a day.

* * *

We raised the white flag and sent Raja Puraji Kika with a brief message to Malik Ayaz:

> 'To the Honourable Malik Ayaz, General of the
> Gujarat Forces.
> Greetings. His Highness, the Maharaj Kumar
> is seriously injured and wishes to sue for peace.
> Could he discuss the terms and conditions of
> surrender as soon as he has recovered?
> Yours truly, Raja Puraji Kika for H.H. Maharaj
> Kumar of Mewar.'

Raja Puraji Kika had to do the honours because Rao Viramdev refused to put his signature to such a shameful document. He along with every commander, officer and soldier in our army felt that we could have fought at least another hour, if not two. It was true that our casualties were high but there was no need to panic. You never could tell, we might have yet turned the tables on Malik Ayaz and his hordes. At least, we would have proved our mettle. This was the first battle the troops were fighting under the Maharaj Kumar's command. What kind of signal was the Rana's eldest son sending to our armies and, more importantly, to the enemy? Who would ever take the Mewar armies seriously again? The Rana had spent a lifetime building a reputation which was the envy and awe of the most powerful kingdoms in the country. And now, with one thoughtless gesture, the heir apparent had brought down this carefully wrought edifice of determination and deterrence. Incidentally, the wounds the Maharaj Kumar had suffered were substantial but not really serious. And which territories was the Maharaj Kumar planning to cede to Gujarat as the price of peace?

'Don't go by his years', Father had recommended me to our senior commanders in those cryptic words. They were coming true. I was proving to be as dependable as a flighty teenager. Flighty indeed, what an apt word. But neither Rao Viramdev nor his fellow-chieftains were in the mood for word play. By now, I had troubles coming to a boil in so many pots, I was having problems deciding which one to look into first. My brother-in-law, the insufferable Rao Raimul whose candidature Father must support for dubious reasons of policy and whose marriage into the family he must regret every time he thought of my poor sister, was busy canvassing support from heads of minor principalities, divisional commanders and the common soldiers for a petition to His Majesty informing him of my disgraceful conduct and asking him to replace me with Rao Viramdev.

'Should I stop the rot, Prince,' Raja Puraji asked me, 'before he incites the army to mutiny?'

'No, not at all. I'm interested in knowing how far he succeeds in his mission. That way we'll get a good idea of the extent of the displeasure of our soldiery and how far it is willing to go. Keep a close eye on him, nevertheless. When the courier leaves with the letter tonight, I want him intercepted and relieved of it. Take the man into custody but make sure that no one learns of it.'

'What game are you playing Maharaj Kumar?' My good old friend Raja Puraji Kika asked me with the first smile of the day.

'No game, Raja. I am in deadly earnest...'

There was no question of my saying more. I could hear Tej baying for me.

'Maharaj Kumar, come out. I publicly accuse you of collusion with the enemy and challenge you to a fight to the death. Let me

215

warn all those assembled here that the Maharaj Kumar is about to hand over Idar and a great big chunk of Mewar to Muzaffar Shah. What pact have you made with Prince Bahadur and his father to gain the throne of Mewar for yourself? You may as well confess for I will not let you leave except on a bier.'

What now? Must I spill my cousin's blood or be killed by a crazed young bull who could not accept the loss of his brother nor let go of the man who had prevented him from taking vengeance? What would you have me do, Lord Eklingji? Will you not still the torment of this young man and make him understand that he is twice as dear to me now that his brother is no more?

'Come out, traitor. Or I'll set your tent on fire and you'll never walk out alive.'

So be it. But by then he had already thrown the lit torch at the sloping roof of Father's tent where I was staying. By the time Raja Puraji Kika and I had rescued the most important documents and run out, the fire was raging. Fortunately, it was a windless day and the rest of the tents were pitched at a distance from Father's so the fire would not spread easily.

Tej who was clearly impressed by his own handiwork, laughed theatrically and brandished his sword in the air.

'See how the rats leave a sinking ship.' I was not quite sure of the implications of his maritime imagery but I went across and spoke to him peremptorily. 'Tej, hold these records for me.' He stretched out his hands almost as a reflex action to pick up the pile of documents. The papers were in his hands, my knee had rammed his crotch and I hit him hard in the face. Tej was in a state of shock, not so much from the impact of my blows, which were vicious enough, as by the dastardliness of my act. I pursued my advantage and did not give him a chance to recover. Before I knocked him senseless with a chop on the back of his neck, I whispered to him, 'I need you alive, you fool – not as my enemy but as my friend and colleague.' He was too drunk with the bashing he had received to comprehend my words. He rolled over. I could see that even if I had not risen in the estimation of my soldiers and my royal peers, I had certainly made a lasting impression on them. They were dumbstruck by how low I could stoop.

216

'Lock him up,' I said to no one in particular but at least seven troopers rushed forward to carry out my orders. 'Rao Viramdev, may I retire to your quarters for a little rest?'

'I'll vacate them instantly, Your Highness,' he said dryly.

'I cannot avail of your hospitality if you are not there to receive me.' I was not about to let the Rao fob me off with cold courtesy when I needed to spend some time with him.

'I will not fail my duties as a host, Your Highness.'

'That is kind of you. Mangal put up another tent for me and fetch me when it's done.'

The Rao's quarters were spartan and severe. He sat stiffly, unable or unwilling to make conversation. I was alienating people with such breathtaking speed, I would soon not have a single friend in the country. How was I going to make headway with the campaign — I found it difficult to persuade myself that it had already begun — without the active cooperation of leaders like Rao Viramdev?

'I know that I haven't done much so far to inspire your confidence but will you, in the privacy of these walls, grant that there was not much to be gained by continuing the battle this afternoon except escalate the casualties on our side?' The Rao looked uncomfortable and tried to clear his throat but I had no desire to put him on the spot. 'All that's so much water under the bridge. Will you be patient with me and my occasionally unorthodox ways for a short while?'

'I cannot answer your question unless I know what you have in mind.'

'I would be less than candid with you if I told you that I had a plan of action.' I was of course being less than candid. Right now I did not want to be pinned down. 'Will you give me time to get my bearings and find my way? All the leaders and the soldiery will take their cue from you. I would too. If you believe in me, they will. And so will I.'

'You are asking for a lot, Maharaj Kumar, and all of it on blind faith.'

'When a newcomer goes looking for a job, he's almost invariably told that they are looking for a man with experience. To labour the obvious, how is he to get experience if no one gives him a job?'

217

'I too want to believe in you, Maharaj Kumar. It looks as if we'll have to invent you by an act of faith,' he smiled for the first time. His smile made my day. It was a passing thing but it lit his face up and it warmed my heart. I wanted to rise in the estimation of this fine old stalwart. He liked me but I knew that respect was a more mature and stable basis for a professional relationship. 'What's next on the agenda, Prince?'

I took a deep breath. 'I was thinking of holding horse-races tomorrow, Your Highness, for our cavalry.'

'For all twenty-three thousand of our cavalry?' There was no surprise in his voice. He merely wanted to get the details right. The act of faith was firmly in place. It was my turn to smile.

That night Mangal intercepted my brother-in-law's letter and brought it to me. Rao Raimul had been hard at work; three thousand soldiers had put their thumbprints to the letter. I was a coward, and an incompetent. I had stayed away from the scene of battle and just when the Mewar forces seemed to be in sight of victory, I had waved a white flag and sued for peace. I was now planning to hand over two of our most prosperous provinces and of course, Idar itself, to Gujarat. The P.S. mentioned that I had tricked the brave Tej who had fought the enemy so valiantly this morning and had, out of spite, attacked him violently and set his tent on fire. The letter ended with a fervent and urgent plea to Father to replace his blot-on-the-fair-name-of-Mewar son lest he do further and permanent damage to the interests of the kingdom.

'Do you think anyone in the enemy forces might be interested in this letter?'

'Who knows,' Mangal kept a straight face, 'they just might.'

'Will you arrange to auction it to the highest bidder?'

'I could try but I can't guarantee a sale.'

We both laughed. 'Don't sell me short, Mangal. And make sure I get the money. If I am going to be slandered, I might as well make some hard cash out of it.'

'What happens then?'

'Nothing. In due time, Sultan Muzaffar Shah will get a copy of it and Father will come by the original.'

'Are you sure you want to risk the letter falling into His Majesty's hands? Those three thousand fingerprints are difficult to ignore.'

'That's a risk I'll have to take. But I cannot deprive Malik Ayaz of it. It will bring him great joy.'

There was a good deal of criticism and resistance to the idea of the competitions on the first day. But there was plenty of food during the day and drinks at night, not to mention professional nautanki plays, and soon everybody was having a good time.

It took four days of round-the-clock racing for the results to come in. There was a terrific festive air in the camp now. It was almost like the annual competitions at Chittor. Swimming, wrestling, archery, night maneouvres, target-oriented spear-throwing during the day and singing and tall-tale telling contests at night. The only variation we introduced was in hand-to-hand combats. Riders and foot soldiers charged headlong towards straw-filled dummies and hacked them. Each soldier got one chance and no more to sever the backbone of the dummy. It looked easy but there was a tough, four inch-thick wet bamboo inside the dummy which gave even the veterans a hard time. The results of all the contests were tabulated and the winners got prizes. We now had a record of who were our fastest riders and who our strongest and most vicious killers.

I stayed inside my new tent all those long, boisterous days and worked without pause. On the third day Malik Ayaz sent his emissary Liaquat Ali to enquire after my wounds and ask when we could meet to finalize the terms of the surrender. Liaquat Ali was kept waiting for four hours during which time doctors went back and forth. He wondered what all the merriment was about when the Maharaj Kumar was so unwell.

'Better a merry army than a mutinous one,' Mangal said laconically and then informed him that the Maharaj Kumar would go over personally to meet the great general the moment he was in better health.

'What kind of injury —?'

'First the terrible blow to the head from one of your soldiers,' Mangal explained to him, 'and then the wound in the stomach which Tej Simha inflicted on him because the Maharaj Kumar sued for peace.'

By the sixth day, I was getting impatient and ill with anxiety. The competitions were over. Liaquat Ali had been to see me again. I would perforce have to go and see Malik Ayaz soon, very soon. What terms was I going to propose to him? Would my brother-in-law Rao Raimul's words come true? Would I be the instrument of Mewar's dismemberment? The Rao had also been active on the rumour front. He was feeding our forces with scenarios of the end of Mewar and its allies thanks to their Maharaj Kumar. Morale was slipping once again. I had to put an end to the rot quickly but didn't know how. Despite his gross insubordination, locking Tej behind bars had not gone down well with the soldiers. Locking up Rao Raimul for sedition was out of the question since he was the reason fifty thousand soldiers and I were here. Rao Viramdev was holding his tongue but I could see that I was trying his patience. Had he made a mistake putting his trust in me? Had I totally miscalculated the turn of events?

My one serious error was that I had not made any contingency plans. It was time I became realistic. I sat down that night and wrote a letter to Father explaining our ignominious defeat and the territories I was proposing to surrender to Gujarat along with all claims to Idar. All our towns and villages were equally dear to us. Even the most barren lands were priceless because of emotional and historical ties. But if we hardened our hearts and looked at the matter in a cold-blooded way, then strategically, politically and economically, the most expendable — that ghastly term stuck in my throat — were Jarrole and Beechabair. Did Father agree with my choice? I tried to weave in an apology for my dismal performance but it was no use. My words sounded either abject and piteous or hollow and flatfooted. I decided to stick to the bare essentials and leave it to his imagination to understand my terrible humiliation.

The next morning, that's the seventh day after the fiasco on the battlefield, we got word that ten thousand Gujarat troops would be leaving for home that afternoon. This was extremely short notice but Malik Ayaz had little choice but to give in to the restiveness of his soldiers. I immediately sent a letter to General Malik Ayaz apologizing for the delay in seeing him and requesting a meeting the following day to discuss the terms and conditions of the instrument of surrender. I have rarely got such a speedy reply. The Gujarat General would be happy to receive the royal visitor at eleven thirty the next morning. Would we be so kind as to have lunch with him? As expected, it was obvious that Malik Ayaz was now in a rush to get back home. He had been away for more than nine months and could look forward to the triumphant welcome that awaited the hero of Gujarat.

We left around two in the afternoon. Raja Puraji Kika, Mangal and twelve others had gone ahead several hours ago. An hour after our departure, I put up my hand and brought the soldiers to a halt. Another couple of hours and it would be pitch dark.

'There are two thousand seven hundred and sixty of us plus Rawal Udai Simha, your ten commanders and me. You have been chosen because you are the swiftest soldiers in our army. We are not even a tidy round figure of three thousand. The Gujarat soldiers who are going home today are ten thousand in number. Which means we are outnumbered three to one. I know that you are all brave warriors. But that's not going to be enough. Each one of you will have to be at least thrice as brave as the enemy merely to survive.' I let that sink in for a full thirty seconds. 'Twenty years ago almost to the day, three thousand of our troops under our venerable Home Minister, the great Lakshman Simha were killed treacherously about sixty miles from here by the Gujarat armies. I don't have to repeat the full story of the terrible and deceitful slaughter. You know it well. I want to know what vengeance means to you. Will you be happy if some day you killed three thousand Gujarat soldiers? I can see the gleam in your eyes. Bravo, you are easily satisfied. You are nothing but tit-for-tat men. If that's all that three thousand of your brothers are worth to you, I suggest we forget Idar and this war, pull up our tents and go home.

'Seven days ago, when I asked for the white flag to be waved, I heard a lot of brave talk. We were down by seven hundred and fifty men and you only wanted to be given a chance to turn defeat into victory. Tomorrow morning, at five thirty you have an appointment with the Gujarat forces. Let's see what all your talk amounts to. I have but one piece of advice for you. It will hold true in the coming skirmish and in any other battle or engagement you are involved in. The secret of victory lies in numbers. Does it take you one blow to kill your opponent or three? If it's three, two other enemy soldiers are going to have a shot at you while you are unable to defend yourself. Besides you are going to tire faster. If it's one blow, then two other enemy soldiers had better look out. There will be those among you who will live to tell your children and their grandchildren how you wounded at least twenty of the enemy single-handed. Now we know who our enemies at home are. Anybody who wounds but does not kill is making certain that his friend and neighbour's life is seriously in danger. If the left hand is injured, the right can still hold a sword and kill. My father, the great Rana Sanga, is living testimony of the man who survived seventy or eighty wounds to kill at least seventy men. We all know how deadly a wounded tiger is. Can you imagine how much more dangerous a wounded enemy soldier is? He nurses his hatred and lives with just one thought. He wants to get even. The only trouble is his vengeance is unquenchable. He can never get even. One more and then one more. And then one more. Think about it. A dead man has no enemies.

'One last word. If from now on any one of you decides to exchange a word with his neighbour, he is going to put two thousand seven hundred and seventy-three of his countrymen in danger. That I'm afraid the rest of us might find unacceptable. Surely you don't want two thousand seven hundred and seventy three of your friends to kill you.' They laughed. 'Godspeed and good luck.'

We took the path parallel to the one taken by the departing Gujarat army. Raja Puraji Kika and Mangal had chosen a site twelve miles from our camp to bivouac. While the men settled down for the night, one of Raja Puraji Kika's men brought Tej over. My cousin looked a little worse for his stay in solitary confinement but I was sure his mood would improve.

'I'm dividing the men equally between Rawal Udai Simha, Raja Puraji Kika and you. That means you have a little over nine hundred soldiers under you.' I turned to my Bhil friend. 'Will you show us the sites, Your Highness?'

For mapping a territory, especially a hilly one there was no one

222

I knew who could compare with Raja Puraji Kika and his men. There might be a forest of seven hundred thousand trees and the Raja would be able to point out the very peepul to which I had tied my horse Befikir seven years ago and under which tree we had had a picnic lunch. He had total geographic recall. Without him we would be lost tomorrow. I realized how confusing the terrain was when I discovered that we were barely a mile from the massive Gujarat encampment. We went up and down over seven low-wooded hills and suddenly the land turned flat.

It was an unbelievably peaceful scene, almost idyllic with the sun going down over the sands in the distance. The soldiers were playing cards, smoking hukkas, chatting with a senior officer who was having a haircut seated next to his tent. You could hear the nervous chatter of the scissors all the way to where we were lying on our bellies. A man has started singing, another joins him. No, the second man is giving a rejoinder to the first man's question. It's a sawaal-jawaab qawwali, a form of improvisation that I love. It's full of wit, sharp comment, philosophical asides and humour. They are singing not a religious qawwali but its secular and lay cousin.

'Why is the beloved more beloved when you are away from home? Why does one miss home only when one is away from home?' The second man keeps the beat with superb clapping while the first singer asks his questions. 'Is there music in the flute?' It's the second singer's turn, 'when you are not blowing in the hole? Is the octave on your lips or on your fingertips as they glide over the reed?' A bulbul tarang accompanies the singers. People are gathering around them now. The first man's response is ready on the instant. 'Either way, who is playing the tune and who is dancing? When we sing who dances, us or the Good Lord himself?' The strings of the bulbul tarang are a limpid cascade of sound, now thoughtful, now bubbling. All those around clap. Did they take classes, have they trained for years to achieve such perfection of rhythm? I look at my companions. I steal a glance at Tej, surely he hasn't forgotten his avowed enemy, how can these unanswerable and timeless queries elicit such intense attention from him? 'Tell me, my friend, what is the velocity of a sneeze?' That evokes gentle laughter. 'And if you know the answer, pray tell me, how many

223

million times is a thought faster than a sneeze?' Are these illiterate troopers or the gurus of sages?

The singing is suddenly drowned by the lowing and keening of cattle. It sends a serrated shiver up my spine. They are killing buffaloes for the evening meal. It is a dreadful and terrible sound, this wailing of animals who know that a horrific death with a ritual of bloodletting is at hand. What if the gate of the pen was not bolted but left wide open? Would they run for their lives? I suspect not. They are mesmerized by their own death. The goats have joined the ghastly chorus. The halal blood gushes out, the heart pumping it out in spurts. You wait for the agony to end, how much blood can one body hold? The animal is in a stupor, it has thrown its head back as if to open wider the single cut the butcher has administered and get it over with. Every once in a while, its lifeless body twitches as if at the last minute it is having second thoughts about dying. Why am I horrified? Will I not eat mutton with relish when I go back to our camp tomorrow? The singers continue undisturbed.

Across, near the centre of the encampment where the commandant of the troops, the much feared Bunde Ali has his quarters, a game of kabbadi has started. One of the youngsters is spinning through the other team with celerity while muttering kabbadi, kabbadi, and flinging his arms and toes all over the place. He flashes past, makes contact with two of the opposing players and gets them out. They have a tricky job here: stay away from him and yet pin him down, till he can no longer say kabbadi, kabbadi. I am making extensive notes of the enemy camp's layout when I see Bunde Ali step out of his tent and join the game. He is a little old but what he lacks in speed, he makes up with cunning. It is evident that his troops are awed by his presence until a young soldier shrugs his shoulders and seems to say to himself 'What the hell' and grabs the great man's leg. Bunde Ali tries desperately to reach the dividing line that will give him a new lease of life. But now the other soldiers are emboldened and fling themselves on him. They hang on to him till his breath has run out and no more kabbadi, kabbadis issue forth from his mouth. Tej is watching Bunde Ali intently.

'Allahu Akbar,' the muezzin calls the faithful to evening prayer.

224

All activity ceases and three-quarters of the troops gather to the west. The cooks, their assistants and the cowherds join them. How beautifully they arrange themselves. Row after row of evenly spaced men, all of them kneeling down, their heads covered, palms raised to seek Allah's blessings. Is the genius of Islam military? Perhaps that explains why it elicits such total obedience. Like sunflowers after the sun has set, the heads bend down in unison. The Hindus in the regiment seem a little lost and go about their business quietly. Only the hens and cocks are oblivious of the solemn proceedings. And the flies. There are thousands of them jostling each other, pushing and shoving, trying to get at the blood that has almost completely disappeared into the earth. Another thousand have settled into the open gash that is fast drying up in the buffalo's neck. God Almighty, the wretched thing is still alive. It shakes its head slowly and they rise like a levitating beehive.

By the time we were back in camp it was getting dark. We conferred for the last time, Rawal Udai Simha, Raja Puraji Kika, Tej, Mangal, the platoon commanders and I. We went over every step, move and countermove, attack and defence tactic. Each com-mander was allotted a specific task and a specific geographical area. He was not to stray from it unless ordered to by me, King Puraji or Rawal Udai Simha or under the most exceptional circumstances. I was willing to bet that there were a hundred contingencies that we had overlooked. And yet, it was of the utmost importance to have a detailed plan and make sure that everyone knew his role and objective in it. I didn't want to just choose the time and place of the confrontation, I didn't want the enemy to have a say in his mode of retreat either. It was critical that we dictate just how, when and where he would retreat.

By nine fifteen the camp was quiet. I don't know if the men were asleep but they had spread out the single bedcloth each one of us was permitted to bring along and covered themselves with a blanket. Dinner had been four big bajra ki rotis, congealed ghee, radish and garlic chutney so hot it would make you weep. You could change the order of the dishes but tomorrow's breakfast and lunch would be the same stuff rolled up in a piece of cloth riding side-saddle along with the leather bottle of water. The wake-up call was for four thirty. There was no way I was going to get sleep unless I did yoga-nidra or shavasan. I lay myself down and took in the sky. It was flat and black and had holes pierced in it. Light leaked out through the tiny dots. I knew many of those holes. We had been taught to read them at school as an aid to finding one's bearings but I didn't think they would give me direction in a spiritual crisis. I closed my eyes and recalled the stars on the closed screen of my eyelids. They would be witness to my death. I started with my big toe, withdrew the sensation from it and the other toes, the heels were dead, then the knees and the thighs, my crotch and belly were a void, the lungs dropped out, then the hands, arms and shoulders. I had disengaged myself and now stood among the stars watching my lifeless body. My feet were a foot and a half apart and my hands had fallen by the sides. A dead man without a bier, flowers and mourners. My head is busier than bazaar-day at Chittor. What decision has Father taken about Vikramaditya? Sunheria's bangles break. My mother is forcing me to eat. The scent of Kausalya's vagina is in my nostrils. What will Father's reaction be when he realizes that I have abandoned orthodox and sensible ways of warfare? Was the Gujarat commander, Bunde Ali, slightly walleyed? Who will take him on tomorrow? Images of my first debacle try to come centrestage but are sent packing by my wife. I erect a whirlpool mandala between my eyes and spin it. As it picks up speed, it draws all thoughts, images, colours, ideas into its vortex. It goes faster and faster till everything collapses in its vertiginous velocity. At its still epicentre is the third eye, the one that never closes and sees everything. Gradually everything comes to a stop. The occasional thought floats down my mind and is washed ashore. The lapping of the void is a soothing sound. It came to me then that we had passed the point of no return. The two thousand seven hundred and ninety-four of us would never be able to join the mass of humanity again. We may mingle with the others, break bread with them, go to mushairas with them, play holi with them, fornicate with their daughters but we would be forever outsiders. We would be bonded together by the unspeakable deeds we were going to

226

commit the next morning.

We were up by four. The horses were fed and the business behind the trees done by twenty past four. Ten minutes for breakfast. At four thirty we had started walking the horses across the seven intervening hills. Perhaps we could have cantered over the first four knolls; the woods might have muffled the sound of the hooves but I was not taking chances. Within fifty minutes we were spread out and lying on our stomachs in the same spot where we had been last evening. We had long since got used to the darkness around us. I wondered why there were only seven sentries guarding the Gujarat encampment on the side closest to us. It took me a while to figure out the answer. As far as they were concerned, the war was over. They had defeated us and were going home. Raja Puraji Kika's men, silent as the beasts they hunted in the jungle took care of those seven with their bows and arrows. They were among the cattle pens now and letting the cattle out. Some of the more stolid of the five hundred buffaloes needed heavy prodding to move. A small contingent of ten Bhils was making its way down to the left where about a half mile away, half the horses of the garrison were tethered. There was a downwind blowing and a dog picked up the scent of the intruders and started barking. In a minute the whole tribe of dogs in the camp would take the cue and alert their companions in Kashmir, Persia and China not to mention Bunde Ali and his armies. Raja Puraji Kika's arrow cut short the dog's alarm. From nowhere five other dogs had turned up. Something about the inert dog warned them and made them whine but not bark. The ground was heavy with dew and I was half-wet as I lay on the grass. There was a low mist rolling over the hills and would soon reach the encampment. The sky was bleaching out in a few places. Any moment now the birds would be up. The leaks in the sky had been plugged by a heavy cloud bank and for a few moments the density of the darkness increased. Who wakes up first when the women are not around? The cooks, the syces or the mullah? What an easygoing, lazy sight an army was when it was on its way home.

There was a bird call, an unseasonal papiha. It was one of Raja Puraji Kika's men telling us that the horses were free. I had debated endlessly with myself whether I should lead the troops or sit back and coordinate the action. I guess at heart I knew all along that I had no option but to set an example in today's treachery.

The troops were divided into three groups. Tej on my left, Rawal Udai Simha on my right. Each one of us commanded nine hundred and odd cavalry. My forces and I would lead the charge. It was Tej and Udai Simha's task to prevent anybody from escaping to either side of us, thus forcing the enemy to retreat in only one direction: directly ahead of us. We wanted all roads to lead south-west.

It was time for me and my contingent to head down softly. When we reached the bottom of the hill, Tej lit the soaked cloth bandaged around the head of the arrow, aimed and stretched the string as far back as it would go. The rest of the officers did the same. At a signal from me the arrows flew forth to their various destinations. Tej's arrow made straight for Bunde Ali's shamiana. It lost altitude fast. I was sure it wouldn't make it. I needn't have worried. It sank into the frilled edge of the shamiana and torched the roof. There were flares whizzing past everywhere. The guard on duty in front of Bunde Ali's residence must have got up to check where the comets were coming from. No one heard from him again. Raja Puraji Kika's arrow had found the soft spot below the sentry's Adam's apple. The sky paled visibly. The seven horses of the Sun-god were in a tearing rush and churning clouds of pink and yellow overhead. The muezzin's cry pierced the still quiet air. (And I thought I had factored in all the imponderables. Bunde Ali's men would be up and headed for prayers in a minute or two.) The sun stuck its head out. I bowed down, did namaskar and said a prayer. Why hadn't the muezzin noticed the pyrotechnics all around? Fires had broken out all over the camp as my heel dug into Befikir's flank. By now the animals in the Gujarat camp were stampeding murderously over sleeping bodies. The deafening noise gave us a tremendous advantage. It spread the impression that a force of about ten thousand cavalry was sweeping through. Twenty of Puraji Kika's men shot out and headed for the second series of stables at the other end of the camp. If they could let loose the horses and camels there, they would add to the pandemonium. My sword was out and I was bending low. I struck anything that woke up, rolled over, moved, stood up, screamed or ran. I hacked, I cut, I chopped, I smashed, I mutilated. The Gujarat soldiers, still only half-awake and bewildered, held up their hands as protection against our swords. The hands and the heads fell on the ground together. I set the pace and rhythm. My men followed. 'Say a prayer for me,' I whispered as I extended myself and smote a frightened and powerless soldier. A diagonal stroke from left of neck to right of waist. A crushing blow from the left shoulder blade that sank down to the thoracic cavity and cleaved the heart. An oblique cut of such grace and power that the head and torso were not aware that they had been severed. An elementary thought crossed my mind as if it were a revelation. An unarmed and unprepared soldier is nothing but a civilian. Rajendra, I promised you two men for every man that was treacherously killed by the Gujarat army under your father's command. Start counting. I hope to pay you back with compound interest. I am any man's equal in treachery and deceit. I don't forget and I don't forgive offences committed against Mewar. Expect the worst of me. I will always improve upon your expectations.

There are few things as infectious as fear, and fear paralyses. The poor helpless clods just stood there shivering and peeing in their pants waiting to be delivered. We did not disappoint them. Men poured out of the flaming tents, then ran back to collect their weapons. Half were asphyxiated, the others returned to put up token resistance. They did not know whether we were real or phantoms. Where had we come from? Wasn't the war over? It was an unequal fight. They were stranded on the ground. We were riding horseback and momentum was on our side. There was a strange ululating sound mixed up in all the crying and screaming. Where was it emanating from, this high-pitched lamenting and wailing? It rose from within me and from all the Mewar troops. It was a ghastly howling, an incredulous and disbelieving cry for mercy, a plea for forgiveness from our prospective victims even as we pierced flesh and cracked bone and skull.

I saw the muezzin then. He was standing unsteadily, his left foot on a dead body, his head aslant to catch the drift of sounds. Every scream was a blow aimed at his person. I knew now why he hadn't noticed the arson in the first few moments. He was blind. He stumbled and fell. I leaned over and gave him a steadying hand. He blessed me. 'What's going on?' he asked me, 'Is it Judgement Day?' 'Not for those who are slain but for the slayers, yes. Lie down quietly, old man, and no one will touch you.' I was impatient to be gone.

Shaan-e-riyasat Bunde Ali was riding towards us at the head of around a thousand men. I eased the pressure on Befikir. We slowed down to a trot. The Shaan-e-riyasat's tunic buttons were undone, his turban was a shade askew and he had not had time to lace up his armour. I had not realized how tall and erect he was. He leaned forward, his sword parallel to the ground. He and his men were a violent whirlwind. They were advancing so rapidly, it was almost as if they were stationary. The sound in my ears was shut off. All the wailing and weeping ceased. I couldn't hear the pounding of the horses either. A thousand horses flexing their muscles and bodies. Black, tawny, dappled, amber, mahogany, the air and skin sparking in the early morning sun. And a thousand horsemen astride them.

The Gujarat horsemen were a tidal force that should have swept everything in its path. Yes, on most other days, they would have.

As rehearsed, my nine hundred men parted in the middle and let Bunde Ali and his men in like much sought-after guests into our homes. The perception of the Gujarat forces though, was that we had given way because they had broken through our ranks. Now my men pressed in upon them, relentlessly walling them in. They could have disregarded the Mewar warriors on their flanks and slipped right out by continuing on their earlier path and then reassembled and charged back. But their minds and thinking were set in a particular mould and they were caught in their rage and the compulsions of vengeance.

It was amazing what a tight little space a thousand riders could be fitted into if you had a mind to do so. They were collapsing in upon themselves. They had no room to move and only the cavalry in the outermost circle was in a position to take us on. They didn't stand a chance. We began to peel layer after layer of the solidly packed Gujarat ball. Meanwhile the claustrophobia proved too much for those at the core. Confused about what was happening

230

outside, they panicked. The outer forces had to now fight both the enemy and the explosive compression from within. At a predetermined signal, my men suddenly released the pressure by providing an outlet in the south-west. The Gujarat contingent pushed and shoved and clubbed their way to attain open space and make their getaway. We were waiting for them, a handful of my horsemen and I. Many escaped but the majority presented such easy targets as they came out single file, we went back to our hacking and chopping.

And what of Shaan-e-riyasat Bunde Ali? What of him? It would be nice to say that the two of us engaged in mortal combat. I would have to turn him into a man of extraordinary prowess and guile to make myself the greater of the two. But only a short-sighted leader can afford the luxury of that kind of petty aggrandizement. Bunde Ali got his four victims. Then one of my braves got him, an ignominious death if he had set his sights on me.

The Gujarat troops were fleeing wildly now, either on foot or on horseback, it didn't matter which. They had lost their nerve as most armies do when blind terror takes possession of them. Horses, cattle, the men and the camels were all headed for the same place under our guidance. They were running for their lives, heading straight for the marshes and bogs in the south-west.

We had cleared a path along the diagonal of the camp. It was left to Rawal Udai Simha and Tej to take care of over two-thirds of the Gujarat forces whom my men and I had not engaged. There were still large pockets of resistance left in the encampment but within an hour from the time we struck the first blow, my colleagues had overrun the enemy and were herding them to the swampy lake of oblivion in parallel streams. Killing is an exhausting and thankless job. Any time our energies slackened, the enemy armies thought that we had had enough and were calling it a day. They instantly slowed down. A great many of them just gave up and sat or lay down. This was intolerable. It only doubled our work. We had to start hacking and slicing in earnest all over again. We could not afford to take prisoners of war. Our supply lines were already extended, and would not be able to bear the additional burden. Besides, we would play directly into the hands of Malik Ayaz and his formidable armies. More to the point, a soldier reprieved is an enemy reborn. It would be folly to think that the quality of mercy would make the defeated forces think kindly of us and treat us leniently at some future date. The idea, if anyone had lost sight of it, was to prove that the age of chivalry was dead among the Rajputs and we could no longer be taken for granted as gullible fools. My objectives were clear and simple: terrorise the Gujarat armies — and any of our friendly neighbours who cared to observe — to a point where they would think twice before they ventured to disturb Idar or any of our other territories. If our current campaign could achieve that limited objective, I would think that we had not done too badly.

One of the retreating soldiers got hold of my right ankle with both his hands and pleaded with me to spare his life. I swung Befikir around hard but the man would not let go.

'Let me live, Prince,' his granite face was pale and beads of sweat dangled at his earlobes like clusters of soap bubbles that a light breeze would send scudding. What is it that happens to human beings when they are in a crowd? They take their cues from the mob and not from the evidence of their eyes. He had enough strength in him to hang in while I dragged him through a full circle. Why did he not pull me down as my attention wavered when through a break in the mist, I saw Tej's forces come riding at gale-wind speeds? I bent down to loosen his grip on my leg. I wish he hadn't spoken. Now he was a person with a past and a present and a future. If he got a chance he would tell me the names of his children, three boys and four girls or vice versa. How could I possibly kill this man? I had a tough time loosening the fingers of his hand. When I was free, I turned and rode away in a hurry. The men were watching me and so was my old friend, Raja Puraji Kika. A few more sentimental fools like me in the Mewar armies and we would be in a fine mess. I galloped back. The soldier looked at me with puzzlement and then with undisguised terror as I raised my sword and brought it down.

Deception, diplomacy, intrigue, prestidigitation, machination, all these and many small and great things, the Flautist had taught me, were the tricks of a king's dharma and trade. But where had I inherited this wanton cruelty from? I remembered then how the great warrior Arjun and his mentor, the Flautist — mine too till a

232

few years ago — had burnt the whole of the Khandava forest and all its inhabitants without cause or provocation. It was one of the strangest episodes in the *Mahabharata*, one that I could not understand, nor make sense of, try as I might. Perhaps that is the point the great epic is trying to make, that life is not explicable, nor does it pass the test of reason; that some, if not much of it, is meaningless. No amount of culture and civilization can subdue or hide the wanton violence in man.

Why do marshes always attract mist and fog? Is there a relationship between bogs and fens and vapours? Thus far and no further. We had arrived. It was time to bear down hard on the enemy, push him over the edge but hold back oneself.

They disappeared, thousands upon thousands of Muzaffar Shah's and Malik Ayaz's braves into the mist. They went happily, relieved that the pursuit and the frantic slaughter were finally waning, if not ceasing altogether. In the twenty or twenty-five minutes that we were there, the fog opened up only once. The sun shone through and lit a couple of acres of the bogs for a minute or two. You do not have to pay for your sins in an afterlife. You start paying for them here and now. Would that the curtain of the low-lying clouds had not rolled back. No fiction can compete with the horrors of reality.

It was downright chilly near the marshes. Those who had gone in set up an infernal racket of screams, cries and bleating. Bodiless hands moved in the air. I saw a man buried up to his nostrils, the water and muck went into his nose, there was no way of knowing whether he was choking, then he sank out of sight. Most of the men thrashed around as if they were swimming for the shore and that only hastened their disappearance. There were no friends here, it was as if the Gujarat soldiers had never seen or known each other or fought wars together. They cursed anybody whose exertions made the sucking and hissing waters shift faster under their feet. I saw two men fighting, slipping, sinking, strangling each other until the lucky one overpowered the other. He hauled himself up on the dead man. He was jubilant as he balanced himself precariously on his victim's shoulders. He was sure he had beaten the odds and would be able to make it safely to solid ground. He let out a triumphant yell. The dead man's shoulders sank further. The man on top placed his right foot on his head. Soon the head was no longer visible and the exhilaration and glee disappeared in the realization that he too would follow his victim's descent.

Elsewhere, when you saw water bubbling you knew that a head was still breathing underneath. As they went down the men cursed or swore or begged forgiveness. 'Tell Fatima I loved her dearly though I scalded her hand with boiling water last year.' 'Tell Ammijaan that her son died a brave death. He killed seventeen enemy soldiers in three wars. Even when we were betrayed by the enemy, I did not once beg for mercy. Call the new baby ...' He was gulping the brackish water with small helpings of air by now.

I had taken it for granted that the last words of men on earth must somehow be profound or terribly moving. I realized how unfounded my expectations were. We are petty, vacuous or vindictive in life. We are not likely to be any different when confronted by death. 'Promise me, Anjuman, promise me, you'll never marry again. If you do, I'll sit on your neck till ....' They all babbled simultaneously. They wished others well or they wished them ill but most of all they cried for help and asked their God to save them.

Those who could have saved them watched in horror and fascination from the hard ground as a pair of legs thrashed and flopped and a man bent his head down with dignity and asked God forgiveness for not being able to turn towards the Kaaba in Mecca and say his last prayers. The saddest were the horses. Bewildered and frightened by the ground that seemed to slip and slither under them, they struggled hard for a couple of minutes craning their necks to see whether there was a way out and then waited silently and resignedly for the end to come. I can still see their forelegs kicking out as if trying to climb a vertical wall, the slow sluggish water fanning out in the air like powdered diamonds in the sun's rays, floating undecidedly and then going down reluctantly, their manes swept from left to right, their handsome heads wondering why we did not help them or put them out of their misery. My men and I watched in silence. There are crimes against humanity and there are crimes against nature and then there are crimes so terrible they do not have a name and we had committed all three of them.

Seven thirty-five in the morning. It was time to leave.

Chapter 19

Was ever an outcome of war so certain? I will wear my saffron saafa, the kind one wears when one is going to certain death in war, smear crimson on my forehead and fight the vile god to the death. But there is no death, only defeat. Daily, hourly, perpetual defeat.

He had abandoned Befikir some days ago. As if that wasn't bad enough, he couldn't now recall where he had misplaced one of his shoes. He sat down and scooped up sand with the remaining shoe and poured it out at the same speed he had seen it run down in an hourglass. There was a foot-high mound in front of him. He must have been playing Father Time for hours, maybe even a couple of days. Before that he had walked for a few days. At every step his foot sank irretrievably into the sand. He fought hard to pull it out but all that frantic activity only made the sand shift. There was a slow hissing sound and the foot was sucked in further. Was he getting a taste of what he had put the Gujarat soldiers through? Was this his final comeuppance? It couldn't be. There was no way he would have an easy and swift end, of that much he was sure.

Something hard was poking sharply into his back. He stretched his hand behind him and pulled out the protruding object. It took him back to the beginning of the Gujarat expedition, to the night before they drove the Gujarat armies into the quagmire. One of Raja Puraji Kika's men was working on a wooden cylinder. The Maharaj Kumar watched fascinated. He was curious about what the final

236

product was going to be but he was damned if he was going to ask the soldier who, once he had acknowledged His Highness' presence, had ignored him. The man was making intricate calculations and measuring out the distance between points on the wooden ferule. Was he a mathematician, a geometrical wizard, would he be able to foretell the movement of the stars with that divining rod? The Maharaj Kumar's curiosity got the better of him. 'If you don't mind my interrupting you, what are you making?'

'This?' the man pointed at the stick. The Maharaj Kumar nodded his head. 'You've been watching me for over a quarter of an hour, why don't you tell me?'

Wise guy. Why would he ask if he had known the answer in the first place? The other soldiers waited expectantly for him to answer. The craftsman had gone back to his markings. The Maharaj Kumar would have liked to walk away nonchalantly, but something held him back. He tried to put on an insouciant face, forced a smile on his tight lips and spoke, 'A magic wand, what else.' Even as the words came forth, he knew he was coming across exactly as he didn't want to: spoilt and ill-tempered. He was amazed to hear the long sound of applause his vacuous reply had elicited. Even the preoccupied artisan-warrior doffed his Bhil cap. The Maharaj Kumar thought it wise to make a getaway before he was asked to solve any more riddles.

*   *   *

Next morning a little before dawn, just before they were about to set out on their dire mission, the Bhil soldier walked up to the Maharaj Kumar. What does the wiseacre want now, he could barely suppress his irritation. He was tense. He was prescient enough to suspect that the day which lay ahead of him was likely to affect his career and fate in ways that it was not in his power to imagine. The Bhil bowed, 'Highness, may the blessings of Eklingji Shiva be upon you.'

'Upon you and all our men too,' the Maharaj Kumar made brisk reply.

'I beg your indulgence for a minute.'

237

'Not now Bhima,' Raja Puraji Kika spoke before the Prince could answer, 'Later, later.'

They were the exact words with which the Maharaj Kumar was going to snub the man. He realized how uncouth and misplaced they would have been in his own mouth. 'It's all right, Raja. I know him. Speak.'

'I have a small gift for you, Maharaj Kumar.' He brought forward his right hand.

'You were very perspicacious last night, Highness.' It sounded like a put down but the Bhil's face was innocent of double-meaning. 'It is a magic wand. Don't underestimate its powers. Breathe into it and it will come alive. It will work its magic on those around you. But more importantly, it will work its magic on you. It will soothe you and bring you peace of mind.'

He waited for the Maharaj Kumar to take the gift. The Prince wanted to break it in two on his knee; or should he hurl the cursed thing into the great unknown distance called space? But the very thought of touching it revolted him. He would rather shove his hand into the bleeding mess of a leper's newly broken stump. Get it out of my sight, you damned fool, get it out of my sight. He was not looking for omens and yet an omen had been visited upon him. Not in a thousand lifetimes could he have thought of a more calamitous augury than the one the man held in his palm.

Fate. There was no escaping fate. Raja Puraji Kika had tried to save the Maharaj Kumar. He had told the man 'Not now, Bhima. Later, later.' But when your time's up and there's a good chance of giving fate the slip, you collar him and get him back.

'Take it, Prince. I didn't know who I was making it for last night,' the man called Bhima was saying, 'but it surely must have your name written on it.'

And yet the Maharaj Kumar would not take it.

'Blow into it, Prince. There's a void inside of it that you can turn into a note and then another and then another till it becomes a tune and a melody and then a raga that can move the very gods.'

It was getting late, his troops were waiting and King Puraji Kika was looking at him with not a little puzzlement. The Prince extended his hand and took the flute. He was about to slip it into his belt

238

(he would break it and disperse the pieces later) when his childhood friend stopped him.

'Your Highness, when you accept a new flute as a gift, you must always play it first.'

You, too, Puraji Kika? And I thought you were my friend. 'I don't know how to play the thing. I don't even know how to make a hole of my lips to blow into it.'

'It doesn't matter. A flute is a friendly, accommodating instrument. Blow somewhere in the vicinity of the first hole,' Bhima was instructing him, 'and you'll hear a clear note.'

The Maharaj Kumar clenched his jaw, lifted the flute and settled his lips over the first hole and clamped his fingers on the other holes. He inhaled deeply and then blew the air out through his lips. There was no sound. Suddenly a cracked, shrill note issued forth followed by a twin-note cacophony. He realized his fingers had slipped.

'There, you are getting the hang of it,' Bhima told him encouragingly.

'You call that music?' the Maharaj Kumar asked him as if he was to blame for the bleating he had produced.

'It will come. One day the notes will come together and sing a song of enchantment. All you need is practice.'

Sure, the Prince said to himself, no doubt, after I throw that damned reed into the marshes.

*   *   *

Weeks and many upheavals later, he was sitting in the middle of nowhere and the flute was still with him. He was sure Mangal was looking all over for him, trying to divert all the nasty rumours about his disappearance that were bound to be floating around in the camp. He was smart, that Mangal, he would slip in the first rumour himself before the gossip mills ran amok. 'Let's not mince words, we all know that the Maharaj Kumar doesn't have the happiest of marriages. So he has a glad eye and a wandering hand. Wouldn't you? No, no, don't call him poor Prince, not in front of me at least. That man, this is just between you, me and the tent pole, the Prince has the raunchiest member under the sun. Let's get this straight,

I don't blame him. What would you do if your wife turned out to be... no point repeating what everybody knows. Just before we came here, Shehzada Bahadur told him of this tawaif from Champaner. He said, "This is no harlot, Maharaj Kumar, this is a jannat ki houri, an apsara, a celestial beauty. Her face is the moon after the rains, her tresses are the nights of longing, her breath is rose petals falling from the weight of the morning dew, in her armpits is the perfume of a thousand mogras, her breasts are snowy peaks with the cherries of Kashmir to nibble on for as long as you wish, and between her thighs," he sighed deeply here, "between her thighs, Highness, is heaven itself, not the first, not the second, but the seventh heaven." From the day we came here, all the Maharaj Kumar could think of was going to Champaner to see this woman. After we crushed the Gujarat forces, there was no stopping him.' Mangal would get some such tale abroad, and let the troops stew in envy and lust.

Where would Mangal look for the Maharaj Kumar? His men would comb every town and village. The desert, Mangal would take upon himself.

The Maharaj Kumar threw the flute up in the air, then twirled it around as if it were a baton. When he had had enough of this juggling, he put it against his lips and blew into it. The notes were clear and well-formed but the tones were disharmonious.

He had had every intention of throwing the bloody reed to the winds on that first day but had forgotten about it in the crush and fury of the battle. When he lay down late that night, it was stuck under him like an extra backbone. From time to time, he wanted to pull it out and at least put it aside but he was dog-tired and couldn't bring himself to make the effort. He knew he was going to get rid of it for sure, either today or one of these days but it had stuck to him like a pariah puppy.

A few days later, a courier had arrived from Chittor. There was a brief but personal letter from the Rana and one with handwriting he could not recognize.

Jai Shri Eklingi

Dear son,

May the blessings of Shri Eklingji keep you from all harm.

There was a fire in your palace but you'll be relieved to know that your wife is safe. We have not been able to ascertain the exact cause of the fire but initial enquiries of the police department seem to suggest that it may have started in your wife's room when the lamp in front of the image of Lord Krishna fell down because of a gust of wind. Her maid from Merta, Kumkum Kanwar, unfortunately perished in the mishap. We are all grateful to God that the Princess suffered no harm beyond some burns.

Your mother sends you her love and blessings. We trust that the war is going well with you and our armies. May the light of the Sun-god shine on you always.

Your Father.

Jai Shri Eklingji

To His Highness, the Maharaj Kumar.

Your friend Leelawati agreed to take dictation from me and write this letter. I will not beat about the bush but come straight to the point. There was a fire on the seventh of this month in the room of Kumkum Kanwar, maid to the Princess, your wife. It started after midnight. It was the Princess who woke up with the screams of her maid and the smell of the smoke and rushed into Kumkum Kanwar's room. She tried to save her but by that time it was too late. The maid tried to keep her mistress away from her, pleading with her that she

241

was past saving but your wife persisted in trying to wrap her with blankets to douse the fire. When the brave girl realized that there was no longer any hope but that her mere presence was jeopardizing the Princess' life, she jumped out of the window. The fall, unlike the fire, brought instantaneous death to Kumkum Kanwar.

The Princess has been badly burnt especially on her hands and forearms. I was away looking after my business in the village when the mishap occurred. As soon as I came back, I discontinued the services of the Raj Vaidya and asked Raja Puraji Kika's physician, Eka, to look after her. Luckily, Shri Eka was in Chittor to receive thanks from His Majesty for saving the life of Shehzada Bahadur. He assured me that herbal poultices will not only heal the Princess' burns but restore her blemishless skin. The first four days she was in great pain but the worst is over and I am happy to tell you that she is now well on the way to recovery.

There are a couple of things about the fire that are puzzling. Kumkum Kanwar invariably went to sleep by nine. She was not in the habit of reading and she always put out the lamp in her room before she went to bed. That particular night could not have been an exception since, as the Princess says, Kumkum, who slept the sleep of stones, could never do so until she had put out all the lights. There was no altar in her room, so the question of the altar light keeling over does not arise. The other curious thing is that none of the wooden furniture in her room is damaged. The fire seems to have begun and raged in her mattress and blanket. The investigation into the causes of the fire is in the hands of the new Deputy Minister for Home Affairs, Prince Vikramaditya. We'll have to wait for his report on the subject to know the facts of the case.

I want you to know that till you return, I will not leave Chittor and will keep an eye on the Princess.

Look after yourself, Maharaj Kumar. Your life is precious to me but even more so to Mewar. At no point can you afford not to be vigilant or put your life at unnecessary risk.

May the flag of Mewar fly high. May you and your armies triumph in this war and may you return safely to our midst.

Blessings.

Yours obediently,

Kausalya.

P.S. This bit is from me, your beloved Leelawati. Father wanted to stop my maths lessons. He said I could learn Sanskrit, history, geography and music and painting but what need did a future housewife have of maths? I went and complained to Dadaji. He said the maths of the heavenly bodies makes the earth go round and the maths of money is what balances the equations of commercial and daily life. Even a housewife must deal in the commerce of daily life. Besides, whether you like it or not, he told Father, maths is in her blood. Are you afraid because she calculates fractional interest faster in her mind than you do on paper? Let her study.

I am working on my presents for you. How about you? What are you getting for me?

Yours forever, yours and only yours,

Leelawati.

*   *   *

In his waking hours and at night the Maharaj Kumar had wished his wife dead. His imagination had run riot and plotted every kind of death for her. Death by drowning, small pox, falling off a horse, a cliff, every kind of accident, the overturning of a carriage, a landslide where a boulder crushed her ribs but kept her alive for a couple of days, death by halal, death by whipping, death by breaking one bone a day, death by hanging, and so on. But the most common form of death in his dreams was a fiery one. And yet when he heard that she had suffered burns and could have died in a fire, he went completely berserk. He was ready to abandon his armies, the war, and the terrible anticipation of the enemy's next move. He would go back to Chittor. Back to his wife. He tied fifteen candles together and held his forearm for hours just above the point where the flames would singe him. What would he have done if she had died? No, that was unacceptable, he wouldn't hear of it; quite simply he would not permit it. Because if something were to happen to her, he would have to put an end to his own life. Hadn't he sworn to protect her the night he got married? He would stand guard in front of her room. He would eschew sleep forever. He would make sure she left the door open. And what if the Flautist came at night as he had seen him do that last night in Chittor? Kill her. Let the flames consume her. Was there a perfume more powerful and heady than the smell of burning flesh? He had a better idea. He himself would set both his wife and the Flautist on fire. Some erotic fire, what?

He went about the business of war with his usual eye for detail without losing sight of the larger perspective. He attended War Council meetings, planned alternate scenarios. He acted normally, he was absolutely normal. He knew he needed to be incarcerated instantly in an asylum.

He had been a judge at the Small Causes Court for years. You did not venture an opinion, let alone judge a case till all the evidence was in. And yet he had to admit that he found the discrepancy between the Rana's and Kausalya's versions disturbing. Neither had been at the scene of action. Whatever he might think or say of the Rana, he knew his father would not lie deliberately. Neither would Kausalya. But the Rana's information was third hand. Kausalya, it was obvious, was conducting on-the-spot enquiries. Second hand reports were fine if the investigator was competent, unbiased and trustworthy. His brother Vikramaditya was not known to possess any one of the three qualities. Granted that the Maharaj Kumar had a jaundiced view of his brother but Kumkum Kanwar's death was hard to explain. She was her mistress's creature and too insignificant to arouse jealousy or rancour. The other possibility was suicide but that seemed unlikely. Her mistress loved her dearly and on the rare occasion when Kumkum Kanwar wanted something, she got it almost instantly. Besides, she was engaged to be married to one of the officers in the Rana's personal guard and was in the throes of first love, hardly a time to kill herself. A fire cannot generate itself. An accidental fire, on the other hand, is always unruly and chaotic and would not limit itself to one person. The furniture and furnishings in the palace were excellent combustible material. It was not likely that they would escape untouched. Try as he might, the Maharaj Kumar could no longer play the objective and dispassionate jurist. He knew that someone had tried to kill the Princess. He may not know who it was but he had a pretty good idea and anyway he was willing to wipe out the whole of Chittor to get back at fate for daring to touch his wife.

Four and a half weeks later there was another letter from Kausalya.

Jai Shri Eklingji

To His Highness, the Maharaj Kumar.
I have failed you. I promised to keep an eye on the Princess but I wasn't vigilant enough. From the day I returned from my village Rohala, I decided to be doubly cautious. After the food-taster had tasted all the dishes, I ate the food and only then served it to the Princess. A week ago, a full twelve hours after the Princess and I had had our lunch, both of us got severe pains and gripes in the stomach and acute diarrhoea. I sent for the Bhil physician Eka but within two hours both of us had lost consciousness because of dehydration and food poisoning. Our condition continued to deteriorate

for forty-eight hours, according to Ekaji. Fortunately, he had been summoned at the very outset and had studied the colour and other signs of our faeces and was able to pinpoint the cause of our sudden and deadly illness. For deadly it was, according to Ekaji. A delayed-action poison had been introduced into our food. But for the Bhil doctor, we would both be dead now.

Both of us are out of danger and on the way to recovery. I assure you that there is no longer any cause for worry. For the time being, my daughter-in-law is cooking the rice soup on which the Princess and I have been living for the past five days. As soon as I have the strength to sit up, I will cook all the meals for your wife myself. I have also called ten of my most faithful and able men to stand guard round-the-clock in your and the Princess' part of the palace. They'll remain here till you come back. The physician informed His Majesty, the Rana, about the attempt on our lives and suggested that Kumkum Kanwar's death may not have been an accident. His Highness has transferred the case from Prince Vikramaditya to Lakshman Simhaji's jurisdiction. He has ordered the arrest of three servants and the cook. For some reason I feel far more safe now on behalf of the Princess. She is truly a brave woman and has not once complained about the terrible calamities that have befallen her since your departure. I'm ashamed that I have not been a better guardian to Her Highness. You are aware that I am not one to give false assurances but I genuinely detect a change in the climate in the palace since Lakshman Simhaji took charge. He has been to see the Princess and me every day and security has been far tighter here than it has been in a long time. As I had suspected, the cook who has been with you since childhood has been found

246

innocent.

Yours obediently,
Kausalya.

P.S. Since you have not bothered to answer my
previous P.S., I refuse to talk to you. Kausalya Ma
has taught me to knit and I have half-completed
a sweater for an unmentionable person.

Love,
Leelawati.

*   *   *

The Maharaj Kumar was in a great hurry. He had nowhere to go,
no one was waiting for him but he had an appointment to keep.
The desert was big, very big. It should be possible to get lost in
it. It was also barren, which is but another word for nothingness.
It was a state of mind and body that he desperately yearned for.
He wandered about. He had much to do. The sand was crinkled
like frozen waves on water. Each wave was precision-contoured and
each ridge of a sand-drift was fine as a strand of hair and unbroken.
It was breathtaking, the work of a mastercraftsman who must have
spent hundreds of years creating this abstract image of perfection
that stretched all the way to infinity. His life's work was cut out for
him. He had to systematically dismantle the work of art, botch it
till it was unrecognizable, churn it back to primal chaos. He took
the first step and smashed his foot into the crest of a wave. He would
work his way to the horizon and then move to the next trough.
It was hard work. Befikir watched him indulgently, then trotted off.
At four in the afternoon he was hit on the head with a sledge-
hammer. He fell down and his brains spilt on the sand. When he
came to, it was night. He should have turned to ice but he was
running a high temperature and sweating and shivering alternately.
He had not realized until now that the stroke in a sunstroke was
a real and physical one and of such disproportionate and violent
force. He was very thirsty but Befikir was nowhere around. He tried
to stand up. His knees buckled and he collapsed.

A shrill cold wind was blowing. Sheets of sand, fine as sheer muslin flapped back and forth. The whole of the desert was in turmoil. Entire sandscapes were being forcibly evicted and were migrating to unknown lands. Tornado sands rose genie-like into the sky. Camels, birds, men and women, carriages, palaces and elephants flew up and slammed into each other.

The light was golden and through the crush of flying objects a golden woman strode towards him with such carnal and loping grace, he raised his hands to greet her. She walked past him. Her yellow chunni was in his hand. He yelled at her to stop but even he couldn't hear himself in all the din around. She turned round and smiled. He thought he would die of her beauty. She ran towards him and fell upon his supine body. She unbuttoned his duglo with her teeth. Where had he seen her before? One of the buttons was in her mouth. She laughed as she shot it at him. It stung him on his exposed chest. He snapped her blouse open. Her hands were at his waist untying the knot of his trousers. He held her tightly as he felt himself come alive. He couldn't get rid of her body-hugging pants. She laughed as her left hand slipped them off. She was sitting on top of him, his hands cupping her breasts. Any moment now she would slip him in.

'Was it my brother Vikramaditya, Queen Karmavati or you,' he asked her as he flung her back, 'who tried to kill her?'

'What difference does it make?'

Her breasts were once again an old pair of socks, her hair a grey nest of vipers and her edentulous mouth chewed upon the air. 'You wanted her dead, didn't you? Does it matter how or who does it?' Bhootani Mata's long, bony hand was playing with his crotch. He tried to throw her off but she was nailed upright to him.

'No, I don't want her dead. I want him killed.'

'We've changed our mind, have we? You were willing to go any lengths to do away with her the last time we met at the Brindabani Temple. I counselled a little more patience, a little more time to think things over but you spat at me. Perhaps the time for vacillation is long past.'

'Don't you dare touch her, you bitch.'

'Language, my friend, mind your language.' Her fingers lengthened and became blades. They went through his heart and pinioned him in the sand. 'Let's not forget you are the supplicant.'

'You are an ineffectual, inefficient and disgusting crone. You botched up everything. You couldn't even get the right person the first time but bumped off poor Kumkum Kanwar. The second time you got Kausalya in addition to my wife but they both survived your singular ineptness. You are a bloody bumbling amateur, Bhootani Mata.'

The Mata caught him by the throat and shook him till his head snapped. 'You ingrate, do you know who I am up against?'

'Don't tell me you expect me to commiserate with you for your failures,' he managed to get the words out despite his broken neck. 'If it was not a god but a mere mortal, why would I have come to you?'

She was gone.

'Leave her alone, you hear, leave her alone.'

*   *   *

When he recovered from the sunstroke, he had no way of knowing how many days had gone by. He realized that he had survived without water only because he had either been in a stupor or unconscious. Befikir was standing near him. How had the horse managed to keep alive? Had he found an oasis or a shallow water hole? He didn't look dehydrated or exhausted. The Maharaj Kumar caught hold of the stirrup and raised himself. He unstrapped the leather bottle that Mangal made sure was always filled with water and tied to the saddle. He could only take a few sips at a time. There had obviously been a heavy sandstorm. The sand puckered north to south now instead of east to west. And a button was missing from his duglo.

That was a long time ago. Befikir was nowhere to be seen. He could not find his other shoe either now. The sun would soon go down and he would once again freeze in the chill silver light of the moon. He placed the flute against his mouth. It was hard to form a hole with lips so drawn, dry and shrunken as his. He blew air out slowly. A crystalline 'sa' in the lowest register. A note of such clarity, depth and weight, it seemed to still the clouds in the sky and the tiny busy creatures weaving in and out of the sands. Sa, re, ga, ma, pa, dha, ni, sa. He went through the full octave and back. Each note was a pearl in the roundness and plenitude of its sound. There is only one art on earth which echoes the perfection of God. It is music. And in music, the most perfect and complete godhood lies within each note. You cannot add to it nor can you subtract from it. It has no reason and no rationale. It is sufficient unto itself. Memories of the ragas he had learnt in childhood flowed through his fingers. He had a gruff, narrow range to his voice. Now there was nothing to stop him from journeying through the three octaves and leaving memories of his stay upon the air and sand of the desert. And the music he made and the journeys he went on were a balm and an elixir and an unguent that brought peace to his battered mind and weary soul.

When the stars came out, Mangal gathered him to his breast and kissed him time and again. And the Prince held his friend Mangal tightly in his arms and would not let go of him.

Chapter 20

𝒫oor Malik Ayaz. He was recalled home in disgrace and disfavour. War is a risky pastime for generals, more so for them than for kings and princes. A sovereign is hardly ever dethroned because he loses a war. A general, if he is lucky, is made head of a police station or put in charge of supplies. But more often than not he is stripped of his rank and job. He may not be banished but it is wiser for him to keep a low profile and retire to his ancestral village. He loves his country dearly but his only hope lies in his successor faring much worse than him. There is then a chance that in time he may be recalled and perhaps even be asked to lead the armies once again.

The time to kick an enemy is when he is on his knees. That way he'll be flat on his stomach and with luck, incapable of getting up again for some time. We could have gone home but someone had to be around to greet Zahir-ul-Mulk, the general appointed to put Mewar and me in our place. Zahir-ul-Mulk, I knew from my docket on him, was a circumspect man. I can't say whether it was my engagements with Malik Ayaz which made him extra careful or he had been instructed by his king to err on the side of caution. Hubris and overconfidence, I warned myself every hour, are the fatal fallout of any victory. Which meant that Zahir-ul-Mulk and I were like two dogs chasing each other's tails but never confronting each other.

I was much clearer now about the strategies I wanted to pursue and the kind of war I wanted to fight than when I had started the campaign. Unless we were left with absolutely no alternative, we would call the shots and if possible, never engage in a head-on battle. In the meantime we practise. I am not a popular commander but the men are beginning to trust me. They are puzzled about why their

251

daily workout is speed-riding and attacking in flight as if they had
lost a battle and were fleeing for their lives. We time the operation
daily. The idea is to get them to ride in formation but faster and
faster. In our training sessions, the putative ratio is invariably in
favour of the enemy. A group of five hundred Mewar soldiers must
take on a thousand and five hundred to two thousand enemy troops.
The next step is to conduct the exercises at night. Rao Viramdev,
Shafi Khan and the rest of the leaders are getting used to my weird
ways but I can still detect a strong undercurrent of resentment
because I have removed gallantry and valour from warfare.

While we prepare for war with Gujarat once again, I ponder
over the war that I am so ill-equipped to fight on the home front.
My brother Vikramaditya is out of prison without so much as a
rigged trial. How, I ask myself, how is it possible that Father, whose
thoughts are straight as an Ashoka tree and can pierce the lush and
snarled undergrowth of his courtiers' machinations, cannot, or
rather will not, see the threat to the throne and the precedent he
is setting for my other brothers and — why am I being coy — me,
in letting Vikramaditya go scot-free?

Is this what love for a woman amounts to? Rani Karmavati is
not to blame. It is her foolish, uxorious husband who does not
merely jump when his wife says jump but smiles ingratiatingly and
asks how high. Can you imagine a greater travesty of justice than
appointing the highest offender of the law its keeper? The security
and policing of Chittor are in the hands of Vikramaditya. The word
is that every petty havaldar, sub-inspector and police inspector,
licensing clerk and petty official has to be bribed before he'll do
his duty.

And now to the one question that has been uppermost in my
mind. What about me? Yes, you heard me right, all you stars and
the sun and the moon, and the leaves on trees, and the restless
waves on the far-off sea and the sand and the birds and beasts and
all the creatures of the earth, what about me, the heir apparent, the
next in line, the would-be-king whose chances grow dimmer by the
minute? There's no one in Chittor who will hold a brief for me
or promote my cause vigorously. There's my mother, the Maharani
who means well and Father is fond of her in the same way that

he likes his dogs and pets. She would not know how to broach the subject of her eldest son and if she did, Father will look quizzically at her and point out that she must be more watchful for she has just dropped a stitch in the nine hundred and seventy-seventh sweater she is knitting for him. Then there's my wife. She was Father's favourite daughter-in-law. If there's one person who could have stood her ground against Queen Karmavati and got Father to consider a point of view at variance with that of his favourite queen, it was my wife. She's Rao Viramdev's niece which fact alone carries not a little weight; she is also self-possessed, has dignity, intelligence and beauty, all of which earned her a rather special place in Father's heart when she first came to Chittor. But it would not occur to her to stay in Father's orbit, cultivate him and insinuate herself into his inner circle. Unfortunately, now, she herself needs something akin to a miracle to reinstate her in Father's good books. Her star, I suspect, has not just plummeted but has, as a matter of fact, dragged me down with it. She has disgraced Mewar and brought dishonour to it as no other princess of the realm has.

There is, of course, one other factor which must certainly weigh heavily against her. She has not delivered herself of a son who will ensure the line of succession. Sadly enough, she has not even proven that she is capable of childbearing.

That leaves but one person in Chittor who could plead my case: the Queen Mother. I believe she would speak up for me but my childless state compared with the prolific output of my brothers and their several wives makes her wonder whether I am man enough. She has good reason to doubt my manhood. After all, I have proved incapable of keeping my wife under control. But even if she set aside her reservations and pushed my claims energetically, I suspect it wouldn't get me very far. Father respects her but she is no match for Vikramaditya's mother, Queen Karmavati.

*　　*　　*

The war with Gujarat is a boon. I may brood but I must work at least sixteen hours a day. I am sure I am not inventing guerilla warfare but I am certainly the first among Rajputs to reinvent the

253

sudden swoop, the savage attack on the flanks, the terrorizing of isolated units, the lightning rearguard action and the just as swift disappearance. The idea, of course, is to avoid a face-to-face confrontation while snapping at the enemy's flesh, sowing chaos and confusion in his ranks, making him tense and nervous by never relaxing the pressure. In short, to play with him tactically, militarily and psychologically while covering one's tracks till he becomes a physical and nervous wreck.

My friend, guide and chief of planning is Raja Puraji Kika. He and his people may call it by some other name but as mountain people, they cut their teeth on guerilla tactics.

Puraji Kika and I have divided our army of twenty-five thousand men (I've sent the rest home) into ten units of two thousand and five hundred each. Each encampment is self-sufficient with its own courier service, stables and other amenities. The distance between any two camps is two or three miles. If there's an emergency or a sudden enemy attack, a dispatch rider can cover the distance within ten minutes on the outside. We change locations frequently, never more than a fortnight at any one place. Of course, this will not prevent Zahir-ul-Mulk from attacking us. But the risk of an attack has been reduced by a factor of ten. We are not just an extremely mobile army, for the time being, we are ten commando units acting with one mind.

Raja Puraji Kika couldn't have wished for better students than Tej, Shafi Khan and me. We were eager learners and theory was almost immediately translated into action and tested. The general belief is that the essence of guerilla warfare is speed and the detour. Puraji Kika told us it is nothing of the sort. Speed and diversionary tactics are absolutely essential but the key to this kind of engagement is your state of mind and your willingness to run. 'You've gone to great lengths to avoid the enemy, and now, at a place and time of your choosing, you are all set to inflict a serious injury upon him and then vanish like mist in the sunlight. The problem invariably arises because after all that trouble and the psychological pressure, you feel you owe it to yourself and your troops to keep an appointment with destiny and attack even if you have a gut feeling that something's amiss. The slightest suspicion that you are being set up and you must have the courage to put your tail between your legs and run.'

Our tactics drove Zahir-ul-Mulk to desperation. He needed to show results, to engage our forces in a decisive battle. He came chasing us only to find that we had moved and were very likely visiting his camp or attacking the tail end of his forces. We were everywhere and yet never to be located.

Our soldiers had begun to get the hang of what Puraji Kika and I were up to, and to enjoy the sense of power and control this low-key style of fighting gave them. They enjoyed the frustration and helplessness of the Gujarat troops who did not know how to hit back at a moving target. They learnt stealth and stillness. They could sit for hours without stirring or exchanging a word. They got used to eating their meals on horseback and trained their horses to hold their neighing and to stand without moving. In time, they might even discover bravery and pride in these clandestine encounters.

It was on the day that Rao Viramdev decided to observe our quicksilver charges that we got mail from Chittor. All of it routine except for one letter in Leelawati's hand. I had begun to think of her letters as harbingers of bad or worse news, the usual case of confusing the messenger with the debacle. What rotten news did Kausalya have for me this time?

Jai Eklingji

To His Highness, the Maharaj Kumar,

About a year ago Sunheria, the washerwoman, asked me to look after the two villages you had gifted her for a fee since she does not have experience in property matters. I told her that I had too much on my hands as it is but I would teach her the basics of poultry farming along with tax collection and accounting so that she need not be dependent on anyone. She spent four hours with me every alternate Monday. A month ago she did not turn up on two consecutive Mondays; nor did she send anyone to explain her absence. This was unlike her. She is keen to be her own woman and is always on time. I went over to her place but she refused to come out. I spoke to her husband. He was hostile and evasive and wanted to know what my relationship with her was. I explained to him that I was the new inspector for laundry and had come in the context of two of the Queen Mother's gold brocade ghagras which were missing. He went on a long tirade about never having been accused of theft in all the seventy years that he had worked for the kings of Mewar. I said I was not accusing him of anything. Besides while he may be innocent, what about his wife? That perked him up. He called her a string of names and vouched that she was a harlot and a thief and begged me to charge her as he had evidence that would lock her up for several lifetimes. His manner and mood changed and he became voluble. After half an hour I cut him short and told him that I would have to interrogate his wife alone. No need, he said, I have not only questioned her but administered severe corporal punishment. That, I told him, was unfortunate since only His Majesty and the courts have the authority to punish and I would have no choice but to report the matter. He was frothing at the mouth by now and rubbing his forehead on my feet pleading with me to ignore his indiscretion. He promised that he would never touch his wife again. I asked him to leave me alone with his wife which he reluctantly did after telling me not to spare her or believe her tales.

I was expecting the worst but I must confess that I was not prepared for the sight that met me. There were wide-open gashes on Sunheria's skull and her body had been worked over with a belt till there was hardly any skin left on it. I put her in my palanquin and brought her home. I got the Raj

him. Our men were dying all around. It was a replay of the attack we had carried out on that first morning when we had rushed the Gujarat battalions going home. One of the Mewar men spotted me keeping a low profile and avoiding battle. He reined in his horse and came directly at me. Some of the Gujarat soldiers were watching me. His first blow fell upon my helmet. The second was aimed at my neck. You should have got me the first time, my friend. I ran my sword through his stomach. He fell forward but managed to cling on to his saddle. I kicked the horse hard in his butt. He took off in the direction of the rapidly retreating Rajput armies.

It was hard work getting close to the General. There was furious fighting around him which I wanted no part of. Zahir-ul-Mulk seemed to slip away from me every time he was within hailing distance. I may have worn a Gujarat soldier's dress but my lateral progress, I was sure, had caught the entire Gujarat contingent's attention. My only hope was that the excitement of killing an unprepared enemy and the pleasure of exacting revenge would keep the Gujaratis preoccupied. How much longer would this take? I knew that Raja Puraji was taking more risks than I. He didn't have my disguise and had to fight for his life while following me.

I was there. I had an inkling of what Abhimanyu must have felt when he pierced the concentric circles of the enemy forces: how will I get out now? But I still had a job ahead of me.

'Get rid of this pest.'

I thought that Zahir-ul-Mulk was talking about me. Were my costume and make-up that transparent? Or, I was about to laugh aloud, was I so incredibly good-looking and distinctive, no make-up could conceal my face?

'Get rid of this pest, you ass,' he repeated pointing to a Bhil soldier alongside Puraji Kika, 'while I take care of the Raja there.'

I said 'Yes, Sire', raised my sword, do it right, pest, this is the only chance you'll ever get. I had to cleave the head from the torso in one clean stroke or the job would only be half-done. Zahir-ul-Mulk must have realized that something was terribly amiss with the angle of my hand and sword as I stood in the stirrups to get extra leverage but by then the blade was on its way down. I had caught him in mid-action. The chained mail hanging from his helmet had

261

risen upward like the wings of a bird as he flew towards Raja Puraji Kika and was about to thrust his sword into him. For the briefest instant, the general's neck was exposed. That was enough time for me to strike. It was a strike without finesse but it did its job. The sword sliced his neck and his head bounced on the shoulder of one of the Gujarat soldiers and fell on the ground a couple of yards from Raja Puraji Kika. His body was slightly askew but still upright. A spasm ran through his hand and the sword dropped from it.

You could see the profile of the cut now. There was far more neck on the right than the left. How is it that two hundred year-old trees don't spurt all over and make a mess of themselves when they are axed? Red rivulets were racing down his armour. The veins in the stump of his neck distended to accommodate the free flow of blood. Where the column of the neck was higher, the blood shot up four or five inches, took a downward turn and subsided. Every time the body twitched, a transparent red bubble formed at the jugular. When it broke, a fine spray fell all around. Already some of the descending streaks had begun to congeal. I had killed count-less people but it was the General's beheaded neck that would keep me company in the future whenever I had a fever and was delirious. The Gujarat troops stood in a stupor, unable to grasp the murder of their commander-in-chief by one of their own. I came to when one of the men whispered 'traitor' and lunged at me. I rammed my sword into the steel armour on the General's chest and saw him keel over. The man had to pull in his horse to avoid trampling the general. I swung my sword wildly and broke through as Raja Puraji speared the head above our colours, held it aloft, and shouted, 'Zahir-ul-Mulk is dead. Zahir-ul-Mulk is dead' and sped away.

It was uncanny, the effect those words had on the Gujarat troops. They stopped dead, even those in pursuit of me. In the few seconds before they came back to life and resumed the chase, I wiped the earth off my face, tore my tunic and yelled to my soldiers, 'Get every one of them.' Raja Puraji Kika galloped back and forth, his voice booming. 'Zahir-ul-Mulk's dead. May his soul rest in peace.' The general's head stood above us all and swung from side to side till

262

the Raja came to a halt next to me. Tej, Shafi and Rao Viramdev joined us. There was no time to waste. 'Let's go,' my voice must have carried to the ends of heaven and hell. 'Let's take the Gujarat camp.'

Chapter 21

We left for Idar early the next morning. Rao Viramdev must have wondered why I was in a hurry but he was far too civil and cultured a man to ask me such a personal question. By nightfall, we were at the gates of this small kingdom which had cost Mewar and its allies so many men, and blocked up a full eighteen months of my life. Both the recently dethroned ruler and the would-be king were with us. My sympathies were with the man who had lost, at least temporarily, his kingdom. I didn't know Bharmal well but what I had seen of him in action I had liked. He was mature and bore his defeat with silent dignity. I was willing to trade my brother-in-law for him and make him our ally. I knew well that while he was alive, Rao Raimul would not be able to sew the seat of his pants to the royal throne. How roundly and warmly I loathed my sister's husband. And yet, however much I blamed him for undoing almost all of us yesterday, I could not absolve myself for taking the greater risk.

I was finally a hero all right. At the end of the day when Rao Bharmal had signed the instrument of surrender and we had disarmed all the Gujarat troops, the Mewar and allied forces took me on their shoulders and bellowed 'Victory to the Maharaj Kumar' and 'Long live the Maharaj Kumar' half the night. I had sought to train them in a new discipline of warfare; I had tried to win them over with friendliness for over a year. Now with one foolish gesture, I had them eating out of my hand. They were willing to become my slaves, do my bidding, march all the way to Delhi that very night and give battle to the Lodi king there. God knows what else they promised me that night. How long will this last, I asked myself. How much time would it take for Vikramaditya to win them over and turn them against me? How quickly would they go back to their old ways of fighting the enemy face to face? But that was beside the point. All the leaders, even Rao Viramdev, had said that nobody but I could have transformed imminent and total defeat into victory. They insisted that while they had all given up, I, alone, was thinking clearly and had apprehended that we were left with no alternative but to take extraordinary measures. But there was a clear alternative, one which I had formulated and reiterated endlessly. Retreat. Save our arses. Run for our lives. I had, of course, ignored my own precept. If one of my deputies had done what I did, I would have stripped him of his rank and banished him from Mewar. How forgiving we are of ourselves. I had endangered my life in a situation that was beyond hopeless. What, pray, would my colleagues have done with our army if I had been killed? Worse, what would have happened had I been discovered and taken prisoner? The very same fate that befell the Gujarat forces when I killed their commander-in-chief would have been ours. A headless army caves in instantly. And with that one unforgivable adolescent gesture, I would have set back guerilla warfare among the Rajputs by a few decades, if not centuries.

If I thought I was in a hurry to get home, Rao Raimul's impatience to assume the throne verged on the ludicrous. He had knocked on the door of my room at five thirty in the morning, asking me to get dressed and come down for his coronation. He had come back initially after intervals of fifteen minutes. By six forty-five he was making his rounds every ten minutes.

'The mahurat, Your Highness, is at nine seventeen in the morning. That's close to four hours from now.'

'Can't we bring it forward?'

'The idea of the mahurat, I believe, is to choose an auspicious time, so that the gods will smile upon you and will not unseat you in a hurry. I trust that you'll find it worth your while to wait a few hours in the hope that your reign over Idar will last many years.' He did not appear to be persuaded by my line of reasoning and was about to speak up when I interrupted. 'Go to your room, Rao Raimul. We'll see you in the coronation hall at eight forty-five sharp.'

I had to hand it to him, he was a blithe spirit, this brother-in-

265

law of mine. I had considered throttling him, giving him a public whipping or arranging an accident whereby he would break his neck after our final attack on the Gujaratis. 'Why weren't you and your men patrolling the camp? What happened?' I had asked him while we sat in Rao Viramdev's tent the previous night to celebrate our victory.

He took a hefty draught of the transparent liquor from Merta that could lay an elephant supine after the third drink. He smiled and asked innocently, 'What happened? About what?' Was he serious? Did he really not know what I was talking about? Or was he putting me on?

'Where were you and your men last night?'

'On guard duty.'

'So why didn't you warn us about Zahir-ul-Mulk's surprise attack?'

He laughed. 'He was not supposed to.'

'The General had talked things over with you, had he?'

'Not him, but we had it from an absolutely reliable source that the Gujarat forces were pulling out and going back because Zahir-ul-Mulk was fed up with your tactics of never waging a straight-forward battle.'

'Why did you not inform us of this invaluable intelligence?'

'I was planning to do so, the next morning. But some of the men from Idar came over and we decided to celebrate our return to Idar and my forthcoming coronation.'

'You were sure of the crown, were you?'

'Yes, of course. How were we to know that our hundred per cent reliable source was planting stories and deliberately misleading us?'

Rao Viramdev who had been silent all the while was looking at my glass or rather, the hand holding it. He saw me now, my hand tightening around the glass as if it were Rao Raimul's neck.

'Another drink for you, Maharaj Kumar?' Did the Rao know that I was about to strike my brother-in-law? 'Oh, I see that while all of us have been guzzling the brew, you have not touched yours yet. Perhaps you find the quality of the distillate a trifle unsatisfactory?' My hand lost its tension slowly.

266

'Forgive me, Your Highness. I'm afraid I got a little carried away with the talk. The liquor from Merta, I'm sure, is a very special one. I know that you've been preserving it for a special occasion.'

'Ah, Maharaj Kumar, I hope you have not been keeping us under surveillance too,' Rao Viramdev laughed his wonderful, gruff and gravelly laugh and we all joined him.

'You should laugh more, Rajkumar,' my brother-in-law advised me.

'Maharaj Kumar,' Rao Viramdev interrupted him. Rao Raimul was forgiven much; his shortcomings were ignored time and again but there was one kind of familiarity Rao Viramdev was not likely to permit him ever.

'Yes, of course. He's my brother, isn't he?"

'That he may be, but he is, first and last, Maharaj Kumar and heir apparent to one and all.'

Rao Raimul was not put out by the snub. 'You have to learn to relax, Maharaj Kumar. Take it easy. Not get so wound up and tense. You'll have to agree that we were right to celebrate last night. After all, am I not about to become King of Idar?'

What was the point of getting angry with this man? He would persevere in being a thorn in our side. And truth to tell, I had begun to suspect that he was not really vicious or diabolical. He was far more dangerous than that. A fool who had been led to believe that the world owed him a crown.

* * *

Either Mangal or the orderly helps me put on my armour when I am about to lead a raiding party or go into full-scale battle. Today for the first time in a year and a half, I am about to deck myself in civilian regalia and I can't do without Kausalya. The thought of Kausalya is a peg of rice liquor with a touch of cinnamon. It sits in my belly and spreads a warm glow. Take care of Sunheria, Leelawati and even that woman they mistakenly call my wife, till I return, Kausalya. And take care of yourself. Tell Sunheria not to give in to despair. We'll be in Chittor soon once we are through with the Rao's coronation.

What has come over me, I am unable to tie my turban today.

267

Stop indulging yourself, Maharaj Kumar, or you are going to be late. There's a knock on the door. Oh God, not Rao Raimul again. The orderly's on his way but I rush past him sword in hand and fling the door open. 'If you bother me once more, Rao...' It's Tej. He's laughing. 'Has he been bothering you too? He woke me up at four.'

'You are looking good enough to be crowned yourself, Tej. Let's get back home and we'll get you married first thing. The virtue of our women is in grievous danger while you are a bachelor.'

Another knock. I open the door swiftly sword still in hand. Rao Viramdev. 'Can't you do something about your brother-in-law, Your Highness? He's been in and out of my room since four thirty wondering if we can bring forward the crowning.'

In an hour and a half the ceremony is over. The priests go through an elaborate ritual, invoke the gods, pacify those who may bear a grudge against Rao Raimul and his ancestors and make hefty offerings to them. Rao Raimul fidgets and grows more and more restless. At last the head priest gets around to holding the royal crown over the Rao's head. But it's not to be yet. There's a series of slokas to be recited. Rao Raimul grabs the priest's forearms and brings the bejewelled turban down. The crown sits askew but the expression on his face is beatific. Oddly enough, I don't grudge him his impatience now. He's waited long enough for this day. The crown is a slippery thing. Most princes go through life waiting futilely for one to land on their heads. Even the lucky ones who manage to become kings are perpetually wary that someone will knock it off. Hang on to your crown, brother-in-law. Nail it to your head. I wish you well. May it bring maturity and wisdom in its wake.

Chapter 22

$\mathcal{W}$e left next morning. By evening we had joined Shafi Khan and the main Mewar army. The Merta, Dungarpur and other forces have gone their separate ways. Rao Viramdev and Rawal Udai Simha have accepted Father's invitation to visit Chittor before they go home and are accompanying me. There's not much chance of Muzaffar Shah attacking the Quartermaster-General and his caravans which now include the Gujarati camels, horses, elephants and vast supplies of victuals, not to mention forty-three thousand soldiers, but I have left behind two divisions to guard them. I prefer to err on the side of caution. In the negotiations that will precede the actual payment of war reparations, Father will use the captured Gujarat forces as a major bargaining counter.

We are making good progress but it's not good enough for me. I would rather be on my own and fly to Chittor. My evidence as a judge of the Small Causes Court which had investigated Sunheria's husband's accusations and found them to be false — albeit at that point in time only — may carry some added weight and help free her. If not, the least I can do is to be there when the trial's over and she's released, and prove her prediction wrong. But I concealed my impatience. It is not seemly for the commander-in-chief and heir apparent to abandon his army and proceed on his own because of a private engagement.

Rao Viramdev tapped me on the shoulder. 'Why don't you go on ahead, Maharaj Kumar? My niece will be happy to see you. She's not a demonstrative woman but I know how much she loves you. She writes about you with such longing and affection in every letter to me.'

This is the first time the old man has brought up the subject of his niece and my wife. I can't quite fathom the reason for this sudden sarcasm. I look at his face to gauge his mood and read his mind and am horrified. He is transparently sincere. Surely he is aware of my wife's antics and what a fine marriage she and I have? What ulterior motive can he have to put on this fine performance? He is puzzled by my silence. Then the simple truth dawns on me. Of course the whole world except him and her close kin knows the truth. Who would dare suggest to this noble and ramrod-straight man that his niece is a common dancing girl and faithless to her husband? I certainly wouldn't.

I took his hand in mine. 'Thank you, Your Highness. I will not forget this kindness. But my place is with our army. Absence ...' I couldn't bring myself to complete the sentence. Good man that he is, he completed the mendacious platitude for me, 'makes the heart grow fonder.'

I can see the ramparts of Chittor in the distance. I feel a faintly perceptible but distinct acceleration in the progress of our troops. Without my prodding him, Befikir too has picked up speed. I thank Eklingji for bringing us safely back home. It is fortunate that we rarely think about the future. Who would venture into battle if he knew that he was destined not to return? Somewhere deep within us, we must believe that death happens only to other people.

The sentries at the fort have seen us and are soon joined by other townsfolk. We are galloping now, a little out of control. We have waited patiently for more than a year and a half for this moment. It doesn't make sense losing our heads when we are almost there. Whether you are returning home from work at your office or from a long campaign, it's in the last five minutes that most accidents occur. Soon we'll be at the Gambhiree and if we continue at this crazy pace, there's going to be one hell of a bottleneck at the bridge. It will be ironic to have economized severely on the death-count in battle, only to die by the hundreds in peacetime and even as we are at the threshold of Chittor.

But we are already at Suraj Pol. This is where for hundreds of years the townspeople of Chittor have gathered and welcomed their triumphant armies with fanfare: flags, flowers and a week of celebrations. There was a deathly silence when we rode in. Neither

Father, the cabinet ministers, the nobles, the queens nor the ladies of Chittor were waiting to greet us. We advanced past straggly groups of men with black flags. Black flags hung from the windows of houses. As we turned into Lakshman Pol there was a crowd of over a thousand men waving black flags. They hung back sullenly. Suddenly a man shouted, 'Down with the butcher and the coward.' That released the tension in the air. 'Shame on the Maharaj Kumar,' someone else cried. 'Long live the Maharana. Long live Prince Vikramaditya.'

Tej had fallen out of line and made for the man who had broken the silence. The crowd lost its voice again. Tej bent down and pulled the man up by the scruff of his neck. 'Who are you calling a coward? A thousand of you won't be a match for His Highness, the Maharaj Kumar.'

'Sure,' a small voice piped up from behind. 'Which fool will not win with deceit, dishonour and guerilla tactics? We are Rajputs here, not cowards.'

Tej had his sword in hand now. Rao Viramdev held Tej's wrist and drew him away. I caught my breath as I glimpsed a young woman trying to make her way towards us but the crowds wouldn't let her pass. Something in the way she carried herself or perhaps it was the way she wore her ghagra and choli was vaguely familiar. She had a delicate nose and her eyes were large quartzes that were lit from within. For once the words intelligence and beauty meant one and the same thing. I had seen her so briefly, I was of course making her up. She was not beautiful in a modern or contemporary way. It seemed to be a face I had seen in one of Rana Kumbha's illustrated books. It turned everything and everyone around out of focus.

Chittor was echoing with a lively ditty. 'Our Maharaj Kumar is a slimy rat. Hurry, hurry. Get a big fat cat. Bury your head in the quicksands of shame. Let's wipe out the coward's and butcher's name. Hurry, hurry, get a big fat cat. Make a meal of the rancid rat. Look at our Vikram, he is a king of cats. Leave it to him, he'll wipe out the whole race of rats.' I searched for the woman as I hummed the words of the song. I couldn't locate her anywhere.

Shafi had lost his head. 'Where were you when Zahir-ul-Mulk

271

and the Gujarat forces surrounded us before dawn? But for the Maharaj Kumar, most of your sons, brothers and fathers would not be returning home today.

The mob was shouting down Shafi and closing in around him. A man got hold of his belt from behind and toppled him. It was Sajjad Hussein, my brother Vikramaditya's companion in conspiracy, whom Mangal had caught with Kali Bijlee and nine other horses outside Chittor in the village of Bagoli. Whoever had planned this reception for us had the demagogue's unerring instinct for the most vulnerable spot in our army. Rawal Udai Simha's wooden leg, the Maharaj Kumar's sudden disappearance from the camp, Tej's arson and revolt, were all grist for the doggerel mill. But the central theme was cowardice and there were a dozen variations on the subject. The dishonourable and dirty tricks the Maharaj Kumar had played on Malik Ayaz and the Gujarat armies, the murder of Zahir-ul-Mulk, the clandestine and dastardly attacks at night, the loss of manhood of the Rajput forces, even Rao Viramdev was not spared for the only night-sortie he went out on. There was a melee and Sajjad Hussein was stabbing Shafi. Our troops had drawn their swords and Tej's right toe had connected with Sajjad Hussein's jaw. A morbid red flower was blooming on Shafi's shirt front. The clangour of sword, shield and armour sounded strange and macabre within the Chittor walls. Sometime back this was just an ugly incident, soon it would look like a civil war. I watched the madness get out of hand as if it was happening not to my people, but to some alien race from another planet.

'You'll stop now,' a soft low voice spoke up. Slowly, very slowly the crowd froze. My wife, all of five feet two inches parted the people and walked towards me. She had a gold plate in her hands and in it were a lamp, kumkum and camphor. She did an arati, put the plate down and touched my feet. 'Welcome home, Maharaj Kumar.' Her voice rang and ricocheted across the ramparts of Chittor. 'Eklingji be praised. You and our friends and our armies have brought honour and victory to Mewar and its allies.' She took her gold chunni in her hands and tore it in two. She folded one half several times over and placed it over Shafi's bleeding wound and tied the other half around his stomach to keep the bandage

firmly in place. 'Take him to our palace and call the Raj Vaidya.'
My men carried Shafi away on a khatiya. She welcomed her uncle,
Rao Viramdev, Rawal Udai Simha, Raja Puraji Kika and Tej and
held out the plate for the men to pass their hands over the flames
of the lamp. Women came out of their homes, garlanded her and
fell at her feet. The prospect of this adoration unsettled her. She
winced and her toes shrank back. Someone said 'Long live the saint-
princess' and soon the whole fortress had taken up the refrain.
Within a short while a lot of the civilian men and our soldiery were
following suit and prostrating themselves before her.

I left my wife to the adulation of the populace and escorted Rao
Viramdev, Rao Udai Simha and Raja Puraji Kika to the Atithi
Palace. I could not look my wife's uncle in the eye. I made sure
that he was comfortably settled before I spoke. 'I beg your forgiveness, Your Highness, for this shameful reception. I do not know
where Father is. He'll be appalled at what happened today.'

Where was Father? Why was he not there to receive guests he
himself had invited? He may not have known that things would go
so completely out of control but wherever he was, I more than
suspected that today's turn of events could not be unknown to him.
Why don't I come right out and say it: granted that my dear brother
Vikramaditya's knack for self-promotion, hired loyalties and genius
for crowd scenes was in evidence everywhere but today's fiasco could
not have taken place without Father's tacit consent. That it was
aimed at me was obvious enough. What was just as clear was that
he wanted to leave no doubt in the minds of his allies that I had
fallen foul of him and to get that message across he was willing
to take the risk of humiliating, if not alienating the very friends who
had fought alongside Mewar. The moment I had articulated the
latter thought to myself, Father's reasoning was no longer a conundrum. Anybody who was associated with the Gujarat campaign
under my command would be wise to disown it and me, and would
have to prove his loyalty to Father anew.

'Maharaj Kumar, speak no more of it and embarrass me further,'
Rao Viramdev halted my train of thought. 'There's little or nothing
I can do to mitigate your disappointment. If there's any shame, it
belongs to the rabble. Let their humbug not cloud the fact that you

conducted an unusual but successful campaign with fewer casualties than we have ever suffered in a major war. The Rana was right to tell us "Don't go by his years. You are in good hands." There's much that my colleagues and I have learnt from you.' He paused and held my eyes. 'You'll find what I am about to tell you particularly ill-timed, even offensive. But if uncalled-for advice was always palatable, it would be useless to give it. Unfortunate as it may be, this reversal, too, will temper the steel in you. A Maharaj Kumar who aspires to the crown after his father's natural death — may Rana Sanga live long and in good health — needs to cultivate a temperament of tensile steel. Both a cynic and a wise man will distrust praise and good luck. Only the wise man has the sense to distrust obloquy and setbacks too. As Bheem learnt from the amulet on his arm, remember, these times too shall pass.'

Yes, these times too shall pass, I said to myself, but who can tell what new and wondrous calamities will follow them? 'You give us sound counsel, Rao Viramdev. I hope it restores my sense of perspective.' I was about to leave when a courier from Father arrived with a note for the Rao. He read it out aloud: 'His Majesty, Maharana Sanga sends you greetings and profound apologies for not being in Chittor to welcome you. We went to Pushkar to give thanks to Lord Brahma for our victory against Gujarat, a victory which we owe in great measure to your stewardship. On our way back we were suddenly indisposed and against our will, had to break journey at Ajmer for a day. We hope to be with you shortly and will make amends for being remiss in our duties as hosts. We trust that the Rajkumar and his wife, your niece will make you feel at home and look after your every need in our absence.

'We are, as always, beholden to Merta for your great and staunch friendship with Mewar. We are sure that with the passage of years, the bonds between our two kingdoms will grow stronger and closer.'

You had to hand it to Father. He was impeccable. What better reason for the host to absent himself from home than to thank the illustrious gods for giving him friends like Rao Viramdev? I wondered if the Rao had reservations about Father's belated apology. He was no man's fool and yet what choice did he have but to swallow the story whole? But there was more to admire in Father's letter.

274

How deftly he had underscored my fall and demoted me from heir apparent to a mere prince ... just in case the Rao had missed the point of today's welcoming ceremony.

My wife and I crossed each other as I left the Atithi Palace. We have been strangers for so long and yet every time I run into her I am awkward, resentful and embarrassed. Her presence unsettles me. As the guilty party, she is naturally on top of the situation and has superb poise. She is self-possessed, lighthearted, and unobtrusively but confidently proud of her husband. Today since she's meeting her uncle, she is glowing. I'll take that back. She always is. A lambent flame, that's how I see her. She bows to me and smiles. My coldness and anger are wasted on her. She doesn't ignore them. The fact is, she is not aware of them. It is not her nature to react. She sets the tone and the pace. How or whether you react is irrelevant. I doubt it if there is a more good-natured, warm and even-tempered human being in Chittor or the whole of Mewar. Neither is there a more deceitful, double-faced and dangerous person than her. I owe her one now. I have no idea how events would have progressed without her this morning. Did she do it consciously or did she merely walk down to greet her uncle and whoever was accompanying him? Whatever the truth of the matter, she had single-handedly averted one of the most dangerous and shameful crises in the history of Mewar. There is no dearth of patricides, villains and other assorted criminals in our annals. But a clash of the populace, albeit a deliberately engineered one, with the Maharaj Kumar and the army is unheard of. How shall I ever repay her?

Talk about surprises, from nautch girl to saint doesn't just strain one's credulity, it reaffirms the axiom that there is no creature more fickle than man. It's one thing to touch a saint's feet once a year and quite another to be married to one. Stranger, saint, wife, what difference does it make to me?

I am still not home and my patience is wearing thin. 'Raja, will you forgive me if I join you later?' I'm not really asking Puraji Kika his permission and he knows it. He smiled and waved me off. Eighteen months is a long time to be away. I want to compare the

Chittor I had so greedily and hastily jotted down in my memory-pad the morning we cremated Rajendra with the current one. Later, later, there would be time enough to investigate both the broad strokes and the nuance. I do not need to goad Befikir. He is in as much of a hurry to reach home as I. 'Where's she?' I looked at Kausalya's face and knew the answer. 'The trial's not over yet? What's taking them so long?' Kausalya shook her head slowly. Kausalya's eyes. You cannot unlock them. They conceal almost as many secrets, suffering and the follies of men as the Gambhiree.

That night I went and bathed in my river. Mother, I screamed silently, unburden me. Her waters neither cleansed me nor proffered me oblivion. I went back and made demented love to Kausalya. I would not stop. I was going to erase the memory of Sunheria. Kausalya held me and bore my assaults in the hope that she could take over some of my anger and bewilderment and stony pain but neither grief nor perhaps any human emotion, can be shared, let alone transferred.

'It's a good thing she went seven days ago. If it had happened just twenty-four hours before you came, you would never have forgiven yourself for not having ridden faster or abridged the distance by some magic.' Kausalya was not one for sugar coatings. Some time later she asked me, 'Do you know what Sunheria said the day she hanged herself? "The Maharaj Kumar is so ignorant of the world. He thinks the court will condone the murder because my husband physically abused me. Does he really believe that human beings are fair and that the courts can handle anything but the most elementary justice? It's not I but the Maharaj Kumar who is a misfit. He's going to learn that there's no place for a good and just person in this world." '

Was I listening to Kausalya? I couldn't make sense of her quiet words or voice. Sunheria had once again spoken in ambiguities. Was she the good and just person or was she referring to me? She had both those qualities in ample measure. As to yours truly, the thought strangely enough, had never occurred to me. I couldn't think of anyone in the changed climate of Chittor barring Kausalya who might even remotely consider me a candidate for fairness and decency. I'm not thinking straight. Kausalya would not back me either, not at all, but for entirely different reasons. She is the true inheritor of the principles of the great Mauryan Prime Minister, Kautilya. The business of a prince, even more so of a Maharaj Kumar, is statecraft. And there's no room for either goodness or justice in statecraft.

I had a feeling that try as I might, the honorific 'butcher' was going to stick to me for life. Did my people really believe that the ethics of civilian life and wartime were the same? War was a Rajput's dharma. When they disowned me, were they simultaneously disowning war? War is about power and supremacy. It is territorial ambition and greed. You cannot fight a war without killing. I did not invent war. I had merely extended its scope and taken it to its logical extremes.

But all that is besides the point. Till Kausalya told me of Sunheria's last words, I had believed that if only Sunheria had trusted me, if only she had waited a little longer, everything would have turned out right. I was no longer so sure. I was out of touch, as was so convincingly proven recently and worse, I was more than willing to delude myself. Perhaps despite Sunheria's unworldliness, she had a far more realistic perception of this world and its two-legged denizens. Maybe the trial would have gone against her and she would have been condemned to hang or spend the rest of her life in prison. Would I have broken the law or taken it in my hands and twisted it to set her free? By ending her life Sunheria had spared me the agony of having to confront my cowardice and convictions about the rule of law. Am I rationalizing after the event? Is there something about life that you know, Sunheria, and I don't? That you cannot trust anyone, least of all yourself? Come back, laundress, I swore at her, come back. You better explain yourself. I have got eighteen months of clothes to wash. Get to work, woman. I want them cleaned of all the blood on my hands, don't forget the collar and the cuffs and my conscience. I don't want to see a single speck of guilt, did you hear me, I won't have anyone suspect that I wiped off ten thousand men one early morning and followed up with several thousand more as the months progressed, go on, bash my clothes, my brains and body till I am a virgin, just the way you were supposed to be despite our sexual discourses over the years and starch me crisp like thin flat steel plate. I will not have you talking in conundrums which I will spend the rest of my life trying to unravel. Get back here, Sunheria. Now. This minute.

✳   ✳   ✳

There was no point trying to sleep. I got up and bathed. It was still dark and the raatranis had not withdrawn into themselves yet. It hit me then that I was home. Perhaps it was the fatigue or the bizarre events of the previous day that left me vulnerable. The scent of the flowers made my head reel. It was as if I had had a drink and was feeling just the right degree of intoxication. The woman who had disappeared behind the throngs of people yesterday came back to me. Where had she gone? Who was she?

Kausalya came over as I was buttoning my angarkha. 'Still can't get the right button in the right buttonhole? What did you do all these months?'

I was a schoolboy and Kausalya was once again buttoning me up. I held her tightly by the hair. She was my oldest memory and yet she was so unbelievably young.

'There,' she smiled, 'the Maharaj Kumar is ready to face the world.' It was my turn to smile. Even if I am not ready, I know that I had better be.

I was standing at the top of the flight of steps of the Palace, my hands full with presents for Adinathji's granddaughter, when I saw yesterday's woman again, the one who couldn't get past the crowd at Suraj Pol, outside the high compound wall. She had her odhani over her head and was walking with quick, determined steps. She had a tall package wrapped in brocade that reached almost to her chin. She looked up and saw me craning. I quickly descended a few steps and withdrew into the shadows.

She was standing against the light in the entrance now. There were tiny sweat-beads on her forehead and above her upper lip and I could hear the susurrus of her breath. As she bent down to put the monster package she was carrying on the floor, I got a glimpse of her shadowy features through her sheer odhani. It was my sister

278

Sumitra.

'Your Highness,' the woman smiled and leapt towards me. I caught her in my arms as the presents were scattered on the steps and the lawns. I lost my balance and tumbled down the stairs. One of my lumbar vertebrae hit the sharp edge of a step and I had twisted my right ankle, what seemed like a full hundred and eighty degrees. I observed the long lines of pain fan out all the way to my eyes and the tips of my toes. Leelawati seemed bent upon fusing our bodies together. Her arms were a shrinking noose around my neck, her face pressed like a dew-laden flower against mine. If sweat is a response to heat and exertion, why is it cooling to the touch? Leelawati's young breasts had scooped out two burning hollows in my chest. They would never fill up again, nor would the fire die. How I loved the brightness of her eyes, the small of her waist and the avidity of her mind and yet my arms turned to lead and sank down. The extreme proximity of Leelawati made me awkward and uneasy.

'I bet you forgot to bring anything for me.'

I looked guilty and crest-fallen.

'Ohhhhhhhh' was followed by a guttural 'uggghhhhh.'

'Sometimes I wonder if I should marry someone so irresponsible and callous.'

'Take my advice,' I sympathized with her, 'don't.'

She looked at me disbelievingly, then realized that I was pulling her leg.

'Nothing can break our marriage now.' She told me sharply. Then her curiosity got the better of her.

'What have you got? Show me, show me, show me.'

I knew that Leelawati would never again leap into my arms. I was willing to bet that this was the last time she and I would play this silly game. I was certain that along with hers, my childhood, too, was coming to an end. Within six months or a year at the most, she would be married off.

'I told you I didn't get anything for you. But take a look, I may have dropped a couple of the rags I got for the gardener's children on the lawns.'

She was off. This is the way I would like to remember Leelawati.

She wraps the odhani around her head and throws it across her left shoulder to keep it in place, lifts her ghagra and runs out. A flurry of mauve shimmering across a field of green. The morning light is a sculptor's chisel and hews out a moving form in razor-sharp outline from the air. Leelawati bends down, stretches her arm, picks up a package and flies away. For truly, Leelawati is a winged bird of infinite and unsuspecting grace who can float on sheer will-power till sundown. A cheeky peahen walks up with mincing steps and pecks at one of the parcels. Leelawati shoos her away with some asperity. She removes her odhani, packs the various big and small packets in it, ties it up and flings it over her shoulder in a gesture that is reminiscent of Sunheria throwing a load of unwashed clothes across her back.

When she returned, Leelawati put her makeshift cloth sack on the floor and held my hands. She rose on her toes and kissed my eyes and forehead. Is she a child or woman? There is an earnestness in her that is unnerving. In that moment, I fear for her. Willingly or unwillingly, someone's going to hurt her grievously.

She opened the cloth purse tucked at her waist and took out four pods of tamarind and a folded paper packet of salt. She passed two tamarinds to me and kept two for herself. The tamarind was a smoky green and though I spiked it with the salt, I would need teeth of stone to withstand its sour impact. I could feel my brains pickling. I wouldn't be able to bite anything for the next couple of days but who gave a damn. Tamarinds and green mangoes have no tomorrow.

'Shall we open your presents or mine first?'
'Yours.'

'Is that blood?' She stared a little disbelievingly at the pennant she herself had embroidered and presented to me and the troops.
'Yes. General Zahir-ul-Mulk's.'
'Did you kill him?'
Perhaps it was not such a wise idea returning the colours to Leelawati. I had forgotten that she and her family were Jains.
'If it upsets you...'

'It is not out of queasiness that I ask but because I wish to record its history for our children and posterity.'

'Yes, I killed Zahir-ul-Mulk by deceit, retrieved a situation fraught with defeat for our forces and brought dishonour to Mewar.' I was appalled at my pettiness and need to wear my heart on my sleeve. What was I looking for, a passionate reassurance from Leelawati that I was brave, unappreciated and much maligned? If she had noticed the change in my mood, she decided to ignore it and moved to the next gift.

'What is it?'

'It's a miracle gadget that will give a sense of direction to your floundering life. Any time you are lost, caught in a quagmire of moral dilemmas, it will show you the way out.'

'Why would I need it? I always know my mind.'

I burst out laughing. 'How you deflate my pomposities, Leelawati. It's a compass to give you geographical directions on a dark and cloudy night when not a star is visible in the sky.'

'Really? It works just as the books say?'

'Yes. Find out for yourself.'

She did, for a full ten minutes. She went out of the pavilion, took various positions in the garden, behind the palace walls, in a dark alcove, under a banyan tree, on the steps where I had stood and watched her. I could almost see the way her mind worked. She was going to surprise the compass and catch it showing west when she was standing squarely north-east.

'Where did you get it?'

'From a sailor who has been around the world, all the way to Venice and whose ship had lost its way on many a storm-tossed night.'

'When shall we go for a picnic in the mountains and jungles? We'll get lost and I'll show you the way back.'

'How about next Thursday?'

'Done. I'll be here at seven in the morning.'

She had already slipped the emerald necklace I had got her around her neck and was trying out the odhani of Egyptian cotton that the sailor had sold to me along with the compass.

'Is that all?' I couldn't figure out why she was suddenly distracted and irritable.

'You are an ingrate, Leelawati,' I tried to laugh off her ill humour, 'a shameless and insatiable ingrate.'

'Better than being a shameless and insatiable show-off like you. There's never an end to the gifts you keep giving me.'

'All right, let's forget your last present.'

'I don't want it. I have got only two presents for you.'

'Do I get my presents or are you planning to keep them for yourself?'

She thought hard but couldn't make up her mind. I had wanted to make her happy but my selfishness had not allowed me to think of how much she enjoyed giving things.

'What are you doing with them anyway?' I tried to rectify matters and grabbed the brocade bundle from her. 'They are mine.'

There were fire and anger in her eyes but she relented. 'Take it. What do I care?' She thrust the package in my hands and turned her back on me. I undid the knot. There was one tall wrapped parcel above a flat one. I opened the flat one. It was a book with a note from Leelawati.

'Dadaji and I read Kautilya's *Arthashastra* together this year. He even made me write a short treatise on it. Father protested this was no reading for a young woman. Dadaji said that if she's got a mind, he would rather that it was filled with knowledge than with gossip or inanities. I have read the *Arthashastra* half a dozen times in the process of copying it for you.'

I flipped the pages of the text she had copied out so meticulously. She had not scratched anything out. If she had made mistakes in copying the Sanskrit text, she had rewritten the whole page. I looked up and caught Leelawati sneaking a look at me. She was obviously pleased with what she saw in my face. I was back in favour.

'Let me have my other present.'

She carefully removed the cloth cover to reveal a bejewelled Veer Vijay turban.

'When they deprived you of your triumph yesterday, I ran home and sat up till this morning making the victory saafa for you.'

'Where did you get all this jewellery?'

'It's all mine.'

282

She was right. When I looked closely, I realized that I had seen most of the jewellery on her at one time or another. Even the gold Chanderi cloth was one of her formal odhanis. On its folds, Leelawati had sewn seven pairs of diamond, ruby, emerald, onyx, jade, topaz and moonstone earrings. Three pairs of gold anklets were strung on the sides. In the front, a little off-centre where the folds criss-crossed each other, she had stuck a meenakari lotus pendant of superb workmanship. Above it stood a heavy paisley-shaped nath that the Maratha women from the west coast wear in their noses. It should have been a mishmash but it was done with a fine eye for colour and design and the effect was exuberant without sacrificing dignity and delicacy.

'What will your family say when they find the jewellery missing?'

'Dadaji knows.'

'What are you waiting for?' For once Leelawati looked blank. 'Fix it on my head.'

'Are you going to wear it?' Leelawati asked in amazement and disbelief.

'Would you prefer it if I locked it in a trunk and put the trunk away in the loft?'

Her smile broke through then and so did her age.

I bent my head down. She pushed back my hair firmly and held it pressed down for a minute. Then she picked up the turban and placed it carefully on my head. She looked at her work and blurted, 'You look just like a Maharaj Kumar.'

'I am. And don't you let yourself or me forget it. On your way back will you hand over my book to Kausalya?'

She gathered all her presents together along with the book. 'Next Thursday.'

'Yes.' She was on her way when I called out to her. 'Do you mind keeping me company up to the stables?'

She held my hand as I limped to Befikir's stall. Mangal was waiting for me impatiently. He tried his best to keep his eyes off my victory turban. I had my say before he could give me his important news.

'There's a durbar at eleven today.'

'How did you know, Sire, that His Majesty was back and had

called a special durbar?'

'He got in with his entourage around midnight. Rao Viramdev is to be awarded our highest honour and title, Mewar Vibhushan, along with twenty villages and three elephants. Raja Puraji Kika will be awarded Mewar Gaurav, ten villages and fifty horses. Rao Udai Simha will receive a Mewar Bhushan, seven villages and thirty horses. Do you want me to go on?'

Mangal frowned. Had his security and intelligence men failed him? Had I given them the slip?

'Did you go and meet your father last night or this morning, Your Highness?'

'I didn't need to, Mangal. Any schoolboy would have guessed as much yesterday itself.'

'Who's that?' Leelawati asked no one in particular about Befikir's young companion.

'That's Nasha.' I told her offhandedly.

'Who?'

'Nasha.' My voice was suddenly cold and harsh. 'I would appreciate it if I wasn't told in the future that you can't go riding with me because your father won't allow you to have a horse.'

'Is he mine?'

'How many dumb questions do I have to answer in one morning?'

My crimes of misdemeanour, omission and commission in this life and all my past and future lives were forgiven and wiped off the record instantly. A dumb-founded Mangal and I were subjected to monstrous bear hugs.

'May I ride him home?'

'Only at a trot and if you'll permit Sapanlal to hold the reins.'

It may be time for me to take up a second career as seer, soothsayer, oracle and prophet but my clairvoyance is not yet foolproof. It had not taken into account a small twist of fate, or should I say foot. (As you can see I may criticize mediocre word play severely but catch me on a bad day and you'll find me indulging in the foulest and most revolting of puns.) The durbar was a full house. Father was not treating the occasion lightly. He had, it was obvious, sent a summons to all the dignitaries in the kingdom to be present for the ceremony. He wanted to make sure that everybody knew who was on the honours list and the one person who was not.

As I entered I heard a low but distinct gasp escape from the assembly of august personages. Only His Majesty can crown you with the golden triumphal turban. Had there been a special private ceremony? Or, as is more likely, did the Maharaj Kumar have the temerity to award himself a triumph? It would have been interesting to see if any of the courtiers had the guts to confront me with a direct question but there was no time since the Minister for Protocol announced Father. We all rose and bowed to our liege. Vikramaditya went over and fussed over him in a proprietary way and helped him sit down. Father wasn't quite sure how to respond to his youngest son's newly-found solicitude since he had managed pretty well on his own all these years but he was in a mellow mood and smiled indulgently though a little uncertainly.

If you wanted to know what was going on behind the scenes at Chittor, there was no point keeping an eye on Father. The key to the drama lay in watching the other players. Look at Rattan, my younger brother. He has not forgiven his mother, me and the powers that be for being born second. He is not a bad sort really. He is intelligent, attentive and hardworking but the setback in the numbers game makes him susceptible to all kinds of slights and insults which most of the time are not intended or given. We keep our distance but there is no genuine animus between us and it is conceivable that the two of us might have been friends under another set of parents and circumstances. Rattan, poor man, is in a bit of a quandary. He had Father all to himself when he was campaigning in Gujarat with him, while the Council of Ministers and I were packing Vikramaditya to Kumbhalgarh prison for treason. Why couldn't he have insinuated himself into Father's good books and become his favourite son? Poor Rattan, he has no idea how to unseat Vikramaditya from Father's affections. He shouldn't be so hard on himself. The fact is, it is an unequal race and Vikramaditya is not the competition.

The competition was sitting across in the Queen's gallery. Rani

285

Karmavati puffed up like a puri deep-frying in hot oil as Father whispered something in Vikramaditya's ear. From total eclipse to rising sun, Vikramaditya may have come a long way since I last saw him but his mother cannot forget that it was almost entirely her handiwork with some excellent planning and help from her confidant Bruhannada. Next to her sat my mother, the Maharani herself. She was beaming with joy. Simple soul that she is, she was happy for Rani Karmavati and Vikramaditya and was blissfully unaware that her own son and heir was not in the running any more. Rani Karmavati scoured the territory for enemies and spotted Rattan. No cause for concern there. He was but further proof of the fact that she had won against heavy odds. Her eyes fell upon me. She smiled, gloating from ear to ear. I realized for the first time why someone like Father must find her hard to resist. She had a harsh kind of beauty but the source of her attraction was a lascivious obstinacy. Women were supposed to give in or give up. She never did. She would outlast us all. I bowed down deeply to her.

Did I detect a smile on Father's face as he took in my golden phenta? What had made me wear it in public? Why did I ask Leelawati to put it on my head when she herself had thought of it as nothing but a private matter between the two of us? Did I wish to assert that regardless of whether Father and the whole of Mewar saw me as a butcher and a coward, I was the architect of the victory over Gujarat? Or was I telling the whole lot of them to go to hell? Rao Viramdev was looking at me expectantly. The durbar was becalmed. Even Father seemed to be waiting patiently for me. What now? Was I expected to make a small speech apologizing for our victory and for fulfilling Father's wishes to set up Rao Raimul on the throne of Idar? Should I go on my knees and thank Father for returning twenty-four hours late and insulting our friends and allies? Should I carry Vikramaditya on my shoulders and tell one and all...

No one, not even Rao Viramdev, could move till I had gone and paid my respects to Father. I may no longer be heir apparent but I was still the eldest and chief of the army that was returning victorious. I hobbled down painfully.

'Are you all right, Prince?' There was concern in Father's voice. 'Why was I not informed about your being wounded?'

I was about to tell him that I was ashamed to return from such a long campaign without much to show for it and had arranged for a minor mishap to overtake me on my way to the court but Vikramaditya didn't give me a chance.

'Nothing of the sort, Your Majesty,' he smiled deprecatingly and hovered a full ten seconds on the edge of the next word before he unburdened himself of the rest of the sentence. The court waited with baited breath and so did I for Vikramaditya to deliver his punch line. 'He was gamboling with the fair Leelawati, the great-grand-daughter of our illustrious Chancellor of the Exchequer, on the lush lawns of the Atithi Palace where he slipped and fell a little foolishly and happily over her. A small price to pay for such delicious company, wouldn't you agree, my friends?' There was a nervous titter from the audience. 'The Veer Vijay saafa he is wearing is a gift from the same lady.'

For some reason the durbar found this last uproarious. Perhaps humour is a matter of expectation and works on a graduated scale. Once you lay the groundwork, even the mildly funny or indifferent lines spoken with enough verve and a casual, throwaway tone will elicit peals of laughter.

My brother had been, as always, more than willing to make somebody else pay the price for an easy laugh. Adinathji would find it difficult, if not impossible, to get Leelawati married now that my brother had light-heartedly suggested that the Maharaj Kumar and the girl had had a romantic assignation which they had not even taken the trouble to conceal. It was of no consequence that Leelawati would soon be one of the most beautiful women in Mewar. It mattered little that Adinathji could pay a king's ransom as his great-granddaughter's dowry. An aspersion, however false or jocular, does not make a girl-woman suspect in Mewar, it proves her guilt beyond any doubt and condemns her. There was not an extra crease in the Chancellor's expressionless face but his rice-flour complexion had gone a dead grey.

'I suggest you apologize to the Chancellor of the Exchequer,' my voice was cold.

My brother looked lost. He had baited me and at the most, expected me to rise to the bait. Instead I had changed the terms of the game itself. Vikramaditya is essentially stupid and tried to make a joke of it even now and sank deeper in his own tasteless mirth.

'Not on, brother, not on. If you have all the fun, it's you who must apologize to our venerable Chancellor.'

I took a step forward. My voice was a metallic whisper. 'You heard me, Prince. You will apologize to Adinathji and his great-granddaughter.'

The Audience Chamber and the people in it had grown eerily quiet and still. I could feel Rani Karmavati's wrath directed against her foolish son who seemed hell-bent on destroying all the years of effort she had put in on his behalf.

'Maharaj Kumar,' it was millenniums since I had heard those two words that had been the compass of all my waking and slumbering hours, 'don't be a cad and ruin such a lovely day. I'm sure the Prince was only joking. He'll apologize to the birds and the bees, the children and adults of Mewar and to this court. How would our beloved Finance Minister like the Prince to apologize?'

Wasn't that brilliant? The son may be an ass but I was no match for his mother. Rani Karmavati had not just checkmated me, she had skillfully retrieved the situation by putting the Finance Minister on the spot. But my brother didn't know how to leave well enough alone.

'Me, apologize? Have you taken leave of your senses, Ma? A Prince of the realm does not apologize to a common moneylender.'

'You are quite right, Prince. You wouldn't normally have to apologize to anyone, commoner, minister or royalty,' Father spoke with a deliberateness that gave added weight to his words. 'But you have behaved abominably. You have insulted this august assembly and an elder who is our friend, guide and financier of last resort. You'll not dishonour a child who is as close to us as our own granddaughter. We suggest that you apologize without further delay.'

Vikramaditya pouted sullenly but did not budge. His mother came down and spoke to the Chancellor.

'If the newly returned Prince had not made such a peevish ado about a little light banter, this happy day would have passed without incident. The people of Mewar have expressed their displeasure with his dastardly exploits and hence he is trying to sow dissension amongst us old friends. I beg you to accept my apologies, Adinathji. Otherwise, we'll ruin this great occasion when so many of our valued allies have come to honour us.'

'We asked your son to apologize, Queen, not you,' Father held his ground but it was clear that the crisis had passed.

'Your Majesty, let bygones be bygones.' Adinathji had totted up the accounts and decided it was wiser to close the books. The damage had already been done. To continue to dwell on the matter would only end up doing further harm to Leelawati. 'With your permission, may I request His Highness, the Maharaj Kumar to complete his interrupted journey (smiles all around) and then call upon the Prime Minister to start reading the honours list?'

I prostrated myself at Father's feet, all six feet one inch of me plus the two feet of my outstretched hands.

'May the blessings of Lord Eklingji be upon you.'

I forgot about my injured ankle and would have lost my balance as I rose, but Father bent down and steadied me. My protestations to the contrary, did I still expect Father to renege on yesterday's events and award me my triumph? Now was the time for Pradhan Pooranmalji to announce my name and hand over the Veer Vijay turban to Father so that he could adorn my head with it. The Prime Minister would then read out the titles, honours, lands and other gifts bestowed upon me by His Majesty. I must have lingered for Pooranmalji felt compelled to call upon Rao Viramdev to come forward. I did not look up and embarrass my wife's uncle. I could feel the tension and puzzlement in Rao Viramdev's walk. Was his niece's future at risk? Had he made the wrong choice by getting her married to a Prince who no longer seemed to be heir apparent? And what was his oldest friend, His Majesty, the Maharana up to? Today's ceremony was going to be more difficult for him than for me. If memory serves me right, I must be the first general in the history of Mewar not to have rated a Veer Vijay after leading our troops to victory.

The day's agenda proceeded without a hitch now but my travails for the day were not over yet. As always, Father was meticulous. After each engagement, a commanding officer was expected to send a list of all those whose contribution went beyond the call of duty. It was a tricky and sensitive task since outstanding courage and bravery was the rule rather than the exception and the officer-in-charge had to work hard to substantiate why one of several of his men was deserving of special mention. In all, two hundred and twenty-seven officers and soldiers received awards. Tej walked off with three, one for himself, one in absentia for his friend Shafi and a posthumous one for his brother Rajendra. Despite the expression on my face which turned from surprise to disbelief to anger to rage to despair, despite every signal that I could summon to warn off Tej after he had touched Father's feet, he walked towards me. Did the dear fool not know that at this moment, he could do no greater disservice to me than acknowledge my presence? He walked slowly and with great deliberation. Please, my friend, please, today's not the occasion to assert your loyalty to me. You were more use to me as an enemy than you are as a friend. Don't do this Tej, don't. He lay his head on my feet. He would not rise till I had lifted him.

Would to God that I was not so transparently fair of complexion. All those years of self-discipline were of no use to me. I went red in the face two hundred and twenty-five times, for Tej had set a precedent which the rest followed sedulously like sheep. No amount of practice, choreography and orchestration could have achieved such a damning and devastating effect. It had the look of not just a premeditated snub, it was as if I was serving Father and the country notice of a time-bound revolt together with a list of the officers and the braves who would lead it under my aegis. How could Father ever trust me? How could he feel safe while I was still alive? I have no idea how the court and the queens and the guests reacted to this absurd turn of events. Were they aghast at this show within a show? Did they think that Father and his advisers had misjudged the temper of the armies and overplayed their hand? Did they believe that I had put up the men to this madness? Would they recommend that I was too dangerous to be allowed to walk the streets again? All I knew was that I dared not look at Father but sensed instinctively that he was watching me in his one-eyed way. One is never sure whether he is sneering at you, lost in his own thoughts, trying to get the dead eye to work again or is just plain sleepy. I waited for him to call the guards and take me into custody.

Chapter 23

On Thursday, I got up at four as always. Kausalya helped me bathe and dress. My foot was larger than a bloated, oversized pumpkin and I had to keep the pain at bay with generous helpings of opium balls stuck between my left cheek and gum.

Seven. Seven-fifteen. Seven-thirty. Eight. Despite the throbbing in my foot, I paced my room, I went down to the garden, I climbed back to my suite of rooms. I was not going to take a no for an answer. Besides, whatever the reason and however serious, Leelawati never misses an appointment. All I had to do was be patient and wait and she would come.

Kausalya had been to the Finance Minister's house four times since eight o'clock.

'Where is she?'

'They don't know. Or rather they tell me a different story each time I ask. First, I asked at the gate. They said she was asleep. The second time I ran into her uncle. "Children," he said vaguely, "you know what they are like. I'm sure she's around playing with her cousins and friends." The next time I went to the kitchen. The cook shook his head. "You won't believe how much tamarind that girl can put away. No wonder she's had the runs for the last two days." "That's a cute story, Sajjonath, but if you don't tell me the truth, you'll no longer get the special discount on the lentils and the vegetables which you pocket and lend at some criminal interest rate to the other servants in the household." "I don't know, Kausalya-mai," he says, "I swear I haven't seen the young mistress since the day Prince Vikramaditya spoke about her in the court." I went back to the sentry. "What's the point of asking me, Mai? Do you think they would let even her cousins or brothers know her whereabouts?

Is there a more tightlipped man in Chittor than the Finance Minister? Maybe she is at Abu, Ranakpur or with her relatives at Chanderi. Your guess is as good as mine."'

'If they had slipped her out, Mangal would have known. I asked him to watch the city gates from the day of the incident at the court. Call Mangal.'

'Your Highness, give it time. She'll surface once things cool down.'

'How do you know they haven't done something to her? How do you know she is alive? Tell the servants to call Mangal.'

A full-grown banyan tree of pain burst forth inside my foot and I lost consciousness under the afternoon sun. Kausalya was bending over me applying cold compresses on my head while her son stood beside her. Mother and son were, as always, studiedly cold with each other.

'The Raj Vaidya's on his way, Maharaj Kumar.'

'Have you found out Leelawati's whereabouts or do you think you and your progeny have been awarded a sinecure in perpetuity?' Why was I asking these inane questions and venting my impotent anger on Mangal? Would I not have done exactly — whatever that was — as Adinathji had secretly arranged, if Leelawati had been my sister or daughter and a prince of the reigning family had cast aspersions on her virtue? Did I not know the moment my brother had spoken that I would never again set eyes upon Leelawati?

'Answer me. Where is she?' There was a thick fog gliding though the stark sunlight in the room but I wasn't willing to let go of Mangal.

'I don't know, Your Highness. My men have kept a record of whoever's gone into or out of the house. We've made enquiries, we've oiled palms. Nobody knows where she is.'

'How convenient, I bet even dear Adinathji is not aware of her whereabouts.'

I knew then that I had lost Leelawati for good.

*   *   *

'Black or white?'

'Black.'

She had been sitting next to the bed for seven days, maybe seven years, I've lost count, but I had not said a word to her. Now without any intention of having converse with her, the word had slipped out of my mouth. She made her move. Either she was a novice or a deep and devious player. So what's new, was there ever any doubt about it, of course she was the latter. I had been foolish enough to respond but I could still go into a huff and back out. I did not, however, want to appear childish and had no alternative but to play. Besides, I was curious about her game. But no more dialogue, that was for sure. She wasn't going to make a fool of me again. It was years since I had exchanged a word with her. I saw no reason to become convivial merely because I was stranded in bed, my foot and ankle in splints and raised nine inches above the rest of my body. She had insisted on bringing my food, filling my glass with water or wine, adjusting the pillow under my head and the bolster under my foot. She had had the gall to suggest, I still can't get over it, that she undress, soap and dry me and help me put on my clothes and spend the nights nursing me. I had put my foot down, don't take that too literally. I had successfully turned a simple hairline crack into a serious fracture by being a hero and carrying on with business as usual with the help of progressively larger doses of opium but I wasn't prepared for the humiliation of facing a wife who would solicitously perform every wifely duty but one. I had, instead, one of my absurd triangular conversations with Kausalya.

'Kausalya, I trust you are not going to a mujra or mushaira tonight and will make it convenient to be in the range of a few hundred feet just in case I fall out of the bed or need to be breast-fed.'

Kausalya must have discovered the code to the future of our planet in a turkey in the Persian carpet on the floor for she stared fixedly at its plumage while my shameless wife almost rolled over with laughter.

'How you embarrass Kausalyamai. No one, not even I, could hope to love you as much as she does and take this nonsense from you.' Greeneyes, as you've no doubt made out, did not need an intermediary.

I won the game of chess but she didn't make a habit of losing. She was an unorthodox player, talk about understatements, she had a bizarre and volatile approach to the game and no qualms about changing her strategy midstream. It was both, a ploy to throw the opponent off his guard and the natural bent of her mind. She took astounding risks, offered an elephant, even the vazir, when there were plenty of other options available, teetered on the edge but was never reckless. She was shrewd, contrary, disciplined in her own perverse fashion and just about the worst loser I have known.

'You cheated, I don't know how you did it, it was somewhere between your seventeenth and nineteenth move,' she flung the chessboard at me. 'Admit it, you are a Shakuni Mama. You were afraid of losing, so you fixed the game.'

Her tantrum was so unexpected and so genuine, I lost control and laughed idiotically. She picked up whatever pawn, camel, king came to hand and flung it hard at me. Tears were streaming down her face. I crossed my arms and covered my head but she got one direct hit on my forehead with a horse. That didn't abate her anger. I doubt it had registered in her mind that I had an inch-long cut above my right eye. I should have stopped laughing but her flying hair, her clogged and sniffling nose, the crazy glint in her eyes added to my mirth.

'You brought the chessboard and the pieces into the room. How could I have fixed them?'

'So what? They are made in Chittor, you must have bribed the craftsman. I guess you didn't even have to do that since you are the Maharaj Kumar. I bet they do it routinely. You wait, let me get a set from Merta, I'll give you such a thrashing, you won't forget it for the rest of your life.'

'You are doing that pretty successfully anyway. And what's to prevent your Merta artisans from loading the pieces in your favour?' It did not take me any effort to regress to her childish level.

'Are you suggesting that there are cheats and liars in Merta? I'll have you know that unlike you, we are an honourable people.' She was advancing towards me now, her rage indistinguishable from her sobbing. That slight, shy and petite woman leaned over me. I was sure she was going to throw me out of the window but with an ever so light flick of her hands, she pushed me off the bed.

'Give me back Kumkum Kanwar. What did they kill her for? She was harmless and innocent. She was about to become a bride when they set her on fire. She looked black and crumpled like charred paper. She looked so dead and helpless when it was me they meant to torch. Oh God, I'm so alone and lonely in your house.'

'I can't move. Something seems to have happened to my other leg. Will you send someone to get the Vaidya?'

* * *

Consider the knee. Without this flexi-joint, we would not be able to sit down, kneel or do a padmasan. There would only be an either/or, a vertical or horizontal posture. Stand up or lie down. Nothing in between. I have no idea how we would ride horses without knees. Steps, staircases, multistories, frankly even first floors, would be inconceivable without knees. Islam would have to invent some other posture for prayers. Wrestling would be out and so would the prospect of putting one's knee in the crotch of some bully or brigand who attacked suddenly. One of my favourite childhood pastimes would have been out too. I would go behind a classmate standing erect or with his legs apart and arms akimbo and shove my knee into the fold of his leg. It always worked. The guy lost his balance or semi-sank and I laughed myself silly till someone came and did the same to me.

And what you may well ask, is the occasion for this ode in praise of knees when there is still no trace of Leelawati? Take my word for it, I'm undone. That accursed woman, the wife and witch of my life, has revealed to me that the knee, at least mine, is an explosive trigger, an aphrodisiac of such phenomenal dimensions that I have driven my companion of infinite patience and indulgence, Kausalya, to despair and exhaustion. I am unquenchably randy and demand satisfaction though I am bedridden, on an hourly, nay, on a half-hourly basis. What infernal perversity led my wife to first break my other leg and then place her moist lips on my exposed knee cap, begging me to forgive her? Perhaps it is an idle mind and my supine posture and two broken legs that are responsible for my unfathomable lubricity. Kausalya who has always maintained and defended the decorum of the home, has finally caved in and smuggled in nocturnal and transient company because I cannot make it to Chandra Mahal. I would be happy or at least painfully wearing myself out if I could plough and till a lonely furrow on rented flesh. But there is no peace even in my own home, my own private chambers. That woman when she is finished with her inordinate outpourings and her devilish swirling of skirts and torrid singing, drops in at the oddest hours. I resolve not to speak. I keep my cool and hold firmly to my stone of silence. It is, needless to say, of no use whatsoever.

Will someone please tell me what I am to make of my life? Is my wife Greeneyes real? Is she nothing but a great actress, a phony all the way? Is she one person or two or many more? Does she love someone else and hurt for me? Is she lying? Does any of this, all that is past and the present and whatever's to come, make sense?

'Want to bet your gold belt with all its rubies and diamonds that I'll beat you?' She had brought back the chess set, the one with the damaged horse.

'No, thank you.'

'Afraid of being beaten?'

'Terribly.'

'What will you bet?' She persisted.

'My box of needles and thread and buttons.'

She stared uncomprehending for a second and then collapsed in waves of laughter. A strange pass, my life had come to. My wife finds my third-rate humour funny.

'You wait, just you wait. I'll clean you out of hearth and home.' She looked defiantly at me. 'But I'm a fair person. Go ahead, ask for anything, anything you want, if not I, but you win the game.'

'Anything?'

'Anything. I don't go back on my word.'

There was something I wanted from her, at least I remember I did a long time ago. Something I had craved and yearned and

297

waited for all these years.

I lost the game. Had I won, would I have asked her? Would she have granted me my wish?

She was a compulsive gambler. We played hundreds of games of chess while I lay on my back in bed. She bet many things. Sometimes she lost. But she never bet 'Anything, ask anything. I don't go back on my word' again.

'Perhaps it may be a good idea to wait a while before you ask His Majesty's permission for us to leave for Kumbhalgarh.'

What was she talking about? We were in the middle of a game. Was I no longer permitted the privacy of my own thoughts? I had not mentioned Kumbhalgarh to anyone. Our games, the only time we had any sort of transactions, were monologues. Hers. How did she know then?

I had no role to perform in Chittor. I was not even an ordinary member on the Gardens and Parks Committee. The projects I had initiated — sewage management, the escape tunnels and the modernization of military technology — were no longer actively pursued. What hurt most was not that they were shelved but that we were willing to cut off our nose to spite our face. Chittor's interests were dismissed merely because my name was associated with those projects. How does one deal with this order of shortsightedness?

I had never had an excess of friends even as a child. After my marriage, I had stopped entertaining almost entirely. Barring Raja Puraji Kika and Rao Viramdev, no one came to visit me. (I'm not counting the Queen Mother and Mother.) Now that both of them had gone to their own kingdoms, my only guest — always uninvited — was my wife. Why stay where one was unwanted? I was an outsider at home. Perhaps I could be at home outside Chittor.

'You feel you'll no longer be seen as a threat if you remove yourself from Chittor. But that's just what the people who have been conspiring against you, want. You wish to leave, they'll say, because you want to foment trouble. Who knows, they'll hint, all those hotheaded people who bowed to you when the victory awards were announced may join you in Kumbhalgarh and you may decide to

298

march against Chittor.'

I held my silence. Whose side was the Flautist's mistress on? Having made me the jester of Mewar, must I now take lessons from her? I had to confess though that I had overlooked the first rule of statecraft. In any matter that concerns your relationship with others, put yourself in the other person's shoes. Get under his skin. View the world and the issues from his point of view. You'll know exactly where the shoe pinches. Now decide whether you want to cut the blood supply off altogether, ease the pain or watch how the situation develops.

'It's not my place to give advice,' that did not seem to deter her though, 'but His Majesty is a good man. He was under great pressure to relieve you of your command. But he did not give in. He let you put your unusual ideas to the test. When you tricked Malik Ayaz and trapped the Gujarat armies in the quagmires, there were public demonstrations for your immediate recall. Both of us know who was behind these, but the dismay and disappointment in the populace were genuine. What was His Majesty to do? How was he to educate his people and his allies about the profound changes you were making in warfare when he himself was in the dark about them? Then you disguised yourself as a Gujarati soldier and killed Zahir-ul-Mulk. After that there was no longer a demand for your recall. They wanted you stripped of rank and office.'

'I am stripped.'

She did not indulge my self-pity.

'I'm not suggesting that your enemies have not won the day. But it may be wise to wait and watch what happens. Sometimes, only sometimes, not always, time will take matters in hand and resolve them.'

That night Kausalya arranged for a rather unusual treat.

'I want you. Not hired help. I want you to crush my head between your breasts or thighs till my putrid brain is flushed out. That way perhaps I'll be finally rid of this obsessive disease.'

She shook her head.

'Are you tired of me?'

She smiled a little ruefully as if I had said something ludicrous and unworthy. 'I'm with you, never more than two rooms away. The disease, Your Highness, is time. This is the first time you have had all the time in the world. If it is a healer, time is also a killer. What you need is a change, a change of faces and companions. I'm a reminder of all your troubles. The two girls will make you forget yourself for a few hours.'

'Two of them?'

'They are twins. They don't operate singly. Double the fun, that's what we do, they told me.'

They couldn't have been very old. Leelawati's age or a couple of years older at the most. Nothing special about that. Most of the people in Mewar are married when they are children. The first period and a girl is allowed to sleep with her husband. The royal family and the highly privileged may not always follow these customs and often wait for the princes and princesses to get into their late teens before conjoining them. But Father has odalisques, not to mention a wife who is maybe twelve or thirteen.

These two, however, were rare birds. They looked young and eager and uncertain and yet every now and then I had the feeling that they had seen more of life than the great sages for whom the past and the future are interchangeable. Their names were Raat and Din. They were identical twins. Their parents, pimp or whoever had named them must have had a juvenile turn of irony or a twisted sense of humour. After a while I began to suspect that they were playing some kind of game with me. If I called Raat and held her hand, she smiled shyly and said 'She's Raat, I'm Din.'

One of them started to unbutton my shirt while the other got down to undoing my trousers.

'Shall I play with myself while Raat takes you? Or if you like you can play with Raat while I let my tongue discover parts of you, you didn't know existed?'

It was like my mother reeling out the names of all the savouries and sweets she could remember as she tried to coax me to eat when I was ill.

'Lie between us and we'll give you a nipple massage. You've never experienced anything like it in your life.'

300

I must have looked a trifle unconvinced.

'I know what you are thinking,' Din smiled knowingly. 'That you can feel a nipple only between your fingers or lips and tongue. But you are wrong. Raat and I have invented this special treat. Your skin will become astringent as an alum-rub and your gooseflesh will be the tremor in the grass when the papiha sings and the monsoon showers scurry through it.'

She let her clothes slither down. How many months had she practised this seemingly triggerless undraping of herself in front of the mirror? Raat thrust herself forward.

'Would you care to undress me, Highness?'

Her hand brushed accidentally against her sister's breast. It was sheer art, this act of casual premeditation and voluptuous provocation. As I undid her blouse, I watched Din's fingers between Raat's legs. Her nipples woke sleepily.

'Hold my breasts, Maharaj Kumar,' Raat told me, 'no, no, don't clasp them. Just place them on the palms of your hands.'

Her voice was a flickering whisper, an erotic invitation as potently compelling as her palm on her sister's breasts. 'They are the apples from the Persian Emperor's orchards, the mangoes from Konkan in Maharashtra. And the red-black grapes, Your Highness, how will you know where they are from unless you bite them?'

Din throbbed like a slow spasm that contracted and released her as her sister put her tongue in her mouth. My hands fell to my sides. The grapes would neither rouse my tongue nor my member. I was disconcerted and disoriented by the mirror images. There was no room for an outsider between these undulating reflections in which it was impossible to tell where simulation began and spontaneity ended.

'Shall we do this a little later?' I asked a shade guiltily.

They looked discouraged but stopped instantly. Their smiles were a little hesitant now, waiting for further instructions.

'Do you divide all tasks, I mean all your work equally?'

'Yes. We never plan but if I take the left, she handles the right. If she starts at the top, I'm already busy working my way up from the toes.'

They smiled constantly but were bereft of humour or playfulness.

They were tirelessly painstaking, ever-willing to do your bidding, persevering even after they had worn themselves to inert fatigue, compulsively good-humoured, extending themselves to any lengths to please the customer. I could not bear thinking about what would happen to them and their self-esteem if they failed to please. Would they kill the customer or commit suicide? They were creatures of such exquisite delicacy and yet so ersatz, an evening with them could go either way: degenerate into excruciating boredom and emptiness or become a bejewelled, if precious experience in a mirror universe. Is it possible, I asked myself, is it possible for an image in a mirror not to have an original? Was there a world where only reflections had life, that there was only antimatter, that we are a shadow world and the universe and creation are not maya or a figment of the imagination but a possibility or an option that cannot be because God lost interest or is lying dead on the edge of some galaxy?

They are singing now. No, Raat sings and Din dances or the other way round. 'There is only one taboo, it is sorrow,' the song tells me. 'There is only one medicine for both the invalid and the healthy. It is love. Because love is the disease. It is the key and the lock, the incarceration that liberates.'

The paradoxes and the antitheses pile up. The banalities never cease to fascinate our poets and their audiences. And yet every now and then, in that synthetic emotion, a live image or irony grabs you and disturbs the tranquil certitudes of one's cynicism. The singing and the dancing may not be extraordinary but they are accomplished to say the least. I'm reminded of the night at Rajendra's and my uncle Lakshman Simhaji's place. Surely I don't expect these pixies or expensively made-up waifs to share the magnificent rolling introspection of Sajani Bai. They have fine antennae, these sisters, they catch the ever-so-fleeting lapse in my attention.

'Our recital does not give you satisfaction, Sire?'

'Much satisfaction, ladies.'

They did not believe me.

'Shall we play the games Prince Bahadur played with us?'

It is a long, long time since I've thought of the Shehzada. Where is he? Still self-exiled in Delhi or back with his father or taking shelter with the Sultan of Malwa? Time has a strange way of playing with

302

the lighting in memories. Clear and sharp lines and features recede at times, the darker recesses come to the fore or gain definition. Perhaps time is a kaleidoscope and never repeats itself. I think of Bahadur now as one of the few friends I have had. We were bound both by life and death. But there was more than that.

'Would you like us to take you in turn? We'll bring you to the brink. It will be unbearable and exquisite and yet we'll make sure that you don't come.'

Sometimes I think of him as a kindred spirit. During the campaign, I often caught myself talking to him. He was not just the enemy. He had, unlike most people, a point of view that he had arrived at after thinking things through. He had a vision for the kingship and the state and the present was but an improvisation towards realization of that objective. He could be narrow, bigoted and chauvinistic but he had the potential to grow and be flexible.

'You could tie us up. We've got a whip. No?'

I had little doubt that despite his being out of favour with Sultan Muzaffar Shah, he would one day assume the throne of Gujarat. Would there be peace between us if I was Maharana of Mewar by then? I doubted it. Malwa was across our borders to the south-east and its king Mahmud Khalji II was erratic and weak. Bahadur was sure to annex it. We were in between. Gujarat was a young kingdom compared to ours. He would go to war with us. At least he was an enemy worth fighting. Guerilla tactics would very likely misfire against him. He was like me. He studied his friends and enemies. He was curious and he didn't forget past defeats and offences.

'He applied a burning cinder to my thigh and twisted Din's arm till she fainted.' The girls had been narrating many a rare pleasure through my reveries. 'Would that please you?'

I had lost them. I seemed to recall that they had at some point switched to Vikramaditya. Did they like pain or did it come with the job? If only they could have broken my brother's or Bahadur's arm or torched their privates. I knew then what was wrong with them. It had never occurred to either of them that someone could and should take the trouble, infinite trouble, to give them pleasure. There was a knock on the door.

'Forgive me, Your Highness.'

'Come in.'

Kausalya opened the doors very slightly. I knew she had her back to me.

'Will you please excuse the young ladies?'

I did not ask what, why, wherefore. Kausalya is not in the habit of intruding on a private party.

'How much time do they have?'

'A minute and a half at the most.'

They did not wait for me to ask, request or order them to leave. The customer's pleasure was the only thing that mattered. Raat, maybe it was Din, tossed her breasts into her blouse and locked them up for the night while the sister tied the strings of her ghagra. They tried to put the musical instruments back in the corner of the room.

'Leave them be. I apologize to both of you. Perhaps some other time. You'll be paid in full, of course.'

They bowed out, their backs to the door till Kausalya pulled them aside and took them to her room. Just in time too.

A heavily cowled person walked in with four guards. Father.

For His Majesty to attempt to disguise himself was like an elephant trying to move about incognito. Who could mistake the limp and the drag and authority of the man?

'Leave us.'

The guards left. Father dragged a seat to my bedside and sat down. I turned on my side to touch his feet. He picked up his bad leg to allow my hand to make contact with it and then put it down.

'May Shri Eklingji's blessings be upon you.' He looked around, then sniffed the air. 'I see that you've had company. I'm relieved that you are not that disabled that you cannot indulge yourself.' Nothing escapes Father. No wonder he outlasted his brothers. 'How is the leg?'

'Improving, thank you.'

'Do the hands and arms come next? Or are you planning to break your neck first?' He smiled. He knew I did not associate wit or laughter with him.

'Your Majesty did not come here to humour me at one in the morning.'

'I came to enquire after your health. You are my son, the eldest as a matter of fact.'

'I never for a moment forget that fact.'

His face clouded and he looked uncomfortable. Perhaps he had hoped to come to the subject of his visit after a few preliminary indirections. But I seemed to have scotched all possibility of light banter.

'It appears nobody else in our kingdom can either. They ask that you be stripped of your rank and titles and imprisoned for life.'

'You are the regent of none other than Lord Eklingji himself, the Maharana of Mewar by divine ordinance. What other opinion can prevail when you are the paramount power in the kingdom?'

'That is unquestionably so, my son. But the key to sovereignty lies in never bringing a critical issue to a head. Put it to the test and you may discover that economics, cultural factors, unforeseen circumstances like droughts, floods and famines, the obedient or indifferent masses, not to mention the vassals, nobility, middlemen and traders, priests and the landed gentry, may tip the balance against you, perchance topple you. The idea is to go with the flow. You may generate the undercurrents, occasionally even swim against the tide, so long as you maintain the formal proprieties.'

What finely reasoned words and how politic. His contention that the court and the populace were clamouring for my imprisonment was clearly far-fetched and for ulterior motives. (I may be powerless and prone but Kausalya, Mangal and my newly discovered counsellor, my wife, have their networks which are far more sensitive to public opinion than Father's inner circle of sycophants, and they would have warned me.) But even if I were to grant the point for the purposes of academic discussion, would Father have the courage and candour to admit that the direction of the tide was generated by Queen Karmavati and her beloved son, my brother Vikramaditya?

'On what charges would they arraign me?'

'Conspiracy and treason against the crown. Affronting the dignity of the court. Egregious and criminal defiance of the most revered traditions of Rajput honour and valour. Inciting subordinate officers and the soldiery from our armies to set up a parallel centre of power. The list goes on.'

305

'In that case His Majesty must forthwith start proceedings against the accused in the highest court of law in the country.'

'Do not presume,' His Majesty did not raise his voice, 'to advise me about how to conduct the business of the state, Prince.'

Why were this man and I at cross-purposes? Even as he snubbed me, I respected his magnificent imperiousness and his sense of the dignity of his office. Openness or the heart-to-heart chat are alien to Father's nature. They are to me too. On the other hand, I could take a calculated risk, and throw myself at his mercy. But I had no intention of falling into the trap Father was so carefully setting up for me. He works out his strategy before any encounter and would surely have considered the possibility of my trying to throw him off guard. Having told me to shut up, he would have to make the next move. That dead eye of his watched me fixedly. Perhaps he would never again talk to me. Perhaps he would leave. Then I saw him do something he reserves for the rarest occasions. It is one of the most disconcerting and effective ploys in his arsenal. He shoved his index finger thoughtfully into the socket of his dead eye and foraged around inside. I sought to keep an impassive face. I think I didn't do too badly but I might as well have screamed or ranted. He savoured the effect he was having on me. He understood that I was willing to tear and gouge out my own eyes just so I could stop his exploration.

'I have a document with me. Sign it and there'll be no more talk of treason, dishonour or whatever from anybody. All your offices will be restored to you. You'll be back in the War Council and you'll be guiding all those projects that are important to the welfare and security of the country.'

'May I see the paper, Father?'

'Of course. Have I not always told you never to sign anything unless you've read it?'

He handed me the paper. It said that I would relinquish the title Maharaj Kumar and all claims to the crown.

'Trust me, son. It's a mere formality. People have short memories. In time they'll forget all the fuss and we can tear up the paper.'

It was odd. I was sorely tempted. He was using all the phony words, the kind that come with 'Danger' written all over them. And yet I believed him.

'Would you have signed it, if Grandfather had asked you to withdraw from the field in favour of your brothers, Uncle Prithviraj and Uncle Jaimal?'

'It's a temporary measure, a mere sop. You have my word.'

'Will you sign a document with words to that effect?'

'Don't be insolent.'

'Frankly, even if you did, I would not put my signature on the paper.'

His voice was low but the threat of retribution was in his good eye. 'This is your last chance, son.'

I thought he would strike me or run his sword through me. He sighed and then rose. He stood with his eyes closed. What a long night it was. Was it also my last night of freedom? His shoulders slumped and he looked old. He walked to the door and opened it. His guards came to attention. He walked back to me. 'What will be, will be.' He touched my forehead. 'Is it true that you were wounded badly seven times on the front and forbade Rao Viramdev from writing to me about it?'

'Minor nicks and cuts, Your Majesty.'

'Now you even lie to your father.'

'When have you ever spoken about your wounds?'

'You are a prophet who's come before his time. An early bird waking up people just a little after the hour of midnight.'

Chapter 24

$\mathcal{J}$t was a morning of sullen and lucid beauty. The Gambhiree was a festering gold rupture in the plains below Chittor. Someone had plucked the sunflower in the sky and torn off the petals and smashed the glowering bulb at the centre. The light was angry pollen scattered from horizon to horizon. It was in a state of constant flux but refused to rise or descend. Soon I would be covered in a patina of yellow dust. It would enter my lungs, burnish them and fill up the holes in my bronchi till all the air had been forced out and I would stand petrified forever in gold in honour of my ancestor, the Sun-god. Gangs of peacocks were out, celebrating the sudden break in the monsoons, fanning out their one-eyed feathers in shimmering waves. The peahens with their acrid scent of sex flew for short bursts and cawed mercilessly while pretending indifference to the frenzied attentions of their future mates.

It had looked as if the rains would never come. The granaries were half empty and the Gambhiree was a cracked bed of stones, pebbles, rusting coins and other detritus of life, an abandoned and shrunken skeleton with the occasional puddle and a ragged trickle of water. They had already started rationing the water and food in the fort. Two and a half months after everybody had given up on the rains, the sky was tarred over, the Sun-god was shut out, the moon and the stars banished and a final darkness closed in on the earth. There was no air to breathe, the birds disappeared and babies choked silently. No rain. The displeasure of the gods with Mewar was obvious. There was only one remedy. Appeasement. A propitious day was chosen by the priests to conduct a mahayagnya for mercy and rains. It took a week of frantic preparations. When the wood, ghee, milk, coconuts, turmeric powder, camphor and kumkum were in place and the fires about to be lit and the darkness lifted, it started to rain. It continued for a month and a half. What were the gods trying to tell us?

It was a beautiful morning if you could hold your breath, or better still, never breathe again for Chittor was in the grip of cholera and the stench of death, debris and excreta was unbearable. I had been in exile in my own home for over seven months. Father was right, people have short memories. I was not ignored, I was forgotten. I'm not quite sure which is more insulting. Those who could afford to, have left Chittor, among them His Majesty, Queen Karmavati and Vikramaditya and most of the court. In a sense I have the run of the capital once again.

The roads are slush, a wild and exuberant mix of rainwater and shit that races along open gutters, clogs them and leaps out with abandon. Nothing new, this. In the summer, the heat cakes and disinfects everything instantly. In the winter, lips chap, the skin cracks and the drainage and sewage waters dry up. In the rains, mud, earth, water and faeces are one gurgling, churning mess. And yet seventeen monsoons have gone by, albeit there were two years of drought, without the visitation of cholera. Why do epidemics occur in some years and not in others? Where do they come from and why do they vanish after they've killed half, sometimes three-fourths of the populace? Three thousand seven hundred and eighteen dead so far. How many more to go before the cholera dies out?

All night long there were cries and screams and moans. It was Vikramaditya's parting gift to me: the cholera, the rumour went, was retribution for what I had done to the Gujarati soldiers in an early dawn attack. The story took hold. The people of Chittor had found their scapegoat. The hostility that Father had spoken of had come to pass. At first they went inside and banged the doors shut if I rode down a street. On two occasions they attacked me. The first time I defended myself with my sword till Mangal joined me and beat them back. The next time, I got off Befikir. Mangal was aghast and told me to get back into saddle, ride home and send reinforcements while he took care of the mob. It had been barely six or seven men when I was spotted. There were at least twenty-five now, a murmuring, maleficent lot waiting for someone to make the first move. 'Only blood will quench the thirst of blood,' a short man shouted and drew his sword. A boy of twelve threw a stone which hit me in the chest. They were milling around me now. A treasonous and criminal act needs to gather momentum before it can be executed. Mangal's sword was about to come down on the man closest to him to divert attention when I raised my hand. He stopped but did not sheathe the sword.

'Kill me,' I said, 'kill me now if it will rid Chittor of cholera. You will do the country a great favour.'

They waited. They had not expected me to be a party to their decision. A white-haired woman with at least fifteen of her thirty-two teeth missing came forward and spoke up.

'Just because there are fifty fools here who are willing to believe any nonsense they are told, it does not mean that you have to follow their example and make an ass of yourself, Your Highness. With your permission, Highness, I want to ask these gentlemen gathered here one question,' the old woman wasn't finished with my would-be assailants or me. 'They are obviously wiser than you are, Maharaj Kumar, so you'll forgive me if I ask them and not you. How should we deal with an enemy? Should we breast-feed the vipers so that they can bury their poisonous fangs in our flesh and wipe us out? I was a wife once who lost her husband. I was a mother who lost her nine sons. I was a grandmother who lost seventeen grandsons, all of them in wars. I had one great-grandson left. When he marched to Gujarat with you, I thought now I'm truly orphaned. But you brought him back, Highness. You got back Idar and you avenged the deaths of three thousand soldiers and Rajendra Simha. Now, if that is not honourable, will these fine gentlemen tell me what is? As for you Maharaj Kumar,' it was my turn to get a dressing down, 'the trouble with you is that you are tough abroad and soft on the people at home. Don't take shelter behind your shyness. In your position, it is no virtue. Get yourself a trumpet and blow it. Where have all the charans and poets who sing of the exploits of heroes gone? If someone's silenced them for their own ends, a little greasing of the palms will unloosen their tongues.' She smiled slyly, and toothlessly. 'How about hiring Joharibai, that's me?' There was a pregnant pause here. 'As of today?' She was a terrific actress with a pungent turn of phrase and was obviously enjoying herself. The audience loved her and burst out laughing.

She laid her forehead on my feet. As I picked her up she looked around at the crowd that was at least four times the earlier group. 'Now bend your head, Maharaj Kumar, so that an old, old crone, so old as a matter of fact that I may just decide never to die, can bless you.' She took my face in her hands. Her palms felt like crumpled paper that was about to disintegrate. 'God bless you, Your Highness.'

The Gambhiree is downgrading its currency from gold to silver as the sun ascends and gets a tighter grip on the day. Will the respite from the rains last? There are few sights as beautiful as the Gambhiree in spate. There's a violence to her that is both terrifying and exhilarating. She's untamed, out of control and lethal. The monsoons are her favourite season. It's easy to see why, the engorged sky bruising and bloodying her, spilling its sperm into her. But enough is enough. If only it will stop raining for a week or ten days, the earth may dry and perhaps the cholera ease a bit.

It's always the same. The first two days the men, women and grown-up children make it to the toilet outside. Thirty, forty times. They spurt and squirt like a fist of fury. They pour out everything they've got, bewildered by the discovery of this raging and writhing python they had thought of as their stomach and intestines. For a couple more days they'll crawl out of the house to defecate. After that they can't move and their shit is thinner than pee. They lie in a stupor of exhaustion, mouths dry and open, the unseeing eyes scanning the ceiling with this thin ribbon of diarrhoea, their only sign of life. Their breathing gets so attenuated, the cart drivers have loaded still-living bodies on four or five occasions.

Following the carts are the scavenger birds. Why did the gods make vultures and their ilk — take hyenas — so grotesquely ugly and repugnant? Is it because they live off death? There is, however, one exception. Have you observed a crow? It is sharp and sly and its black coat is shining and slick. You may not like it but it's a compact hustler, a bird of the world. The vulture now is an altogether

311

different story. Difficult to find a more bedraggled, seedy and uncouth creature. Nothing arouses it except the sight of food. Then too it gets up grudgingly and eats with an expression of extreme distaste. It must be hard work to consume against its will. But this is one task it will not shirk. Even with a full and bursting belly, it continues to work its way through whatever carrion there is, never mind if it takes another hour or a full day.

The sun is on the run again. Dirty, smudged clouds the colour of ash are blowing in from the east and a slow, warm and sticky rain has begun to fall. The raindrops are bloated leeches reluctant to move. They cling to the skin and when they are pulled off forcibly, they leave behind a powdery charcoal film. This is not a rain that washes you clean. It fogs your mind and leaves you feeling soiled.

The peahens must have grown weary of play-acting or they've realized that if they play demure any longer, the cocks will walk away and they'll have to wait till next year to have a good time. Suddenly there's a flurry of activity. The petulance, shyness, mincing and don't-touch-me are forsaken for an instant and the males are all over, atop their partners. I watch their frantic goings-on from the window of the palace. Do they not know the gravity of the occasion? Do they not see death stalking the land?

'Lakshman Simhaji sends you his greetings. Would you do him the favour of going to his office immediately?' the servant's voice was apologetic.

The peacocks had an expression of smug and brimming fulfillment as they rested deep inside their womenfolk. I turned back from the window and followed the man to the Defence Minister's office.

'I want you and the Princess to leave Chittor immediately,' Lakshman Simhaji came straight to the point.

'On what grounds, Uncle?'

'On what grounds?' He was puzzled and a little irritated by my question. 'Isn't that obvious? Your lives are at risk, that's why.'

'From whom?'

'What's come over you, Maharaj Kumar? I always thought of you as one of our most sensible young men who would never put

312

his or anybody else's life in unnecessary danger.' I still didn't get his drift. 'From the cholera, what else?' He saw the look of relief on my face and laughed. 'What did you think?'

'I don't know what to think anymore, Uncle.'

'You've begun to see red everywhere which is not unreasonable, considering ...' He didn't finish the sentence. 'Somebody else in your position would most likely have done something thoughtless and wild. Now, is it settled that you and your wife will leave tomorrow morning?'

'I cannot vouch for my wife, you'll have to talk to her and see what she has to say. But I have work here.'

'If you don't go, you know very well the Princess won't go either.'

'She may not go even if I do which I have no intention of doing. She has commitments here.'

'There's no work here that the health officers cannot manage.'

'Which health officers, Uncle? We don't even have a secretariat of health, let alone a ministry. The five officers appointed were transferred from the ministries of revenue and agriculture. They are not trained or motivated and have neither enough powers nor money.'

'That's not true, I've blocked off five percent of this year's defence budget to combat this epidemic.'

'I'm not finished yet, Uncle. Two of the officers are dead.'

'That's precisely it. I cannot in all conscience permit the same fate to overtake the heir apparent. It took me three weeks to persuade His Majesty to leave Chittor. I'm not going to spend another three weeks trying to cajole you into leaving.' He was out of breath and those soft baby jowls on his face were in a tizzy with anger.

'I do not underestimate your concern for our well-being. I'm grateful to you for having forced Father to go away. Had I been His Majesty's only son, I would have considered it my duty to preserve my life and secure the future of Mewar. But the line of succession has, in the event of my demise, six princes of the blood. Someone from the royal family must be in Chittor if our people are not to feel abandoned and lose morale and heart altogether.'

'I am of the royal family,' his voice was a dangerous rumble. He had drawn himself up straight and was in full possession of his dignity.

'So you are, Uncle. If the capital is still running, it is because of your presence and leadership. But I am the son of His Majesty, for better or worse, the eldest one and I would like to stay with our people. And if you'll permit me, to work under you.' Lest I compromise his relationship with Father, I immediately added, 'Only in an unofficial capacity.'

I think my uncle was genuinely touched and so became even gruffer than normal. 'You were always obstinate as a mule. No point trying to din some sense into you at this late age.'

✳ ✳ ✳

Perhaps every crisis needs a saviour. My wife fitted the role perfectly in this time of pestilence. She had begun to have a substantial following. And it was not just women who flocked around her. The survivors in town including patients who had the strength to move, joined her at the Brindabani Temple at seven in the morning and at night for arati. She and I hardly saw each other since she camped out most of the day and sometimes part of the night in front of the Flautist and prayed to him to come to the succour of Chittor.

Kausalya had requisitioned an old property close to the Brindabani Temple and converted it into a children's orphanage. She named it Nandanvan. Never one for light talk, she became more and more silent. Sometimes she would come home and bury her head in my shoulder. That was the only way I would know that there had been an unusual number of deaths at the children's home or that one of the children she had grown attached to or worked round-the-clock to save, had not made it. We made love at times. She never said no. Perhaps it gave her something else to think about as it did for me. The peacocks, I realized, were not alone. We make love regardless of grief, indifference, death, happiness, pain.

One Thursday evening I took the civil engineer to Nandanvan. Kausalya had told me a few nights before that the roof of the orphanage had sprung many leaks and in some places it was merely a matter of time before the rafters, supports and tiles came crashing down. We were late and riding at a good clip because the roads were almost empty. Who would venture out after seven these days?

So I thought. I was wrong. The deserted roads, at least in this one instance, had nothing to do with the epidemic. Everybody in Chittor, dead or alive, young or old, civilian and soldier, whores, pimps, men, women and children, everybody was at the Brindabani Temple. Was it the Flautist's feast? Had the idols been stolen, was there an accident? There wasn't room to move. The Temple and the wide Maharana Kumbha Path were filled to overflowing. Some of the people were shivering but being drenched or ill with fever did not bother them. The crowds saw me and took hold of Befikir's reins. No Joharibai to the rescue this time, not even the intrepid and loyal Mangal to defend me against a mob of thousands. My companion too was made to dismount.

'Leave him alone. Only I'm accountable.' Nobody paid me any heed. They merely parted to make way for me. I did not know that the cycle of birth and death can take place in the same life. Hell is not some other place and some other life. It is going through the same, terrible experiences again and again. I was at the steps. I had heard that voice years ago, I had heard it today as we turned into the Maharana Kumbha avenue and rode down at a gallop but my mind would not admit its reality. Was it the same song? Frankly, I don't recall. Yes, you do, every word of it and you know damn well, this one's different. One step at a time, Maharaj Kumar, one step and one more and you'll be on top of Mount Kailash. There she was strumming the ektara with her fingers, her eyes closed and her body whirling and rotating in a trance. When she came to the refrain, all those thousands of people picked it up and lifted it heavenwards. They repeated it lustily again and again till at some predetermined signal, she went on to the next verse.

> What is a flower, if it cannot bloom?
> What is air if it cannot fill the lungs?
> What is water if it cannot quench thirst?
> What is the sun if it cannot give the body heat?
> What is a body if it cannot give pleasure?

(Trust her, trust her to treat the sensual and the spiritual as one and the same.)

What is a prayer if it cannot rise to heaven?
What is a saviour if he will not save?
Oh Lord, save us, save us, save us.
It took a hundred crimes for you to act against Shishupal.
We've committed a hundred and one. Where are you?
It took the disrobing of Draupadi for you to show up.
We were born naked. Where are you, where are you?
When the wrath of Indra, the king of gods, started the
     deluge,
You lifted a little finger and saved Brindaban. Where
     are you now?
Oh Lord, save us, save us, save us.
Save us from cholera, save us from the plague, save us
     from harm.
What is a saviour if he will not save?

She had worked herself to such a pitch and frenzy in the midst of
the last 'save us, save us' refrain, she collapsed and fell in a heap.
No one moved, then one by one they went and touched her feet.
There should have been a scramble but they formed a queue. How
the times had changed. Nautch girl, slut, the royal whore, the people
of Chittor had called her every dirty name in the language. When
they ran out of them, they invented new ones. Finally her name
itself became synonymous with the faithless wife as mine became
interchangeable with cuckold. Now she was called Chhoti Sant Mai.
If you are exposed long enough, time will get you inured to anything.
The distance between a full stomach and starvation, the normal and
the abnormal, the done and the forbidden, affluence and poverty
is nothing but habit. I had blushed and raged and kicked the plate
of food from her hands when she sang and danced. The last time
I was here, the acid in my belly had burned a hole in my head.
I had given orders that she be confined to her rooms in the palace.
Now when she sings, I don't get into a rage or even shrug my
shoulders. I shut my ears and shut up. Frankly, I've ceased to be
bothered. She goes her way and I mine.
     She came to. She cringed. She sat up, then stood up. She tried

316

to cover her feet with her ghagra, then with her hands, it was no use. They put a coin in the plate and touched her feet with their hands or their foreheads.

'Not mine, not mine, it's his feet, the Lord's feet you must pray at.'

They smiled and moved on. If her feet were inaccessible, they touched the ground she had stood on. If only, I thought, if only Queen Karmavati and Vikramaditya could have been here. Who, after all, had loved her more and wished her better? The priests alone had not changed. They had thought her conduct shameless that fateful Janmashtami day. They had smirked and sneered at her then. They hated her now. I looked at the head priest of the temple. There was loathing and fear in his eyes.

The Little Saint as everyone called my wife now, had usurped their temple and their importance. The Chief Mahant raised his hands. The crowds inside, and as the word was passed around, the people outside, fell silent. 'The priesthood of Chittor has decided to initiate a month-long Sankat-Vighna Yagnya to rid our capital city of the terrible pestilence that has wrought unimaginable havoc,' the priest's voice rang out like a challenge, daring any one, especially the Princess to contradict him. 'The community of priests will take turns round the clock and invoke the gods, appease them and ask for their blessings. We will not rest till they lend a favourable ear to our prayers. The Sankat-Vighna Yagnya is the most powerful antidote available to man against the evil spirits. We give you our word.'

A small voice from the crowds outside piped up, 'The Little Saint is our Yagnya. She is the fire that will cleanse this land ... and all of you.'

It's a wonder that little wiseacre did not bring the Brindabani Temple crashing down. The people laughed as they hadn't for months.

'We will vanquish,' the Chief Mahant's voice rose above the din, 'this evil force that is amongst us.'

Who did he mean? Who was he referring to? The cholera? The little man who had got a laugh out of the public? Or my wife who it would appear did not need the mediation of priests to approach

317

God and was on a first-name basis with Him? Few royal couples had the kind and number of enemies that my wife and I had. We could now count the priests of Chittor amongst them.

'Long Live the Little Saint,' a woman shouted and the cry was taken up by everybody. There was no stopping them.

✳ ✳ ✳

When the civil engineer and I had examined the orphanage at length, he said, 'This is going to cost a lot of money.'

'That's all right. The children need a roof over their heads not just during the crisis but on a permanent basis. Will you give me an estimate by tomorrow?'

'Yes, the building's in bad shape and needs immediate attention.'

'Kausalya, will you ask the Princess to see Lakshman Simhaji with the estimate? Tell her to suggest that the money could come from the plate at her aratis at the Brindabani Temple.'

I may not have had a smile on my face as I said that but deep down I had a feeling of poetic justice and gloating, that for once the temple priests would be paying out of their own coffers for something worthwhile. My pleasures, as you can see, come cheap. But what an enormous price Chittor and I would have to pay for that, the small change of satisfaction. Do you have any idea how many thousands of tons of milk, butter, ghee, fruits and food were poured over the gods and into the fires of the Yagnya, how much wood was consumed, how many lambs sacrificed, how much saffron ground, how many coconuts cracked, how many cooks kept busy night and day? Who are we appeasing and why? Tell me the charge first, sirs, prove it and then declare the punishment. Everything is conjecture, speculation and suspicion. Droughts, famines, floods, epidemics, too much and too little, defeat, deprivation, whether it's personal or universal suffering, the explanation's always the same: we must have done something wrong, terribly wrong. Nobody knows what the crime is, your guess is as good as mine. If we don't know the wrong, how can we correct it? What did my sister Sumitra do, what did Sunheria die for, what is Leelawati's crime?

The notion that the gods can be bought has always seemed dubious and abhorrent to me. There's nothing novel about that thought, I'm sure the sages have said it often and far better. But we continue to pacify the divinities regardless.

The people of Chittor attended the Little Saint's overwrought prayer sessions. She sang and danced and they could join in and she didn't ask for a copper tanka and they could follow her words and the songs were simple and striking and sharp with barbs and insights and the turn of phrase was familiar yet surprising in its juxtapositions and sincerity and emotion and the tunes she set them to were on everybody's lips. But they also went to the Yagnya. They couldn't understand a word of the Sanskrit and even if they could, most of the priests concatenated three or four lines, sometimes an entire verse of a sutra in one breath, so it came out garbled and rushed, maybe even the gods would have a problem deciphering it but the good people of Chittor attended the Yagnya off and on, dropped some money and felt good. It was a great spectacle, this ritual, and besides, it was best to play it safe.

All things come to pass. (Give a pregnant and substantial pause here, then move to the next sentence.) In time. A lovely, ambiguous word that: pass. All things come to be? Or is it that all things that are, are ephemeral, they disappear and vanish? Or are both interpretations right?

In due time the fury of the cholera abated. People were still dying but the numbers were going down. What had broken the back of the epidemic? Do these vile things also have life cycles? Had the Sankat-Vighna Yagnya which went on for a full thirty days as promised by the priests forced the hand of the gods? Or was it my wife's prayers which did it? The people of Chittor, whoever's left that is, certainly think it's the latter. The gods may have recalled the curse and saved us but they did so only because the Little Saint asked them, especially the Flautist, to intervene. Whoever or whatever it was who had put an end to the disease, I was willing to go on my knees and thank the powers that be that the nightmare was over.

Chapter 25

 Beware the paramour. In times of need, he'll abandon you with greater alacrity than your enemies.

It was almost at the end, in the very last stages of the epidemic that the Maharaj Kumar's consort caught the infection. She didn't let on the first few days. Maybe it was her time of the month, Kausalya thought. Or she was exhausted, so were they all, except that she had always been so delicate. Soon it was no longer possible to conceal it and the Raj Vaidya was called to treat her. Frankly, as far as her husband was concerned, that was a mere formality. After all, her lover and her god wasn't going to allow her to die. He had, if one was to believe the claims made on his behalf, put a halt to the rampant death in Chittor because the Little Saint had asked him to. The days passed and the rotting thin watery smell seeped from her apartment into the Maharaj Kumar's suite of rooms. He could hear her retching. The sound was almost inaudible now, but there was no cause for worry. Unless they appear at the eleventh hour, the Prince thought, they won't be taken for gods. If you recall, the Flautist didn't turn up to rescue Draupadi till the Kauravas were well into disrobing her. The Blue One had been, there's no question about it, fully cognizant of the disgraceful behaviour of the villains and the silence of all the elders in the assembly hall while they watched the undressing of Draupadi patiently. But if you are to make a lasting impression, the timing of your entry is of the essence. The Flautist would arrive all right ... but only in the very nick of time.

In the meantime the town was rife with rumours. Actually it was the same rumour with a number of variations. The Little Saint had made a deal with the gods: her life in return for the lives of the people at Chittor. Within a couple of days it was no longer a rumour, it was the absolute, certified truth. Crowds of people stood outside the main palace walls at all hours waiting for half-hourly bulletins about her health. The rains had stopped and the vultures had almost disappeared but when the Prince looked out of the window, he was sure that the birds had congregated outside the palace. The fact was that the Little Saint's devotees were not really waiting. They knew for certain that his wife would die. Like good carrion-eaters, they wanted to be there in time for the big event.

That night Kausalya knocked and asked permission to come into his suite. He was impatient with her formality.

'What is it?'

'Your Highness, would you care to come and see her just this once? She has been in a coma for more than twenty-four hours. She's come to for a minute. I think she would be happy to see you.'

He would have sniggered mirthlessly but for the fact that Kausalya would not look him in the eye.

'What do you expect me to do?'

'I doubt it if she'll make it till morrow.'

He was about to say don't exaggerate when Kausalya said, 'Please.' There was something in that voice, something in that word that sounded alien on Kausalya's tongue. He strode past her, perhaps ran, he didn't recall and was at his wife's bedside. She looked younger than the day he first saw her. She had lost so much weight, she was, he had no doubt in his mind about it, an apparition. A wraith-like figure that would flicker a few more times and then withdraw into wherever orphaned waifs disappear. She smiled or did he imagine it? Her hand rose a millimetre, he was daydreaming. He went to her bed and knelt down. He picked up her hand and cradled it. Her lips moved. Did it matter that he was hallucinating? He drew close to her till his left ear was almost touching her lips.

'Forgive me, Highness. No man and no god could have borne the pain and suffering I have inflicted upon you. No man and no god has your fortitude or your dignity. You did not deserve someone as cold and ungrateful as I. But that is fate. You did not disown me or your fate. I will not forget your kindness. This may sound like a bad joke but to the very limits of my soul and beyond it, I have loved you. A strange love, but love nevertheless. Thank you.'

Her voice petered out. Her eyes clouded. He felt her pulse. If he imagined hard enough he could feel it once every fifteen or twenty seconds. He felt nothing. In all those vast spaces in the whorls of his fingers, in the tiny honeycomb holes of his lungs, in the chambers of his heart, and in the cosmos which was too small to fit into a tiny wedge of his head, there was silence and nothingness. And then the first tiny glimmer of a wave rose. It was followed by another and another, till it became a tidal wave. And it was nothing but one superstructure of anger toppling the one before. How could her lover, the one for whom she had made a cuckold and laughing-stock of him, how could he have abandoned her? Where was his miracle? The time for a theatrical entry was well past. Where was that god, that shameless, cavalier Flautist who had ditched thousands of women and was now, true to form and legend, ditching his wife? What difference did it make to him, one woman less or more?

All the difference in the world to me, though, the Maharaj Kumar thought. Because whatever your peeve and however great your grievance, you don't abandon the people who are yours.

'Water, lemon, salt, honey. Three blankets.' Did he whisper, did he scream? Within minutes the retainers had brought the things he had asked for. He covered her cold body and forced a few teaspoons of fresh lime juice into her mouth.

'The Raj Vaidya has said that she's not to be fed under any circumstances,' one of the maids ventured to tell him.

'Leave me. No one will enter these rooms without my orders. Tell Kausalya Mai to make kanji every four hours and a quarter glass of fruit juice every two hours. I want one more bed in the room. Leave two buckets of water here, one with hot water and the other with khas grass, mind you, not the attar of khas. And bring plenty of soft towels.'

Whenever she was fed, she threw up what seemed like twice the quantity. Every hour or so her bedsheet and mattress were wet with a few drops of faeces. Which is why the school of medicine to which the Raj Vaidya and almost all other doctors belonged, believed that any liquids aggravated the condition and hastened death. The only time a patient was force-fed with liquids was when the medicinal powders had to be given either with water or honey. As to food, semisolid and solid, the patient usually didn't want it and the doctors advised against it even during a routine fever. The other school, whose followers could be counted on the fingers of one hand, thought that at the best of times, life without fluids and semi-solids was impossible. In a severely debilitated condition, they believed, a zero-diet would be suicidal. The disease seemed to kill either way, but the Maharaj Kumar was inclined to think that if you didn't give fuel to the body how would it have the wherewithal to fight the disease?

It had been a highly contentious issue not just between the two sets of doctors, but between His Highness and the proponents of the starvation diet. Fortunately, the poor could not afford doctors most of the time and were blissfully unaware of the controversy. They drank water or refrained from doing so depending on their frame of mind and energy levels.

Though she was semi-comatose and listless, the Princess resisted all offers of sustenance but the Maharaj Kumar was firm and persistent. Often she refused to open her mouth. He held the teaspoon of juice at her lips for minutes on end. When she continued in her obstinacy, he blackmailed her.

'I've no objection to your suffering but I don't see why I should be made to hold a spoon till my hand falls off.'

If she could, she opened her eyes and looked at him piteously or with anger and loathing. It was pointless. He was willing to stoop to any means to force that damned juice and honey down her throat. One thing was certain, the only reason she survived that first night was because she had to wake up to retch and puke everything he fed her. He turned her on her side, wiped her mouth and body with a wet cloth when the vomit dribbled down her blouse and cleaned the cleavage between her buttocks gently when she had soiled herself. He changed her clothes and picked her up. This was when he realized that she would not require a change of clothes again. She was so weightless and her breathing so laboured, it was a matter of an hour or two before she receded into everlasting oblivion. He felt discouraged and hopeless. It was his pathological hatred of the Flautist that kept him going. Because if he didn't, it would mean that her lover had once again beaten him. He put her on the other bed, so that the bedsheet and the jute cloth under the first could be removed.

For days she hovered in a twilight zone.

'Please,' she said, 'please let go of me.'

He smiled to himself. How could he, for years now her betrayal of him was the only thing that had kept him going. What would he do without her?

'Get up. Stop stalling. Is there no end to your selfishness? I haven't done any work since you decided to indulge yourself. The children from the orphanage are dying and so are all the other sick people. Don't you think it's about time you got up and took care of them?'

She closed her eyes. Why had he gone out of his mind when she had spurned him on their wedding night? She had the same bulges or projections that Sunheria, Kausalya or any woman had. They might be higher or lower, bigger or smaller, loose and dangling or firm and steady, but they were all breasts with a springy centrepiece and the same went for the slit in the middle. Wasn't Kausalya good enough for him? Under normal circumstances he would have married two or three other princesses by now anyway. There had been more than enough offers and on two occasions the Maharana had been genuinely upset with him because not only were these important political alliances, the girls were supposed to be exceptionally attractive and talented. Even Rao Viramdev had suggested that he marry Rao Ganga's granddaughter after the Rao's death. It would be a gesture of appreciation of the services of the deceased to Mewar and strengthen the bonds between the two kingdoms. Besides, his wife's uncle assured him that the girl did not have an iota of malice in her; just an inexhaustible supply of sweetness and vivacity.

No, the Maharaj Kumar still couldn't fathom what all the fuss was about. Once you had discounted extremes of caricature like buck teeth, squint eyes and exaggerated tics, why were some men and women more desirable and in demand than others? What was so special about his wife except that she had said no to him? Look at her now. She had shrivelled and her legendary transparent complexion was the colour of the slate he had used as a child. There wasn't enough skin to go around and it seemed as if it was about to split open. Those breasts which had driven him to a voyeuristic sexual frenzy the night he had caught her in flagrante delicto were dry and creased and pitiably small.

A phosphorescent green and mouldy syrup oozed out of her mouth. He wiped it with a piece of cloth. It smelled sour and looked poisonous enough to bore a hole through the palace floor. Was this the cholera or were these the final remains in her stomach? Was the Flautist watching? Would he want to make love to this woman again? Down below beyond the tall security wall of the palace, the crowds were singing one of her songs.

> In death and in life, I'm yours, yours alone.
> Take me. Do what you will with me.
> As stone or stray dog, as roach or rose, as fish or fowl,
> Whatever the shape of reincarnation, I'm yours, yours
>   alone.
> You are free to reject me: I will never deny you.
> Beware, my beloved, of the pleasures of my body and
>   soul.
> You are mine, mine alone.
> I'm your bride, your mistress, your slave.
> Has it occurred to you, my Lord,
> that you can only take and I can only give?
>
> You've had your day. Time to listen to me now.
> A god is but a stone till a devotee comes along
> and paints it vermillion.
> In death and in life, I'm yours, yours alone.
> Take me. Do what you will with me.

The irony of the situation made him smile. There was a time when it would have made him run his sword through her and

325

himself. She was in his arms and even as she was breathing her last, she was embracing someone else. Kausalya brought the rice broth, more like rice soup with a bit of chicken stock for nourishment. His hand shook as he took the bowl from her.

'Sleep a little, Highness, I'll feed her.'

'I'm more pigheaded than you are. I don't give in to her pleas to drink the kanji some other time.'

He took a tablespoon of the translucent broth and tilted it in his wife's mouth which was always half-open these days so she could get as much air as possible. She gagged and it trickled down. When she had settled down, he started again.

'I'll be firm with her. You've been here for seven days and nursed her night and day. If you should fall ill, I'll not be able to look after two patients.'

He ran his hand over his chin and face. There was a good growth of stubble there. Should he grow a beard? He looked at Kausalya. She was not about to give in and she was right. He gave her the bowl and went and lay down on the other bed. His wife was dead. She was fortunate to die before her husband, so Kausalya bathed her and draped her wedding ghagra around her. He walked ahead of the bier, the clay pot of agni in his hand. The whole of Chittor, even the priests from the Brindabani Temple had come to say goodbye to her. All the way down to the banks of the river, they sang the songs they had learnt from her. They placed her gently on the logs. She lay silent and serene as if waiting expectantly. He remembered his wedding day. It was the first time he had seen her and he had promised her many things. He had not fulfilled any of those vows. He had no business letting her go. He lit the torch from the fire in the earthen pot and touched the edge of her ghagra and then the logs. The flames caught instantly and surged upwards. The Flautist rose from them. He smiled. 'The time for miracles, my friend, may I call you that,' he asked the Maharaj Kumar superciliously, 'is not the eleventh hour. It is the twelfth.' He passed his hand over the flames and they retreated and died down. He kissed her lips. 'Wake up, dearest.' She opened her eyes. They were suffused with an infinite love. He picked her up in his arms and they ascended to the sky.

'She hasn't thrown up the last three times I've fed her,' Kausalya told him.

'How long have I been asleep?'

'Eleven hours, no, more like twelve.'

The razor slipped out of his hand at least three times and nicked him badly.

'I should let it slit your throat.' There was nobody in the room but he knew who it was. Bhootani Mata was slashing his body, long clean gashes from which the blood welled up eagerly. 'I warned you it was no easy task. What you wanted me to do was to overturn the very scheme of the universe, interfere with the private affairs of the gods themselves.' The razor was going for his face now. 'But you wouldn't listen. You said you didn't give a damn about the costs or the consequences. You wanted the job done and quote, "no excuses, please". I tried for years but anything and everything I attempted misfired. She got away. This time around I didn't take any chances. I don't want any more wrong blood on my hands. I planned for months, I worked out every single detail. Nothing could go wrong. I gave her cholera. And what do you do on the night that she's supposed to breathe her last? You suddenly enter the picture. You countermand the doctor's instructions, you force-feed her, you wipe her mouth and clean her arse, you sit in that room with its noxious fumes and you nurse her. You fuck up all my efforts and you bring her back from the dead. I should have given you the shits, not her. That way I would have got rid of all my problems once and for all.'

'Didn't want the wrong blood on your hands, you said and you killed half of Chittor to get at one little defenceless woman? Nine and half thousand dead as of last count and you call that a surefire hit? Even the gods won't be able to save us from your precision.'

'She may have those thugs up there in heaven taking care of her, but I've got you, you little twerp. Nobody here or in the heavens wants to protect you. Frankly almost everybody would give his right arm, including His Majesty who's already lost his other, to be rid of you. But that would be too easy. You are so clever and smart, nobody, not even an army of your worst enemies could wish you the kind of troubles you bring upon your own head. I'm going to sit in the wings and savour every setback, every humiliation you invent for yourself.'

Chapter 26

$\mathcal{W}$ithin a week, Greeneyes was walking about the house. On the tenth day she visited the orphanage. Rather, she intended to. The people of Chittor had got word that the Little Saint had resurfaced and stopped her at the Brindabani Temple. They forced the priests to bring out the image of the Flautist and installed it outside. From there on it was chaos. No Diwali, no festival, no birth, no victory in Chittor had ever been celebrated the way the Little Saint's return was. They made her sing, they danced. They sang her songs, they carried her in a palanquin round the city. They stopped traffic, everything came to a halt. Offices were closed and shops shuttered. Everybody including the Commissioner of Police, the security guards, even some priests laid their heads at her feet. My uncle, my very own gruff and undeviatingly practical and hard-nosed uncle was about to bend down (don't ask me how, the fort would have collapsed with his weight; we wouldn't have known how to lift him and would have had to bury him there in front of the Temple) when the wise woman that my wife is, touched his feet and said, 'Not you, Your Highness. Do not embarrass me in front of all these people.' Wisdom or discretion prevailed but only for a minute. For the whole city now had two pairs of feet to touch: the Saint's and Lakshman Simhaji's.

The procession had to stop at every house where there was a married woman. The woman of the house lit a lamp and performed an arati. It was evening by the time they had come full circle and were back at the Brindabani Temple. Every street and home was lit with clay lamps, everybody was distributing sweets to everybody. Someone suggested that the Little Saint be weighed in gold. Within minutes my wife was sitting in one plate of a balance that had been

329

transported from one of the godowns for storing grain. Bangles, studs, ear and nose rings, anklets, belts, chokers, necklaces fell into the other plate and slowly, imperceptibly my wife began to rise. It was a thrilling sight, the ascension of the Little Saint; soon the two pans were level with each other and yet they kept piling the gold ornaments and jewellery. My wife was up in the air now. 'You must stop,' she cried. 'You must stop now.' But nobody listened to her. Suddenly the sky lit up with fireworks, the Police Commissioner's gift to the city. For a full hour lighted fountains rose in the air. Rubies and diamonds and emeralds exploded in the most stunning patterns. You would have thought that the crowds would wind up and head for home after that spectacular show. But the revelries continued. The men and women and children sang songs, danced, and drank bhang. The Little Saint was made to sing the folk songs of Merta. Jugglers, nautanki actors and actresses, acrobats, charans, anybody with some talent put up a five or ten-minute show to entertain the crowds and themselves. At the end of each act, they clapped with gusto, regardless of how accomplished or boring or unconsciously funny the participants had been. My wife begged to be let off. They allowed her to go after the morning arati to the Flautist.

The next day Chittor was officially declared safe and the gates thrown open for the commerce of life to resume after months of isolation. The bridge over the Gambhiree was busy day and night. The families who had left Chittor during the blight — bless them, for what would we have done if we had had to feed and look after thousands more — came back home one by one. Soon Father and the Court too returned. Life was back to normal.

I got my marching orders within ten days. I was to proceed to Kumbhalgarh forthwith with my wife, the 'with' was underlined, and supervise the repairs on the fortifications in consultation with the governor of the fort, Rawat Sumer Simha.

Now who could say Father didn't have a sense of humour? Kumbhalgarh, built by my great-grandfather, Maharana Kumbha, was not just one of the finest forts in the whole of Mewar, it was not even fifty years old and in superb condition. I was not quite sure who was being transferred this time, me, my wife or both?

Obviously word about the change in the status of the nautch girl had reached Queen Karmavati and my brother Vikramaditya. I must say that I couldn't blame the pair of them for taking remedial measures immediately. If push came to shove, I could be tried for treason, jailed or exiled. On what charges were they going to try my wife? It would be difficult to convict or slander a saint. Even the priests who were no partisans of the Little Saint had vetoed a suggestion from Queen Karmavati to ban the evening prayers which she led, as too risky. Bump her off and she would become an instant martyr. Her death would redound to my greater glory and there was a remote chance that I might become popular despite the fine job they had done in terms of character-assassination. The best solution, for the time being at least, was to contain the damage. Get the Little Saint out of Chittor. People might forget her, she could have an accident, anything was possible once she was out of sight.

I love Chittor and never tire of it but I was relieved to be leaving it this time. If I was going to be marginalized, I might as well be away from the centre of action. My wife and I packed our stuff within a day. I went over after dinner to tell Father that I was leaving the next day. He was preoccupied or at least pretended to be.

'I see that you are recovered completely.' I didn't bother to remind him that I had been all right for at least seven or eight months. 'So what are your plans for Kumbhalgarh?'

'To follow your orders, Your Majesty. Fortify the fortifications of Kumbhalgarh.'

He ignored my little jibe.

'You do that. We'll come and inspect the fort when we have work in that area.'

'Thank you, Father.'

The farewell ceremony was over without undue pain to either party. I decided to ride around a bit before returning home. I went to the stables and got Befikir. Whatever had happened to Nasha, the stallion colt I had got for Leelawati? Funny, how I remembered her so often and yet had quite forgotten that beautiful horse.

'Do you really want to come to Kumbhalgarh, Mangal? It's going to be boring as hell.'

'Yes, Sire.'

'Yes what?'

'I want to come with you.'

'You are my closest associate, Mangal. We hardly ever talk, that's because you are privy to almost everything that I do. Without you I would have been dead several times over by now. I can be contrary and at such times, I take advantage of the one thing that you've given me unstintingly, steadfast loyalty. I had plans for both of us, Mangal, good, solid, challenging plans that would have made our country's future more secure. But there's no future with me. For the time being at least or perhaps for good, they are through with me at Chittor. It's absurd for me to tell you this since you are far better informed about matters and far more in advance than I am. You would be an asset to any of the ministers in the cabinet. I could talk to Lakshman Simhaji before I leave tomorrow. He would be delighted to have you with him. It's likely that the Commissioner of Police here may be transferred. There I go again, telling you things that you are familiar with. I can't think of a more capable and honest person for that position than you. That department needs to be overhauled, no, almost reinvented. You would do it brilliantly. Shall I talk to Uncle?'

'No, Sire.'

'Don't be pigheaded, Mangal. You have to think of your career. Besides, Chittor and Mewar would benefit from your expertise and experience. And if, with some luck, I am back in favour, we'll be together again, an inseparable pair. Stay Mangal, think of your wife, most of all, of your future.'

'Sire, I beg you not to think ill of me for speaking candidly. But you leave me no option. We were born at around the same time and that's how our fates got locked together. We were suckled by the same mother and my future became inseparable from yours. You've been good to me and I have risen faster than most. I would like to be of use to our country, not in some vague romantic way, but in a concrete and hardheaded fashion. It's one of the many things I learnt from you. No heroics, just deliver the goods as efficiently and economically as you can. But I am a marked man.

I know you believe that there is only one camp and it's called Mewar but not everybody sees it from your angle. They think I'm your man and I'm automatically suspect. We are like lepers, Your Highness, anybody who's seen with us gets tainted.

'I will always be suspect. The inference will always be that I am your agent. Unlike you, they cannot separate a job from the employer. They do not understand that one doesn't owe loyalty to a person but to the job and the institution. So, if you don't mind, I'll take my chances with you.'

He smiled but I was in no mood to reciprocate. We had never in our entire lives had such a long conversation. Even at school, my interests came before his. I was his responsibility. He always kept himself in the background. For the first time I felt guilty for keeping him in tacit bondage. Would Tej, Shafi and all the other fine people who had worked with me share the same fate as Mangal?

We got going again at a canter. The sky was ebony and the moon was two days short of fullness. There were so many stars playing fireflies that the sky seemed abuzz. Three-quarters of Chittor was already asleep. The silver shikhara of the Eklingji Temple shone like the beam from a lighthouse. The complex of palaces, the city centre, the houses of the shopkeepers and workers looked like faces whose eyes had been scooped out. The pools of water, Chaturang Maurya Talab, Sasbahu Kund, Fateh Lake, were shimmering sheets of mercury which blinded the sight.

'How about a quick dip, Mangal?'

We raced all the way down to the Gambhiree. The river was cold and speeding. Both of us knew where the dangerous currents were but you could never take the river for granted. If you were foolish enough to swim in her in the monsoons or immediately after, she would teach you a lesson in treachery. Every year at least five or six people, especially youngsters who thought they could outsmart her, lost their lives. We swam from bank to bank and back. It was exhilarating to have to work hard to swim in a straight line and not be towed away. We were shivering when we put on our clothes again.

'What time is departure tomorrow, Sire?'

'Seven. Are you bringing your wife with you?'

333

'If it's all right with you, Maharaj Kumar.'
'I wouldn't have it any other way.'

When I opened the door to my bedroom there was only one lamp with a barely visible flame burning. I closed the door and headed for the lamp to turn up the wick. I didn't make it.

'Maharaj Kumar.'

I knew the voice but it was from another life and from some other planet. Was this an emissary from Vikramaditya? It was a smart move to send a woman to ambush me. I should have been more careful. I should have known instantly when I entered the room that something was wrong. Whose voice was it? If it was familiar why did it sound so alien? I turned around and froze. The reflexes in my adam's apple had stopped functioning. I couldn't swallow. I couldn't move. She was pale the way someone who has been deprived of the life-giving light and warmth of the Sun-god is bleached and sucked of colour. Somehow in the process, the girl-child in her had also been wrung out. She was a full-grown woman of such tortured and aching beauty that I had trouble steadying myself. Leelawati stood still. I took her in my arms. I kissed her hair, her forehead, ears, eyes, cheeks, chin, the sides of her neck, everywhere except on the mouth. It was not an embrace, it was a futile attempt to plug the numb hollow that had been at the pit of my stomach since the day she had disappeared. She did not reciprocate, she would not speak. What has happened to me? I shake my head and try to kill her with my manic hugging, then I shake my head again. Stop it, I tell myself but I continue to look into her dead eyes.

'Don't move,' I told her and fetched the lamp. I lit all the other lamps in the room till she was bathed in light. I led her to the bed and made her sit down. She did not resist. Had she become a marionette? Was she dead? There was no point sitting next to her. I would not be able to look at those burnt-out eyes that held me transfixed. I knelt on the floor. She tried to get up, form demands that the Maharaj Kumar sit at a greater height than everybody except the Maharana and the Maharani. I forced her down.

'I looked everywhere for you for days and weeks. I thought you were dead.'

'I would have killed to find you.' It was not a reproach, merely a matter-of-fact statement of the truth. 'I nearly did strangle the maid in charge of me. That's when my great-grandfather had me tied up.'

'Where were you?'

'In Chittor but in some other house. I do not wish to talk about the past year.'

I looked at her feet and ankles. They had shrunk. You could see the marks of the silk scarves that had bound her to the legs of a chair or bed. I took her hands in mine. Her wrists were swollen and the skin looked livid.

'I could have killed myself but I thought what would happen to you?'

I could no longer meet her eyes.

'Then I heard that you were being sent to Kumbhalgarh tomorrow.'

I hugged her legs and buried my head between her knees.

'My great-grandfather Adinathji fixed my wedding for next Thursday the moment he learnt of your impending departure.'

This was the last time. I would never get to see Leelawati again. I was about to say something as stupid as congratulations. I believe Leelawati would have run out, grabbed a knife and plunged it into me if I had. There was no telling what those dead eyes could do.

'Marry me, Maharaj Kumar.'

I felt my neck snap sharply as the hangman kicked the plank from under my feet.

'It's a mere formality. You know we are already married.'

Why didn't I give her the knife or pull out my dagger from the scabbard and ask her to kill me? Anything, anything under the sun to avoid having to answer her.

'No, I can't.'

'Take me with you, Maharaj Kumar.'

And yet once again I said, 'No, I can't.'

She came and sat in my lap then. This time she put her arms around me and kissed me on the forehead and then on the lips. I did not respond. She took out a small silver box from the pocket in her ghagra and opened it. It had kumkum the colour of blood in it. She took a pinch and put it on my forehead.

'I'm a woman now capable of bearing children.' She plunged her index finger into the kumkum and put a large tika between her eyes, a little above the bridge of the nose. Now with her thumb and index finger, she limned a bloodline in the parting of her hair. 'I was and will always be married to you and to you alone. See, it's public knowledge for the first time.'

How can the tiniest of earrings or a little stone stuck on the nose highlight the entire face? Why does a thin almost invisible gold chain around the waist spark such a charge of sensuality in a woman? How can a simple and bold red dot make a woman regal and imperious and change the terms of her beauty? Leelawati laid her head on my feet. 'Bless me Maharaj Kumar.' And I did not utter a word to this woman who was dearer to me than .... never mind, what comparison can do justice to my twisted and strange love for Leelawati.

She rose to her full height. 'Now I too will bless you, my husband and Highness. May you always stay out of harm's way. May you bring glory to Mewar. And may you return quickly to my arms.'

There was a smile on her face. She had erased the year of solitary confinement and the tied hands and ankles from her face, if not her mind. Then she left.

Chapter 27

$\mathcal{J}$ did not envy Rawat Sumer Simha, the Governor of Kumbhalgarh, the task of looking after me and my party. He had to tread a delicate and ambiguous line. I was in disgrace and the governor had to keep a watch on me and make certain that I was not up to any mischief. The problem was that I was a Prince of the royal family and what was worse, since no official directive had yet been issued to the contrary, still the Maharaj Kumar. I guess one of his major fears must have been that I would interfere with the governance of the province. Within a month, he realized that I had no interest in his affairs, civilian, military, administrative or others. I did not visit his office once or attend any official functions. I did not qualify as a hedonist or voluptuary either in his eyes. He hinted from time to time that he could arrange for me to have some company.

'This may look like a backwater to you city folks but you'll be amazed at the delights and pleasures Kumbhalgarh has to offer,' he leered knowingly, 'to even the most discerning or jaded palate.'

A musical recital perhaps? The game in the forest was excellent. Would I care to go on a hunt?

'I seem to have run out of ideas. Why don't you tell me what you would like to do?'

'Nothing.'

'Nothing?'

He was bemused. Was I suffering from depression? Had I renounced the material life? Or was it an elaborate front to hide some grand evil scheme against the Crown or the country? It was a thesis worth pursuing since he didn't want to be caught off guard but he must have come up against a dead end. I had no visitors,

I had left strict instructions with Tej, Shafi and my other lieutenants that even if they happened to be next door, they were not to visit me. I wrote no letters, I received none except one. It was an invitation to Leelawati's wedding. It came the night before the event along with a gracious note from Adinathji regretting that the wedding had been fixed at very short notice. He hoped, however, that I would be able to attend it.

I did not mix with anyone in the fort or outside. If the Governor invited me and my wife for a private dinner, I never refused and made it a point to return the gesture. The rest of the time I wrote, I walked, I rode, I read. Rawat Sumer Simha may have adduced that I was a man who had lost all sense of direction and was fast turning into a vegetable. He was right. I did not wish to attract any attention to myself. I wanted to be left alone and forgotten.

My great-grandfather, Kumbha, had gone on a binge in his day and dotted the country with thirty-five magnificent citadels. But there was only one Kumbhalgarh and you can see why. It is one of the greatest fortresses built in the last few centuries. Made from black stone, Kumbhalgarh is indomitable and barring treachery, impenetrable. The fortress walls are as high and wide as roads. In the monsoons it makes far better sense to transport supplies over the flat top of the parapet walls than for the horses to get mired in the dirt tracks. The black stone is beautifully cut and precision-laid. It gives no purchase to an attacker's ropes or to the monkey-men who are trained to dart up the flanks while the main body of soldiers pretends to batter down the main gate. I believe that Kumbhalgarh could withstand a siege for a year or two without any problems of shortages. Its land mass is as big as any middle-sized city. It has huge farming areas and can grow almost everything we need. Which explains why no one has so far laid siege to the fort.

Rana Kumbha, they say, was a giant of a man. The Charans, in their heroic and panegyric poetry, would have us believe that he was tall as a banyan tree and just as wide. He ate an omelette of thirty-six eggs for breakfast. Lunch was a dozen tandoori chickens, a full deer or boar, six goats, five litres of rabadi, seventy-two makai ki roti, sixty-four jilebis, not to mention seven varieties of vegetables and four kinds of lentils. His duglo, the longer version of which is the Muslim angarkha, required seventeen yards of cloth and the knee-length trousers that were buttoned at the calves had a waist of fourteen yards, ungathered. Everything in Kumbhalgarh seems to have been inspired by his girth and height. The Palace, our rooms in it, the bathing facilities, even the stairs have been designed for larger-than-life men and women. From my rooms you can see the Aravalli mountain ranges which link so much of Mewar but it's the view of the plains which redefines one's notion of the horizon. On a clear day, one is apt to believe that you can see forever simply because the concept of a horizon almost breaks down. You can sit at the window in my room and believe that you are in the midst of the greatest desert in the world or in the middle of the ocean. Cross over to the other side of the Palace, and you can keep a watch on the traffic entering and leaving the main gate. That's exactly what Rana Kumbha did. He kept a watch on the watchmen and made sure that they were securing the fort from the enemy. Beyond, seven or eight hundred yards away is the great Eklingji Temple. This is where my great-grandfather sat and prayed. Every corner in the Palace, every tree, roadside shrine or temple, the river and the lake bear a memory of the man who built the fort. In my room there's a desk where the Rana sat and wrote his treatises on music. When he wanted to test any of the principles he was enunciating or elucidating, he went over to the veena which sits in a glass case now and played for hours and substantially extended the vocabulary and scope of the instrument. Three-quarters of a mile from the Eklingji Temple is a tamarind tree which according to the Rana was specially blessed. I find this noteworthy because in Hindu tradition it is the banyan or peepul tree under which one gains enlightenment or which is a place of worship and meditation and bestows boons upon you. Rana Kumbha was a great respecter of tradition but he saw it as a river and not as a dead pool of beliefs. Every spring, runnel and rivulet added to the richness and breadth of the river and so when he came across anything which caught his fancy, was beneficial to his people, or medicinal or just plain beautiful to behold, he appropriated it and incorporated it into the Mewar tradition. The tamarind tree is where he meditated. He found it cool and soothing and the leaves of the tree aesthetically pleasing. He would sit for hours here with his legs folded in padmasan, eyes closed and the third eye of the mind open. Before and after the meditation he took a dip in the well nearby and then walked back talking to any stranger and passer-by, asking after their health and crops and what they thought of the new taxes and the state of the country. You can see why he was universally liked for though he was truly one of the most learned kings in the history of Mewar, he was not pedantic and never lost touch with the source of his strength, his own people.

While the Rana meditated under the tamarind tree, Uda, they say, stabbed him in the heart thrice. Others point to the well next to the tree and describe how the son waited for the Rana to close his eyes as he poured the bucket of water over his head and in that instant pushed his father down the long, long neck of the well and then had it covered because the broken and fractured Rana was too obstreperous. He was a good swimmer and might take forever to die. There are other stories about how Uda tricked and slew his father or had someone else do the job for him. The only thing we know for sure was that the murderer was the Rana's very own son. Does it matter how he did it?

Father had sent me to Kumbhalgarh to get my wife and me out of the way but there was no point disregarding the specific task he had set me. It took a full week for Mangal and me to inspect the wall and instruct the stonecutters and builders about the cosmetic repairs. I did one more thing before going into complete retirement. It would be shortsighted and foolhardy to believe that whenever an enemy decided to take a shot at attacking the fort, he would be kind enough to knock on the front door. It would be much easier for a group of just seven to ten smart commandos to infiltrate the fort from a remote corner and open a couple of gates from inside. You have to see the fort with your own eyes to realize how big it is. I drew up a scheme to construct eight tall watchtowers along the wall of the fort. That would cover Kumbhalgarh from every angle and make it a little more safe. The Governor pondered if there was a catch somewhere and stalled. I surmised that it would take about six weeks for Father's reply to arrive. Within a month, I had got his approval. I supervised the work once a week but did not lift a finger after that bit of effort.

I have no idea how my wife kept herself busy. Arati was at six in the evening at the Blue One's temple and if you wanted to meet her without prior appointment, all you had to do was turn up at around five thirty or quarter to six and you would kill two birds with one stone: have a darshan of the Blue One and meet the Little Saint. I was a trifle anxious about the scandal that the Princess might cause but I need not have worried. The Little Saint's fame had preceded her and crowds of people from within the fort and from the nearby villages used to start gathering from five in the evening. It had finally begun to dawn upon me that Greeneyes was no longer a local personality, very likely she was a Mewar heroine whose fame and songs had begun to spread to other states beyond our frontiers. The people here were certainly singing her songs before they had heard her in person. In a few years' time Father should hand over the command of our troops to my wife. She'll sing and dance and the people of Gujarat, Malwa, Vijayanagar and Delhi will catch the fever, disown their kings and follow her wherever she goes. It's a good thing our gods are an egalitarian lot and not jealous and insecure because if one were to measure the shift towards the Flautist since my wife was canonized, he's currently at least fifty percent more popular than the other big divinities including the presiding deity of Mewar, Shri Eklingji himself. Fortunately, we are a polytheistic people and are given to playing it safe by visiting all the gods once in a while. Even so, at least for the time being the Blue One's future is hitched directly to my wife's fate and influence.

At Kumbhalgarh, it's taken just three months for the Governor's family to have turned devotees of the Little Saint. No disrespect meant to the Governor, his large and genuinely friendly wife or any of the other big and small parties involved, but it's as if they can no longer go to the toilet, have a bath, name a child, tell lies, get amorous, amass wealth, go on a journey or have an affair or an old-fashioned familial quarrel without asking the Little Saint's permission. I know I'm exaggerating a bit but only a bit. While she is very often blissfully unaware of what's going on around her, or so she pretends, they touch her feet when she has so often begged them not to. She shrinks from any attention to her person and directs all and sundry to the one who is the recipient of all her attention: the Flautist. And that's the strangest part, they dote on her, wait hours in the rain and freezing cold for her to turn up and yet they never seem to listen to her. They were all so busy adoring her, who had the time to pay any heed to what she was saying?

And what about me? I who straddle two stools, worship the earthly icons of the gods and yet feel the profundity of the Upanishadic concepts such as the one that is the corner-stone of my yogic meditation: 'So' hum'; I am that. It is a truly staggering and daring thought, this interchangeability or, to be precise, the oneness that the individual living creature shares with the cosmos and the Almighty. Or if you like with the higher consciousness or creative force. And yet if you were to probe further and not be lulled by these lofty platitudes, what is the meaning of the word 'that' in 'I am that'? Who knows, each one of us must negotiate the word on his own and to the best of his or her abilities. I sometimes like to think that if everything is animated by God or a higher consciousness, then the utterly pointless death of a child is as much 'that' as a flower which is about to bloom. My wife's physical and spiritual passion for the Flautist is 'that' and so is the hunger of a man who has not eaten for five days or the pain, the insurmountable and unbearable pain of a tumour. Rani Karmavati's conniving against me or the Little Saint as well as my drowning all the thousands of soldiers in the swamps is 'that'. 'That' is grief as much as it is happiness. If I am 'that', then I am all these things and every single object, emotion, experience and memory in the universe. It is a fine thought as large as the mind which is the most capacious thing in the world. But what about good and evil then? If my individual actions can affect and change the complexion of 'that', then I bear the responsibility for the state of the cosmos or universal consciousness. All of us starting from me must be extremely careful and selective about what we choose to do. Is that the outer limit of a deluded solipsism and megalomania or is it the highest and noblest concept of dharma and our roles in life?

What about the gods, what is their function? And is the meaning of the word 'Almighty' altered because of its interaction with us? And yet if 'that' is these and every other simultaneity including the time-space continuum, then is it all just a conceit, one that has ceased to have any significance? I do not know. There are no answers. Or rather each one must find or invent his own.

Perhaps that was the reason that I had gone back to music. Now that is a reality without reason, rationale or explanation. Who pulls the strings, why are we moved, why do we feel transported to a different world? Who knows? What difference does it make?

*   *   *

I sat at my desk, picked up the thick stack of papers and laid my head on it. Paper was the transmitter of vidya. Anything related to knowledge deserved the highest respect. I recalled my teacher whacking me with a cane on my shin-bone when my toe accidentally touched a book. I myself would do the same now if I became a father and my child showed disrespect to any object of learning. I breathed deeply the bouquet of the off-white paper from Ahmedabad. How fine it was, almost translucent and yet it had great longevity, if you didn't go out of your way to abuse it. I divided the papers into two exact halves and drew the diagram that a teacher draws on each student's slate on his first day at school. Draw a circle and extend the line all the way down to the left, now continue the stroke to the right and end with an upward flourish. Crisscross the pattern in a descending order nine times and what you had was a graphic symbol of Saraswati. When the ink sketching the goddess of learning had dried, I chanted a prayer asking for her blessing.

The agenda was to write two books. I wrote my autobiography on odd dates and the massive introduction to Shafi's book on *The Art and Science of Retreat* on even dates. The second book, I knew, would be a major contribution to the state of current thinking on warfare. Shafi had got down to the nitty-gritty and dealt with seventy possible scenarios of fleeing. What the book needed was a full-scale treatment of the philosophy of defeat and retreat. No king could use defeat as a ploy for losing a battle and winning a war, unless he effectively conditioned the populace and soldiery to think of long-term objectives. My first task, perhaps doomed from the start, was to remove the stigma from the word 'flight' and then from the act itself.

343

Despite its highly controversial subject, I was certain there was a genuine need for Shafi's book. People would read it, argue about it and perchance even take it seriously. I was nowhere as sure about my reasons for writing my memoirs. Was I so disheartened, I asked myself, that I needed an apologia? My transformation from Maharaj Kumar to a nobody was now almost complete and that deck of cards called the fates would have to be shuffled to a freak statistic for me to be in the running again. But it had nothing to do with self-esteem. The mediocre will often find solace in identifying a scapegoat, even if it means pointing the finger at themselves. I may have been down but the almost extinct Maharaj Kumar had no intention of giving up. If the opportunity presented itself, I would fix that deck of cards in my favour. If, as His Majesty had suggested, the heir apparent was ahead of his times, I must learn the art of hurrying my countrymen slowly. I had to take a cold, dispassionate look at my life, find out where I had gone wrong and calculate how I could make a different but more propitious set of moves.

There are no dress rehearsals in life, but sometimes if one is observant and lucky, one can detect patterns in it. The idea is not to make the same mistake the second time around but allow someone else to do it. Would I today pursue Vikramaditya's treason trial with such single-mindedness or do Queen Karmavati a favour she could never forget and let her handle her son while he collaborated ineffectually with the enemy and conspired against his own country? Admittedly, there was no worse enemy in the country than the Queen but as an ally, albeit an unreliable ally, one could occasionally make her careless, get her to miscalculate or perhaps even come to an understanding with her. Perhaps it was too late to build bridges with her. But there was still the steadfast Vikramaditya. One could always depend on him to be devious without always knowing where his self-interest lay.

Here indeed was a fecund field, a source that I had left completely untapped. But the motivation for the autobiography went a little further than the search for lost and new opportunities or even introspection. The past was with my countrymen every moment of their lives. History for them was that fabled second chance. They could rework the past and get it right this time around. It was an

344

act of faith and invention where defeats turned to glory; courage, bravery and heroism were chosen above vision or long-term gains and enmity was more precious than alliances. Best of all, you did not have to tot up the accounts and pay for the grandeur of your delusions or the vacuity of your mistakes. To them five hundred years ago was the same as yesterday, an episode outside the orbit of time. The past was never your responsibility. It was not the sum-total of mankind's wisdom, errors and insights. It was not the torch that lit the darkness and choices of today. My memoirs would try to go against the grain and break with tradition. If personal history was an inheritance, then I would leave behind a record that would allow the next generation, including my children, to understand how their fathers and forefathers negotiated the turns and twists of diplomacy and the business of the state; how they failed, what mistakes they made and how they picked up the pieces and started anew.

I wrote as usual with a long, firm and neat hand. But the language and the thought processes of the two texts were different without any conscious intention on my part. The prose of the 'Retreats' text was formal and precise. I composed entire paragraphs, often several pages in my head and then transferred them to the page. I had worked out the architecture of the book in advance during the long months of my confinement in bed. Since I was dealing with a taboo subject, I had to spend far more time rein-forcing the foundation or over-engineering it, to use the town planner's technical vocabulary, so that it could withstand the full force of the backlash of orthodoxy and dogma. I knew which were the load-bearing chapters, the keystones of my thesis and made sure that both the vista and the goal were visible from every angle, jharokha and balcony: a retreat is a strategy to save lives and live to fight and win another day. It may be a feint, an attempt to await reinforcements or regroup resources; or a side show while the real action takes place elsewhere; or it might be a close call where your only chance of survival is to put your tail between your legs, pull in and streamline your body so that your getaway is swift and effective.

I did not have a plan for my memoirs but its language came

as a shock to me. I tried to resist it, at times tore up page after page but finally gave in. I realized for the first time that my mind was a two-tongued instrument: an austere, distanced and deliberative high Mewari for the purposes of ratiocination and logic; and a cross between the language of the court and the colourful, pungent and coruscating dialect of the eunuchs, servants and maids in the palace. I had no intention of striving for a cold and clinical objectivity (that kind of honesty, I was more than aware, was a sham and unreadable to boot) but I was amazed to discover such a strong, personal tone in my narrative. I am not a man to let my guard down, whatever the occasion or provocation. Or so I thought. Instead here I was, if not baring my soul, certainly throwing my usual habit and mask of caution to the winds, telling it all, taking swipes at myself and at my relatives including Father, meditating, digressing despite an ingrained habit of disciplined progression. I was alarmed by this openness and my willingness to express an opinion on any and every matter. Should I abandon the project? Was it getting out of hand? I had to admit that it was. But to censor it would be tantamount to a kind of doctoring. I would be just as guilty of a normative version of the past as the charans and their ilk. And not to write at all would mean that I, too, believed that truth was a good slogan but not to be confronted in the corridors of real life; that it emasculated us instead of enlightening and endowing us with a quality of rigour and introspection. I smiled wryly and decided to carry on. Maybe I was enjoying myself too much to stop.

Chapter 28

 To combat a god, one must become one. (Or at least masquerade as one.)

$\mathcal{H}$e was returning from a seven-mile walk along the parapet of the fort at eleven at night when he saw his wife sitting at the Flautist's temple. He turned towards the palace but something about her made him go back. She sat still, her eyes closed. This was unusual, to say the least. One of the stories about her said that not just her feet but even her skirt and plait would never come to rest. There was a strange expression on her face. He knew he wasn't making sense but he could only call it joyous, ecstatic tranquillity. She was no longer of this earth or of this world.

He was sure that the light from the solitary lamp was playing tricks with her face. He drew closer to her. There was a light flowing from her, not just from her eyes which were shut anyway, but from her entire body. It had lit her from within and she had become transparent. He realized that it did not make any difference whether he gave credence to what he saw or didn't. Nothing could touch her. She was a circle and a completeness. All else was without. She was in communion with something that was beyond comprehension. Only someone touched by the divine could be so insensible and self-absorbed. What was she thinking about? That was a silly question. She seemed beyond thought. He would never be able to penetrate the mystery at the centre of her being. But that, he suspected, is the nature of the mystical experience. It is a one-to-one rapport. The rest of the world was, perforce, shut out. To an outsider, the saint's world was quintessentially solipsistic, but that was missing the point. There was no outside for her.

He felt an odd desire. He wanted to cup his hands and gather the light emanating from her.

✳   ✳   ✳

Late that night, he took off his clothes and stood in front of the full-length, vertical mirror. He poured five tablespoons of indigo powder into a shallow bowl and carefully mixed it with two tumblers of water. It was time to spread out four large gunnysacks in the centre of the room. Must be careful not to stain the floor or the walls. He dipped the thick brush he had bought into the indigo solution, pressed the bristles against the curving sides of the bowl and let the excess water flow back. He stood in front of the mirror, studied his reflection without much curiosity and applied the first stroke. Was it the water which was cold or the feel of indigo against his skin? He felt like an actor working with make-up. It was a slow process. He was in no hurry. He wanted to do it right. Under the arm pits, behind the ears, between his buttocks and over his crotch, on the ups and dips of the vertebrae of his backbone, he did not want a speck or line of his own skin to escape his eye. He examined himself in the mirror. A sliver of white showed between his littlest toe and the second-last one. One daub and that was done. He turned around. The back, the three ribs behind his right arm had been the most difficult but all that effort and attention to detail had paid off. He stood still for ten minutes. The paint was dry but he wanted to make sure. He picked up the yellow silk pitambar. It felt soft and rich and subdued. He tied it around his waist. Next, the finely meshed gold belt. Now the headband. He tucked in his hair carefully under it and then stuck the peacock feather a little off-centre above his right eye. One last look. He collected his flute, the one that the Bhil soldier from Raja Puraji Kika's army had gifted him, and left.

He opened the door to her room almost imperceptibly. She was sleeping. He started to play softly. He had no raga or tune in mind. The notes came effortlessly. Heart, soul, mind and flute were one. He played on. The sound of the reed had a deep, full and fine-grained texture. Music was the smoke from a joss stick. He could see its lines rising and spiralling mysteriously. She turned on her side, semi-awake, then lapsed back into sleep. The notes seemed to drift in and out of her consciousness. She lay on her back and covered her face with her chunni. A lazy smile as diaphanous as the song he was playing parted her lips. She was awake now. The smile played mischievously around her eyes but she would not open them.

'I'm not at home. Might as well go back to all your other women. Guess you didn't have the time to look in on me when I had that slight fever and a touch of diarrhoea and kept throwing up as if I didn't want any of my mortal remains left behind. Oh, please, please do me a favour. Spare me your cosmic reasons, matters of state and other excuses. It really doesn't matter. After all, it wasn't anything. I was on my deathbed and everybody had given up on me, he certainly had, the poor dear man, how he looked after me, night and day and cleaned my mess, he didn't leave my bedside, not for a minute, nor did he sleep. But that's nothing to get worked up about, is it? I might have died but as you are about to tell me, I didn't. Then what's all the fuss about? Let's not have a scene, oh please, we are decent, civilized people here. You are quite right. Let's call it a day. We had good times, some great ones too but that's all over. You go your way now and I'll go mine and never the twain shall meet.'

He tucked the flute in his belt, turned around and started to walk away. She was working herself up into a regular tantrum. He could expect flying objects any moment now.

'Can you hear me? Cat got your tongue? Don't you have anything to say in your own defence, never mind if not a word of it is true? Don't you have any shame? An iota of human feeling? You think you can concoct all those stories and expect me to believe them? Forget it. I'm through with you once and for all.'

He was out of the door when she ran after him.

'Hold me, hold me. Don't talk, don't say a word.'

By eight the next evening, night, really, since it got kohl-dark by six, he was standing naked again in front of the mirror and applying the indigo solution.

*　　*　　*

'Stand in it.'

He wasn't quite sure what she meant.

'Move, stupid. I can't wait all night long. And why have you stopped playing?'

As usual she had not lit any lamps and his foot landed on the rim of the large twenty-two carat gold platter. He steadied himself and took up the Bhil air where he had left off. She fetched a gold lota with a long spout.

'What's the matter with you today? Have you forgotten how you normally stand when playing the flute?'

He hurriedly crossed his right foot over the left one. To his consternation she began to pour water and wash his feet. The game's up, he said to himself as his heart fibrillated wildly. He watched mesmerized as the indigo from his left foot began to run.

'Now the right foot. Careful, don't keel over. Wouldn't bother me if you dislocated your hip,' she looked up at him and laughed, 'but I don't want my neck broken.'

Did she really not know who he was? Was she indulging him? Or herself? Was it all make-believe, some arcane tableau that they had both decided to participate in? Surely she knew.

'Step out,' she wiped his feet dry with her pallu. 'I'll water the Tulsi plant with this holy water in the morning. She'll be pleased and flower as if it were spring.' She laid her head on his feet, clutched his ankles and stretched out on her stomach. 'Bless me, O Lord. Never did I dare to presume that I would be worthy of you. Never did I imagine that you would choose me as your beloved. Is it all a dream?' She craned her neck, her eyes looking into his with adoration. 'Let me pinch you and make sure that you are real.' She raised her right hand, dug her nails into his calf muscle and pulled it back till he cried in agony. 'Did that hurt?' She looked genuinely surprised. 'How strange, then you really are real. That will teach you never to abandon me for that Radha woman or anyone else.'

She plucked the peacock feather from his headband. What now, he wondered. He didn't have to wait long to find out. It was soft and insubstantial-as-air like the Dhaka mulmul of her chunni. Perhaps it really was drafts and undercurrents of a rarefied ether and not a feather at all. He would have preferred the steel tines of a rake to drag through his flesh. A strange torture it was, a

350

smothering, unbearable caress that seemed to test the limits of his endurance. He was not sure whether the eye of the feather touched him but it generated a charge that slid and prowled under his skin and left him bruised and raw. How was he going to reconcile the contradiction of the rutting of the peacocks in the time of cholera and the rapture of their dance on his body today?

Sometimes after lunch, they played cards or Mamta brought the multi-coloured game of checkers and unrolled it like a carpet. His Highness would have preferred to have played without stakes but his wife insisted that money was what made the games fun and exciting. They hadn't ever discussed it or cast lots but the pairs got fixed soon after they arrived in Kumbhalgarh. The Princess and Mangal were partners against Mamta and the Maharaj Kumar. As the days passed, one thing became clear: the three of them were completely outclassed and outmanoeuvred by the Princess. She looked what she was, a little saint whose innocence shone through like burnished armour while she masterminded every devious scheme of self-advancement, buccaneering and profiteering known to man or woman and many unknown to both.

It was impossible to grasp the enormity of her mendacity, the subtlety of her finger-work and her sense of aggrieved outrage when she was caught red-handed. Her rapacity was as great as her inexhaustible charm. She may be dealt the worst hand of cards, she may have had a run of one plus one every time she threw the dice for the last four hours but she always managed to be ahead of the others. Her standard ploy was a diversionary tactic: she dropped her odhani, the screw of her earring clattered down, something had got into her eye, would someone please use the end of his or her kerchief to get it out. By the time she had rearranged her odhani, retrieved the gold screw or someone had located the boulder lodged between her eyelid and eye, the complexion of the game had changed beyond recognition: her hand of cards had improved to the point where she collected the prize money or her coins were way ahead of the others. On the rare occasions when no ruse worked and all seemed lost, she would get an attack of hiccups or sneezes and accidentally scatter the coins on the cloth board.

'Damn that fly,' she slapped her chest hard, 'it's been bothering me since we started playing.'

The Maharaj Kumar leaned over and gripped her hand. The side of his wrist rested on her breasts.

'And pray, what do you think you are doing, Your Highness?'

'Just helping you catch that fly.' He squeezed her hand. Beads of sweat broke out on her upper lip.

'Let go of my hand, Highness.'

'I will. Once you let me have the fly.' He kneaded the bones of her hand till you could hear them crack a mile away. Her eyes smouldered with pain and anger but her fist remained tightly closed. Mangal and his wife looked at this family squabble in alarm. They had never seen the Maharaj Kumar so adamant. It was obvious he was hurting her.

If the back of my wrist, the Maharaj Kumar thought, can recognize that softly pounding breast of hers, surely she can identify her nocturnal visitor. The appearance of normality, the feigned amnesia of couples who, a couple of moments back had been locked in each other's arms, had always struck him as the quintessential duplicity of mankind.

The card fell from her hand. Mangal picked it up to reassure himself that it was real paper and not a trick his eyes were playing on him. Husband, wife and the Maharaj Kumar collapsed with laughter. The Princess was not amused.

'You planted that card in my hand, Highness. You are an abominable cheat.'

She threw her cards down and stomped out of the room. Mamta ran after her and brought her back after much pleading and coaxing. They resumed the game. That little detour seemed to have improved the quality of her cards enormously.

Chapter 29

The news from home and the rest of the kingdom has been mixed. The freak monsoons of the previous year, and the unseasonal flooding have ruined the crops. The economy is in bad shape and there's a major recession on in the country. The farmers need money to buy seed but the exchequer's almost empty and the Finance Minister Adinathji is unable to advance any loans. Under the circumstances, Father's done what most monarchs in the world would: encroached on our neighbour's lands, marauded, plundered and wherever possible, annexed territory. The choice was between the Sultanates of Delhi and Malwa. Father, as is his wont, weighed the pros and cons and took a shrewd decision. He opted for the former. Both Delhi and Malwa have lost their energy and vigour and are on their last legs. Ibrahim Lodi of Delhi and Mahmud Khalji of Malwa, are kings bereft of ideas and unable to control their nobles and vassals. Malwa would have been a walkover but for the fact that Mahmud Khalji has a prime minister whom he distrusts but who happens to be both a Rajput and very capable. His name's Medini Rai. It is, as I have said repeatedly, Father's greatness that unlike his predecessors, he does not choose to commit any hostile acts, let alone start a war with Rajputs. As a consequence, the Sultan of Delhi has been receiving news for the last few months about Rana Sanga helping himself to big chunks of Lodi land.

The Sultan is a deeply suspicious man and regards almost all the high-ranking men in his own kingdom as potential enemies. It is a condition that is as trying for him as it is for those upon whom his suspicion falls. His victims lose their lands, families and heads but the victimizer too must pay a terrible price: his support at home dwindles, his ubiquitous doubts become self-fulfilling and the toxins of insecurity must surely eat into his very soul. If the platitude 'trust breeds trust' is even halfway credible, then the reverse must also be true. If Ibrahim Lodi has ignored Father's depredations it's because he's been too busy quelling a series of revolts of his deputies in outlying provinces. He finally managed to put down the internal threats to his throne or at least keep them in abeyance, and rode posthaste to confront the Rana.

Queen Karmavati pestered and pursued Father till the day he left, trying to get him to appoint Vikramaditya governor of Chittor while he was away but Father was not to be swayed. He appointed my younger brother Rattan governor, and took Vikramaditya with him to the battlefront. Court gossip has it that Queen Karmavati has fallen out of favour and Rattan is now being groomed as heir apparent. It may well turn out that Rattan will ascend the throne after Father but it would be shortsighted to underestimate the Queen's power and influence. It is more than likely that Father took Vikramaditya with him to keep him away from mischief at Chittor while also making certain that he got exposure to a real war. (Incidentally, Mangal's sources say that the Queen gave in only after Father had made some kind of deal with her though nobody knows what the terms of the agreement were. I can only vouchsafe two things. One, that she didn't plead my case as heir apparent and two, that we are bound to find out the substance of the covenant in due time.)

The Delhi and Mewar forces collided against each other near the village of Khatoli on the borders of Haravati. The battle lasted five hours at the end of which the Delhi army decided that flight was the better part of valour and took to its heels. Father was shrewd enough to take a Lodi prince prisoner. He was released after the Sultan paid a ransom which ensured that while Mewar may not feast the rest of the year, we would at least be able to eat from time to time.

* * *

I was giving the finishing touches to my two hundred and seven page introduction to Shafi's book when there was a knock on the door. Whichever servant was knocking was in for the bawling of

354

his or her lifetime.

'Come in.' The door opened. 'What the...'

It was my wife looking brand-new after a bath. Her eyes were alight. What awful mischief was she up to?

'Shall I complete the sentence for you?'

'You know very well that I'm not to be disturbed between seven thirty and twelve thirty in the mornings.'

'Not even in an emergency?'

'What's happened?'

'Got you, didn't I? You are such a spoilsport. Surely I'm allowed to ruin your routine once every eighteen months.'

'No.'

'Come on, I'll race you to Ranakpur.'

'I bet on all fours.'

'Very funny. Get up. Mangal and Mamta are waiting in the courtyard.'

'Have you ...' I stopped short again. I had become a one-response man. Every time my wife suggested one of her impromptu projects, she didn't have any others, my reaction was to ask her whether she had gone mad. Didn't I know by now that she was born that way? She was certifiably insane. It was an infectious kind of craziness. Mangal, Mamta and I were also suffering from advanced symptoms.

'How are we going?'

'We'll ride, how else?'

'You'll ride?'

'And beat you to it.'

'And what do I get if you lose?'

'My bangles.'

'I have them. Remember, you lost them at cards.'

'You cheated.'

'You should talk.'

As usual she turned the question right back at me.

'What are you betting?'

I looked out of the window. 'The flowers from the parijat tree.'

She stared at me quizzically for a long time and then at the tree which covered the ground with hundreds of red-stemmed white flowers every morning.

'You are the most generous human being I have known. Don't move. I'm going to take out your nazar. I said sit still. I don't want anyone casting the evil eye on you.'

I had long since stopped trying to make sense of my wife. She brought two plates, one with burning coals and the other with salt, red chillies and all the other paraphernalia and made me close my eyes. I could feel the air swish and lap in my face as she moved her closed fists back and forth around my head and muttered something. She opened the fists and let the contents fall into the plate on the floor. They crackled and sputtered and spattered angrily.

'May I open my eyes?'

'May all your enemies die a terrible death,' she was in a temper. The firecrackers were still bursting, if anything even more virulently. 'See, see how much ill they've been wishing you. I'm to blame. I should have taken drastic action a long time ago. You watch me, Highness, nobody will come between you and His Majesty again. I'll take care of you, I'll vanquish all your enemies.'

Dear God, did she not know who she would have to destroy first?

* * *

We were travelling incognito. Greeneyes had got picnic lunches packed for us. I had informed the Governor of our last minute plans and he looked a bit uncertain. Would Father approve? Was our trip as innocent as we were making it out to be? What if something should happen to us? Why the incognito? He was ambivalent about the Princess and Mamta riding with us. It seemed to reassure him that we couldn't be up to much mischief since we were with our wives, but he would have preferred it if they had ridden in palanquins instead of roughing it out. What put his mind at rest was my request that four of his men go ahead and set up tents for us. My reasoning was elementary. He would have to send somebody or the other to keep a watch on us anyway. Might as well get them to do a little work.

The road between Kumbhalgarh and Ranakpur is hilly and heavily wooded. The sun was out in his full glory but it was still several months to May when the rock of the Aravali ranges would

356

heat up like fat in a griddle. We must have ridden for over two hours when the Princess who was ahead of us — why should I exhaust Befikir today, I figured I would conserve his energies for the final spurt — raised her right hand and brought us to a halt. To everybody's surprise she took a bow and arrow from Mangal. She patted her horse on the neck and quieted him down. Had she sighted a tiger or a lion? Unlikely at this hour but not impossible. This was, after all, game country. Mangal had got his spear while I readied my bow and arrow. Greeneyes sat straight and still, then quietly fixed the arrow to the bow and pulled the string taut. We could see the herd of barasinghas grazing on an open grass patch to the left of the road ahead now. Did she know what a barasingha weighs? If the buck was wounded and not killed, it could rush her and lift her and her horse all the way to heaven.

What was she waiting for?

It was clear soon enough. She wanted the odds to be even. She would take a shot at him only if he had as much of a chance to maul or kill her as she had with him. Of all varieties of deer, the barasingha is, by far, my favourite. One look at him and it was obvious why the Princess had chosen him. The twelve-antlered one stood out, literally, head and shoulders above the rest of his tribe. His complexion was a russet gold. Even in the dark it would shine like a nimbus around him. He was at least five feet tall, that's not counting his horns. He was lean and tight and without a gram of fat. The sinews on his legs were made of steel cables. They had three specific tasks: to charge; to round up his kinsfolk and retreat if his tribe was in danger; and to hold firmly to the earth when a contender to his throne locked horns with him. He had a neck like the double-barrelled thighs of a Gujarat wrestler. Every now and then he twitched his epidermis to get rid of a fly. But it was his eyes that set him apart from everyone else. They were keenly intelligent and kept a casual but vigilant watch over his wards. They were aloof and full of hauteur. Thus far, they said, and no more. The message was clear. Don't trifle with me.

He stared at the Princess for a long time and then turned his head dismissively. What you do is your business just so long as you leave my people alone. He grazed for a minute and looked up again.

357

This time he sensed that the woman across was waiting for him. He pawed the ground furiously in a show of strength hoping that wiser counsel would prevail and she would leave him alone. It also gave him a couple of seconds to decide on his course of action. She was still watching his every move. It was clear to him now that he was the target. The least he could do was make it a moving one. He bolted. It was a magnificent sight as he took off, his front legs folded, his body including his rear legs straight as the arrow he hoped to elude. It was a smart move. He had alerted his people against present and imminent danger. There was a left to right stampede now. My wife looked motionless even though she swivelled a full 180 degrees, keeping the speeding beast in the dead centre of her vision. There was no slack in her backbone, neck or the muscles of her arms. The thunder was deafening and the duststorm obscured the view. He was out of sight now. She waited. He must have taken a three-quarter turn for he was back. He had accelerated his speed. There was a barely audible zing of the bow string and the arrow was out of sight. We waited till the entire herd of two hundred or so deer had disappeared and the dust had settled. He was lying on his side, the beast; the arrow had pierced his heart. He had died instantly.

'Where did you learn to shoot like that, Highness?' Mangal asked the Princess as she pulled out the arrow.

'It was a fluke,' the Princess said self-deprecatingly.

'No fluke this.'

'My uncle taught me.' She was embarrassed by the attention she was attracting. 'Let's keep a leg and give the rest away to the villagers nearby.'

I was not overeager to meet anybody. Not that the villagers would recognize me but one couldn't discount the possibility that someone might have touched the Little Saint's feet or danced with her in Kumbhalgarh or Chittor. It would put unnecessary stress on the Governor and we would soon have welcome committees waiting for us at every village and hundreds, if not thousands of villagers would accompany us all the way to Ranakpur. But the barasingha had been downed and there was enough meat there to feed seventy to eighty people. There was nothing to be done but locate the closest village.

I was reluctant to leave the women by themselves but my wife, as usual, had the last word.

'I can take care of myself and Mamta.'

We discovered a hamlet three quarters of a mile away and spoke to the village headman and his friends. Barasingha meat is a rare treat reserved for feast days. The villagers were delighted with our gift and only too happy to help us carry their dinner home. They hitched two of their biggest bullocks and we were about to ride out with six young men when the headman asked whether we would stay for an impromptu lunch of paunk. It was an offer I was unlikely to refuse even on my deathbed.

Paunk is no ordinary food. It is ambrosia and an enigma. Which mortal would have thought of using crisp vermicelli savouries made from chickpea flour as a foil to the lightly roasted green and succulent corn of jowar picked fresh from the farm? Eaten soft and crunchy, it is deadly and unpredictable but spike it with lemon and what you get is a collision and collusion of sweet, sour, and salty that's likely to go down as one of the high points of one's life.

When was I going to get to know my people? The men were tall and erect and handsome and the women were shy and beautiful. (This is, I realize, the paunk speaking but it also happens to be the truth.) They were hospitable and loved company. We sat on a dhurrie under the open sky. They wanted to know where we came from.

'Chittor,' we told them.

'We knew it,' they said. 'You look like people from the centre of power, though you may for all we know, be powerless. But that busy, purposeful look is Chittor, no question about it. And the accent is a dead giveaway. And what is your name?'

'Sisodia.'

'Not related, we trust, to the royal family. If you were what would you be doing with the likes of us? But you never know, some princes like to travel incognito and keep a watch on their people. Hope you are not some of them.'

'Sure we are. Can't you tell from our haughty demeanour? Better watch what you say.' My wife pointed to me, 'That man's making mental notes of everything you say because he is the Maharaj Kumar

359

and I'm the Princess.'

They found this very funny. They slapped each other on the back and the women giggled and nudged my wife on the shoulder. They bowed to us and fanned us and got into the spirit of things.

'Your Highness, my daughter needs a husband. We'll give you three cows and a dozen hens. What do you say, will you take her off our hands and make her the Queen of Mewar when, long live His Majesty, you become the king? The first one we believe is a saint but no queen.'

'Saint?' That was my wife again. 'They call her a strumpet and a nautch girl.'

'Really? The Maharaj Kumar need never worry about our darling daughter singing or dancing. She has no ear for music and has paddles for feet. But she's docile as a cow, cooks a fine meal, washes clothes and gives a back massage that crushes your bones but makes you fit within minutes. There she is, the one who's got her head covered by her mother's chunni.' The girl withdrew further behind her mother and chewed on the cloth of her chunni. 'No, seriously, what do your parents do? Perhaps you have a younger brother who might fancy her.'

How much do you earn? And your parents? How many siblings? Fourteen sisters? We can't manage to get rid of one. Didn't your mother bury any in the sand? They were incredible. They had no problems asking strangers about their ancestors, their property, their troubles and the most intimate details of their lives.

'Why haven't you got your daughter married yet?' Greeneyes asked the headman.

'We found a good boy for her last year but we had a bad crop and what with taxes, we couldn't afford the dowry. The boy's parents wouldn't wait and got him married to someone else.'

'Don't you put money aside for a lean year?' I asked.

'We do but if we give that as taxes what do we eat the whole year? The Maharana, I'm sure has his share of problems but it would help if he could devise a more equitable system of taxes. More in the good years and less in the bad ones.'

'You think that will clear your debts and you'll be happy then?' I asked laughingly.

360

'Of course not. Only dumb animals don't complain. Human beings always have one reason or the other to complain about.'

It was time to go. The Governor's men would be waiting for us after they had pitched our tents at Zajora. If we weren't there in a couple of hours, they would be sure to think that we had decamped and would rush back to Kumbhalgarh and inform the Governor.

✳   ✳   ✳

I woke everybody at one thirty. The men from Kumbhalgarh dismantled the tents and we took off almost immediately. I had not been to Ranakpur before and I wanted to see it in the first light at dawn. The road rose steadily through hills and mountains and was densely wooded. We were on the outskirts of the village by five. We bathed in a frisky rivulet which would disappear at the first sign of summer. The water was a shock to the system. I could hear my blood rush back and forth, take hair-pin turns, speed up to my brains and plunge to my toes across my body to warm me. We put on fresh clothes and stood at the base of the temple.

Ranakpur is consecrated to the Tirthankar after whom Leelawati's great-grandfather, Adinathji was named. It was built during the golden age of architecture in Mewar, but not by my great-grandfather Kumbha. When the temple was complete, Rana Kumbha visited it. He thought it extraordinarily beautiful. He regretted that not he, but one of the men in his employ, his Jain Finance Minister, had built it. But all was not lost. He would build a Victory Pillar in marble inside the temple which would put the Treasurer's work in the shade. The Jain poets are discreet about the Minister's response to this grotesque suggestion. Whatever his private feelings, there was no way the Treasurer could say 'no' to his sovereign. The plan, side and front elevations, the interlocking and intricate carvings, everything was worked out and approved by the Rana and work was begun. But try as he might, and mighty as he was, there was no completing the pillar. As a matter of fact, even today what I see is an enormous square-based eyesore that does not even reach the ceiling of the first floor.

We took off our shoes at the bottom of the wide flight of stairs, almost the width of a middling street in Chittor and climbed to the plinth. Suddenly the sun struck and crept in like the first wave of a flow tide near Surat. It seeped into the marble and retreated as a wisp of cloud swept over the nascent sun way below the horizon. There was no one else there at this hour. Within minutes the sunlight streamed in like a river in flood. At the extreme corner of the building are rounded bulwarks as at any fort except that these are much shorter. Ranged across the entire plinth are enclosure walls that are really a series of miniature temples housing subsidiary luminaries from the Jain pantheon. Four beautifully proportioned central gateways interrupt the shrines on all four sides. It is impossible to gauge how stupendously large and complex the temple is until you get to the very heart of the edifice. And, yet, that too is a limited and partial view for one has not yet climbed to the first and then the second storey.

Jain saviours in the panels stand or sit, stiff and erect, compellingly directing one's attention to their large, shining, unblinking eyes. The quadruple image of Adinath in the core chamber at the very top is no exception. You may close your eyes but you always know that the first Tirthankar's eyes are within you, not outside.

The Ranakpur temple was a revelation. It opened my eyes to possibilities that had not occurred to me. Hindu temples come in many shapes and sizes. The spire may be small, large or sometimes totally dispensed with but the garbha griha, the sanctum sanctorum where the image of the deity resides, is almost always the heart of darkness. It symbolizes the impenetrable mystery of divinity. It is the primal womb, a tight and closed blackness, a claustrophobic and intimidating place which only the intermediaries between the deity and the layman, the brahmins, may negotiate. The Jain temple at Ranakpur turned the Hindu concept on its head. It brought things out in the open. Instead of the subterranean and the secretive, light and air were the elements of the divine here. The white marble was part of that openness. It had the swirl and speed of milk being poured.

The Ranakpur temple may be dedicated to Adinath, the first Tirthankar. And yet if you ask me, it is a celebration of the Sun-god. Its thrust and impulse are light and its goal is enlightenment.

362

It is unlike any temple I know. It is not its incredible sprawl, the marble mass or the exquisite carving which are central to the conception of the temple. As the temple rises tier upon tier, there are no walls but pillars that let the light and the air mingle and merge with the structure and stone. By themselves, the latter would have made the temple heavy and obdurate and earthbound. What I saw instead was the transubstantiation of marble into light. By making light a structural and integral part of the architecture, the Adinath temple had beams, shafts, columns and walls of light, and floated in the air.

The Adinath temple, as I was to discover, was not one, but a hundred, a thousand and a hundred thousand temples. By dawn, noon, by twilight, by the hour, by the minute, by full moon and the other phases of the moon, there's a different Adinath temple. The speed, weight and shape of a cloud can alter it. Rain, shadow, lightning and thunder reshuffle and reinvent it. It does not celebrate conquest or victory. I do not know whether Rana Kumbha's treasurer was singing a paean to the power of money or hoping to etch his name on the continuum of time. It doesn't matter. It is an aspiration and striving towards openness and freedom. It is a flight and an ascension. It dares you to assay the unknown, to reach out beyond yourself.

I sat down in the lotus position. I doubt if I was conscious of what I was doing. The light of my ancestor, the Sun-god suffused me. 'So' hum'. I am that. I breathed in 'so' ' and breathed out 'hum'. And I too was transubstantiated. I was the marble and the light and the air. And then the temple lost its walls and all that was left was consciousness, an indivisibility and oneness with all things living and unliving.

What am I doing in a Jain temple? Why did Mahavir, who founded Jainism, and Buddha find Hinduism inadequate and look to other ways for moksha or nirvana as Buddha would call it? Why did they reject violence so totally? Did it not amount to denying one of our deepest human impulses? Was that one of the reasons why Hinduism has reasserted itself in our land and squeezed Buddhism till there's only one drop of it left in Sri Lanka? Jainism, it is true, survives but only in a marginal way.

363

Violence is first and last about power. When two pairs of antlers are locked into each other, it is to decide who controls power. Jainism is even more extreme than Buddhism in its stance on violence. Its monks and nuns often wear white masks over their noses and mouths to avoid killing the infinitesimal forms of life floating around in the air. But it sometimes seems to me that they have only replaced violence with finance. It is still very much the pursuit of power. And yet even I, one of the bloodiest mass murderers in history, must confess to the temptation of peace, the peace of mind that must come from renouncing violence.

There is no gainsaying both the Buddhist and the Blue God's analysis of the human condition. It is desire, the life of the senses, attachment and ignorance which suck us deeper and deeper into the quagmire of unhappiness, misery and more desire, and keep turning the wheel of reincarnation ceaselessly. But Buddha's compassion, vision and understanding are all the more remarkable because even after enlightenment, he refrained from saying that his is the one and only way; follow it. Quite the contrary, he tells anyone who is interested that the golden mean and discipline are what worked for him but each of us must discover on our own whether they are valid for us. If not, we must seek our own way out of the maze of life, death and rebirth. The detachment that Buddha preached is, like all teachings, open to different interpretations. It is true that your chances of meeting with an accident go down perceptibly if you do not stir out of the house and cross the street or join the army and go to war. Needless to say, your chances of not meeting with that accident will not just improve dramatically but become fool-proof and fail-safe if you commit suicide. But if detachment is really fear of failure and hence never putting oneself to the test, or if it's fear of being hurt, humiliated or rejected, then one is closing all doors to life, to the possibilities of happiness, pain, dejection, achievement and experience. Reincarnation may be on the cards for most of us but we live this particular life, whether it is maya or whatever else, only once. This is our only chance to engage it.

Excess is the language of adolescence. We do not have to posit life as extremes or polarities, as either close to nothing or surfeit.

364

The thought of the afterlife or lives or even nirvana does not mean that we have to miss out on this life.

*   *   *

I woke up with a song the next morning. It was not on my lips but on my wife's. I looked around for her but she wasn't in the room.

It was dark outside and a low wind scuttled through the scrub. I ran up the stairs of the temple in one breath and sat down against a pillar. A chill light flowed from inside. It came to me then that marble is nothing but frozen moonlight. My bodily processes slowed down, my temperature dropped, my breathing became subdued and I found myself retreating or rather, distancing myself from the ups and downs in my life that had exercised me so inordinately; from my family, Father, wife, Queen Karmavati, Vikramaditya.

I do not know how to describe my wife's homage, song, offering or whatever one wishes to call it. I think it was an invitation and an invocation to the Sun-god. It was not entirely bereft of words but almost so. This was unusual since my wife's preferred mode of expressing religious fervour is poetry. Her singing and dancing were but variations and extensions of her lyrics. If the purest form of music, its very essence and distillate are the singing human voice, why do we debase it with words? Since I'm not a singer and am not likely to found my own school of classical music, I doubt whether alaapi will ever become the centrepiece of a recital. I had never discussed my concept of the alaap with my wife and yet here she was, not expounding but singing it. Was it the Ranakpur temple? Or did she and I think alike at least on this one single subject?

It was strange weather for this season. When I looked through the open interstices in the tiers of the temple, I saw black clouds grinding their teeth and itching for a fight. There was vicious thunder from time to time. It looked like rain but the banks of clouds stacked up like unsteady boulders would not let the sun, lightning or rain through. My wife started out thoughtfully with a quiet, unhurried exploration of her mind. It was a diverse landscape, asymmetrical but not chaotic. Cold, empty oceans stretched forever and yet sprouted gentle fires where you could warm your hands.

365

Macabre winds blew over dead cities bringing messages of longing and unfulfilled desires. But even here there were transparent blue pools of water where you could rest for an hour or a couple of nights. If you climbed the hills, the horizon slipped under your feet and moved behind you so that the future was something that had occurred in a long-forgotten past. A fog floated in now and you couldn't see the present but there was no panic for if there was one polestar in this universe, it was faith and hope.

My wife called out to the sun, her song was impatient and imperious. But it could also implore and plead, use any kind of guile to push aside the rock-clouds. I closed my eyes.

She changed her tactics. Her voice grew soft and sinuous and hinted at secret trysts. It ingratiated itself into the chinks and fissures, became frisky and intimate and slipped in and out of the rock precipice in the sky. It withdrew into the cellars and underworlds of the earth, lingered like mist and then started back. It gained momentum rapidly, wave rolled into urgent wave, fought its way out into the open, built into a roaring wall of water that would brook no obstacle and hurled itself at the black impregnable dome. Nothing happened. Then there was a fearsome creaking sound and the sky tottered and crashed down. The sun broke through the temple, not a nascent, tentative one but a full-blown, unstoppable golden orb. The carvings, the pillars, the mandapas, the staggered levels of the temple, the full marble structure and the two of us inside turned into light. My wife's song was pure joy. The temple tilted, and we were airborne. We flew at the speed of light and were at the heart of the stillness that is the universe.

✳   ✳   ✳

Messengers from Chittor were waiting for us at the bottom of the steps to the temple. The Sultan of Delhi had engaged the Mewar forces a second· time and had been routed once again. We were to return to the capital immediately. We rode hard and spent the next night at Kumbhalgarh. In the early morning I went down to the gardens and collected the showers of parijat flowers, five hundred of them, in the cloth of my saafa and poured them over Greeneyes. She woke up and looked in wonderment at the profusion of flowers on her person and all over the floor She gathered them in the palms of her hands time and again, flung her head back and let them fall over her face, her long, diaphanous neck, her breasts and the rest of her body.

'I wish we didn't have to leave. You'll never bring me parijats again.'

'Yes, I will. I've taken a branch of the tree from here.'

Chapter 30

*T*hings had not changed much. Father pleaded indisposition when I asked for an audience to lay my head at his feet. Why had he called me back?

When I went to the Victory Hall in the evening, a bandaged effigy masquerading as a human being dragged himself to the throne. His face was sewn up. Some Delhi soldiers had tried to sever his dead arm and the one good leg had been sliced open in the thigh. We all rose and bowed. He looked at us with what a stranger would call a one-eyed sneer but which was in fact one of his more amiable expressions and, to everyone's consternation, raised his good hand over his head and bowed deeply to all of us. Had one of the enemy blows affected his brain? No Rana will raise his hand above his shoulder in salutation; how could His Majesty possibly bow to his subjects and subordinates? The court stood awkwardly not knowing how to respond. But the surprises were just beginning. He bade us sit down in our accustomed places. And then, like all the other nobles, took his seat on the floor next to the throne.

The courtiers and the vassals couldn't contain themselves. They whispered about the mental health of His Majesty and his fitness to rule. I stepped out and prostrated myself before Father. That was the only way I could distract the court's attention. He was brusque: 'May Lord Eklingji's blessings be upon you.' My wife took in the situation and followed me. It was a little unusual for the Princess to pay her respects to His Majesty in open court but it was turning out to be a memorably unorthodox day. Father was chatting with my wife.

'Never seen a ghost before, have you, Princess?'

'I've seen worse, Your Majesty. From tomorrow I'll cook for you and heal you within fifteen days.'

'What would the Little Saint know of cooking?'

'Even the gods come to eat Merta food from me, Sire.'

'I might just take you up on that, Princess.'

'You don't have a choice, Majesty.' And added softly, 'Shall I help you sit on the throne?'

He smiled and shook his head.

When the whispered confabulation was over, Father addressed the court.

'My lords, raos, rawats, rajas, the highest and the mightiest in the land, friends and people of Mewar,' his voice was low and rich in emotion, 'we welcome you. We are honoured that you are with us to share this great and happy victory. This is the second time that we have inflicted a heavy defeat upon the Sultanate of Delhi. Ibrahim Lodi has not only sued for peace but has agreed to all our terms and conditions. We could not have done this without your help, cooperation and loyalty to Mewar. We are truly thankful to you. Before we proceed to the banquet hall and then to the victory celebrations, including a mushaira and fireworks display, I have a small announcement to make.

'My lords, you are all familiar with our Hindu customs and culture.' The voice had suddenly changed. You could have heard it all the way to the ancient coronation field two miles away. 'We do not worship a damaged idol.' He paused. Like everyone else, I too wondered what the hell he was talking about. 'A scratch, even a slight chip, and the holy image is holy no more. We no longer offer it prayers. It is no longer garlanded, and we no more fall at its feet. The divinity has withdrawn from it and we install a new image. My noble friends, I stand before you today like a broken and desecrated image. Victory has taken its toll. I am broken and injured from head to toe. It has been a great honour to lead Mewar all these years but it is a wise king who knows when it is time to retire. I beg you to grant me leave to relinquish my crown. Relieve me of my royal duties and appoint a new, whole and unblemished sovereign instead of me. All I ask you is to bestow a not too opulent maintenance upon me, just enough to keep body and soul together and allow me to serve our state of Mewar like any other warrior

369

noble and lord in this assembly for the rest of my life.'

I could have gagged. Bravo. Hooray. Cheers. If that wasn't superb theatre, I don't know anything about acting any more. Oh the modesty, the humility and the magnanimity of the man. There were tears in Rajput eyes, young and ancient. You might have the full deck of cards but Father has always got an extra card up his sleeve that's sure to wipe you out. I could hear a murmur rising. I could tell it was about to turn into a thundering chorus. The credulous fools didn't even pause to ask themselves why after all these years of victories and bodily injuries, His Majesty had chosen this moment to offer his resignation. What was he up to? What game was he playing? Why not say it in plain language, what did the great big idol of Mewar want? But why was I rushing things? The cat was bound to pop out of the bag in a few minutes. If Father was trying to prove his popularity, he had made his point. They were raising hell, yelling the great big hall down, vying with each other to proclaim their loyalty. It was wonderful to watch my brother Vikramaditya, who not too many years ago had tried to unseat Father, now racing ahead of everyone else and in a frenzy of filial love swearing to slit his own throat if His Majesty stepped down.

I had, needless to say, painted myself into a corner. I had no one to blame but myself. If you are a public personality and wish to remain so, you can't afford to shy away from showmanship. It's not enough to be honest and loyal, frankly it doesn't matter if you are not, so long as you are perceived to be so. Why was I tongue-tied, why couldn't I compete with the rest of them and tell Father that I wouldn't permit him to retire from kingship when that was the truth and nothing but? If you like, let's take a more cynical view. What would happen if he threw it all up and walked away? What if they appointed, at his bidding, Vikramaditya as his successor? Anyway you looked at it, I had little choice but to bray along with the others. It was too late now. I had let my diffidence and dislike for exhibitionism get the better of me. Besides, I was being unfair to the majority of Mewar's vassals and friends. Whatever their private ambitions, they respected Father and believed in him and his leadership. I caught my uncle Lakshman Simhaji looking at me quizzically. He was my father's colleague and contemporary. He could afford to hold his tongue. No one would question his intentions.

Two minutes of 'nays' would have made the point but His Majesty let them go on for over five minutes. It fell upon Rawat Rattan Simha of Salumbar to refute His Majesty's transparently rhetorical argument. With what earnestness and enthusiasm he took up his task. There was not a shadow of dissembling or sham in the good man. Like almost all the other grandees, he believed that his liege meant every word he uttered and would renounce both royal title and function. How suavely Father had manoeuvred his vassalage and courtiers exactly where he wanted.

We were kings by divine right, the earthly regents of Lord Eklingji who is none other than the great Shiva himself. By the simple device of a simile, Father had entered highly dangerous and dubious waters and arrogated divinity to himself. And yet here were Rawat Rattan Simha and the other elders falling over each other trying to explain with more and more convoluted ratiocination why he must continue to occupy the throne and perform the duties that devolve upon the Maharana.

'We submit to Your Majesty that your excessive sense of modesty, your untiring and persistent endeavours to put the interest of the state above all else, and your regard for the court have clouded your mind like the opaque tissue of a cataract and thus engendered the subtlest misapprehensions and misconceptions in it. We beg you to allow us to remove the scales from your eyes. The injuries His Majesty has received are the mark of the legendary heroism and valour that every Rajput thirsts after. They were earned in the line of the highest duty to the state while vanquishing the enemy and ensuring the pride of victory for Mewar and its friends. You are not the lesser from loss of limbs or your wounds. Far from diminishing your reputation and stature, they crown you with the most illustrious laurels and enhance the glory and fame of Mewar. More than ever before you are the paradigm of divinity.'

The bombast was forgivable. The lord of Salumbar had a difficult task and he was trying to impress his liege. How we get carried away by words. Who is to keep track and count of the rights and prerogatives we give away of our own accord in our eagerness to make gods of men? Further vociferous cheering followed. Finally, Rao Viramdev stepped forward and raised his hand. He waited till the last voice had died down.

'Your Majesty, you have heard the verdict of the people of Mewar, of the raos and rawats, of the princes and the court officials. We've gathered here to celebrate our victory over the Delhi Sultanate. I beg you not to turn it into a grievous defeat.' Thereupon, Rao Viramdev and the other chieftains including Raja Puraji Kika got up and took His Majesty by the hand and placed him on the unoccupied throne.

Father demurred. Father protested. Father acquiesced.

'What can I say? To refuse now would be tantamount to abusing your trust in me and my office. There is only one thing that sustains any kingship: the faith and goodwill of its people. I'm overwhelmed by your regard for me. I am beholden to you and hope that I shall continue to be worthy of your great trust.' When the applause had subsided, Father spoke softly. 'I have but one small request.' 'Yes, yes,' the courtiers and the whole assembly shouted, 'we'll lay down our lives for you, Sire.' His Majesty had something a little less straightforward and obvious than the mere gift of life on his mind. We had come to the point of this whole elaborate exercise. 'It is our wish that the fort and province of Ranthambhor be bestowed upon Prince Vikramaditya and his brother Prince Uday Simha as jagirs.'

Where had all the hurrahs and bellowing and 'Anything, absolutely anything, Sire, it is yours to ask and ours to give' vanished? The court sat stunned. His Majesty was breaking with tradition and the sanctity that attaches to protocol that had been deliberately constructed over hundreds of years. He would get away with it, no doubt about it, but it was evident that in his moment of triumph Father had overplayed his hand. He had misjudged the mood of his court: his lords, nobles and rajas were willing to back him all the way but not the caprice and favouritism of an overbearing and overindulged queen. By giving in to her, Father was willing to risk alienating his closest allies. But there was more to follow. Having gone out on a limb for Queen Karmavati's two sons, the younger one still a child, and asked for a special and extraordinary dispensation for them, Father felt compelled to safeguard their interests further.

Rani Karmavati may have been a foolish queen but she was no fool. The jagir of Ranthambhor was not only a considerable territory, it was one of our most prestigious provinces. She must have suspected that her beloved Vikramaditya may not be up to the task of defending that fine stronghold.

'I would like to ask His Highness, Hada Surajmal to be the guardian of the two Princes in Ranthambhor.'

Hada Surajmal sat impassively, only the ticking of the pulse in his tight-set jaw giving away his surprise, anger and discomfiture at Father's request. Queen Karmavati and the Hada had nothing, absolutely nothing in common but the fact that they were siblings. Hada Surajmal was curt, haughty, painfully upright and exceedingly sensitive to the possibility that his position and privileges may be construed to be a consequence of his sister's marriage to His Majesty. He loathed his nephew Vikramaditya. If he could, he would never have visited Chittor. He did not stay at the Palace but with friends of his in the capital. He was one of our most important and valued allies. He was also one of the three or four people in Mewar who could stand up to Father.

'Your Majesty, the interests of Mewar are paramount to me.' He then looked pointedly at me. 'As such my loyalty to the throne forbids me from undertaking a commitment that may perchance lead to a conflict of interests.'

I found it droll that the Hada should glower at me. Since I no longer figured in the line of succession, there would certainly be no conflict of interest between his nephews, especially Vikramaditya and me.

'Your Highness,' Father answered in an unaccustomedly appeasing tone, 'I doubt that such an extreme exigency will arise. But let me reassure you that should there ever be a divergence of interests, the well-being of Mewar will take precedence over all else.'

Hada Surajmal had little choice but to accept the assignment.

'As you wish, Majesty, but,' he was not about to give in without protest, 'I hope I have made it amply clear that I would find it intolerable to be put in an untenable position.'

373

Father smiled and refrained from comment. 'One last matter and we'll proceed with the festivities. We have recalled our eldest son from Kumbhalgarh. As of tomorrow he'll be appointed governor of Chittor and will assist me in the War Council.'

A single audible gasp escaped from the Queen's enclosure. While my favourite mother's confidant, the eunuch Bruhannada maintained an impassive expression, she had not been able to contain herself. It was followed by much thumping and clapping from the court. I'm often lectured in glowing terms about the innate wisdom of the common man. It is pointed out that regardless of temporary lapses, it rests on a solid foundation of pragmatism, hardheaded sense and the good of the community. It's a nice thesis and patently false. The common man is just as fickle, shortsighted, sensible or otherwise as the nobility gathered in this court. We are deluding ourselves when we say man is a rational animal. If we are to understand him, or ourselves rather, we must look to impulse, the mood of the moment, the herd mentality and a cursed unwillingness to weigh the consequences of our actions. There was indeed a simple explanation for the sudden show of affection for me. When indifferent tidings come on the heels of bad news, they are greeted as if there has been a turn in fortunes that one has prayed and yearned for every hour of one's life.

I would have to be a tetchy prig to be piqued by the newfound enthusiasm of the courtiers for me and their attempts to catch my eye and convey their congratulations. I smiled back at them but my thoughts were elsewhere. That old fox, His Majesty, was in good shape and at his devious best. You had to hand it to him. He had fooled even his favourite queen who had put him up to gifting the kingdom and purse of Ranthambhor to her own children. That susurrus of surprise from her was not for dramatic effect. It was the genuine article. She had got what she wanted but Father had proved once again that he was the master of the stalemate. He had obviously left Queen Karmavati in the dark about the new move he had planned and had thwarted both Vikramaditya and me. Our fortunes had improved but we were no better off than we were. You can't please everybody, a king certainly can't, Father had said to me when I was a child. He had forgotten to mention the other half of that proposition. You can displease everybody and get some peace of mind for yourself. The whole court, including the Queen, was at liberty to keep guessing who Father had in mind as his successor while the princes could keep themselves busy scheming and intriguing against each other and with some luck kill each other off.

*　　*　　*

So far, two of the administrative officers working for me have taken it upon themselves to tell me that they did things differently. I have quietly and half seriously reminded them that things haven't changed but have gone back to being the same as they were. My style may not have changed but my hours have. I hope it is only till such time as I finish catching up. Otherwise I will have given the lie to my maxim that whether you work eight or twenty hours, the quantum of work that gets done on a normal day is the same.

Vikramaditya had spent all his time on the second set of administrative services he set up. The parallel economy, the parallel police force, the parallel food and agricultural department, the parallel trade and commerce ministry and so on. That left the original infrastructure in a shambles. My younger brother, Rattan, who was given charge of Chittor when Father was out campaigning against Sultan Ibrahim Lodi, did not wish to rock the boat. His concept of the job was an interim one, a holding operation till Father returned. His chief concern was to keep the machinery of the state working.

I am supposed to be working right under Father's nose. That should leave me paralyzed but I prefer to think that it gives me a free hand. After all, his subjects are bound to take it for granted that he is keeping an eye on me. For one interminable month I debated whether I should take action against the officers who ran the parallel government and whose dereliction of duty had few precedents in our history. Tej and Shafi had enough documented evidence against them, especially the senior members, to keep them in jail for at least a couple of lives. I knew it was the right thing to do to set a precedent and a deterrent. But wisdom, I felt at this juncture, did not lie in taking punitive action. I would be raking up a lot of old issues and making the whole administration nervous. It would be seen as vengeful instead of just and fair and I would paralyse the civil services. Perhaps I was taking the easier way out, letting sleeping dogs lie. (As in most cases where higher-ups are involved, the moving force behind the colossal corruption in the state would go scot-free.) I declared amnesty for all and sundry in my mind. But anybody who slipped up henceforth would pay a heavy price for wrongs past and present.

There is no addiction like work and routine. After barely five weeks in Chittor, I find it difficult to recall that I have been out of circulation for close to three years, one in Chittor and nearly two in Kumbhalgarh.

I ask myself how this extended period of enforced marginalization and inactivity has affected me? Do human beings ever change? Do calamities, crises, sudden loss of self-esteem, and the meaning of one's life, the death of one's closest friends or relatives transform one in obvious as well as subtle ways? Do our goals alter? Is there a larger vision of life? Do our unhappy experiences make us more understanding of people and their foibles? One could go on with the list of possibilities for a couple of pages. But one question alone will suffice. Do they make us better human beings? I find the thought that great upheavals and traumas may leave us untouched at the very core of our beings, even as we protest to the contrary, devastating, though I suspect that that is where the truth lies. I'm not making any large generalizations nor do I claim to have made a deep study of the subject. I can only speak for myself. I find that I'm still as intent on being Maharaj Kumar as I ever was. There's one thing and one thing alone that I want above all else: it is the crown after Father's death. Secondly, I'm still utterly and inseparably attached to worldly ambitions like enlarging our kingdom to the boundaries of the oceans, and that's the very least I would aim for. Take those two things away and what is left of me? My wife, Kausalya, Leelawati, my good friends Raja Puraji Kika, Tej and Shafi matter to me, but the meaning of my life does not revolve around them.

I am, as even my well-wishers are constrained to admit, a man with not one, but numerous hobby horses. The intervening lost years have brought a new sense of urgency so that I'm now trying to ride astride all of them simultaneously. Everything has a rhythm and a momentum. A little too early or too late and you fall on your face. I am beginning to appreciate more and more the importance of the auspicious moment. Why is timing so important for a project? Because mankind would like a tree to bear fruit before planting the seed. We would all want Victory Towers dedicated to ourselves without laying deep and solid foundations. The propitious moment is rarely the next day or the next minute. It is a week, months or even years away. It forces you to get your wits together, to analyse data, assess the chances of success, check whether you've got your facts right and check and double-check who is likely to go along with you, who'll go against you and who'll sit on the fence. Plan your strategy to the last detail and then know when to seize the auspicious moment. Ripeness is all. Or phrasing it a little more practically and personally, catch Father and his senior advisers at the right moment. Even in matters of state when sometimes the very survival of the polity may be at stake, never underestimate the effect of the favourable moment. Without it, as with both pointless haste and procrastination, all will come to nought.

At the third cabinet meeting since my return, the town planner, Sahasmal and I pushed through the water and sewage schemes without needing exceptional skills in persuasion. I'll attempt the tunnel project only when Sahasmal has devised a foolproof system of ventilating the passages.

That brought me to the third and most pressing of my self-imposed tasks: reliable information regarding ordnance and weapons knowhow and the latest military strategies. Instead of making a case for each individual project, I had temporarily circumvented most of the problems by clubbing all of them under the title of Intelligence. All I did was to get Father's approval for Mangal's appointment as head of the intelligence services. Father was of the view that as Mewar's territories grew, there was a need to recruit more agents and of course, increase the budget for the department substantially. What Mangal and I did with the budget was my business and responsibility so long as the security of the state was not compromised.

Mewar's intelligence services were at an all-time low. Let me rephrase that. The reports from our various agents kept coming in

377

regularly. But in the absence of an active and centralized guiding authority, a clear-cut enunciation of goals and special subjects of interest, our agents stuck to traditional areas of observation, enquiry, infiltration and reporting. There was no system for gauging the value of the reports. Not only was the enemy as busy as we were planting false information, but, as in most fields where immediate means of verification are not available, the only way an agent can raise his importance is to inflate dangers and threats — better still, invent them and inculcate a chronic crisis mentality. Matters got completely out of hand and inextricably complicated when the competitive element was added to the spy scenario.

Agents rarely knew the contents submitted by other members in the service but they did not wish to take any chances. They turned master storytellers. In the majority of the reports, even dry ones like the enemy's crop situation or the numerical strength of a garrison, they turned themselves into heroes. They took on the might of Delhi, Gujarat, Malwa or any of our other opponents single-handed; the odds would be stacked a thousand to one but they secured the information and came out alive.

But you cannot blame the agents. It was our systems which were at fault. For a while after Mangal took over, things seemed to go from bad to worse. Had I made a mistake in choosing him? It's one thing to take care of the Maharaj Kumar, pick up whatever gossip and rumour you can and protect His Highness, and quite another to take over the reins of a demoralized intelligence service, enthuse its members while always keeping alive the threat of disciplinary action and most important of all, deliver valuable and trustworthy information. Maybe Mangal was out of his depth. Two months into the post, almost all reports from his agents had ceased. Then every once in a while he started sending me pages written in Turki, some of them in a childish script, some in exquisite calligraphy along with an execrable and indecipherable scrawl which was meant to be a translation of the Turki. I had little desire and even less patience to unravel the meaning from bits and pieces of what was clearly someone else's diary. They were rarely connected and I did not get a feel for the diarist or the way his mind worked. Besides, I also had the strange feeling that if I continued reading,

378

I would become a voyeur. A diary by definition is a chronicle of past events. Detailed descriptive passages about flowers and fruits; nocturnal raids which were nothing but dacoities in plain language; the one-time bane of my life, poetry, though I must confess that in the last couple of years, constant exposure has worn me down to the point that I am not only receptive to it but even look forward to it occasionally. But poetry in Turki where assonance and wordplay run riot and the translator is not always capable of handling the multiple layers of meaning? No, thank you. Constant troubles with uncles, cousins and half-brothers, as if I don't have enough of my own. Drinking parties followed by remorse at having imbibed.

What interest would Father have in an indigent man who was a maruader, with literate and cultured tastes, in some distant land? I stopped going through the scraps. I had now at least seven or ten of them, some of them two lines long, others a paragraph while a couple went on for a page. I put them away in a desk and decided to call Mangal and ask him why he was wasting my time with a Turki diary, and how did he expect me to brief His Majesty and the War Council three weeks from now when all other reports from our agents in Delhi, Malwa, Gujarat and elsewhere had dried up.

My irritation with Mangal kept rising but for some reason I was loath to summon him. (The scraps of Turki with their translation have now gone up to twenty-one.) There was only one thing for me to do. When I get mad with a written report, I sit down with a pen, go over the text line by line and then tear apart the writer's facts and assessment, his lack of interest, his woolly language and ask him to redo the report within a day or two. I sat down with paper and quill and the excerpts and got ready to blast Mangal. If he thought he could take me for granted just because we had grown up together since childhood and because I was dependent on him, he was making a mistake.

If anybody was mistaken, it was not Mangal but I. I wrote furiously and scathingly. By the seventh note a pattern had begun to emerge; by the eleventh excerpt I was hooked. I couldn't have enough.

'In the name of God, the Merciful, the Compassionate.

'In the month of Ramzan of the year 1494 and in the twelfth year of my age, I became a ruler in the country of Farghana.

'Farghana is situated in the fifth climate and at the limit of settled habitation. On the east it has Kashghar; on the west, Samarkand; on the south, the mountains of the Badakhshan border; on the north, though in former times there must have been towns such as Almaligh, Almatu and Yangi which in books they write Taraz, at the present all is desolate, no settled population whatever remaining, because of the Moghuls and the Auzbegs.'

'Farghana has seven separate townships, five on the south and two on the north of the Saihun river.

'Of those on the south, one is Andijan. It has a central position and is the capital of the Farghana country. It produces much grain, fruits in abundance, excellent grapes and melons. In the melon season it is not customary to sell them out at the beds. Better than the Andijan nashpati, there is none. After Samarkand and Kesh, the fort of Andijan is the largest in Transoxiana. It has three gates. Its citadel is on its south side. Into it water goes by nine channels; out of it, it is strange that none comes at even a single place. Round the outer edge of the ditch runs a gravelled highway; the width of this highway divides the fort from the suburbs surrounding it.

'Andijan has good hunting and fowling; its pheasants grow so surprisingly fat that rumour has it four people could not finish one they were eating with its stew.'

'It passed through my mind that to wander from mountain to mountain, homeless and houseless, had nothing to recommend it.'

'I do not write this in order to make complaint; I have written the plain truth. I do not set these matters down in order to make known my own deserts; I have set down exactly what has happened. In this History I have held firmly to it that the truth should be reached in every matter, and that every act should be recorded precisely as it occurred. From this it follows that I have set down of good and bad whatever is known, concerning father and older brother, kins-

380

man and stranger; of them all I have set down carefully the known virtues and defects. Let the reader accept my excuse; let the reader pass on from the place of severity!'

'Umar Sheikh Mirza, my father, was a short, stout, round-bearded and fleshy-faced person. He used to wear his tunic so very tight that to fasten the strings he had to draw his belly in and, if he let himself out after tying them, they often tore away. He was not choice in dress or food.

'He was very generous; in truth, his character rose altogether to the height of generosity. He was affable, eloquent and sweet-spoken, daring and bold.'

'A middling archer, he was strong in the fist; not a man but fell to his blow. Through his ambition, peace was exchanged often for war, friendliness for hostility.'

'It has been mentioned that the fort of Akhsi is situated above a deep ravine; along this ravine stand the palace buildings, and from it, on Monday, Ramzan four, Umar Sheikh Mirza flew with his pigeons and their house, and became a falcon.'

'Without a glance at the fewness of our men, we had the nagarets sounded, and putting our trust in God moved with face set for our opponent Muquim.

    For few or many God is full strength,
    No man has might in His court.

'How often, God willing it, a small force has vanquished a large one! Learning from the nagarets that we were approaching, Muquim forgot his fixed plan and took the road to flight. God brought it right.'

'As the Bajauris were rebels and at enmity with the people of Islam, and as, by reason of the heathenish and hostile customs prevailing in their midst, the very name of Islam was rooted out from their tribe, they were put to general massacre and their wives and children were made captive. At a guess, more than three thousand men went to their death; as the fight did not reach to the eastern side of the fort, a few got away there.

'The fort taken, we entered and inspected it. On the walls, in houses, streets and alleys, the dead lay in what numbers! Comers and goers to and fro were passing over the bodies.'

'After taking Bajaur by storm in two to three gari, and making a general massacre of its people, we went on into Bhira. Bhira we neither overran nor plundered; we imposed a ransom on its people, taking from them in money and goods to the value of four lakhs of shahrukhis and having shared this out to the army and auxiliaries, returned to Kabul.'

There was more, all of it jagged and piecemeal. There were various references to defeats, ignominious flights from whichever place served as a temporary home, repeated mention of the enormous pleasure the diarist took in swimming in any kind of climate. He was constantly on the move, from Samarkand to Kabul to Kandahar to Samarkand and other places. There were times when the band of men following him was less than two hundred.

I suspect that there were two reasons why Mangal wanted me to look at the transcripts. The first was that the diarist never gave up. Defeat rejuvenated him. There was something in his character which drew people to him despite repeated defeats, failures and dethronings. The second feature could have a direct bearing on Mewar itself. The man had crossed the River Indus. Granted that it was more in the nature of a swift desperado raid on Bajaur for what appeared to be religious reasons and the collection of a substantial ransom from the people of Bhira. Having tested the waters of Hindustan and found them inviting, he had made a second incursion from his base in Kabul.

Perhaps Father knew of his visits. He is news to me since I was dead to the world in Kumbhalgarh. Innumerable Muslim chieftains, kings and padshahs have come through the Khyber Pass, pillaged the land around the Indus and sometimes as far down as Delhi, defaced temples and massacred people in the hundreds of thousands but most of them have gone back for the simple reason that they were transient marauders and their only purpose was plunder and booty. Only a few stayed behind. Delhi has been under Afghan rule for generations. Hardly anyone remembers that their ancestors crossed the high passes in the Hindukush without any clear-cut idea of settling down in India. This man (why is Mangal keeping his name in the dark?) will bear watching closely.

There is however one other reason, call it intangible, whimsical or absurd, why I'm drawn to the diarist. I see myself in him. I too take notes and since Kumbhalgarh, have begun to turn them into an autobiography of sorts. You will find the passage where he speaks about writing the truth without regard to how one comes across, on the flyleaf of my own memoirs. Of course the language and specifics may differ but the sentiment is exactly the same. I read about the pleasure the man takes in swimming across rivers and I see myself. He is fond of his father but does not care if the pen portrait is not always complimentary to the subject. There's something else, something dour and dark and disturbing. He leaves his conscience and sentiments out of the picture and the diary, when he commits mass murder. I feel a closeness to the man that makes me feel that I'm familiar with his mind. As we all know, or at least ought to know, the one simple way a commander can ensure defeat and disaster is for him to go by his intuition alone.

Having said that, let me not underplay the sharp and unbridgeable differences between us. There is a truly scary sentence which occurs again and again in his writing. 'God brought it right.' I am a believer in our gods. I may no longer have any serious dialogue or transaction with the Flautist, but I cannot imagine starting a day or ending it without saying a prayer to Lord Eklingji. And yet my relationship with God is distant, formal and more a matter of protocol and habit. The diarist on the other hand has an extraordinary faith, the kind of compelling faith that can almost bend and coerce God to rise to his expectations. Don't take me literally; the wandering diarist would find this blasphemous in the extreme. But there is something about his tone and his absolute and unshakable trust in God which must surely give pause to even the Almighty.

There is a side effect of this belief which can have the gravest consequences for us. If he ever comes to Hindustan with long-term plans of settling down, he'll want to be a ghazi, a holy warrior of God who fights against infidels and heathens like us in Mewar. Will

383

he keep off the Muslim kingdoms like Malwa and Gujarat or will his territorial ambitions run them over? This is speculation but there's more to it than foolish imaginings. Since my return, I have been pondering the Hindu-Muslim divide. If Mewar is to grow and expand, one of our major tasks will have to do with making Muslims feel secure in a Hindu kingdom. They must have as much of a stake in Mewar's future as the Jains or Hindus. How, I keep wondering, do we ensure a dichotomy whereby God and faith remain at home and the state takes first priority in public life?

That evening Mangal sent his 'confidential and top secret' file home to me.

Your Highness,

Now that you've been through the notes that I have been sending you over a period of months and studied them carefully (the man has me followed round the clock; I can't pee without one of his men noting down the time and place and colour of the fluid), I feel free to present my report. I'm aware that I have tested your patience and put you in a predicament by not having yet submitted my very first report for the coming cabinet meeting. It is true that I have also been avoiding you but that was because I did not wish to have converse with you till you had independently made up your mind about those excerpts.

A word before I come to the report. I know you've been wondering why I have not submitted most of the reports sent by our agents. Their veracity was, frankly, doubtful and I wished to spend time with each agent and get a feel for the man, his quirks, his level of insecurity and his need to justify his patriotism. I wanted to encourage them in their endeavours and discourage them from what can perhaps be termed as parallel truths. I gained their confidence by putting them at ease over a series of meetings. Then I went over their previous reports. I gave them my assessment of the ratios of truth and fabrication they contained and told them that they were free to contradict my assessment so long as they produced corroboration for their stories.

Ten days from now, I believe, intelligence reports will once again appear on your table. Each will come marked with its priority rating and also a rating for veracity. Over and above these two parameters, every once in a while you'll come across a comment like 'Facts and data unreliable but agent's feel for the situation is insightful and should not be discounted.' It is in the nature of a spy's job that nothing can be guaranteed, not even his lies; for every once in a while you'll discover that his fabrications have been substantiated by the turn of events.

Now to the report.

Name of subject : Zahiru'd-din Muhammad Babur

Designation : King of Kabul

Sources : Dictation or copying exercises given by Zahiru'd-din Muhammad Babur to his nine-year-old cousin, Haidar. Also scraps of paper on which Babur's amanuensis tested his quill, ink and handwriting before making a copy of the diary under Babur's supervision or sheets thrown into the waste paper basket because of spelling and other errors committed during the course of copying.

Ancestry : On his father's side Babur is the great-great-grandson of Timur the Lame. On his mother's, Babur is descended from Chaghatai Khan, second son of the Mongol conqueror, Jenghiz Khan.

Rajputs and even the Lodis of Delhi may regard Timur and Jenghiz Khan as barbarians but that is the outsider's point of view. For Babur it is a matter of the highest pride that the blood of these two conquerors flows in his veins.

Most of his life Babur has been on the run. In 1497, at the age of fourteen he captured his ancestral home, Samarkand. The expedition proved prohibitively expensive since within a hundred days, he lost both his own kingdom Farghana, and Samarkand as well.

In 1499, Babur recovered Farghana but the year after he had to share it with his brother Jehangir.

In the year 1500, Babur recaptured Samarkand. Within a few months, he had once again lost it. Homeless for three years, in 1504 Babur took possession of Kabul which he made his capital. In 1511 Babur again mounted the throne of Samarkand only to vacate it in May 1512.

In 1519, Babur first crossed the Indus and took Bajaur fort. In

1520, he invaded India for the third time, attacked the Gakkai tribe, quashed a rebellion at Bhira and reached Sialkot.

There is clearly a pattern here. In his diary, Babur keeps referring to Samarkand, the place that Timur used as his home base, and to Delhi which Timur invaded in 1398.

Timur always had Samarkand to return to. Babur captured Samarkand thrice and thrice he has had to relinquish it. Even Kabul he may lose one of these days. India is infinitely bigger, infinitely richer, and has the added attraction of being peopled by infidels. If he decides to take Delhi, he serves both Allah's purposes and his own.

Conclusion : Adversity does not faze Babur. Wherever he goes, whether it is Samarkand, Kandahar or Kabul, he quickly establishes a court and gathers poets and artisans around him. Since he is a man of his word, he arouses strong loyalty in his men. He is swift both to attack and retreat. Some of his most impressive victories have been won by a mere thousand to twelve hundred men. It is not inconceivable that he will go into battle with just two hundred men and yet come out triumphant. He has a keen interest in weapons technology and is constantly trying to acquire and incorporate it in his military strategy. He has, it is said, acquired a new kind of weapon called cannons and a Turkish artilleryman called Ustad Ali who casts them. We await more information on these firearms.

Recommended action :

1. Babur, to follow your own precepts, will bear watching.

2. Go all out to obtain samples of the new weaponry.

3. Demonstrate how this new weaponry operates to His Majesty.

4. Get a big budget sanctioned to place large orders for guns and cannons.

5. Build our offensive and defensive strategies around these weapons.

6. Train our army personnel in the use of these firearms.

7. Ensure that our investment in technology is not a one-shot exercise but a continuous one so that at every point it is our enemy who is at a disadvantage against us and not the other way round.

8. Accessing ordnance know-how from foreign sources as an

386

initial measure is fine but in the long run, we'll have to steep ourselves in the new knowledge and learn to stand on our own feet, the idea being that future advances in the field come from us.

*　　*　　*

Is there any room for doubt that Mangal and I fed at the same breast after you've read his report? He may be more terse than I but that's because the format of a briefing demands brevity, clarity, a conclusion and a line of action. I doubt if I will ever have to rework a Mangal-report before presenting it to Father. Will Mangal's recommendations have the desired effect on Father? After all, I have been saying the same things to His Majesty for the last seven or eight years. There is no denying, however, that Mangal's action-scenario is now anchored to an actual set of circumstances while what I've been talking about was really a matter of policy. I hope the War Council meetings are not going to get stuck in a discussion about how Mangal's suggestions devolve upon a series of assumptions: one, the ruler of Kabul plans to come into India again; two, at some point in time he'll give battle to the Sultan of Delhi; and three, our own borders and kingdom will then be threatened by him.

On the other hand, there is no gainsaying that even if Babur ventures into India, it may once again be for a quick hit-and-run money-making raid. Or he may leave Delhi alone now and decide to try to regain Samarkand which seems to have become almost an obsessive symbol of legitimacy and nostalgia for him. He could also lose his head, literally.

Babur has already been to India twice. Mangal's implicit guess is that Babur will some time or other make further forays into India. I would go along with Mangal's analysis for the simple reason that Mangal weighs his words carefully before he speaks out. I doubt if Kabul will contain Babur's ambition. He will find it difficult, if not impossible, to resist the temptation of India. But the question to ask is whether we want to plan our armament strategy contingent upon a single enemy's plans to invade India. Of course, we have to be prepared for any contingency including an invasion from the north-west. But more to the point we have to be better equipped and better prepared because we ourselves have territorial ambitions.

It seems hard to believe that I am actually holding pages of matter written God-knows-where, Farghana, Samarkand, Kandahar or Kabul in my hands and that they are the words of a king whose ancestors hailed from the distant kingdom of Turkey. How could they have travelled so far? Is it a big hoax? We don't have any foolproof method of verifying the authenticity of the documents unless of course I send an emissary to the current king of Kabul and enquire whether the notes I have in front of me are his own. And yet I suspect that the words are true and come from a man of great resolve and vision, a man whose sense of self is neither inflated nor modest, but matter-of-fact.

For some reason I keep going back to two passages, one about Andijan in Farghana and the other about his father. There is a quiet warmth in the tone of writing which could only come from someone who is deeply attached to his country. And yet it is devoid of the sentimentality that accompanies most writing about one's home-land, especially if one is an exile. It makes the reader want to go and explore the place for oneself. 'Into the citadel at Andijan water goes by nine channels; out of it, it is strange that none comes at even a single place.' What happens to the water? Where does it go? Has it been collected underground year after year? (Like a bump on the head, does the citadel keep rising? Will Andijan burst open like a pod one of these days with the pressure of all that water under it?) Take the puzzling passage about Umar Sheikh Mirza and his pigeons at the Akhsi fort. I went over it at least a dozen times before I realized that Babur's father had gone to see his pigeons in the dovecote when the side of the mountain ledge seems to have collapsed, and in death Umar Sheikh 'became a falcon'.

The less said about my dislike of hunting the better but I must confess that I want to go to Andijan to check out the pheasants there. Why has Babur switched to rumour when it's obvious that he has done enough hunting and fowling himself to know the facts except to pull our leg with some fabled and fat-bird stew that four

388

people cannot finish? I've always had a fondness for humour. But the kind of humour that really gets to me is the straight-faced variety where unless you are on your guard you don't detect the tongue in the cheek.

Can you imagine any charan, poet or even historian from Mewar writing so candidly, objectively and affectionately about His Majesty, the Maharana, for instance? Frankly, I can't see any of my brothers, cousins or uncles managing it either. No whitewashing, no genuflecting, no obsequious toadying, just a quick sketch done with superb self-assurance. It's obvious that the man is not afraid of being critical because he does not believe that the act of appraisal or judging someone rules out affection or high regard.

How often does one hear even our seniormost officials prefacing their remarks with the proviso, 'Please don't misunderstand me, the last thing I want to be is judgmental.' Why have they been appointed to senior positions with so many people reporting to them, if they are not expected to analyse and assess situations and human beings with the utmost rigour and ruthlessness? Rigour and ruthlessness do not preclude sympathy with another's point of view. But it is impossible to take decisions, often critical ones, or to deal with one's enemies, friends, peers, juniors, seniors or wife and children unless one evaluates their and one's own strengths, weaknesses and blind spots.

*   *   *

'And what if I don't get your report within the next ten days?' I knew what Mangal's answer was going to be but I wanted to make him squirm. 'What shall I tell the cabinet and our friendly neighbours? Should I tell the former that they should postpone the business of the state of Mewar and the latter that they delay any plans to attack Mewar because Mangal isn't ready to brief the Security Council yet?'

'You'll have it within the next ten days, Your Highness.' He didn't blanch, I should have known that too.

'I'm much beholden to you.' That was shabby and utterly uncalled for but it did the trick. There was a crack in the stone-face for a fraction of a second. Perhaps underneath it, the man may actually have winced. 'That will be all.'

He prepared to leave, not reacting to my childish snubs.

'Mangal, that was excellent work. How did you get hold of the stuff?'

Mangal smiled. 'From a sweeper.'

I laughed. 'Bravo. The laugh's on me this time. Let's have the truth now.'

'It is the truth, Your Highness.'

'Come off ....' I realized that he was not joking.

'One of the local operatives told me laughingly one day over samosas that times had changed. "Sweepers," he said, "would soon be doing better than jagirdars." "How's that?" I asked him. "Have you ever got a parcel from abroad?" he asked me sarcastically. I shook my head. "Shyam Dulare, the sweeper at the Prime Minister, Pooranmalji's home, gets them." "From where?" "How would I know? All I can tell you is that some passing mendicant delivers them." I think Your Highness has guessed the rest.'

'I may have but I wouldn't mind it if you spelt out the details. How did Shyam Dulare get access to the Kabul court?'

'Shyam Dulare, it turns out, has a cousin Pyarelal who worked in Bajaur. When Bajaur was sacked, Pyarelal and his family were spared because Pyarelal said to the commandant of the occupying army, "In the name of God, the Merciful, the Compassionate, is it not true that the Prophet has forbidden the faithful to kill those gentiles and pagans who have discovered the true Lord, Allah himself?" The commandant smiled and asked, "Have you discovered the Lord and Master of the Universe or is it that you've discovered that your life is worth nothing unless you profess to the faith of the Prophet and of His Highness Zahiru'd-din Muhammad Babur?" "And what if the latter be the truth," the sweeper's cousin replied cheekily, "will you question the diverse and manifold ways in which Allah causes the blind to see and the deaf to hear and the mute to speak, and the unenlightened to see the light and the deceived to forsake their deceptions and the hypocrites to abandon their hypocrisy? For if you do, then is it not obvious that you consider yourself wiser than Allah himself and is there any crime greater than placing yourself above the All-knowing and the All-perceiving who hath wrought this earth and all living and dead things in it, the waves in the sea and the colours on the birds and the dome of the sky and the rains that water the earth and quench our thirst and bring forth grain a thousandfold from one seed?" And the commandant stayed the sword in his hand as it was about to slay Pyarelal and took him to his king, Babur himself, and told him of the miracle of the words from the sweeper's tongue, for verily they were words that the Holy Book itself would recognize and honour. And Babur lifted the sweeper up by the hands and said, "From today this man shall be my brother in the faith and work in my house." And thus it came to be.'

'Mangal, will you spare us the archaic language?'

'It was the language in which Shyam Dulare told me this lofty tale.'

'Shyam Dulare, it appears however, has not been converted yet.'

'Pyarelal, now known as Karim Muhammad, is working on it.'

'And is the two-way traffic a phenomenon that occurred after Pyarelal's conversion or was Shyam Dulare sharing documents and information from the Pradhan Pooranmalji's home from earlier times?'

Mangal no longer seemed to enjoy the raconteur's job. 'Shyam Dulare's conduit has been functioning for a long time, Highness. The information has been going to the Delhi, Gujarat and Bajaur courts and to Medini Rai at Malwa.'

'That's a relief. At least Shyam Dulare is impartial to money and the colour of its religion. Is our Prime Minister Pooranmalji involved in this affair?'

'So far I have not found any evidence to suggest that.'

'Is that "so far" a hedge against future discoveries or are you holding something back?'

'So long as I am in charge of the intelligence portfolio, forgive the impertinence, Highness, I'll use the phrase "so far" in your context too if ever you were under investigation.'

'I believe you would, Mangal, and that is one of the reasons why you and not someone else is holding the job. And what are we doing about Shyam Dulare?'

'Paying him money, feeding him information and keeping him

391

under surveillance.'

'How do we know he'll not raise the price for the next instalment of these scraps of papers?'

'We know for certain, Sire. He has already raised his price.'

'Despite the fact that he's committed treason?'

'He knows that we need him alive if we wish to continue getting information from him.'

'How do we know that Babur is not deliberately feeding this information to Pyarelal to misguide us?'

'It's a possibility that I have considered but I don't think we need worry too much about it. We are unlikely to get current intelligence on the man and his plans anyway unless he comes geographically closer to us. Barring you, Highness, nobody would be interested in knowing whether Babur has a hernia, whether he sleeps late and how long his hangovers last. I also know that you are going to ask me to research the military strategies of his ancestors Timur and Jenghiz Khan.'

'Mangal are you planning to make all speech from the Maharaj Kumar redundant? Let me warn you I won't have it. Do you have anything on Shyam Dulare?'

Maharaj Kumar. The words had slipped from my mouth. I thought I was going to be facetious. Instead I was aghast to find that somewhere in my mind I still hoped to be next in the line of succession.

'All we have, Highness,' Mangal deliberately changed the subject, 'is a slight deterrent.'

I wondered if Mangal had taken to archness. 'And what may that be?'

'We have taken one of his children in custody.'

'This is not a police state, Mangal.' I was genuinely horrified.

'You can't have it both ways, Highness.' That shut me and my hypocrisy effectively. 'The boy is getting an education, something inconceivable for a sweeper's child. Besides, the child is no guarantee. Shyam Dulare may turn around and say "Go ahead, kill him. I'm young enough to have more."'

'Who's doing the translation from the Turki?'

'Pyarelal or Karim Muhammad as he is known now.'

'Mangal, what about the original? Is it really Turki or gibberish?'

'It is Turki, Sire, and as you must have realized, Karim Muhammad is not a bad translator at all.'

*　*　*

'How long do you plan to avoid me?'

'We run into each other four to seven times a day.'

'You no longer wish to see me, Kausalya?'

'You have other commitments now, Sire.'

'I was foolish enough to lose you once. I don't intend to make the same mistake again.'

Kausalya did not prise open my fingers from around her wrist but there was a distant ache in her eyes, a resolve to suffer the pain of severance now rather than live on false hope and defer the loss of closeness and intimacy. She was too proud to tell me that if I had wanted to, I could have walked into her room months ago. I thought of the hundreds of women in the palace waiting for their lovers or husbands. How many months and years would they keep vigil? Who would scotch their loneliness? Very likely they knew who their men were spending the night with. There is no measure to the bitterness and heartbreak of the zenana. How does it feel to be rejected daily? Was death the only way out?

'Your Highness, one request. No kindness, please. Nor a visit out of a sense of duty.'

Kausalya had redrawn the boundaries and there was no crossing them. The tension between her and me ebbed away without either of us noticing it.

'Why don't you sit down, take my head in your lap, locate, pick and squash the eleven thousand lice from my hair as you did when I was a child and then knock some sense into my head?'

There's no difference between dogs and men. We'll circle around ourselves half a million times, check the place where we want to deposit ourselves as we've done for the last eleven years and then ease ourselves into it. There's surely a trough or dip the size of the back of my head on the inside slope of Kausalya's right breast. I know this place well, I have chatted long hours looking at the underside of Kausalya's chin, wondering if her skin is inherently blemishless or she has some esoteric unguent that strips away stray, sharp hairs from the roots before they appear. I have fallen asleep in that hollow while Kausalya's been busy tracing a rao's or sultan's family tree for me or unravelling the bitter roots of enmity between two Rajput families who'll even today kill each other without any idea of the original grievance.

The bells of the Brindabani temple are pealing away.

The gods no longer materialize on earth, at least not in Kali Yuga, this most fallen of ages. Divine intervention, I must confess, seems a matter of hearsay, faith and credulity. The only miracles in life are wrought by time. My wife sings and dances at six every evening now and the prayer meetings are often attended by none other than His Majesty. Plans are afoot to enlarge both the temple complex and compound to hold fifty thousand people. Marble lattices wrought with workmanship that's comparable to the exquisite silver filigree jewellery that Chittor is so renowned for, now screen the billowing storms that my wife's skirts generate for the Blue God.

Frankly, Chittor has little reason to complain. The pilgrim and tourist traffic in the citadel has gone up by a hundred and fifty percent since we got back from Kumbhalgarh and shows no sign of abating. Caravans of people from Chanderi, Champaner, Jaipur, Delhi, Agra, Mathura, Ahmedabad, Raisen, Daulatabad, Pune, Vijayanagar, even the valley of Kashmir come by bullock and camel cart, by palanquin and on horseback. Those who can't afford fancy transport, load their bedding and a couple of utensils on their heads and walk all the way to Chittor. My wife, as the finance ministry was discovering, is not just a rare and living treasure, she is Chittor's biggest economic asset. All these years, it was Father's vision and diplomacy that tried to bring disparate geographical and historical Rajput interests together. Today the nexus between the Little Saint, the Flautist and His Majesty has bound Rajput, Bhil, Hindu, Jain and Muslim in a manner that would have been almost inconceivable a few years ago.

While the Little Saint is lost in the adoration of the Flautist or preoccupied with household chores, Chittor or rather, all of Mewar is busy mythologizing her. Already there are enough stories of her purity and piety, of her conversations with the Blue God, and of her miraculous escapes from the attempts on her life to fill up at least a couple of volumes. The latest has to do with Swami Rupa Goswami, the highly renowned ascetic and disciple of the late Chaitanya Mahaprabhu, who was arguably the greatest poet-saint and adherent of the Flautist.

When Rupa Goswami was passing through Chittor a few months ago, he stayed, as almost all Vaishnavaite holy men do, at the Brindabani Mandir. My wife, who believes that knowledge and salvation, if not enlightenment, can come only through the offices of a teacher and in the company of sages, went to meet the Goswami the next day. As a severe ascetic and one who had sworn off women, the swami refused to see the Little Saint. He was certain that she was not just a much indulged Princess but, very likely, an impostor whose public displays of devotion and other antics like dancing and singing were nothing but a ploy to gain attention. Rupa Goswami had a formidable reputation but the Princess neither lost her composure nor was she dismayed. She merely expressed surprise that he was a man. For if he was, what right did he have to enter Brindaban? Did the Goswami not know that there was but one male in the universe and that was the Blue One and all others, barring none, were women?

What was the Little Saint talking about? I'm completely out of my depth when my wife switches to this kind of highly esoteric symbolism. But the Goswami seems to have got her drift and instead of bristling at her snub, he realized that here was an enlightened bhakta who had grasped the essence of the Lord. He agreed to see the Princess.

What does Queen Karmavati have to say about my wife's rising star? She has certainly made Vikramaditya the strongest contender to the Mewar throne, working up a groundswell on his behalf in Ranthambhor and its environs; one can feel her presence and her hand shaping, recasting and interfering with the affairs of Chittor almost daily. And yet, however puissant her long-distance reach may be, it has not been able to prevent my wife from becoming almost indispensable to Father. The keys of the stores, the royal jewels, His Majesty's cupboards and chests of clothes, shoes, saafas, in short, of the Palace itself hang from the silver clasp which she so casually tucks into the waist of her ghagra. She may look a little bemused, other-worldly and on an altogether higher spiritual plane than any of us mortals but as the entire hierarchy of eunuchs, palace bureaucracy, staff, servants and the seraglio were discovering, not much escapes her. If sweetness of temper does not yield results, she is tough and adamant. If anyone thought that feminine delicacy would prevent her from confronting difficult or personal subjects, they were much mistaken. Whether it's bodily functions, illness, awkward or exotic sexual proclivities, usury or blackmail, feuding and intrigue, her lack of guile allows her to come straight to the point and tick a person off when necessary without leaving a bad taste in the mouth.

None of us eats less, the standard of cuisine hasn't slipped nor is there any parsimony in the upkeep of the palace and yet expenses are down by close to thirty per cent.

How she finds time in such a busy schedule to look after palace affairs, serve Father meals, lay out his clothes and massage that battered body of his which is in perpetual pain, entertain him with stories about her childhood, her grandfather Rao Duda, and her uncle Rao Viramdev, sing to him when he is feeling out of sorts, or play cards with him, and yet not be harried or rushed or short-tempered is not just a mystery but cause for alarm in the likes of me and all those whose use of time can never aspire to even a quarter of her efficiency. It would appear that she has discovered another talent. She can unobtrusively slip in an opinion on political or state matters but unlike Queen Karmavati she always allows Father to think that the idea has originated from him.

Did I detect Father's deep and rumbling baritone in the chorus which accompanied my wife's first bhajan of the evening? He may be king, but at the Brindabani Mandir the devotees have no qualms drowning His Majesty's voice. Kausalya and I had the whole evening to ourselves. The devotional songs to the Blue God and the arati would go on for another hour at the very least. It would be nine thirty or ten at night before the Princess returned after serving Father dinner and reading out a couple of chapters from the *Gita*.

How quickly one reverted to old ways and the wrinkles and creases of habit returned. It was as if there was a break in time and I had slipped into my premarital mode. I told Kausalya about my day. The Security Council meeting was scheduled for eleven in the morning but Father sent for me at ten. We had a visitor from abroad that day, all the way from Portugal. His Majesty was sitting for a portrait when I arrived. Portraiture is an alien art-form to us. Our painting tends towards types and traditional subjects but in the last decade or so some visitors from France and Italy have brought along pictures of their kings and doges and now some of our artists have begun to adapt this style of painting. The result is a quaint hybrid that can be occasionally quite pleasing.

The miniature artist Chand Rai had posed Father with his face in profile to avoid the absent eye. Father looked intimidating and haughty. He was sitting astride a wooden ledge covered with heavy red brocade and the royal saddle. His right hand was covered in a leather glove and raised to the level of his seventh rib. Saathi, His Majesty's horse, and his falcon Aakash would be painted in later. Right now the artist was concentrating on getting the flowers on Father's angarkha right. Father was a painter's ideal subject. He could sit for hours without moving or what is more trying, talking, for as the artist often explained to our guests, lip movements not only changed the features, expression and composition of the face continually but affected the posture of the body.

The painting, I must add, has been in the works for the last seven years. If you look closely, you'll realize that Father's wearing a duglo that is yellow, not blue and the flowers on it are not mogras but green chaphas. The portrait, as you've guessed, is a decoy. Father likes to get the measure of outsiders who visit the court. He is averse to talking at the best of times but is decidedly tongue-tied and maintains an aloofness on such occasions while his courtiers chat up the visitor till the man has furnished us his entire life-story and a detailed account of his sovereign's nocturnal escapades and plans for travel and war. Chand Rai was the only person in Mewar or anywhere else who could with impunity tell His Majesty to shut up. 'Your humble servant, Chand Rai, begs your forgiveness for his impertinence of speech but Your Majesty will do posterity a signal service if he holds his tongue and allows me to get on with the painting.'

Every once in two or three years a wanderer or trader from Italy, Turkey, Spain, Portugal or Britain stopped over in Chittor and spent a week or two, sometimes even a month with us. Conversation is not always easy but there is a universal language that we all share: commerce. The merchants got gold from across the seas and exchanged it for cloth, pepper, cinnamon or whatever was in demand at home. Our guest this time is a little different. Manuel de Paiva Bobela da Costa was here in a semiofficial capacity. At the very end of the last century, I think it was 1498, a Portuguese admiral called Vasco da Gama rounded the Cape of Good Hope and discovered the sea route from Europe to India. Since then the Portuguese have been visiting the country regularly and have even set up small bases on the western littoral. This year oddly enough has seen three governors: Duarte de Menses, Vasco da Gama (I must ask da Costa whether this da Gama is the same man who landed in Calicut in 1498) and Henrique de Menses. Today's visitor has been sent by the Portuguese Governor of Goa, Henrique de Menses, as a roving ambassador to explore the possibility of commercial links with local kingdoms. Or at least that's his story.

Mewar was certainly interested in commerce with the Portuguese, if possible the kind where we sold more than what we bought from them. The problem was, we were not quite sure what the Portuguese were interested in. Instead of establishing trading houses or factories as they prefer to call them, they have been using force and building forts, the first one at Cochin and the second at Cannanore. In 1510 they took Goa. Not exactly a mercantile activity, would you agree? If that doesn't give you pause, there's far more disconcerting news tucked away in the title of the Portuguese king. Dom Manuel I of Portugal took the title 'Lord of the Conquest, Navigation and Commerce of Ethiopia, Arabia, Persia and of India' almost immediately after Vasco da Gama's discovery of the sea-passage to India. It would seem that the present Portuguese king, Joao III, wishes to conquer and rule India from a distance of four thousand miles. So far it's primarily the western seaboard that has been feeling the effects of the Portuguese presence in the Indian Ocean but we

398

haven't escaped entirely either. As Lord of the Sea in Asia, Joao III or to be precise, his governor Henrique de .Menses has been patrolling the seas and levying a customs duty on any ship, Indian or foreign plying the waters. Which means that anybody including us who has cargo in those ships has to pay a surcharge to the shipowners who then have to pass it on to the Portuguese.

The Portuguese are either extraordinarily tightfisted or have an extremely low opinion of their hosts in India. Manuel de Paiva Bobela da Costa brought for His Majesty a painting of their God as a child in the arms of his mother. The mother is thin, long-faced and unrelievedly morose while her son has an infant's chubby body and a mop of curly hair but a bizarre and disconcertingly adult face. In his left hand is a globe with a diamond-studded cross on it. In the top left and right corners are winged creatures called angels. In the background, off centre to the right, is an echo of the cross motif but this time it's a wooden one. Impaled on it with thick nails is an emaciated man with every rib in his chest sticking out painfully. The ambassador informed us that this man was none other than the lady's son grown up. His face is even sadder than the mother's. He wears a diadem of thorns and in the middle of his chest is a glowing and ethereal heart. A rather strange concept of God, to say the least. Gods, I have always assumed, are all-powerful. This one, however, needs help and succour desperately. You would need to have a strong stomach to live with this tearful and gloomy mother and child, apart from a God who is in perpetual pain.

The painting was shown to Father who passed it on to me and I offered it to the Prime Minister, Pooranmalji. I couldn't bring myself to make any comment about the picture but Pooranmalji is far more sophisticated than I. He held the framed painting in his hands, studied it and nodded his head slowly as if gradually imbibing the symbolism and poetry. He gave it to the court clerk with instructions to send it to His Majesty's palace. 'Careful, very careful. Make sure that it's packaged properly before it leaves these premises. Please thank His Majesty King Joao for his fine gift to His Majesty Rana Sangram Simha, Your Excellency. We have, I'm afraid, a very insignificant offering, nothing that can compare with the exquisite artistry, not to mention the sacredness, of your painting.'

I knew that tone of voice well. The Pradhan Mantri had anticipated the niggardly present from the Portuguese king and his
representative in India, a painting churned out from one of the
studios in Lisbon like a thousand or ten thousand others and was
about to snub the ambassador and his sovereign with an artefact
of overwhelming superiority. What he pulled out from a cloth
wrapping that was itself a hundred times the cost of the picture was
a soft white shatoosh shawl. It must have taken a year and a half
to weave.

'Drape it around your shoulder, Your Excellency.' Pooranmalji
handed the shawl to the visitor. The ambassador was perhaps a little
disconcerted by the lightness of the shatoosh but acquiesced to
Pooranmalji's request. 'Will someone there fetch a mirror for His
Excellency?'

We were in the middle of winter. The shawl was only a little
heavier than a Chanderi odhani but by the time they had fetched
the mirror, the ambassador was sweating. 'Even if it's snowing, that
one shawl should keep His Majesty Joao warm.'

As His Excellency removed the shawl from his shoulders and
folded it absent-mindedly, Pooranmalji pressed home his advantage.

'Let me do it for you, Sir,' the PM eased the shatoosh out of
the visitor's hands. 'We are under severe pressure, Your Excellency,
to impose duties on all imports. We have resisted all such requests
so far but I'm afraid ....'

The Pradhan had no intention of completing that sentence. I
had wondered why Father had asked me to attend this particular
session of the durbar. Perhaps he had wanted to fill in the lacunae
in his eldest son's education. Diplomatic converse, its symbolic and
strategic withdrawals, its innuendoes and weightages, and the things
left unsaid fascinated and intrigued me. I knew I was inept at it
but not averse to learning from a master like Pooranmalji.

Who was the Pradhanji fooling? Who was putting pressure on
him? The populace of Mewar, the merchants, the Minister of the
Exchequer, His Majesty? Father scarcely ever interfered in trade
policy, and Adinathji at the Exchequer and the PM had an equation
that rarely required speech or spelling out things. I suspected that
Pooranmalji was improvising but I wouldn't bet on that. After all

these years I had not managed to get the hang of the PM's arithmetic and mind. I guess that is the mark of the true diplomat and statesman.

'Your Highness,' the Portuguese ambassador picked up the slack where Pooranmalji had left off, 'I trust that this is not in retaliation for the customs duties our inspectors have been charging occasionally.'

'Have they? I have to admit,' the PM was as silken as the stole on his shoulders, 'that age is catching up with me. I have been a trifle out of touch with things of late. But His Majesty Rana Sangram Simha certainly does not believe in petty retaliation.'

'I had no intention of insinuating that at all,' the ambassador was stammering.

'I'm sure you didn't.'

'I'll speak to His Honour the Governor and suggest in the strongest terms that customs duties not be charged on Mewar goods.'

'That is most gracious of you, Your Excellency. Now tell us more about your country. Is it true that when one of you is invited to dinner at a friend's, you have to carry your own, what's the eating instrument called, fork?'

The ambassador's ear lobes were a hot shade of red and I had the feeling that he would have liked to terminate the meeting.

'Oh, that's only among the poor where the male of the family takes his fork along with him.'

'And the wife and children, they do not eat as guests?'

'Oh, they do, they do, but with their fingers since forks are a luxury for them.'

The foreign visitor was saying his thank you's and taking his leave when I interrupted him. 'Your Excellency, we are, as you are well aware, land-lubbers and know next to nothing about seafaring or ships. We believe you have some of the most advanced ships in the world with tonnages as high as a thousand.'

'We certainly do, Your Highness,' de Paiva Bobela da Costa relaxed for the first time that day. 'We would be happy to supply you with ships.'

'Where would we ply them, Your Excellency?'

He was not about to let go a business opportunity. 'You can rent them out to the coastal traders. I'm sure there's money in it.'

'It's an interesting proposal. We need to look into it. Perhaps His Majesty, the Rana may appoint a commission to do a report. I was wondering what kind of guns your ships are equipped with?'

'Cannons, Sire. Anywhere between eight to twelve between port and starboard. I'm afraid I won't be able to give any more details because such matters are generally left to sailors in our country.'

'No offence meant, Your Excellency. But would you use these same cannons for land warfare?'

'Not the same, Your Highness, much larger ones.'

'And would their primary function be to defend your forts and citadels?'

'That would be but one use to which they are put. As I am sure you well know, they are our first line of offence as well as defence. We would take them anywhere we are to give battle.'

'Yes, of course. And would you be as interested in selling these cannons as you were in selling your ships?'

'This is the first time anyone's broached the subject with me. I'm sure His Honour, the Governor of India, I mean of the Indian outposts, would be interested in looking at such a proposition.'

'Would you consult him and let us know?'

I was sure that this was a decision that the Governor Henrique de Menses could not take without consulting his sovereign. It was a long shot and getting a reply could take anywhere between a year and a year and a half but I didn't see any harm in starting the ball rolling.

*   *   *

It was the first time Mangal was briefing His Majesty and his Council as Head of Intelligence. He was not fazed by the gravity of the occasion and was just as precise and to the point as he had been with me. He did a quick survey of our neighbours, friends and foes, sketched what they were up to, the state of stability or otherwise in their kingdom and the threat they posed to Mewar.

Zahiru'd-din Muhammad Babur, the king of Kabul, Mangal next told us, had invaded Hindustan again after almost four years, secured Lahore and Punjab and returned home. Nearer home, there are signs that Sultan Mahmud Khalji II of Malwa, egged on by Muzaffar Shah of Gujarat, has initiated moves to get his troops together for a war with his erstwhile Prime Minister Medini Rai within the next few months.

'The King of Kabul,' Father spoke more to himself than to the other members of the Security Council, 'we can safely ignore so long as the Sultan Ibrahim Lodi rules Delhi. The foreigner Babur cannot get at us unless he first crashes through the barrier of Delhi. But what do you suggest we do about the Sultan of Malwa, Pradhanji?'

'Mahmud Khalji would like to wipe out all trace of Medini Rai from the face of the earth. We could sit back and await the outcome philosophically.'

'Without us, you well know,' Lakshman Simhaji, as usual, was easy prey to the Prime Minister's needling bait, 'Medini Rai does not stand a chance.'

'In that case the Rai should be willing to pay whatever price we put on our help.'

'The Sultan bears a grievance against Medini Rai but in this instance, the Rai is only a pretext. Make no mistake, Mahmud Khalji is coming after us. If we ditch the Rai this time, we'll not only lose an ally but we'll be the weaker for it. Our friends will never trust us again.'

'And who paid the bill the last time when our troops rushed to the Rai's aid?'

'Whatever the reasons for it, we were of little use to him since we arrived late. They say he lost twenty, maybe even forty thousand men when the combined forces of Muzaffar Shah and Mahmud Khalji took the Mandu fort and ordered a massacre.'

'Won't Mahmud Khalji have to foot all the bills if Medini Rai defeats him with our help?' That was Adinathji. With one rather simple query he had made the sparring between the Prime Minister and Lakshman Simhaji redundant and gone straight to the heart of the matter.

'Shall we alert our allies and fix a date with them for a War Council?' Lakshman Simhaji asked Father.

'A little premature for that yet. Let Medini Rai ask for our help

403

first.' His Majesty then turned his dead eye on me. 'But perhaps the Prince has a different view of the matter.'

And I thought I was going to keep a low profile, hold my tongue, fall in line with whatever was decided by the elders and be a good boy whom nobody would notice.

'No, no views, Your Majesty.'

'Do you expect us to believe that a young man of your keen intelligence, Highness,' Pooranmalji had his lip turned a little sardonically without losing his indulgent prime ministerial smile, 'has no views on such weighty matters as a likely war with our neighbours?'

'Your Highness, perhaps my phrasing was a little vague. What I meant was that I'm in agreement with the views of the Security Council.'

'Sire,' Adinathji did not smile indulgently as he looked me in the eyes, 'you are as much part of the Security Council as any one of us.'

'Your Highness,' Lakshman Simhaji patted me on the back and broke into a guffaw, 'we all know that you think we are all, no offence meant, Your Majesty, a bunch of old fools. And perhaps with good reason too, at times.' Even Father smiled then. Only my uncle could get away with such impertinence. 'But you owe it to the Security Council and Mewar to give us the benefit of your views.'

Was I to continue with my protestations or speak my mind?

'I believe that the Security Council has decided on a wise course of action for any other response would be so unorthodox as to be unthinkable.'

'Highness, if you don't think the unthinkable at your age, you certainly won't at mine. Why else would His Majesty have appointed you to the Council but to be confronted with a point of view that is, occasionally, radically different from his and ours?'

Did Father really want to hear my half-baked and wild opinions? He had put me in a spot and Lakshman Simhaji had attributed an openness to him which he may not want to live up to. He had no choice now. He would have to sit patiently and listen to his son's bizarre ideas.

'Mangal told us that Muzaffar Shah of Gujarat is cajoling

Mahmud Khalji to go to war with us. It is my guess that this time around, come what may, the Sultan of Gujarat will not contribute anything to the Malwa war efforts beyond encouraging words. Is it possible then to expend our energies on a more gainful enterprise?'

'And what would that be?' the Pradhanji did not bother to conceal his disdain.

'Zahiru'd-din Muhammad Babur has so far made four sorties into Punjab, each one deeper than the previous one. It would stand to reason that his next stop is Delhi. It could be argued that like his Turki ancestor, Timur and other invaders from the northwest, he may come on a flying raid, sack the city and return. The question is what if he has other ideas on the subject? Kabul is his kingdom but whatever the attractions of that cold mountain principality, it is neither the hub of power nor does it have the wealth of Hindustan. Do we let him take a shot at Delhi or do we ride into Delhi, gain possession of the tottering Lodi empire and take control?'

I would rather not use that hackneyed phrase 'stunned silence' but nothing else will do. It was Father who finally broke the quiet.

'And in the meanwhile we let Mahmud Khalji walk into Chittor?'

'No, Your Majesty. While you assume the crown of Delhi, Medini Rai and I will harass and destroy the Malwa forces with quicksilver attacks.'

'Aren't you forgetting one of the first principles of war: never open two fronts simultaneously?'

'I have no intention of doing that, Highness,' I told Lakshman Simhaji. 'There will be only one front, one of our choosing against the Delhi Sultan. Our objectives in Malwa will be limited: take a highly trained, mobile force and keep the Malwa armies preoccupied and off-balance. After you've taken Delhi, the initiative will have passed on to us and we could enlarge the scope of our tactics in Malwa.'

'Do you believe that taking over Delhi will be such an easy task?'

'No, Your Majesty. Nobody clings to life as persistently as a dying patient. But if we don't annex Delhi, someone else will. Besides, I do not think our troops will have difficulty defeating Ibrahim Lodi under your leadership.'

'If that last sentiment had come from someone else, I would have told him, "Sycophancy won't get you anywhere" but I believe you mean business. Let's think over the Prince's proposals, shall we?'

Would Father really think over my proposals?

*   *   *

Kausalya was giving me her variation of a head massage. I think she was happy that my visit was not a token gesture. She sank her hand into my hair, pulled it gently but long and then let go of it. It brought back memories of my childhood when she would put me to sleep by playing with my hair. It was amazing what a relaxing and soporific effect this innocuous scrabbling in the scalp had on me.

'Your Highness, I don't need to tell you how much I enjoy it when you tell me stories of the affairs at court and especially your comments about people but surely you didn't come over to tell me about the Portuguese visitor.'

'Why Kausalya,' I was horrified, 'are you trying to suggest that I'm a calculating mercenary who never does anything without an ulterior motive? I'm truly offended.'

'I'm not suggesting anything of the kind, Sire,' How rare it was to see Kausalya in a light and bantering mood. 'I believe it would offend you no end if you ever caught yourself in a selfless act or discovered that you were doing something for the sheer pleasure of it.'

Just as I was leaving I asked her, 'Tell me about Mahmud Khalji II and Medini Rai.'

There is no greater living hero among the Rajputs than Medini Rai (I doubt if anyone remembers what his real name is since Medini, the title the Sultan of Malwa gave him, has stuck for good.) Father may be more respected, his word certainly carries far more weight; even raos and rajas will think ten times before they cross him but Medini Rai, despite his precipitous fall from power, is a legend. I remember Kausalya coming back from Mandu where she had gone to visit some cousin telling me when I was fourteen and grieving about three pimples on my left cheek, 'May you have more of those pustules, Maharaj Kumar. Imagine being perpetually

406

conscious of and handicapped by the kind of good looks that Medini Rai has.'

After all those years I needed to brush up on Medini Rai. Who was this Rajput who had appeared almost from nowhere, hitched his star to that of Mahmud Khalji when he had been abandoned by everyone else, reversed the fortunes of his king, risen to the pinnacle of power as prime minister of Malwa and then been hounded out of the kingdom by the very man whom he had restored to the throne? What was the cause of the falling out between the king and Medini Rai? And why did Mahmud Khalji see the Rai as a threat despite his downfall? Would Medini Rai seek our help even though the last time he had asked for it we had failed to come to his aid in time?

'Do you want the long-winded version or a quick sketch with highlights?' Kausalya asked me.

'The shorter one for the time being with some detailing and colour after Medini Rai comes on the scene.'

This is what Kausalya told me. It's not verbatim, and it's got asides from me, but it's close.

Mahmud Khalji II's grandfather was called Ghiyath-ud-din. (I can't resist telling you that he's reputed to have had fifteen thousand women in his seraglio, one thousand of whom were his personal guards. I wrote the figures in words because I was sure that you would think that I had slipped up and added a couple of zeroes for effect.)

Unlike his grandfather, Mahmud Khalji II was a weak and childish man who was incapable of keeping his own counsel or acting decisively. He believed every story, rumour or whiff of gossip floating in the air and was overeager to lend an ear to any amir or nobleman inclined to low or high intrigue.

Soon Mahmud Khalji was a king without a kingdom. His younger brother captured Mandu and usurped the throne. The Sultan's followers abandoned him and it seemed he would never regain his crown.

Enter Rai Chand Purabia, a Rajput from the east whose past

is a mystery. Why would any man want to join his fortunes to those of a king whose situation seemed hopeless and beyond repair? Was it faith in his destiny or was it hubris and unbridled arrogance that made the Rai think he could reverse Mahmud Khalji's run of bad luck and reinstate the king on his throne at Mandu? How many troops did he have? Kausalya didn't have the answers to those questions. I certainly didn't and I doubt whether too many people in Mewar or Malwa for that matter had any inkling either. Be that as it may, the cloud over Mahmud lifted almost overnight.

Rai Chand Purabia was no practitioner of black magic, he did not have the reputation of being the greatest general this side of the Narbada, but he had certainly managed to get the planets of the zodiac in the most auspicious conjunction possible. When the armies of the two rival Sultans of Malwa finally met, Rai Chand routed the usurper.

Mahmud Khalji was grateful to the man who had rescued him when his fortunes were at their nadir. He appointed him vazir and gave him the title by which he is known all over the country: Medini Rai. Perhaps the Sultan was incapable of having any but hothouse friendships. The vazir could do no wrong. Mahmud Khalji's admiration and his reliance upon the Rai waxed without let.

The Rai too, it would appear, had not learnt any lessons from his predecessors. Perhaps that's what power does, it makes you blind to the obvious. He could not perceive the portents of his own decline and fall. Did the Rai really believe that Mahmud Khalji would not realize that he had become a mere plaything, especially when there was no dearth of malcontents and disaffected nobles to steer their vacillating sovereign into troubled waters? Events came full circle when some of the Sultan's favourites under instructions from him made an attempt on the vazir's life. Medini Rai was badly wounded but survived. The infuriated Rajputs under the Rai's son attacked the royal palace. The king and his guard stoutly defended his home and put the Rajputs to flight. In the ensuing melee, the Rai's son was killed. Despite his terrible personal loss, not to mention the injury to his person, Medini Rai wrote to the Sultan: 'As during my whole life I have never done anything but wish for your welfare, and act faithfully to my salt, I have carried my life in safety from the wounds. If in reality, the affairs of the kingdom can be better regulated by my being put to death, I have no objection to even that.' It was the kind of petition that most nobles who had offended their liege wrote to gain forgiveness. Did Medini Rai mean what he wrote? (Kausalya said she wouldn't put it past him.)

There was a rapprochement between the king and his vazir but it did not take a clairvoyant to see that it was not to last. Medini Rai had saved the king when he was on the run. Now the king was on the run from the same man. He left Mandu one night and sought refuge with Muzaffar Shah of Gujarat.

When Medini Rai heard that the combined armies of Mahmud Khalji and Muzaffar Shah were marching towards Mandu, he left his capital in the care of his deputy and set out for the Mewar court to seek Father's help. But before Father and Medini Rai could reach the Malwa capital they got news that the Mandu fort had been reduced and that Muzaffar Shah had ordered a massacre in which twenty thousand soldiers, forty according to some estimates, were killed.

That was some time ago. Mahmud Khalji no longer had the Gujarat Sultan, Muzaffar Shah, by his side but he reckoned rightly that if he didn't destroy the Rai, who had gone to Gagrone, soon, it would be too late.

Chapter 31

 Identical twins are close. But true enemies are closer.

One of the first things the Maharaj Kumar did when Mangal, Mamta, the Princess and he got back to Chittor was to plant the parijat sapling in the large courtyard in his wing of the palace. He would have liked to have dug a hole in the dead centre of the plot but that was not possible because that spot belonged to the Tulsi plant which every housewife worships since there is no woman as adamantine in her fidelity to her husband as Tulsi. He chose a corner not too close to the wall so that the parijat would have plenty of room to spread its wings. Every morning, as soon as he had had his bath and said his prayers, he took a watering can (he could hear the eunuchs and the maids giggling and calling him royal mali) and poured water slowly around the branch that he hoped would take root and flower.

Close to a month passed but instead of the first green shoots showing up, the plant seemed to die on the Prince. He dug it out and turned the soil over. Seven days later he knew there was no hope. Some people, he told himself, have green thumbs, others have the gift of death. He had meant that statement to be facetious but he felt as if someone had struck that dead runt of a branch into his heart.

The gardener had been watching him for days but had refrained from proffering advice. The Prince was glad to be left alone but resentful that the man had not had the decency to resuscitate the dry stick that meant so much to him.

410

'Is there any fertilizer,' the Maharaj Kumar did not want to admit defeat, yet he had no choice but to approach the expert and ask his opinion, 'that could give this plant a second life? A kind of ambrosia?'

'I'm afraid no ambrosia works on the dead. It can only bestow immortality on the living. But that plant doesn't need fertilizer. You've burnt it with too much watching and attention. Talking to trees is fine but you can't water a little baby plant three or four times a night, cuddle and pet it and then threaten it with dire consequences if it doesn't start showing results instantly.'

The Prince would have liked to throttle the man. The gardener however had not finished with his homily. 'Learn to leave nature well enough alone with just the occasional nurturing. Perhaps it might take heart and rise from its ashes yet.'

The Maharaj Kumar expected that the gardener would at least now suggest that he would take over the task of rejuvenating the parijat. No such offer was forthcoming.

'Would you be so kind as to undertake the care of this plant for me?'

'Certainly, Sire, I believe that's what I'm paid for.'

If only the parijat would die the next week, the Prince thought, and I could with a clean conscience sack the swine or maybe have him beheaded in public. But within a couple of days the stick had regained colour; within a week it was sporting seven incipient leaves and within seven months the courtyard was littered with parijat flowers. He collected the flowers every morning at dawn and showered the half-asleep Princess with them. Sometimes he wove them into her plait or threaded them into a garland and put it around her neck.

* * *

The room was an impenetrable cube of darkness, but he knew that she was not there. He was seized by a raging and unfathomable fear. He fell on his knees, groped with his hands till he had made contact with the bed. She was not lying on it. He slipped under it, lay immobile on his belly and closed his eyes tight. He had an overwhelming urge to throw a tantrum, go out of control and never be

411

reasonable again. He lifted the bed on his back as he rose up. Had Bhootani Mata finally succeeded? Had she done his wife in? He was crawling on all fours, the bed a battering ram that crashed into the walls of the room. Then an even more grisly idea struck him. She had run away with someone else. He dropped the bed and lay still. He would not get up. Now or ever. They would find him in the morning, an unevenly painted blue corpse with ghastly natural flesh-coloured lips. And what about her? Was he going to let her get away with it?

He saw red phosphorescent footprints; he had been in such a panic that he hadn't noticed them. He recognized the imprint of those small, delicate feet: the large dot that was the big toe and the four descending ones that were the other toes; the sharply etched ball of the foot extending into a solid land mass that receded into the curving shoreline of the instep and rounded off into the heel.

As he walked into the courtyard there was a loud bang. He stepped aside swiftly to dodge a likely blow. She had burst a paper bag bulging with air and was doubled over with laughter. Was this the woman they called the Little Saint? She was a child, that's what she was. The smallest and sometimes the silliest acts gave her pleasure. What was unsettling was that she had this strange gift of transmitting joy, turning others into little children, swinging god-crazed dancers or overearnest, adult devotees.

She took his hand in hers and placed it inside her choli. 'Is it possible, is it possible,' she spoke rapidly as if time and air were running out, 'to fall in love all over again every day with the same person? Am I not blessed as no other woman is? Play, play, play the flute, O Lord and still my pulse and enlarge my heart for I need room to accommodate my love for you. Make my heart as wide as the cosmos, no, make it a dozen cosmoses. Play, my beloved one.'

Cosmos? A dozen cosmoses? Beloved? How could she get away with these quaint archaisms, worse, mean every one of them and make one believe in them? He played the Basant Bahar, an urgent call to spring.

'Here,' she had two dandiyas in her hand.

'What should I do with them?'

'You should ask. You know it better than anyone else.'

He was about to say, 'No, please. I don't know how to dance. And frankly I don't think a prince of the House of Mewar should indulge in —' but fortunately realized the absurdity of saying anything of the sort. The eldest prince and would-be Maharaj Kumar had indulged himself enough and more. He had done things that most princes would disown instantly. And besides, his wife was not one to take a 'no' once she had decided upon a course of action. He took the two sticks in his hands. They were overlaid with a patina of black lacquer through which gold vines and leaves with red flowers shone in the dark. She slipped her right hand into the patch-pocket on her skirt and brought out another pair of dandiyas. The pattern here was the exact reverse of his: a gold bed on which the black vines interwove and flowered.

She started singing a traditional song as she raised her hands and struck her dandiyas on the beat. He followed her cue but a little clumsily. She waited for his sticks to make contact with hers but his timing was off and so was his placement.

'Will you stop playing the fool?' she pulled him up sharply. 'When I come in from the right, you don't do the same. You have to move in from the left.' She saw the bewilderment on his face and her tone softened. 'How could you have forgotten the dandiya raas? It's your dance. You invented it.'

He looked down shamefacedly.

'Let me show you. One two three, raise your dandiyas to the right, knock knock knock. One two three, dandiyas to the left, knock knock knock. One two three, our dandiyas meet, knock knock knock. Now lower the sticks and repeat the same pattern. Let's try it once. There, you're getting it. You just pretended you didn't know. How beautifully you play the dandiya raas. No wonder that vixen Radha and the gopis from Mathura can't keep their hands off you. But you try anything funny behind my back, my friend, and I'll break your legs with these very same dandiyas.'

He tried not to listen to the song. The gopis were, as usual, filling their pots with water on the banks of the Jamuna when the god with a thousand names took out a catapult and one by one broke the pots on their heads and ogled at the drenched ladies. How were they to go home with wet, transparent clothes that revealed all?

413

Madhusudana alias the Flautist, everyone knew was shameless but they were honourable, decent women, some of them with husbands and children, and all of them had spotless reputations. How were they to face their families and pray, what explanation were they to give?

How he loathed these songs. Didn't the bards of India have anything else to write about? There were thousands of songs about the divine eve-teaser and every day someone or the other was adding to the genre. In plaintive, vexed or patently false angry voices, the women complained about him. They pleaded with him to stop stealing their clothes, implored him not to flirt with them in full public view and spray colours on them during the Holi festival; would he please leave them alone once and for all? No more, no more, no more, they said when they meant more, more, more and please don't stop. If he turned his back on them, instead of rejoicing they went berserk with grief. They pined, they fretted, they had nervous breakdowns. Frankly, if they were painful when their modesty was compromised, they were unbearable when they were wailing with lovesickness.

Who, he wondered, wrote these songs of soft pornography, and suggestiveness, these songs which were keyholes through which peeping toms — that came to almost the entire male population — lead a fantasy double-life? The voice and persona of the lyrics was that of women but the majority of writers were men. And yet, given half a chance, any housewife who could manage a rhyme, would dash off a song about 'Look Ma, see how the Flautist is undoing my plait and pulling my pallu.' Sure, it was a convention and the poets were working within a framework and the words and images had deep metaphysical significance (a likely story if he had ever heard one), but the curious thing was that the overwhelming majority of the singers were women. Were they too as repressed as the men? What was the lure of this god? It was not just the women who fantasized about him, the entire population of the country carried on one continuous love affair with him. Nobody sang steamy overwrought songs to Rama, Vishnu or Shiva. What was the source of the irresistible attraction of the peacock-feathered god? How was he able to get away with the very things that would land any other man in jail for life? Did the women, in their heart of hearts, want to walk the streets with see-through, wet blouses and wait for some dashing young man with a peacock feather in his phenta to tug at their odhanis?

Whatever the ironies and paradoxes, he was convinced the Flautist was wish-fulfillment for both men and women.

But even as he excoriated the banality of the besotted love songs to the Flautist, he was drawn to the beat and lilt of the music. His wife, as was her wont, was pouring her soul and incredible voice into the hori. She kept you off-balance because you never knew what to expect from even the most familiar song when she was rendering it. There was fire and ferocity in her voice which dropped suddenly to whispered intimacies and passionate pleading. He remembered the pichwai paintings he had seen from childhood. Their subject was almost always the dance of the Flautist; never alone of course, but with a hundred or thousand shepherdesses. The women did not have to wait in a queue or share their beloved. He was sufficient unto all of them without having to divide his time amongst them. There were always as many Flautists as there were gopis in the picture. He was sure he had walked into a pichwai painting except that the Princess had taken care to eliminate the competition altogether.

The raas was a sensuous, circular dance which after the first half hour invariably got on your nerves. You went slow or you went fast but either way it got to be the most monotonous and repetitive dance you could think of. He was damned if he would go round in circles by rote. He had no option but to improvise. What he did was to follow the same principle that's used in playing the pakhawaj drum. The taal had twelve or sixteen beats. On the face of it once you chose the taal, there was no escaping its constricting scheme till eternity. And yet a taal allowed an almost unimaginable degree of freedom. You could do almost anything you wanted so long as you touched base every twelve or sixteen beats dead on time.

The Princess was carrying on sedately and routinely when he switched tracks and changed the coordinates of the dance. He thought his wife looked disoriented and was bound to miss a beat but she was on to him.

'You want a fight, my friend,' she whispered, 'you are going to regret it.' She smiled, her body language changed. She was lightning alert, watchful and ready to spring into action. Her limbs were loose, she rocked almost imperceptibly while she calculated her partner-opponent's next move. There was glee in her green eyes and she looked like a cat about to play with her quarry before polishing it off. She beat a tattoo with her sticks and signalled that she was entering the fray.

What if somebody saw him? He would be a fine sight for the gossip mills. His eyes darted and took in the windows and dark corners of the palace. The retainers, the gardeners, not to mention Queen Karmavati's flunkies and spies were bound to be watching. He thought he saw a shadow slither away. Why was he lying to himself? There was no one around, not for all these weeks and months since he had got back from Kumbhalgarh because Kausalya made sure every night that all the maids, eunuchs and numerous other busybodies were flushed out and put to work in some other wing of the palace.

'I worry about you, Maharaj Kumar. Look at the dark circles around your eyes,' Bhootani Mata was suspended like a bat from the ceiling of a balcony in the palace. There was no purchase for her fingers but she seemed to hang in there without any difficulty. 'How you burn the midnight oil. You do bring out the worst clichés in one. Pray, where is everybody? Has there been a plague in the palace? There's not a soul around except of course that old faithful retainer of yours, I forget her name. Was she your nurse or the one who first slipped your member between her legs? What's her name? It's at the tip of my tongue.'

'You remember her name just as clearly as you remember every damn thing you ought to forget. I suggest you stay clear of her.'

'My, my, we are sensitive about Kausalya to this day. But why is she keeping guard? What's going on here?'

'Why don't you mind your own business?'

'But you are my business. My one and only business for the time being.' She looked at the Princess and then him. 'Isn't this romantic? Never seen anybody so besotted with his enemy. What would I not give to exchange places with the lady?' Bhootani Mata opened her crotch. 'Peer into the void and see the cosmos at a glance, Maharaj Kumar. All the pleasures and treasures of this and every other universe await you. Do you like that internal rhyme? Of course you don't. You have no ear for poetry, not even bad poetry.'

He spat into the black hole. 'What are you doing here?'

'Casting the proverbial evil eye.' She laughed. It was an evil sound, something that came straight from the heart. 'Let me invoke a benediction upon you. May everything you touch, turn to ashes. May all those who are dear to you, rue the day they came within your ambit.'

Chapter 32

$\mathcal{R}$aja Puraji Kika and I may be soulmates but it's mostly a long-distance closeness. Besides, even when we are together, neither of us is very voluble. What we share is taciturnity and silence. I often ask myself if I am incapable of making, and more important, keeping friends. And yet perhaps my state of almost total friendlessness is good training for kingship. For a king may have many companions but no friends. However much the poets and romantics may protest, friendship and favouritism go hand in hand. And where there's favouritism, it's not long before a king or a dynasty heads for a fall. I hear people say that the best relationship between a father and son is that of friendship. I have no doubt about it. But I think Father is wise to keep all his sons at a distance. Fondness is often nothing but foolishness. You can only say 'no' to people who cannot blackmail you emotionally. And a king must needs say 'no' several times a day. When it comes to jobs, for instance, there's a limit to them. You can't, it's obvious, have two prime ministers or two commanders-in-chief. But even in the lower echelons where the posts are not so limited, you can only appoint a restricted number of people for otherwise, both the concept of 'officer' and 'the chain of command' become meaningless and the strain on your exchequer intolerable.

That leaves Mangal. He is the only companion I have in my professional dealings and the closest thing to a friend under the circumstances. I wonder if I have degraded the notion of friendship. For me it seems to boil down to respect for ability, the willingness to pursue a goal with imagination, originality and economy. There's something about doing a job well that is akin to art. In his sphere of action, Mangal is indeed an artist. Even so, one of my fears about the bits and pieces of paper that have been coming down from the court in Kabul is their authenticity. I guess what is at the back of my mind is the staggering rise in fake miniatures and relics in Mewar in the last few years since my wife's elevation to sainthood. Our two most well-known miniaturists are Ajeet Solanki and Sharafat Ali. On an average anywhere between twenty and forty paintings of the Little Saint singing, playing the ektara, dancing with the Flautist are sold outside the Brindabani Mandir every day and all are signed Ajeet or Sharafat. But the miniature industry is a fraction of the relic business. There's so much of the Princess' hair sold daily that she should have gone bald seven times over by now.

My anxiety about the Babur-notes has been that some clever trader who is fluent in Turki is in league with Shyam Dulare and Pyarelal and is making a small fortune by selling forgeries and fabrications. Mangal had decided on his own to double-check at the very source. It must have required a great deal of ingenuity, deviousness and perseverance but he has slowly established a network that extends up to Kabul and has infiltrated the king's quarters. Babur, it turns out, does have a much younger cousin called Haider of whom he is very fond. Despite his sojourns to India, various battles with neighbours and rebels, not to mention civilian and administrative matters, he has taken it upon himself to supervise the education of the youngster. As a matter of fact there are some subjects like calligraphy, reading, the art of writing letters and poetry for which Babur alone is his teacher. As for tangible proof, Mangal has furnished that too. He has managed to obtain, steal would be more correct, the ceramic vessel inside Haider's bejewelled inkpot (which is a present from Babur) and the quill which Haider used. Both the ink and the strokes, angle and width of the quill match the ones in the stolen diary entries.

Let me quote some of the highlights from the material that Shyam Dulare has been passing on to Mangal over the past year or so. They are longer and far more substantial than the earlier ones.

Here's an entry about his first marriage at the age of sixteen.

'Ayisha-sultan Begum whom my father and hers, i.e. my uncle, Al-Ahmed Mirza had betrothed to me, came to Khujand and I took her in the month of Sha'ban. Though I was not ill-disposed towards

419

her, yet, this being my first marriage, out of modesty and bashfulness, I used to see her once in ten, fifteen or twenty days. Later on when even my first inclination did not last, my bashfulness increased. Then my mother Khanim used to send me, once a month or every forty days, with driving and driving, dunnings and worryings.'

Babur is smitten with an adolescent but deep infatuation, the only one of its kind, it would appear, in his entire life.

'In those leisurely days I discovered in myself a strange inclination, nay! as the verse says, "I maddened and afflicted myself" for a boy in the camp-bazaar, his very name, Baburi, fitting in. Up till then I had no inclination for anyone, indeed of love and desire, either by hearsay or experience, I had not heard, I had not talked. At that time I composed Persian couplets, one or two at a time; this is one of them:

May none be as I, humbled and wretched and love-sick;
No beloved as thou art to me, cruel and careless.

'From time to time Baburi used to come to my presence but out of modesty and bashfulness, I could never look straight at him; how then could I make conversation and recital? In my joy and agitation I could not thank him for coming; how was it possible for me to reproach him with going away? What power had I to command the duty of service to myself? One day during that time of desire and passion when I was going with companions along a lane and suddenly met him face to face, I got into such a state of confusion that I almost went right off. To look straight at him or to put words together was impossible. With a hundred torments and shames, I went on. A Persian couplet of Muhammad Sabih's came into my mind:

I am abashed with shame when I see my friend;
My companions look at me, I look the other way.

'That couplet suited the case wonderfully well. In that frothing-up of desire and passion, and under that stress of youthful folly, I used to wander, bare-head, barefoot, through street and lane, orchard and vineyard. I showed civility neither to friend nor stranger, took no care for myself or others.

420

Out of myself desire rushed me, unknowing
That this is so with the lover of a fairy-face.

'Sometimes like the madmen, I used to wander alone over hill and plain; sometimes I betook myself to gardens and the suburbs, lane by lane. My wandering was not of my choice, not I decided whether to go or stay.

Nor power to go was mine, nor power to stay;
I was just what you made me, o thief of my heart.'

Would I who am as much a warrior as Babur, have been candid and so explicit about a homosexual longing even in the privacy of my own diary? I doubt if I will ever distrust Babur's word.

I feel like a peeping tom. What would be my reaction if I discovered that someone was privy not just to my actions (you can't live in the palace and expect privacy) but to my thoughts and writings? Diaries, at least those that are not written deviously with an ulterior motive and for public consumption, I'm convinced are far more revealing than a face-to-face encounter or even a long acquaintance with the person. One thing is certain: the more I get to know Babur, the more I want to know him. Why must religion be such an unbridgeable divide? I would have liked to meet him, perhaps, even be friends with him.

My train of thought was broken off. I heard a heavy dragging step and the scurrying of retainers. It couldn't be. His Majesty. It was late and Father had hurriedly thrown a duglo over his shoulders. My head was resting on his feet when his good hand reached down and tousled my hair, an unusual gesture on Father's part, to say the least. Had I finally come of age, had he discovered that his eldest son was not a bad sort after all or, more likely, was he favourably disposed towards me because of his affection for the Little Saint?

My wife brought a silver lota of water and poured him a glass.

'A missive's just arrived from Medini Rai. His former liege, the Sultan of Malwa, has laid siege to Gagrone at the head of forty thousand troops and three hundred elephants. The Rai's son Hem Karan is holding the fort. Supplies are running out and he doesn't have enough warriors to defend the citadel.'

'Where is Medini Rai?' I asked.

'At Dharampur waiting for assistance from us. Who should we

421

appoint commander and how many troops can we muster in a short time?'

'How long can Prince Hem Karan last out in Gagrone?' Had Father really come to consult me about who I thought was the best man for the job — he had never done so in the past — or did he have something else in mind?

'Seven days, maybe eight. After that he will have to declare Kesariyabana: open the gates and march with his men to certain death. Who is going to be our man, son?'

'There's only one person I can think of.'

I had not realized that my wife was now His Majesty's military adviser. Neither it would seem, had Father, for he looked as surprised as I.

'And who may that be? You, Princess?' Father had obviously decided to indulge the Princess but I felt she was trying his patience.

'Don't underestimate me, Your Majesty.' There was a smile on my wife's face but she was also giving notice that she would not brook it if anyone took her lightly. 'Prince Vikramaditya. He's aggressive and a doer; and most crucial of all, he has the killer instinct. Come what may, he'll rescue Prince Hem Karan and his men.'

'He's all those things, Princess, but he's also a hothead. Not the ideal qualification on this campaign when you need to think clearly and yet act swiftly and decisively.'

'That sounds like the profile of Rattan Simha,' Greeneyes, it was becoming clear was not about to shut up. 'He's thoughtful, dependable and experienced. He'll deliver Gagrone.'

What was the Little Saint up to? Was she really backing my brothers? I had the uneasy feeling that the more earnest she looked, the less trustworthy she was. Was she leading Father on or was His Majesty merely playing along because he too had a hidden agenda?

'You wouldn't recommend your husband for the job?'

'His Highness? No. He's good but he has too many unorthodox ideas. If the commanders of Mewar are uncomfortable with his methods, imagine poor Medini Rai's reaction. I'm sure he'll think we are letting him down once again.'

'That's curious. That's what I thought too. But it's the Rai who

422

has asked for your husband.'

My wife had gone through this elaborate charade, it was clear now, to try and get Father to nominate me to lead the Mewar armies against Malwa. But as usual His Majesty had already made up his mind.

'That settles it then. Will you excuse me, Majesty? I'll pack His Highness' things.'

'Do I take second place in your affections merely because your husband is going to war? Am I to eat my meal alone tonight, then?' Father smiled. It is clear that my wife knows Father better than I am ever likely to.

'Not a chance, Majesty. I know you are looking forward to spending all the money that you made off me last night by cheating me at cards. But I intend to win everything back with compound interest.'

'I keep telling your wife that she's got married into the wrong family. Rao Viramdev should have given her in marriage to one of Adinathji's grandsons. She's no saint, this woman. She has a moneylender's heart, mind and soul.'

Greeneyes stomped out melodramatically. Father, needless to say, was delighted with his daughter-in-law's histrionics.

'What is the strength of Medini Rai's army?' Father got back to business.

'I believe it's around ten thousand, Majesty. If the Rais from the east join him and Silhadi brings his forces, they would swell by another ten thousand. But Mahmud Khalji has chosen his time well. Silhadi and the other rais, while being favourably inclined, will, I suspect, play a waiting game and not commit their troops for fear of another defeat at the hands of the Sultan.'

'Mahmud Khalji didn't beat them alone the last time. If Muzaffar Shah of Gujarat hadn't taken the lead, I am sure that Medini Rai would have defeated Mahmud Khalji.'

'More than likely but that's an academic question now. Mangal tells me that the Rai and his Rajputs lost not twenty thousand of their men but closer to forty thousand including most of the senior commanders.'

'How many troops do you wish to take with you?'

'Three thousand. All of it cavalry.'

'I would caution you against arrogance, my son.'

'I believe time is of the essence on this occasion. If we try to put together an army of twenty or thirty thousand, it will take at least ten to twelve days and another week to arrange supplies. By that time, it will be too late to help either Prince Hem Karan or Medini Rai.

'Tej and Shafi have been working for the past year and a quarter on a kind of flash-force. Most of the soldiers have fought alongside me in the past but the idea was to train them in a different kind of discipline and make them into a task force that is so tightly knit that they think and act as a highly trained raiding party and are yet almost impenetrable. They've been fighting mock battles so far. This will be a good time to test their skills. Besides, I hope that the news of the Mewar men joining Medini Rai will encourage his allies to stop vacillating and proceed directly to Gagrone.'

'I trust you know what you are doing. I wish you success. When do you leave?'

'Seven hundred and fifty men will leave tonight. I'll speak to Tej and Shafi right away. They'll go singly and without attracting attention to themselves. They'll conceal their weapons and will move out as farmers or as pilgrims returning after taking a darshan of the Little Saint. One thousand five hundred will wend their way in the daytime tomorrow. And the remaining tomorrow night. We'll meet up in Dharampur.'

'You had planned all this in advance, hadn't you?'

'When Mangal said at the Security Council meeting some weeks ago that there was much troop movement in and around Mandu, I felt that Mahmud Khalji might be plotting a sudden attack. But frankly, Tej and Shafi's task force is meant to be in a state of preparedness at all times.'

'Has Mangal been leaking all the reports he makes to me to you?' Father had a smile on his face but I knew that we had reached the trickiest part of our meeting. After all, he must have known from day one that Tej and Shafi were instructing our troops at the training ground behind the Khatan Rani Palace.

'Mangal's loyalties are to the Rana and Mewar, Your Majesty.

424

Mangal did not part with any information to which the Security Council was not privy.'

'What would we do without Mangal?'

'I trust we'll never have to do without him.'

'One small matter, son. I suggest you ensure that the Sultan of Malwa survives the battle.'

You can never trust Father or rather you can trust him a hundred point seven percent as Adinathji's tribe is fond of saying. Father had pulled this same trick on me before but I never seem to learn. Instead of summoning me, he had come over in person. He had put me at ease with his banter with the Princess, asked me honest probing questions, then taken the offensive and put me in the dock about Mangal's and my integrity and when I was vastly relieved that I had risen to the occasion and had made the grade, he had, in passing, revealed the reason for his visit.

Had Medini Rai really asked for my services? Maybe he had. Maybe Father had put him up to it. It doesn't matter. His Majesty was, as usual, playing two or three games simultaneously. Queen Karmavati has been clamouring for the past six months to come back to Chittor: she had realized that while she thought that she had inveigled His Majesty into doing her bidding, Father, dear Father, had sidelined her. In the meantime, my wife and Father had become close. I don't think this was a conscious, calculated move on the part of either of them but once it had happened, Father was not averse to bending the friendship to his own purposes. The Queen would be recalled but held in check by the Princess. I was to be removed from the scene, given an important mission, perhaps even a second chance to try out my unorthodox ideas but clearly put on a very short leash. I was firmly told to stay off what I perceived to be the objective of the exercise: eliminate Mahmud Khalji and conquer Malwa.

His Majesty was not ready, at least not yet, to wipe out a dynasty and take control of a new kingdom. Perhaps he has sound reasons, he wants to build and integrate a strong Rajput confederacy first, perhaps he doesn't think that we have the trained manpower to staff a new bureaucracy and the top posts or more importantly to police the new state and quell revolts and rebellions. He may be

425

right. But I believe a king may wait too long for the opportune moment. When the time is ripe, it may be too late and one may forfeit the chance altogether.

Chapter 33

'*H*ighness,' Medini Rai walked briskly towards me. He had not had time to put on his saafa and was carrying it in his hands, 'forgive me for not coming to receive you. We were not expecting you for another week. If only you had sent a courier ahead of you, I would have ridden hard and met you at the border.'

There was a silver streak in his slightly dishevelled hair cutting across his head like a vein of mica in the noon sun. He ran his hand over the shock of thick hair and pushed it back as he put on the turban. He was not putting me on or flattering me, he would have ridden seventy miles to greet me.

'I bring you greetings from His Majesty, the Rana, and a detailed letter. With me, are my deputies from Mewar, Tej Simha and Shafi Khan. I believe that all three thousand of our soldiers have been in Dharampur since early this morning.'

'That seems unlikely, Maharaj Kumar. If the Mewar troops had arrived, I would have heard of it from my commanders. Or perhaps not,' he smiled deprecatingly as he looked at our clothes. 'Were they also travelling incognito in villagers' clothes?'

'I'm afraid, yes. We did not want to arouse Sultan Mahmud Khalji's suspicions. As a further precaution they must all have gone east, west and north before turning south-east. How many days will it take for the Sultan to turn around and confront us at Dharampur?'

'Four to seven days if he rides with his army. But why would he forsake the prize at hand and come looking for us?'

'I may be wrong but it is my guess that once the Sultan learns that the Mewar forces have joined you, he'll appreciate that Gagrone is likely to be an extremely ephemeral possession. If he takes it, he might find us besieging him in a couple of days. That might prove to be galling since Prince Hem Karan and his men have exhausted all supplies and it may take a while before the Sultan can restock the granaries. If, however, you feel that we should proceed forthwith to Gagrone and relieve the siege and the Prince, we can leave in an hour's time.'

He pondered over my two scenarios for a long time. 'I am anxious for Prince Hem Karan and my people but it would be unforgivable if that consideration led me to take an unwise step. It is likely that there is a slim chance, a chance nevertheless, that your prognosis is sound. Besides I doubt that thirteen thousand troops will be sufficient to relieve Gagrone.'

'In that case we have time for a quick bath prior to conferring with you and the heads of your army. Highness, may I make bold to ask you a candid question: when you wrote to His Majesty for assistance, why did you ask for me?'

'Before I make answer, I must ask you, Maharaj Kumar, not to take offence if I return your candour with just as much honesty. I asked for you because they tell me you are an unreasonable man. That if it was possible, you would like to win a war without losing a single one of your soldiers. They say you are a man without scruples, that you have no qualms attacking an enemy from the rear and in the dark. They say you play your cards so close to the chest that even your commanders sometimes learn of major engagements just a few hours before they are to take place. They say you walk at all times with your tail between your legs and will retreat at the slightest pretext. They tell me that you are unpredictable and change your plans without notice. They also say that you are a liar and are not to be trusted by your enemies and if you had any friends, they would be wise to keep you at an arm's length. That is why I chose you, Maharaj Kumar.'

When we met again, I showed Medini Rai the letter I had written and asked him to send it to the Sultan by the fastest set of couriers at his disposal.

428

It was a friendly letter.

To

His Majesty, Mahmud Khalji, Sultan of Malwa.

His Majesty, Rana Sangram Simha, the citizens of Mewar, Hindu, Muslim and Jain, and I, the Maharaj Kumar of Mewar, send you and the populace of Malwa our greetings. We wish you a long, happy and healthy reign.

I am sure that your sources have already informed you that fifty thousand of Mewar's soldiers are camped some fifteen miles from Dharampur and await your arrival with a growing sense of impatience. My men will soon be joined by His Highness Rao Medini Rai, His Highness Silhadi, Their Highnesses Chand Rai, Arjun Rai, Jai Rai, Rai Pithora's son Indrasen Rai, and their troops. All in all, over seventy thousand soldiery will be gathered to welcome you amongst us.

Our only wish is peace. Our only gift to the people of Malwa is the hand of friendship. We believe that you too are tired of all the internecine squabbles and wars within Malwa and are just as keen to sign a pact of peace with His Highness, Medini Rai, Mewar and the other Rais of the east. May no Mewar or Malwa blood be spilt henceforth. May our children grow up and grow old as brothers.

Think of us kindly, Your Majesty.

Ever at your service, etc.

The Maharaj Kumar

P.S. Ajeet Simha, His Highness Medini Rai's head of intelligence, tells us that the intent of your visit to Gagrone is bellicose. How can that be possible, we ask him even as we scoff at him, does he not know that you are a wise man and a man of peace?

Does he not know, we further ask him, that a confrontation with Mewar will not only cost the Sultan the lives of tens of thousands of men as it did Muzaffar Shah, the Sultan of Gujarat, but several provinces of precious Malwa territory, for while we are generous in friendship, excessively so, we are also ruthless with our enemies. But we know that Ajeet Simha is a foolish man, and you will not suffer fools.

'What if he accepts your offer, Highness?'

'Why, then, Sire, we'll wine him and dine him, throw a feast such as Gagrone and Malwa have never witnessed and sign a peace treaty with him whereby Chanderi is awarded to you as your fiefdom. Anyone who dares break the terms of the treaty will stand to lose his entire kingdom. But while I pray that the Sultan will see sense, I suspect he'll feel honour bound, having come so far, to wage war with you.'

'And what if he wins? Neither His Highness Silhadi nor the other rais have shown much enthusiasm to join us. And I'm afraid as of this moment your forces amount to a little over three thousand and not fifty thousand.'

'If we lose, my father, the Rana will not forgive me for letting you down. If on the other hand I had decided to bring thirty thousand men with me, it would have taken us at least twenty to twenty-five days and that delay may have cost you Gagrone and your son Hem Karan. That was a risk I did not wish to take.'

'In that case, it is for my people and me to do your bidding while making you responsible for both victory and defeat.'

* * *

The meeting with Medini Rai's commanders was not the most pleasant but not unsatisfactory. Whether the Rai agreed with me or not, whether he believed that I was dangerous or deranged, he held his counsel and allowed me to conduct the meeting without contradicting or questioning my oddest assertions. Our first task was to spread the word and make people believe that we were arranging

430

accommodation for fifty thousand soldiers behind two stocky peaks of the branch of the Aravali mountains called Dhola Maru. We requisitioned every single tent in Dharampur and in the neighbouring areas and placed an order for another hundred, delivery within two days. Next we rounded up all the dogs in the vicinity and penned them in the military camp. Dharampur is well known for its monkey population. There were thousands of them; in a good year a third of the crops is eaten by them. They are much hated and though there's no law against killing them, hardly anybody does, since they are said to be descendants of Hanumanji. Notices were put up in all the villages that His Highness the Maharaj Kumar would pay a tanka to anybody who delivered ten dogs or monkeys to the army stores.

'Army stores?' His Highness's second-in-command Karan Rai sounded perplexed. 'What would they do with them?'

'The soldiers will as usual cook for themselves but what will an army of fifty thousand feed on? I'm afraid there's not much game left in this region after last year's drought.'

'On monkeys, Maharaj Kumar?' Karan Rai looked genuinely horrified.

'The brains of live monkeys are considered a rare delicacy in China, Karanji.'

'You have odd tastes in food,' he looked revolted, 'to say the least. My troops certainly will not touch the stuff.'

'The Mewar armies, I'm afraid, cannot afford to be choosy. When on a campaign, they'll eat elephant meat or rats if need be. On the Gujarat campaign, when there was an acute shortage of food because of a drought, our armies and I had snakes, mongoose and roasted red ants for a week.'

I believe Karan Rai would have liked to ask me to pack up my bags and leave but since Medini Rai kept an impassive face, he had no choice but to shut up. I turned round to Shiraz Ali, the man Mangal had deputed as intelligence officer for the campaign and asked him to spread the word in the Khalji camp that any enemy soldiers who were taken prisoner would be blinded and put to work instead of oxen in the oil presses or the flour mills. Alternatively, they would be emasculated and despatched to labour in the coalmines whence as everyone knew no one ever returned alive. Their mothers, wives, sons and daughters would be prostituted; they would be made to participate in unnatural and beastly acts and then when they were no longer of any use, put to death. Needless to say, their lands would be confiscated by us and auctioned off to the highest bidder.

On the other hand, if a Khalji soldier joined the Mewar army or went back home, he would be given a handsome reward: two months' salary in advance on reporting to our war office in Dharampur and a beast of burden or a cow, as per his wishes, at the end of the war.

'Surely you don't mean that about the old parents and the wives and children being prostituted, do you, Your Highness? Or that business about unnatural acts?' one of Karanji's lieutenants smiled indulgently and tried to humour me.

'Why not?' I was short with him.

'Because we are not like them, we are civilized.'

'No, you're right, we are not like them. They are about to discover that there is no deed so heinous and depraved that we will not perform it. Let me explain the arithmetic to you gentlemen. Our interest charges currently stand at 300 percent. As you know Mewar lost 3,000 soldiers to Gujarat a long time ago. Some years later Mewar destroyed 10,000 Gujarati troops in one morning alone. His Highness Medini Rai lost 39,917 men at Mandu. One way or the other, Mahmud Khalji is about to find three times that number, civilian or military, male or female, wiped out from his kingdom.'

The Rai's War Council sat chewing upon that information in silent consternation.

'One last question, Highness.' Karan Rai was not about to let go of me that easily. 'When do the rest of your fifty thousand soldiers arrive?'

'Within the week. Shiraz Ali and his men will bring them to the encampment directly along the Neelkanth bypass so that they won't disturb the peace of the civilian populace. They are good people, Karanji,' I smiled deprecatingly, 'but like any other troops a little frisky.'

In the end Karan Rai and his deputies did the job of vilifying us far more effectively than any fifth column or disinformation service could have. There was a wave of revulsion in the city: a couple of occasions when our men were abused and one incident of stone-throwing. Medini Rai ordered the miscreants whipped but we thought it wise to remain inside the camp limits from then on and not venture out unless something pressing demanded our attention in the city. I have to grant that my brother Vikramaditya, too, had his uses. But for him, I would never have known the potential of innuendo and rumour. By the third day there was not a dog on the streets of Dharampur. No, we hadn't eaten them all yet (though I was more than willing to, they were making such an unholy cacophony in the encampment at nights, or worse, keening for some mate in Badrinath or Bajaur.) The townspeople had either shooed them away or locked them up in their courtyards and houses, so that those devilish Mewaris wouldn't get at them.

✱　　✱　　✱

Late one night, I believe it was the fourth day since our arrival, Medini Rai came to our camp. There was another man with him. The Rai seemed a little overwrought and unable to speak. Oh God, please, not bad news. Don't let Prince Hem Karan die. Had Gagrone fallen? Had I committed the one unforgivable crime for a commander: overconfidence? Why had I not played it safe and ridden with the Rai to Gagrone and relieved the pressure on the fort?

'Highness, there are debts that one is unable to repay.' Medini Rai was inside the tent by now. 'This is one debt I have no wish whatsoever to be free of. I shall be beholden to you till my dying day. You have given me back my son, Hem Karan, and all my people who were beleaguered in Gagrone.'

I gave thanks to our family deity, Eklingji, that the Sultan had given credence to my story about the fifty thousand Mewar troops. We could expect him any time now but that was fine with me. I hugged Karan I don't know how long. I sat him down next to me but within minutes, he was fast asleep.

'Take him under your wing, Maharaj Kumar. I think you are a hero to him and he would like to walk in your footsteps.'

God forbid. Today's heroes are tomorrow's villains. But I would be happy if there was one other Rajput apart from Tej and Shafi who thought that all life was not about the art of dying.

What was the Sultan of Malwa up to? It was close to three weeks since he had lifted the siege of Gagrone and there was still no sign of him. He should have followed on the heels of Prince Hem Karan and overrun us. Was he waiting for reinforcements? Was he far shrewder than I had given him credit for? Was he paying me back in the same coin by preying upon our fears? If he was, he was doing a good job of it. He had Medini Rai, Hem Karan, Tej and Shafi, all our men and me stewing in a gruel of doubt and speculation and fear, wondering what his next move was going to be.

It was time, I thought, to test the waters; if possible, jangle the Sultan's nerves and get a reaction out of him. We would play cat and mouse with him, hopefully he would be mouse. We chose three thousand of Medini Rai's men, put them together with our troops and divided them into four groups of fifteen hundred men. At no time would more than two task forces go out on sorties. Tej and Shafi were put in charge while Prince Hem Karan and Karan Rai were to assist them till they had learnt the ropes. After that they would have independent command.

'You are on your own,' I told the four men. 'Don't try to figure out how I would act or wonder whether I'll approve of your actions. You will be on the spot and therefore the best judges of what needs to be done. Two rules. Don't take the enemy head on. Whenever possible, strike simultaneously but in different locations. Sow confusion and panic among the enemy. The idea is to decimate their men. Lose one of our men without good reason and you'll be charged with culpable homicide. Godspeed.'

Chapter 34

$\mathcal{I}$ got news from home mostly from Mangal. The first phase of the water and sewage system was coming along nicely. Lakshman Simhaji had had a stroke but was recovering fast. The royal barber's wife had tried to cut off her husband's member with one of his razors since he had got himself a mistress. The barber Madanlal is inordinately proud of his wife and is more than willing to show his mutilated manhood to all and sundry including His Majesty. The extension work on the Brindabani Temple had been completed and though there had been much protestation against His Majesty attending the evening arati there from some sources in the palace, he continued his visits. The King of Kabul, Zahiru'd-din Muhammad Babur, was riding hard towards Hindustan with the ostensible purpose of restoring order in Punjab. Mangal sent me some more of his notes. 'They don't always make sense,' Mangal wrote, 'but that's because our source there picks up whatever he can and they are almost invariably out of context.' Sometimes I resolve to ask Babur himself for clarifications and annotations when we get together one of these days and are sitting outside his tent of an evening and drinking the wine which he so often talks of renouncing.

'Marching from that ground, we dismounted over against Kahraj, at the mouth of the valleys of Kahraj and Peshgram. Snow fell ankle-deep while we were on that ground; it would seem to be rare for snow to fall thereabouts, for people were much surprised. In agreement with Sultan Wais of Sawad there was laid on the Kahraj people an impost of four thousand assloads of rice for the use of the army, and he himself was sent to collect it. Never before had those rude mountaineers borne such a burden; they could not give all the grain and were brought to ruin.'

This is a curious entry. Babur's ancestors were nomadic tribes and the flying raid where you stole grain, women, wealth in the form of horses, camels, cattle and jewellery and if you had the time after wholesale massacres, set the township or encampment on fire was routine. But Babur seems by nature a more circumspect and just man. He does not give idle offence and prefers not to antagonize people needlessly. Did he miscalculate and suddenly fall short of supplies? Even if he did, why not pay the going price of grain and make certain that those mountain-farmers and their families too did not starve?

It was, however, Babur's next entry, which would destroy my sleep once and for all. It proved Mangal's and my worst fears true.

'The various flocks and herds belonging to the country people were close round our camp. As it was always in my heart to possess Hindustan, and as these several countries, Bhira, Khushab, Chinab and Chimut had once been held by the Turk, I pictured them as my own and was resolved to get them into my hands, whether peacefully or by force. For these reasons it being imperative to treat these hillmen well, this following order was given: "Do no hurt or harm to the flocks and herds of these people, nor even to their cotton-ends and broken needles!" '

What followed was even more revealing.

'People were always saying, "It could do no harm to send an envoy, for peace's sake, to countries that once depended on the Turk." Accordingly on Thursday the 1st of Rabi 'u' 'lawwal, Mulla Murshid was appointed to go to Sultan Ibrahim of Delhi (the next line and a half are illegible) ... I sent him a goshawk and asked for the countries which from of old had depended on the Turk. Mulla Murshid was given charge of writings for Daulat Khan and writings for Sultan Ibrahim; matters were sent also by word of mouth; and he was given leave to go. Far from sense and wisdom, shut off from judgement and counsel must people in Hindustan be, the Afghans above all; for they could not move and make stand like a foe, nor did they know ways and rules of friendliness. Daulat Khan kept my man several days in Lahore without seeing him himself or speeding him on to Sultan Ibrahim; and he came back

436

to Kabul a few months later without bringing a reply.'

It was a specious argument yet perfectly sound. Babur had grasped the central truth behind governance. At the heart of civilized life was a contract; real or concocted, articulated or subterranean, did not matter. The form was all. Its perception was the source of all power and order in a state. It kept chaos at bay. It is the sole underpinning of a monarchy or any other system of rule whereby the many obey the fiat of a few.

We Sisodias are, as you know, but regents of the supreme power of Shiva and that is the source of the authority vested in my family. Why do people pay taxes, offer their wrists for manacling when the kotwal or even an ordinary policeman shows up at the door to arrest a man who is accused of committing a theft or murder? Because the offices of taxation and law and all instruments of government are but conduits of the power which flows from that covenant, contract or whatever you choose to call it. It is because of the putative authority of that binding abstraction that Babur is so bent on invoking the validity of his claim to the Delhi throne through his ancestor Timur. It did not matter that the legal status of that claim is highly dubious and at best, far-fetched. The lame Turk, Timur, was more a whirlwind dacoit, a hit-and-run marauder than a king in these parts. He swept through Delhi in 1399. Babur needed a pretext to stake a claim to Delhi and Timur's flying visit over a hundred years ago to the place was reason enough.

Having decided to take possession of Hindustan at some future date by the simple expedient of his distant relationship with Timur (the Lame Scourge had, after all, many sons and grandsons and legions of great-grandsons and who was to say which of the current crop of the fifth generation of cousins was the legal heir to Delhi), Babur was now willing to be generous with Sultan Ibrahim and make a deal with him: a goshawk in exchange for the Sultanate of Delhi and all the territories that Timur had run over. A fair and just bargain and barter by any count, wouldn't you agree?

I was marvelling at the audacity and the gall, the political acuity and chicanery of the King of Kabul and chuckling to myself when the Chief of Security walked in.

'I beg your forgiveness, Highness, but ....' I raised my hand to cut the preliminaries short. If I had given orders that I was not to be disturbed and he had still had the temerity to do so, he must have had good reason. 'There's a lady come to see you.'

I smiled. Only one kind of lady visits an encampment close to the battlefield. 'I'm touched by your solicitude but when I am desirous of female company, I'll let you know.'

'Highness, she says she's a relative of yours, a very close one.'

I did not have time to tell myself that I had three guesses; the first one was Queen Karmavati, the second Greeneyes and the third .... She was standing in front of me.

I knew I was hallucinating. For close to four years, I have repressed one single thought. I have done the one thing I consider the most cowardly deed that mankind is capable of: deny my love. Had I killed her it would have been a kindness. Instead I let her live and killed her spirit.

She touched my feet. 'Bless me, my Lord.'

I raised her up. 'What are you doing in Dharampur, Leelawati?'

Ah, the converse of princes. Was there a banality that I would not dredge from my infinite store of small talk?

'Mahmud Khalji asked my husband to come from our home in Mandu to discuss the matter of an urgent loan. I came along with him and thought I would make a small detour and visit you.'

'Do you accompany your husband wherever he goes?'

'He is a financier,' she smiled, 'I'm a moneylender with a stateswoman's head. In important and complex matters, he has discovered that it profits him to consult me.'

'And what advice did you give him?'

'The Sultan believes that your forte is the lightning attack. It wounds and debilitates but does not destroy and can be effective only on a long-term basis. He is banking on your not having staying power this time for why else would you bring along an army of fifty thousand?

'He'll not give battle to you on land which has hills and deep ravines. On flatland he's persuaded that he can beat you just as Malik Ayaz did on that first encounter near Idar. I think it's smart thinking on the Sultan's part. But I told my husband the problem's not the Sultan but you. You are the most parsimonious royal in

438

the country when it comes to state funds and manpower. I find it difficult to believe that you were able to muster and move such large forces in so short a time. And even if you did, I doubt it if you would want to commit so much money and time against the Sultan. Malwa would be good to pocket if it happened to drop into your lap, but my guess is that Delhi is the prize you have your eye on.'

'So what do you think is my game plan on this campaign?'

'I have no idea, Highness. I'm not sure you have anything specific in mind either.'

I kept a deadpan face or so I hoped but I had the feeling that I was being undressed, not just my body but the innermost recesses of my mind.

'There's only one thing I'm certain about. You are entirely without any loyalty to any one particular military theory or ideology. And that's what makes you so unpredictable and dangerous.'

'So should your spouse bet his money on the Sultan or not?'

'Highness, we are not Rajputs,' she laughed a matter-of-fact, unmalicious laugh. 'It's never all or nothing for us. We invariably hedge our bets and always cover our risks. The Sultan, as you well know, is badly strapped for funds and is already in debt.' She smiled mischievously. 'I'm sure Mangal and his men have told you the exact sum to the last decimal point. Now is obviously the time to extract an extra fractional percentage point. But all that is piffle. The only pertinent question is will Mewar be satisfied with defeating the Sultan or does it want to grab the whole of Malwa this time? Because if it's the latter, we stand to lose everything, the previous debt monies as well as the contemplated current loan. Let me frame the crux of the problem: what is the objective of the Mewar campaign; more specifically, who has formulated it, His Majesty, the Rana or you?' She did not take her eyes off me. 'I'm betting my money on His Majesty. Which is why I've told my husband to put together a cartel of financiers from Gujarat, Vijayanagar and the east and lend money to the Sultan. That way we don't take undue risks and yet collect commission on the loans given by the cartel. Does that confirm your conclusions about the lending policies of my husband's house?'

She had not given away anything I did not already know or would not have found out in a couple of days. I had not forgotten that she had one of the keenest heads in Mewar but to see her break up a problem into its various subdivisions, address each one of them and then make a clean sweep of the lot with a composite solution was like watching a master make his moves at a dense and convoluted game of chess.

I shook my head slowly. 'If only your grandfather had married you to someone from Mewar, Chittor rather than the Sultan, would have benefitted immeasurably from that swift and shrewd brain of yours which leaves nothing to chance.'

'I am married to Mewar, Maharaj Kumar. It may have escaped you, but I'm not likely to forget it ever.' She let that sink in. 'I am back for good this time.'

'Not exactly the happiest time for banter, Leelawati.'

'I'm in earnest, Your Highness.' Unhurriedly but with an economy of movement that was like pressing a lever to open hidden passages and vistas, she unsheathed herself. 'Take me, Sire.'

She was more serene and self-possessed in her nakedness than the supernaturally calm larger-than-life image of Lord Mahavir in her grandfather Adinathji's courtyard. I closed my eyes. She stood inside them.

In Lakshman Simhaji's library, there's a priceless illustrated copy of Vatsayan's *Kamasutra*. In it is a picture of a woman's face. The head is thrown back. Her eyes are closed with the pleasure of anticipation, her lips are moist and a little open. At the end of her expectant yearning is the index finger of a man, perhaps it is of a woman. The lips will close upon the finger, the tongue will wet, flicker and swirl around it. Gently the lips will suck at the prathama, draw it in and release it.

And yet, and yet Vatsayan and his artist have not seen Leelawati's toes.

There is nothing, absolutely nothing one cannot do without in life. All wants are dispensable so long as one can absent oneself. What happens if you discover a dark and urgent longing in your chest that runs all the way from front to back, a hole that you pack with the rest of your life, state-work, lovemaking, the tunnels under Chittor, writing diaries and military manuals, wars and warcouncils; and yet you never make any progress? The hole stays as it is, you

440

carry it wherever you go, no great ache, just an emptiness and a suspicion that you have betrayed both Leelawati and yourself.

If it is politic, I have no problems lying with a straight face. But I am not given to lying to myself, at least not consciously. And yet through the intervening years whenever I have struggled to erase the thought of Leelawati, I have asked myself what she means to me, what is the relationship that our stations and roles in life permit. Some questions I can answer, others I cannot do anything about. But there are also areas where I am not able to sort out the boundaries of prevarication, responsibility and that very real and just as intractable entity called the truth-of-the-matter.

I loved Leelawati when she was a child. She was precocious, lovely, vivacious and fond of me (that always helps). Despite my great affection for her, I was perhaps patronizing towards her as adults are wont to be. I did not doubt the intensity of her attachment to me but I read it as puppy love. My brother Vikramaditya did not mind ruining Leelawati's name and future just so long as he could get at me. That effectively dropped the curtain on my relationship with Leelawati. But even if Vikramaditya had not intervened, would matters have been any different between Leelawati and me? How much was I responsible for her fate? Given the fact that we were Rajputs and her family Jains and that her great-grandfather was not just minister of the exchequer but also the most powerful financier in the kingdom, could we have continued to be anything but formal and distant friends after she grew up? We are not a closed and oppressive society in Mewar, but men and women who are not married to each other do not meet except socially.

'And what about your husband?'

Where was my ancestor, the Sun-god? Would he not turn his flammable gaze upon me and rid Leelawati of a man who would rather stammer inanities than do her bidding?

'I'm a virgin, Maharaj Kumar.'

My face must have shown some sign of humanity and perhaps even astonishment.

'No fault of his, Sire, he's a whole man. Unfortunately for him, he is also a staunch believer in the tenets of Jainism. In the early years of our marriage when he tried to force his attentions upon

441

me, I would tell him that if he touched me, I would kill his favourite singing bird, Geet, the mynah he fed with his own hands every day and the blood of the bird would be on his head. He's besotted with me, Maharaj Kumar but he is a true Jain and even for love of me, he'll not spill blood.'

'Go back to your husband, Leelawati,' I could barely whisper the words, 'Make him happy.'

'I'm yours and no one else's.'

'I'm truly touched, Leelawati. Nobody has paid me a greater compliment.' I was choosing my words with care so that they had just the right degree of pleasant anonymity. The sand of fraudulence and chicanery blocked my mouth and try as I might, I could not be rid of it. 'Your cruelty and denial can kill a man, Leelawati. You must stop this foolishness.'

'You need an heir, Highness. The Little Saint is too self-centred to give you one. We'll have children, boys and girls and I'll make you a fine wife and colleague.' She got hold of my hands then and clutched them tightly. 'I'll wipe out all the terrible years of your first marriage. I'll make you happy.'

I did not doubt her but I would not let go of my cussed silence.

'You don't give a damn about my husband. Is it because of the Princess? Haven't you learnt yet that she loves someone else? Always has?'

You are doing all right, my friend. You need no longer practise pretending being a stone in the mirror. You've become one.

'Why then, Maharaj Kumar? Why?'

Chapter 35

*T*he news from Tej, Shafi and Hem was encouraging. They were everywhere and nowhere. Northern and eastern Malwa were as much a part of Sultan Mahmud's territories as Mandu but the Sultan was distinctly at a disadvantage in these parts. Medini Rai and the other rais were locals and closer to the hearts of the people.

There was no denying that the boys' campaign of harassment was steadily wearing down the enemy. All food was rapidly disappearing from the market. When the Malwa troops forcibly extracted grain, lentils or salt from the food merchants and villagers, retribution from Tej or Hem was swift and severe. Often it was meted out even as the soldiers were heading back for their camp.

All in all, I should have been a satisfied man, if not a happy one. Instead I was growing more and more uneasy. Mahmud Khalji had sent an urgent missive to the Delhi Sultan asking for monetary and military assistance against us. I knew that I had no reason to fear Ibrahim Lodi of Delhi. If he could find the time to respond, it would be to beg off. And that was the source of all my anxiety, edginess and helplessness. How far had the Moghul Babur come into India by now? Would the Sultan of Delhi be able to stand up to him? I felt trapped and was in a hurry to be back in Chittor. A bad state of mind to take critical decisions and fight an enemy whose forces outnumbered ours three to one.

Then Mangal's right-hand man Shiraz Ali intercepted a letter from Sultan Muzaffar Shah. A Gujarat force, ten thousand strong was riding full speed for Dharampur. That certainly made me forget even the Moghul. We would make a nice sitting target caught between the Malwa and Gujarat armies. There's a time to fight and a time for flight. Our only hope was to gather whatever we could of our baggage, and run all the way to Mewar or perhaps to Chittor itself.

I went over to the Rai's palace, had the briefest meeting I have ever had with a senior leader of such standing, five minutes all told, came out, ordered all real and phony camps to be dismantled by four in the afternoon, and sent word by courier to Shafi, Tej and Hem to forget goodbyes and other niceties and pull out.

Before Medini Rai and I led our troops out of Dharampur in an unseemly hurry we made sure that word got out that we were off to Mandu to visit the absent Sultan.

An army can't ride like the devil as a search party or a small band of men can but we did a middling imitation. We rode three nights, the guerrilla warriors joined us on the second night. On the fourth day the Rai and I scouted the territory, chose level ground in a valley encircled on all sides by decent-sized mountains, the kind you can climb on horseback in half an hour. The next morning we got word that His Highness Suraj Rai, one of Medini Rai's vacillating allies was joining us at the head of five thousand troops. I doubt if I have ever been a greater hypocrite than on this occasion; I was so relieved I could have rushed up to him and embraced him as if he was my friend Raja Puraji Kika himself. Instead I was civil, courteous but distant. I was not going to welcome him with open arms and thank him for taking his time.

Over the campfire in the evening, he asked the question that had been weighing on his mind all day.

'Where are the rest of the troops?' He tried to make the question sound as casual as possible.

I kept silent. Medini Rai gestured off-handedly to the mountains behind us.

'They'll come out at the right time.'

We were having dinner when Silhadi sought permission to have an audience with the Rai and the Maharaj Kumar of Mewar.

'This is a rare privilege, Highness. We have fought side by side with His Majesty, the Rana, but we hear the son is every bit a match for his father,' Silhadi's voice was glossy as china silk but without character or sincerity.

'Our admiration is mutual, then. His Majesty has spoken often of you but I did not think that you would honour us with a visit after all these months.'

My little dart did not miss its mark but Silhadi was not about to be fazed. He would let me know that we were beholden to him.

'Not a mere personal visit, Highness, a train of seven thousand gallant men is following on my heels to be of assistance to you.'

'Then we are doubly honoured and you are doubly welcome. Won't you join us for dinner?'

I watched him play with the partridge pickle and the sarson ka sag on his plate. In the lamplight, he had a reptilian charm. I had the odd feeling that he would be a good happy-go-lucky friend so long as the weather did not change and the stars were favourable. Which was not really as much of an adverse comment as it sounds. It is a happy circumstance for mankind that things rarely come to the crunch and friendships are not put to the test often.

Just then Shiraz Ali asked to have a word with me.

Suraj Rai made his excuses about not realizing how late it was and Silhadi discovered that he was exhausted after such a long day.

When they left, I beckoned Shiraz Ali in.

'The Sultan and his armies will be here by one in the afternoon, two at the latest.'

*   *   *

Shiraz Ali's timing was off by half an hour. The Sultan was in a hurry to save his capital from the Mewari marauders and must have left his overnight camp by six in the morning. They had made good progress. Elephants, camels, cavalry and infantry had trudged for six or seven hours when they entered the enchanted circle of the mountains. The much-hated Gujarat division of five thousand horse permanently posted in Malwa ostensibly to safeguard Sultan Mahmud Khalji from his own people rode in first followed by the rest of the Malwa army. We should have been closing in on Mandu, the Malwa capital. What in the devil's name were we doing in battle formation some eighty miles from Dharampur? And where were the fifty or sixty thousand Mewari troops? There were not even ten thousand massed together in the valley. The Sultan raised his hand for his armies to come to a halt. For the next hour they kept pouring in and arranged themselves in respectable units: the camel corps, cavalry and infantry. The Sultan and his commanders had had time to look around by now. They were puzzled. Silhadi's men were atop the northern mountains, Suraj Rai's on the western heights and close to seven thousand of Medini Rai's men stood guard above the southern slopes. Exactly how many troops were there in the mountains? Thirty, forty, sixty – or barely ten thousand? What were they doing up there instead of being with their brothers in the valley? Did Medini Rai and the Maharaj Kumar of Mewar want to take on the Sultan's forty-five thousand with a force of a mere seven or eight thousand? There had to be a catch. The Sultan could mow down the entire cavalry on the ground in an hour, or hour and a half at the most. But then those thousands of troops on the ridges of the mountains whose numbers it was impossible to ascertain could swoop down and draw a deadly noose around the Malwa armies. Or had we taken up these positions merely as a temporary decoy so that while we delayed the Sultan, the greater part of our armies would race to Mandu and capture it?

It was an odd tableau. Two enemies ranged against each other, one tired after riding for close to seven hours and hungry to boot, the other full-bellied and fresh, and neither willing to make the first move. The Malwa Sultan seemed to be paralyzed. I thought it was time to relieve his agony. Tej detached himself and taking a position ahead of the Rai and me, and barely seventy feet from the Sultan, took out a scroll tied in red brocade.

'Can you hear me, Your Majesty?' Pause. 'Because if you can't, I will draw closer to you.' He did not wait for an answer but went forward another twenty feet or so. 'His Highness Medini Rai, His Highness the Maharaj Kumar of Mewar, His Highness Silhadi and His Highness Suraj Rai send you greetings from His Majesty Rana Sangram Simha of Mewar. His Majesty, the Rana wishes you a long and healthy and prosperous reign. Which is why he wishes to stress again that he bears you only goodwill and would avoid confrontation with you. It is his belief that both the people of Malwa and Mewar desire peace and that it is a foreign power which wishes to lord it over you, and which is instigating you to fight against Mewar and its allies.

446

'Ask your soldiers, enquire of your farmers and villagers, listen to your townspeople, they'll tell you they would be rid of the Gujarati forces who treat your sovereign land as a vassalage and its people as second-class citizenry. They want to be left alone. They wish for peace.

'All His Majesty, the Rana, asks for is fairness and justice. Give Chanderi to the man who helped you regain your throne and your lost capital and who was your closest ally and friend, His Highness Medini Rai. As the Sultan of Malwa, you alone have the power to make a generous peace with their Highnesses, Silhadi and Suraj Rai. As to reparations to Mewar for our troubles, we can work them out as two great nations in a spirit of amity and goodwill.

'Once again we wish to extend our hand towards you. Will you hold it forever in friendship?'

Tej stopped and looked up at the Sultan and his commanders and then at the common people and soldiers of Malwa whom neither their Sultan nor any previous Maharana had ever taken cognizance of before.

'Make peace, Your Majesty, or you'll rue this day for the rest of your life. This we promise you. This we swear, that seven thousand five hundred Mewar and allied men, unnatural men without conscience or human heart, fed on that which no civilized men will eat, dog and monkey meat, which makes them invincible and beyond the reach of Yama, will ride forth and slaughter, destroy and erase without trace all Malwa soldiers here present.

'No idle threat, this, Your Majesty. For how else can you explain the preternatural confidence that permits us to ask the host of our armies to stand aloof and still on distant heights instead of joining fierce battle with the enemy?

'Think, Your Majesty. If we do not receive a friendly reply within ten minutes, you and you alone will be accountable for the deaths of forty-five thousand innocent soldiers.'

As a parting gesture, Tej rode up to where His Majesty the Sultan sat on the howdah of his royal elephant, rolled back the scroll, tied the strings into a neat knot, bowed deeply, handed it to the monarch of Malwa and joined us. Medini Rai and I retreated to the sidelines while Tej, Shafi and Hem Karan took command of the three divisions into which the army had been divided.

I had woken up in the morning and broken my resolve not to send Hem Karan into battle and risk his death. I did not wish to test his good luck any further but we are warriors and sentimentality is but another word for fear and I had to learn to live with my fears, not close my eyes to them.

'The war we have initiated and pursued so far is a war of nerves,' I had told our soldiers in the morning. 'One you cannot see and which seems either like child's play or a waste of time. There is, however, some proof that it works. You cannot deny that Prince Hem Karan and his braves are with us without our having shed any blood. But the war of nerves is first and last an aid to conventional and guerrilla warfare. Its purpose is to break the backbone of the enemy, his morale, before we attack. Have we succeeded? I don't know. You alone can bring in the results of that experiment this afternoon.

'Your swords are seven inches longer and yet weigh a little less than the conventional sword that the Sultan's men use. They are lighter but not a whit less sturdy and thirty percent more tensile. In short, your reach and efficacy are greater.

'Prince Tej and his men will stay behind with us. They are our emergency group. If you can't force the Sultan's men back into the narrow orifice from which they issue forth, if we find instead they have us on the run, then of course we'll call down the troops from the mountaintops. Do you want that to happen? Our new allies are opportunists. They have joined us after all these months only because they think our chances are good and they can share the fruits of war and glory with us. Seems a bit unfair to me that you do all the work and they arrive to collect the laurels.

'Can so few beat so many of the enemy? I think so. Go forth and make history. Godspeed.'

The Sultan's ten minutes were over. Fifty massive ladles, with forty-foot long handles which had been pinned down to the ground sprang up suddenly like behemoth shot-putting arms and flung out great comets of whooshing, hurtling fireballs. I doubt if these oil-soaked cloth and cotton wool-bound rocks did much physical damage to the enemy but they did cause pandemonium in his ranks.

The ladles had been staggered and placed strategically after much testing the previous day so that the fire barrage would catapult all over the enemy.

At the height of this inflammable rain, Shafi and his men formed themselves into a tight triangle and headed for the Gujarati division. Their programme was limited: destroy the Gujarat cavalry within thirty minutes. Simultaneously a hundred megaphones addressed the Sultan's men. 'Malwa brothers, we have no intention of killing you. Drop your arms and withdraw to the sides. No one will raise his weapon against you. Brother will not fight brother.'

It would make a rather elegant story if I could report that the Malwa troops watched from the wings while Shafi and his men struck and ravaged Muzaffar Shah's Gujarati troops. Nothing of the sort happened. Most of them swung valiantly into action. But there was hesitation and few things work as effectively in the enemy's favour as a divided state of mind. For a brief moment but long enough for our purposes, the Gujaratis felt isolated. They were good, experienced warriors and slashed out for the kill but discovered seven inches of deadly extra blade had overtaken and dismembered them.

All armies are made up of companies of men led by an amir, rao, raja, sardar or whatever honorific the vassal may bear. Feuds and rivalries, between two villages, royal houses, subcastes, or religious groups are invariably transferred and carried on to the battlefield regardless of who the common enemy is. Hem Karan's men slipped in and exploited the cracks, drove in wedges and left them wide open and then as those long, long blades cut down men like grass in late autumn, the Sultan's men began to lose heart. Soon they were in earnest retreat. The battle, however, was not going according to my plan. We had been fighting for an hour and ten minutes but we were behind schedule. We were behind schedule because of one man, Sultan Mahmud Khalji himself.

I have seen some good warriors in my time, Father, Rao Viramdev, Rao Ganga, Malik Ayaz, but they were not in the same class as the Sultan on that day. The Sultan was heroic and murderously effective. We could have swords a yard longer, but no tactic could trap him. His own men were already rallying around him.

Another forty-five minutes and visibility would be poor and the day would end with neither a decisive winner or loser.

Tej, Medini Rai and I set out with five hundred men. Within minutes we were engaged in hand-to-hand combat. Then I was face to face with the Sultan. I had lied to myself. He was good, very good but that was not why I had joined the fray. I wanted him dead so that we could appropriate Malwa and put an end to the foolishness that could very likely have already lost us Delhi. Mahmud Khalji was mine to finish off despite the circle of magic that had made him invulnerable so far. My sword was about to fall on him when I saw the Rai shaking his head and looking askance at me. It was an accident, I wanted to tell him, come on Highness, this much you owe me, back me up and tell a lie to His Majesty, the Rana, for your own sake and the sake of Mewar. We don't need a victory over Malwa, think about it, we need an annexation. A permanent one. But by then the moment was past. The Sultan brought his sword down on me, I lunged to the right. The blade glanced off, struck sparks upon my chainmail and sank into the flesh of my left arm. He must have struck an artery for blood shot out and hosed his face. His eyes closed. I must have blacked out for when I came to my sword had fallen to the ground. How quickly blood congeals. He was trying frantically to open his eyes and rid them of the glue that blood is. I took the tip of the Sultan's sword in my mailed right hand. It was difficult to get a grip on it. I had little choice but to bring my left hand into play. I suddenly rose and leaning forward for better leverage drove the hilt of his sword with such force into his chest that he teetered and keeled over. He lay awkwardly on the ground, one of his feet tangled in the stirrup. I dismounted. My sword was in my hand and I had my right foot on the Sultan's chest. For safety's sake, the sword tip rested in the hollow under his adam's apple, the same spot where many, many years ago Father had cold-bloodedly stabbed my mother's throat when a chicken bone had got stuck in it. He wiped the blood from his eyes and face and looked at me.

'Why, Maharaj Kumar? Why the moment of hesitation? It was either you or me.' He had a childish voice, not unpleasant but the kind that would make you go back after a picnic to check whether that dreamy-eyed little boy had got left behind. 'I certainly wouldn't have spared you had my sword not missed its mark.'

I smiled. Dreamy-eyed people, I had learnt through experience, can be a shade more deadly than even mercenaries.

What should I tell the Sultan? That I was a boy of seven who did not disobey my Father?

When in trouble, always pull out the most egregious rhetoric.

'One does not strike so valiant a warrior, Sire.'

Perhaps it's time I gave up being a prince and took up my true vocation: become a court chronicler or charan turning defeats and stalemates into triumphs.

Chapter 36

I am like a schoolboy, I am always rushing home. From Idar, from Kumbhalgarh and now from Dharampur. It's as if I need to pretend that there's always something of moment, a crisis that cannot be resolved without my intercession, beckoning me. Am I stupid, am I incapable of learning that no human intervention can alter fate? Perhaps. But the day I acquire that wisdom, or rather, accept its behest, I will be unfit to be king. There's indeed a time to let go. I'll tell you when that is: when I am dead and gone.

There's a desperation to my impatience this time, however, which is new. I have no idea what it is that I expect to forestall but I have half a mind, make it three-quarters, to leave all the rais, sultans and princes, behind and ride Befikir non-stop to Chittor. And if Befikir collapses, I'm willing to run the last fifty or seventy miles to knock on Mangal's door. News, Mangal, give me news.

I've taken to meditation twice a day, instead of just once along with the rest of my yoga. I'm afraid I'm not doing too well. Babur intersects my attempts at equilibrium with parabolas, ellipses, trajectories and tangents that fragment and dislocate my mind and leave me feeling jangled. Fortunately, everybody else is in good spirits and ignores me.

It was difficult to tell whether the Sultan saw himself as a prisoner of war or as a guest of honour. Barring the occasional flash of temper, he was easy to like and did not have Prince Bahadur's arrogance. He had only one problem. He was in the wrong profession. He would have made an excellent shopkeeper selling diamonds or saris. He had a story for every occasion and could talk you into anything. He was jolly, convivial and willing to listen as much as he liked to talk. Even the lowliest soldier or sweeper could go up to him and tell him about his first amatory conquest or the death of his six-month-old son. The Sultan had a genuine capacity to share in the joy, sorrows and perplexities of the populace, a rare gift for a king. Unfortunately, that was one of his few royal qualities. When in power Mahmud Khalji tried hard to be Sultan but he failed miserably. Now he was just a soldier, albeit a royal hostage, and he no longer had to play-act. You could see how relieved he was to be himself and what a good time he was having.

We were still close to three days from home when we got the news that Muzaffar Shah of Gujarat had died and his eldest son, Sikandar, had ascended the throne. Where was my one-time friend and guest Prince Bahadur? Was he still wandering around in search of a following and the crown? Had the new king of Gujarat, Sultan Sikandar issued a fatwa for his brother's head? One thing was certain, so long as Bahadur was alive, neither Sikandar nor any of his other brothers could rest easy.

I needn't have bothered to rush home. Delhi had fallen to Babur. Sultan Ibrahim Lodi and the King of Kabul had done battle in Panipat and the Sultan was no more. How simple it sounded when the courier read out the message. Was that all it took, a few words from a breathless rider to capture the most important crown in Hindustan? Was this the calamity that I had frantically hoped to avert by speeding to Chittor? Not Babur, but we, Father, should have fought Sultan Ibrahim Lodi and taken Delhi.

Five times Babur had negotiated the frozen, inhospitable passes of the Hindukush mountains and crossed the Khyber Pass and each time he had progressed further into Hindustan. How many years had I been following Babur's career? All I had to do now was ride to Delhi and see the new Padshah face to face. Frankly, I knew that I wouldn't even have to do that any more. I had little doubt that we were destined to meet sooner or later.

* * *

The Malwa campaign was everything I could have asked for. It got me the triumph I had so longed for after we had reinstalled Rao Raimul on the throne of Idar. Three-quarters of the township of Chittor crossed the bridge over the Gambhiree and were waiting

453

behind the entire court and the Maharana of Chittor. His Majesty alighted from his elephant and took two steps towards Raja Medini Rai and me. This was contrary to all protocol and a signal honour. The Maharana stands firm and rooted to the ground regardless of the gravity, urgency or joy of the occasion. Whatever the rank of a vassal or prince, it is he who must step forward and bow to the sovereign. Medini Rai was about to bend forward to receive His Majesty's blessings when Father placed his hand on the Rai's shoulder to restrain him.

'May Lord Eklingji look upon you always with favour. You do Mewar and us great honour by visiting us immediately after defeating His Majesty, the Sultan of Malwa.' Father turned his head a fraction and the Pradhan Pooranmalji placed the victory turban in his hands. 'Never in the history of the Rajputs have so few overwhelmed so many. It is our privilege to bestow the Veer Vijay saafa on such a victor.'

'Your Majesty, there is no greater honour for a Rajput than the Veer Vijay of Mewar. I shall wear it proudly always. But I must in all honesty confess that the credit for this remarkable victory is due not to me but to the Maharaj Kumar and as such the Veer Vijay is rightfully his and not mine.'

The Mewar court seemed to hold its breath, wondering whether this was excessive generosity or crass ingratitude on the part of Rao Medini Rai. Father, however, was in no humour to take offence and lightly chided the Rai.

'Your Highness, this war effort may have emptied our coffers somewhat but our Minister of the Exchequer, the venerable Adinathji, tells me that things may look up a little now that His Majesty Mahmud Khalji may pump some life and lucre into our treasury. We may, therefore, be able to afford a separate Veer Vijay saafa for our son.'

Pooranmalji was already holding the second saafa which Father set on my head.

'They tell me that you acquitted yourself rather well, son and have brought a rare and precious gift for me. Your mother and I and the Little Saint are proud of you.'

The solid regiments of soldiers behind us parted as Tej and Shafi escorted His Majesty, Mahmud Khalji.

'Your Majesty, we are happy to present His Majesty, the Sultan of Malwa.'

The Sultan was not sure how much back-bending he had to do in front of the man who was at least temporarily his master and whose captive he now was. But Father could afford to be the soul of graciousness today. 'We cannot tell your Majesty, how honoured we are to have so exalted a personage visit Mewar. Chittor throws its doors open to you and bids you welcome. We trust you will not find our hospitality wanting at any time.'

The Sultan decided that it was wise to bow before his captor now. The crowds went wild after that. It was Jai Maharana, Jai Raja Medini Rai and Jai Maharaj Kumar for a full ten days. Mother was a little bemused by the sudden change in my fortunes. She kissed me on the forehead and cheek and asked me, 'Did you really beat that evil-looking man?'

'No, Your Majesty. Our armies did. And I'm afraid we must all look more than a little evil to him. He appears a little lost to me.'

'Well, so long as you are safe, I'm happy. Have you eaten, son?'

I could not help smiling then. My dear simple mother. I think she was the only one who put our victory in perspective.

'I'm not impressed,' Queen Karmavati bestowed one of her dire benedictions upon me. 'Those who have meteoric rises have meteoric falls.'

But I'll grant you this, Queen of all my ill-wishers, I, too, am not impressed by my victory. Don't get me wrong. It was not an inconsequential battle and the prelude to the actual conflict was excellent training and experience. But we've subdued Malwa, not conquered it. And a new man sits on the throne of Delhi.

*   *   *

Babur is, at least for the time being, distant and unreal for the people of Mewar. There is an euphoria at home which even I find hard to resist. Sultan Mahmud Khalji has ceded Mandasaur to us. Medini Rai is now Rao of Chanderi and Silhadi has been awarded the jagirs of Bhilsa, Raisen and Sarangpur. Victory celebrations in Chittor have always lasted for seven days. This time His Majesty has decreed that the festivities be extended to ten days. Was the Maharana making amends for the triumph I was deprived of the previous time, or was he underscoring a point to my brother Vikramaditya who has arrived from Ranthambhor without his permission?

'It is a pleasure, albeit an unwarranted one, Prince Vikramaditya, to see you in the capital,' Father had refused to see my brother privately and had chosen to speak to him at the durbar held to honour the victors of the Malwa campaign, 'but I believe the invitation we had sent was for your uncle Surajmal. Are we to understand that Ranthambhor is unguarded and if an enemy had an eye on it, could seize it without much resistance?'

'The blame, Your Majesty, is entirely mine,' Queen Karmavati spoke before her son had a chance to say something foolish. 'I missed him terribly and I knew that his brother, the Maharaj Kumar,' she snatched my hand, 'would be most upset if Prince Vikram was not here to share his joy and celebrate his victory.'

Nice move, my never-say-die second mother.

'This assembly finds your maternal yearning most affecting, madam. It is for mothers to call their sons back and for fathers to send them away.'

The Queen let go of my hand and before I knew what she was up to embraced me with a theatrical flourish. 'May your star rise to the meridian, Maharaj Kumar, and if it were possible, higher still. Take care of your little brother, Prince Vikramaditya.'

If anyone was in dire need of care, it was I. I felt I'd just received the hug of death.

From across the room I saw my wife looking at me. She was deliberately keeping a low profile and staying in the background. Not just the humble people of Mewar but even the courtiers can forget where they are and do the unthinkable: turn their backs on His Majesty and prostrate themselves at the Little Saint's feet.

I thought I could handle my brother's sudden surge of fraternal affection but I had a premonition that the relationship between Father and Queen Karmavati had reached some kind of turning point. It was likely that she still shared his bed more often than any other queen or concubine but I had the inexplicable feeling that she had broken free of him. In the past, however peeved or aggrieved she was with him, he was the final arbiter; she would perforce turn to him for redressal and a sly reinveigling into his affection. She was, I suspected, past desperation now. Perhaps my wife's ascendency had something to do with it though I was sure that the Queen knew from her spies that there was nothing sexual afoot between the Princess and His Majesty and that the Little Saint did not fancy politicking. This is extremely simplistic. I mention it merely because the Queen believed at some deep gut level that the way to control a man was through sex. Time was running out and if she did not make a decisive move, her son Vikramaditya might find it difficult to gain the throne of Mewar.

I feared her but at the moment my fears were on behalf of Father.

Chapter 37

The essence of life is not cause and effect. It is perversity. There is no telling the consequences of one's actions. As you sow, so shall you reap has a neat ring to it but you are making a grievous mistake if you put your faith in that kind of cheap sentiment. There are no just deserts. The wages of sin are not necessarily hell and the path of goodness is often lined with treachery for the world is predicated upon the principle of randomness.

Who would have imagined that Medini Rai of all people would do me in?

'I do not need to protest in what high esteem I hold you and your family, Highness. Do not ask me to give you reasons for it but I beg you, do not do this.'

'It's rather late for that, Maharaj Kumar. The deed is as good as done. The Rana himself has given his approval.'

The Rai had called me over to the Atithi Palace for a drink and we were sitting on the terrace in the chill evening air.

'I do not know how to phrase this, but perhaps you feel beholden for what Mewar did for you.'

'Nobody's forcing my hand. I am grateful to you and to His Majesty. But is it not possible that I might have developed a fondness for you over the past few months?'

'I do not take this honour lightly, nor am I ungrateful, but I hear the drums beating in Babur's camp calling us to war. Perhaps we can take up the matter after Mewar and its allies decide on a course of action.'

'If we resolve to confront the new ruler at Delhi, as I suspect we will, then will you ask us to wait for the outcome of the war?'

'It would be reasonable to assume that, wouldn't you agree? Not everybody returns from war.'

'Precisely. If I do not return, I would like you to be the shield and light for my family.'

'That we already are, Highness, even without the formality of an alliance between the two families.'

Perhaps I spoke that last sentence a trifle too eagerly for Medini Rai laughed out loud.

'We know how devoted you are to the Princess from Merta but a saint is no substitute for a wife. My daughter is a loving girl, Sire. She would have brought cheer to any home, but Chittor has a special place in her heart. She worships you since you rescued both her brother and her father.'

'I do not wish to sit at an altar. One saint in the family is more than enough.'

The Rai was as taken aback by the sharpness in my voice as I was.

'My daughter thinks the world of the Princess and aspires like most of our countrymen to be her companion and confidante but she is no saint, Highness. You'll find a woman in your bed, one made of ordinary flesh and blood.'

The only one apart from me who was against my second marriage was Queen Karmavati.

'Mark my words,' she interrupted Father and me while we went over the guest list, 'he'll make a mess of it. That wouldn't upset me so much except that he will ruin our relationship with Medini Rai.' Then she turned to me. 'We know what you intellectuals are like, you cup your hand over your ear and you think you hear the sea. Still waters don't always run deep, Maharaj Kumar, it's usually just wind in an empty tunnel.'

I am, as usual, intrigued by the Queen's linguistic reconditeness. It matters little that my second mother's words will not bear close scrutiny. There's an aphoristic condensation in her turn of phrase. What it succeeds in doing is to set up a chain of dissonant images that are compelling because they seem to share a common thread or belong to a family of metaphors. Is Mother at heart a poet? She

459

appears to be saying something deep even when we don't understand her or worse, when she is talking gibberish. She is not through with me yet.

'Do I need to tell you which vessels make the most clatter? You'll rue the day you get married, Prince. God help the poor girl.'

'If you are finished with prophesying, Madam,' Father remarked impatiently, 'the Prince and I could get back to more pressing and mundane business.'

Is it possible that venom and loathing incinerate deception, politesse and euphemism and go straight to the heart of the matter? The Queen certainly saw the future better than my misgivings allowed me to.

My wife Sugandha had disowned the burden of her father's looks when she was born but there was something engaging about her innocence and her wish to please and be liked. Medini Rai had not exaggerated when he had advised me that she was made of flesh and blood. She was not chubby but there was a softness in her that was disconcerting. I was convinced that if I pressed my index finger into her arm or the knot at her navel, her flesh would gently wash and settle over it and I would not see my fist again.

I am convinced now that wedding nights don't suit me. This is not belated wisdom but short of running from the marriage ceremony, I had done everything in my power to resist a second betrothal. I was gauche, if not downright offensive with the Rai, and anyone but my father-in-law (how strangely that phrase sits on my tongue) would have taken umbrage and not just withdrawn the offer of his daughter's hand but nursed a lasting and vindictive grudge against Mewar. The Rai, however, thinks of me as his friend and well-wisher. How long will it take him to discover his mistake? And what form will his regret assume?

And what about the Little Saint? What kind of equation does she have with my new wife? As always I have no clue. A week before the marriage, she came into my study and announced rather theatrically, 'I'll be vacating my rooms.'

'Why?'

'You may not suspect it but I'm not exactly unaware of the momentous event which is about to overtake Mewar.'

460

Did I detect a note of mockery in her voice or was it really the sarcasm of the wounded? Not only has my wife been the keenest backer of the concept of bigamy, she has practised what she teaches. A wife-in-law (is that what a wife calls her husband's second wife?) would ease the pressure of domestic duties on Greeneyes, not to mention free her from the onerous task of making small talk with the said husband so that she could devote herself full-time to the Flautist.

'You'll want your privacy with the lady.'

'I'm not the first nor will I be the last in the Mewar royal family to get remarried.'

'What if I want to?'

'Want to what? '

She knew I was being deliberately obtuse but she was not fazed.

'Remarry?'

'There are enough rooms in the palace and I believe a wing has been redone.' I continued to talk at cross purposes.

I had, however, merely played into her hands but it was too late to do anything about it.

'For whom? Me or you?'

I have neither the skill nor the quick-wittedness for the lethal riposte and thus failed to point out that with or without a separate wing, her assignations and affairs of the heart had continued undeterred.

I sometimes wonder if my wife is a conundrum without a key. Or if there was one, it's been lost a long time ago. For what does one make of the Princess' behaviour with my new wife? It must have been a week after my second wedding. I was coming home from work when I saw Sugandha calling out 'wait, wait, wait' to the Little Saint. Greeneyes stopped at the bottom of the stairs and allowed Sugandha to catch up with her.

'Can I come with you to the temple?'

'The correct verb is "may". You can come to the temple with me but you may not.' The Rai's daughter was too naive to take offence at the Little Saint's pedantic snub.

'Why?'

'Your place is with your husband, not in my hair.'

Why is Greeneyes, for the first time since I got married to her, going out of her way to make enemies? Has my luck suddenly taken a turn for the better? Has she become jealous and possessive?

Sugandha looked at my wife, then at me, ran up the stairs and locked herself up in her room. If she expected me to take her side, she was mistaken. I was not about to arbitrate between my two wives or encourage a race between them for the number one position.

The Little Saint may have accelerated the alienation of the Rai's daughter, but however loath I may be, I must give credit where it is due: to me and me alone. I did not will it so, quite the contrary. But what use are good intentions if all we end up doing is to subvert their results?

*   *   *

I had decided to go through the marriage ceremony with stoicism and detachment. Instead I got involved. My Sanskrit is not what it used to be but I was pleased to note halfway through the rituals that I could make sense of many of the stotras and verses. There was a young priest who reinvented the language by a simple trick, perhaps the right word is insight. He did not reproduce a text he had learnt by rote. He spoke Sanskrit as if he was talking an easy Mewari. The key to Sanskrit, the pundits never tire of telling us, is crystalline diction. They are right, absolutely right. What they forget to mention is that diction will make sense only if it is illuminated by understanding. Eschew meaning and context and even your mother tongue will sound dead. The most condensed and closely reasoned or lyrical verse, the priest seemed to suggest, is not so much rhyme or metre as it is spoken language.

Who killed Sanskrit? How does a language die? It wasn't as if a cataclysm had wiped out the populace of the country or the Muslims had decreed one day that Arabic or Afghani would replace the mother of our languages. Was language like a woman from the zenana that we could abandon any time we felt like it? Would Sanskrit have survived if not just the brahmins and the court, but all castes had spoken it? Will the language of Mewar also die? Along with geography and religion, a mother tongue is the destiny of a people. I have the strange feeling that man created language but now

462

it creates us. This is too big a thought. Am I talking rubbish? I need to examine this interaction closely.

Suddenly my bride and I were alone in the bedroom. Sugandha had her back to me. It was a scene that every Mewari couple has re-enacted on its first night together. It was the time, I had a feeling, when the fate of most marriages is decided. Please, don't be afraid. I won't touch you. I won't touch you till the day you ask me to share the bed with you. I give you my word. I've got some alta powder with which I'll stain the sheet so that when the maid comes to clean the room tomorrow, she'll not carry any tales. I'll just remove one blanket from the bed and sleep in the corner here.

I stood in front of the door unable to move and kept going over the same sentences over and over again till she finally turned around and looked at me. I could hear her pulse from where I stood. I thought I detected a passing smile as she looked at me expectantly. I realized then that my internal monologue was misplaced. She wanted me to do my husbandly duty by her. I was overtaken by the same desire I had seen in her eyes. I walked up to her and gently undressed her. I played with her till both she and I were fully aroused. She had closed her eyes and waited for me. She might as well have waited for me till she was dead. I could not perform.

I watched myself in horror as I shrank into myself. I was in an impotent rage. My world had lost its moorings. What was left of life if I could not depend on sheer, straightforward lust? There is no certainty more immediate than the hardness at the crotch. And now even that was taken away from me. Unable to cope with the betrayal of my body, I began to rail and rant at my new bride. She drew her knees to her chin and made a tight ball of herself. She waited for me to strike her as she cowered. I did not raise my hand but I could not stop my ranting.

I hated marriage, I said, I had done everything possible to spare her and myself the pain and indignity of being together. But does anybody listen? Everybody but me knows what is best for me. I have no idea what connections, or rather disconnections, my mind was making but I brought Babur and the coming war with him into the picture. I was surrounded by enemies on all sides, did she know that? All my brothers had an eye on the crown. Did she want it too? And what if the legal heir didn't get it? Was she going to blame me for it? There was no end to people's expectations of me. I'm not superman, is that clear? I couldn't guarantee her the throne or anything. Did she know that people thought I was a coward?

It was obvious that she was responsible for everything that had gone wrong with my life from the time I was born, perhaps even when I was in my mother's womb. There was more, much more but the fact was, nothing was going to cover the gaping hole of my inadequacy. I knew I had to shut up, this was Medini Rai's daughter and my wife, for better or worse, in sickness and in health. Did I doubt it for a moment that Sugandha would run to her father and tell him all? Did I wish to wreck Mewar's friendship with the Rai at such a critical time?

'Forgive me, Sire, forgive me for hurting you.' She still had her head between her knees and I couldn't hear her clearly.

'What? Don't mutter, woman,' I lashed at her with renewed fury, 'speak up, I am man enough to take whatever you have to say.' By now my one-track mind had deciphered her words and I was even more incensed than before. 'I'm treating you like a swine and you want forgiveness? Oh God, how I hate these martyrs. Can't you stand up for yourself and tell me to shut up and leave you alone?'

I was dressing with my back to her (I had got my dignity and prudishness back) when she pulled my belt towards her. Before I knew what was happening she had got my scimitar out of the scabbard, held her hand over the bedsheet and cut her index finger.

*　　*　　*

I was working on a speech for the passing out parade at the Gurukul, when Mangal walked in with a shade more urgency to his step than is his wont.

The curious fact is, even when Mangal is silent, everybody listens to him. I'm no exception. Long before he became head of intelligence, it went against Mangal's grain to reveal what was going on in his mind. The natural rider to that article of faith has been an impassive exterior, an economy of body movement and zero degree of excitability. But there is a paradox here. Despite his stoniness, Mangal is approachable, very much so, otherwise he would be

464

useless at his job. I think his unique quality is that he lets you think you have a special rapport and reciprocal relationship with him without ever allowing you to discover how wrong you are. He will not show his hand even after the game's over. How could he? All through our childhood, not that things are very different today either, I hogged the attention, I was the one who had moods and tantrums. He had to pretend that that was all right, that it was a perfectly just world and that he was without feelings or likes and dislikes. But I don't want to grieve overmuch about Mangal's deprived childhood. It has made him the best listener in Mewar and perhaps the second most powerful person in the kingdom.

I looked at the note he had placed on my table. It was addressed to me but I couldn't make out who it was from, since the handwriting was unfamiliar and the seal was smudged.

> To
> His Highness, the Maharaj Kumar of Mewar
> Greetings.
> Would you do us the kindness to see us? We await
> you outside the city limits.
> Yours,
> Prince Bahadur.

'Is Shehzada Bahadur really waiting for us?'

'In the shade of the rain tree outside the banyan grove, Highness.'

'Any chance of an ambush?'

'I doubt it, Sire. He has only eleven of his companions with him.'

'They were twenty-seven the last time he was here.'

'I believe the Shehzada is much reduced in circumstance.'

I have mixed feelings about Bahadur. I should hate him and a part of me does for what he did to Rajendra, however provoked he may have been, and yet I cannot deny my fondness for him. There is a quickening in my pulse and a repressed excitement at the thought of seeing a friend I had not imagined I would run into again, except perhaps on the battlefield. I will of course not allow

465

myself to articulate the one question that needs to be asked: of all people in the world not excluding my new friend and likely enemy, the Padshah of Delhi himself, what is Bahadur doing on the outskirts of Chittor?

Mangal was right. Time has not been kind to the Shehzada. He had always been self-indulgent but he had taken care in the past to camouflage the cruel streak in him with humour and easy, likeable ways. But he had either given up the attempt or he no longer cared that he now had the air of a dyspeptic lout.

His deep-set eyes had turned beady and watched you shiftily. They measured your good fortune against his. Disappointed ambition, hard times and a wavering faith in his destiny had made him bitter and given him an evil eye. He could and did wish you all the ill in the world. The most unsettling change in him was that he could no longer focus on or attend to anything for more than a few minutes. He would ask you a question, start to listen intently and lose interest. He was a man who was through with impatience and would go over the edge any day now.

We embraced each other. He had obviously been drinking steadily. Liquor is like garlic. Its miasma and stale smell envelop the whole body.

'Are you surprised to see me, Highness?'

'Pleased to see you would be more precise.'

'You were always the perfect gentleman, Maharaj Kumar. And how has life been treating you?'

'The usual ups and downs.' I wondered if we were going to exchange banalities for the next couple of days.

'Have you finally been officially declared as the successor to His Majesty, the Rana?'

'No, Highness. But His Majesty has, God willing, many more useful years left to him.'

'My old man's dead but I'm still not the Sultan of Gujarat.'

'I was sorry to hear about His Majesty's death. But take heart, Prince. If it's written that you'll be the sovereign, then no power on earth can prevent it. Our best wishes are always with you.'

'But is it written, Maharaj Kumar?' he asked me with not so much vehemence as rancour.

466

'Shehzada, I, too, am just as keen to decipher the hieroglyphics of destiny as you are.'

'Highness,' his tone changed suddenly, 'I'm a homeless man looking for a home. We were on our way to Malwa when we were told that you had not only defeated the Malwa armies but taken Sultan Mahmud Khalji prisoner. You've shut the door of Malwa on my face. Without the Sultan there, they'll not give me asylum.'

I refrained from telling Bahadur that had the Sultan been in Malwa, he would have been even less welcome there than in Mewar. Gujarat and Malwa had been allies recently but I don't think Sultan Mahmud had any illusions about Gujarat's intentions. The slightest provocation and the late lamented Muzaffar Shah or now his son, Sikander, would swallow Malwa whole and without a burp.

'I'm fed up with going from pillar to post. I need a temporary home. Will you let bygones be bygones?'

'I do not live in the past, Shehzada. You've known my views for a long time. Gujarat and Mewar need to be friends and at peace. If anything, I believe that even more now. If it was up to me, you could stay with us as long as you wanted. But I must be candid with you. The people of Mewar will not welcome you. Not after what happened on your last visit.'

'Are you saying no to me, Highness, even though I'm begging you to give me asylum?'

'I've no say in the matter, Shehzada. However, I'll arrange for you to rest and recover incognito in one of our villages for the next couple of days. I'll also give you a loan of ten thousand tankas from my personal funds to be paid back when you can.'

'I'll accept your hospitality,' Bahadur told me imperiously. I have to admit that he made me feel that I was the recipient of his benevolence and largesse. 'Your generosity, however, is misplaced, Highness. I have an elephant's memory. I'll not forget that you refused me shelter. Beware, Maharaj Kumar, you sent ten thousand Gujarati men to their death by deceit. You masqueraded as a Gujarati soldier and killed Malik Ayaz. You took Idar back. No one has ever inflicted such a devastating defeat upon Gujarat. Vengeance is mine, Maharaj Kumar. Mark my words. I'll hound you from village to village and town to town and I will overrun the whole

467

of Mewar.'

I couldn't help smiling. Was this the talk of a supplicant or of an autocrat at the peak of his power?

'You are tired and at the end of your patience. But your luck will turn, hopefully very soon, and then your elephant's memory will remind you of all the good things that transpired between you and me. If ever there was a chance of two hereditary enemies coming together, becoming friends and fighting for peace, it is Gujarat and Mewar.'

'And what of honour and vengeance?'

'Why not try an honourable peace, Prince? Its consequences are little short of wondrous. It will give us the time and the funds to build new cities and renovate old ones. It will attract artists and musicians to our courts. I may then even find time for my favourite obsession: the sewers of Mewar.'

He smiled tentatively. 'You think so?'

'Yes. I believe that with both my heart and head.'

'Khuda hafiz, Maharaj Kumar.'

'Khuda hafiz, Shehzada. Till we meet again.'

*   *   *

On the morning of the last day of the victory festivities, the Sultan of Malwa, Medini Rai and the Rana of Mewar signed a peace treaty. That night Sajani Bai sang for us at the palace.

Normally Kausalya would have looked after the arrangements since I was the host but Kausalya has ditched me. She was not there to greet me when I returned to Chittor.

'She sent Mamta a message about a month ago saying that she was going to her village on some pressing business. We have not heard from her since then,' Mangal said.

'Does she know that I am back?'

'I suppose she does.'

Why do my conversations with Mangal about his mother always turn obtuse and cagey?

'What's that supposed to mean? Don't be supercilious with me, Mangal. Does she know or doesn't she?'

'I don't know, Sire. Would you like me to send for her?'

'Yes.'

Two days later he was back.

'She's not in the village, Maharaj Kumar.'

'Where the hell is she?'

'I don't know. Ghanikhama Durbar, but I need hardly tell you that my mother is an independent woman and not answerable to me.'

'Did she go some place else after visiting the village?'

'She never did go to the village.'

'So where did she go?'

'I have reported her missing to the police. They are combing the city and checking out with their underworld connections. I have spoken personally to the Inspector-General. He's sending messengers with mother's description to every town and city in the kingdom.'

'Is she all right, Mangal?'

I had to get a grip on myself. What was Mangal supposed to say? Mother's missing for over five weeks now but she's doing fine?

'I have alerted our intelligence network too, Highness. I took the liberty of borrowing one of her portraits from your collection and have asked one of the artists at the temple to make a dozen copies of it.'

'Thank you Mangal. I appreciate this.'

Mangal smiled wryly. 'We may not always get along, Highness, but she is my mother and I'm concerned about her.'

'You are right. Let me know if you hear anything. Anything at all.'

I needn't have worried about the hospitality and the protocol for the guests. In my absence the Princess routinely managed dinners and banquets for anywhere between twenty-five and two thousand five hundred people. She plans and organizes while Mangal's wife, Mamta, executes her orders. You'll find more than a trace of Merta cuisine at the palace these days but as always the Princess makes sure that no one can accuse her of partisanship by introducing some Delhi or Ahmedabadi dishes in the meals. Since that night's recital

469

was in honour of His Majesty Mahmud Khalji, the menu for the dinner was Malwa all the way. My wife's grapevine was obviously a sound one for the Malwa King was delighted with the meal and in terrific back-slapping humour. I, too, must have been feeling lightheaded and expansive for I was caught unawares when he disingenuously slipped in a query while we were walking after dinner to the Rana Kumbha hall where the concerts in the palace are held.

'Now that it's merely a memory of little consequence, perhaps you may care to tell me whether you brought an army of fifty thousand along with you on the Malwa campaign or was it only a bluff?'

When I think back on it, it was a good thing that I had not rehearsed my answer beforehand for my look of surprise had nothing false about it. I recall Medini Rai who was accompanying us slowing down and awaiting my reply with as much curiosity as the Sultan himself.

'It was, Your Majesty, not a bluff so much as a rounding off of numbers.'

'How much?' the Sultan paused almost as if he was asking himself whether he really wanted to know the truth. 'How much of a rounding off are we talking about here?'

'We were forty-seven thousand seven hundred Mewaris, which didn't sound half as impressive as fifty thousand, so we padded the figure a little bit. Why, why do you ask, Majesty?'

He looked relieved. 'I thought someone mentioned yesterday that you had taken the latitude of adding a zero and had turned forty-five hundred soldiers into forty-five thousand.'

'I would like my children to believe that I was heroic, almost supernaturally so, but I don't want to be the laughingstock of Mewar, Sire. Soldiers are the worst liars in the world but I do believe that your source was overdoing things a bit.'

The Sultan hadn't finished with me yet. 'And how would you explain so large an army covering so great a distance in so short a time? Three days to be precise?'

I tried to avoid answering that one. 'You don't really want to know, Majesty.'

'I do.'

470

'It was an egregious lie and you've caught me out. It was a matter of dropping a zero this time. His Highness Medini Rai asked for assistance from his Majesty, the Rana, immediately after you left Mandu. We had a little time, so we divided ourselves into ten groups, each one leaving after an interval of two or three days and never by exactly the same route.'

I knew what the next question was going to be.

'And the business of dog and monkey eating, is that true?'

'Entirely. It's something we learnt from a Chinese traveller who visited us some years ago. Their belief is that the meats of these animals, especially the brains of monkeys, increases aggression and virility to the power of ten. That explains why so few of us were able to take on so many of you.'

'That is disgusting. A dog is a man's best friend. For no gain on earth would I consume dog or monkey flesh. I feel like throwing up.'

He didn't. One thing I was certain of: when he went home to Malwa, he would order monkey brains at least once a day. The Sultan took his duties of servicing his seraglio a trifle more seriously than the care and administration of his kingdom.

'I cannot begin to tell you how honoured and touched I am that the people and princes of Mewar have recalled me to their midst. My salutations to His Majesty, the Rana. My adaabs to His Majesty the Sultan of Malwa. My special greetings to His Highness, the Maharaj Kumar and His Highness, Lakshman Simhaji. Each and every one in this august assembly is special to me. I will name each one of you separately and singly when we are alone, one to one, just the two of us,' Sajani Bai paused. What alternative did she have? She had brought down the whole house and they were never going to cease clapping. She had not lost any of her magnificence. She had the royal audience waiting on her every word, and more than her words, on her every gesture, for it is with her nazakat and nakhra that she is the equal of any king or emperor. 'But before I sing for you, I am going to ask a favour from a very special patron of the fine arts. On behalf of all of us lovers of music, I am going

471

to ask His Highness Raja Medini Rai to render a song for us.'

If you think the men went berserk, then you should have heard the women. They would have put to shame the entire populace of stalwart ladies working in our red light district. Catcalls, hooting, howling, ululations, clapping. Soon they had joined hands and trooped down to where His Highness Medini Rai was sitting and formed a circle around him and danced an impromptu dandiya. The Raja raised his hands several times to quieten the audience, then gave up.

> Don't be shy
> Medini Rai
> Don't be shy
> Sing us a lori, hori or thumri
> Else we'll follow you to Chanderi
> Sing us a lori, hori or thumri.

The Raja of Chanderi smiled and the women of Chittor sighed and swooned.

'There's no point, none whatsoever, in pleading with me to sing,' his smile grew bigger and the dimples in his cheeks were deep enough to play parallel games of gilli-danda. 'Did you people really think that I was going to let you go without singing with Sajani Bai?'

> Listen now, cut out the weeping, nip it in the bud.
> It's only a story, even if the people in it were real,
>   like me and you.
> Nothing new about it, just a boy and a girl and some
>   spilt blood.
> Listen now, cut out the weeping, nip it in the bud.
> After all, neither you nor I are Dhola or Maru, are
>   you?

Sajani Bai closed her eyes for the lovers Dhola and Maru and for my dead cousin, Rajendra, who had died while listening to the song. How innocently Medini Rai of Chanderi had opened wounds

472

that had not yet had time to develop scar tissue. Sajani Bai kept us waiting and wondering, would she sing on or would she move on to another song ? Then her clear, source-of-the-Ganges voice dug into the wound and drew blood and cleansed us all.

> Death will not part them, so the song tells us with
>   authority.
> How would you know, songster, did you die and check
>   out your story?
> Speak not to me of the afterlife, it's the here and now
>   I'm interested in.
> Can you make Dhola Maru come alive, uncross the
>   stars, change the ending?
> If not, cut out the weeping; better still, shut up and do
>   our bidding.
> Say what you will, the story will be told, Dhola Maru
>   may live only in the retelling.

Sajani Bai stopped and looked around. This was not unusual. Our singers and instrumentalists, even classical ones, will interrupt a taan, a raga, bhajan or folk song to recount its history, tell an anecdote, give a comparative analysis of the way different singers or schools treat the same words, or comment and philosophize about any matter whatsoever. Instead Sajani Bai zeroed in on me.

'Does not our song give you pleasure, Maharaj Kumar?'

'It does, madam, but I cannot deny that it awakens painful memories.'

'And you fear that some terrible catastrophe will follow as on the previous occasion? But there is no cause and effect operative here, Sire. If we consign a song to amnesia because of the burden of our own memories, then it is possible that an entire people will push a dastardly act or even the life of one of their own into the black hole of oblivion merely to seek forgetfulness and absolution.'

'Do you really think one can wipe out people and events that easily?'

'We rework our own memories and reinvent ourselves to suit our tastes and predilections every day. Who is to notice a hiatus in history a few centuries down the road?'

'Why is it so important,' Father spoke almost inaudibly, 'to remember, Sajani Bai?'

'Because otherwise our lives would be lies and we may never tell our children to speak the truth again.'

'Will you be the remembrancer of Chittor, Sajani Bai?'

'I would be honoured, Your Majesty.'

'Then the truth will never be in jeopardy, at least not in Mewar.'

A regal pronouncement, eminently suited to such a public occasion and yet even as fond hopes go, I thought His Majesty was getting a little carried away.

Chapter 38

*T*he good times had idled by. The party was over. It was time to get back to work. What next, heir apparent, question mark; husband of the Little Saint; black sheep, black cloud on horizon, source of all ills, one and only hurdle to kingship, for Queen Karmavati and Vikramaditya; friend in absentia to Raja Puraji Kika; bully and repeatedly beholden to Mangal; lover and looking desperately for Kausalya; plaything of Bhootani Mata stroke who is she stroke fate, stroke the void; indefatigable voyeur and reader of crumbs and leaves from Babur's diary; murderer of ten thousand innocent (are there such beings on earth?) Gujarati soldiers; dysfunctional husband of Medini Rai's daughter; hypocrite and destroyer of the one woman who is fit to be his wife and future queen of Mewar, Leelawati. What next, Prince? Any more fillers, any more homilies? Yes, yes, yes. Anything to put off facing up to the enormity of the question mark that is the future. To complicate matters, there isn't at any one moment in time, one future but many futures.

*   *   *

Future number one: What do we do with the Sultan of Malwa?

At the cabinet meeting to which Medini Rai and Silhadi were invited as special advisers, this simple matter was debated for four and a half hours. The Pradhan Pooranmalji and Silhadi were of the same view but for different reasons. Pooranmalji felt that we should hold the Sultan hostage and prisoner for six months and thereby ensure that all war reparations were cleared. Silhadi was convinced, along with nine-tenths of Mewar, that we were being foolishly lenient and lax. Khalji, that ... (expletive deleted), ought to be clapped in a dungeon and left there for a year or two. Had we forgotten the forty thousand massacred at Mandu, the humiliation that Rao Medini Rai and the other Purabiya Rajputs had suffered at the hands of the feckless sovereign, etc. etc?

Lakshman Simhaji was remarkable that day. My uncle kept a lid on his impatience till Silhadi had finished his diatribe. Further amazements were in store for us. The most upright and outspoken man in Chittor forbore to remind Silhadi that he had sat on the fence till the very last minute; that at least partly because of his procrastination, Rao Medini Rai could well have lost Gagrone, Prince Hem Karan and his followers, and that for this extraordinary contribution to the Malwa campaign, Silhadi had been awarded no less than three jagirs. Instead, Lakshman Simhaji was at his courteous best.

'Do you suggest then that we leave Malwa headless for a year or two? Chaos will ensue. Nature cannot endure a vacuum. The Sultan has brothers and an adopted nephew who would be king. Civil war is not an unthinkable possibility.'

'Good. We'll carve up Malwa and take what is ours.'

'What is yours is a moot point, Highness. But even if you did manage to grab whatever you could on a first come, first served basis, do you think Gujarat or Malwa's other neighbours will sit tight and watch as spectators? Won't they jump into the fray and want a piece of Malwa?'

'Perhaps I am speaking out of place but it might help if we could know our minds first before we decide upon the Sultan's fate.' That soft voice which went for the jugular couldn't be anyone else's but Adinathji's. As Finance Minister he would listen to all your raving and ranting and then suggest, humbly always, that you compute the cost before you act. 'What is it that we want? Vengeance and short-term gains? Or do we wish to secure peace so that we can build and strengthen our own fiefdoms? If the latter, then stability is the first prerequisite. Stability, however ephemeral and illusory, will come from law and the natural order of things. Which would seem to suggest that the earlier the sovereign of Malwa returns to his throne and his people, the more we stand to benefit.'

'Are you going to swallow this specious reasoning, Highness?' Silhadi Rai turned upon Medini Rai as if the Mewaris were con-

476

spiring against the two of them. 'They can mouth such fine and noble sentiments for one reason and one reason alone: because they didn't lose a single man, woman or child that day when Muzaffar Shah of Gujarat and his obsequious, knee-scraping, toadying host, the rat of Malwa, fell upon forty thousand of our family members and put them to the sword. Have you not wondered every waking night since then about one thing: what kept the Mewar forces from coming to your rescue? Lakshman Simhaji says that they left as soon as they got word. Maybe I am willing to give him the benefit of the doubt, but the fact is they were not there when they could have made the difference between life and death for forty thousand of our people.

'I have seen the smile of sheer gratitude appear on your face every time the Maharaj Kumar greets you. Gagrone was in dire distress and about to fall to the Khalji menace and all Lakshman Simhaji could spare for the relief of Prince Hem Karan and Gagrone was three thousand five hundred men. The Maharaj Kumar told the Sultan that he headed a force of forty-seven thousand seven hundred men and the fool believed him. But you and I were not born yesterday and we aren't taken in by these childish fabrications. Granted, the bluff worked. It was a fluke and lady luck was his mistress for that day. But what if that idiot Sultan had called the bluff? Where would we have been today? Think about it, Rao. It won't bear thinking.

'Lakshman Simhaji and the Jain Minister of the Exchequer want us to be politic and diplomatic, they appeal to the statesmen in us and ask us to let the Sultan go back home. I say no. I trust false gratitude will not overwhelm you and you too will say no. Let the Khalji pig rot in prison till doomsday.'

Before Medini Rai had a chance to recover from Silhadi's onslaught, His Majesty intervened.

'Your Highnesses, Medini Rai and Silhadi Rai, we must beg your indulgence. We have known the grievous loss you suffered and we've grieved bitterly for it. What we perhaps failed to appreciate fully was the intensity of your feelings against His Majesty the Sultan of Malwa. But it has been our experience that a military defeat is in itself so devastating a blow to the enemy that any further humiliation

477

beyond territorial and war reparations is counterproductive.

'You are, however, our allies and our dear friends. Beyond all else, Mewar values the strength that issues from a commonality of interest, a shared heritage and principles, and respect for each other's deepest and innermost feelings. The Sultan, we assure you, will remain our prisoner.

'It has been a long and overwrought day. I'm sure you want to rest a while. To our honoured guests, I say this, stay as long as you wish. Chittor cannot pretend to be your first home but it begs you to treat it rightfully as your second home.'

Was ever a royal conference dismissed with greater finesse? Most meetings end with the participants exchanging notes, lingering and loitering before they part. That day we took our leave of each other instantly and went our separate ways. I am not quite sure what Silhadi stood to gain from his performance but there wasn't much mystery about his methods or motivation. He had ostensibly targeted the axis running through Lakshman Simhaji, Adinathji and me and sown, or at least made an overheated attempt to sow, dissension between Medini Rai and us but his real quarry was the Rana.

Who had put Silhadi up to such a barely-concealed attack on His Majesty? Do I set my long-cherished scruples aside and hint without saying a word (how does one do that?) to Mangal to put Queen Karmavati under surveillance? And if the man is already doing it, for who is more protective of the Rana than Mangal, how do I elicit the information? Worse still, if there is bad news, what action can one take against His Majesty's favourite queen?

✳   ✳   ✳

Future number two: the parijat tree.

My tree is dying. There are plenty of leaves yet on the branches and every morning there are still drifts of parijat blossoms on the dew-drenched ground. But I know that my friend has turned its back on me. I have no idea what unspoken covenant I have broken, what unwritten law of nature I have transgressed or in what way I have disappointed my joyous companion of the mornings. Who knows what pain we cause our dearest ones? And yet I tell you, tree, however grave the error of my ways, it cannot compare with the

478

hurt you inflict when you shrink at the sight of me.

I can see you shrivelling, the sap slowing down, the heart growing fainter. Even in terminal cases, the doctors have told me that if the will to live is strong, both the disease and death are kept in abeyance. Who or what killed your will?

What is it, tree? Speak to me. You were like a three-hundred-armed goddess and your bounty was prodigal as a summer shower, day in and day out. I remember the leap of joy in your face and the goose-pimples on your body the first morning after I returned from the Malwa campaign. A thousand parijats leapt down and covered me; not even the pet dogs I had when I was a child have missed me so and made me feel so welcome. And now, barely ten weeks later, you are willing to fold your three hundred hands, withdraw into your tight little cocoon and bid goodbye to the concourse of creation, birds and worms and bees which nested in your breast.

No fever, no bruises, no symptoms and yet I know that something happened, something terrible.

Can we talk this over? I guess not. You can't talk to someone's back, to someone who's stopped listening.

I've brought Befikir's manure and buried it under the topsoil. I turn the earth every two days. I water the ground myself. I have rushed back sometimes even during office hours like an anxious parent or lover. I have played you the flute for hours. I've hugged you tightly and said I'll not let you go. You were but a fledgeling shoot when I brought you from Kumbhalgarh. I don't know whether you missed home; or the terrain and nourishment here are different from those where you were born. You almost died but you didn't give up. You were a tough fighter. Do you know how young you were when you started flowering? Queens and princes and the most beautiful odalisques would stand and gaze in wonder. I thought when I grow old, I would sit in your shade and let your flowers drizzle on me.

Has the thing I fear most happened? Is there death in my touch?

Has that Bhootani Mata been here? Has she cast the evil eye on you?

*   *   *

479

Future number three: How do we greet Sultan Bahadur Shah?

If you believe that you are the captain of your own destiny, I'll tell you that I share your view. And were your friend, neighbour and wife to warn me that it's all ultimately in the infinite number of hands that fate has, I'll concur energetically with them, too. Look at what happened to Sikander Shah, Sultan of Gujarat, and you'll begin to see that nothing makes sense and that's the way it was meant to be. The essence of fate and God is to move not only in mysterious ways but to be incomprehensible.

Sultan Muzaffar Shah died on March 16th, 1526. Two months and nine days later on May 25th, his son Sultan Sikander Shah was no more. They say he had an evil disposition and his slave Imad-ul-mulk, acting in concert with others, strangled him to death.

I remember the day Shehzada Bahadur rose out of the morning mist while I stood at the window of the top storey of the Victory Tower and took in the panoramic view. He had spent years in search of that elusive headgear, the crown of his father. Now in a trice, one of those storybook quirks of fortune had decreed that the golden orb come looking for him. Imagine, Prince Bahadur had been in touch with Babur and was contemplating joining him, when an envoy from Gujarat came to receive him and invite him to sit on his father's throne.

Congratulations, Sultan Bahadur Shah. I rejoice in your good fortune.

The Sultan's first act on ascending the throne was to pass a sentence of death on the slave Imad-ul-Mulk who had disposed of his brother, and on the amirs who had instigated him.

I would like to send an embassy of goodwill and gifts to the new Sultan and when the time is ripe, remind him of the peace treaty that we had talked of so often. Perhaps we can go beyond that and sign a military pact in case of an act of war on either of our kingdoms by an enemy. What chance do I stand of persuading the members of the cabinet to proffer a hand of friendship to the new Sultan of Gujarat?

The only chance I may have is to cite the Babur factor.

* * *

Future number four: Will someone please tell me what His Majesty, the Rana, is up to?

If Babur had been like the other visitors who invaded Hindustan from the north-west, he would have plundered Delhi, left a few hundred thousand dead or maimed, taken back slaves along with famous craftsmen and artisans, and the crown of Delhi would have passed on to Mahmud Lodi who unlike his brother Sultan Ibrahim, had escaped unhurt from Panipat. For the time being, however, Mahmud Lodi has had to be content with being the Sultan of Hindustan in absentia only. War and misfortune, I'm aware, are reputed to make strange bedfellows but Father has not only offered Mahmud Lodi asylum but struck an alliance with him to drive out Babur. Wherefore such misplaced haste and enthusiasm to make a commitment and to a former enemy at that? What happened to the classic rules of wait-and-watch when a new man comes into the neighbourhood, especially one who is aggressive and flush with victory? Does Father wish to dare Babur, see how far he can go? But if you think that His Majesty was deliberately going out of his way to provoke the new Padshah of Delhi, you haven't heard the rest of the story.

Father has taken and occupied the formidable fortress of Kandar and driven away its ruler, Hasan. That, however, was merely a foretaste of things to come. Like a desperado running out of time, he has been picking up towns and cities from the erstwhile Lodi kingdom. The tally as of now is two hundred new territories, some minor and trifling, others substantial. The spoils of war, they call them. But the fact is, the spoils did not belong to His Majesty. The Rana neither fought nor won the war against Ibrahim Lodi; Babur did. All this landgrabbing has also led to a lot of displacement. In some cases Muslim chiefs have been replaced by Hindus, not all of whom are tolerant and open-minded. What we are ensuring is that all these malcontents will gravitate to Babur and start looking upon him as their leader and saviour. While Father's helping himself to whatever he can, the two most interested parties, Mahmud Lodi and Babur, are watching the dismemberment of what they consider their territory with growing resentment. The former can do little about it, at least for the time being. The latter can, and I suspect, will.

A war with Babur at some point or another, may be inevitable but does His Majesty want, what other conclusion can one draw, a war right away? (Why now? Delhi was there for the taking all these years but he turned a deaf ear to my pleas.) This seems unnecessary and foolhardy. The Padshah is eminently capable of seeing sense and self-interest. All we've got to do, at least for the moment, is propose a pact from a position of strength whereby both sides respect the boundaries between the two kingdoms.

* * *

Future number five: Kausalya.

I ask the same stupid questions of Mangal every two or three days, sometimes twice or thrice on the same day.

'How do you mean it seems that she's disappeared? This is Chittor, Mangal, the capital of Mewar, not some ancient village where the natives are still savages. I'm telling you, she can't disappear. It doesn't make sense. You are not doing your job, that's what it is.'

'I checked with the police, Sire. They showed me their records. Every year from Chittor alone close to seventy people are found missing and are never heard of again.

'Mangal don't give me this....' I have to stop abusing him. What's the matter with me? I'm edgy, crabbed and short with everyone and not just on my bad days. All that meditation and talking to myself gets me nowhere. I'm still screaming. 'You are the head of intelligence, I got Father to appoint you. And you can't find your own mother. Everyday you give me the same,' I switched the word just in time, 'story. Instead why don't you find her?'

'I'm trying, Highness. I have contacted the Malwa, Gujarat and Delhi police. My people have been questioning pilgrims returning from Kashi, Mathura, Prayag, Kedarnath, Madurai. I haven't given up.'

'Did Mamta have a fight with her? Did you say something nasty to her?'

'You know Mamta, Highness. Mother was never close friends with anybody and Mamta was no exception. But Mamta never had

482

the courage to raise her eyes to look at Mother and talk to her. The last time Mother came over, she seemed pleased that Mamta was carrying.'

'When is the baby due?'

'Another month, Highness.'

'You had better find Kausalya before that, hadn't you? I mean what's she going to say if she was not there for her grandchild's birth?'

'I'll do anything to find her.'

'Do you remember what they told us when they couldn't find Leelawati? They said she had been smuggled out of Chittor or Adinathji had done away with her. We couldn't find her but she was right here in the fort. Imagine my humiliation when she turned up pale and starved and said that I would have found her if I had tried hard enough to look for her. Search every house in Chittor, Mangal, every hut. I'll speak to the Commissioner of Police.'

'I already have. His Majesty signed the search warrant. We are combing the third muhalla now.'

'Don't leave out the houses of the rich. Don't leave anybody out. And what about your underworld connections?'

'They doubt that she was kidnapped or murdered for her jewellery or for a ransom. They usually know about these matters and they haven't heard anything.'

I knew I would start again tomorrow. Talking distractedly and in circles got me nowhere but that was my only way of keeping her alive. It occurred to me then that barring that one foolish mistake on my part, Kausalya and I had never fought. I can't explain this but my image of her was of her riding a tigress. Things always got murky at this point. Was she the tigress or was she the lady who rode one? Or was she both?

I was her's and to keep me she would share me with whoever I wanted.

I felt unprotected without her. What was the point of being Maharaj Kumar if I couldn't even look after my own?

Where are you, Bhootani Mata? What have you done with Kausalya?

*　　*　　*

Future number six: the Padshah of Delhi.

Things may change but since the time Babur defeated Sultan Ibrahim Lodi and occupied Delhi there was really only one future for Mewar: the resolution of our relationship with the Moghul king. Our allies as well as all our other small and big enemies knew this. On the 17th of October, Father has called all the leading Rajput, Muslim and Bhil princes and kings to a War Council to confer and to decide upon the future course of action.

I'm not quite able to answer the question why the whole confederacy of Rajputs and many Muslim jagirdars, amirs and kings had invested Babur with such importance and were persuaded to think that the threat to their lands would come from him. Till very recently he was nothing but a minor, displaced king who had after many wanderings and vicissitudes secured the inconsequential throne at Kabul. Did Delhi have something to do with it? Was it the defeat and death of the Delhi Sultan at the battle of Panipat that enhanced his reputation and made him the focus and centre of our lives? Or was it his avowed claim, repeated almost like a mantra, that he would take possession of Hindustan? I'm certain that there are many answers to these questions and yet I doubt if anyone will ever be able to give one that is wholly convincing.

Since the Moghul Padshah has been preoccupied with travel, battles, messages to and from Kabul, embassies to distant kingdoms, and his administrative duties have doubled if not tripled, one would have expected the entries in his diary to have dried up entirely or become perfunctory. But the conquest and annexation of a kingdom at least thirty to fifty times larger than his eyrie in the Hindukush mountains seems to have had exactly the reverse effect. Perhaps he has more than a couple of amanuenses and calligraphists to take notes and make copies.

Hindustan certainly excites his curiosity, disdain, opprobrium and sense of wonder. He sounds more self-assured now — and with good reason — but his self-importance hasn't drowned his wit or sharpness of observation. And as always, he is one of the most objective reporters of geography and scenery, people and their habits and mores, that I have come across. But more of that some other time. What concerns Mewar now is his mood, tone of voice and strategy at Panipat.

'After dispatching the light troops against Ghazi Khan, I put my foot in the stirrup of resolution, set my hand on the rein of trust in God, and moved against Sultan Ibrahim....in possession of whose throne at that time were the Delhi capital and the dominions of Hindustan, whose standing army was a hundred thousand, whose elephants and whose begs' elephants were about a thousand.

'When everything was ready, all the begs with such braves as had had experience in military affairs were summoned to a General Council where opinion found decision at this: Panipat is there with its crowded houses and suburbs. It would be on one side of us; our other sides must be protected by carts and mantelets behind which our foot and matchlockmen would stand. With so much settled we marched forward, halted one night on the way, and reached Panipat on Thursday the 12th of April.'

I drew sketches and diagrams to understand the schematics of Babur's defence, the placement of his army and his strategy. He had ordered every man in his army to collect carts. The final tally came to seven hundred carts. The idea was to treat even the open battlefield as a moveable fortress. The carts and mobile shields of thickets of branches called mantelets were tied tightly together in front of the infantry to form a protective barrier. Ibrahim Lodi's men would have to breach it to come to grips with Babur's forces, an interregnum in which the Delhi cavalry and infantry would suffer heavy casualties. Babur had secured the right flank by using the town of Panipat and its suburbs as an impregnable wall. On his left and elsewhere Babur had dug ditches. At intervals of an arrow's flight, there was enough space left open for a hundred or two hundred horsemen to sally forth. All this was not only very interesting but an eye opener. Where the Turki tactics differed from Sultan Ibrahim's — and our own — concepts of defence was in extending the principle of fortification to every point of the battlefield itself. The ditch, for instance, was nothing but the moat around the fort.

485

'From the time that Sultan Ibrahim's blackness first appeared, he moved swiftly, straight for us, without a check, until he saw the dark mass of our men, when he pulled up and, observing our formation and array, made as if asking, "To stand or not? To advance or not?" They could not stand; nor could they make their former swift advance.

'Our orders were for the turning-parties to wheel from right and left to the enemy's rear, to discharge arrows and to engage in the fight; and for the right and left wings to advance and join battle with him ... Orders were given for Muhammadi Kukuldash, Shah Mansur Barlas, Yumas-i-ali and Abdullah to engage those facing them in front of centre. From that same position Ustad Ali-quli made good discharge of firingi shots; Mustafa the commissary for his part made excellent discharge of zarb-zan shots from the left hand of the centre. Our right, left, centre and turning parties having surrounded the enemy, rained arrows down on him and fought ungrudgingly .... By God's mercy and kindness, this difficult affair was made easy for us! In one half-day, that armed mass was laid upon the earth. Five or six thousand men were killed in one place close to Ibrahim. Our estimate of the other dead, lying all over the field, was fifteen to sixteen thousand, but it came to be known, later in Agra from the statement of Hindustanis, that forty or fifty thousand may have died in that battle.'

Firingi and zarb-zan. I was finally face to face with the new technology. Unlike us, Babur was not only using matchlocks routinely, he had field-cannons for that's what those two marvellous-sounding words signified. Forget casting them, just buying and transporting them from abroad would take at least a year or a year and a half. No point thinking about that time-frame now. The important thing was to find out who would sell them to us and order them instantly. Lakshman Simhaji was my ally in this matter and he has asked Mangal to make enquiries with the Portuguese and the Persians.

Mangal has been instructed to buy at least half a dozen of these field-guns from whoever was willing to supply them to us.

Here is the strangest note I have come across so far in the Padshah's diaries:

486

'While we were still in Kabul, Rana Sanga had sent an envoy to testify to his good wishes and to propose the plan: "If the honoured Padshah will come towards Delhi from that side, I from this will move on Agra." But I beat Ibrahim, I took Delhi and Agra, and up to now that Pagan has given no sign soever of moving.'

Was I to give credence to this entry? And if I did, for my experience and assessment so far are that Babur is not given to fabricating stories, what does one make of Father? What could his motives be and what did he expect to gain? Did he really believe, as did so many of my ancestors and Rajput brethren, only to discover without fail how grievously mistaken they were, that my enemy's enemy is my friend? Did the Rana of Mewar wish to invite a foreigner into Hindustan merely in the hope of splitting the bounty of war and perhaps even the Delhi Sultanate? Did His Majesty have so little confidence in his army and his leadership that despite being the most powerful sovereign in the region, he felt he needed the help of Babur to reduce a decadent and debauched Ibrahim Lodi whose hold on the Delhi Sultanate was fast slipping? But there was something even more inexplicable: why make an offer if you have no intention of backing it with action? That, it would seem evident to anyone, is the surest way of turning an unknown king into the worst kind of vindictive enemy.

But the deed is done and it is so much water under the bridge.

There is no dearth of malcontents in Agra and so we are never short of reliable information about Babur's court from Mangal's agents in the city. Every Monday morning, sometimes during the week too, Mangal sends reports with quotes and analyses, revenue figures, military movements, who's in favour and who's not and an update about the thinking and debates in Agra regarding Mewar. One thing is clear, that while Babur views us with extreme hostility, he is fortunately preoccupied with troubles nearer his new home. The peasantry and the previous soldiery are afraid of Babur and his men. More importantly, almost every Afghan amir in the service of the late Sultan is in either open or insidious rebellion against the Padshah. Babur's son Humayun had already ridden to Junpur in the east to subdue some of the more troublesome rebels. All this is to the good. We need to buy as much time as possible to get

487

those field-cannons, purchase at least ten thousand matchlocks and train our men in their use and we need to do some major rethinking about both attack and defence strategies against Babur's battle tactics.

But the omens don't augur well. It is my habit to give Mewar's enemies their due and to take even the weakest of them seriously. Babur, however, is in a class by himself. As I got to know him from the odds and ends from his diaries, I grew not just to like him but to respect him. I felt he would make a good friend and a worthy enemy. But in the last few months he has begun to exhibit facets that I find disturbing. These are doubtless a consequence of his faith, but faith, it seems to me, must be tempered by wisdom and tolerance, especially if you are a king. Babur's language has undergone a radical change since he came to Hindustan. It is only while talking about a war with us that he repeatedly speaks of a Holy War. What then does one call his wars with Ibrahim Lodi and all the other Shia and Sunni chieftans, not to mention kings and sultans?

It seems sad, not to say counterproductive, if one has only contempt for the people one has conquered, and all one wants to do is to dash, to quote Babur, the gods of the idolaters. Follow this path and you'll never look upon the vanquished as your own subjects and will not want to take care of them as a father must. If a king is to be strong he must be close to his people. They must all feel that he is their shield and sword regardless of their religion or caste or creed. Anybody who thinks that these are new-fangled ideas is a fool. Any enlightened leader will tell you that this is but self-interest, for in division lie the seeds of the destruction of your kingdom.

Even at the time when Babur attacked Bajaur on one of his earliest forays into India, he thought of himself as a defender of 'the Faith'. He reverted to the ways of his ancestor Timur, sacked the town and massacred all the denizens, barring the few who managed to escape to the east, because they were not true believers. Now that he's assumed the throne in Delhi, he has begun to cast himself in the role of a Ghazi, Avenger in the name of God. Strange word that, avenger. For what slights and grievances, does Babur wish to exact vengeance from infidels on whom he has never set eyes nor had any social or other commerce? Our only crime seems to arise from an accident: that we were born to another faith.

Since his victory over Sultan Ibrahim Lodi, the Padshah has been razing temples and building mosques on the same sites or if time and funds are short, converting Hindu places of worship to that of Islam.

Nothing special about that. We've done the same with Buddhist sacred places as well as mosques, as the Muslims have been doing with our temples since they first invaded India.

This is truly one of the great mysteries of life. Why this obssessive need to occupy the very precincts of a defeated belief? However, while the relationship between Hinduism and Buddhism may have been adversarial, they did not think of each other as tainted or unholy. But what could be more profane for Islam than the idolatrous temples of Hindu gods?

I've heard it said that the conqueror will forcibly take over the geographic site of another faith because there is an inherent sacred quality to the place which he wishes to appropriate. There is as much substance to this reasoning as there is sophistry. Perhaps a far simpler explanation will suffice. It is the naked assertion of brute power. The victor is signalling that the old order is dead and letting his new subjects know who the new master is.

Chapter 39

 There is but one male and his name is the Flautist.

The night of his debacle with Sugandha, he went straight to the Little Saint's room.

'Where have you been?' she grabbed his arm and shook him. She was in a rage of impatience and had difficulty speaking. 'How you make me suffer. How can you be so cruel and heartless?'

Was he late? They hadn't fixed a time for their tryst last night, they never did. As far as he could make out, he had arrived at about the same time, give or take a minute or two, as he had done all these nights.

'What is the matter?'

'You should ask.'

Was it the Flautist's birthday? Couldn't have been, or the whole of Chittor would be celebrating it. He must have looked blank for now she was incensed.

'You have forgotten, you really have.' She stamped hard on his foot. 'It's Holi.'

Alarms went off in his head like a series of violent firecrackers. How could it have escaped him? Self-preservation alone would have dictated that he keep his eyes glued to the calendar. What was he going to do? He had thought about the spring festival since the first day he had walked into her room when they were in Kumbhalgarh. It was not the coloured powder that he dreaded but the coloured water. He could see the blue of his skin trickle down leaving him

490

naked and exposed as she sprayed him with a brass syringe. Should he take the offensive, rush her and daub her with vermillion, yellow, mauve, green and violet powder, fling some of it in her eyes and make his escape?

'Stand still and put on this blouse.'

There was no doubt about it. She really had lost her mind. 'Why would I want to wear a blouse?'

'Because you are a woman today.'

As simple as that.

'Didn't you tell Rupa Goswami that there's only one male in the world and that's the Blue One, and the rest are women?'

'Men and women have genders. Gods are simultaneous. Which is why like Ardhanareshwar, you are both man and woman. You should know that better than anyone else.'

'That doesn't make sense.'

'Life is not meant to. Ambivalence is the essence of life. Or rather ambiguity is. Besides you never have problems wearing a woman's clothes when you are with your favourite milkmaid, Radha. Radha this and Radha that. Even your name gets changed to Radhekrishna.'

There was no way, absolutely none, that he was going to wear a blouse. He was a Prince, perhaps even heir apparent. Can you imagine the Maharaj Kumar of Mewar as a transvestite? If his bumpy and highly fluctuating fortunes had not already put paid to his ambitions, this new wrinkle would certainly seal his fate.

He was a fool, he told himself. How come he hadn't realized all these years that it was a conspiracy? Was his wife, in reality, in league with Vikramaditya and Queen Karmavati? The pieces suddenly began to fall in place. The Princess and the Queen had hatched the plot from the very beginning, from the time she had married the Maharaj Kumar. Queen Karmavati had pretended to hate the Princess while the two of them worked hand in hand. Even as his wife set him up and humiliated him at every stage, made him Mewar's number one cuckold and brought public obloquy upon the house of the Rana, the Queen howled for her blood and played the role of the Princess' enemy with a deliberate lack of subtlety, so that it appeared to be in character with her public image, and thus accelerated his descent into ignominy. Now his wife was about to administer the final and fatal blow: expose him as a closet queen. Queen Karmavati would do the rest. This time he would lose the kingship for good.

She took hold of his right hand and slipped his arm into the blouse and then did the same with the left. 'Turn around,' she tied the strings of the backless choli and gave him a once-over. 'Seems to fit okay, what do you think?' She didn't wait for his response. 'Wait, wait a minute. I've got the order of things all wrong.' She tugged at the knot of the blouse and pulled it off again. She ran out of the room and brought back a razor. What now, did she want to shave his head off? She tested the blade on her left index finger and then in swift firm strokes shaved his arms, armpits, chest and back.

'What are you doing?' he whispered in disbelief.

She was short with him. 'How can a woman have hair in the wrong places?'

Her hand was light and yet he twitched uncontrollably as if she was removing chunks of his flesh.

'What is it? Why are you shivering so?' She ran her hand over his body gently and soothed him. Now she undid his dhoti. He stood there naked. He had not felt so humiliated, not even when the people of Chittor had booed him when he and his armies had returned from the Gujarat campaign. He wondered whether she intended to parade him through the main avenues of the city. Or was she going to cut his member off to make a full woman of him? She slid the razor over his underbelly, the triangular patch of hair he had just above the buttocks and then over his legs. What was she doing? More to the point, what was he doing? Why didn't he snatch the razor from her and slice off her hand?

It was time to dress him. First the black silk skirt with a soft Dhaka cotton lining, then the red and black bandhani blouse and finally a red chunni. He had to admit that she had an eye for colour. She brought out her jewellery box, parted his hair in the middle and pinned a gold chain in the divide so that the minakari pendant hung over his forehead. Now the glass bangles, black, red and gold to match the colours of his clothes. He was certain that she would not be able to get them beyond the knuckles. He was wrong. Like Sunheria, she too pretended that the hand and wrist are boneless and all you had to do was gently massage them and then slip the bangles up almost as an afterthought. The anklets posed even less of a problem. She hooked two of them together, pulled up his skirt and tied them above his feet.

'How lovely you look.'

He stared at his image in the mirror she had fetched. But for the ghastly uneven blue with the red-pink lips sticking out and the flat breasts, he could easily have passed as a woman.

She dropped her own clothes in a hurry. What now? She laughed out loud when she saw the bemused look in his eyes.

With astonishing speed she tied his pitambar around her waist. She was right, he was stupid. If he was Radha (perish the thought, his wife would not hesitate to slit his throat if she thought he was confusing her with her legendary rival), if he was Greeneyes, then she was the Flautist. She stuck the peacock feather into her headband.

How far would the Little Saint go down this dangerous path? He had vaguely heard of the weird practices of the fringe sects who worshipped the Blue God. Make-believe was the crux of their adoration and they took turns at being the Flautist. Gender was a fuzzy line and they crossed it continually. Surely at some point such sexual indulgence could become an end in itself and lead to some bizarre perversions and decadence?

The Princess crossed her forearms and held his crossed hands in hers. She began to go round slowly. He didn't quite know what she had in mind but he followed her. They were face to face and still he had the feeling that they were stalking each other. What game of cat and mouse had she devised this time? Nothing of the sort, he soon realized, all she was doing was playing kikli. Their hands locked into each other, feet barely lifting off the ground as they circled. They gradually accelerated their velocity. The palace walls, the parijat tree, the Victory Tower, the tulsi plant hurtled past and just as swiftly reappeared. Faster and faster they went, each leaning as far back and away from the other as possible. Their chunnis slipped, skirts flared and the sky see-sawed madly. He felt a strange

sense of elation, the sweat leapt off their bodies, they had gone to
the limits of their energy and then beyond and yet would never stop.

He envied the simplicity of her universe where everything she
did or thought of was an act of devotion. Sex was worship and so
was looking after his father and cheating while playing cards and
laughter and standing on the swing and tossing the earth back and
forth and singing and dancing. Her whole life, the highs and the
lows, the tantrums and the pleasures, everything was an offering as
much to herself as to her god. She was the essence of the Flautist's
idea of a karmayogi, or rather, yogin for whom the life of action
made life worth living. She engaged life as if there was no tomorrow.
Perhaps moksha lies in not thinking about the afterlife.

'My Prince,' Bhootani Mata was standing demurely behind the
parijat tree.

'Haven't seen you for so long, I had begun to fear that you had
met with an accident.' He had still not learnt there was no point
being sarcastic with her.

'Did you miss me that much? But you should know by now that
I'm always within hailing distance. Frankly I am, like your beloved,
lodged in your heart.'

'I advise you to keep off my wife if you know what's good for
you.'

'May I refresh your memory, Highness, it was I who suggested
to you, while you were whining and importuning me on an hourly
basis, that you should not just keep off your dear wife but,' Bhootani
Mata smiled reproachfully, 'forget her altogether. I am pleased to
see that there has been a radical change in your wife's fortunes. The
country no longer thinks of her as a whore. Little Saint, isn't that
what they call her these days? The townspeople would be most
impressed by the Little Saint's saintly acts every night.'

'Spare us your sarcasm.'

'Don't wince, Maharaj Kumar. You will agree that there has been
a rapprochement among parties who one would have wagered,
would become friends only when heaven and hell change places.
You look bored, Prince, and impatient to be rid of me.'

'Can we come to the point? I have other matters to attend to.'

'I do not wish to delay your dalliance. Let me give you the good news. From now on anybody who has had the misfortune to have come in contact with you is under threat. People who are totally unaware of the pact that you made with me will pay the price for your sins and the vagaries of your mind. I hope you rot with guilt and the enormity of the havoc you will unleash on innocents. We'll get even yet, Highness. I must take your leave now.'

She turned to leave. He knew she wasn't finished with him.

'Oh, how could I forget? I say, aren't you going to ask me about the parijat tree and Kausalya?'

'No.'

'You don't care?'

'Let's just say that I don't care to give you credit for whatever's happened to them.'

'You think, my friend, that the earth opened and swallowed Kausalya just as it did Sita in the story books and your parijat dropped dead out of exhaustion one sunny morning?'

'You are getting to be a megalomaniac, Bhootani Mata. Do you want me to believe that the drought in Vijayanagar this year, Babur's victory at Panipat, the latest Portuguese ship sinking near Surat, are all your doing? If that's the case, why don't you play with your equals, the Flautist, for instance? You are like all the third-rate babas, gurus and saviours of the world. All you can do is play upon the fears of men and women. But I'm through with fear, fear of what you can do to me.'

His feet had begun to shrink and worse, he no longer minded the bangles on his arms. He had the distinct feeling that he had grown small and delicate. If he had been horrified at the thought of masquerading as a transvestite, why was he not incensed that his step had become light and his torso lissom? Or were the reasons for this quite simple and banal? That at heart he was a woman or perhaps all human beings are really bisexual? What was the source of a person's sex? Did clothes play a role in it? Could he really get under a woman's skin merely by wearing a ghagra and choli? All these years he had believed that the only difference between men and women was their bodies. But were their minds made differently too? What does it mean to be a woman? Is it long, flowing hair tied in a plait or knot, is it the fullness in the breasts, is it patience and nurturing as much as strength and intelligence? What is the most complete and sufficient idea that mankind has had? God. And yet if you assign sex to God, then he or she too becomes finite and incomplete.

Her choli and chunni were wet. She saw him looking at her and the wheeling, careening sky stopped abruptly. She slipped into his arms. He tried to hug her tightly but her liquefying flesh kept slipping away, he went out of his mind with that slithery touch, he wanted to annihilate the separateness of their bodies and become one with her. There was no way they could hold on to each other. She bent down, scrabbled in the ground, stood up and frantically rubbed earth on herself and him. The scent of the wet earth cleared his head.

Spring was in the air and her flesh broke out imperceptibly into tendrils that grew into vines. They entwined themselves around her arms and breasts and spread out over her thighs and calves and toes. And all the while, tiny green leaves stirred and essayed forth. And shyly, ever so slowly, yellow and red buds crept out and almost soundlessly popped open. He stretched a finger to touch flower and leaf. Before he knew it, the green had leapt over and entwined itself around his hand and drew him to the creeper-woman. Nothing, he knew then, could break them asunder.

It was then that she called out to him, 'Krishna Kanhaiyya, Krishna Kanhaiyya.'

Chapter 40

$\mathcal{I}$ should have seen it coming but my vaunted prescience was malfunctioning or has it been just a matter of guesswork and some luck posing as clairvoyance all these years? Political considerations alone should have forced me to go back to my second wife but I felt as disinclined as Babur was with his first. His mother, he says in his diaries, cajoled him to visit his bride at least once in forty days. My mother lived in a world of her own and was not overeager to engage with life. She was aware that I had recently remarried but it would not have occurred to her to ask me how things were between me and my second wife. I had a severe case of conscience but try as I might I could not bring myself to visit Sugandha.

Any new wife in the Palace is treated as an antagonist by the zenana. (Perhaps it's the same in any royal family.) What she faces is the equivalent of ragging at the military academy. Not a day passes in the first few months when you are not snubbed, humiliated and made a fool of. Sugandha could have easily weathered all the needling and found that, like most underdogs, she too had her champions. But thanks to the example set by the Little Saint, the women of the biggest club in Chittor, the seraglio, cut her dead. Sugandha is naive, spoilt and comes from a family that has made much of her — perhaps because she is the only one who did not inherit the Medini looks — and she went to pieces when she was left alone.

My second mother stepped into this vacuum of extreme isolation and took Sugandha in hand. She did not fawn or fuss over her. She made her part of her entourage. She was firm and supportive and made her feel wanted by giving her a role in the scheme of

497

the royal firmament. There was an inevitability about what happened next and yet I kept watching as if I were a spectator at a dark comedy of errors. There may have been some truth in the rumour that the Queen had played procuress in this instance but there was no denying that I had driven my wife into Vikramaditya's arms.

Vikramaditya had come back from Ranthambhor, to use his own words, because he was fed up with the backwaters and needed to be revitalized at the fount of Chittor. He was never a private person and the thought of keeping a confidence was alien to him. The conquest of my wife, Sugandha, was not exactly a rare victory but it was ample ammunition against me, and he was certainly not about to underplay his victory or my lack of manliness. Chittor had indeed worked wonders on him. He had drunk long at the fount and decided that he could never have enough and had extended his stay indefinitely. He was in great spirits and so was Sugandha. Scandal seemed to suit my second wife. People had suddenly begun to take note of her and it restored her self-esteem. Queen Karmavati knew she was playing a dangerous game but it was clear that it was part of her plan to raise the stakes and underline her independence from His Majesty.

My own response to discovering that I was a cuckold a second time round was mixed and did not entirely do me credit. Sugandha was young, she was having a good time and I wanted to root for her because she had had the satisfaction of getting back at me. I also felt protective towards her. Our poets never tire of telling us that life is short and I wanted to warn Sugandha that my brother's fancy for a woman is even shorter. Besides, did she not understand that she was a mere pawn in the devious hands of my second mother. But somewhere I was also relieved. Hem Karan, who had only a few months ago begged me to allow him to stay behind in Chittor and train under me, had become frosty after my marriage to his sister. His sneer was aimed as much at himself as at me. How could he have worshipped me as his saviour when I was not even man enough to do justice to his sister? Now that Sugandha had got even and dishonoured the house of Mewar (carrying on with your brother-in-law was nothing special in the royal household, flaunting the relationship was), Hem Karan did not have the courage

498

to look me in the eye. I could now absolve myself of guilt or at least pretend to. Hem Karan's discomfiture was balm to my soul. The more egregious and shameless Vikramaditya and Sugandha were, the cleaner my conscience.

I was seeking martyrdom, nothing less. I wanted my forbearance and quiet dignity to be perceived as heroic and turn the whole of Mewar against my brother and wife. Humiliation was not a new sensation for me. Few people in Chittor have had my experience and expertise in it. And yet, despite the fact that I had crystallized my objectives so clearly, it took hours of coaxing myself in the morning before I could muster the courage to show my face to the members of my extended family, or worse, make a public appearance.

Let me not, however, downplay the other unfortunate side effects. I was growing progressively more ineffectual in my work and in the chain of command as the days passed by. I had proven my worth on the battlefield repeatedly but nobody was in the mood to recognize that. If you are no good in bed, you are no good. End of matter.

The marital bed is where people think your kingly capabilities are measured and proven. I had been given a second chance and I had failed to make good once again. What use are your administrative or military gifts if you can't take your pleasure with your wife nor control her?

About a month ago, I heard an altercation between brother and sister in repressed voices. Or rather the brother was trying to have a whispered conversation while Sugandha made it a point to take the town of Chittor into confidence.

'You are not going on the hunt, if your husband's not there with you.'

'I'm not? Watch me.'

'Think of the consequences, Sugandha. We are allies, we are related and we are beholden to them for our lives, for our freedom and for Chanderi. If we are ever again in trouble, no Rajput rao or rawat, certainly not the Maharana, will come to our help.'

'The Maharana needs our help against Babur, not the other way round. Besides, I'm not about to sacrifice my life either for you or Father. Father got me into this mess but only I can get myself out of it.'

'In that case I have no alternative but to accompany you.'

I heard a hearty unmistakable laugh then. 'Chaperone a married woman, not a bad idea at all.'

Vikramaditya was warming up to the thought. 'Will you watch while we...'

Hem Karan left in a huff. He kept his word though and for the sake of the proprieties, whatever they were in this instance, went to the hunt with his sister.

One night, soon after the hunt, Sugandha packed her bags and left. Greeneyes was waiting for her at the door leading out of our suite of rooms.

'Where are you going?'

'Where do you think I'm going?'

'I could hazard a guess but I'd rather you told me.'

Sugandha could have left in the forenoon or even in the evening when I was at work and the Little Saint was doing arati at the Brindabani temple. But that wouldn't have served her purpose. She did not wish to do things behind my back, or to put it uncharitably, she wished to make me privy to all the sordid details of her newfound private life.

'I'm moving in with Prince Vikramaditya.'

'I don't think that's such a good idea, my dear.'

'Don't "my dear" me.'

'What you do with your time is your business but your place is in your husband's home.'

'What husband? That man who can't...?'

'I believe we share the same husband. I will not have you speak ill of His Highness, the Maharaj Kumar.'

'You are welcome to him. I'm off. I would rather be honest than a hypocrite.'

'Kingship is an institution. Content is of the essence. But in its absence, form will have to do in the hope that content will follow. Leave your things where they were.'

'And pray, what will you do if I don't?'

The Little Saint's voice was matter-of-fact. 'I'll break your leg and lock up your room from outside.'

'That won't stop me. When I'm recovered I'll leave.'

'No, you won't. I'll break your leg again.'

My second wife refrained from testing the Little Saint's resolve.

*   *   *

We had celebrated our victory over Malwa but in the press of events, Father had kept putting off the thanksgiving ceremony that the Rana must perform in Pushkar. Lord Brahma is the most benign and low-key of gods but nobody dare forget that he is no less than the Creator of the universe itself. The visit to Pushkar is, however, a little more than the obligatory obeisance done at the site where Brahma care-lessly dropped a lotus blossom as he was wondering where to perform a yagnya. The Pushkar lake is not just one of the holiest places in the country, second only to the Mansarovar waters in the Himalayas for its sanctity and cleansing powers, it is a truly en-chanted arbour in the desert and a great favourite with my family.

Father and I had planned to ride by ourselves when Greeneyes decided to join us.

'I'm afraid that's not possible, since we plan to ride non-stop and be back within a week to prepare for the War Council meeting.'

'I can ride with the fastest,' my wife had made up her mind on the subject. 'Ask the Maharaj Kumar. I beat him in a race to Ranakpur.' I was about to protest and tell her that was not true but thought the better of it.

Suddenly Pushkar has become the event of the year. By the next day anybody in the Palace who had a horse with two and a half legs and could sit on it, was coming along with us. Father tried to put his foot down and tell the women that we were not going on a picnic but on holy duty, but by this time things had gone well beyond his control. My mother, the Maharani herself was going and so were Queen Karmavati, her son and his mistress.

Nobody officially asked her but Greeneyes took charge of this extended outing. A caravan would leave with our luggage before us. Four days of travel, the fifth and sixth day in Pushkar and four days for the return journey. There was a dress code for each day for both the men and women. Dhaka, Paithani, Ikkat and Balucheri in the evenings on the first four days, white on the first day at Pushkar and purple on the second day. Trust the Little Saint to raise the temperature of what was turning out to be a mammoth picnic by these impromptu ploys and rules that had no point to them except to put the palace ladies into a frenzy of preparation.

You would imagine that the royal women were not exactly impoverished as far as clothes were concerned. But suddenly there were no purple blouses, Dhakas, whites or Balucheris in the harem and it was impossible to have a conversation or a few hours of sleep at night. The place was a madhouse. The whole of the cloth market at Chittor had taken up residence in the Palace and cloth merchants visited the seraglio round-the-clock. Tailors, maids, eunuchs, along with Queen Karmavati and the rest of the ladies were cutting and sewing, opening up cholis and letting down hems of ghagras. My only consolation was that by the day of our departure, most of the ladies and their menfolk were bound to drop out. I couldn't have been more mistaken.

We take it for granted that crises bring people together. A Rajput state is in a perpetual state of crisis and by that logic, we should be the most closely-knit people in the world. But the bonding of war and calamity has its source in fear. And fear is the most destructive of human emotions. It corrodes the soul and the camaraderie it breeds is a false and forced one. I do not know whether the bliss of those first four days will stay with us and make us more tolerant of each other but one thing I'll vouch for. Pain may be the only reality but if mankind had any sense it would pursue the delusion called happiness. All the philosophers and poets who tell us that pain and suffering have a place and purpose in the cosmic order of things are welcome to them. They are frauds. We justify pain because we do not know what to make of it, nor do we have any choice but to bear it. Happiness alone can make us momentarily larger than ourselves. Not always, but at least occasionally, it can break our obsession with the self.

The trip to Pushkar was idyllic. There were a hundred and seventeen of us. The women sang in the evenings, the children played and gambolled, the sunrises and sunsets were a little beyond sensational and my wife Sugandha carried on with Vikramaditya.

I wrote that last paragraph and paused. It has just the right degree of urbane aloofness, quick brush strokes and images laced with a slight world-weariness. The romantic setting and resonance are nicely undermined by a lighthearted realistic detail in the last clause of the last sentence. But it's a pose. And if there's one thing Pushkar brought home to me and perhaps to all of us, it was the devastating barrenness of the roles we play.

However much we may deny it, we deal in the currency of stereotypes. We do not see people, leave alone our wives, children, secretaries, mistresses, ministers, we only have converse with our preconceptions of them. On the way to Pushkar, I accidentally discovered my family, my extended family.

We were sitting around the campfire on the first evening when I heard a startlingly authentic imitation of my voice.

'I'm afraid I can't take any credit for our victory over Malwa. His Highness, Medini Rai was the Commander-in-Chief and it was his leadership that made all the difference. Part of the credit must also go to Prince Hem Karan. He is young, committed and a brilliant fighter. I would be doing a disservice to Mewar and its allies if I didn't mention the gallantry, the tactical ingenuity and ferocity of my friends, Shafi and Tej. It would be unforgivable on my part if I didn't bow my head before the valour, speed and single-mindedness of our soldiers. Last but not least, how could we possibly have won the great battle without the help of His Majesty, the Sultan of Malwa? If he hadn't lost, what victory would we be celebrating today? Under the circumstances, I'm constrained, nay, I've no option but to return the greatest honour Mewar can bestow on a warrior, the triumph we call Veer Vijay.

'I beg of you not to misunderstand me. I'm not ungrateful nor do I wish to insult the great people of Mewar or His Majesty, the Maharana.' My sister-in-law, Rattan Simha's wife, paused then. When the audience finally stopped laughing, she said, 'Long live the Maharana and may he prosper for ever. As an earnest of my gratitude to you all, I would, however, like you to know that under duress I will accept the Crown anytime.'

Could this be the shy and stammering Deepmala, my first brother's fifth wife, to whom I've never said more than 'hello' perhaps seven times in the last four years? Surely she must be one of the sharpest observers of the political scene in Mewar. No, not just of the political scene; she next did a devastating portrait of Queen Karmavati lending money to a concubine after taking over her property, which was worth at least a thousand times the amount borrowed, as security and then charging some unheard-of interest. She followed that with a dialogue between a maid and Vikramaditya. The maid pleads measles, menstruation, her husband, her duties as maid-in-waiting to Greeneyes, brain fever, a visit from a mother-in-law and several other reasons for her inability to meet the Prince in the rose garden and is delighted when Vikramaditya overcomes every obstacle and seduces her.

Poor Vikram, he'll make fun of the whole world but becomes apoplectic when he himself is targeted for some ribaldry. He went through all the colours of the spectrum and snarled 'never, never' when his sister-in-law touched his feet and asked for his forgiveness. His mother was far more diplomatic and blessed her step daughter-in-law.

'Ah Highness, you laughed the loudest,' Deepmala whispered when she came around to me, 'forgive the impertinence but do you really like being made an ass of or are you the biggest hypocrite in this gathering?'

'Both, Princess, both,' I told her as I handed her my ruby ring.

'Stick with the second, Highness. It will take you far.'

I doubt if there's a better impresario in Mewar than the Little Saint. Deepmala was just the first of her surprises. On the second day, she lined up Tej as a magician (he cut up Greeneyes with a saw, threw up her bleeding limbs in the air and at the audience and put them back together) and believe it or not, my second wife.

What was Sugandha going to perform? After she sat down on the stage along with a concubine, two servants brought a veena and a pakhawaj. The veena is an unwieldy instrument with its large and small hollowed-out resonating gourds and I had a malicious vision of my second wife sitting astride the central beam and playing horsie, horsie.

Let me come clean and confess that I love the veena more than most musical instruments and I did not wish her to ruin my pleasure by playing indifferently.

Sugandha, however, was no longer diffident or defiant. Her opening meditation was short but she made up for it by a subtle and sinuous vilambit. It took me a while to get the hang of what she was doing. She was not a purist the way zealots tend to be. Since her teacher was from the south, her training and discipline were evident in her conception and her phrasing but the natural bent of her mind resisted the ironclad Karnataka format. The tension between the two impulses was a liberating one. She did not always succeed in what she was trying to do but that was because she was young and inexperienced. What was important was that she could create an air of mystery and excitement, so that you were curious to see whether she could make it worth your while to stay.

She did not disappoint me or the rest of the audience.

There were two shows in the evenings, the one presented by Greeneyes and the one in the sky. If you are Brahma, the Creator of the universe, you can spit on all the laws of aesthetics, tell the theoreticians to stuff their mouths with all their talk of the balance of colour and the painterly palette. In the evenings, Brahma dipped his palms, palms wide enough to hold the entire universe in them, into a cauldron of raging colours and flung them helter-skelter at the horizon.

I'm a classicist by nature. My own life, writing and other excesses may give the lie to that claim but that does not alter the bent of my mind. Austerity, clean lines, wide vistas and, above all, clarity and going to the essence of things is what I respond to. The god of Pushkar is an exhibitionist, he's garish, profligate and prodigal, he can't stop showing off, he's tasteless, he's self-indulgent, he exaggerates beyond the farthest limits of hyperbole, but none of it matters, not at all. Because, however disparate and contrary his palette, the only thing that matters is, does it work? The answer is yes, yes and yes again. It shouldn't but it does. Don't take my word for it, come to Pushkar and see it for yourself.

505

He does black sunsets, this god, the poisonous black that dripped from the serpent Vasuki when the gods and the demons churned the oceans in search of ambrosia. In a span of twenty minutes, he starts multiple interplanetary fires and douses them with the most gentle and soothing of unguents; whips up sandstorms that turn into rain and flash floods. It is a seamless transformation, the texture of Chanderi cotton becomes the heavy silk of Kanchipuram, ochre pales to azure. Now you know where all the Rajput contradictions, extremes and clichés come from: fire and ice, rock and fluid, arrogance and extreme politeness. Yes, at Pushkar you can get sunsets in black and white too.

Did my wife know something about the desert light that I didn't? Was that the reason why she made everyone wear white the first day at Pushkar? Perhaps it was the interplay between the sun and sand that made all things translucent: men, women and temples. Mirages had more substance than any of us. The slightest breeze, I was sure, would make us disintegrate and waft us into the holy lake.

The Pushkar waters. Now there is a mystery. If they can purify us and cleanse all our sins, then reincarnation is a lie or at least redundant. We could all snap the cycle of rebirth and achieve moksha with just one dip in the Pushkar. The trip to Mecca achieves something similar for Muslims, and the Christians, I'm told, can draw a veil over their sins by the mere act of confession and repentance. I sometimes think that Buddhism is the toughest religion in the world. It not only eschews all talk of god but does not allow any instant remedies. Responsibility for one's own acts is its only metaphysics.

So did I forgo the immersion in the Pushkar? Would you? I may be a doubter, a frequent one at that, but I am hypocrite enough to play it safe and take my chances with the sacred waters. No, that is too facile an answer. Washing one's sins is wishing them away. Yet I've never doubted the healing and cleansing power of the lake. I held my breath and stayed underwater till my mind had gone dead.

When the Sun-god touched the red spire of the Brahma temple,

Father and I entered the gate where the swan of Brahma keeps an eye on all his devotees. We lay prostrate in front of the Creator. I was grateful to Brahma for the life he had breathed into me, for Hem Karan's escape from Gagrone and the victory he bestowed on us against the Sultan of Malwa and yet, even as I thanked him, my thoughts kept wandering to the Padshah in Delhi. Would that I had Babur's total faith and confidence in his God. When he lost, did he say 'God made it come wrong' or did he consider defeats the price he had to pay for his sins? Would my hesitation to ask my Creator to intervene in the war that we must surely fight with the Moghul one of these days and make it come right, affect the outcome of the war itself?

His Majesty and I stood at the head of the stairs of the temple for a moment. The lake had the sheen and stillness of milk on which the cream was congealing. The family was out now and along with the summer pavilions, was dressed in radiant white. The light and air seemed to be filtered through gauze and Dhaka muslin. Barring a lecture in the morning, Greeneyes had set the day aside for a long and lazy picnic by the lakeside.

I was in two minds about going for the talk. There are two topics that I scrupulously avoid, not always successfully, but I try. One is the weather. Mewar is either singeing dry and hot or corrosively dry and cold. There's nothing more to say about it.

The other subject is the eunuchs in the Palace. I'm physically uneasy in the presence of eunuchs. This is not their fault. They are certainly more sinned against than sinning but they are a dangerous lot. They bring a steamy, hothouse air wherever they are. They scheme, intrigue and machinate not with a purpose but as the end-all and be-all of their lives. Where they are, there is trouble, often grievous trouble. Today's talk is by Bruhannada, the most powerful, arrogant and devious of the breed at Chittor. It may perhaps tell you something about the man or whatever gender you wish to assign to him, that as Rani Karmavati's chief eunuch and closest confidant, cabinet ministers as well as visiting rajas and rawats seek an audience with him. I have resolutely eschewed his company all these years and am inclined to do so today but the subject intrigues me: Self-denial in the *Mahabharata*.

The shamiana was full by the time I got there. I forgot to mention that while Bruhannada's looks may not appeal to me, he is singularly goodlooking and can be delightful company when he wants. Bruhannada knew his *Mahabharata* better than most of us and he had a thesis to propound. He chose Bhishma, the greatest celibate in the epic as the symbol of an abstemiousness that is not of one's own choosing. This is of course a bit of a grey area. As you are well aware, Bhishma's ageing father Shantanu fell in love with the beauteous Satyavati but she would not agree to the marriage unless her son and not Bhishma inherited the throne. Shantanu would not ask his son for this terrible sacrifice, yet Bhishma not only renounced the throne but took a vow of eternal celibacy.

Without saying it in as many words, Bruhannada seemed to suggest parallels between Bhishma and the eunuchs. No, he went even further. He hinted that they shared a common lineage. Both must suffer a neutered fate. He did not of course stop there. It is what you make of this imposed condition that brings the question of choice into play. You would be entirely justified if you spent your entire life railing against your misfortune. But there is another option. Rise above your fate. Internalize your calamity and give it a heroic dimension as Bhishma did. It was a thoughtful disquisition and its central insight applied to all of us since there is no man born who is not handicapped in one way or another. So it is up to us to make the best of a botched job.

After breakfast we went to the Mrikanda Muni Kund which grants the boon of wisdom. It is close to the most wooded spot on the rim of the lake and also the most secluded. I knew that it would be a long time before I spent such a quiet day again and I wanted to make the most of it. My brothers Vikramaditya and Rattan and their nine children, Tej, Mangal and I played seven tiles and peet-pitai. After the games I swam for a long time and then lay on my back on the bank. There's no more soothing sound in the world than the slow, unintrusive, soft swish of water against the shore. Every now and then I would turn on my side and look at the ladies in the distance. Was this all my family? I had rarely seen so many beautiful women together. They were playing hide-and-seek, some of them were making garlands while others chatted or scolded the children. The sound of their voices seemed to come from a long way off. I let my hand fall drowsily in the water.

'Which ... which ... which-whee-whee-which?' No other bird but the black-and-chestnut crested bunting, the pathar chidiya could be so cheerfully inquisitive about life. If there's a pond or a river nearby, there's bound to be a red munia around. The munia reminds me of a child. It is a musical bird which is always short of breath. This one too sang a discontinuous and feeble song. Where had I been all these years? How could I have ignored a world that Raja Puraji Kika had opened up for me when we were at school together and would go bird watching on holidays? That black and orange chestnut bird pecking at spiders and insects is, I think, a redstart. It's too busy eating to call out its sharp and short whit ... whit ... whit. I was watching that shy winter visitor, the blue throat feeding on caterpillars and beetles in the reeds when I must have fallen asleep.

I don't know how long I had been dozing. The sound of voices in the background had almost completely died down. Everybody must have had lunch and lain down for a siesta. I did not want to open my eyes but I had the strange feeling that somebody was watching me. It was Sugandha. She was on her knees, crouching, with her arms tightly wound around herself. Every half a minute or so her body jerked, her throat and tongue worked hard to release some deep and unmentionable grief and yet could only let out an occasional hiccup-like sound. But it was her eyes that held me. They wouldn't look at me. There was a terror in them that made them dart and flit from the trees to the lake to the sky and then to the rise and fall of my belly. I sat up slowly and gently, very gently placed my hand on her shoulder. Her body tensed at my touch and I thought she would roll her eyes and fall to the ground in a fit of epilepsy or hysteria.

Whatever it was that was on her mind, why would she want to come to me? Vikramaditya was her friend, no sarcasm meant, and she should have gone to him. I stroked her back barely touching her at first and then firmly. The spasms that were shaking her to the very pit of her stomach had reduced in intensity but she still could not speak. She took my hand in hers and we walked for a minute. Some terrible urgency seemed to take hold of her then and

509

she began to run till we came to a break in the trees around a slight detour in the line of the lake. A body with its head resting on its chest was immersed three-quarters in the shallow water. A watery red had spread all around it and the white of the clothes had gone a dirty brown. I lifted the head. It was Bruhannada.

I pulled him out with some effort. His right leg had got stuck in the mud and he was heavy with all that water soaked into his clothes. There were multiple stab wounds all over his chest, none in the back, and his privates or whatever passes for them in eunuchs had been slashed repeatedly. Why would anybody, I wondered, want to mutilate the genitalia of a eunuch? His lips were the ashen grey of the dead and I couldn't get a pulse on him but when I put my ear to his chest, I thought I detected a faint but erratic heartbeat.

'Will you stay with him while I get some help?' I asked Sugandha.

'Don't leave me alone.'

'He needs medical help urgently.'

'He may be dead by the time you get it.'

'That's a chance we'll have to take.'

When I got back, my second wife was no longer there.

* * *

Greeneyes had planned for two days at Pushkar. We had all been so happy and carefree, Father was even considering extending our stay by another day. Perhaps paradise is always short-lived. The water at Pushkar had suddenly curdled and the summer pavilions had lost their exuberance. The women were huddled together around the Little Saint. She had taken charge as usual and had already given orders to pull up the tents. Father appointed Rattan to oversee the journey back while Mangal, he and I took off for home.

'Mangal will handle the investigation,' Father told me as we were about to enter Chittor, 'while you will conduct the trial.'

'Mangal's not in the Home Ministry, Your Majesty, and I'm merely a judge in the Small Causes Court.'

'I'm aware of who's in what department, Prince. This is a Palace matter and I want it to stay within the Palace. I also want the culprits brought to justice speedily. You had better do a good job.'

'I beg of you, Majesty. I'm part of the family. The purposes of justice may be served better if an outsider was appointed.'

'We need to get to the bottom of things. It's because an outsider may be intimidated that I'm appointing you. Now will you get on with the job or will you continue to tell me how to do mine?'

Chapter 41

'They are afraid of us, there's no question about that. Why else would Babur recall his son Humayun to Delhi from Junpur?' Silhadi asked the question of no one in particular at the War Council. He was in great spirits and seemed to have forgotten the uncalled-for tantrum he had thrown the last time he was at Chittor. (It was also likely that he did not find this an opportune moment to ask why and on whose authority the Sultan of Malwa had been sent back to his own kingdom with an escort, a week after the Rai's departure.)

'Would you not recall your right hand man to be with you,' my wife's uncle, Rao Viramdev, asked Silhadi,' if this Council decided that we should march against the Padshah?'

'I would, naturally.'

'Should Babur then conclude that the Rajputs fear him?'

The Prime Minister changed the subject before Silhadi realized that he had been trapped by his own words and became nasty.

'Did you know that both Babur and Ibrahim Lodi, the Delhi Sultan, had solicited Mewar's help before the battle of Panipat? I think we are all agreed that the loose confederacy which holds Mewar and its friends together is today the mightiest power in this part of Hindustan. Let us strike while the iron is hot. Let us give battle to Babur as soon as we can.'

The War Council, it appeared, did not wish to debate the matter of war or weigh the advantages and demerits of putting off the confrontation for a while, maybe even for a couple of years. They were impatient to go and finish off Babur.

'Before one takes such an important decision,' I asked a little hesitantly, directing my query to Rao Viramdev in the hope that he would consider the issue on its merits and not in the heat of

512

the moment, 'would it not help if we investigated how so small a force as Babur's defeated the numerically vastly superior armies of Ibrahim Lodi?'

'Why is that such a puzzle?' It was Lakshman Simhaji who fielded my question. 'Hadn't you told us for years that the Delhi dynasty was a spent force and ready to crumble?'

'Besides,' Prime Minister Pooranmalji had a broad grin on his face, 'did you not but recently prove beyond the shadow of a doubt how a tiny band of dedicated warriors lead by Rao Medini Rai and you could defeat the combined armies of Malwa and Gujarat?'

'I mean no disrespect to the courage and valour of the Rajput armies but ask a mere hypothetical question. What is to prevent Padshah Babur from repeating the same feat as ours and giving a drubbing to the combined Mewar armies?'

The Prime Minister was patient with me. 'Because unlike Delhi and Malwa, Mewar is at the peak of its power. Never have the Rajputs been so united and their hegemony so undisputed.'

'You were trying to tell us something, Maharaj Kumar,' Rao Viramdev revived my earlier point. 'The Lodi empire may have been in bad shape but the Sultan undoubtedly had a formidable war machine. What would you say were the causes of his defeat?'

'Four reasons. The Moghul bows are better designed and their steel arrows have greater penetrating power. Unlike us, they make extensive and routine use of matchlocks. One can shoot from a greater distance and yet be far more accurate and deadly than with arrows. They don't just come with superior conventional arms, they build fortifications on the battlefield itself.' I drew the diagrams of Babur's battle plan at Panipat and explained how his strategy worked. 'Fourth, the Padshah uses new deadly weapons called field-cannons which discharge huge flying stone balls at high speeds from great distances into the midst of the enemy. The cannon balls played havoc long before Ibrahim Lodi's forces could engage Babur's cavalry or infantry.'

'You call wagons tied together, ditches and walls of packed branches fortifications?' Silhadi asked me disdainfully. 'Our elephants will trample them down.'

'Ibrahim Lodi had a thousand elephants.'

513

'How many cannons does the Padshah have?' Rao Viramdev again.

'Three or four, I'm not sure about the precise number. But he has employed a Turkish master artilleryman and cannon-builder called Ustad Ali-quli who has recently cast an enormous mortar. It is calculated that the new cannon will lob its stone shots sixteen hundred paces.'

'And what do you recommend should be our course of action?' Rao Viramdev kept the discussion on course.

'Play for time.'

'To what purpose?'

'We have been making enquiries. There seems to be a good chance that the Portuguese may sell us four field-guns within a year or year and a half. That will give us time to buy at least a couple of thousand matchlocks and work out a strategy that will bypass Babur's portable fortifications.'

'What kind of strategy would that be, Maharaj Kumar?' Raja Puraji Kika pinned me down. 'You have obviously given it some thought.'

'Eschew all confrontations. If hostilities cannot be avoided, harry and harass. Strike at the flanks and disappear.'

'We thought you had grown out of your fun and games phase when you fought a conventional battle with the Malwa Sultan. Time to get serious, Maharaj Kumar, this is war we are talking about.'

Raja Puraji Kika ignored Silhadi's dig at me. 'How long could you carry on with these tactics? The Padshah, as you've convinced us, is nobody's fool.'

'We would fall back on this evasive strategy only as a last resort. I am fully seized of the fact that at some point, not in the immediate future but as soon as our arsenals are on par, we must meet the Padshah head on.'

'I keep thinking that it couldn't have been just four cannons and a thousand matchlocks that ran Ibrahim Lodi to the ground,' Rao Medini Rai spoke as if he had been puzzling over the issue for some time. 'There was a serious problem of morale amongst the Sultan's troops. He had alienated the majority of his people and most of his amirs and generals were at odds with him. I believe that with us the Padshah will face a united army whose leaders are acting in concert and share common goals and aspirations.'

'I cannot gainsay the truth of the points you have made, Highness. We are a large, strong and united force. Cohesion and compactness will come with extensive drilling and practice as we discovered on our last campaign. What harm could ensue from some procrastination that would also make us stronger in small and big firearms?'

'And how will you hold off the Padshah till then?'

'By a diplomatic offensive. We send an embassy to Agra bearing gifts for the Padshah, Shehzada Humayun and others in the royal household. We congratulate Babur and make friendly overtures; if need be, even discuss boundaries and borders with him. It will throw him off balance and he'll be confused about our intentions.'

'Are you suggesting that after months of a hostile build-up, the Padshah is going to be fooled by your transparent ploys?' Silhadi was perhaps rightly scornful.

'It's worth a try. He has so many revolts, rebellions and other problems on his hands, I believe Babur too would be happy to get a respite from what he calls the infidel problem of Mewar.'

'You are right, Maharaj Kumar, time is of the essence. The best time to attack an enemy is when his house is not in order. If we don't engage the enemy now, he'll gain the upper hand. If we are the paramount power in the country, surely we must behave like one?' Pooranmalji reasoned patiently with me.

'Is it settled then,' it was the first time Father had spoken that day, 'that we move swiftly against the Padshah?'

I should have known better. His Majesty had made up his mind before calling the meeting of the War Council.

*   *   *

I saw Rao Medini Rai and Raja Puraji Kika off that afternoon.

'Why is it that half of Chittor is always dug up?' Medini Rai asked me as we rode down.

'We are trying to set up an aqueduct system like the one they have in Vijayanagar.'

'That's the reason why he doesn't want to go to war, Highness,'

515

Raja Puraji Kika told the Rao. 'Because he thinks funds will get diverted from his pet project.'

'I hadn't thought about that but you are right. Everything will come to a standstill till we get back.'

'So you think this is going to be the big one?' Medini Rai asked me.

'I suspect it is. What do you think?'

'This new man in Agra is like a fever that keeps rising higher and higher. I hope all of us are not going to be delirious by the time we get to the battlefield.' Medini Rai was right. We could think of nothing but Babur. 'Our allies seem to be raring to go. That kind of excitement and confidence can't do us any harm. Why didn't you mention the fanatic frenzy with which Babur's approaching this war?'

'I was hoping to slow down the pace of the discussion from excessive patriotism to a rational level. Any talk of Babur's extreme stance would have made them want to go to war today.'

'That doesn't answer the question of how we are going to combat it.' Medini Rai stopped me short.

'Do you have any ideas?'

'Perhaps we too should make it a religious war?'

'And lose the support of the Muslim kings and populace?'

'So what do we do?'

'There are only two checkmates to a Holy War. Enlist as many Muslims as we can on our side. Make merit the only criteria for advancement and not religion. Secondly, and that's what I was holding out for throughout the meeting: technologically, we have to be, if not ahead, at least on par, and militarily, we have to think and move like a single unit instead of ten companies moving in ten directions.' The Rai listened intently but it was what I had to say next that made him frown grimly. 'Do you know what Babur says about us? "Swordsmen though some Hindustanis may be, most of them are ignorant and unskilled in military move and stand, in soldierly counsel and procedure." We have to prove him wrong.'

'It would appear that I was in error to suggest that Ibrahim Lodi was as much to blame as Babur's brilliant management of the limited resources at his disposal.' I was glad to see that Medini Rai had

516

the courage to have second thoughts. 'It also diverted attention from Babur's technological superiority in arms.'

'Only slightly, for everybody at the Council thinks the field-cannons and matchlocks will not do serious damage to our forces.'

'I owe you and His Majesty the Rana an apology for another matter. It is long overdue. I believe His Highness, Silhadi, got carried away the last time when we met to decide the fate of the Sultan of Malwa. I am not lacking in appreciation of what I owe you, Highness. Without you I may have lost my son and Gagrone and we certainly would not have won the battle.'

'You need not have worried on that count, Highness. I am not likely to confuse Silhadi with you.'

*　　*　　*

I was working late at the office (we all were, there's so little time before we set off) when Father came to see me.

'I think a clarification would be in order. I did not write to the Moghul Padshah as his diary suggests. It was he who asked me.'

'It doesn't matter who asked whom, Your Majesty. What matters is that Babur feels betrayed because you wrote to him that we would support him and attack Agra from the south. He is the kind of man who does not forget a grievance easily. I suspect he'll bring an extra degree of malevolence to this conflict not just because we are pagans but because he wishes to settle other scores with us.'

'My calculations were based on a different set of assumptions. I was counting on Ibrahim Lodi beating Babur's lesser forces but in the process suffering unacceptably heavy casualties. On the other hand, if Babur defeated the Delhi Sultan, he would collect a huge sum and at best, annex a province or two. Either way, I felt that the ideal time for us to attack Ibrahim Lodi was after his brush with Babur. Who would have guessed that Babur would occupy Delhi?'

It never ceases to amaze me how we disregard people's avowed intentions. Copies of the translation of the bits and pieces of Babur's diaries had been sent to all the cabinet members. Surely Father knew that Babur had announced a long time ago that he viewed the Delhi Sultanate as his since his ancestor Timur had conquered it some generations ago.

'Perhaps we were a shade naive.' That's about as close to admitting a mistake as His Majesty had ever come.

'You did not stop there. After the battle of Panipat, you made Ibrahim Lodi's brother Mahmud, who's next in line for the succession of the Delhi throne, welcome in Chittor. Then you took Kandar which belonged to the Delhi Sultanate and which Babur considers his territory since he beat Sultan Ibrahim Lodi. As if all that was not enough, you've also surreptitiously occupied another hundred and ninety or is it two hundred other towns and villages that Babur thinks belong to him. We cannot deny, Father, that we have given Babur grave provocation.' I laughed then. 'I suspect that was your intention.'

'I wouldn't go so far as to quite put it that way.'

'It's of no consequence now, Father. The Padshah is in Agra and there is no avoiding the conflict, but if you will forgive my harking back to the same point, will you even now reconsider postponing it?'

'If I didn't know you as one of the toughest generals in the history of the Rajputs, I would say that you've lost your nerve. This excessive caution is making you faint of heart. The more we delay, the stronger he'll get. Now is the time to strike while the Padshah is still unsettled and the Lodi vassals are busy fomenting revolts everywhere.'

Chapter 42

'Who, Mangal, who?'

It was seventeen days since 'the accident' as the court bulletin preferred to call it.

'Could be any one of a hundred and fourteen people.'

I looked sharply at Mangal. Why not a round hundred or ninety-three out of the hundred and seventeen who went to Pushkar? Mangal tends to get flippant when he wants to be cagey. But he meant what he said and he was right. Queen Karmavati's chief eunuch was not just powerful, he used that power to hurt and destroy people. He liked the women in the zenana to be beholden to him so that at some critical moment he could ask for an exorbitant favour or exact a terrible price. He could be charming but always with an ulterior motive and even the queens were afraid of him. Mangal was right, barring Queen Karmavati and Vikramaditya, all of us at Pushkar could have borne the eunuch grievous ill will.

'Has he regained consciousness?'

'No.'

'Has his condition stabilized?'

'No, the doctor says he's bled profusely plus his system has suffered a terrible trauma. There's no saying yet whether he'll make it or not.'

'There was not a single slash or wound on Bruhannada's back. He knew who was attacking him but did not retaliate or defend himself. Nor did he try to run away. All he seems to have done is to shield himself from the blows with his hands and arms. Do you think he believed he deserved to die?'

'Perhaps.' It was monosyllabic day for Mangal.

'Who was it, Mangal, who? You think it was someone so

powerful that Bruhannada felt he had no choice but to take an assault on his person without raising his hand in self-defense?'

'The thought has crossed my mind, Highness.'

'Will you stop acting officious with me and be more forthcoming? This was a crime committed within hailing distance of His Majesty. Anybody who could get to Bruhannada could have got to His Majesty.'

'The police are aware of the lapse in security, Highness, but they are not happy that I've been given charge of the investigation and are not exactly being cooperative.'

'Do you think someone's putting the screws on them?'

'It's possible.'

'Have you talked to Rani Karmavati?'

'She informed me that she was under no compulsion to speak to me since I was in Intelligence and not with the police. But she did finally give me an audience yesterday.'

'And?'

'She was short with me. Would I not have told you if I knew who did it, she asked me.'

'Does she suspect anybody?'

'Everybody, she said, everybody.'

'You think she's coming clean?'

'I don't know.'

'Have you questioned my second wife?'

Mangal looked blankly at me.

'Don't play games with me, Mangal. She was the one who found the mutilated man.'

'She said she had skipped her bath in the morning because it was cold and was going to take one in the afternoon in a quiet place since the water would be tolerably warm then.'

'Do you believe her story?'

'I have no reason to doubt it, Sire.' I thought I could read Mangal's mind and even hear him say, 'Why don't you ask your wife and get all the details first-hand yourself?'

'Did she see anybody else around?'

'She said no.'

520

I was irritable and frustrated. I knew I was making Mangal do all the dirty work because I didn't expect the Police Commissioner and his men to come up with answers. This was a Palace matter and they would be out of their depth. But all either he or I had turned up so far were blind alleys and blanks.

'Let me know if something comes up.'

'The Queen, it appears, has asked her maid-in-waiting, Urvashi, to go back to her home in Bundi.'

'A falling-out with one of her maids is nothing new for Queen Karmavati.'

'The word is that Urvashi may have missed her period two months running.'

'Why would I be interested in Urvashi's menstrual cycle? This won't be the first or last time that my brother Vikramaditya has cohabited with one of his mother's ladies.'

'But it would be a precedent of sorts if the lady is really pregnant with Prince Vikramaditya's child and is being sent away from Chittor.'

'I don't get the connection Mangal.'

'It bothers me that I can't get the link either, Sire.'

'Maybe there's none and you are reading too much into the Queen's displeasure. Why not accost the lady while she's wending her way home and check matters out?'

'I intend to, Highness.'

Mangal must have been halfway to his office block when I ran after him.

'Where have you kept him, Mangal?'

'In one of the rooms in the quarantine section in the Atithi Palace, Highness. I've posted one of my own men there.'

'Can we move him without anyone coming to know of it?'

'I believe Rasikabai rents some of her outhouses behind Tamarind Lane to visitors from out of town.'

'Transfer him there but not before you've got a completely bandaged double who can take solitary confinement for a couple of weeks at the minimum, maybe a month.'

'When do you want it done?'

'Tonight if possible. Keep at least half a dozen alternative accommodations in mind. We'll move the eunuch as often as necessary.'

The rear wing of the Atithi Palace which houses the infectious diseases section went up in flames two days after we transferred Bruhannada. His replacement was lucky to have got away with only twenty-five percent burns.

From day one I had been going over the same question over and over again: Why would anyone want to crosshatch the genitalia of a eunuch? It didn't make sense. Defacement of Bruhannada's face, that I could understand. One could apprehend some kind of motive there. The chief eunuch was a goodlooking man and conscious of it. If anyone wanted to get back at him, the face might be a good place to start. I was not sure who we were looking for. Was it a personal thing or a political vendetta? Was it a man or a woman? And whoever it was or they were, why would the eunuch not defend himself?

Mangal and I went for a swim in the Gambhiree where we had decided to meet every night while we struggled to sort out the Bruhannada case. It was the only place where we could have some privacy. We were running out of time. Father was getting impatient, the matter of the Padshah of Delhi demanded Mangal's and my full attention and the atmosphere in the Palace reminded me of that evening in the Gujarat campaign when I had watched a buffalo's throat being slit while the rest of the cattle awaited their turn in cowering anticipation.

The ladies in the zenana would not take a bath or go to the toilet except in groups of three or more. A curtain or shadow moving was enough to start one of them screaming and within seconds the whole lot would be convinced that they were about to be murdered, and ran shrieking for cover. It's not as if Chittor is innocent of crime. We have our share of wife-beatings, thefts, stabbings, highway robberies, and murders. But something about the viciousness and brutality of the attack on the eunuch seemed to have caught the imagination of the women and made them terribly nervous and fearful.

The hijadas of the city who share their genderless state with the royal eunuchs in the palace, have adopted Bruhannada as their patron and are going to take out a silent procession at ten tomorrow morning and march around the city both as a mark of respect and as a way of highlighting their plight. This is indeed a curious turn of events which would surprise no person more than the said Bruhannada whose worst nightmare, along with that of all the eunuchs in the royal household, is to be confused with the hijadas. What is more curious and to the point is that I have been deputed to safeguard a man for whom I bear nothing but the most unmitigated antipathy.

Both Mangal and I have always suspected that the brains and subtlety behind Queen Karmavati's schemes belong to her chief eunuch. He knows what he wants and knows how to go about getting it. He also has that rarest of gifts: sustained application. He wants to be kingmaker and the power who rules from behind the scene. He has chosen his vehicle carefully. He may not love Vikramaditya as much as his mother does but he loves him far more wisely.

Now when he was at the peak of his powers and was perhaps the most feared person in the Palace, who would dare to touch him and why would he let them?

'Rani Karmavati called me over today and told me to hand over Bruhannada to her since I was incapable of taking care of him.'

'Why didn't you tell her that it was too late to do anything about it now, Mangal?'

'I did. I even gave her his ashes and bones. She smiled and told me to tell these old wives' tales to my wife or some other credulous fool. She had no intention of allowing me to murder the chief of her household staff.'

I was about to ask Mangal who was snitching on us when I realized the folly of the question. Nothing, absolutely nothing escapes Queen Karmavati's ears.

'What about her maid-in-waiting, Urvashi, have you questioned her?'

'She won't talk, Highness.'

'Is she pregnant?'

'The midwife is convinced she is.'

'Is it Vikramaditya's baby?'

'I doubt it. Since she wouldn't talk I threatened to call Prince Vikramaditya. Do that, she said, and I'll kill myself. She meant it, I think.'

'Let her go to her parent's place in Bundi, Mangal. If Vikram or his mother find out that we waylaid her, I'm sure they'll tell His Majesty that we tried to molest her.'

'I would like to keep her for another week or two though.'

'Why?'

'As I was about to terminate my interview with Urvashi, she enquired after Bruhannada.'

'Why not, the whole world's talking about him?'

'Still, it's a little odd that of all the people in the world, she should ask after him.'

'Have it your way. Just make sure neither Vikram nor his mother find out where she is. Are you shifting the eunuch tonight?'

'I already have. Whoever's out to get him is as well-informed about his whereabouts as Queen Karmavati.'

'What does the Raj Vaidya say? When will he gain consciousness?'

'He's not hazarding any guesses.'

'I keep getting the feeling that we are missing something. What do you have on the Chief Eunuch?'

'Nothing much really. When Prince Vikramaditya felt like a change of pace, he sodomized the eunuch from time to time.'

'Does Bruhannada have another lover? Some young boy or another prince?'

'I don't think so. Sex doesn't seem to interest him much, not even with His Highness.'

'Do you think we are barking up the wrong tree? Maybe it's not a sex crime at all. Whoever did it wanted us to think it was.'

'So what kind of crime was it?'

We were back to where we had started. Nowhere.

524

That night when I got back home after the swim, there was no light in my room. The Bruhannada fever had got to me. My hand was on the hilt of my sword. I waited for my eyes to adjust to the darkness when two hands clutched at my ankles.

'I beg you not to put on the light.'

It was hardly a voice, just the broken remnants of a person transiting into the nether world. What if I had heard Sugandha's voice half a second later? Who would have believed that I had killed my faithless wife by accident?

I dropped my sword and picked her up.

'Please don't look at me.'

Even in the darkness of the room, the purple of her bruises glinted like the shot colours in a Kanchipuram silk. Her body had swollen grotesquely.

'Who did this to you, Sugandha?'

'It doesn't matter. There is no punishment in hell commensurate to the shame I have brought upon your name.' Her flesh shifted like heavy liquid in my arms. She groaned in pain.

'Hold me tight. Promise me you'll never let go of me. Never.'

I felt such unbearable love and tenderness for her then, I was willing to foolishly promise her anything, declare bondage to her for the rest of my life as reparation for having let her down. And yet something held me back. Was this pity for her or for myself?

I looked at her baby face. Oh God, what had I done to this childish and childlike woman? How could I have allowed her to go to Vikramaditya? Did I not know that my brother would not be able to resist the soft invitation of her flesh to damage and disrupt it? Suddenly I saw myself for what I was: a petty, vindictive man who was relieved that his wife was committing adultery so that he could have a clean conscience and be free of any guilt towards his father-in-law. What had my brother gone and done to her? What did Rajput honour expect of me? Should I challenge Vikram to a swordfight, should I split his head and spill his brains, should I tear off his clothes in public and force him to walk naked on the streets of Mewar? And yet the only infamy I thought he was worthy of was the worst kind of un-Rajput conduct: stab him from behind and carve his heart out and see the bloody thing palpitate like a fish flapping and tossing for air on land. And yet I was aware I would do none of these things. Instead I would be circumspect, there was enough scandal attached to my name like shit to the sole of a sandal. I would tell myself that I did not need to shove my foot any deeper than I already had. I would be heroic in my self-restraint and find any excuse not to confront Vikram.

I felt a wave of such revulsion against myself, I tried to smother it by crushing my wife in my embrace. Her lips brushed mine and her breasts clamoured against me.

Why is it that the oldest questions we ask about ourselves never have answers? Where do violence and pain stop and sex start? Is lovemaking nothing but loneliness trying to break out?

'Princess,' I asked her afterwards when I lay quietly against her breasts, 'why did my brother fly off into a rage today?'

'He's been doing it every day. It's just that it got out of hand today. His temper has been unstable since Pushkar. He's afraid that I know something.'

'Do you?'

'Would you believe me if I told you?'

'Yes, I would.'

'I don't know what I'm supposed to know.'

There was good news the next day. Bruhannada had regained consciousness.

I looked in on him, enquired after his health and left. I thought I would give him another day, let him regain his strength but I also had some less than honourable motives. He was a smart man, he had a pretty shrewd idea about how the world worked but he was also arrogant. He didn't just know it all, he knew better. He would expect to be put through a round-the-clock grilling immediately. Be a good idea, I thought, to leave him alone and make him wonder what was going on. A little uncertainty never did anybody any harm.

'How long have you known?' I asked Mangal.

'Known what, Highness?'

526

'You know what or who I am referring to.'

'I'm no mind reader and you, Highness, are getting more and more cryptic.'

'Don't try my patience, Mangal.' I had not been able to wipe that invisible grin off his face though there was one appearing on mine now. 'I'm going to have to take you down a peg or two, very soon. Now, are you going to talk or be evasive for some more time?'

'A couple of days, Highness, though it's still just a hunch. But it would appear you are more knowledgeable than I am.'

'Just a hunch, Mangal, same as you. Nothing more. We still need proof.'

Our conversation must have sounded like pure nonsense to any passing listener but Mangal and I were so much together, I just took it for granted that he had access to my innermost thoughts. Well, I hope not the whole lot.

I knew that Sugandha had lied to me last night. She was privy to something that my brother Vikram was afraid she might share with me or someone else. I didn't think she was dissembling or that Vikram had put her up to it. My guess was that she was trying to protect me. Like most people who rush to conclusions, Vikram is, by nature, deeply suspicious. But he has a limited and straightforward mind which is not given to analysis or working a thought through. Unless Sugandha had been in the know of something, it would not occur to him to try to shut her up. I could be wrong but I suspected that she had run into Vikram at the wrong time on the day of the crime. I wanted to test my thesis with Mangal but as usual he's far better at these matters than I and had zeroed in on the suspect much earlier than I. But even Mangal had no answer to one question: why would Vikram want to kill his staunchest ally? If His Majesty were to ask me to submit a report to him tomorrow, there was no way I could tell him that Vikramaditya was our prime suspect. I would merely come across as a man who was trying to frame his brother because of an ancient vendetta.

It was past eleven forty when I got back home at night. Sugandha would not allow me to light the lamp.

'How long do you plan to stay in the dark?'

'I'm not a vain woman, Highness. I am also not the prettiest

527

of women,' she told me with a simplicity that was not feigned. 'I do not want to lose whatever little affection you may bear for me by seeing me in the state that I am in. You shouldn't have provoked your brother, Highness. You do not know what a vengeful and dangerous man he is.'

Sugandha was referring to a short expedition that I had taken the previous morning. There was consternation amongst Vikramaditya's security guards and his retinue of servants as Mangal and I strode unannounced into his palace in the morning. His aide-de-camp was so flabbergasted that he asked me, 'Who should I say is calling?' I ignored him and walked into my brother's bed-chambers. He was still in bed with some woman from Rasikabai's establishment who made a considerable fuss about her dignity and honour being compromised. I threw her clothes at her and asked her to leave.

'Who do you think you are that you can order a guest of mine out of my house?' Vikram yelled at me. 'Guards. ADC.'

Who-shall-I-say-is-calling had not recovered from seeing me stomp in but had had the presence of mind to follow us in case his master was in danger. I waited till the lady had left.

'Shut up, Vikram, and listen to me carefully. If you raise your hand on my wife again; if you are anywhere within a hundred yards of her even by accident; if either you or your hired hands try anything funny with her; no, let me state it a little more precisely: if anything should happen to her, typhoid, pneumonia, a fall from a horse, an innocuous fire lit under her, or a poison that finds its way into her food, I will hold you personally responsible and I will kill you. Regardless of the consequences.' I turned around to his ADC, guards and servants and asked them, 'Do you get my drift?'

'Hey, cuckold, which of your faithless wives are you referring to?'

I went over to Vikramaditya's bed. For some reason he pulled the blanket up to his throat as if to cover his modesty. I slapped his face hard with the back of my hand.

'Now, why didn't I do that all these years?' I asked myself in puzzlement. 'Either one, Vikram, either of them.'

✳   ✳   ✳

'I don't think he'll dare touch you, Sugandha.'

'It's not me I'm worried about. Your life's at risk.'

'May I ask a favour of you, Princess?'

'Are you trying to change the subject, Highness?'

'No. It's something that occurred to me yesterday.'

'What is it?'

'Will you teach me to play the veena?'

'You are making fun of me, aren't you?'

I shook my head.

'You mean it?'

'Yes. I don't think any other instrument barring the sarod has the richness of sound and depth that the veena has. Did you know that my great-grandfather Rana Kumbha was not just a fine veena player but that he wrote several books on music?'

'I know. I had to study him.'

I laughed. 'Did you hate him?'

'He does have a rather ponderous style and takes forever to come to the point. But it's curious, now that nobody's forcing me to study him or to play the instrument, I've been going back to him. He takes a different tack from all the classical thinkers who have written about music. He makes you rethink many of the things that you take for granted.'

'I'll let you in on a secret. I've not read him so far.'

'But you must.'

'I will. But first the lessons.'

'When do you want to start?'

'Tomorrow morning at six, is that all right with you?'

'I've never woken up that early.'

'We can drop the idea then.'

'Highness, you'll make a good wife of me yet. I'll be ready at six.'

The question of course is whether I would make a good husband.

Impotence is a strange thing. It may strike you just once in a lifetime but you are a marked man. You live in perpetual fear of when it will visit you again. You learn for the first time that the body is no longer your creature; you are its plaything. It's a terrible and terrifying realization but there's worse to come. It doesn't make sense, it is totally and utterly irrational but no defeat on the battle-field or anywhere else can eat at the heart of a man as the fear of being let down by his member. One of these days, it doesn't matter when, it'll happen again and I will begin to resent Sugandha for revealing my failure to me. Will I end up hating her? Who knows, for the time being happy days are here again.

How little it took to make Sugandha happy. A bit of attention and affection and she would follow me around everywhere and do whatever I wanted.

'Highness, I've something to confess. I lied to you yesterday.' Sugandha had made me lie on my stomach and without my asking her to, she was massaging my back and neck. My face was deep in the mattress and my answer came out a little garbled.

'What did you say?' She bent down to hear me better.

'I said I know.'

'You know? How?'

'I surmised that my brother was, in his usual friendly fashion, warning you to keep whatever you had seen that day, under your odhani. Or else ...'

'He said if I told you anything, or anybody else, he would kill you.'

'And what would you tell me that could provoke him to fratricide?'

'Do you really want to hear this? I'm afraid of losing you all over again.'

'It's up to you and me not to let the foolishness of the past come between us again.'

She was quiet for a minute before she spoke. 'We had an assignation in the woods near the Mrikand Muni Kund Ghat. I had lost my mind in those days, I was impatient to be with the Prince and arrived a good twenty minutes before I was supposed to. I heard his voice, it had a demented tone to it and I couldn't move. I couldn't see him but I heard him repeat the same sentence over and over again. "Let's see how you can ..." she hesitated, 'you really want to know what he said?'

530

'Yes, it may be important.'

'Let's see how you can fuck anybody anymore.'

'Did you hear a scuffle?'

'No. The Prince began to cry then like a child who's terribly afraid. I ran out and I held him to me saying "Everything's fine, don't worry" and he said "What's fine, you stupid fool?" and then he turned on me and asked me, "What are you doing here so early? Weren't we supposed to have met when the hour struck two? Can't you ever do what you are told?" He struck me then and walked away in a huff.'

We had made progress, I would finally be able to report to Father that we had identified the culprit and yet in some ways we were now in greater darkness than when we had started out.

Why had my brother fallen out with the eunuch? What did he mean by 'Let's see how you can fuck anybody anymore?' It was indeed an odd expletive to use about a eunuch. Or was Vikram using the four-letter word figuratively? Perhaps he was incensed that Bruhannada had tried to harm or ruin someone dear to him.

I was fairly certain that the murder attempt had come as a shock to Queen Karmavati as it had to the rest of us. Not only was she deeply upset by the near-fatal assault on her favourite eunuch and adviser, it appeared that there was for the first time, serious dissension between mother and son.

But the Queen's perception of the situation had altered radically since then. Vikramaditya had been able to persuade her that while the doubly castrated eunuch lived, he posed an unacceptable threat to both of them. What did Bruhannada know that was so dangerous?

One thing I'll vouch for almost blindly: Vikramaditya and his mother have misjudged their own retainer. He's not the type who talks or tattles.

'Do you think coercion will make me blabber?' the eunuch asked me with a thin sardonic smile that sat slightly unbalanced on his face.

My answer was matter-of-fact. 'I don't think so. But that's what the people who tried to murder you, not once but on four occasions, seem to believe and would therefore like to shut you up for good.'

'What is your interest in this case then, Highness?' His asthma was acting up and he had to sip hot water to ease his breathlessness but he had lost neither his hauteur nor self-assurance.

'His Majesty has put me in charge of the case so that whoever assaulted you is brought to justice.'

'Fine word that, justice. Nobody brought anyone to book when I was violated and neutered as a child. Why should anyone take interest in the same act and consider it a criminal offence now?'

'I cannot put the past to rights, Bruhannada, but I will endeavour to do so with the present.'

'Good luck to you, Highness, but I must take you into confidence and tell you that it was a suicide attempt on my part.' He was once again in full control of the situation and he was enjoying playing with me. I saw little point in continuing the conversation.

I wished him a quick recovery and was about to leave when Mangal escorted my brother's one-time odalisque, Urvashi, in. It was a long shot but Mangal wanted it to be a surprise for both Bruhannada and Urvashi.

It was.

Bruhannada lost his poise but only just. For a second his mask of supercilious urbanity cracked but he recovered it almost instantly. Urvashi was far more spontaneous. There was no stopping her joy as she rushed into his arms. 'Oh God, you are alive, you are safe.'

One can discount Mangal's hunches only at one's own peril. He had thought there was something between the Queen's maid and her chief eunuch and he was right. The question was, what was that something?

I made my exit then.

∗   ∗   ∗

I thought it would be a good idea to keep up the pressure on the chief eunuch.

'Are you moving me every day to make a show of how endangered my life is?' It was obvious Bruhannada had regained his flippant spirits by the next day.

'Maybe. Would you rather that you stayed in the same place?'

'No, I'll play along. I'm just as fond of the theatre as you are.'

'I found your talk on the *Mahabharata* thought-provoking. It raised some important issues.'

'Highness,' the chief eunuch shook his head coyly from side to side, 'flattery won't get us anywhere.'

'Where would I go with you, Bruhannada? Your life's come to a dead end.' I said that without malice but it had the desired effect. 'If you'll allow me to, I want to go back to the subject of your speech. May I?'

'Yes,' he was a little less sure of himself now, 'Yes, please.'

'I think our countrymen have a rather warped idea of loyalty. Bhishma is the ultimate icon of our notion of sacrifice and loyalty. But it might have helped if he had ventured to question his beliefs. Is he recommending that we abdicate ethical choice and thus abandon the responsibility for our acts? Do we stick to people, however mistaken or evil they may be, merely because we were born on their side or have familial bonds or should we owe our loyalty, not to people or institutions but to values? Bhishma may have served humanity better if he had had the courage not to follow tradition blindly but to weigh in on the side of right, especially because he was perceived as a man of great moral fibre.'

'You've got it wrong, Highness. Go back to your *Gita*. Whichever side of the river you are born, the *Gita*-god tells us, whichever caste or profession you belong to, be true to it.'

'So he does, Bruhannanda, so he does. But gods too may be wrong occasionally and one must have the courage to go against them, perhaps even contravene their fiat.'

'Beware Maharaj Kumar, you are overreaching and inviting the wrath of the gods. Bhishma, I would have you remember, is the expression of the highest integrity.'

'Integrity, I'm afraid, is not enough Bruhannada. Only when it is in the right cause, is it worthwhile.'

'You would rewrite the *Mahabharata* then, Maharaj Kumar?'

'I believe you were doing the same when you traced the eunuch lineage to Bhishma.'

'Where is this chatter leading us, Highness? I'm not interested in making any deals with you unless I can secure the future of my wife and child. I want an assurance with the full weight of the royal imprimatur behind it that no harm will come to Urvashi and the child she bears. I want it stated unambiguously that my child will not be a concubine if it's a daughter or a eunuch if it's a boy. As you can see the bloody surgeons, barbarians really, could not even do a clean job of it on me.'

'No deal, Bruhannada.' I let that sink in while I tried to grasp the fact that Bruhannada was the father of Urvashi's foetus. 'We don't bargain with anyone by holding women and children to ransom. His Majesty will give you his word that no harm will come to Urvashi and your son or daughter regardless of what transpires between you and me,'

I had had enough of the man's trade-offs and deals. When I was at the door, I turned around. 'Have you ever tried exercising your right to make a moral choice, Bruhannada? You'll be amazed, truth too, has its lures and gratifications. More to the point, probity needs a Bhishma.'

Did I really mean any of this nonsense? You'll be surprised.

$$* \quad * \quad *$$

'When did you learn that the male principle in you had not been fully extirpated?'

'I was puzzled when I had the occasional nightly emission in my teens but did not think that it contravened my genderless status.'

'Would you define the approximate interval between two emissions?'

'Anywhere between four and seven months.'

Bruhannada's hearing was in its third day. Since the commission sat in secret, Mangal had to take down the deposition of the victim. At the end of each day, the eunuch went over his testimony to check whether he had been misquoted and then signed the original.

'Did your perception of your gender alter when you grew to maturity?'

'I wasn't certain but around the time I was twenty-five, it occurred to me that maybe I was not all eunuch.'

'Why did you not report this to the concerned authorities?'

534

'Every eunuch has just one regret and just one dream: that he has no gender, and wishes that he had. If I was even occasionally a man, I was not about to deliberately destroy my good fortune. Besides I wasn't sure of my status since I never dared discuss it with anyone.'

'When did you come to know Urvashi?'

'About ten years ago when she first came to Chittor and was put in my charge.'

'Did you know that she was Prince Vikramaditya's mistress?'

'Yes, but only for the first month. After that he lost interest in her.'

'When did you start seeing her?'

'Seven years ago.'

'Did the Prince ask for her while you were secretly carrying on with her?'

'Not once, Sire. He had declared that she was so shy and frigid that he would dismiss me if I ever brought her name into our conversations or suggested that he bed her.'

'When did you discover that Urvashi was pregnant?'

'About four months ago. I didn't believe her at first when she told me that she had missed her period. But there was no mistaking it in the second month. Urvashi was really pregnant.'

'How did you know it was your baby?'

'It is my business to know who sleeps with whom in Queen Karmavati's and the Prince's palaces.'

'How did you plan to handle Urvashi's pregnancy in the seraglio?'

'I thought I would send her to her parents' place after the third month.'

'When did the Prince discover that Urvashi was pregnant?'

'He did not, at least not then. Later despite my best precautions, he caught me with her in the second month of her pregnancy.'

'What did he say to you?'

'My master finds the bizarre highly provocative and becomes maniacally excitable.'

'Did the Prince requisition your services in bed after he discovered your relationship with Urvashi?'

If the eunuch was disconcerted by my switch in subjects, he didn't show it.

'He thought I was a freak of some sort and couldn't leave me alone.'

'Was the Prince's interest in Urvashi rekindled when he came to know of your affair with her?'

The eunuch, or rather the former eunuch closed his eyes then. It was the first time since I began to question him that he showed any sign of emotion.

'It was no affair, Highness. Urvashi and I were secretly married a long time ago.'

'I'll make a note of that. But that is not the answer to my question.'

'The Prince was incensed that Urvashi had responded to a eunuch and not to a real man like him. At first he only hinted at getting back with her. Then a few weeks later he said she had better visit him. I told him that I had engaged two virgins for him for that night. Stop stalling, he said, I want Urvashi, do you understand that, nobody else. I told him then that Urvashi was my wife. I should have known better for that only seemed to provoke him all the more. He had her. Not once but again and again. I won't use the word hate because it is so inadequate but the more she withdrew into herself and resisted, the more he wanted her.'

'Did you have any inkling that he planned to kill you?'

'My master is an impulsive man, Sire. Sometimes I think he's truly deranged. He had been friendly and even considerate on our way to Pushkar. He insisted that I share his tent with him. He asked me to see him after lunch when everybody was either asleep or sailing on the lake. I thought he wanted his pleasure with me and started to undress when he attacked me.'

'Why did you not defend yourself?'

'I've eaten the salt of this house, Highness. I cannot be disloyal to it.'

We had come to the end of the investigation. I had little sympathy for Bruhannada but I respected the way he had conducted himself. There was a bad taste in my mouth and it was mostly due

536

to my brother. What does one do with people like Vikram? Self-indulgence is bad enough. But combine it with power and your appetite for brutality and evil becomes boundless. Your pleasure is the only law and in its pursuit you may ruin a stranger as readily as your closest companion.

Bruhannada had encouraged my brother to think that his wishes took precedence over all else. He had been his pimp and procurer in matters of state as much as in his indulgences. I could be a moral prig and rejoice in the fact that Bruhannada had got his dues. I now had the power to lock up the eunuch for good. But the intolerance and wilful blindness of the self-righteous is far more dangerous and dehumanizing than the rampant destructiveness of someone like Vikram.

'Why are the Queen and her son trying so hard to kill you now? What threat can you pose to them?'

'The best of friends make the worst enemies, Highness.'

There was no point pursuing the matter. Bruhannada had proved that he was not afraid of dying, nor was he about to abandon loyalty to the two people he had loved most.

'What do you plan to do with me, Sire?'

'You broke the law of this land and of this house, Bruhannada, and under normal circumstances, you would either lose your head or be incarcerated for life. But you've already paid a terrible price. I intend to recommend to His Majesty to let you go in peace.'

He looked at me quizzically and then laughed, 'Do you expect me to believe you? We've been enemies so long, you'll take your time with your vengeance.'

'I may dislike you, Bruhannada, but don't confuse me with you or your friends. The purpose of justice is not settling personal scores or vengeance. I believe you'll be out as soon as His Majesty signs your release papers.'

'That's neatly done. You'll wash your hands off me knowing that Prince Vikramaditya will do the dirty work for you: finish me and my wife.'

'The state will relocate you wherever you want. In or outside Mewar. You and your wife will be given a new identity and some

537

money to start a new life. Though I believe you won't really be needing the latter since you are one of the richest men in Mewar.'

Mangal informed me that it would take him about a week to make the arrangements for Bruhannada's and Urvashi's migration. I had half a mind to ask him where he was planning to settle the couple but I knew what his answer would be: why do you want to know? He would of course be right. Ignorance, in some cases, is the better half of wisdom. And what about Vikramaditya, I wanted to ask Father, what did he plan to do with this barbaric murderer masquerading as his son and a prince of the realm? But of course I didn't do anything of the sort. I didn't want to be told to mind my own business or worse, that Vikram had been asked to read stories to the children in Nandanvan, the state orphanage at Chittor for three consecutive evenings as atonement for his crime.

I had fortunately little time for this kind of asinine carping. I was always behind in my work these days and there was also the question of Sugandha. She was now truly alone. Her one-time patroness, the Queen, had abandoned her and so had the Queen's son. The Little Saint, I'm afraid, was behaving in a singularly unsaintly manner. I thought I had detected a thaw in their relationship when Greeneyes had recruited Sugandha for the veena recital on our journey to Pushkar. But Sugandha's break with Vikram and the consequent rapprochement between her and me had rekindled the antipathy in Greeneyes. And since Greeneyes cut Sugandha dead or ignored her, the other women in the seraglio made it a point to ostracize her too. Who, after all, would risk the Little Saint's displeasure now?

I started going home for lunch just to keep Sugandha company. She would be loath to let go of me and I got into the habit of sitting down for a second veena lesson with her. Her face would light up at such times and she would cling to me gratefully. But the pleasure of this companionship was short-lived. I came home one day to find the Little Saint waiting for me.

'Sugandha won't be serving you lunch any more.'

'Why not? Is she unwell?'

'You need not perturb yourself unduly on her behalf. She is strong as a buffalo and shares many of the creature's habits, one of them being laziness.'

'I am not interested in her pedigree. Where is she?'

'Doing a little bit of work for a change. I have asked her to supervise the annual cleaning of the ladies' quarters.'

I was not about to interfere in zenana politics and left but Sugandha was not home the next day either.

'Don't you think, Highness,' Greeneyes was there to greet me again, 'that Mewar would benefit if you sacrificed your post-prandial dalliance?'

'When I need counsel about how to conduct the affairs of my office, I will hire your services, Madam. In the meantime, I would appreciate it if you refrained from offering advice gratis.'

I was about to ask her to send for Sugandha when I thought the better of it. Both the Little Saint and the rest of the zenana would only humiliate and isolate her further.

'May I suggest Your Highness, that pity is no substitute for love? Nor is duty.'

Was she a mind reader, this woman who would not be my wife nor would allow anybody else to be? She knew she had scored a direct hit and smiled her saintly smile.

Chapter 43

The day before Bruhannada and his wife were to leave Chittor, he sent me a message asking if we could meet.

'Forgive me, Highness, for not coming myself but as you know it is not wise for me to stir out.'

I was not a little impatient with Bruhannada since I thought that that unpleasant chapter was closed and found it distasteful to be reminded that, as expected, His Majesty had taken no action against his favourite son.

'I've been pondering about what you said to me some time ago, Sire. What would have happened if the most honourable man in the *Mahabharata* had thrown his weight with the righteous?'

'I'm afraid, Bruhannada, that we'll have to find a more opportune moment to discuss that academic question. And that moment, as you know, will not be available to us since you leave tomorrow.'

'Would you say that a conspiracy to destabilize the sovereign power of Mewar is an academic issue?'

The eunuch's breathing may have been laboured and laced with much asthmatic wheezing but perhaps that only helped to augment the effect of his words. I kept a deadpan face but I was sure that Bruhannada knew that I was merely putting on a bad show and was in reality instantly alert and all attention.

'Will you record my testimony, Highness, or would you rather that His Majesty constituted the highest court in the land?'

'If it's treason we are talking about, then I must, as you know, first inform His Majesty. Before I do that, I'm duty bound to ask you to reconsider. For if you are implicated in a conspiracy, turning a witness for the state will not necessarily protect you nor will it grant you immunity.'

'I appreciate your warning, Highness, but do you really believe I would take such a major step, a step from which there is no turning back, without due thought?'

'No, Bruhannada,' I found myself strangely subdued, 'Few people get a second chance at life. Now you are tempting the fates for the third time. What will happen to your wife Urvashi and to your unborn child?'

'I'll take you briefly through a series of contradictory propositions. But that is the logic of my mind at this stage in my life and that is how I arrived at my decision. I'm now truly what I started out my career as: a eunuch. Urvashi is a kind and gentle woman. In time she, too, will tire of a husband who can give her no pleasure.' Bruhannada paused to drink some hot water. When the congestion in his throat and chest eased a bit, he went on. 'I'm not very good at being an object of pity, Sire, but in truth, what will kill me is my own bitterness against what my life has become.

'You may find it difficult to give credence to this but there is no vengeance in me. My destiny and the source of my power lay in my loyalty. However reluctant I may have been to face up to it, you've challenged my notion of loyalty. I need to find out if I can still make my life worthwhile.'

I've always found eunuch flesh repulsive and yet I caught myself laying my hand on Bruhannada's shoulder. 'You are a courageous man, Bruhannada.'

The weight of all the obvious ironies of the moment was a little overpowering. Barring a victory over the Moghul Babur, I could not have wished for a greater boon from the god of my house, Shri Eklingji, than a confession from the man who Mangal and I suspected had masterminded Queen Karmavati's plans to secure the future for Vikram. And yet there was something disturbing, if not devastating, about Bruhannada's loss of faith and fidelity which I would always find difficult to come to terms with. If only the Queen and her son had known and trusted their retainer a little better, it would never have occurred to him to reconsider his loyalty to them; no, not even after my brother had tried to butcher the eunuch.

How many of us know when to leave things well enough alone?

* * *

I watched my associate justices take their places with a curious sense of detachment. Had I been in a facetious frame of mind I would have said that it was the same old gang: Pooranmalji, the Pradhan; my uncle Lakshman Simhaji and the Finance Minister, Adinathji. I had forgotten how many years had passed since we had met for Vikramaditya's treason trial. Like a lot of men who bald early, Lakshman Simhaji had always grown the hair on the side of his head long so that he could train it to cover his pate. But there was so little hair left above his ears now that it stuck out like a cat's whiskers. Pooranmalji had become frail and there were cataracts in both his eyes. There was still not a wrinkle in Leelawati's great-grandfather's skin but the light had gone out of it and Adinathji's movements were slow and unsteady. It struck me then that while other people age in our eyes, we ourselves never do. You'll invariably find the elderly referring to a contemporary as that old man, forgetting that they themselves are close to ninety.

How did the other three members on the bench view me? Did they see me as older and worn out, but without a line of wisdom on my forehead? Was I the official court cuckold for them, the prince who would take a new wife only on condition that she would lie with somebody else?

How did Father see me for that matter? Was I the harbinger of black tidings or was I the bad news itself? He had sat in his office for the longest time yesterday without uttering a word. I knew he wanted to pace up and down, close his eyes tight and ask me to get out and not show my unlucky face again. But he was the king and he was trapped in the finality of his own authority.

'How do you know this is not a ploy on the eunuch's part to go scot-free?'

'Bruhannada is a free man, Majesty. You pardoned him and set him free.'

'He wants revenge, that's what it is. He wants to get back at the ... No, that doesn't make sense because he would lose his own head in the process.'

'No, it does, Majesty. The thought had occurred to me that the eunuch hated his former masters so much that he was willing to destroy them even if it cost him his own life. But he will have to furnish proof for everything he says and the court will verify all his allegations.'

'Have you fixed the venue?'

'Not yet. Mangal would prefer to select the place only after you appoint the judges who will constitute the bench under you and fix the date.'

'Never delay a good action; but the unpleasant ones, perform them even faster. The proceedings will start tomorrow. You'll preside over the same court that heard Rao Balech's plaint against Prince Vikramaditya.'

'Me?' I asked incredulously. 'Your Majesty is the Chief Justice of Mewar. This is a matter that only you can decide.'

'Do I notice a certain amount of discomfiture, Prince? Since you have aspirations to the throne, I'm sure you'll have to be doubly careful in assessing the evidence.'

'What if the case has ramifications not just for Mewar but for the whole confederacy?'

Father turned his good eye upon me. I was not certain whether I saw loathing there or the confirmation of fear. I realized that I had gone too far.

'What makes you think that?'

'Bruhannada is an ambitious but circumspect man, Majesty. He would not stake both his reputation and life that lightly.'

'Whatever the truth,' there was a chill in Father's voice which suggested that he had made his truce with the demons inside him, 'I'll stand by you, Prince. Consult me when you need to.'

I have no idea where Mangal had stowed the eunuch on the previous night but I was relieved to see him enter the private durbar-room in the Atithi Palace with four of Mangal's men. Bruhannada had obviously spent as restless a night as I had. His face was drawn and he had the tortured look of a man who had tried hard to still the ghosts of his past but had not succeeded. The only indication that his asthma may have acted up last night was a shortness of breath and the occasional involuntary nasal wheeze. Mangal had remembered to keep the lota of hot water next to the eunuch's seat but Bruhannada's voice was steady as he took the oath of truth on the *Gita*. He knew that he was centre-stage but that knowledge seemed to quieten him instead of making him theatrical.

'Swearing on the *Gita* does not make testimony proof from prevarication.' I could barely hear the Prime Minister, his voice was lower than a whisper but there was no mistaking the virulence in it. It was no idle threat but an earnest of imminent danger and damnation. 'However distasteful it may be, perjury is an inescapable feature of the judicial process. We are not conducting a trial but today's hearings may lead to one or several of them. You have come forward of your own free will and, I take it, are about to make grievous charges. They may ruin reputations, they may unseat people and heads may fall. Be warned, that any tampering with the evidence or distortion of the truth, any statement which may not withstand verification, will earn you the highest penalty in the land. Your body will be dismembered, your limbs flung in the eight directions of the universe and your head impaled on the Ram Pol as warning to all those who would accuse others for their own gain or to get even with their enemies.'

I do not believe any of the judges of the Court of Last Resort were likely to take their task lightly but the weight of Pooranmalji's words was crushing and all of us were a little awed and subdued. All except Bruhannada. He cleared his throat and spoke in measured language.

'I do not take the Honourable Prime Minister's words lightly. I put it to you that I am seized of the gravity of the charges I am about to make. I stand here not only as accuser but as one of the chief accused.

'Fourteen months ago, I was asked to get together a group of the most trustworthy people from within and without Mewar who were deeply dissatisfied with the state of affairs in our kingdom. My sponsors were concerned about the growing power of His Highness, the Maharaj Kumar, a man who they thought had brought dishonour to Mewar. They were worried about the way His Majesty, Maharana Sanga, had come to depend more and more on him. They feared that His Majesty was becoming senile and were anxious about the issue of succession. They wished to save Mewar from the

Maharaj Kumar by appointing a candidate of their choice to the throne. Over the next eleven months, I travelled extensively and secretly met some of the most powerful and disaffected nobles, vassals and allies of Mewar and put together a committee of seventeen people. As chief convener, the first ground rule I laid down for all our communications was that under no circumstances would we put anything on paper. Our plan of action was to undermine the authority of both His Majesty and His Highness, the Maharaj Kumar, at every possible opportunity but not interfere with the course of events until the Padshah of Delhi and Mewar and its allies had met and the outcome of the battle was known. If we lost, we did not need proof that His Majesty was ineffectual and incapable of leading the nation. If he won, we would have to rethink our tactics.

'I'm now open to questioning.'

There was a rasp to Bruhannada's voice and he was overtaken by a fit of acute coughing. When he was able to breathe, he poured himself some hot water from the lota and drank from it. Even as he sipped the first few drops, Mangal looked at the copper container as if he was mesmerized by it and sprang up, 'Don't drink the water, don't drink.'

It was far too late, the tumbler had fallen from Bruhannada's hand and he was choking. Seven interminable gasps and only the whites of his eyes showed and he was dead.

Looking back, I keep asking myself if matters may have stood differently with Sugandha had I been a little more attentive when I got back from Bruhannada's funeral on the day, or rather, night of the hearing. It was late, past three thirty in the morning by the time we briefed His Majesty, informed Bruhannada's wife Urvashi and as the parting irony, I poured the ghee over the wood blocks and lit the pyre. Mine were the last words over the dead man's body.

'There is no man of greater integrity, the *Mahabharata* tells us, than Bhishma. Bhishma was Bruhannada's ideal in life. There is little doubt that Bhishma's patience, self-control and abstinence were tried as no man's were. Yet when it came to loyalty, I doubt if even the great Bhishma was tested as harshly as Bruhannada was. He came through without any consciousness of doing something special, something almost superhuman. He did it because he believed in the teachings of the *Gita*: because it was his duty and nothing more.

'But that is not where his greatness lay. His valour and his daring lay in the quality of his mind and soul. He had that rarest of gifts: he could question the very principles which had been the polestar of his life and which had nearly cost him his life. Not, mind you, out of vindictiveness or a sense of despair and disillusionment, but because he perceived the possibility of a more honourable and meaningful loyalty than the one he had been practising: a faith in just causes and the value of right over wrong.

'He could be accused of overreaching. Anyone who challenges accepted wisdom, is. The sad truth is that it cost him his life without his being able to test his new concept of duty.

'Was he greater than Bhishma? That is an irrelevant and meaningless question. What matters is that he may have made not just all of us but even the great Bhishma rethink the notion of loyalty.

'There are not too many people about whom we can say that.'

And then I sang out, loud and clear, in the morning darkness the words of the *Gita* that I had heard on a thousand occasions and which only gained in meaning and vision instead of losing their edge, the more I heard them.

> The soul is never born, it does not ever die;
> Never having come to be, it will never cease to be
> Unborn, immortal, perennial, the pristine soul
> Survives even after the body is slain.

> When a man casts out old clothes,
> He must perforce wear new garments.
> So does the soul discard old bodies
> And enters new ones.

Swords cannot cleave through it,
Fire cannot burn it,
Water cannot wet it,
Wind cannot dry it.

Never to be cut, never incinerated,
Never wet, nor dry ever
Ever-present, immovable, eternal,
It is steadfast and perpetual.

Death comes to all who are born.
The dead too cannot escape birth.
If both birth and death are inevitable,
Wherefore wilt thou mourn?

Sugandha was asleep leaning against the banister of the landing to the first floor when I came home. I wondered if Greeneyes had locked her out. Not another silent cold war, please, I said to myself though I had no reason to complain since Sugandha never tattled against the Little Saint or anybody else in the zenana. I removed my shoes and walked up on my toes but that didn't prevent her from waking up.

She smiled as she looked down on me.

'I'm pregnant.'

Her hand reached out to touch me. I shrank back from her since I had not yet had the mandatory bath after a funeral. I tried to explain my reasons later but they sounded like an apology and the damage was done.

'You think it's your brother's?'

'What?'

'The baby.'

'I hadn't thought about it.' I had. This is perhaps a despicable observation but I tend to think the worst about myself or anybody else before I think better about either party.

'You did. It is not. I don't think so.' Her face crumbled. I had wrung the joy out of her good news. She turned away from me and walked towards her own rooms.

'Are you telling me that you know what's in my mind better than I do?' I wanted to make amends to this daughter of Medini Rai so badly that I got myself in worse straits.

'You are a good actor, Highness, but there are times when the acting shows. I know you'll never be sure whose child I bear.'

I changed tactics once again and called out to her. 'Sugandha, you've given me the only good news of a day when almost everything I have heard was not just bad but disastrous. Please don't ruin this little happiness.'

She was instantly contrite. 'I'm sorry. I am. You really believe me?'

'Yes. Yes, I do.' Maybe I meant it too. I certainly had no wish to break our friendship with Medini Rai or destroy the peace in the kingdom as no less a god than Shri Rama had done when he doubted the chastity of his own wife because of a dhobi's suspicion. I did not want to take any more chances with Sugandha and wrapped my impure hands around her.

✳   ✳   ✳

Will somebody enlighten me about the way the human mind works? From the day I got married to her, Greeneyes has told me to keep off her. Now I'm married the second time, never mind that it was against my wishes, and all she spends her time doing is wooing me. Her tactics are out of the ordinary, to say the least, and she has an unusual arsenal. She was born with a flair for colour and cloth but all these years she has been casual about them. Forgive the banality but it is the only way to describe her intentions, she now dresses to kill. The last seven days she has gone on a rampage of green. She can carry any colour, a garish yellow or a tinselly brown to devastating effect but it is green that looks lethal on her. She is well aware of this and has a hundred, more likely two hundred odhanis, ghagras and cholis in shades of green.

She makes it a point to be around fully dressed before I go to work. I may ignore her (no, that's not possible) but I must say that I am not a little amused by her: why attempt to seduce someone who was hers the day he first saw her and has never shown any signs of changing his mind? Poor Sugandha never did stand a chance against the Princess of Merta but frankly there was not a woman from the zenana who was a match for Greeneyes in this avatar.

What did the Little Saint want? Was it even remotely possible that she missed me? Or was she insecure that she was about to lose her position as prospective Maharani if at some time in the future I became the Rana of Mewar? Why else would she be jealous of Sugandha's pregnancy and want to break my already shaky marriage?

Greeneyes put a halt to guerilla combat with my second wife when she discovered that Sugandha was pregnant. It was open war now.

She let it be known that there was no guaranteeing that even Vikramaditya was the father of the child in Sugandha's womb. Who, after all, was to know how widely my second wife had spread her infidelity? To cast Sugandha as villain, it was essential for Greeneyes to make a paragon of me. She was, as can be expected of so capable a woman, up to the demands of the task. My deification was well under way, but most of the mud and calumny would not unfortunately adhere to Sugandha. My first wife had set a trap for herself from which she could not escape. The more she talked about the paternity of my second wife's foetus, the more smug Sugandha became.

'I can't quite recall who the father of the child is, whether it was an eunuch, the gardener or the milkman,' Sugandha seemed to puzzle over it when she ran into Greeneyes. 'Whoever's responsible for it, I'm going to deliver one of these days. Can you muster up even a false pregnancy, Princess, after all these years?'

Suddenly there was a desperation and hurt in Greeneyes that she could not conceal and which Sugandha latched on to instinctively. Greeneyes could carp and insinuate as much as she wanted, all Sugandha had to do was to get more pregnant by the day.

Do you remember the advice that Kautilya (the very same one whose treatise on the art of governance Leelawati had copied with such care for me) gave to a king? It is not wise for a prince or king to trust anyone. It was dinned into my head in the Military Academy and I practised it up to a point when I grew up and started aspiring to the kingship. I realize now that I was faking it. My heart really hadn't been in it. No longer though. Bruhannada had not died in vain. It is his legacy to me that I suspect everyone now. Who were the seventeen conspirators who were lying low but were even now working towards destabilizing Mewar and getting rid of both His Majesty and me?

In my more cynical moments, I am convinced that it would have been far better for His Majesty, Mangal and me and the three judges of the tribunal if Bruhannada had not attempted to be heroic and outdo Bhishma. He is dead and gone and none of us is any the wiser. Mangal has offered to resign since Bruhannada died under his nominal care. Urvashi has been sent off to her parents and I doubt if anyone gives a damn whether Bruhannada fathered a son or daughter or a genderless creature. That leaves Vikramaditya. His Majesty seems to have finally, if feebly, woken up to the threat posed by this son of his and has despatched him to Ranthambhor and kept him under house arrest there. I believe Queen Karmavati protested vociferously that Vikramaditya had only done what any prince barring the ball-less (her word) Maharaj Kumar would have when he discovered that Bruhannada had broken the eunuchs' code of conduct.

Father, however, did not pursue the little matter of the conspiracy since we had nothing but the eunuch's word for it and that, as he had mentioned before the treason-hearing began, may well have been nothing more than a vendetta. Did His Majesty really believe that cock-and-bull story even after Bruhannada had been snuffed out before he could reveal any names?

But Father's right. We needed proof, dates, plans, names and anything and everything connected with the conspiracy. We could easily have got them and more, if only His Majesty was willing to use a little bit of persuasion and pressure on my brother. It is almost axiomatic that those who get pleasure by inflicting pain upon others are rarely any good when they are at the receiving end. I am not suggesting for a moment that Vikramaditya is not every bit as brave as any Rajput. But an armed confrontation like a battle is nothing but carefully orchestrated mass frenzy. There is usually enough time to prepare oneself mentally, let the juices flow and be prepared to kill or be killed (we never entertain the thought of being maimed) within a matter of four to six hours.

Torture, especially torture by your own people, however, is an altogether different proposition. There's incredulity that your own friends and relatives can turn on you, do all kinds of inhuman things to you and the fact that nothing is time-bound or barred. It may take a day, a week or months and there's no telling if they'll stop at anything.

You need a different kind of temperament, rather than sustained physical endurance to come through unbroken from such an experience. Frankly, I doubt if it would take much to get Vikram talking. The one thing that my brother is almost pathologically allergic to, is being alone. Put him in solitary confinement for a couple of days, three on the outside and he'll spill his guts without much coaxing. He can't think long-term and will dump even his mother if he feels hemmed in and hopeless.

I was sorely tempted to take some extralegal measures and intercept the progress of my brother to Ranthambhor. A small detour wouldn't inconvenience him too much and we would soon be privy to all the details of the treason plot. I will never know whether I lacked the daring to do something unorthodox or I behaved sensibly. Perhaps this is the fatal flaw in me, that I do not have it in me to do what is necessary, whatever the cost. If I captured Vikram, I could take the information I elicited from him to His Majesty and confront him with the sordid details of the plot that mother and son and the other nobles involved had hatched. But where would that leave me? Father would feel cornered. He would be forced to recognize that I had had the courage to do something he could not face up to and he would have no alternative but to take action against his favourite queen and Vikram. All to the good. He would know who among the vassals and allies, were his friends and who his enemies. But he would never forgive me for taking the initiative and countermanding his orders. And worse still, for putting him in a spot. He would never trust me again. My only realistic option was to interrogate my brother and then kill him 'accidentally'. I would then know who the enemies within the kingdom and the confederacy were. Mangal's men would take over from there, put them under surveillance and catch them red-handed.

Of course, the plan could misfire but perhaps it was worth trying. Instead I went to Father again.

'Mewar may soon face its deadliest enemy to date, Your Majesty. The Padshah at Delhi is likely to exploit any weakness within our ranks. The eunuch's death will have been in vain if despite his warnings, we do not identify the people who have been plotting against the state and expose the conspiracy. We need to take the severest action against them.'

'Let us for a moment assume that Bruhannada was telling the truth, but barring resurrecting him, I have no idea how we could come by the names of the people involved in the conspiracy.'

'We could,' I paused since I was not sure of Father's reaction, 'question Vikramaditya.'

'Summon him back from Ranthambhor?'

'Or we could send a team of interrogators.'

'And how do you plan to elicit this information?'

'Isolation and a few threats might do the trick.'

'But if necessary you would not hesitate to use third degree methods?'

I thought about it for a moment: Should I tell the truth or not?

'Yes,' he seemed to be talking to himself, 'I believe you would not hesitate to eliminate your brother in the so-called interest of the state even if he is innocent.'

'That is untrue and unjust, Your Majesty.'

'Is it? Both my elder brothers tried to sacrifice me in their self-interest.'

I was appalled by Father's equivocation, if not outright mendacity. This was the first time that he had ever mentioned his brothers and the internecine struggle for succession. He had the gall to compare my desire to pursue the perpetrators of the plot against him and Mewar with his brothers Prithviraj and Jaimal's murderous race for the throne. He was obviously identifying with Vikramaditya since both of them happened to be younger brothers and third in the line of succession. For him, however great my brother's faults or crimes, he would always be the underdog. That may help explain

552

Father's behaviour with me over the years but it was a disturbing comment on human frailty. Here was a thoughtful, sensible and astute man who had steered his people and state through some explosive and trying times and was preparing to meet his most dangerous adversary. And yet this very paradigm of a king could not think straight and was willing to allow the most shallow and sentimental paternal feelings to endanger the fate of his own country.

'We have banished Vikramaditya, that is warning enough to all those who would indulge in treason against us. Let sleeping dogs lie, son, at least till we have defeated this Moghul upstart.'

I had nothing more to say to my father.

'You are, I'm told, about to become a father soon. You'll judge me less harshly when you have children of your own and not all of them are as exemplary as you are and some of them try your patience to the breaking point.'

Eklingji Shiva, what is my dharma? What is my duty to the state, to the people of Mewar, to the confederacy of Muslim and Hindu allies and to myself? I'm not just a kshatriya, I have aspirations to the crown. If it is my duty to preserve and protect Mewar, then how should I conduct myself? Should I not ignore His Majesty's tepid response to the plot and take matters into my own hands? Corner my brother and whatever the cost, get the information out of him? What will it gain a man if he loses his kingdom to say that he had the responsibility but not the power and authority to contravene the Rana's command and act on his own?

There is another unanswered question underlying all these. Why did I approach Father except to ward off all possibility of my having to deal with Vikram and if need be, eliminate him?

Chapter 44

*H*ad I really been that preoccupied formulating the new tax proposals to finance the war that I hadn't noticed the night descend? How could that be, surely it wasn't more than two and a half hours since I had come to office? There was something wrong, terribly wrong. How could the bird-sounds have died so suddenly? And where had all the people of Chittor disappeared: the children playing marbles and spinning tops on the streets; the steady, hypnotic swing, bash and splash of clothes at the dhobi ghat on the river; the vegetable, fruit, pearl and precious-stone vendors calling out and hectoring passers-by and of course the continuous quarrying of stone for Sahasmal's water and sewage system?

I felt uneasy and decided to find out what was going on. There was not a cat or dog, bird, child or grown-up on the streets. A knot of terror was tightening at the pit of my stomach. Even during the cholera or my grandfather, Rana Raimul's funeral, there wasn't such an eerie silence. Had Babur stolen into Chittor and like Allauddin Khilji, run his sword through all living things in the city and massacred them? Was Father all right? I started to run dementedly calling out for Mangal I know not why.

And then I looked up at the sky.

In the dead centre of the starless night was a perfect black full moon with a fuzzy halo around it. What was it, this evil bindi in the forehead of the sky?

My good friend and protector Mangal, papers in hand, ran in the dark to save me from whatever demons were pursuing me.

'Highness, please,' Mangal was yelling at me, 'don't look at the solar eclipse.' He threw his hands around my eyes and buried my head in his chest. 'Are you all right, Maharaj Kumar?'

554

A total solar eclipse. Couldn't the Sun-god have chosen another time and place for his own annihilation? What was my ancestor trying to tell me? Was it the most unambiguous message the god of light was sending us about how inauspicious a time we had chosen to meet the Moghul menace? But the eclipse must have been on simultaneously in Agra and the Padshah too must have seen it. Whose side was the Sun-god on? Did the conjunction of the sun and the moon signify doom for Mewar or the Moghul Padshah? I didn't know and I didn't care. This was one time when I was going to use the full weight and thrust of superstition to try and postpone the forthcoming engagement with Babur.

'What were you doing staring at the eclipse, Sire? We must get the Raj Vaidya to treat your eyes immediately.'

'Later, later. I must meet His Majesty first.' There were flaming circles at the centre of my eyes and I stumbled as I ran but there was no stopping me.

'Your Majesty,' I was a little breathless, 'I urge you to heed the signs and omens. I beg you, let wiser counsel prevail. Our ancestor, the Sun-god himself is warning us that this is not an opportune moment to take on the Moghul Padshah.'

'Quite the contrary, my son,' His Majesty laughed and patted me on the back. 'Our ancestor has sent us a messenger who has just told us that Babur is dying.'

Everything's come to a halt. There's a moratorium on war preparations. You would think we were celebrating Diwali in December. The clerks stopped writing in mid-sentence, the stable-master who had shod three of a horse's hooves abandoned the fourth, the sword-makers have doused the smithy, tied up the forges and gone to the nautanki. Believe it or not, they are distributing sweetmeats in some localities. Even the government offices and cabinet ministers who've been working overtime for three months running have taken the last two days off. The bells in the temples ring all day long and everybody including all our Muslim brothers are giving thanks.

Sultan Ibrahim Lodi's mother whom the Moghul usurper had kept, out of kindness to an old woman, under his own roof at Agra, had got one of her retainers to poison the Padshah. Babur has been vomiting copiously for over twenty-four hours.

'Any moment now,' Shafi's father told me, 'the Padshah will breathe his last, may his soul fly to heaven.'

He was followed by none other than His Majesty. If there's a problem to discuss, instead of standing on his dignity and summoning me, he drops by and the two of us clear both the problem and the file on the spot ninety-five per cent of the time.

'You should have summoned me, Majesty.'

'Summon you for what? It's a holiday, albeit an unofficial one. You and Mangal are the only two people in Chittor who are still at work.'

I smiled and got up and gave my chair to him.

'You are such a pessimist, son. Why do you think Babur won't die or isn't already dead?'

'The old lady's retainer, I suspect, botched the job. In poison cases if you are not dead within twelve hours, you'll very likely survive.'

'What makes you so sure?'

'I don't know whether God is on his side or not, but he has survived all these years on faith and his faith seems capable of seeing him through many a tight spot. Cats have nine lives, Father; Babur has already run through nineteen or maybe twenty-nine.'

'Are you feeling fatalistic about this campaign, son?'

'No. I just don't want to leave anything to chance.'

'In that case, I, too, better get back to work.'

'Father, before you leave, may I ask you a question?'

'You may.'

'Who did you wish to appoint governor of Chittor and acting head of Mewar while we are away?'

'I've been puzzling over it for weeks without coming to any conclusion. When the cat's away not only will the mice be at play, other cats too will be eyeing our territory. I tried to broach the subject to my old friend, Lakshman Simhaji, but this time he is adamant. He wants to be by my blind side so that he can see for me and protect me. Who did you have in mind?'

'Mangal Simha.'

556

'Have you learnt of the whereabouts of his mother yet?'

'No, Your Majesty.'

'He's a fine man, unblinkered, ruthless and fair. And utterly loyal to the throne. But they won't have him. He is young and is not directly descended from royal blood. If that was all, he might still stand a chance. But Rao Pooranmalji, our Pradhanji, would take grievous offence if he was not appointed acting head of Mewar. I have, however, a solution. I'll appoint Mangal governor of Chittor. That way no one will be upset and Mangal can keep an eye on things internal and external.'

*   *   *

There's something punitive about the way I play the veena these days; more like an act of repentance and a desperate seeking for forgiveness, if not absolution from Sugandha. I practise whenever I can. Since I have no free time during the day, I have to cut into my hours of sleep. I guess the fact that I am more than proficient at the flute and have some acquaintance with classical theories of music must have its advantages. My fingers no longer bleed since they are developing protective calluses and barring glissandos, my fingerwork is improving almost by the day. If I continue to work at it as hard as I have been for the past few months, Rana Kumbha, the master veena player, may even approve of his great-grandson following in his footsteps from wherever his soul is wandering.

I have realized now that I am at heart, an inveterate show-off and exhibitionist. If I was a little more accomplished at the instrument, I would go public today and hold professional concerts in the courts of all the leading rajas and get myself invited to the durbars of the Sultan of Gujarat, maybe, even play for the new Padshah of Delhi. Unfortunately, my desire for unceasing applause is not commensurate with my talent, at least not yet. Every time my ambition gets the better of my commonsense and I want to perform for a select group of music lovers, I think of my guru and in her unobtrusive and gentle way, she shakes her head and advises me to be patient.

Now that's curious, this is the first time it has registered in my mind that the word 'patient' must stem from suffering and so relate to the sick and the ailing. It is they who are expected to be forbearing and to have the patience and fortitude required to recover. Or die. I have no idea why Sugandha was patient, patient as hardly anybody I've known has been. Why did she not cry and howl, rend the skies, smash everything in sight, stab and assault anyone who had the good fortune to be healthy and walking? Why did she bear such unconscionable pain? I know that one has no choice in the matter but isn't that the very reason why she should have screamed and sworn at the gods? Did she not know that mankind may be powerless but the impotent too can curse and imprecate? Who knows, sometimes even the gods must fear the wrath of creatures who cannot retaliate. Sugandha was a fool. She bore her fate magnificently. What heroism is there in bearing pain? All pain humiliates and debases. The least she could have done was to make all of Chittor witness to the pettiness and nastiness of our Maker.

As all of us hovered over her, His Majesty, Queen Karmavati, her brother, Hem Karan and her father who had been summoned, it slowly became evident that there was no hope for her. Yes, even the Little Saint and I watched her in silent complicity, grateful that she had been struck and not us. Oh, make no mistake, we grieved and we sympathized and we tossed in our beds full of remorse and disquiet. Greeneyes pursued and pressurized the Flautist with her prayers and implorings till he probably fled the Palace, Chittor and maybe the cosmos itself but without so much as a glance at Sugandha.

And I, what did I do? I bet I bled internally, my backbone and brains cracked with the sheer weight of my megalomaniac guilt. I had little doubt that it was I who was responsible for Sugandha's condition. The betrayal of my member was just the beginning. It was my seed, or was it Vikramaditya's, which was lodged in her, waiting to explode in her Fallopian tube. What if Sugandha had lived and given birth to a fine, healthy Rajput prince or princess whose patrimony would always be in doubt? Perhaps I could exercise my benevolence and concern and anguish only because Sugandha had decided to die.

The night before she died, she looked at me and asked, 'I am dying and so is our child because I was unfaithful to you, isn't that so?'

'That's not true,' I yelled maniacally at her, 'that's not true at all. There is no justice on earth, no tit-for-tat. Because if there was, Vikramaditya should have died a long time ago and I'll have to die at least ten thousand times for all the people I murdered on the Idar campaign and once more for the way I treated you.'

But she was past listening. The foetus inside her was being strangled and making sure that she paid with her life for making it suffer.

Besides, she wouldn't have believed me anyway.

*　　*　　*

It must have been six in the morning. The fiery orbs which came between me and everything I saw on the day of the eclipse are my constant companions now, even when I close my eyes and sleep. I've consulted the Raj Vaidya repeatedly. He has given me eye drops with camphor and other herbs which are supposed to be soothing but they do not put out the fire. He is evasive when I ask him how long the effects of the eclipse will last. Has the Sun-god taken the light from my eyes and turned his back on me? I had had about two hours' sleep and was taking a bath when a maid knocked on the door.

'The Commissioner of Police has sent a man to ask whether he can come and see you in an hour and a half. The messenger says that the Commissioner has found a suspect who may be the woman you have been looking for.'

'Tell the man I'll be at the police station in seven minutes.'

I was damned if I was going to wait an hour and a half to see the Police Commissioner's suspect. I had never thought of Kausalya as a suspect. I was still wet and in a tearing hurry, an apt phrase, because I tore my duglo trying to get my right arm into it. I buttoned up as I mounted Befikir and was at the police chowki in less than seven minutes. It was dark inside the police station but the lady certainly looked like Kausalya, a little frailer than I remembered her and her hair was turning grey but hard times could have done that. Her clothes were unwashed and her hair uncombed. She would not look at me, not because she was afraid but because she was not interested in me or anything else for that matter.

'Where did they find her?' I asked the policeman on duty.

'One of Mangal Simhaji's agents spotted her at Rishikesh.'

'Leave us alone.' The woman rose and started to go with the policeman but she tripped.

'Why have you tied her up?'

'That was the way she was brought here. I guess she didn't want to come to Chittor.'

'Untie her.'

It took a while to undo the knot. The woman was patient but the moment she was free of the rope, she walked out. The policeman ran after her and brought her back.

'I would like to talk to you.' She sat down neither reluctantly nor happily. She seemed past emotion. 'Are you hungry? Would you like something to eat?'

'No.'

'What is your name?'

'No name.'

'Where do you come from?'

'From wherever I was.'

'May I ask where you are going?'

'It doesn't make a difference.'

'Do you have any children?'

'May I go back to my dog? He must be waiting for me in Rishikesh.' Her language, tone and accent were so nondescript, they certainly weren't giving any clues.

'What's his name?'

'Anand.'

'That's a strange name for a dog.'

'Not at all. That's what he is, the happiness of my life.' She came over to me and suddenly held my arm. I could feel her right hand through the rent in my sleeve. 'Please let me go back to my Anand. Please.'

I had been wondering if I would have to do a body check. What was I going to tell the policeman, the Commissioner of Police, His Majesty, Mangal or the lady herself? I want to see you naked. Would you please make love to me? It was not Kausalya, the woman's hands told me that. Just to make sure, I took her hands in mine. They had gentle, soft palms but they were not Kausalya's.

Mangal walked in then.

'I'm sorry I'm late. I was held up in a meeting. Is it my mother?'

'You tell me.'

He hesitated. Did he wish to tell me that I knew her far better than he would ever know her? If he did, he phrased it differently.

'I have not lived with Mother for close to fourteen years now. She looks like her but I don't know.'

'She's not.'

I gave the woman some money, enough for her and her dog Anand to live off for the next couple of years.

'Do you wish to go back to Rishikesh?'

'If that's where Anand is.'

I called the policeman and asked him to send her back with any group of pilgrims doing the rounds of the sacred places in the north.

'Don't you ever sleep, Mangal?'

'About as much as you, Sire. Just got a message that Babur is rushing reinforcements to the fort at Bayana since he thinks that it may be under threat from us.'

'Who's heading the troops?'

'Muhammad Sultan Mirza, Yumas-i-ali, Shah Mansur Barlas, Kitta Beg, Qismati and Bujka.'

Babur, as you've made out by now, did not succumb to the poison though it appears that he has had a close shave and that he gave profuse thanks to God for saving his life.

✳ ✳ ✳

Since my secretary was down with malaria, I had to open the letters myself when the mail-bag arrived. Letters from grain merchants about supplies for the war; the dealer of horses says that there'll be a shortfall of four hundred and seventy; the armoury at Raisen wants money in advance for five thousand swords. There are about thirty or thirty-five others. But the one I opened next had no official seal on it. It was marked personal. I knew the handwriting but couldn't put a name to it.

561

To

His Highness, the Maharaj Kumar,

May Lord Eklingji be your armour and inspiration. May he always look after you and keep you safe.

My condolences to you on the death of your second wife. I did not know her and will speak neither ill nor glowingly of her. She is, however, not the reason for this letter.

I have asked myself the definition of a wife and/or friend since the time we last met and I have to confess that I have found myself wanting. If we don't speak the truth for fear of hurting our closest friends, then we let down both our friends and ourselves. I remember your telling me as a child that we have to earn our friendships. I am both friend and wife to you and if I wish to remain so, I must speak up now. If you are my friend and husband, you, too, will understand that even if my words are harsh, you must consider them on their merit and not be peeved or discomfited or think that I am jealous or about to abandon you.

Kausalya did not speak to you about it. The Princess doesn't mention it. Sunheria is dead but I suspect she would not have broached the subject with you either. I will.

There is nothing between you and the Princess. There never was and there never will be. Proximity may have brought you closer, it certainly has me and my husband. It was in your power to do violence to her and force her to be a wife to you in bed and in life. But you are a proud man and will not stoop to coercion. She is then, at best, your friend and no more.

You do not know after all these years if you love your wife, or are besotted with her because she loves someone else. The only reason you hanker

562

after her is because she rejected you. You cannot forgive one thing and one thing alone, that she rejected you for someone else. That is the only reason you hate her and yearn ceaselessly for her.

No living creature can be more self-centred than saints. They are self-sufficient. There is no life beyond themselves. When they need you, they use you. There is no malice in them, nor is there memory.

There has been enough self-deception. It is time to put an end to it.

You know as well as I that it is inviting trouble, if not destruction on your head if you fight two wars on two fronts simultaneously. You are in the direct line of kingship. Your wife's lover is not your enemy. Babur is. The Moghul deserves all your wiliness, obstinacy, imagination, innovation and most of all, flexibility. Hardly anyone, I'm certain, shares your views about how to tackle him. You are alone as you've always been. Which is why you must make sure that you persevere and overcome despite your foes at home and despite people who mean well but do not know how to secure the interests of Mewar.

Let the Princess be. Leave her to her god.

There are, you used to tell me, two Flautists. The warrior and the lover. We need to study the warrior. Instead the Princess's pursuit of her paramour has made the philanderer Blue God the paradigm for Mewar. This is sad. We are a warrior race, not a tribe of adulterers and gay blades dallying with maids in our sylvan dales.

It would be timely to remind the Mewari people that the Flautist's greatest achievement is the *Bhagavad Gita*. Its avowed purpose was to tell a warrior called Arjun to stop shilly-shallying, to take up arms and to fight the righteous battle.

One last thing. You are my husband. I love you as I have loved no man or woman. You are the most lonely man I know. You love me and need me. If I strive to be worthy of you, you too, I trust, will want to be worthy of me. I'm a good, strong and sensible woman. I'll be your partner in life and share your burdens and joys at work. I am a patient woman but don't try my patience long. It is not infinite.

Defeat the Padshah and on your way back, take me home.

May the Sun-god shine on you always.

Leelawati.

Chapter 45

 You can get under the skin of a woman and perhaps even become one with her. But slip inside a god and there's the devil to pay.

'Krishna Kanhaiyya, Krishna Kanhaiyya,' she had called him. He had decided that night that he would never, not even on pain of death, enter her bed. And yet here he was, going through the blue charade again.

But something was wrong. Soon after he applied the indigo solution, his body started to swell. He was consumed by a strange pathological itching. He had never had long nails but he drew deep furroughs through his flesh. Scratch as hard as he might, he could not assuage the itching. He kept jabbing his fingers, plunging them all the way in and gouging out ribbons of his skin and digging deeper still, the ruts criss-crossing each other like wagon tracks during the monsoons on the slushy streets of Chittor. The deep lesions on his flesh were suppurating now, a yellow-green ooze, the colour of ripening guavas dripping from all over his body.

The indigo, he realized, did not agree with him. Every night he had pretended to be the Blue God, he had played the flute just like him, danced the dandiya and even turned into a woman just like him. Surely, he had told himself a thousand times, his wife knew it was all make believe. One of these days he was going to take off his mask, no more indigo, no more silk pitambar, just his naked flesh and they would cohabit as husband and wife. And yet on the night of his second wedding when she had suddenly called him by the god's name, he felt as if she had mutilated and dismembered him. He might as well have joined the ranks of the eunuchs in the palace and rubbed mustard or groundnut oil on the breasts of the queens and slid his finger back and forth inside the vaginas of the odalisques but apart from a memory of ancient times, he would have felt no tug between his legs.

She didn't love him, he didn't figure in her night life. The person she held in her arms, talked to, played with and found new ways to love was not him but her lover and god. She was not aware of him, so he wasn't even a lie. She had never seen through his game, it was he who had decided to deceive himself, that was all. There was a tight red anger stuck like a spear deep inside his cortex. It blinded him but that didn't matter. He could still destroy everything in and out of sight. He would kill his faithless wife come what may. What did that witch Bhootani Mata know of rage and vengeance? Shiva was his god and his family deity. He would learn the Tandava from him, an exhilarating joyous dance of death and destruction. Yes, he would dance and with each step he would crush a continent and overturn an ocean. He would wipe out the earth and the birds and the fish and the trees and all of mankind. And then move to the gods, not all of them, just the Blue One.

The battle with Babur was child's play compared to the war he would wage against the Peacock-feathered One. There was only one thing to be done and he would have to do it himself, not leave it to Bhootani Mata. He would do it, come what may, that was a promise to himself and the god. Just let the fracas with the Padshah get over.

His skin had erupted and begun to fester. There were violent open sores across his body, red welts that grew and tried to reach out to each other and become one. The sour, intoxicating smell of putrescence and corruption fermented like an evil brew. Sometimes he would stop scratching himself out of exhaustion but then another subterranean wave of itching would start at the edge of his right toe or roll forward from his belly button, and the leftover stub of his genitals would rankle with rot.

He was inflamed and raw and in terrible pain. When he came to, she had his head in her lap and was nursing him. She wiped his brow and forced open his lips and let her saliva dribble into his mouth. Leave me be, get away from me; go to your Flautist, he was shouting at the top of his lungs yet there was no sound from his tongue. I don't want to see your face again, you two-timing god's bride. No more, I'm through with you. Once and forever. How he loathed her, he would fling her down from the Victory Tower or the parapet wall of the fortress.

She opened her mouth and sucked and drew out the putrefaction from his wounds gently and the cold flame of her tongue soothed and sank over the length of his body bringing a momentary forgetfulness.

The fever abated and there was a respite in the gruesome itching. Run, Maharaj Kumar, run; run before the woman bewitches you and you are trapped again. He tried to move away from her but he had neither the energy nor the will.

'Give me your fever,' she said, 'I'll quench this raging fire and share all your pain and suffering and go out of my mind with joy, my Blue One.'

He knew then that he was finished with his wife.

He sat up painfully. He turned his back upon her and walked out of the room.

*　　*　　*

The day before the Maharaj Kumar left for the war, he found the door to the Little Saint's room half open. The first time he had intruded upon her, she was lost in the ecstasies of love. He had almost not gone to the Idar war then. Keep off. Put blinkers on your eyes and move on. Before you know it, she'll have worked her black magic on you and you'll refuse to keep your appointment, the most important one of your life, with Babur. He pushed the door a little. The hinges creaked but she didn't hear the rusty sound. She was sitting in front of the Flautist and he could see her profile. She was wearing a raging mustard Sangamneri choli and ghagra topped with a bottle-green Venkatgiri chunni over her head. She picked up a marigold garland and put it around her neck. Then another and another. She dipped her thumb in turmeric powder and put it on her forehead and then added a vermillion sindoor.

567

She smashed a coconut on the floor. It broke into two perfect halves. She placed them in front of herself.

She closed her eyes.

'Worship me,' she told the Flautist. 'There's as much of the divine in me as in you.'

There. She had done it. Said the unsayable. The Maharaj Kumar was appalled by the gall and audacity of it. And yet he had to admit that it was the most logical and natural thing for her to say. Hadn't he recited and believed in the mantra 'So' hum' all his grown-up years? 'I am that'; that which pervades, inspires and encompasses the universe. And yet they had been nothing but empty shells of words. The Little Saint's faith had made the final leap. She could change roles with the Flautist. She was the substance and the power and the force that was God.

Chapter 46

What a splendid sight it was to see the full panoply, the pomp and glory of the Mewar armies as they marched past and Father took the salute. (Today is cliché day. At heart I am a worse romantic than any Mewari.) What proud, tall, handsome men our soldiers are. They are wearing such brilliantly colourful clothes, you would think they were going to a marriage. First the cavalry, then the camel corps, the elephant brigade and the foot soldiers. Bows across the shoulders, arrows in their quivers at the back, swords at the waists and spears in their hands. Finally the matchlock company of a hundred men. The Mewar troops are followed by the armies of many of the allies who have already joined us. The pageantry and magnificence of the procession seem to go on forever. Is sheer size a virtue or a disadvantage? The sight of so massive an army, serried upon serried ranks of fierce soldiers, can overwhelm and paralyse an enemy. But it also precludes flexibility and mobility and makes you the perfect target if the enemy is armed with guns, great and small. Anywhere he fires he is going to reap a crop of dead men. Suddenly our soldiers didn't seem so formidable.

There I go again with my misgivings. I've been watching myself for the past few months. I seem to have become brittle and fragmented. This is not the final battle, I tell myself sharply. We'll do our damnedest to win it and put the Padshah to flight all the way to Kabul. If by any chance we don't succeed this time, it will only be a temporary reversal. We'll have learnt a lesson and will be far smarter, shrewder and better-equipped the next time. Let's go, Maharaj Kumar, let's go. Let's get on with the job and terminate the enemy for good.

The Princess was waving out absent-mindedly, not to anyone in particular. Did she know that her husband, the legal one, was going to fight a war? Did it make a difference to her? I suspected she was preoccupied with matters of greater moment, nothing less than god himself.

The war, I had to admit, had some things to recommend it. I had avoided her for the past two and a half weeks as scrupulously as possible but not always successfully. Now I was going away and there was no chance of running into her or seeing her face even accidentally. There was nothing I wished for more fervently than freedom from her.

*   *   *

Fifty miles from Bayana, Mangal's words came back to me: The Padshah Babur was sending a substantial party to reinforce his garrison at the fort since he thought that it might be at risk from us. Perhaps we shouldn't disappoint him. It might help create the right kind of climate before the war.

It was doubtful that Father would approve of my harebrained scheme at the eleventh hour but I decided to chance it. Having said no to my big plea, he was willing to indulge me in inconsequential matters. I'm being unfair to him. I think he liked the idea of introducing an intimidatory note prior to the main campaign.

'Once you are in secure possession of the fort, we'll join you. We'll leave for Mandakur together.'

I did not ask Father why he didn't consider the possibility that Babur's men might butcher our small party.

Tej, Shafi and I left with five hundred cavalry. We knew the lay of the land better than the Padshah's men. We had worked together and had developed a rapport that was almost akin to knowing each other's minds. We took the shortest possible route, made good time and got there a good eleven hours before Babur's begs and men. We fell upon them just as the governor of the Bayana fort opened the great gates for the reinforcements that Babur had sent. Luck was very much on our side and we made the best of it. Within an hour the enemy had lost several of their soldiers and company commanders and we had stormed the fortress. Sangur Khan Janjuha never saw the light of day again. And the formidable

Kotta Khan had nearly overwhelmed one of our soldiers when he snatched a sword from the enemy and slashed the Khan across his shoulder.

Looking back, though, Bayana may not have been such a wise idea. The very success of that sortie may have made us a little overconfident. It certainly sent a wave of panic through Babur's soldiery and commanders and forced the Padshah to take a decision that had the gravest consequence on the outcome of the war.

We were waiting for His Majesty and the rest of our armies when I realized that I had left Chittor without saying my farewells to the Gambhiree and without taking my standard tour of the fort and its environs from the Victory Tower. Was I too losing my cool and calm? Father had agreed to my suggestion that life should continue normally at home and that the work on the water systems and the tunnels should proceed as planned. The only hitch was that I had forgotten to hand over to the town planner His Majesty's sealed order asking Adinathji to release monies for the job. It was locked in the second compartment of my desk at the office. I must remember to send the key with the next courier going to Chittor.

His Majesty and our allies were in great spirits when they arrived. They felt the fall of Bayana was an auspicious omen. Father appointed Rao Pranmal to the governorship of our latest acquisition and early the next morning we were off. We had made excellent progress so far and I was elated that His Majesty wished to press home our advantage. The less time Babur got to prepare, the better our chances of making a clean sweep of the enemy. Besides the word was that the Padshah's camp was badly demoralized because of our lightning attack.

Then the Rana did something which I cannot explain to this day.

Babur had initially pitched his camp at Mandakur between Agra and Sikri. His soldiers had set up tents and his heavy artillery was in place when he realized that the plain did not have an adequate water supply and decided to move to Fatehpur Sikri by the side of the lake. If we marched north-east from Bayana for barely a day,

571

or a day and a half if we wanted to take in the scenic beauty around, of which there is none, we would be in Sikri face to face with the Padshah's forces. But instead of pressing on and catching the enemy unawares while he was still unpacking, Father chose to go north-west and halted at Bhusawar. I doubt if my children or anybody else will believe this, but Father's reasons were that he wanted to cut off Babur's lines of supply. Couldn't His Majesty think straight any longer and do simple calculations? Had he gone out of his bloody .... Never mind, what was the point of fuming, it only makes you feel more impotent. That delay cost us close to a month. The Padshah couldn't have asked for a more obliging foe.

Shiraz Ali, our chief field-intelligence officer, told us that Babur had chosen the flatland next to the village of Khanua which is about ten miles from Sikri as the site for the battlefield. Setting about his job with a civil engineer's precision, he positioned his field-cannons up front facing the enemy. They rested on wheeled tripods of wood which also gave shelter to the gunners. Behind them he placed his wagons, seven or eight yards separating one from the other. He secured the wagons with solid iron chains and tested them repeatedly to make certain that they were held tightly and firmly. That was his second line of defence behind which his artillery, the men with the matchlocks, took shelter. Where the carts did not offer protection, Babur had his deputy, Khurasani and local spadesmen and miners dig ditches.

The storming of Bayana had sent shock waves through Babur's forces. Tales of our fierceness and valour spread through the Padshah's camp. Added to that, the astrologer, Muhammad Sharif, who had recently arrived from Kabul prophesied: 'Mars is in the west these days; who comes into the fight from the east will be defeated.' Try as he might Babur could not allay the anxieties and fears of his men. His response to the crisis was typical. He was completely unmoved by all this talk of defeat and decided to make the two most dramatic gestures of his life. I have little doubt that it was done in good faith but like all great leaders, he also has a superb sense of timing and theatre. The first was to renounce his greatest addiction: wine. Babur issued and had posted a farman over his dominions. It is written in a florid style and full of bombast, obviously not the work of the diarist I knew but one of his secretaries or priests. Here are some excerpts from it.

'In that glorious hour when we had put on the garb of the holy warrior and had encamped with the army of Islam over against the infidels in order to slay them, I received a secret inspiration and heard an infallible voice say *"Is not the time yet come unto those who believe, that their hearts should humbly submit to the admonition of God, and that truth which hath been revealed?"* Thereupon we set ourselves to extirpate the things of wickedness ... And I made public the resolution to abstain from wine, which had been hidden in the treasury of my breast. The victorious servants, in accordance with the illustrious order, dashed upon the earth of contempt and destruction the flagons and cups, and the other utensils in gold and silver, which in their number and their brilliance were like the stars of the firmament. They dashed them in pieces as, God willing! soon will be dashed the gods of the idolaters — and they distributed the fragments among the poor and needy.'

That last bit was not the only philanthropic measure Babur took. In a bid to enlist the support of the Muslim populace of his kingdom he decreed that no Mussalman would henceforth have to pay tax.

And yet even this great pledge and sacrifice did not seem to have had the desired effect. There is a note from Babur's diary that Shiraz Ali sent me:

'At length after I had made enquiry concerning people's want of heart and had seen their slackness for myself, a plan occurred to me, I summoned all the begs and braves and said to them:

"Begs and Braves! ... Better than life with a bad name, is death with a good one.

Well is it with me, if I die with good name!

A good name must I have, since the body is death.

"God the Most High has allotted us such happiness and has created for us such good fortune that we die as martyrs, we kill as avengers of His cause. Therefore must each of you take oath upon His Holy Word that he will not think of turning his face from this foe, or withdraw from this deadly encounter so long as life is not

573

rent from his body." All those present, beg and retainer, great and small, took the Holy Book joyfully into their hands and made vow and compact to this purport.'

When we finally arrived at Khanua, Babur was ready and waiting for us.

Chapter 47

*A*t the final meeting of the War Council on the night before the battle, the mood was buoyant, even jocular. Most of the talk was about how small the Padshah's army was and whether the ditches had been dug to bury the Moghul dead. The members of the Council had got used to my being the only one to introduce a sour note in the proceedings. They humoured me but I didn't know how to give up.

'The only battle plan we have is to soften the enemy under the feet of our thousand elephants and then to follow this up by getting the four seemingly monolithic blocks of our army to move forward and attack. We have no overall strategy, no way to monitor the progress of the war and to make continuous adjustments to exploit the weaknesses of the enemy and break his nerve or to rush help and reinforcements wherever we are taking a beating. The first prerequisite for this is an overview where you can see the moment-to-moment developments taking place on the entire battlefield. You then have information to which people on the ground, both your own and the enemy's, are not privy. We have a huge army. If we can place a man at a vantage point, he can move bits and pieces of the army backwards, sideways or even trap the enemy in a pincer movement. I believe that we can even now with this one advantage alone use the sheer weight of numbers to crush the better-equipped and fortified Moghul forces.'

'Where is the hill or height nearby from where one can get the kind of panoramic view you speak of, Highness?' Hasan Khan of Mewat asked me.

'There isn't, Sire. Which is why my men and I have built a mobile observation tower. It is sturdy and portable since it has

575

wheels and it will always be just beyond the reach of the cannon balls.'

'How high is it?' Rao Medini Rai was the other person who had been paying close attention to me.

'Fifty feet.'

'And you see yourself up there ordering all of us around, including His Majesty?' Silhadi was doing target practice on me again.

'There is only one person whose vision we all respect because he has not merely Mewar's interests at heart but those of the entire confederacy of Muslims and Rajputs gathered here today. He has fought and won more wars than any one of us. His experience and expertise are our biggest resource. He alone is fit to analyse and interpret the overview and decide what action needs to be taken. A series of couriers will stand along the main ladder and pass his messages swiftly to different parts of our armies and their leaders.

'There is one more consideration. For us, in Mewar, the life of the most insignificant soldier is priceless. You are our dearest friends and doubly precious to us. It is our fervent hope that at the end of the day tomorrow, we'll embrace every member of this Council in celebration of victory. Which is why it is important that His Majesty guide and not fall prey to a random shot or arrow or the sword of a Moghul trooper.'

'There's no question about it.' Rao Viramdev had not only caught the drift of my circuitous speech but realized that he, and not I, must articulate the sentiment that amongst all of us His Majesty's life was the least dispensable. 'We cannot afford to put His Majesty's life at risk for entirely selfish reasons. If he conducts the war in the manner the Maharaj Kumar has suggested, then we can get the better of the Padshah.'

'That is a brilliant strategy. We'll yet teach Babur that we, too, are fighting a jehad.' The Chief of Mewat, Hasan Khan, had reason to believe that as a Mussalman he too was fighting a Holy War. 'Not only that, we must guard His Majesty's life at any cost.'

There were yeas and murmurs all around.

'A Rajput king, that, too, the Maharana of Mewar run from the battlefield as if he were a frightened chicken or a woman in a ghagra and choli? What an absurd idea. What message will we be sending to Babur and his troops? That His Majesty's afraid of him?'

'Quite the contrary, the message is that if there's a leader who's in total control of the war, then he, and he alone will win the day.'

I knew that my proposal had already been defeated. Silhadi had diagnosed Father's rawest nerve and pressed on it. Ever since the day, so many years ago, when he had fled, badly wounded and with one eyeball hanging out, from the unexpected and dastardly attack by his brothers, there was no man in Mewar as sensitive to the charge of cowardice as Father.

'And pray, how will you explain His Majesty's absence to our own armies? What kind of example will the Maharana be setting?'

'If each of us, His Majesty's closest allies and advisers takes his men into confidence, I've little doubt that they will understand our strategy and support it fully.'

Rao Viramdev made good sense but Father was not about to tell Silhadi that he refused to be provoked by his needling but would act according to what he felt was best for the future of the confederacy. 'I thank you all for your concern for my safety but my place is with our forces. No more about the observation tower now, it's time to retire for the night.'

'It's not concern for you, Your Majesty,' this was the closest I had come to an open disagreement with Father, 'we need a leader who will lead us, not one who is lost among a lakh and twenty thousand soldiers.'

'Maharaj Kumar, I did say that the subject was closed, did I not? There are enough capable leaders here who can lead our armies as well as I.'

*   *   *

March the seventeenth, fifteen twenty-seven. It was cold when I got up. Most of the fires the soldiers had lit the previous night had died down. As I sat up, I may have startled a scarlet minivet which had roosted on a low branch of the tree under which I had spent the night. It took off in that first light, a shrouded scarlet-red meteor rising into the sky instead of hurtling from it. Red would be the colour of the day.

577

I felt rested. I did not have any anxieties about what lay ahead of us. For a brief moment, I had the feeling that Babur and I were mirror images. Which was the real person and which the reflection? I was sure he, too, was composed and steadfast of intent. He too would be up and bathing with cold water. Perhaps it would not matter if we changed places. I looked around. Is this what they mean when they talk about an ocean of people? Mewari and allied troops were sprawled all the way to the horizon.

Bath, yoga, meditation, breakfast, I got into my armour and was on the battlefield. I could see the cannons in the distance. I wondered why Tej, Shafi, Hem Karan and I hadn't gone across in the night and rolled them over to our side. Both the armies were in position now. The minivet swept past, east to west with a couple of worms in its beak. It was indifferent to our hectic preparations. War was for fools called men. It had more urgent matters on hand. I had seen two minivet chicks sitting in their nest. All the while their father was away, and he would be gone for a good fifteen minutes at a time, the idiot fledgelings kept their beaks open, ever ready for some delicacy to fall into their mouths. The Moghul armies were barricaded behind an unsightly line of wagons and ditches. Where was the Padshah? Would I recognize the man I knew better than most of my colleagues in Mewar? I rode back to the observation tower which had been set up just in case Father changed his mind. The army carpenters had built it in three parts. The lowest was twenty-five feet high. It was on wheels with a platform on top. The next one was fifteen feet tall, flat-topped and had wheels that could be removed easily. The top section was heavily armoured except for open slits at eye level all around. It looked a trifle awkward but it served its purpose. I climbed up to the top storey.

I had a better view of the battlefield now. There was a hole the size of the eclipse in the centre of my vision. My eyesight fluctuated, sometimes from hour to hour. There was no logic to it. On good days, I could see almost normally; at other times while my peripheral vision was passable, I could only see vague, bleached and burnt images when I looked straight ahead. A fine way to go into battle with Padshah Babur; I would have to request him to step aside so I could see him clearly. I'm sure there will be a school of historians in the future who will put forward the theory that the black sun in my vision was not due to chance or bad luck. Somewhere deep inside me, they would say, I wanted to dissociate myself from the war, which is why I had deliberately arranged an accident. Fortunately, while I will fight to kill as many of the enemy as I always do, our allied forces are packed with some of the fiercest warriors in history, and if I grope and blink and stumble, it shouldn't make too much of a difference to the outcome of the battle.

Ours was the classic battle formation. It had been the same for I don't know how many hundreds of years: a semicircle of elephants behind which were ranged three densely packed armies. Mewar's vassals and feudal chiefs stood in the centre while the allies were massed to the right and left. Behind this impenetrable phalanx were His Majesty, the Mewar and allied generals, and when I climbed down, there would be me. Placed in the middle behind us was another solid block of our back-up soldiers. Somewhere in the centre of the Moghul armies a little before their reserve force was a huddle of men. One of them, I was certain, was Babur.

It suddenly occurred to me that I had lost count of the number of years I had been carrying on my conversations with Leelawati. What a pompous ass I was not to have seen what was in front of my nose. I had blamed myself for my sister Sumitra's death. If only I had taken her limp seriously ... if only I had disobeyed Father and asked the surgeon to amputate her leg ... Leelawati was my expiation, the price I had decided to pay for my guilt. Better late than never. Enough was enough. I didn't give a damn any longer whether the social mores of Mewar allowed a marriage between a Rajput and a Jain. At worst, there would be a scandal. That would be tough to handle. But my wife had tutored me in such matters. I had better send a courier in the evening to Leelawati telling her that she need no longer be patient with me. I was coming to fetch her from Mandu. Or if I couldn't get away, Mangal would escort her back.

I climbed down and went back to my post a few hundred yards from Father. It was nine thirty. Suddenly there was an earth-shattering sound and a celestial missile sped towards us like the wrath of God. Its thunderous rumble was accompanied by a thin

579

slithering sound that penetrated the eardrum and lodged in the brain like a vibrating needle which jangled every nerve in the body. Where Rao Raj and Rawat Somnath were, there was now a crater five foot deep and three foot wide. The war had begun but the Rajput armies were petrified in their places. I frankly don't think they were terrified as much as confused and bewildered. Where were these flying missiles coming from? Six more landed at various points and all we could do was to wait patiently for the one with our names written on it to land in our midst and kill us. Fortunately Rao Medini Rai and Rao Maldev were leading our left front and after the first moment of disorientation took off against Babur's right wing. That seemed to snap our men out of their paralysis. There was incessant fire from the matchlock battalion of the Padshah. They were not aiming particularly well but the shots picked our men at random in the hundreds. Medini Rai and Maldev made a battering ram of their forces and did not let up the pressure. On the other side Akhil Raj, Raimul Rathod and Hasan Khan Mewati engaged the Padshah's left wing. Babur's men had begun to cave in under their relentless attack when one of the Padshah's flying flanks arrived to their rescue. The two sides were now equally matched and would have been locked together till evening but for the havoc wrought by the matchlocks. Soon the Moghuls were on the offensive and there was a wide crack between the right wing and the centre of the Rajputs.

Boom. Boom. Boom. Boom. You can make that sound with your mouth. Not at all scary, is it? Hear one of those cannons shattering your eardrums and you lose all confidence and sense of purpose. It's worth pointing out that the cannons didn't do extensive damage to our people; after all, the Padshah had only seven of them and it takes a while before the gunpowder compartment cools and you can clean the barrel, reload it and fire. What pulverized us was the sound of those hot balls flying in the air and landing with a strangely repressed, and hence so much the more fearful, thud as they dug into the earth. Plus the terror of not knowing when and where the next stone-death would fall. What happened then? I have no idea. I was far too preoccupied with the immediate business of galvanizing our men and fighting the Moghul menace through the air and on the ground to have any concept of the overall picture.

The matchlocks kept picking on us, ticking off one soldier at a time. You rarely knew where the bullet was coming from except when it hit you. In any case, what difference would it have made even if a soldier knew who was firing the musket? His best chance was to hurl his spear at the opponent but before he had extended his arm backwards for leverage, the bullet would have blown his brains away or nestled nicely in his heart or gone right through his upper intestine or if he was lucky, lodged in his thigh.

One bullet at a time, it should take a month or two to kill or cripple a hundred and twenty thousand, give or take a few thousand, Mewari or allied soldiers. But let's do a little arithmetic here. My guess is that five thousand of Babur's soldiers had muskets, perhaps seven thousand, but the conservative number will do. I think the Padshah saw our hundred and twenty thousand-headed behemoth ranged against him and said a prayer of thanks to his God. Barring his first line of musketeers, he asked them to point their guns at an angle of 45 degrees. The bullets shot out and curved down at us at 80 to 105 yards per second. Even a bullet flying at barely 65 yards a second will penetrate the skull. No need to aim at all. Just cock your gun and fire.

Our men kept advancing and falling steadily hour after hour. Again it was not the bullets that inflicted such fearful casualties upon us. What the new weapons technology did was to destroy our morale by the middle of the second hour. By itself a cannon ball could kill maybe two or five soldiers at the most, and that, too, if they were huddling together in the path of the ball as it landed. But it was its impact on earth which could be far more deadly. Thousands of tiny, medium and big shards of rocks, roots, branches and jagged chunks of earth were dislodged and flew at great velocities into our midst. We were blinded, knocked down, stupefied. And yet I wouldn't have minded the pandemonium around me so much if I could have strangled the throats of all the soldiers, mostly ours.

I had never heard the likes of the cries and shrieks and the weeping and the screaming that day. The disbelief of an arm separating from the shoulder and hitting the ground; the horror of a spear twisting spirally in the belly; the appalling pain of a shoulder blade cracking as a sword cleaved through it and continued its progress till it breached the backbone, disconnecting the seventh vertebra from the eighth; the amazement of discovering an arrow that was stuck in the neck like a weather vane; the realization that the hole where the floating ribs and liver should have been was a clear air passage all the way to the back. Above all, the gasp of astonishment and the sharp break in the intake of breath as death closed in. I was a veteran of wars and the suffering of the men in this war was no different from that of all the others. Wherefore my surprise and intolerance? Was it because my sight was impaired and my hearing that much keener? Or did I react harshly because every one of those agonizing calls only confirmed our rout?

And now they were coming back, those asphyxiating ten thousand Gujarati soldiers, from the misty marshes and bogs on that early morning, phalanx upon phalanx, ten thousand faces caught timelessly in anguish with soundless open mouths. Smile, I begged them, smile. We are paying for what we did to you. See the hands, legs, hearts, pancreas, kidneys and innards flailing and flung to the winds. Breathe easy now, we have to pay for our karma, sometimes in this very life itself. Take pleasure while you can. This is revenge, my friends, the sweetest satisfaction life can offer. But they did not smile and the twisted faces and the horror would not pass. All day long, as the wounded fell and the dead piled up helter-skelter and graceless, some of them with their chests, stomachs and privates exposed, the ghoulish Gujarati troops watched silently. If not absolution, I yelled, give me oblivion. They did not hear me, or if they did, they were not about to oblige me.

Babur had done his homework carefully. He knew we were not one army but at least fifty armies. He concentrated on ripping open the slight and insecure seams that held together our various forces. He put pressure along these fault lines till we came apart. That was not very difficult. We didn't have a unified discipline (Shafi, Tej and Hem Karan's seven or ten thousand men could have been a single lethal force but the men were attached to different divisions), whereas Babur's twenty thousand had fought at least five wars in India alone and were compact units which the Padshah handled like a master juggler.

Think of a game of chess. At the start we were facing each other, pawns, king, elephants, vazir, horses, on either side. Halfway through the game Babur had moved his pieces so skillfully and swiftly we were under attack on all sides, and losing our men at a staggering pace. Among the leaders Sajja Chundawat, Rawat Jagga Sarangdev, my uncle Lakshman Simha, Rawat Bagh, Sajja Ajja and Karamchand, Chandra Bhan Chauhan, Bhopat Rai, Dalpat and Manik Chandra were all dead. The Moghuls had even captured the Rana's colours but Karan Simha Dodia rescued them at the cost of his life.

We were in desperate straits. Perhaps it might have been a good idea to use strategy three from Shafi's book of retreats: 'Slowly and unobtrusively back out, scatter and meet at a predetermined place where the enemy would not pursue you. Then if all is not lost, take a long detour, mass behind the enemy and attack.' No one among our leaders, however, had taken into account a defeat, let alone a retreat, so there was no question of a premeditated and orderly withdrawal. In the meantime, His Majesty saw the dismal fate of our troops and decided to commit the most foolish blunder of his life. He took it upon himself to rally and inspire them. He exposed himself between two divisions when a random arrow laid him low. It was a mortal blow but you forget that after eighty-seven or ninety wounds to his person, His Majesty was immortal. We raised him gently from the ground, he was unconscious and losing a lot of blood, and transported him in a litter to a distant place called Baswa just in case Babur himself came looking for him or sent someone else to finish him.

I have only two more things to report. We had removed Father in as clandestine a manner as possible because we did not wish either of the armies, ours or Babur's to know about His Majesty's departure. The elders appointed Raja Rana Ajja, Chunder of Halwad, to lead the battle in Father's absence. They hoped that once Raja Rana Ajja was seated on Father's elephant, no one would notice the difference. It is difficult for anyone to impersonate Father, you would have to lose an eye and have a few dead limbs. I had my doubts if Rana Ajja could double for the real Rana but anything was worth a try and I was all for it. All the emblems of sovereignty including the chhatra were in place on Father's elephant and war

583

was resumed. We had hoped that since we had acted quickly, word of Father's injury would not get around. It was at precisely this moment that Silhadi deserted us and joined Babur. He also did us the favour of telling the Padshah that a makeshift pretender was sitting on the Rana's elephant. I should have been incensed by his treachery but I took the news matter-of-factly. Silhadi liked being on the winning side. Besides, his presence or absence wasn't going to make much difference. The end was nigh.

In the evening the Padshah ordered the heads of the enemy to be gathered and raised in a column. I was not there to see this ghastly victory tower but they told me that it was a little higher than the fifty foot tall observation tower I had built for His Majesty and just as secure.

Chapter 48

$\mathcal{J}$ reached the palace on the hill at Baswa late at night. There weren't too many people with Father. Perhaps it made sense to abandon ship, if I may use a maritime image for a land-bound conflict. Even the few people who were there looked coldly at me and gave me a wide berth. (Is my unconscious switch to seafaring imagery trying to tell me something? Do I wish to leave the shores of this land for good?) Since I had been so insistent that we postpone the battle of Khanua by a year or two and they had all vetoed my arguments, I'm somehow or other held responsible for today's rout.

'We were worried about you. I'm so thankful that you could make it in one piece,' Rao Medini Rai greeted me.

'How's Father?'

'Considering the injuries he's suffered, very well indeed. When he came to, he wanted his armour and horse, so he could get back to the battle. He's very weak but has been asking for you every five minutes.'

'I told Prince Hem Karan, Tej and Shafi to arrange for the wounded to be moved here once the Padshah's men leave the field. They should be with us by morning at the latest.'

Father suddenly looks so frail and small. His lips and skin were ashen and his pulse uneven. I sat numbly next to him. My tongue seemed to have gone dead.

'Are you disappointed in your father, son?'

I would prefer His Majesty to be distant and curt with me. 'I will be disappointed if you are not up in the next seven days. There's a great deal of work to be done before we take on the Padshah again.'

'You warned me at every step but I would not listen to you.'

'Do you know the kind of people I can't stand the sight of? The I-had-told-you-so types.'

'So what do you suggest we do now?'

'I'm in earnest, Your Majesty. I'll nurse you back to good health in a week's time, or ten days on the outside. We'll be back in Chittor in fifteen days and get down to work.'

'I'm not going to Chittor.' I almost didn't hear him.

'Not now, Your Majesty. A little later when you are feeling better. We need to look at our finances. We'll have to come to some kind of terms with the Padshah. I suggest we be friendly with him from now on for a year or two. By next July or August we'll have got the field-cannons. Six months or a year's practice with them and the matchlocks, and some sound rethinking about how to deploy our forces and we'll be ready for Babur.'

Who was I trying to cheer up? Father or myself? And yet I meant every word I said.

'Didn't you hear what I said?' His Majesty sounded peeved with me, 'I'm not going to Chittor until I've vanquished the Padshah.'

I could barely keep myself from smiling. 'But that's precisely why we have to get back. We need to be at home. The Rana must be on his throne with the full machinery and dignity of his office behind him for us to marshal our resources and launch our next attack upon the Moghul intruder.'

'When I gained consciousness this afternoon, I took a vow in front of our allies.'

'We'll go back on it. Nobody's going to hold it against you. You were, after all, in shock and had lost an incredible amount of blood.'

'Don't you understand?' He turned his head away. 'I cannot show my face at home.'

'This is not the first time that Mewar has been given a thrashing and it won't be the last. Look at Babur, he made a career of defeat but he hung on till he had forced the fates and fortune to change his luck.

'I'm not going home.'

'You rest now. We'll talk about it tomorrow.'

The mood at Baswa was, at first, a little down, at times even downright morose. But just the fact of a number of people in the small palace had given it a busy, purposeful air. Now, all of a sudden, Baswa has become eerily quiet. My father-in-law, Medini Rai had to rush to Chanderi when word reached us that the Rai's capital was under threat from Babur. The Padshah of Delhi was moving swiftly, annexing smaller kingdoms and principalities and there was a good deal of uncertainty about who he would attack next. Almost overnight all our allies, Amber, Jodhpur, Sirohi, left for their homes fearing that Babur might turn his attention to them.

There are just thirty of us now in Baswa: Father, me and Rawat Ram Simha, chief of the elite security force of twenty guards attached to His Majesty. The soldiers play cards, chess or sleep when they are not on duty but there's no denying that morale is tepid.

Like me, the soldiers want to go home. We suffer from the same malaise, boredom.

Some days ago, my mother wrote saying that she was coming to Baswa to be with the Rana and keep house for him. Father sent her a curt note telling her that he would prefer it if she looked after her home in Chittor rather than take care of somebody else's palace in Baswa.

A month has passed and I've still not been able to persuade Father to return to Chittor.

'Who's going to look after the administration, the civilian, military and financial affairs of the kingdom? A sovereign state cannot and must not function without a sovereign.'

'The Prime Minister and Mangal are quite capable of looking after Mewar. No man, be he prince or pauper, is indispensable.'

'Mangal has been sending a courier almost every day asking us to come back. Are you reading his reports, Your Majesty? There's serious trouble brewing in the capital. Vikramaditya and Her Highness, Queen Karmavati, are now openly talking of removing the Pradhan, Pooranmalji, from office. If you don't show up in Chittor right away and take the reins of the kingdom in your hands, it will be too late.'

'Too late for what?'

'The war's been over for weeks. Your subjects can't understand why you won't return and take charge. Pooranmalji is old and feeble. Now more than ever Mewar needs a firm sense of direction. What they have got instead are a lot of rumours and fear of what the future holds in store. You must go back before the machinery of the state breaks down altogether.'

'Is that really why you want me to go back? Is it because you want me to wear the crown or because you wish to secure it for yourself?'

'You are the crown. Which is why you must go back and take charge of your throne. Of course I want the crown. I am the first-born and the Maharaj Kumar. It will descend from your head to mine but only after you have lived a full life and long after you have driven the Padshah back into the Hindukush mountains.'

What had happened to Father? Was it that last wound and the injury to his head as he fainted and fell from his elephant? Or had he lost his nerve? Did he really believe that the people of Mewar would scoff at him? Even if they did, did he not know that hired hands are but parrots, they'll repeat anything they are taught? I am impatient and irritable with Father because I know time is running out. But that doesn't in any way mitigate the fact that I'm being crass and unreasonable. He has suffered a terrible defeat and it is little wonder that his spirit has been crushed.

*　　*　　*

Two days later, I sat down to write to Leelawati. It had taken me over a month but I had finally got down to it. I may have got a little carried away before the battle but I had not changed my mind about one thing: if she would have me despite the defeat the Padshah had inflicted upon us, we could start living together. It was, however, not going to be easy. What would she tell her husband? Would she run away? Her great-grandfather would probably resign the moment he learnt of our intentions. That was all right with me. We owed him so much money, perhaps that would get written off. Besides Leelawati could take over his job. No, facetiousness apart, it was going to be difficult, almost insurmountably so. Was a Rajput prince, a Maharaj Kumar in this instance, allowed to marry someone else's wife? More to the point, could the Maharaj Kumar marry below his station, and that, too, a Jain moneylender's daughter? No. That was unthinkable. Well then, we would have to set a precedent. There was, of course, the question of His Majesty's approval. And then there was Queen Karmavati. But I needn't worry on the last count. Leelawati would be more than a match for the Queen.

How had this romantic streak suddenly shown up in me? Why was I fantasizing like an adolescent? Was I out of my mind? It no longer mattered. One of these days I would be king. I needed a woman who would manage not just the home and be the mother of my children but also take care of the finances of the kingdom and be queen to Mewar.

I heard Father's footsteps. 'We'll leave the day after tomorrow at seven in the morning for Chittor, Maharaj Kumar. Enough loitering and lingering. I'm like the patient whose only ailment is that he likes to stay in bed. We must get back to work as you suggested.'

Maharaj Kumar. How many years had I waited to hear those two words from His Majesty?

'I'll tell Ram Simha to have everything ready for departure by tomorrow evening.'

I called the Chief of the Security Guard, Rawat Ram Simha, and told him about the Rana's decision. His old and lined face broke into a smile.

'Shri Eklingji be praised that His Majesty has recovered his will. We'll teach that King of Kabul a lesson yet.'

'King of Delhi,' I reminded him.

'Not for long. His Majesty will send him back to his mountain hide-out soon enough.'

The guards had gathered around us by now and it was as if we had already vanquished Babur. 'Long live His Majesty, long live Mewar,' they cried again and again till the Rana showed up on the balcony and waved to them.

*　　*　　*

Why hasn't Mangal written or sent word in the last four days? Even if it's a three-line note, he sends a letter and a report every day. Is he all right? In the past few weeks it seems that things have come to a breaking point between Queen Karmavati and the Little Saint. Life teaches me a hundred things every day, and I forget ninety-nine of them, sometimes all hundred of them. I forgot once again never to take anything for granted, least of all the power and permanence of the great. My wife is the second most powerful person in Chittor, or Mewar for that matter, and I am even willing to wager that she can have her way in any matter, be it religious or secular. Fifteen days ago, she went to the Brindabani Temple for the evening arati and found the gates closed. Queen Karmavati and the priests who have always hated her, especially after she gained sainthood and the loyalty of the populace, had joined hands and declared that the shikhara of the temple was about to collapse and was a hazard to the devotees of the Blue One, especially the Little Saint. As our greatest spiritual treasure, it was their duty to safeguard the Little Saint's life and hence until further notice, entrance to the temple was barred to one and all.

How I wish Queen Karmavati was my ally and not my enemy. She would make sure that I overcame any hurdle and sooner or later got my hands on the crown. It's not even a year since the Brindabani Temple underwent extensive repairs and its wings and grounds were enlarged sevenfold. And now suddenly they discover that the steeple is unsafe. Bravo, second mother. Incidentally, guess which civil engineer signed the order regarding the structural problem and closure of the temple? My friend, the town planner Sahasmal seems to have joined the other camp. Perhaps Queen Karmavati will commission him to build a victory tower higher than Rana Kumbha's celebrating her triumphs.

My wife, in the meantime, has taken off for Mathura, the hometown of her beloved.

Chapter 49

That afternoon a party of seven came over from Mewar to meet His Majesty. Father was delighted with the company and the attention. Baswa is a godforsaken place though its ruler, Rao Himmat Simha, has been gracious and hospitable and has even moved out to a smaller palace ten miles from here so that Father doesn't feel that he is in the Rao's way. The Rao rides by every day to make sure that Father is comfortable and doesn't lack anything. Unfortunately the only thing lacking, neither Rao Himmat nor I can offer the Rana. Father wants his friends and companions, lively conversation and bustle, the intimacy of women, anything that will take his mind off the catastrophic tragedy at Khanua. Frankly, I still haven't grasped the magnitude and depth of either the slaughter or the defeat.

I must confess that I am a little surprised by this unexpected invasion from Mewar. Where were they all these weeks? Why this sudden concern and solicitude? That's not being quite fair to our guests. They had explained the purpose of their visit almost as soon as they came. They want His Majesty to go back with them to Chittor.

Rao Bhoopat Simha, Rawat Manik Bhan and the five others are not my favourite people at court. They are trustworthy in one sense. You always know which way the wind is blowing by the company they abandon or keep. His Majesty, I observed wryly to myself, must be back in favour at Chittor.

'We are not going to take a no from you, Your Majesty,' Bhoopat Simha told father. 'We are taking you back with us tomorrow.'

It did Father good to know that he was awaited impatiently in Chittor.

'Not tomorrow, I have to say thank you and goodbye to my host who'll be visiting tomorrow evening. But day after tomorrow's fine. I must be fated to return to Chittor. It's only an hour ago that I told the Maharaj Kumar that we'll be heading for home in a couple of days.'

'Let's drink to that, Majesty. Rawat Manik Bhan shot a deer on the way here especially for you, since you are fond of venison.'

Father was beaming now and placed his hand on Bhoopat Simha's shoulder. 'That is grand. I am touched that you remembered.'

'Then we are going to touch you again,' Bhoopat Simha seemed pleased with his play on words. 'We've also brought your favourite liquor.'

The servants got glasses and Rawat Manik Bhan poured drinks for all of us.

'Your Highness, Maharaj Kumar, I need hardly mention that you are our second guest of honour at dinner tonight.'

I would have thought of excusing myself anyway since our age-groups are different, no, that's not the reason, I don't fancy the company of sycophants and this band of seven was laying it on a bit too thick for my liking. Fortunately I had a valid reason. 'I would have loved to but I've promised the villagers that I would go to a bhavai with them this evening and then eat with them later.'

They looked genuinely disappointed. 'We'll leave some venison for you. You could have a bit of it when you get back, just a taste. Fortunately, the weather's still cold and the venison will keep for a couple of days at least.'

'Thank you, that's kind of you.'

'Rawat Ram Simha, I hope you have no prior engagement?'

'My only appointment is to be at the side of my liege,' the chief of the elite guard said a little sententiously but there was no doubting the sincerity of his words.

'Noble words, Rawat. Did you know, Your Majesty, that the Security Chief and I were in the same batch at the military academy?'

'Yes, I remember. Distinctly. I was two years your junior,' Father's face crinkled mischievously, 'and I recall the thrashing I got because you went and told my father, the Rana, that I was warming myself inside a whore's skirts in Tamarind Lane when I should have been at the academy.'

Bhoopat Simha went red in the face.

'That's because,' the Chief of Security chipped in, 'he wanted to be nesting where you were.'

'Shame on you, Rawat Ram Simha, for revealing my secrets,' Bhoopat Simha had more than recovered his equanimity. 'We are going to have such a feast tonight, you'll remember it for a lifetime.' He went to the window and shouted to the guards. 'You there, dig a fire-pit. I'm going to roast the finest venison in Mewar. All of you are invited for drinks and dinner. We will celebrate His Majesty's imminent return to Chittor.'

I could see that it was going to be a very boisterous party that evening.

'That reminds me, how are the Prime Minister, Pooranmalji and Mangal Simha?' I asked as I was about to return to my room.

'Very well, very well indeed and looking forward to seeing His Majesty and you.'

*   *   *

The bhavai was rambunctious. I hadn't laughed so much for years. The gods came in for some hilarious spoofing as they always do in our folk theatre and there was some sharp political satire which incidentally included His Majesty and me. We were out of jobs and looking desperately for employment. We were found unfit as cooks, washermen, syces, construction workers, jewellers and carpenters because we had no skills whatsoever and always had our hands in the till. Finally it was discovered that we had more wives and women than we needed or could handle and the people of our kingdom set us up in business as pimps.

I was having dinner with the village elders at the mukhiya's place when one of the servants announced that I had a visitor.

'Ask him to wait. I'll be out in a few minutes.'

The man was back in a moment. 'He says it's urgent.'

My hosts accompanied me out. It was dark and I couldn't see the man's face. He prostrated himself and touched my feet.

'Ghanikhama, Durbar. Forgive me for disturbing your dinner.'

593

The accent was clearly bureaucratic Chittor. A minion serving the seven who were visiting His Majesty? I was short with him.

'What is it?'

'My name is Ishwar Simha. I've come from Chittor.'

'Then why did you not wait for me at the Baswa Palace?'

'I asked one of the villagers for directions and he said you were here. Sire, may I have a word with you alone?'

I could see him a little better now. His clothes were dirty, the dust and sweat had dried on his face leaving it a dark, earthy brown. His turban was wrapped around his arm. He was shaky on his feet and I had to steady him. The cloth of the turban was wet and sticky. There was something a little too theatrical about his bandage and his appearance.

What message could this man possibly have for me? Was he really alone? Was I being set up? Where was his horse? How come after all these weeks, there was such an influx of people from Chittor? I dug deep into his arm. The wound was real. The blood welled up and he passed out. The villagers carried him into the house.

'Bring me some hot water, please. Then leave us alone.'

There was a deep gash in his arm, clearly a wound from a sword. I undid his turban, tore open his sleeve and washed his wound and face.

'Who sent you?' I asked him when he opened his eyes. If he was a messenger, then the earlier I learnt his mission, the better.

'Shiraz Ali, Highness. I was to warn His Majesty and you that Rao Bhoopat Simha, Rao Manik Bhan and five others were on their way to Baswa.'

'Does Shiraz Ali apprehend danger to His Majesty?'

'He said that you were to be vigilant and not to let His Majesty out of your sight.'

'A little late for that. His Majesty has been with them for hours.'

'I've been remiss in my duty to His Majesty and you. I deserve to forfeit my life.'

'Let me be the judge of that. Just answer my questions. What took you so long?'

'I was followed by Prince Vikramaditya's men. They wounded

594

my horse at Chandor and I had to abandon him.'

'Is that when you got the wound on your arm?'

'No, Sire. That was later when I tried to take every byway I could to reach Baswa.'

'Where's Mangal Simha?'

'His body was found four days ago in the Gambhiree, seven miles downstream from Chittor. It was badly mutilated and unrecognizable. His wife was able to identify him by his ring.'

'Thank you, my friend. Wait here for me. Don't leave till I get back.'

'There's one other thing, Sire. The day before Mangal Simha died, he gave a letter addressed to you to Shiraz Ali for safekeeping. He said if something should happen to him, Shiraz Ali was to hand it over to you.'

I pocketed the letter and I asked my hosts to feed the messenger.

Somewhere in my heart, I thought that I knew the ways of the world, that I had taken the measure of good and evil and nothing could surprise me. It was clear now that I knew little or nothing about human nature. How else could I have been so blind? And yet, even as I asked myself this futile question, I found it difficult, if not impossible to believe that Queen Karmavati's and Vikramaditya's ambition would dare to touch the person of His Majesty.

Was my father still alive? There was only one way to find out.

The visitors would be waiting for me to ride back to the palace. I left Befikir at the village. I took long detours and got to the back of the palace. It was quiet as death but so it was every night in this loneliest of places. Were Shiraz Ali's and my fears unfounded? A little bit of patience, however, revealed one of Father's visitors standing guard in the shadows of the servants' entrance. I've never missed my bow and arrow as much as I did that night.

'Jagte raho. May God keep an eye on us.' My voice sounded strange in that thick silence. The man on duty was out of the doorway, his sword in hand. Did I make a convincing sentry? I was still far away. Besides, a night watchman couldn't have been such an unfamiliar sight. Every palace, village and city had at least one who went around on the hour till daybreak. I walked steadily towards him.

'Jagte raho. All is well.'

He relaxed but the sword was still out. I was alongside him now. 'May God keep an eye on us.'

My left hand was on his mouth and my dagger in his heart.

I lifted him up and dragged him to the stables. He was heavy and it was a relief to set him down. The horses stirred softly as the dim light from the oil lamp in the courtyard threw my shadow on them. I unlatched the gate to the stables and led the horses out one by one.

Time to start a minor conflagration. I went back and picked up the lamp (not much oil left in it) and let it drop in the hay. It was a terrible way of repaying our host for his hospitality but I had no other means of flushing out our visitors. Within minutes the overhead beams of the stable and some of the rafters in the left wing of the palace were in flames. The horses were terror-stricken and running wildly into the woods at the back. A few of the servants were up and shouting frantically. Three of His Majesty's security guards joined them now and ran to the well to fetch water.

I was standing in the recess behind the stairs when the visitors came tearing down. Should I take on all seven of them? Six now to be precise. It was hardly the time for heroics.

'The horses, save the horses,' they screamed at each other as they rushed out of the building.

I waited for His Majesty. He did not follow our guests down the stairs. Nor did Rawat Ram Simha, the Security Chief. What had happened to the rest of the elite guard?

Where are you, Father?

I climbed the stairs reluctantly. Lord Eklingji, let him be lost in the oblivion of nocturnal sleep and not in the other one that lasts forever. The door to his room was open, the lamps still brightly lit. Even from where I stood his lips looked green. The poison had worked but not painlessly. His right hand was a claw trying to tear open his throat, his eyes seemed to be searching for air but the rictus of pain and horror on his face suggested that all the air in the world would not do him any good. I went over and closed his eyes and mouth. Dear God, how swiftly is a man dead and cold. Forgive me, Father, I'll grieve for you later.

The venison and a little bit of pepper powder in a bowl were waiting for me in my room.

I went to check on the security chief and his band of men merely to confirm my suspicions. The visitors from Chittor had indeed served a feast, a feast of death. It was not difficult to guess why they themselves had not suffered the same fate. The poison, as any primer on statecraft and intrigue will tell you, was not in the venison but in the pepper powder that we Rajputs sprinkle so liberally on our food, especially roast meats. All you had to do was to avoid the pepper and you were fine. The three guards downstairs who were trying to douse the fire had obviously skipped the pepper.

For sycophants and toadies there's nothing more important than self-interest and survival. The murderers would come looking for me only after they had located their horses and secured their own safe return.

I was back in the village. Everybody was asleep. I wasn't sure if the messenger, Ishwar Simha, would still be waiting for me at the village headman's house. I needn't have worried. Mangal did not hire men who are false or faint of heart. Life without Mangal, now that was one possibility that had never occurred to me.

'Your Highness, how is His Majesty?'

'Dead.'

He was about to commiserate with me but I stopped him short.

'I will give you some sealed papers. Deliver them to Sajani Bai, the court singer at Chittor. Here's my necklace. It will make it worth your trouble. Now wait outside and keep watch.'

When he went out, I undid the seal on Mangal's letter.

It was an almost illegible scribble.

Jai Shri Eklingji

A very brief letter, Your Highness. I suspect the very worst is about to befall Mewar. There is a plot

597

underfoot to murder His Majesty and you. Do please take the most extreme measures to safeguard both your lives.

There is another matter that I must now share with you since it is likely that I too have been targeted by Prince Vikramaditya's men. I'm aware that you'll never forgive me once you've learnt the contents of the accompanying letter. But I gave my word to my mother and so must suffer the one thing I cannot bear: your displeasure.

Fly, Your Highness, fly.

Your servant, Mangal

I moved to the other letter.

To His Highness, the Maharaj Kumar,

May Lord Eklingji shower his blessings upon you and preserve you from all harm.

I've asked Mangal to write this note for me. He's the only person to whom I can trust the contents of this letter.

You were Mewar's and my great hope. The future of Mewar belonged to you. You were mine but my ambitions for you were my ambitions for our country. I am a very possessive woman. But I knew that if I were to keep you, I would have to let go of you.

I had prepared myself for your marriage from the day I first breast-fed you. But nothing could have prepared me for the Princess. She was a devoted wife but not to you. It took me a long time to realize this but I finally understood that she would destroy Mewar. The saddest part in all this was the influence she had over you. You seemed to lose your mind when you were with her. She would not give you a son and she made you the laughingstock of Mewar. It was a matter of time before both the Mewaris and our allies lost all respect for you.

I warned the Princess and asked her to mend her ways. She paid me no heed. I decided to take action. Your enemies had had the same thought but they messed up the job. Instead of the Princess, they killed her maid, the innocent Kumkum Kanwar.

I planned the Princess' death far more meticulously. I also took good care not to be caught. I poisoned her food as well as mine except that the dose I gave her was at least ten times stronger than the one I had. Since I was also a victim, nobody suspected me. Unfortunately I too did not succeed in ridding Mewar of the Princess.

Is it an evil force or the gods who protect her? Sometimes I wonder if they are not the same thing. I have no regrets about my actions. The Princess and you have come closer over the years. But no good will come of it because your relationship is based on a lie. I am powerless to save you. Needless to say you do not wish to be saved. You can't even see that it is you and not she who stands to lose everything.

The legend of the Little Saint will become greater with every passing year. The whole world loves a lover. Love and overheated poetry will make her immortal. As for you, Highness, if Queen Karmavati and Vikramaditya don't get you, the Princess and her lover will. Either way, they'll wipe out your memory.

You were meant for greater things, Highness. You have it in you to be the greatest Rajput ruler the country has seen. You have the vision and wiliness to beat all our enemies and become Maharana of the whole of India. Can you break with your wife? Only then will you be able to get the better of your brother and his mother and concentrate on Babur and our other enemies.

Will you do it? I know in my heart that you will not. There is only one woman for you. It is the Princess. It would have helped if she had loved you too. But no matter. You seem to do it for both of you.

I'm leaving, Prince. There is no place in Mewar for a murderess, not even a failed one. But neither can I stand by and watch your fall.

I pray that you'll prove me wrong.

Your servant,

Kausalya.

I have almost finished my last entry. In a minute now I'll seal these bits of my memoirs and hand them over to the messenger and ask him to head for Chittor. It's merely a matter of time before His Majesty's assassins come for me. But I still have one job to do, something I have been postponing for years, but which can no longer wait. I have to settle scores with someone at the temple.

Besides, if I can help it I won't be an easy target for Queen Karmavati, Vikramaditya or their six lackeys yet. Don't forget I still have Befikir, and the mountains and Raja Puraji Kika are not far from here. And I am longing to be in Leelawati's arms.

Why do I keep deceiving myself?

There's no question in my mind that both Kausalya and Leelawati are dead right. Their counsel is irrefutable. If I am to make something of myself, I must turn my back on that woman. Banish her from my life.

Yes. I must.

But there is only one woman for me. It is not Leelawati and it is not Kausalya. It is my wife. I will follow her to Brindaban, to Mathura, to the gates of hell, even to heaven if the gods will have me.

Epilogue

 I am the missing page that is not missed, the hiatus that may be skipped.

*N*o one saw or heard from the Maharaj Kumar again. There were many stories floating around about the manner of his disappearance. One said that the six butchers, the henchmen of Queen Karmavati and Prince Vikramaditya, killed him. Another maintained that the Maharaj Kumar escaped to Mandu and eloped with Leelawati into the mountains where Raja Puraji Kika held sway. Yet another said that he had been spotted in Mathura. He had become a mendicant and was one of the group of people who followed the Little Saint wherever she went. The fourth version seemed to suggest something more complicated.

Pursued by the six, the Maharaj Kumar ran to the temple of the Flautist at Baswa. He had on his kesariya bana, the turban of the final confrontation. 'Even the gods,' he muttered, 'must get their just deserts.'

The marble image of the Flautist at Baswa was not half as big as the one at the Brindabani Temple in Chittor but it had a rare beauty and though the Maharaj Kumar found it difficult to admit, the god was possessed of a sense of peace that was, of all things, ironically, reassuring. The folds of the pitambar were as delicately carved as the waves in the sand the Maharaj Kumar had destroyed when he was missing for seven days during the Idar campaign. The carved peacock feather was stuck jauntily in the headband and was so delicate, it was nearly transparent. But it was the expression on the face and the way he held his head that struck a chord in the Maharaj Kumar. He could have almost mistaken the Flautist for himself. He was playing the flute and the song he was seeking had closed his eyes. There is no truer meditation than music and no journey of discovery greater than that of looking within.

A fine time to dwell on the aesthetics of sculpture and its resonances. No more procrastination. No more. They say god dwells in all things, the Prince told himself. He must surely be present in his own image.

Take the sword out of the scabbard. Raise the right hand above your left shoulder. Now look him in the face, don't worry, he won't open his eyes and he won't stop playing the flute. Then suddenly, with lightning speed bring the right hand down, left to right, one clean stroke and his head should be rolling on the floor.

'How long will you nurse this enmity? How long will you fight this personal war? And to what purpose? Do you not know that you and I are one? My flute and song are on your lips. We love the same woman. Why, you fool, no power on earth can separate or divide us.'

Was the Blue One equivocating, the Maharaj Kumar asked himself. He was after all a god of infinite mendacity. He would prevaricate, dissemble, stoop to almost anything to get out of a tight spot or to gain a point. Wasn't that one of the reasons why the Maharaj Kumar had thought him one of the greatest statesmen of all time and hoped that the people of Mewar would learn the art of diplomacy and war from him?

The Prince was in two minds. Should he raise his hand and strike him dead? Or ...

He brought his double-edged sword down, swift and hard just as he had imagined he would. Was his hand stayed in mid-air? Did it at least make a slight nick in the beatifically smiling face or torso of the marble Flautist? Sajani Bai is silent on the subject.

The six were already closing in on him, swords ready for the kill. It was then that the Flautist embraced the Maharaj Kumar.

Terror and astonishment struck the six men. One minute the Maharaj Kumar was there, the next he had become invisible. Had they been dreaming? There was just the end of the Maharaj Kumar's turban, the kesariya bana, showing outside the lower left edge of the Flautist's chest.

Every time anybody walks into the temple, the cloth caught in the seamless marble stirs slightly with the draft in the air.

Afterword

The last thing I wanted to do was to write a book of historical veracity. I was writing a novel, not a history. I was willing to invent geography and climate, rework the pedigrees and origins of gods and goddesses, start revolts and epidemics, improvise anecdotes and economic conditions and fiddle with dates. As luck would have it, I didn't get a chance to play around too much except in the case of the chief protagonist, since he is a person about whom we know nothing but the fact that he was born, married and died. His only claim to fame was that he was betrothed to a princess who is perhaps the most remembered and quoted woman in Indian history, right down to our own times.

If, despite my intentions, a substantial quantum of history has inveigled itself into the novel, it is because both the princess and her husband lived in momentous times. He was heir apparent of Mewar, the most powerful Rajput state in the early sixteenth century. His father, Rana Sanga, had for the first time in generations managed to unite the perpetually feuding and warring Rajput king-doms and principalities. He was surrounded on three sides by hostile forces. To the north-east was the Lodi dynasty whose Afghan rulers called themselves, rather ambitiously, Sultans of Hindustan. On Sanga's left in the south-west was the kingdom of Gujarat headed by Muzaffar Shah II. To the south-east was Sultan Mahmud Khalji II of Malwa.

The state of research about Mewar is not exemplary but available history books suggest that Muzaffar Shah's second son, Shehzada Bahadur took asylum in Mewar. He was treated generously but things went sour when, at a party, the Shehzada killed a prince related to the royal family. The Queen Mother had grown fond of

604

Prince Bahadur. It was she who intervened and saved his life. Mewar fought with Gujarat mainly over a principality called Idar. In a battle with Malwa, Mewar defeated Sultan Mahmud Khalji and took him prisoner.

It was around the early 1520s that Babur began to make his presence felt in India. He made, in all, five forays into Hindustan, the first expedition having taken place in 1516. Both Babur and the contemporary Mewar chronicles agree that there was some correspondence between Sanga and Babur about attacking Ibrahim Lodi simultaneously, one from the Panipat end, the other from the Agra side.

Most British and Indian historians usually underplay Babur's battle with the Rajputs at Khanua and dismiss it in a sentence or paragraph. They tend to see Delhi as the focus of power in India. This was primarily because the Moghul dynasty that Babur founded ruled mostly from Delhi. But Babur's perception of Maharana Sanga and the Rajputs was vastly different.

After Babur defeated Sultan Ibrahim Lodi at the famous second battle of Panipat, the Padshah annexed Delhi and Agra, and gradually subdued the rest of the Lodi empire. It is worth remembering that Ibrahim Lodi was a much-hated man even amongst his own relatives, vassals and amirs and the Lodi Sultanate was already in the process of disintegrating. Babur knew that his most crucial trial of strength lay ahead. The real power in that region lay with Rana Sanga and the alliance of Hindu and Muslim rajas and chiefs. Babur's soldiers wanted to go back home to Kabul and as he himself writes, they were intimidated by the combined forces of Rana Sanga and his allies and extremely reluctant to engage them. Babur had to resort to extraordinary measures to persuade his soldiers to fight a battle to the death.

The importance of the battle of Khanua where the two armies met is generally underrated. The fate, not just of Padshah Babur, Rana Sanga and his friends, but of India was at stake. It is no exaggeration to say that the history of India may have been very different but for that battle. At the same time any conjectures about its future course if Babur had lost are idle and futile.

After his defeat at Khanua, Rana Sanga vowed not to return to

Chittor till he had defeated Babur. It is during this interregnum, many historians believe, that he was poisoned, though it is not clear who was behind this crime.

Colonel Todd, in his *Annals of Rajasthan*, and other historians share the view that Sanga was a uxorious husband and that Queen Karmavati had an excessive and unhealthy influence over him. If Prince Vikramaditya, along with his brother, was awarded the kingdom of Ranthambhor while the Rana was at the peak of his career, the credit for this highly irregular gift must go to his mother. Vikramaditya was degenerate and power-hungry, with hardly any redeeming features and proved to be a rotten king. Both the Queen and her son did not do Mewar proud.

So much for the facts.

As for the rest, storytellers are liars. We all know that.

Historical Note

*A*ll that work and effort Queen Karmavati had put in was not in vain. Vikramaditya became the Rana of Chittor. Not for very long but that is beside the point. Chittor was only a shadow of its former puissant self and the Maharaj Kumar's one-time guest, Sultan Bahadur Shah, laid siege to the fort. Ironically, Queen Karmavati sent frantic messages to Babur's son, Humayun who was now the Moghul Padshah, to come to Chittor's rescue. For a while it appeared that he might arrive with his forces and relieve Chittor. He never did. When there was no hope, Queen Karmavati and thirteen thousand of the Chittor women, saved their honour by jumping into the fires of johar.

*   *   *

The Turkish chief, Babur, who had not started out from Transoxiana with the intention of becoming the Padshah of Hindustan, founded one of the most memorable dynasties in the world, the house of the great Moghuls.

His most significant contribution to India and to civilization was his grandson, the Emperor Akbar. Akbar was a contemporary of Queen Elizabeth I. His grandfather would have been proud of him. He extended the empire to practically two-thirds of India. He was a great builder and founded his new capital at Fatehpur Sikri close to Khanua where Babur had defeated Rana Sanga. But his finest achievement was something that his grandfather would not have been too happy about. He appointed Hindus, Muslims, Jains and Zoroastrians to the highest military and civilian posts in the empire. He believed that different faiths could coexist. As a matter of fact he tried to found a new religion, Din-i-Ilahi, which was a synthesis

607

of what he thought was the best in the different faiths. He was completely illiterate. Enlightenment and tolerance, it would seem, have little to do with being lettered or unlettered.

His son Jehangir ruled from 1605 to 1627. It was during his tenure that the British established their first settlement in Surat. Akbar's grandson, Shah Jehan was the great builder of the Moghul dynasty. He built the Agra fort, the Red Fort in Delhi and one of the most beautiful monuments in the world, the mausoleum of his wife, the Taj Mahal.

*　　*　　*

Sultan Bahadur Shah of Gujarat eventually swallowed up both Chittor and Malwa. When Babur's son Humayun decided to invade Gujarat, Bahadur sought the help of the Portuguese in exchange for the seven islands of Bombay which were part of Gujarat then. It is said that the Portuguese invited him on one of their ships at Surat and while he was doing the royal tour, fore and aft, starboard and port or whatever they call these things in Portuguese, they arranged an accident that did him in.

*　　*　　*

Saints in India do not, perforce, have to be celibate as in Western tradition. Nor do they have to perform miracles to be canonized. In the mystical Bhakti ethos, which signalled a sharp break with the totalitarian brahmin control of God and religious rituals, anybody from high caste Hindus to grocers and traders to mendicants and untouchables like cobblers or potters, had access to the Almighty. All that was needed was intense devotion and God was yours. It is a peculiar feature of this intimate rapport with God (He went by all kinds of names, Ram, Vitthal, Krishna, Shiva), that the Bhakti mystics from all over India felt an almost compelling need to converse with the Lord in poetry. A great number of them wrote truly superb verse, lyrical, passionate, colloquial, abstruse, rigorous, humorous, romantic, austere, complex, playful. The subject was always the same: Him. He was father, friend, lover, companion, soul mate. He was not high and mighty. You could tease him, order him, wake him up at any time of day or night. You could do all these

things because you believed in the oneness of God; that there w.
no dividing line between Him and you.

Kabir, Dnyaneshwar, Krishna Chaitanya, Thyagaraj, Tukaram,
Lulla, Namdev, Narsi Bhagat. And then there was the Little Saint,
Meera. Unlike the others, she was the only one who was a princess.
She was born around 1498 and married Rana Sanga's son, the
Maharaj Kumar, Bhoj Raj, in 1516. Her affair, albeit with a god
was a scandal. She was constantly criticized and persecuted for it
in the Palace. In one of the lyrics ascribed to her, she calls upon
the Flautist to rescue her from her sister-in-law, mother-in-law and
the Rana (Vikramaditya?). Perhaps they really did attempt to kill her
by giving her poison or in some other way.

It is impossible to separate biographical detail from the legends
and myths that grew around her name. The Indian imagination
responded warmly to the romantic story of the Princess and her
divine paramour, and her travails with her in-laws. She was a fairly
prolific writer. Her love poetry was in the confessional mode and
she has innumerable imitators even in this day and age. Her imagery,
the turn of phrase and her work are part of the conscious and
unconscious vocabulary of Indians. You can recognize her picture
anywhere. Krishna is the yogi. She is the jogan or devotee. She is
always in white and thrumming a one-stringed instrument. She
never looks out at the world. She is lost in her god and is dancing
in a trance in front of him.

The Little Saint, as we all know, became a very big saint. The
measure of life in India is the commercial cinema. Indian cinema
keeps going back to the Little Saint time and again. The Krishna-
cults including the Hare Krishna sects in New York, Moscow,
London and elsewhere owe not a little to Greeneyes. In the 1980s,
it was discovered that like Saint Joan of Arc, she was one of the
earliest feminists. Meera is the subject of plays, dances, poetry and
painting. Her bhajans, love-poetry and other kinds of verse are sung
all over the country. More singers have recorded her songs than
those of any other poet or saint The other great Bhakti saints of
India may have been intellectually more robust than her but their
fame is mostly regional. Her name is on almost every Indian's lips.